YOUNG MILES

LOIS McMASTER BUJOLD

YOUNG MILES

This is a work of fiction. All the characters and events portrayed in this book are fictional, and any resemblance to real people or incidents is purely coincidental.

A Baen Books Original

Baen Publishing Enterprises
P.O. Box 1403
Riverdale, NY 10471
www.baen.com

ISBN: 0-7434-3616-4

Cover art by Larry Dixon

First paperback printing, July 2003

Library of Congress Catalog Number 97-2168

Distributed by Simon & Schuster
1230 Avenue of the Americas
New York, NY 10020

Production by Windhaven® Press, Auburn, NH
Printed in the United States of America

Contents

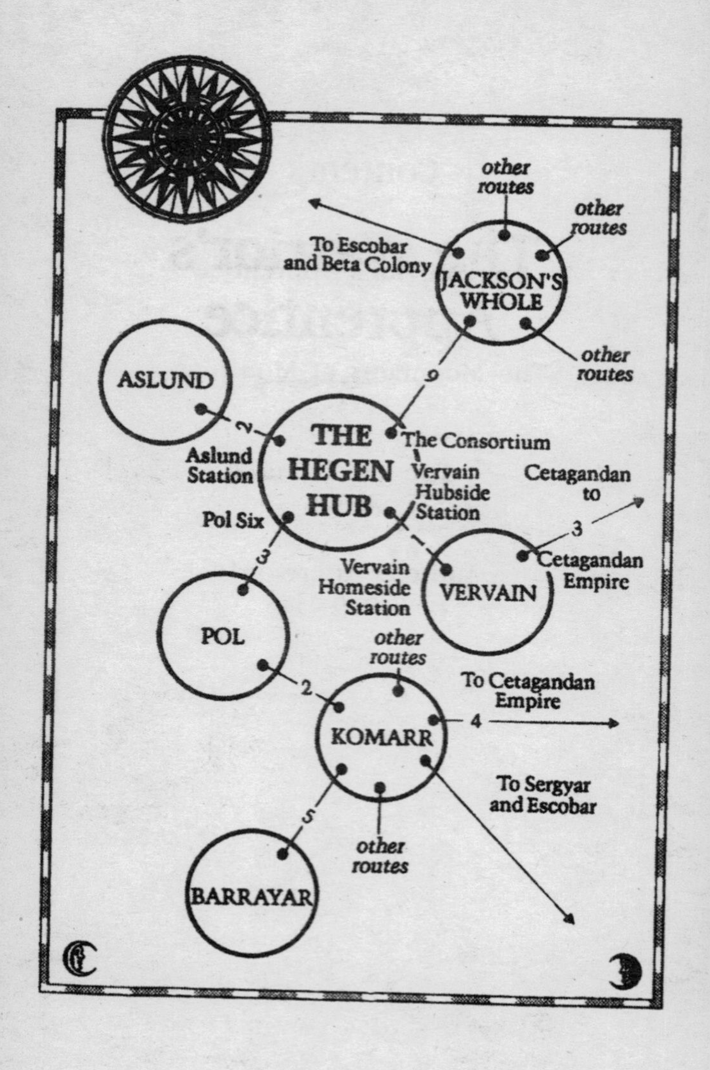
other routes
other routes
To Escobar and Beta Colony
JACKSON'S WHOLE
other routes
ASLUND
6
2
THE HEGEN HUB
The Consortium
Aslund Station
Vervain Hubside Station
Cetagandan to
Pol Six
3
1
3
Cetagandan Empire
Vervain Homeside Station
VERVAIN
POL
other routes
To Cetagandan Empire
2
4
KOMARR
To Sergyar and Escobar
5
other routes
BARRAYAR

The Warrior's Apprentice

For Lillian Stewart Carl

CHAPTER ONE

The tall and dour non-com wore Imperial dress greens and carried his communications panel like a field marshall's baton. He slapped it absently against his thigh and raked the group of young men before him with a gaze of dry contempt. Challenging.

All part of the game, Miles told himself. He stood in the crisp autumn breeze and tried not to shiver in his shorts and running shoes. Nothing to put you off balance like being nearly naked when all about you look ready for one of Emperor Gregor's reviews—although, in all fairness, the majority here were dressed the same as himself. The noncom proctoring the tests merely seemed like a one-man crowd. Miles measured him, wondering what conscious or unconscious tricks of body language he used to achieve that air of icy competence. Something to be learned there . . .

"You will run in pairs," the non-com instructed. He did not seem to raise his voice, but somehow it was pitched to carry to the ends of the lines. Another effective trick, Miles thought; it reminded him of that habit of his father's, of dropping his voice to a whisper when speaking in a rage. It locked attention.

"The timing of the five-kilometer run begins immediately upon completion of the last phase of the obstacle course; remember it." The non-com began counting off pairs.

The eliminations for officers' candidacy in the Barrayaran Imperial Military Service took a grueling week. Five days of written and oral examinations were behind Miles now. The hardest part was over, everybody said. There was almost an air of relaxation among the young men around him. There was more talking and joking in the group, exaggerated complaints about the difficulty of the exams, the withering wit of the examining officers, the poor food, interrupted sleep, surprise distractions during the testing. Self-congratulatory complaints, these, among the survivors. They looked forward to the physical tests as a game. Recess, perhaps. The hardest part was over—for everyone but Miles.

He stood to his full height, such as it was, and stretched, as if to pull his crooked spine out straight by force of will. He gave a little upward jerk of his chin, as if balancing his too-large head, a head meant for a man over six feet, on his just-under-five-foot frame, and narrowed his eyes at the obstacle course. It began with a concrete wall, five meters high, topped with iron spikes. Climbing it would be no problem, there was nothing wrong with his muscles, it was the coming down that worried him. The bones, always the damn bones . . .

"Kosigan, Kostolitz," the noncom called, passing in front of him. Miles's brows snapped down and he gave the non-com a sharp upward glance, then controlled his gaze to a blank straightness. The omission of the honorific before his name was policy, not insult. All classes stood equal in the Emperor's service now. A good policy. His own father endorsed it.

Grandfather bitched, to be sure, but that unreconstructed old man had begun his Imperial service when its principal arm was horse cavalry and each officer trained his own military apprentices. To have addressed him in those days as Kosigan, without the Vor, might have resulted in a duel. Now his grandson sought entrance to a military academy, off planet style, and training in the tactics of energy weapons, wormhole exits, and planetary defense. And stood shoulder to shoulder with boys who would not have been permitted to polish his sword in the old days.

Not quite shoulder to shoulder, Miles reflected dryly, stealing a sidelong glance up at the candidates on either side of him. The one he had been paired with for the obstacle course, what's his name, Kostolitz, caught the glance and looked back down with ill-concealed curiosity. Miles's eye level gave him a fine opportunity to study the fellow's excellent biceps. The non-com signalled fall out for those not running the obstacle course immediately. Miles and his companion sat on the ground.

"I've been seeing you around all week," offered Kostolitz. "What the hell is that thing on your leg?"

Miles controlled his irritation with the ease of long practice. God knew he did stand out in a crowd, particularly this crowd. At least Kostolitz did not make hex signs at him, like a certain decrepit old countrywoman down at Vorkosigan Surleau. In some of the more remote and undeveloped regions on Barrayar, such as deep in the Dendarii Mountains in the Vorkosigans' own district, infanticide was still practiced for defects as mild as a harelip, despite sporadic efforts from the more enlightened centers of authority to stamp it out. He glanced down at the pair of gleaming metal rods paralleling his left leg between knee and ankle that had remained secretly beneath his trouser leg until this day.

"Leg brace," he replied, polite but unencouraging.

Kostolitz continued to stare. "What for?"

"Temporary. I have a couple of brittle bones there. Keeps me from breaking them, until the surgeon's quite sure I'm done growing. Then I get them replaced with synthetics."

"That's weird," commented Kostolitz. "Is it a disease, or what?" Under the guise of shifting his weight, he moved just slightly farther from Miles.

Unclean, unclean, thought Miles wildly; should I ring a bell? I ought to tell him it's contagious—I was six-foot-four this time last year . . . He sighed away the temptation. "My mother was exposed to a poison gas when she was pregnant with me. She pulled through all right, but it wrecked my bone growth."

"Huh. Didn't they give you any medical treatment?"

"Oh, sure. I've had an Inquisition's worth. That's why I can walk around today, instead of being carried in a bucket."

Kostolitz looked mildly revolted, but stopped trying to sidle subtly upwind. "How did you ever get past the medicals? I thought there was a minimum height rule."

"It was waived, pending my test results."

"Oh." Kostolitz digested this.

Miles returned his attention to the test ahead. He should be able to pick up some time on that belly-crawl under the laser fire; good, he would need it on the five-kilometer run. Lack of height, and a permanent limp from a left leg shorter, after more fractures than he could remember, by a good four centimeters than his right, would slow him down. No help for it. Tomorrow would be better; tomorrow was the endurance phase.

The herd of long-legged gangling boys around him could unquestionably beat him on the sprint. He fully expected to be anchor man on the first 25-kilometer leg tomorrow, probably the second as well, but after 75 kilometers most would be flagging as the real pain mounted. I am a professional of pain, Kostolitz, he thought to his rival. Tomorrow, after about kilometer 100, I'll ask you to repeat those questions of yours—if you have the breath to spare. . . .

Bloody hell, let's pay attention to business, not this dink. A five-meter drop—perhaps it would be better to go around, take a zero on that part. But his overall score was bound to be relatively poor. He hated to part with a single point unnecessarily, and at the very beginning, too. He was going to need every one of them. Skipping the wall would cut into his narrow safety margin—

"You really expect to pass the physicals?" asked Kostolitz, looking around. "I mean, above the 50th percentile?"

"No."

Kostolitz looked baffled. "Then what the hell's the point?"

"I don't have to pass it; just make something near a decent score."

Kostolitz's eyebrows rose. "Whose ass do you have to kiss to get a deal like that? Gregor Vorbarra's?"

There was an undercurrent of incipient jealousy in his tone, class-conscious suspicion. Miles's jaw clamped. Let us not bring up the subject of fathers . . .

"How do you plan to get in without passing?" Kostolitz persisted, eyes narrowing. His nostrils flared at the scent of privilege, like an animal alert for blood.

Practice politics, Miles told himself. That too should be in your blood, like war. "I petitioned," Miles explained patiently, "to have my scores averaged instead of taken separately. I expect my writtens to bring up my physicals."

"That far up? You'd need a damn near perfect score!"

"That's right," Miles snarled.

"Kosigan, Kostolitz," another uniformed proctor called. They entered the starting area.

"It's a little hard on me, you know," Kostolitz complained.

"Why? It hasn't got a thing to do with you. None of your business at all," Miles added pointedly.

"We're put in pairs to pace each other. How will I know how I'm doing?"

"Oh, don't feel you have to keep up with me," Miles purred.

Kostolitz's brows lowered with annoyance.

They were chivvied into place. Miles glanced across the parade ground at a distant knot of men waiting and watching; a few military relatives, and the liveried retainers of the handful of Counts' sons present today. There was a pair of hard-looking men in the blue and gold of the Vorpatrils; his cousin Ivan must be around here somewhere.

And there was Bothari, tall as a mountain and lean as a knife, in the brown and silver of the Vorkosigans. Miles raised his chin in a barely perceptible salute. Bothari, 100 meters away, caught the gesture and changed his stance from at ease to a silent parade rest in acknowledgment.

A couple of testing officers, the noncom, and a pair of proctors from the course were huddled together at a distance. Some gesticulations, a look in Miles's direction; a debate, it seemed. It concluded. The proctors returned to their stations, one of the officers started the next pair of boys over the course, and the noncom approached Miles and his companion. He looked uneasy. Miles schooled his features to cool attention.

"Kosigan," the noncom began, voice carefully neutral. "You're going to have to take off the leg brace. Artificial aids not permitted for the test."

A dozen counter-arguments sprang up in Miles's mind. He tightened his lips on them. This noncom was in a sense his commanding officer; Miles knew for certain that more than physical performance was being evaluated today. "Yes, sir." The noncom looked faintly relieved.

"May I give it to my man?" asked Miles. He threatened the noncom with his eyes—if not, I'm going to stick you with it, and you'll have to cart it around the rest of the day—see how conspicuous it makes *you* feel . . .

"Certainly, sir," said the noncom. The "sir" was a slip; the non-com knew who he was, of course. A small wolfish smile slid across Miles's mouth, and vanished. Miles gave Bothari a high sign, and the liveried bodyguard trotted over obediently. "You may not converse with him," the noncom warned.

"Yes, sir," acknowledged Miles. He sat on the ground and unclipped the much-loathed apparatus. Good; a kilo less to carry. He tossed it up to Bothari, who caught it one-handed, and squirmed back to his feet. Bothari, correctly, offered him no hand up.

Seeing his bodyguard and the noncom together, the noncom suddenly bothered Miles less. The proctor looked shorter, somehow, and younger; even a little soft. Bothari was taller, leaner, much older, a lot uglier, and considerably meaner-looking. But then, Bothari had been a noncom himself when this proctor had been a toddler.

Narrow jaw, hooked beak of a nose, eyes of a nondescript color set too close together; Miles looked up at his liveried retainer's face with a loving pride of possession. He glanced toward the obstacle course and let his eyes pass over Bothari's. Bothari glanced at it too, pursed his lips, tucked the brace firmly under his arm, and gave a slight shake of his head directed, apparently, at the middle distance. Miles's mouth twitched. Bothari sighed, and trotted back to the waiting area.

So Bothari advised caution. But then, Bothari's job was to keep him intact, not advance his career—no, unfair, Miles chided himself. No one had been of more service in the preparations for this frantic week than Bothari. He'd spent endless time on training, pushing Miles's body to its too-soon-found limits, unflaggingly devoted to his charge's passionate obsession. My first command, thought Miles. My private army.

Kostolitz stared after Bothari. He identified the livery at last, it seemed, for he looked back at Miles in startled illumination.

"So, that's who you are," he said, with a jealous awe. "No wonder you got a deal on the tests."

Miles smiled tightly at the implied insult. The tension crawled up his back. He groped for some suitably scathing retort, but they were being motioned to the starting mark.

Kostolitz's deductive faculty crunched on, it seemed, for he added sardonically, "And so that's why the Lord Regent never made the bid for the Imperium!"

"Time mark," said the proctor, "now!"

And they were off. Kostolitz sprinted ahead of Miles instantly. You'd better run, you witless bastard, because if I can catch you, I'm going to kill you—Miles galloped after him, feeling like a cow in a horse race.

The wall, the bloody wall—Kostolitz was grunting halfway up it when Miles arrived. At least he could show this working-class hero how to climb. He swarmed up it as if the tiny toe and finger holds were great steps, his muscles powered—over-powered—by his fury. To his satisfaction, he reached the top ahead of Kostolitz. He looked down, and stopped abruptly, perched gingerly among the spikes.

The proctor was watching closely. Kostolitz caught up with Miles, his face suffused with effort. "A Vor, scared of heights?" Kostolitz gasped, with a grinning glare over his shoulder. He flung himself off, hit the sand with an authoritative impact, recovered his balance, and dashed off.

Precious seconds would be wasted climbing down like some arthritic little old lady—perhaps if he hit the ground rolling—the proctor was staring—Kostolitz had already reached the next obstacle—Miles jumped.

Time seemed to stretch itself, as he plummeted toward the sand, especially to allow him the full sick savor of his mistake. He hit the sand with the familiar shattering crack.

And sat, blinking stupidly at the pain. He would not cry out—at least, the detached observer in the back of his brain commented sardonically, you can't blame it on the brace—this time you've managed to break both of them.

His legs began to swell and discolor, mottled white and flushed. He pulled himself along until they were stretched out straight, and bent over a moment, hiding his face in his knees. Face buried, he permitted himself one silent rictus scream. He did not swear. The vilest terms he knew seemed wholly inadequate to the occasion.

The proctor, awakening to the fact that he was not going to stand up, started toward him. Miles pulled himself across the sand, out of the path of the next pair of candidates, and waited patiently for Bothari.

He had all the time in the world, now.

✧ ✧ ✧

Miles decided he definitely didn't like the new antigrav crutches, even though they were worn invisibly inside his clothing. They gave his walk a slithery uncertainty that made him feel spastic. He would have preferred a good old-fashioned stick, or better yet a sword-stick like Captain Koudelka's that one could drive into the ground with a satisfying thunk at each step, as if spearing some suitable enemy—Kostolitz, for example. He paused to gather his balance before tackling the steps to Vorkosigan House.

Minute particles in their worn granite scintillated warmly in the autumn morning light, in spite of the industrial haze that hung over the capital city of Vorbarr Sultana. A racket from farther down the street marked where a similar mansion was being demolished to make way for a modern building. Miles glanced up to the high-rise directly across the street; a figure moved against the roofline. The battlements had changed, but the watchful soldiers still stalked along them.

Bothari, looming silently beside him, bent suddenly to retrieve a lost coin from the walkway. He placed it carefully in his left pocket. The dedicated pocket.

One corner of Miles's mouth lifted, and his eyes warmed with amusement. "Still the dowry?"

"Of course," said Bothari serenely. His voice was deep bass, monotonous in cadence. One had to know him a long time to interpret its expressionlessness. Miles knew every minute variation in its timbre as a man knows his own room in the dark.

"You've been pinching tenth-marks for Elena as long as I can remember. Dowries went out with the horse cavalry, for God's sake. Even the Vor marry without them these days. This isn't the Time of Isolation." Miles made his mockery gentle in tone, carefully fitted to

Bothari's obsession. Bothari, after all, had always treated Miles's ridiculous craze seriously.

"I mean her to have everything right and proper."

"You ought to have enough saved up to buy Gregor Vorbarra by now," said Miles, thinking of the hundreds of small economies his bodyguard had practiced before him, over the years, for the sake of his daughter's dowry.

"Shouldn't joke about the Emperor." Bothari depressed this random stab at humor firmly, as it deserved. Miles sighed and began to work his way cautiously up the steps, legs stiff in their plastic immobilizers.

The painkillers he'd taken before he'd left the military infirmary were beginning to wear off. He felt unutterably weary. The night had been a sleepless one, sitting up under local anesthetics, talking and joking with the surgeon as he puttered endlessly, piecing the minute shattered fragments of bone back together like an unusually obstreperous jigsaw puzzle. I put on a pretty good show, Miles reassured himself; but he longed to get offstage and collapse. Just a couple more acts to go.

"What kind of fellow are you planning to shop for?" Miles probed delicately during a pause in his climb.

"An officer," Bothari said firmly.

Miles's smile twisted. So that's the pinnacle of your ambition, too, Sergeant? he inquired silently. "Not too soon, I trust."

Bothari snorted. "Of course not. She's only . . ." He paused, the creases deepening between his narrow eyes. "Time's gone by . . ." his mutter trailed off.

Miles negotiated the steps successfully, and entered Vorkosigan House, bracing for relatives. The first was to be his mother, it seemed; that was no problem. She appeared at the foot of the great staircase in the front hall as the door was opened for him by a uniformed servant-cum-guard. Lady Vorkosigan was a middle-aged woman, the fiery red of her hair quenched by natural grey, her height neatly disguising a few extra kilos' weight. She was breathing a bit heavily; probably had run downstairs when he was spotted approaching. They exchanged a brief hug. Her eyes were grave and unjudgmental.

"Father here?" he asked.

"No. He and Minister Quintillan are down at headquarters, arm-wrestling with the General Staff about their budget this morning. He said to give you his love and tell you he'd try to be here for lunch."

"He, ah—hasn't told Grandfather about yesterday yet, has he?"

"No—I really think you should have let him, though. It's been rather awkward this morning."

"I'll bet." He gazed up at the stairs. It was more than his bad legs that made them seem mountainous. Well, let's get the worst over with first . . . "Upstairs, is he?"

"In his rooms. Although he actually took a walk in the garden this morning, I'm glad to say."

"Mm." Miles started working his way upstairs.

"Lift tube," said Bothari.

"Oh, hell, it's only one flight."

"Surgeon said you're to stay off them as much as possible."

Miles's mother awarded Bothari an approving smile, which he acknowledged blandly with a murmured, "Milady." Miles shrugged grudgingly and headed for the back of the house instead.

"Miles," said his mother as he passed, "don't, ah . . . He's very old, he's not too well, and he hasn't had to be polite to anybody in years—just take him on his own terms, all right?"

"You know I do." He grinned ironically, to prove how unaffected he proposed to be. Her lips curved in return, but her eyes remained grave.

He met Elena Bothari, coming out of his grandfather's chambers. His bodyguard greeted his daughter with a silent nod, and won for himself one of her rather shy smiles.

For the thousandth time Miles wondered how such an ugly man could have produced such a beautiful daughter. Every one of his features was echoed in her face, but richly transmuted. At eighteen she was tall, like her father, fully six feet to his six-and-a-half; but while he was whipcord lean and tense, she was slim and vibrant. His nose a beak, hers an elegant aquiline profile; his face too narrow, hers with the air of some perfectly-bred aristocratic sight-hound, a borzoi or a greyhound. Perhaps it was the eyes that made the difference; hers were dark and lustrous, alert, but without his constantly shifting, unsmiling watchfulness. Or the hair; his greying, clipped in his habitual military burr, hers long, dark, straight-shining. A gargoyle and a saint, by the same sculptor, facing each other across some ancient cathedral portal.

Miles shook himself from his trance. Her eyes met his briefly, and her smile faded. He straightened up from his tired slouch and produced a false smile for her, hoping to lure her real one back. Not too soon, Sergeant . . .

"Oh, good, I'm so glad you're here," she greeted him. "It's been gruesome this morning."

"Has he been crotchety?"

"No, cheerful. Playing Strat-O with me and paying no attention—do you know, I almost beat him? Telling his war stories and wondering about you—if he'd had a map of your course, he'd have been sticking pins in it to mark your imaginary progress . . . I don't have to stay, do I?"

"No, of course not."

Elena twitched a relieved smile at him, and trailed off down the corridor, casting one disquieted look back over her shoulder.

Miles took a breath, and stepped across General Count Piotr Vorkosigan's inner threshold.

CHAPTER TWO

The old man was out of bed, shaved and crisply dressed for the day. He sat up in a chair, gazing pensively out the window overlooking his back garden. He glanced up with a frown at the interrupter of his meditations, saw that it was Miles, and smiled broadly.

"Ah, come, boy . . ." He gestured at the chair Miles guessed Elena had recently vacated. The old man's smile became tinged with puzzlement. "By God, have I lost a day somewhere? I thought this was the day you were out on that one-hundred-kilometer trot up and down Mt. Sencele."

"No, sir, you haven't lost a day." Miles eased into the chair. Bothari set another before him and pointed at his feet. Miles started to lift them, but the effort was sabotaged by a particularly savage twinge of pain. "Yeah, put 'em up, Sergeant," Miles acquiesced wearily. Bothari helped him place the offending feet at the medically correct angle and withdrew, strategically,

Miles thought, to stand at attention by the door. The old Count watched this pantomime, understanding dawning painfully in his face.

"What have you done, boy?" he sighed.

Let's make it quick and painless, like a beheading . . . "Jumped off a wall in the obstacle course yesterday and broke both my legs. Washed myself out of the physical tests completely. The others—well, they don't matter now."

"So you came home."

"So I came home."

"Ah." The old man drummed his long gnarled fingers once on the arm of the chair. "Ah." He shifted uncomfortably in his seat and thinned his lips, staring out the window, not looking at Miles. His fingers drummed again. "It's all the fault of this damned creeping democratism," he burst out querulously. "A lot of imported off-planet nonsense. Your father did not do Barrayar a service to encourage it. He had a fine opportunity to stamp it out when he was Regent—which he wasted totally, as far as I can see . . ." he trailed off. "In love with off-planet notions, off-planet women," he echoed himself more faintly. "I blame your mother, you know. Always pushing that egalitarian tripe . . ."

"Oh, come on," Miles was stirred to object. "Mother's as apolitical as you can get and still be conscious and walking around."

"Thank God, or she'd be running Barrayar today. I've never seen your father cross her yet. Well, well, it could have been worse . . ." The old man shifted again, twisting in his pain of spirit as Miles had in his pain of body.

Miles lay in his chair, making no effort to defend the issue or himself. The Count could be trusted to argue himself down, taking both parts, in a little time.

"We must bend with the times, I suppose. We must

all bend with the times. Shopkeepers' sons are great soldiers, now. God knows, I commanded a few in my day. Did I ever tell you about the fellow, when we were fighting the Cetagandans up in the Dendarii Mountains back behind Vorkosigan Surleau—best guerilla lieutenant I ever had. I wasn't much older than you, then. He killed more Cetagandans that year . . . His father had been a tailor. A tailor, back when it was all cut and stitched by hand, hunched over all the little detailing . . ." He sighed for the irretrievable past. "What was the fellow's name . . ."

"Tesslev," supplied Miles. He raised his eyebrows quizzically at his feet. Perhaps I shall be a tailor, then. I'm built for it. But they're as obsolete as Counts, now.

"Tesslev, yes, that was it. He died horribly when they caught his patrol. Brave man, brave man . . ." Silence fell between them for a time.

The old Count spotted a straw, and clutched at it. "Was the test fairly administered? You never know, these days—some plebeian with a personal ax to grind . . ."

Miles shook his head, and moved quickly to cut this fantasy down before it had a chance to grow and flower. "Quite fair. It was me. I let myself get rattled, didn't pay attention to what I was doing. I failed because I wasn't good enough. Period."

The old man twisted his lips in sour negation. His hand closed angrily, and opened hopelessly. "In the old days no one would have dared question your right . . ."

"In the old days the cost of my incompetence would have been paid in other men's lives. This is more efficient, I believe." Miles's voice was flat.

"Well . . ." The old man stared unseeingly out the window. "Well—times change. Barrayar has changed. It underwent a world of change between the time I was ten and the time I was twenty. And another between the time I was twenty and forty. Nothing was the same . . . And another between the time I was forty and eighty. This weak, degenerate generation—even their sins are watered down. The old pirates of my father's day could have eaten them all for breakfast and digested their bones before lunch . . . Do you know, I shall be the first Count Vorkosigan to die in bed in nine generations?" He paused, gaze still fixed, and whispered half to himself, "God, I've grown weary of change. The very thought of enduring another new world dismays me. Dismays me."

"Sir," said Miles gently.

The old man looked up quickly. "Not your fault, boy, not your fault. You were caught in the wheels of change and chance just like the rest of us. It was pure chance, that the assassin chose that particular poison to try and kill your father. He wasn't even aiming for your mother. You've done well despite it. We—we just expected too much of you, that's all. Let no one say you have not done well."

"Thank you, sir."

The silence lengthened unbearably. The room was growing warm. Miles's head ached from lack of sleep, and he felt nauseated from the combination of hunger and medications. He clambered awkwardly to his feet. "If you'll excuse me, sir . . ."

The old man waved a hand in dismissal. "Yes, you must have things to do . . ." He paused again, and looked at Miles quizzically. "What are you going to do now? It seems very strange to me. We have always been Vor, the warriors, even when war changed with the rest of it . . ."

He looked so shrunken, down in his chair. Miles pulled himself together into a semblance of cheerfulness. "Well, you know, there's always the other aristocratic line to fall back on. If I can't be a Service grunt, I'll be a town clown. I plan to be a famous epicure and lover of women. More fun than soldiering any day."

His grandfather fell in with his humor. "Yes, I always envied the breed—go to, boy . . ." He smiled, but Miles felt it was as forced as his own. It was a lie anyway—"drone" was a swear word in the old man's vocabulary. Miles collected Bothari and made his own escape.

Miles sat hunched in a battered armchair in a small private parlor overlooking the street side of the great old mansion, feet up, eyes closed. It was a seldom used room; there was a good chance of being left alone to brood in peace. He had never come to a more complete halt, a drained blankness numb even to pain. So much passion expended for nothing—a lifetime of nothing stretching endlessly into the future—because of a split second's stupid, angry self-consciousness. . . .

There was a throat-clearing noise behind him, and a diffident voice; "Hi, Miles."

His eyes flicked open, and he felt suddenly a little less like a wounded animal hiding in its hole. "Elena! I gather you came up from Vorkosigan Surleau with Mother last night. Come on in."

She perched near him on the arm of another chair. "Yes, she knows what a treat it is for me to come to the capital. I almost feel like she's my mother, sometimes."

"Tell her that. It would please her."

"Do you really think so?" she asked shyly.

"Absolutely." He shook himself into alertness. Perhaps not a totally empty future . . .

She chewed gently on her lower lip, large eyes drinking in his face. "You look absolutely smashed."

He would not bleed on Elena. He banished his blackness in self-mockery, leaning back expansively and grinning. "Literally. Too true. I'll get over it. You, ah—heard all about it, I suppose."

"Yes. Did, um, it go all right with my lord Count?"

"Oh, sure. I'm the only grandson he's got, after all. Puts me in an excellent position—I can get away with anything."

"Did he ask you about changing your name?"

He stared. "What?"

"To the usual patronymic. He'd been talking about, when you—oh." She cut herself off, but Miles caught the full import of her half revelation.

"Oh, ho—when I became an officer, was he finally planning to break down and allow me my heir's names? Sweet of him—seventeen years after the fact." He stifled a sick anger beneath an ironic grin.

"I never understood what that was all about."

"What, my name—Miles Naismith, after my mother's father, instead of Piotr Miles, after both? It all goes back to that uproar when I was born. Apparently, after my parents had recovered from the soltoxin gas and they found out what the fetal damage was going to be—I'm not supposed to know this, by the way—Grandfather was all for an abortion. Got in a big fight with my parents—well, with Mother, I suppose, and Father caught in the middle—and when my father backed her up and faced him down, he got huffy and asked his name not be given me. He calmed down later, when he found I wasn't a total disaster." He smirked, and drummed his fingers on the chair arm. "So he was thinking of swallowing his words, was he? Perhaps it's just as well I washed out. He might have choked." He closed his teeth on further bitterness, and wished he could call back his last speech. No point in being more ugly in front of Elena than he already was.

"I know how hard you studied for it. I—I'm sorry."

He feigned a surface humor. "Not half as sorry as I am. I wish you could have taken my physicals. Between us we'd make a hell of an officer."

Something of the old frankness they had shared as children escaped her lips suddenly. "Yes, but by Barrayaran standards I'm more handicapped than you—I'm female. I wouldn't even be permitted to petition to take the tests."

His eyebrows lifted in wry agreement. "I know. Absurd. With what your father's taught you, all you'd need is a course in heavy weapons and you could roll right over nine-tenths of the fellows I saw out there. Think of it—Sergeant Elena Bothari."

She chilled. "Now you're teasing."

"Just speaking as one civilian to another," he half-apologized.

She nodded dark agreement, then brightened with remembered purpose. "Oh. Your mother sent me to get you for lunch."

"Ah." He pushed himself to his feet with a sibilant grunt. "There's an officer no one disobeys. The Admiral's Captain."

Elena smiled at the image. "Yes. Now, she was an officer for the Betans, and no one thinks she's strange, or criticizes her for wanting to break the rules."

"On the contrary. She's so strange nobody even thinks of trying to include her in the rules. She just goes on doing things her own way."

"I wish I were Betan," said Elena glumly.

"Oh, make no mistake—she's strange by Betan standards, too. Although I think you would like Beta Colony, parts of it," he mused.

"I'll never get off planet."

He eyed her sapiently. "What's got you down?"

She shrugged. "Oh, well, you know my father. He's such a conservative. He ought to have been born two hundred years ago. You're the only person I know who doesn't think he's weird. He's so paranoid."

"I know—but it's a very useful quality in a bodyguard. His pathological suspiciousness has saved my life twice."

"You should have been born two hundred years ago, too."

"No, thanks. I'd have been slain at birth."

"Well, there is that," she admitted. "Anyway, just out of the blue this morning he started talking about arranging my marriage."

Miles stopped abruptly, and glanced up at her. "Really. What did he say?"

"Not much." She shrugged. "He just mentioned it. I wish—I don't know. I wish my mother were alive."

"Ah. Well . . . There's always my mother, if you want somebody to talk to. Or—or me. You can talk to me, can't you?"

She smiled gratefully. "Thanks." They came to the stairs. She paused; he waited.

"He never talks about my mother anymore, you know? Hasn't since I was about twelve. He used to tell me long stories—well, long for him—about her. I wonder if he's beginning to forget her."

"I shouldn't think so. I see him more than you do. He's never so much as looked at another woman," Miles offered reassuringly.

They started down the stairs. His aching legs did not move properly; he had to do a kind of penguin shuffle to achieve the steps. He glanced up at Elena self-consciously, and grasped the rail firmly.

"Shouldn't you be taking the lift tube?" she asked suddenly, watching his uncertain placement of his feet.

Don't you start treating me like a cripple, too . . . He glanced down the railing's gleaming helix. "They told me to stay off my legs. Didn't specify how . . ." He hopped up on the banister, and shot her a wicked grin over his shoulder.

Her face reflected mixed amusement and horror. "Miles, you lunatic! If you fall off that, you'll break every bone in your body—"

He slid away from her, picking up speed rapidly. She cantered down the stairs after him, laughing; he lost her around the curvature. His grin died as he saw what awaited him at the bottom. "Oh, hell . . ." He was going too fast to brake . . .

"What the—"

"Watch out!"

He tumbled off the railing at the bottom of the staircase into the frantic clutch of a stocky, grey-haired man in officer's dress greens. They both scrambled to their feet as Elena arrived, out of breath, on the tessellated pavement of the front hall. Miles could feel the anguished heat in his face, and knew it was scarlet. The stocky man looked bemused. A second officer, a tall man with captain's tabs on the collar of his uniform, leaned on a walking stick and gave a brief surprised laugh.

Miles collected himself, coming more-or-less to attention. "Good afternoon, Father," he said coolly. He gave a little aggressive lift to his chin, defying anyone to comment on his unorthodox entrance.

Admiral Lord Aral Vorkosigan, Prime Minister of Barrayar in the service of Emperor Gregor Vorbarra, formerly Lord Regent of same, straightened his uniform jacket and cleared his throat. "Good afternoon, son." Only his eyes laughed. "I'm, ah—glad to see your injuries were not too serious."

Miles shrugged, secretly relieved to be spared more sardonic comments in public. "The usual."

"Excuse me a moment. Ah, good afternoon, Elena. Koudelka—what did you think of those ship cost figures of Admiral Hessman's?"

"I thought they went by awfully fast," replied the Captain.

"You thought so too, eh?"

"Do you think he's hiding something in them?"

"Perhaps. But what? His party budget? Is the contractor his brother-in-law? Or sheer slop? Peculation, or merely inefficiency? I'll put Illyan on the first possibility—I want you on the second. Put the squeeze on those numbers."

"They'll scream. They were screaming today."

"Don't believe it. I used to do those proposals myself when I was on the General Staff. I know how much garbage goes into them. They're not really hurting until their voices go up at least two octaves."

Captain Koudelka grinned, and bowed himself out with a brief nod at Miles and Elena, and a very sketchy salute.

Miles and his father were left looking at each other, neither wishing to be the first to open the issue that lay between them. As if by mutual agreement, Lord Vorkosigan said only, "Well, am I late for lunch?"

"Just been called, I think, sir."

"Let us go in, then . . ." He made a little abortive lift of his arm, as if to offer his injured son assistance, but then clasped his hands tactfully behind his back. They walked on side by side, slowly.

Miles lay propped up in bed, still dressed for the day, with his legs stretched out correctly before him. He eyed them distastefully. Rebellious provinces—mutinous troops—quisling saboteurs . . . He should get up one more time, and wash and change to night clothes, but the effort required seemed heroic. No hero he. He was reminded of that fellow Grandfather told about, who accidentally shot his own horse out from under himself in the cavalry charge—called for another, and then did it again.

So his own words, it appeared, had set Sergeant Bothari thinking in just the channel Miles least desired. Elena's image turned before his inner eye—the delicate aquiline profile, great dark eyes—cool length of leg, warm flare of hip—she looked, he thought, like a Countess in a drama. If only he could cast her in the role in reality . . . But such a Count!

An aristocrat in a play, to be sure. The deformed were invariably cast as plotting villains in Barrayaran drama. If he couldn't be a soldier, perhaps he had a future as a villain. "I'll carry the wench off," he muttered, experimentally dropping his voice half an octave, "and lock her in my dungeon."

His voice returned to its normal pitch with a regretful sigh. "Except I haven't got a dungeon. It would have to be the closet. Grandfather's right, we are a reduced generation. Anyway, they'd just rent a hero to rescue her. Some tall piece of meat—Kostolitz, maybe. And you know how those fights always come out—"

He slid to his feet and pantomimed across the room, Kostolitz's swords against—say—Miles's morningstar. A morningstar was a proper villainous weapon. It gave the concept of one's personal space some real authority. Stabbed, he died in Elena's arms as she swooned in grief—no, she'd be in Kostolitz's arms, celebrating.

Miles's eye fell on an antique mirror, clasped in a carven stand. "Capering dwarf," he growled. He had a sudden urge to smash it with his naked fists, shattered glass and blood flying—but the sound would bring the hall guard, and packs of relatives, and demands for explanation. He jerked the mirror around to face the wall instead, and flopped onto the bed.

Lying back, he gave the problem more serious attention. He tried to imagine himself, rightly and properly, asking his father to be his go-between to Sergeant Bothari. Horrific. He sighed, and writhed vainly for a more comfortable position. Only seventeen, too young to marry even by Barrayaran standards, and quite unemployed, now—it would be years, probably, before he would be in a sufficiently independent position to offer for Elena against parental backing. Surely she would be snapped up long before then.

And Elena herself . . . What was in it for her? What pleasure, to be climbed all over by an ugly, twisted shrimp—to be stared at in public, in a world where native custom and imported medicine combined ruthlessly to eliminate even the mildest physical deformity—doubly stared at, because of their ludicrous contrast? Could the dubious privileges of an obsolete rank more drained of meaning with each passing year make up for that? A rank totally without meaning off Barrayar, he knew—in eighteen years of residence here, his own mother had never come to regard the Vor system as anything other than a planet-wide mass hallucination.

There came a double rap upon his door. Authoritatively firm; courteously brief. Miles smiled ironically, sighed, and sat up.

"Come in, Father."

Lord Vorkosigan poked his head around the carved door frame. "Still dressed? It's late. You should be getting some rest." Somewhat inconsistently, he let himself in and pulled up a desk chair, turning it around and sitting astride it, arms comfortably athwart its back. He was still dressed himself, Miles noted, in the dress greens he wore every working day. Now that he was but Prime Minister, and not Regent and therefore titular commander of the armed forces, Miles wondered if the old Admiral's uniform was still correct. Or had it simply grown to him?

"I, ah," his father began, and paused. He cleared his throat, delicately. "I was wondering what your thinking was now, for your next step. Your alternate plans."

Miles's lips tightened, and he shrugged. "There never were any alternate plans. I'd planned to succeed. More fool I."

Lord Vorkosigan tilted his head in negation. "If it's any consolation, you were very close. I talked to the selection board commander today. Do you—want to know your score on the writtens?"

"I thought they never released those. Just an alphabetical list: in or out."

Lord Vorkosigan spread his hand, offering. Miles shook his head. "Let it go. It doesn't matter. It was hopeless from the beginning. I was just too stiff-necked to admit it."

"Not so. We all knew it would be difficult. But I would never have let you put that much effort on something I thought impossible."

"I must have inherited the neck from you."

They exchanged a brief, ironic nod. "Well, you couldn't have had it from your mother," Lord Vorkosigan admitted.

"She's not—disappointed, is she?"

"Hardly. You know her lack of enthusiasm for the military. Hired killers, she called us once. Almost the first thing she ever said to me." He looked fondly reminiscent.

Miles grinned in spite of himself. "She really said that to you?"

Lord Vorkosigan grinned back. "Oh, yes. But she married me anyway, so perhaps it wasn't all that heartfelt." He grew more serious. "It's true, though. If I had any doubts about your potential as an officer—"

Miles stiffened inwardly.

"—it was perhaps in that area. To kill a man, it helps

if you can first take away his face. A neat mental trick. Handy for a soldier. I'm not sure you have the narrowness of vision required. You can't help seeing all around. You're like your mother, you always have that clear view of the back of your own head."

"Never knew you for narrow, sir."

"Ah, but I lost the trick of it. That's why I went into politics." Lord Vorkosigan smiled, but the smile faded. "To your cost, I'm afraid."

The remark triggered a painful memory. "Sir," asked Miles hesitantly, "is that why you never made the bid for the Imperium that everyone was expecting? Because your heir was—" a vague gesture at his body silently implied the forbidden term, *deformed.*

Lord Vorkosigan's brows drew together. His voice dropped suddenly to near a whisper, making Miles jump. "Who has said so?"

"Nobody," Miles replied nervously.

His father flung himself out of his chair and snapped back and forth across the room. "Never," he hissed, "let anyone say so. It is an insult to both our honors. I gave my oath to Ezar Vorbarra on his deathbed to serve his grandson—and I have done so. Period. End of argument."

Miles smiled placatingly. "I wasn't arguing."

Lord Vorkosigan looked around, and gave vent to a short chuckle. "Sorry. You just hit my jitter trigger. Not your fault, boy." He sat back down, controlled again. "You know how I feel about the Imperium. The witch's christening gift, accursed. Try telling *them* that, though. . . ." He shook his head.

"Surely Gregor can't suspect you of ambition. You've done more for him than anyone, right through Vordarian's Pretendership, the Third Cetagandan War, the Komarr Revolt—he wouldn't even be here today—"

Lord Vorkosigan grimaced. "Gregor is in a rather tender state of mind at the moment. Just come to full power—and by my oath, it is real power—and itching, after sixteen years of being governed by what he refers to privately as 'the old geezers,' to try its limits. I have no wish to set myself up as a target."

"Oh, come on. Gregor's not so faithless."

"No, indeed, but he is under a great many new pressures that I can no longer protect—" he cut himself off with a fist-closing gesture. "Just alternate plans. Which brings us, I hope, back to the original question."

Miles rubbed his face tiredly, pressing fingertips against his eyes. "I don't know, sir."

"You could," said Lord Vorkosigan neutrally, "ask Gregor for an Imperial order."

"What, shove me into the Service by force? By the sort of political favoritism you've stood against all your life?" Miles sighed. "If I were going to get in that way, I should have done it first, before failing the tests. Now—no. No."

"But," Lord Vorkosigan went on earnestly, "you have too much talent and energy to waste on idleness. There are other forms of service. I wanted to put an idea or two to you. Just to think on."

"Go ahead."

"Officer, or not, you will be Count Vorkosigan someday." He held up a hand as Miles opened his mouth to object. "Someday. You will inevitably have a place in the government, always barring revolution or some other social catastrophe. You will represent our ancestral district. A district which has, frankly, been shamefully neglected. Your grandfather's recent illness isn't the only reason. I've been taken up with the press of other work, and before that we both pursued military careers—"

Tell me about it, Miles thought wearily.

"The end result is, there is a lot of work to be done there. Now, with a bit of legal training—"

"A *lawyer?*" Miles said, aghast. "You want me to be a lawyer? That's as bad as being a tailor—"

"Beg pardon?" asked Lord Vorkosigan, missing the connection.

"Never mind. Something Grandfather said."

"Actually, I hadn't planned to mention the idea to your grandfather." Lord Vorkosigan cleared his throat. "But given some grounding in government principles, I thought you might, ah, deputize for your grandfather in the district. Government was never all warfare, even in the Time of Isolation, you know."

Sounds like you've been thinking about it for a while, Miles thought resentfully. Did you ever *really* believe I could make the grade, Father? He looked at Lord Vorkosigan more doubtfully. "There's not anything you're not telling me, is there, sir? About your—health, or anything?"

"Oh, no," Lord Vorkosigan reassured him. "Although in my line of work, you never know from one day to the next."

I wonder, thought Miles warily, what else is going on between Gregor and my father? I have a queasy feeling I'm getting about ten percent of the real story . . .

Lord Vorkosigan blew out his breath, and smiled. "Well. I'm keeping you from your rest, which you need at this point." He rose.

"I wasn't sleepy, sir."

"Do you want me to get you anything to help . . . ?" Lord Vorkosigan offered, cautiously tender.

"No, I have some painkillers they gave me at the infirmary. Two of those and I'll be swimming in slow motion." Miles made flippers of his hands, and rolled his eyes back.

Lord Vorkosigan nodded, and withdrew.

Miles lay back and tried to recapture Elena in his mind. But the cold breath of political reality blown in with his father withered his fantasies, like frost out of season. He swung to his feet and shuffled to his bathroom for a dose of his slow-motion medicine.

Two down, and a swallow of water. All of them, whispered something from the back of his brain, and you could come to a complete stop . . . He banged the nearly full container back onto the shelf.

His eyes gave back a muted spark from the bathroom mirror. "Grandfather is right. The only way to go down is fighting."

He returned to bed, to relive his moment of error on the wall in an endless loop until sleep relieved him of himself.

CHAPTER THREE

Miles was awakened in a dim grey light by a servant apprehensively touching his shoulder.

"Lord Vorkosigan? Lord Vorkosigan?" the man murmured.

Miles peered through slitted eyes, feeling thick with sleep, as though moving under water. What hour—and why was the idiot miscalling him by his father's title? New, was he? No . . .

Cold consciousness washed over him, and his stomach knotted, as the full significance of the man's words penetrated. He sat up, head swimming, heart sinking. "What?"

"The—y—your father requests you dress and join him downstairs immediately." The man's tumbling tongue confirmed his fear.

It was the hour before dawn. Yellow lamps made small warm pools within the library as Miles entered. The windows were blue-grey cold translucent rectangles, balanced on the cusp of night, neither transmitting light from without nor reflecting it from within. His father stood, half-dressed in uniform trousers, shirt, and slippers, talking in a grave undertone with two men. Their personal physician, and an aide in the uniform of the Imperial Residence. His father—Count Vorkosigan?—looked up to meet his eyes.

"Grandfather, sir?" asked Miles softly.

The new Count nodded. "Very quietly, in his sleep, about two hours ago. He felt no pain, I think." His father's voice was low and clear, without tremor, but his face seemed more lined than usual, almost furrowed. Set, expressionless; the determined commander. Situation under control. Only his eyes, and only now and then, through a passing trick of angle, held the look of some stricken and bewildered child. The eyes frightened Miles far more than the stern mouth.

Miles's own vision blurred, and he brushed the foolish water from his eyes with the back of his hand in a brusque, angry swipe. "God damn it," he choked numbly. He had never felt smaller.

His father focused on him uncertainly. "I—" he began. "He's been hanging by a thread for months, you know that . . ."

And I cut that thread yesterday, Miles thought miserably. I'm sorry. . . . But he said only, "Yes, sir."

The funeral for the old hero was nearly a State occasion. Three days of panoply and pantomime, thought Miles wearily; what's it all for? Proper clothing was produced, hastily, in somber correct black. Vorkosigan House became a chaotic staging-area for forays into public set-pieces. The lying-in-state at Vorhartung Castle, where the Council of Counts met. The eulogies. The procession, which was nearly a parade, thanks to the loan from Gregor Vorbarra of a military band in dress uniform and a contingent of his purely decorative horse cavalry. The interment.

Miles had thought his grandfather was the last of his generation. Not quite, it seemed, for the damnedest set of ancient creaking martinets and their crones, in black like napping crows, came creeping from whatever woodwork they'd been lurking in. Miles, grimly polite, endured their shocked and pitying stares when introduced as Piotr Vorkosigan's grandson, and their interminable reminiscences about people he'd never heard of, who'd died before he was born, and of whom—he sincerely hoped—he would never hear again.

Even after the last spadeful of dirt had been packed down, it was not ended. Vorkosigan House was invaded, that afternoon and evening, by hordes of—you couldn't call them well-wishers, exactly, he reflected—but friends, acquaintances, military men, public men, their wives, the courteous, the curious, and more relatives than he cared to think about.

Count and Countess Vorkosigan were nailed downstairs. Social duty was always yoked, for his father, to political duty, and so was doubly inescapable. But when his cousin Ivan Vorpatril arrived, in tow of his mother Lady Vorpatril, Miles determined to escape to the only bolt-hole left not occupied by enemy forces. Ivan had passed his candidacy exams, Miles had heard; he didn't think he could tolerate the details. He plucked a couple of gaudy blooms from a funeral floral display in passing, and fled by lift tube to the top floor, and refuge.

Miles knocked on the carved wood door. "Who's there?" Elena's voice floated through faintly. He tried the enamel-patterned knob, found it unlocked, and snaked a hand waving the flowers around the door. Her voice added, "Oh, come in, Miles."

He bobbed around the door, lean in black, and grinned tentatively. She was sitting in an antique chair by her window. "How did you know it was me?" Miles asked.

"Well, it was either you or—nobody brings me flowers on their knees." Her eye lingered a moment on the doorknob, unconsciously revealing the height scale used for her deduction.

Miles promptly dropped to his knees and quick-marched across the rug, to present his offering with a flourish. "Voila!" he cried, surprising a laugh from her. His legs protested this abuse by going into painful cramping spasms. "Ah . . ." He cleared his throat, and added in a much smaller voice, "Do you suppose you could help me up? These damn grav-crutches . . ."

"Oh, dear." Elena assisted him on to her narrow bed, made him put his legs out straight, and returned to her chair.

Miles looked around the tiny bedroom. "Is this closet the best we can do for you?"

"I like it. I like the window on the street," she assured him. "It's bigger than my father's room here." She tested the flowers' scent, a musty green odor. Miles immediately regretted not sorting through to find some of the more perfumy kind. She looked up at him in sudden suspicion. "Miles, where did you get these?"

He flushed, faintly guilty. "Borrowed 'em from Grandfather. Believe me, they'll never be missed. It's a jungle down there."

She shook her head helplessly. "You're incorrigible." But she smiled.

"You don't mind?" he asked anxiously. "I thought you'd get more enjoyment from them than he would, at this point."

"Just so nobody thinks I filched them myself!"

"Refer them to me," he offered grandly. He jerked

up his chin. She was gazing into the flowers' delicate structure more somberly. "Now what are you thinking? Sad thoughts?"

"Honestly, my face might as well be a window."

"Not at all. Your face is more like—like water. All reflections and shifting lights—I never know what's lurking in the depths." He dropped his voice at the end, to indicate the mystery of the depths.

Elena smiled derisively, then sighed seriously. "I was just thinking—I've never put flowers on my mother's grave."

He brightened at the prospect of a project. "Do you want to? We could slip out the back—load up a cart or two—nobody'd notice . . ."

"Certainly not!" she said indignantly. "This is quite bad enough of you." She turned the flowers in the light from the window, silvered from the chill autumn cloudiness. "Anyway, I don't know where it is."

"Oh? How strange. As fixated as the Sergeant is on your mother, I'd have thought he'd be just the pilgrimage type. Maybe he doesn't like to think about her death, though."

"You're right about that. I asked him about it once, to go and see where she's buried and so on, and it was like talking to a wall. You know how he can be."

"Yes, very like a wall. Particularly when it falls on someone." A theorizing gleam lit Miles's eye. "Maybe it's guilt. Maybe she was one of those rare women who die in childbirth—she did die about the time you were born, didn't she?"

"He said it was a flyer accident."

"Oh."

"But another time he said she'd drowned."

"Hm?" The gleam deepened to a persistent smoulder. "If she'd ditched her flyer in a river or something, they could both be true. Or if he ditched it . . ."

Elena shivered. Miles caught it, and castigated himself inwardly for being an insensitive clod. "Oh, sorry. Didn't mean to—I'm in a gruesome mood today, I'm afraid," he apologized. "It's all this blasted black." He flapped his elbows in imitation of a carrion bird.

He lapsed into introspective quiet for a time, meditating on the ceremonies of death. Elena fell in with his silence, gazing wistfully down on the darkly glittering throng of Barrayar's upper class, passing in and out four floors below her window.

"We could find out," he said suddenly, startling her from her reverie.

"What?"

"Where your mother's buried. And we wouldn't even have to ask anyone."

"How?"

He grinned, swinging to his feet. "I'm not going to say. You'd go all wobbly on me, like that time we went spelunking down at Vorkosigan Surleau and found the old guerilla weapons cache. You'll never get another chance in your life to drive one of those old tanks, you know."

She made doubtful noises. Apparently her memory of the incident was vivid and awful, even though she had avoided being caught in the landslide. But she followed.

They entered the darkened downstairs library cautiously. Miles paused to brace the duty guard outside it with an off-color smirk, lowering his voice confidentially. "Suppose you could sort of rattle the door if anyone comes, Corporal? We'd, ah—rather not have any surprise interruptions."

The duty guard's return smirk was knowing. "Of course, Lord Mi—Lord Vorkosigan." He eyed Elena with fresh speculation, one eyebrow quirking.

"Miles," Elena whispered furiously as the door swung closed, cutting off the steady murmur of voices, clink of glass and silver, soft tread of feet from Piotr Vorkosigan's wake that penetrated from nearby rooms. "Do you realize what he's going to think?"

"Evil to him who evil thinks," he flung gaily over his shoulder. "Just so he doesn't think of this . . ." He palmed the lock to the comconsole, with its double-scrambled links to military headquarters and the Imperial Residence, that sat incongruously before the carved marble fireplace. Elena's mouth fell open in astonishment as its force screen parted. A few passes of his hands brought the holovid plates to life.

"I thought that was top security!" she gasped.

"'Tis. But Captain Koudelka was giving me a little tutoring on the side, before, when I was—" a bitter smile, a jerk of the wrist, "studying. He used to tap into the battle computers—the real ones, at headquarters—and run simulations for me. I thought he might not have remembered to unkey me . . ." He was half-absorbed, entering a tattoo of complex directions.

"What are you doing?" she asked nervously.

"Entering Captain Koudelka's access code. To get military records."

"Ye gods, Miles!"

"Don't worry about it." He patted her hand. "We're in here necking, remember? Nobody's likely to come in here tonight but Captain Koudelka, and he won't mind that. We can't miss. Thought I'd start with your father's Service record. Ah, here . . ." The holovid plate threw up a flat screen and began displaying written records. "There's bound to be something about your mother on it, that we can use to unravel," he paused, sitting back puzzled, "the mystery . . ." He flipped through several screens.

"What?" Elena agitated.

"Thought I'd peek into near the time you were born—I thought he'd quit the Service just before, right?"

"Right."

"Did he ever say he was involuntarily medically discharged?"

"No . . ." She peered over his shoulder. "That's funny. It doesn't say why."

"Tell you what's funnier. His entire record for most of the preceding year is sealed. Your time. And the code on it—very hot. I can't crack it without triggering a double-check, which would end—yes, that's Captain Illyan's personal mark. I definitely don't want to talk to him." He quailed at the thought of accidentally summoning the attention of Barrayar's Chief of Imperial Security.

"Definitely," croaked Elena, staring at him in fascination.

"Well, let's do some time-travelling," Miles pattered on. "Back, back . . . Your father doesn't seem to have gotten along too well with this Commodore Vorrutyer fellow."

Elena perked with interest. "Was that the same as the Admiral Vorrutyer who was killed at Escobar?"

"Um . . . Yes, Ges Vorrutyer. Hm." Bothari had been the commodore's batman, it appeared, for several years. Miles was surprised. He'd had the vague impression that Bothari had served under his father as a ground combat soldier since the beginning of time. Bothari's service with Vorrutyer ended in a constellation of reprimands, black marks, discipline parades, and sealed medical reports. Miles, conscious of Elena staring over his shoulder, whipped past these quickly. Oddly inconsistent. Some, bizarrely petty, were marked with ferocious punishments. Others, astonishingly serious—had Bothari really held an engineering tech at plasma-arc-point in a lavatory for sixteen hours? and for God's sake, why?—disappeared into the medical reports and resulted in no discipline at all.

Going farther into the past, the record steadied. A lot of combat in his twenties. Commendations, citations for being wounded, more commendations. Excellent marks in basic training. Recruiting records. "Recruiting was a lot simpler in those days," Miles said enviously.

"Oh! Are my grandparents on that?" asked Elena eagerly. "He never talks about them, either. I gather his mother died when he was rather young. He's never even told me her name."

"Marusia," Miles sounded out, peering. "Fuzzy photostat."

"That's pretty," said Elena, sounding pleased. "And his father's?"

Whoops, thought Miles. The recopied photostat was not so fuzzy that he couldn't make out the blunt, uncapitalized "unknown" printed in some forgotten clerk's hand. Miles swallowed, realizing at last why a certain insulting epithet seemed to get under Bothari's skin when all others were allowed to roll off, patiently disdained.

"Maybe I can make it out," Elena offered, misinterpreting his delay.

The screen went blank at a twitch of his hand. "Konstantine," Miles declared firmly, without hesitation. "Same as his. But both his parents were dead by the time he joined the Service."

"Konstantine Bothari junior," Elena mused. "Hm."

Miles stared into the blank screen, and suppressed an urge to scream with frustration. Another damned artificial social wedge driven between himself and Elena. A father who was a bastard was about as far from being "right and proper" for a young Barrayaran virgin as anything he could think of. And it was obviously no secret—his father must know, and God knew how many hundreds of other people besides. Equally obviously, Elena did not. She was rightfully proud of her father, his elite service, his position of high trust. Miles knew how painfully hard she struggled sometimes for some expression of approval from the old stone carving. How strange to realize that pain might cut both ways—did Bothari then dread the loss of that scarcely acknowledged admiration? Well, the Sergeant's semi-secret was safe with him.

He flipped, fast-forward, through the years of Bothari's life. "Still no sign of your mother," he said to Elena. "She must be under that seal. Damn, and I thought this was going to be easy." He stared thoughtfully into space. "Try hospital records. Deaths, births—you sure you were born here in Vorbarr Sultana?"

"As far as I know."

Several minutes of tedious search produced records on a fair number of Botharis, none related to the Sergeant or Elena in any way. "Ah ha!" Miles broke out suddenly. "I know what I haven't tried. Imp Mil!"

"They don't have an obstetrics department," Elena said doubtfully.

"But if an accident—soldier's wife and all that—maybe she was rushed to the nearest facility, and the Imperial Military Hospital was it . . ." He crooned over the machine. "Searching, searching . . . huh!"

"Did you find me?" she asked excitedly.

"No—I found me." He flipped over screen after screen of documentation. "What a scramble it must have been, making military research clean up after its own product. Lucky for me they'd imported those uterine replicators—yes, there they are—they could never have tried some of those treatments *in vivo*, they'd have killed Mother. There's good old Dr. Vaagen—ah ha! So he was in military research, before.

Makes sense—I guess he was their poison expert. I wish I'd known more about this when I was a kid, I could have agitated for two birthdays, one when Mother had the cesarian, and one when they finally popped me out of the replicator."

"Which did they choose?"

"Cesarian day. I'm glad. Makes me only six months younger than you are. Otherwise you'd be nearly a year older—and I've been warned about older women . . ." This babble won a smile at last, and he relaxed a little.

He paused, staring at the screen with slitted eyes, then entered another search query. "That's weird," he muttered.

"What?"

"A secret military medical research project—with my father as project director, no less."

"I never knew he was in research too," said Elena, sounding enormously impressed. "He sure got around."

"That's what's curious. He was a Staff tactician. Never had anything to do with research, as far as I know." A by-now-familiar code appeared at his next inquiry. "Blast! Another seal. Ask a simple question, get a simple brick wall . . . There's Dr. Vaagen, hand-in-rubber-glove with Father. Vaagen must have been doing the actual work, then. That explains that. I want under that seal, damn it . . ." He whistled a soundless tune, staring into space, fingers drumming.

Elena began to look dampened. "You're getting that mulish look," she observed nervously. "Maybe we should just let it go. It doesn't really matter by now."

"Illyan's mark's not on this one. It might be enough . . ."

Elena bit her lip. "Look, Miles, it's not really—" But he was already launched. "What are you doing?"

"Trying one of Father's old access codes. I'm pretty sure of it, all but a few digits."

Elena gulped.

"Jackpot!" Miles cried softly, as the screen began disgorging data at last. He read avidly. "So that's where those uterine replicators came from! They brought them back from Escobar, after the invasion failed. The spoils of war, by God. Seventeen of them, loaded and working. They must have seemed like really high tech, in their day. I wonder if we looted them?"

Elena paled. "Miles—they weren't doing human experiments or, or anything like that, were they? Surely your father wouldn't have countenanced . . ."

"I don't know. Dr. Vaagen can be pretty, um, one-track, about his research . . ." Relief eased his voice. "Oh, I see what was going on. Look here . . ." The holoscreen began scrolling yet another file in midair; he waved his fingers through it. "They were all sent to the Imperial Service Orphanage. They must have been some children of our men killed at Escobar."

Elena's voice tensed. "Children of *men* killed at Escobar? But where are their mothers?"

They stared at each other. "But we've never had any women in the Service, except for a few civilian medtechs," began Miles.

Elena's long fingers closed urgently on his shoulder. "Look at the dates."

He scrolled the file again.

"Miles," she hissed.

"Yes, I see it." He stopped the screen. "Female infant released to the custody of Admiral Aral Vorkosigan. Not sent to the orphanage with the rest."

"The date—Miles, that's my birthday!"

He unpeeled her fingers. "Yes, I know. Don't crush my collarbone, please."

"Could it be me? Is it me?" Her face tightened with hope and dismay.

"I—it's all numbers, you see," he said cautiously.

"But there's plenty of medical identification—footprints, retinal, blood type—stick your foot over here."

Elena hopped about, removing shoes and hose. Miles helped her place her right foot over the holovid plate. He restrained himself with a twitching effort from running a hand up that incredible silken length of thigh, blooming from her rumpled skirts. Skin like an orchid petal. He bit his lips; pain, pain would help him to focus. Damn tight trousers anyway. He hoped she wouldn't notice . . .

Setting up the optical laser check helped his focus rather better. A flickering red light played over her sole for a few seconds. He set the machine to comparing whorls and ridges. "Allowing for the change from infant to adult—my God, Elena, it is you!" He preened. If he couldn't be a soldier, perhaps he had a future as a detective. . . .

Elena's dark gaze transfixed him. "But what does it mean?" Her face congealed suddenly. "Don't I have—was I—am I some kind of clone, or manufactured?" She blinked suddenly liquid eyes, and her voice trembled. "I don't have a mother? No mother, and it was all just—"

The triumph of his successful identification seeped out of him at her distress. Clod! Now he'd turned her dream mother into a nightmare—no, it was her own flying imagination that was doing that. "Uh, uh—no, certainly not! What an idea! You're obviously your father's daughter—no insult intended—it just means your mother was killed at Escobar, instead of here. And furthermore," he sprang up to declaim dramatically, "this makes you my long-lost sister!"

"Huh?" said Elena, bewildered.

"Sure. Or—anyway, there's a 1/17th chance that we came out of the same replicator." He spun about her, conjuring farce against her terrors. "My 1/17th twin sister! It must be Act V! Take heart, this means you're bound to marry the Prince in the next scene!"

She laughed through her tears. The door rattled ominously. The corporal outside declaimed with unnecessary volume, "Good evening, sir!"

"Shoes! My shoes! Give me back my stockings!" hissed Elena.

Miles thrust them at her, killed the comconsole, and sealed it with one frantic, fluid motion. He catapulted onto the sofa, grabbed Elena about the waist and carried her down with him. She giggled and swore at him, struggling with her second shoe. One tear was still making a glistening track down her cheek.

He slipped a hand up into her shining hair, and bent her face toward his. "We better make this look good. I don't want to arouse Captain Koudelka's suspicions." He hesitated, his grin fading into seriousness. Her lips melted onto his.

The lights flicked on; they sprang apart. He peered up over her shoulder, and forgot for a moment how to exhale.

Captain Koudelka. Sergeant Bothari. *And* Count Vorkosigan.

Captain Koudelka looked suffused, a slight upward curl escaping from one corner of his mouth as if from enormous inward pressure. He glanced sideways at his companions, and tamped it out. The Sergeant's craggy face was icy. The Count was darkening rapidly.

Miles finally found something to do with all the air he'd taken in. "All right," he said in a firm didactic tone, "Now, after 'Grant me this boon,' on the next line you say, 'With all my heart; and much it joys me too, to see you are become so penitent.'" He glanced up most impenitently at his father. "Good evening, sir. Are we taking up your space? We can go practice elsewhere . . ."

"Yes, let's," Elena squeaked, picking up her cue with alacrity. She produced a rather inane smile for the three adults as Miles towed her safely past. Captain Koudelka returned the smile with all his heart. The Count somehow managed to smile at her and frown menacingly at Miles at the same time. The Sergeant's frown was democratically universal. The duty guard's smirk broadened to a muffled snicker as they fled down the hall.

"Can't miss, eh?" Elena snarled out of the corner of her mouth at Miles as they rose up the lift tube.

He executed a pirouette in midair, shamelessly. "A strategic withdrawal in good order; what more can you ask for being out-gunned, out-numbered, and out-ranked? We were just practicing that old play. Very cultural. Who could possibly object? I think I'm a genius."

"I think you're an idiot," she said fiercely. "My other stocking is hanging over the back of your shoulder."

"Oh." He twisted his neck for a look, and plucked off the filmy, clinging garment. He held it out to her with a sickly, apologetic smile. "I guess that didn't look too good."

She glared at him and snatched it back. "And now I'm going to get lectured at—he treats every male that comes near me like a potential rapist anyway—he'll probably forbid me to speak to you, too, now. Or send me back to the country forever . . ." Her eyes were swimming for their lives. They reached the door. "And on top of that, he's—he's *lied* to me about my mother—"

She fled into her bedroom, slamming the door so hard that she came close to taking off a few fingers from the hand Miles was raising in protest. He leaned against the door and called through the heavy carved wood anxiously. "You don't know that! There's undoubtedly some perfectly logical explanation—I'll get it figured out—"

"Go AWAY!" her muffled wail came back.

He shuffled uncertainly around the hall for a few more minutes, hoping for a second chance, but the door remained uncompromisingly blank and silent. After a time he became conscious of the stiff figure of the floor duty guard at the end of the corridor. The man was politely not looking at him. The Prime Minister's security detail was, after all, among the most discreet, as well as the most alert, available. Miles swore under his breath, and shuffled back to the lift tube.

CHAPTER FOUR

Miles ran into his mother in the back passage downstairs.

"Have you seen your father lately, heart?" Countess Vorkosigan asked him.

"Yes," unfortunately, "he went into the library with Captain Koudelka and the Sergeant."

"Sneaking off for a drink," she analyzed wryly, "with his old troopers. Well, I can't blame him. He's so tired. It's been a ghastly day. And I know he hasn't gotten enough sleep." She looked him over penetratingly. "How have you been sleeping?"

Miles shrugged. "All right."

"Mm. I'd better go catch him before he has more than one—ethanol has an unfortunate tendency to make him blunt, and that egg-sucker Count Vordrozda just arrived, in company with Admiral Hessman. He'll have trouble ahead if those two are getting in bed together."

"I shouldn't think the far right could muster that much support, with all the old soldiers solidly behind Father."

"Oh, Vordrozda's not a rightist at heart. He's just personally ambitious, and he'll ride any pony that's going his way. He's been oozing around Gregor for months . . ." Anger sparked in her grey eyes. "Flattery and innuendo, oblique criticisms and these nasty little barbs stuck in all the boy's self-doubts—I've watched him at work. I don't like him," she said positively.

Miles grinned. "I never would have guessed. But surely you don't have to worry about Gregor." His mother's habit of referring to the Emperor as if he were her rather backward adopted child always tickled him. In a sense it was true, as the former Regent had been Gregor's personal as well as political guardian during his minority.

She grimaced. "Vordrozda's not the only one who wouldn't hesitate to corrupt the boy in any area he could sink his claws into—moral, political, what you will—if he thought it would advance himself one centimeter, and damn the long range good of Barrayar—or of Gregor, for that matter." Miles recognized this instantly as a quote from his mother's sole political oracle, his father. "I don't know why these people can't write a constitution. Oral law—what a way to try and run an interstellar power." This was homegrown opinion, pure Betan.

"Father's been in power so long," said Miles equably. "I think it would take a gravity torpedo blast to shift him out of office."

"That's been tried," remarked Countess Vorkosigan, growing abstracted. "I wish he'd get serious about retiring. We've been lucky so far," her eye fell on him wistfully, "—mostly."

She's tired too, Miles thought.

"The politicking never stops," she added, staring at the floor. "Not even for his father's funeral." She brightened wickedly. "Nor do his relations. If you see him before I do, tell him Alys Vorpatril's looking for him. That'll make his day—no, better not. We'd never be able to find him, then."

Miles raised his brows. "What does Aunt Vorpatril want him to do for her now?"

"Well, ever since Lord Vorpatril died she's been expecting him to stand in loco parentis to that idiot Ivan, which is fine, up to a point. But she nailed me a while ago, when she couldn't find Aral—seems she wants Aral to stand the boy up in a corner somewhere and brace him for—er—swiving the servant girls, which ought to embarrass them both thoroughly. I've never understood why these people won't clip their kids' tubes and turn them loose at age twelve to work out their own damnation, like sensible folk. You may as well try to stop a sandstorm with a windsock . . ." She went off toward the library, muttering her favorite swear-word under her breath, "Barrayarans!"

Wet darkness had fallen outside, turning the windows into dim mirrors of the subdued and mannered revelry within Vorkosigan House. Miles stared into his own reflection in passing; dark hair, grey eyes, pale shadowed face, features too sharp and strongly marked to satisfy aesthetics. And an idiot, to boot.

The hour reminded him of dinner, probably cancelled due to the press of events. He determined to forage among the canapés, and collect enough to sustain a strategic retreat back to his bedroom for the rest of the evening. He peered around a hall arch, to be sure none of the dreaded geriatric set were nearby. The room appeared to contain only middle-aged people he didn't know. He nipped over to a table, and began stuffing food into a fine fabric napkin.

"Stay away from those purple things," a familiar, affable voice warned in a whisper. "I think they're some kind of seaweed. Is your mother on a nutrition kick again?"

Miles looked up into the open, annoyingly handsome face of his second cousin, Ivan Vorpatril. Ivan too held a napkin, filled close to capacity. His eyes looked slightly hunted. A peculiar bulge interrupted the smooth lines of his brand-new cadet's uniform jacket.

Miles nodded toward the bulge, and whispered in astonishment, "Are they letting you carry a weapon already?"

"Hell, no." Ivan flicked the jacket open after a conspiratorial glance around, probably for Lady Vorpatril. "It's a bottle of your father's wine. Got it from one of the servants before he'd poured it into those itty-bitty glasses. Say—any chance of you being my native guide to some out-of-the-way corner of this mausoleum? The duty guards don't let you wander around by yourself, upstairs. The wine is good, the food is good, except for those purple things, but my God, the company at this party . . . !"

Miles nodded agreement in principle, even though he was inclined to include Ivan himself in the category of *my God the company*. "All right. You pick up another bottle of wine," that should be enough to anesthetize him to tolerance, "and I'll let you hide out in my bedroom. That's where I was going anyway. Meet you by the lift tube."

Miles stretched out his legs on his bed with a sigh as Ivan pooled their picnic and opened the first bottle of wine. Ivan emptied a generous third of the bottle into each of the two bathroom tumblers, and handed one to his crippled cousin.

"I saw old Bothari carrying you off the other day." Ivan nodded toward the injured legs, and took a refreshing gulp. Grandfather, Miles thought, would have had a fit to see that particular vintage treated so cavalierly. He took a more respectful sip himself, by way of libation to the old man's ghost, even though Grandfather's tart assertion that Miles couldn't tell a good vintage from last Tuesday's washwater was not far off the mark. "Too bad," Ivan went on cheerfully. "You're really the lucky one, though."

"Oh?" muttered Miles, closing his teeth on a canape.

"Hell yes. Training starts tomorrow, y'know—"

"So I've heard."

"—I've got to report to my dormitory by midnight at the latest. Thought I was going to spend my last night as a free man partying, but instead I got stuck here. Mother, y'know. But tomorrow we take our preliminary oaths to the Emperor, and by God! if I'll let her treat me like a boy after that!" He paused to consume a small stuffed sandwich. "Think of me, out running around in the rain at dawn tomorrow, while you're tucked away all cozy in here . . ."

"Oh, I will." Miles took another sip, and another.

"Only two breaks in three years," Ivan rambled on between bites. "I might as well be a condemned prisoner. No wonder they call it service. Servitude is more like it." Another gulp, to wash down a meat-stuffed pastry. "But your time is all your own—you can do whatever you want with it."

"Every minute," agreed Miles blandly. Neither the Emperor nor anyone else demanded his service. He couldn't sell it—couldn't give it away. . . .

Ivan, blessedly, fell silent for a few minutes,

refueling. After a time he said hesitantly. "No chance of your father coming up here, is there?"

Miles jerked up his chin. "What, you're not afraid of him, are you?"

Ivan snorted. "The man turns entire General Staffs to pudding, for God's sake. I'm just the Emperor's rawest recruit. Doesn't he terrify you?"

Miles considered the question seriously. "Not exactly, no. Not in the way you mean."

Ivan rolled his eyes heavenward in disbelief.

"Actually," added Miles, thinking back to the recent scene in the library, "if you're trying to duck him this might not be the best place, tonight."

"Oh?" Ivan swirled his wine in the bottom of his cup. "I've always had the feeling he doesn't like me," he added glumly.

"Oh, he doesn't mind you," said Miles, taking pity. "At least as you appear on his horizon at all. Although I think I was fourteen before I found out that Ivan wasn't your middle name." Miles cut himself off. That-idiot-Ivan was beginning a lifetime of Imperial service tomorrow. Lucky-Miles was emphatically not. He took another gulp of wine, and longed for sleep. They finished the canapes, and Ivan emptied the first bottle and opened the second.

There came an authoritative double knock on the door. Ivan sprang to his feet. "Oh, hell, that's not him, is it?"

"A junior officer," said Miles, "is required to stand and salute when a senior officer enters. Not hide under the bed."

"I wasn't thinking of hiding under the bed!" said Ivan, stung. "Just in the bathroom."

"Don't bother. I guarantee there'll be so much covering fire you'll be able to retreat totally unnoticed." Miles raised his voice. "Come!"

It was indeed Count Vorkosigan. He pinned his son with eyes cold and grey as a glacier on a sunless day, and began without preamble, "Miles, what did you do to make that girl cr—" He broke off as his gaze passed over Ivan, standing at attention like a man stuffed. Count Vorkosigan's voice returned to a more normal growl. "Oh, hell. I was hoping to avoid tripping over you tonight. Figured you'd be getting safely drunk in a corner on my wine—"

Ivan saluted nervously. "Sir. Uncle Aral. Did, um, did my mother speak with you, sir?"

"Yes," Count Vorkosigan sighed. Ivan paled. Miles realized Ivan did not see the amusement in the hooded set of his father's eyelids.

Miles ran a finger pensively around the lip of the empty wine bottle. "Ivan has been commiserating me upon my injuries, sir." Ivan nodded confirmation.

"I see," said Count Vorkosigan dryly—and Miles felt he really did. The coldness sublimated altogether. Count Vorkosigan sighed again, and addressed Ivan in a tone of gentle, rhetorical complaint. "Going on fifty years of military and political service, and what am I? A boogey-man, used to frighten boys into good behavior—like the Baba Yaga, who only eats the bad little children." He spread his arms, and added sardonically, "Boo. Consider yourself chastized, and take yourself off. Go, boy."

"Yes, sir." Ivan saluted again, looking decidedly relieved.

"And stop saluting me," Count Vorkosigan added more sharply. "You're not an officer yet." He seemed to notice Ivan's uniform for the first time. "As a matter of fact—"

"Yes, sir. No, sir." Ivan began to salute again, stopped himself, looked confused, and fled. Count Vorkosigan's lips twitched.

And I never thought I'd be grateful to Ivan, Miles mused. "You were saying, sir?" he prompted.

It took Count Vorkosigan a moment to collect his thoughts after the diversion provided by his young relative. He opened again, more quietly. "Why was Elena crying, son? You weren't, ah, harassing her, were you?"

"No, sir. I know what it looked like, but it wasn't. I'll give you my word, if you like."

"Not necessary." Count Vorkosigan pulled up a chair. "I trust you were not emulating that idiot Ivan. But, ah—your mother's Betan sexual philosophy has its place—on Beta Colony. Perhaps here too, someday. But I should like to emphasize that Elena Bothari is not a suitable test case."

"Why not?" said Miles suddenly. Count Vorkosigan raised his eyebrows. "I mean," Miles explained quickly, "why should she be so—so constrained? She gets duenna'd to death. She could be anything. She's bright, and she's, she's good-looking, and she could break me in half—why shouldn't she get a better education, for instance? The Sergeant isn't planning any higher education for her at all. Everything he's saved is for dowry. And he never lets her go anyplace. She'd get more out of travel—hell, she'd appreciate it a thousand times more than any other girl I know." He paused, a little breathless.

Count Vorkosigan pursed his lips, and ran his hand thoughtfully across the chair back. "This is all very true. But Elena—means enormously more to the Sergeant than I think you are aware. She is a symbol to him, of everything he imagines . . . I'm not sure how to put this. She is an important source of order in his life. I owe it to him to protect that order."

"Yes, yes, right and proper, I know," said Miles impatiently. "But you can't owe everything to him and nothing to her!"

Count Vorkosigan looked disturbed, and began again. "I owe him my life, Miles. And your mother's. In a very real sense, everything I've been and done for Barrayar in the last eighteen years is owed to him. And I owe him your life, twice over, since then, and so my sanity—what there is of it, as your mother would say. If he chooses to call in that debt, there's no bottom to it." He rubbed his lips introspectively. "Also—it won't hurt to emphasize this anyway—I'd much prefer to avoid any kind of scandal in my household at the moment. My adversaries are always groping for a handle on me, some lever to move me. I beg you will not let yourself become one."

And what the hell is going on in the government this week? Miles wondered anew. Not that anybody's likely to tell me. Lord Miles Naismith Vorkosigan. Occupation: security risk. Hobbies: falling off walls, disappointing sick old men to death, making girls cry . . . He longed to patch things up with Elena, at least. But the only thing he could think of that might put her imagination-generated terrors to rest would be actually finding that blasted grave, and as near as he could figure, it had to be on Escobar, mixed in with those of the six or seven thousand war dead left behind so long ago.

Between opening his mouth, and speaking, the plan possessed him. The result was that he forgot what he'd been about to say, and sat with his mouth open a moment. Count Vorkosigan raised his eyebrows in courteous inquiry. What Miles finally said instead was, "Has anyone heard from Grandmother Naismith lately?"

Count Vorkosigan's eyes narrowed. "Curious that you should mention her. Your mother has spoken of her quite frequently in the last few days."

"Makes sense, under the circumstances. Although

Grandmother's such a healthy old bird—all Betans expect to live to be 120, I guess. They think it's one of their civil rights."

Miles's Betan grandmother, seven wormhole jumps and three weeks' travel time away by the most direct route—via Escobar. A carefully chosen commercial passenger liner might well include a layover at Escobar. Time for a little tourism—time for a little research. It could be done subtly enough, even with Bothari hanging over his shoulder. What could be more natural than for a boy interested in military history to make a pilgrimage to the cemeteries of his Emperor's soldiers, maybe even burn a death offering? "Sir," he began, "do you suppose I could—"

And, "Son," Count Vorkosigan began at the same moment, "How would you like to deputize for your mother—"

"I beg your pardon," and "Go ahead, sir."

"I was about to say," continued the Count, "that this might be a very opportune time for you to visit your Grandmother Naismith again. It's been what, almost two years since you were to Beta Colony? And while Betans may expect to live to be 120—well, you never know."

Miles untangled his tongue, and managed not to lurch. "What a wonderful idea! Uh—could I take Elena?"

There went the eyebrows again. "What?"

Miles swung to his feet, and shuffled back and forth across the room, unable to contain his outpouring of schemes in stillness. Give Elena a trip off-planet? My God, he'd be a hero in her eyes, a sheer two meters tall, like Vorthalia the Bold. "Yes, sure—why not? Bothari will be with me anyway—who could be a more right and proper chaperone than her own father? Who could object?"

"Bothari," said Count Vorkosigan bluntly. "I can't imagine him warming to the thought of exposing Elena to Beta Colony. After all, he's seen it. And coming from you, ah, just at the moment, I'm not at all sure he'd perceive it as a proper invitation."

"Mm." Shuffle, turn, shuffle. Flash! "Then I won't invite her."

"Ah." Count Vorkosigan relaxed. "Wise, I'm sure . . ."

"I'll have Mother invite her. Let's see him object to that!"

Count Vorkosigan emitted a surprised laugh. "Underhanded, boy!" But his tone was approving. Miles's heart lifted.

"This trip idea was really hers, wasn't it, sir?" Miles said.

"Well—yes," Count Vorkosigan admitted. "But in fact, I was glad she suggested it. It would—ease my mind, to have you safe on Beta Colony for the next few months." He rose. "You must excuse me. Duty calls. I have to go feel up that rampant creeper Vordrozda, for the greater glory of the Empire." His expression of distaste spoke volumes. "Frankly, I'd rather be getting drunk in a corner with that idiot Ivan—or talking to you." His father's eyes were warm upon him.

"Your work comes first, of course, sir. I understand that."

Count Vorkosigan paused, and gave him a peculiar look. "Then you understand nothing. My work has been a blight on you from the very beginning. I'm sorry, sorry it made such a mess for you—"

Mess of you, thought Miles. *Say what you really mean, damn it.*

"—I never meant it to be so." A nod, and he withdrew.

Apologizing to me again, thought Miles miserably.

For me. He keeps telling me I'm all right—and then apologizing. Inconsistent, Father.

He shuffled back and forth across the room again, and his pain burst into speech. He flung his words against the deaf door, "I'll make you take back that apology! I am all right, damn it! I'll make you see it. I'll stuff you so full of pride in me there'll be no room left for your precious guilt! I swear by my word as Vorkosigan. I swear it, Father," his voice fell to a whisper, "Grandfather. Somehow, I don't know how . . ."

He took another turn around his chamber, collapsing back into himself, cold and desperately sleepy. A mess of crumbs, an empty wine bottle, an open full one. Silence.

"Talking to yourself in an empty room again, I see," he whispered. "A very bad sign, you know."

His legs hurt. He cradled the second bottle, and took it with him to lie down.

CHAPTER FIVE

"Well, well, well," said the sleek Betan customs agent, in sarcastic simulation of good cheer. "If it isn't Sergeant Bothari of Barrayar. And what did you bring me this time, Sergeant? A few nuclear antipersonnel mines, overlooked in your back pocket? A maser cannon or two, accidentally mixed up with your shaving kit? A gravitic imploder, slipped somehow into your boot?"

The Sergeant answered this sally with something between a growl and a grunt.

Miles grinned, and dredged his memory for the agent's name. "Good afternoon, Officer Timmons. Still working the line, are you? I thought for sure you'd be in administration by now."

The agent gave Miles a somewhat more courteous nod of greeting. "Good afternoon, Lord Vorkosigan. Well, civil service, you know." He sorted through their documents and plugged a data disc into his viewer. "Your stunner permits are in order.

Now if you will please step, one at a time, through this scanner?"

Sergeant Bothari frowned at the machine glumly, and sniffed disdain. Miles tried to catch his eye, but he was studiously finding something of interest in midair somewhere. On the suspicion, Miles said, "Elena and I first, I think."

Elena passed through with a stiff uncertain smile like a person holding still too long for a photograph, then continued to look eagerly around. Even if it was only a rather bleak underground customs entry port, it was another planet. Miles hoped Beta Colony would make up for the disappointing fizzle of the Escobar layover.

Two days of records searches and trudging through neglected military cemeteries in the rain, pretending to Bothari a passion for historical detail, had produced no maternal grave or cenotaph after all. Elena had seemed more relieved than disappointed by the failure of their covert search.

"You see?" she had whispered to Miles. "Father *didn't* lie to me. You have a hyper imagination."

The Sergeant's own bored reaction to the tour clinched the argument; Miles conceded. And yet . . .

It was his hyper imagination, maybe. The less they found the more queasy Miles became. Were they looking in the wrong army's cemetery? Miles's own mother had changed allegiances to return to Barrayar with his father; maybe Bothari's romance had not taken so prosperous a turn. But if that were so, should they even be looking in cemeteries? Maybe he should be hunting Elena's mother in the comm link directory. . . . He did not quite dare suggest it.

He wished he had not been so intimidated by the conspiracy of silence surrounding Elena's birth as to refrain from pumping Countess Vorkosigan. Well, when they returned home he would screw up his courage and demand the truth of her, and let her wisdom guide him as to how much to pass on to Bothari's daughter.

For now, Miles stepped after Elena through the scanner, enjoying her air of wonder, and looking forward like a magician to pulling Beta Colony out of a hat for her delight.

The Sergeant stepped through the machine. It gave a rude blat.

Agent Timmons shook his head and sighed. "You never give up, do you, Sergeant?"

"Ah, if I may interrupt," said Miles, "the lady and I are cleared, are we not?" Receiving a nod, he retrieved their stunners and his own travel documentation. "I'll show Elena around the shuttleport, then, while you two are discussing your, er, differences. You can bring the luggage when he gets done with it, Sergeant. Meet you in the main concourse."

"You will not—" began Bothari.

"We'll be perfectly all right," Miles assured him airily. He grasped Elena's elbow and hustled her off before his bodyguard could marshall further objections.

Elena looked back over her shoulder. "Is my father really trying to smuggle in an illegal weapon?"

"Weapons. I expect so," said Miles apologetically. "I don't authorize it, and it never works, but I guess he feels undressed without deadly force. If the Betans are as good at spotting everyone else's goods as they are at spotting ours, we really don't have anything to worry about."

He watched her, sideways, as they entered the main concourse, and had the satisfaction of seeing her catch her breath. Golden light, at once brilliant and comfortable, spun down from a huge high vault upon a great tropical garden, dark with foliage, vibrant with flowers and birds, murmurous with fountains.

"It's like stepping into a giant terrarium," she commented. "I feel like a little horned hopper."

"Exactly," he agreed. "The Silica Zoo maintains it. One of their extended habitats."

They strolled toward an area given over to small shops. He steered Elena carefully along, trying to pick out things she might enjoy, and avoid catastrophic culture shock. That sex-aids shop, for example, was probably a little too much for her first hour on the planet, no matter how attractive the pink when she blushed. However, they spent a pleasant few minutes in a most extraordinary pet store. His good sense barely restrained him from making her an awkward present of a large ruffed Tau Cetan beaded lizard, bright as jewelry, that caught her eye. It had rather strict dietary requirements, and besides, Miles was not quite sure if the 50-kilo beast could be housebroken. They wandered along a balcony overlooking the great garden, and he bought them rational ice creams, instead. They sat on the bench lining the railing to eat.

"Everything seems so free, here," Elena said, licking her fingers and looking around with shining eyes. "You don't see soldiers and guards all over the place. A woman—a woman could be anything here."

"Depends on what you mean by free," said Miles. "They put up with rules we'd never tolerate at home. You should see everyone fall into place during a power outage drill, or a sandstorm alarm. They have no margin for—I don't know how to put it. Social failures?"

Elena gave him a baffled smile, not understanding. "But everyone arranges their own marriages."

"But did you know you have to have a permit to have a child here? The first one is free, but after that . . ."

"That's absurd," she remarked absently. "How could

they possibly enforce it?" She evidently felt her question to be rather bold, for she took a quick glance around, to be sure the Sergeant was nowhere near.

Miles echoed her glance. "Permanent contraceptive implants, for the women and hermaphrodites. You need the permit to get it removed. It's the custom, at puberty—a girl gets her implant, and her ears pierced, and her, er, um—" Miles discovered he was not immune to pinkness himself—he went on in a rush, "her hymen cut, all on the same visit to the doctor. There's usually a family party—sort of a rite of passage. That's how you can tell if a girl's available, the ears. . . ."

He had her entire attention, now. Her hands stole to her earrings, and she went not merely pink, but red. "Miles! Are they going to think *I'm*—"

"Well, it's just that—if anyone bothers you, I mean if your father or I aren't around, don't be afraid to tell them to take themselves off. They will. They don't mean it as an insult, here. But I figured I'd better warn you." He gnawed a knuckle, eyes crinkling. "You know, if you intend to walk around for the next six weeks with your hands over your ears . . ."

She replaced her hands hastily in her lap, and glowered at him.

"It can get awfully peculiar, I know," he offered apologetically. A scorching memory of just how peculiar disturbed him for a moment.

He had been fifteen on his year-long school visit to Beta Colony, and he'd found himself for the first time in his life with what looked like unlimited possibilities for sexual intimacy. This illusion had crashed and burned very quickly, as he found the most fascinating girls already taken. The rest seemed about equally divided among good Samaritans, the kinky/curious, hermaphrodites, and boys.

He did not care to be an object of charity, and he found himself too Barrayaran for the last two categories, although Betan enough not to mind them for others. A short affair with a girl from the kinky/curious category was enough. Her fascination with the peculiarities of his body made him, in the end, more self-conscious than the most open revulsion he had experienced on Barrayar, with its fierce prejudice against deformity. Anyway, after finding his sexual parts disappointingly normal, the girl had drifted off.

The affair had ended, for Miles, in a terrifying black depression that had deepened for weeks, culminating at last late one night in the third, and most secret, time the Sergeant had saved his life. He had cut Bothari twice, in their silent struggle for the knife, exerting hysterical strength against the Sergeant's frightened caution of breaking his bones. The tall man had finally achieved a grip that held him, and held him, until he broke down at last, weeping his self-hatred into the Sergeant's bloodied breast until exhaustion finally stilled him. The man who'd carried him as a child, before he first walked at age four, then carried him like a child to bed. Bothari treated his own wounds, and never referred to the incident again.

Age fifteen had not been a very good year. Miles was determined not to repeat it. His hand tightened on the balcony railing, in a mood of objectless resolve. Objectless, like himself; therefore useless. He frowned into the black well of this thought, and for a moment even Beta Colony's glitter seemed dull and grey.

Four Betans stood nearby, arguing in a vociferous undertone. Miles turned half around, to get a better view of the speakers past Elena's elbow. Elena began to speak, something about his abstraction. He shook his head, and held up a hand, begging silence. She subsided, watching him curiously.

"Damn it," a heavy man in a green sarong was saying, "I don't care how you do it, but I want that lunatic pried out of my ship. Can't you rush him?"

The woman in the uniform of Betan Security shook her head. "Look, Calhoun, why should I risk my people's lives for a ship that's practically scrap anyway? It's not as if he was holding hostages or something."

"I have a salvage team tied up waiting that's collecting time-and-a-half for overtime. He's been up there three days—he's got to sleep sometime, or take a leak or some goddamn thing," argued the civilian.

"If he's as hopped-up crazy as you claim, nothing would be more likely to trigger his blowing it than a rush. Wait him out." The security woman turned to a man in the dove-grey and black uniform of one of the larger commercial spacelines. Silver hair in his sideburns echoed the triple silver circles of his pilot's neurological implant on midforehead and temples. "Or talk him out. You know him, he's a member of your union, can't you do anything with him?"

"Oh, no you don't," objected the pilot officer. "You're not shoving this one off on me. He doesn't want to talk to me anyway, he's made that clear."

"You're on the Board this year, you ought to have some authority with him—threaten to revoke his pilot's certification or something."

"Arde Mayhew may still be in the Brotherhood, but he's two years in arrears on his dues, his license is on shaky ground already, and frankly, I think this episode is going to cook it. The whole point of this bananarama in the first place is that once the last of the RG ships goes for scrap," the pilot officer nodded toward the bulky civilian, "he isn't going to be a pilot anymore. He's been medically rejected for a new implant—it wouldn't do him any good even if he had the money. And I know damn well he doesn't. He tried to borrow rent money from me last week. At least, he said it was for rent. More likely for that swill he drinks."

"Did you give it to him?" asked the woman in the blue uniform of a shuttleport administrator.

"Well—yes," replied the pilot officer moodily. "But I told him it was absolutely the last. Anyway . . ." he frowned at his boots, then burst out, "I'd rather see him go out in a blaze of glory than die of being beached! I know how I'd feel if I knew I'd never make a jump again . . ." He compressed his lips, defensive-aggressive, at the shuttleport administrator.

"All pilots are crazy," muttered the security woman. "Comes from getting their brains pierced."

So Miles eavesdropped, shamelessly fascinated. The man they were discussing was a fellow-freak, it seemed, a loser in trouble. A wormhole jump pilot with an obsolete coupler system running through his brain, soon to be technologically unemployed, holed up in his old ship, fending off the wrecking crews—how? Miles wondered.

"A blaze of traffic hazards, you mean," complained the shuttleport administrator. "If he makes good on his threats, there'll be junk pelting all through the inner orbits for days. We'd have to shut down—clean it up—" she turned to the civilian, completing the circle, "and you'd better believe it won't be charged to my department! I'll see your company gets the bill if I have to take it all the way to JusDep."

The salvage operator paled, then went red. "Your department permitted that hot-wired freak-head access to my ship in the first place," he snarled.

"He said he'd left some personal effects," she defended. "We didn't know he had anything like this in mind."

Miles pictured the man, huddled in his dim recess, stripped of allies, like the last survivor of a hopeless siege. His hand clenched unconsciously. His ancestor, General Count Selig Vorkosigan, had raised the famous siege of Vorkosigan Surleau with no more than a handful of picked retainers and subterfuge, it was said.

"Elena," he whispered fiercely, stilling her restlessness, "follow my lead, and say nothing."

"Hm?" she murmured, startled.

"Ah, good, Miss Bothari, you're here," he said loudly, as if he had just arrived. He gathered her up and marched up to the group.

He knew he confused strangers as to his age. At first glance, his height led them to underestimate it. At second, his face, slightly dark from a tendency to heavy beard growth in spite of close shaving, and prematurely set from long intimacy with pain, led them to overestimate. He'd found he could tip the balance either way at will, by a simple change of mannerisms. He summoned ten generations of warriors to his back, and produced his most austere smile.

"Good afternoon, ladies, gentlemen," he hailed them. Four stares greeted him, variously nonplused. His urbanity almost crumpled under the onslaught, but he held the line. "I was told one of you could tell me where to find Pilot Officer Arde Mayhew."

"Who the devil are you?" growled the salvage operator, apparently voicing the thought of them all.

Miles bowed smoothly, barely restraining himself from swirling an imaginary cape. "Lord Miles Vorkosigan, of Barrayar, at your service. This is my associate, Miss Bothari. I couldn't help overhearing—I believe I might be of assistance to you all, if you will permit me . . ." Beside him, Elena raised puzzled eyebrows at her new, if vague, official status.

"Look, kid," began the shuttleport administrator.

Miles glanced up from lowered brows, shooting her his best imitation General Count Piotr Vorkosigan military glare.

"—sir," she corrected herself. "Just, uh—just what do you want with Pilot Officer Mayhew?"

Miles gave an upward jerk of his chin. "I have been commissioned to discharge a debt to him." Self-commissioned, about ten seconds ago . . .

"Somebody owes money *to* Arde?" asked the salvage operator, amazed.

Miles drew himself up, looking offended. "Not money," he growled, as though he never touched the sordid stuff. "It's a debt of honor."

The shuttleport administrator looked cautiously impressed; the pilot officer, pleased. The security woman looked dubious. The salvage operator looked extremely dubious. "How does that help me?" he asked bluntly.

"I can talk Pilot Officer Mayhew out of your ship," said Miles, seeing his path opening before him, "if you'll provide me with the means of meeting him face-to-face." Elena gulped; he quelled her with a narrow, sideways flick of a glance.

The four Betans looked one to another, as if responsibility could be shuffled off by eye contact. Finally the pilot officer said, "Well, what the hell. Does anybody have a better idea?"

In the control chair of the personnel shuttle the grey-haired senior pilot officer spoke—once again—into his comconsole. "Arde? Arde, this is Van. Answer me, please? I've brought up somebody to talk things over with you. He's going to come on board. All right, Arde? You're not going to do anything foolish now, are you?"

Silence was his sole reply. "Is he receiving you?" asked Miles.

"His comconsole is. Whether he's got the volume turned up, or is there, or awake, or—or alive, is anybody's guess."

"I'm alive," growled a thick voice suddenly from the speaker, making them both start. There was no video. "But you won't be, Van, if you try to board my ship, you double-crossing son of a bitch."

"I won't try," promised the senior pilot officer. "Just Mister, uh, Lord Vorkosigan, here."

There was a moody silence, if the static-spattered hiss could be so described. "He doesn't work for that bloodsucker Calhoun, does he?" asked the speaker suspiciously.

"He doesn't work for anybody," Van soothed.

"Not for the Mental Health Board? Nobody's going to get near *me* with a damn dart gun—I'll blow us all to hell, first . . ."

"He's not even Betan. He's a Barrayaran. Says he's been looking for you."

Another silence. Then the voice, uncertain, querulous, "I don't owe any Barrayarans—I don't think . . . I don't even know any Barrayarans."

There was an odd feeling of pressure, and a gentle click from the exterior of the hull, as they came in contact with the old freighter. The pilot waved a finger by way of signal at Miles, and Miles made the hatch connections secure. "Ready," he called.

"You sure you want to do this?" whispered the pilot officer.

Miles nodded. It had been a minor miracle, escaping the protection of Bothari. He licked his lips, and grinned, enjoying the exhilaration of weightlessness and fear. He trusted Elena would prevent any unnecessary alarm, planetside.

Miles opened the hatch. There was a puff of air, as

the pressure within the two ships equalized. He stared into a pitch-dark tunnel. "Got a hand light?"

"On the rack there." The pilot officer pointed.

Provided, Miles floated cautiously into the tube. The darkness skulked ahead of him, hiding in corners and cross corridors, and crowding in behind him as he passed. He threaded his way toward the Navigation and Communications Room, where his quarry was presumed to be lurking. The distance was actually short—the crew's quarters were small, most of the ship being given over to cargo space—but the absolute silence gave the journey a subjective stretch. Zero-gee was now having its usual effect on making him regret the last thing he'd eaten. Vanilla, he thought; I should have had vanilla.

There was a dim light ahead, spilling into the corridor from an open hatch. Miles cleared his throat, loudly, as he approached. It might be better not to startle the man, all things considered.

"Pilot Officer Mayhew?" he called softly, and pulled himself to the door. "My name is Miles Vorkosigan, and I'm looking for—looking for—" What the devil was he looking for? Oh, well. Wing it. "I'm looking for desperate men," he finished in style.

Pilot Officer Mayhew sat strapped in his pilot's chair in a mournful huddle. Clutched in his lap were his pilot's headset, a half-full liter squeeze bottle of a gurgling liquid of a brilliant and poisonous green, and a box hastily connected by a spaghetti-mass of wiring to a half-gutted control panel and topped by a toggle switch. Quite as fascinating as the toggle box was a dark, slender, and by Betan law very illegal little needle gun. Mayhew blinked puffed and red-rimmed eyes at the apparition in his doorway, and rubbed a hand—still holding the lethal needler—over a three-day beard stubble. "Oh, yeah?" he replied vaguely.

Miles was temporarily distracted by the needler. "How did you ever get that through Betan customs?" he asked in a tone of genuine admiration. "I've never been able to carry so much as a slingshot past 'em."

Mayhew stared at the needler in his hand as if he'd just discovered it, like a wart grown unnoticed. "Bought it at Jackson's Whole once. I've never tried to take it off the ship. I suppose they'd take it away from me, if I tried. They take everything away from you, down there." He sighed.

Miles eased into the room, and arranged himself cross-legged in midair, in what he hoped was a nice, nonthreatening sort of listening posture. "How did you ever get into this fix?" he asked, with a nod around that included the ship, the situation, and Mayhew's lap-full of objects.

Mayhew shrugged. "Rotten luck. I've always had rotten luck. That accident with the RG 88—it was the moisture from those busted amphor tubes that soaked those dal bags that swelled and split the bulkhead and started the whole thing. The 'port cargo master didn't even get a slap on the wrist. Damn it, what I did or didn't have to drink wouldn't have made a damn bit of difference!" He sniffed, and drew a sleeve across his flushed face, looking alarmingly as if he were about to weep. It was a very disturbing thing to see in a man pushing, Miles estimated, forty years of age. Mayhew took a swig from his bottle instead, then with some dim remnant of courtesy offered it to Miles.

Miles smiled politely and took it. Should he grab this chance to dump it out, in the interests of sobering Mayhew up? There were drawbacks to the idea, in free fall. It would have to be dumped into something else, if he were not to spend his visit dodging flying blobs of whatever-it-was. Hard to make it look like an accident. While he mulled, he sampled it, in the interests of scientific inquiry.

He barely managed not to choke it into free fall, atomized. Thick, green herbal, sweet as syrup—he nearly gagged on the sweetness—perhaps 60% pure ethanol. But what was the rest of it? It burned down his esophagus, making him feel suddenly like an animated display of the digestive system, with all the different parts picked out in colored lights. Respectfully, he wiped the mouthpiece on his sleeve and handed the bottle to its owner, who tucked it back under his arm.

"Thanks," Miles gasped. Mayhew nodded. "So how," Miles aspirated, then cleared his throat to a more normal tone, "what are you planning to do next? What are you demanding?"

"Demanding?" said Mayhew. "Next? I don't—I'm just not going to let that cannibal Calhoun murder my ship. There isn't—there isn't any next." He rocked the box with the toggle switch on his lap, a miserable madonna. "Have you ever been red?" he asked suddenly.

Miles had a confused vision of ancient Earth political parties. "No, I'm Vor," he said, not sure if that was the right response. But it seemed not to matter. Mayhew soliloquized on.

"Red. The color red. Pure light I was, once, on the jump to some little hole of a place called Hespari II. There's no experience in life like a jump. If you've never ridden the lights in your brain—colors no man's ever put a name to—there are no words for it. Better than dreams, or nightmares—better than a woman—better than food or drink or sleep or breath—and they pay us for it! Poor deluded suckers, with nothing under their skulls but protoplasm . . ." He peered blurrily at Miles. "Oh, sorry. Nothing personal.

You're just not a pilot. I never took a cargo to Hespari again." He focused on Miles a little more clearly. "Say, you're a mess, aren't you?"

"Not as much of a mess as you are," Miles replied frankly, nettled.

"Mm," the pilot agreed. He passed his bottle back.

Curious stuff, thought Miles. Whatever was in it seemed to be counteracting the usual effect ethanol had on him of putting him to sleep. He felt warm and energetic, as if it flowed right down to his fingers and toes. It was probably how Mayhew had kept awake for three days, alone in this deserted can.

"So," Miles went on scornfully, "you haven't got a battle plan. You haven't asked for a million Betan dollars in small unmarked slips, or threatened to drop the ship through the roof of the shuttleport, or taken hostages, or—or *anything* constructive at all. You're just sitting up here, killing time and your bottle, and wasting your opportunities, for want of a little resolve, or imagination, or something."

Mayhew blinked at this unexpected point of view. "By God, Van told the truth for once. You're *not* from the Mental Health Board. . . . I could take you hostage," he offered placatingly, swinging the needler toward Miles.

"No, don't do that," said Miles hastily. "I can't explain, but—they'd overreact, down there. It's a bad idea."

"Oh." The needler's aim drifted off. "But anyway, don't you see," he tapped his headset, attempting to explain, "what I want, they can't give me? I want to ride the jumps. And I can't, not any more."

"Only in this ship, I gather."

"This ship is going for scrap," his despair was flat, unexpectedly rational, "just as soon as I can't stay awake any more."

"That's a useless attitude," scoffed Miles. "Apply a little logic to the problem, at least. I mean like this. You want to be a jump pilot. You can only be a jump pilot for an RG ship. This is the last RG ship. Ergo, what you need is this ship. So get it. Be a pilot-owner. Run your own cargos. Simple, see? May I have some more of that stuff, please?" One got used to the ghastly taste quite quickly, Miles found.

Mayhew shook his head, clutching his despair and his toggle box to him like a familiar, comforting child's toy. "I tried. I've tried everything. I thought I had a loan. It folded, and anyway, Calhoun outbid me."

"Oh." Miles passed the bottle back, feeling deflated. He gazed at the pilot, to whom he was now floating at right angles. "Well, all I know is, you can't give up. Shur—surrender besmirches the honor of the Vor." He began to hum a little, a snatch of some half-remembered childhood ballad: "The Siege of Silver Moon." It had a Vor lord in it, he recalled, and a beautiful witch-woman who rode in a magic flying mortar; they had pounded their enemies' bones in it, at the end. "Gimme another drink. I want to think. 'If thou wilt swear thyself to me, thy liege lord true to thee I'll be . . .'"

"Huh?" said Mayhew.

Miles realized he'd been singing aloud, albeit softly. "Nothing, sorry." He floated in silence a few minutes longer. "That's the trouble with the Betan system," he said after a time. "Nobody takes personal responsibility for anyone. It's all these faceless fictional corporate entities—government by ghosts. What you need is a liege lord, to take sword in hand and slice through all the red tape. Just like Vorthalia the Bold and the Thicket of Thorns."

"What I need is a drink," said Mayhew glumly.

"Hm? Oh, sorry." Miles handed the bottle back. An

idea was forming up in the back of his mind, like a nebula just starting to contract. A little more mass, and it would start to glow, a proto star. . . . "I have it!" he cried, straightening out suddenly, and accidently giving himself an unwanted spin.

Mayhew flinched, nearly firing his needler through the floor. He glanced uncertainly at the squeeze bottle. "No, I have it," he corrected.

Miles overcame the spin. "We'd better do this from here. The first principle of strategy—never give up an advantage. Can I use your comconsole?"

"What for?"

"I," said Miles grandly, "am going to buy this ship. And then I shall hire *you* to pilot it."

Mayhew stared in bewilderment, looking from Miles to the bottle and back. "You got that much money?"

"Mm . . . Well, I have *assets* . . ."

A few minutes' work with the comconsole brought the salvage operator's face on the screen. Miles put his proposition succinctly. Calhoun's expression went from disbelief to outrage.

"You call that a compromise?" he cried. "At cost! And backed by—I'm not a damned real estate broker!"

"Mr. Calhoun," said Miles sweetly, "may I point out, the choice is not between my note and this ship. The choice is between my note and a rain of glowing debris."

"If I find out you're in collusion with that—"

"Never met him before today," Miles disclaimed.

"What's wrong with the land?" asked Calhoun suspiciously. "Besides being on Barrayar, I mean."

"It's like fertile farm country," Miles answered, not quite directly. "Wooded—one hundred centimeters of rain a year—" that ought to fetch a Betan, "barely three hundred kilometers from the capital."

Downwind, fortunately for the capital. "And I own it absolutely. Just inherited it from my grandfather recently. Go ahead and check it through the Barrayaran Embassy. Check the climate plats."

"This rainfall—it's not all on the same day or something, is it?"

"Of course not," replied Miles, straightening indignantly. Not easy, in free fall. "Ancestral land—it's been in my family for ten generations. You can believe I'll make every effort to cover that note before I'll let my home ground fall from my hands—"

Calhoun rubbed his chin irritably. "Cost plus twenty-five percent," he suggested.

"Ten percent."

"Twenty."

"Ten, or I'll let you deal directly with Pilot Officer Mayhew."

"All right," groaned Calhoun, "ten percent."

"Done!"

It was not quite that easy, of course. But thanks to the efficiency of the Betans' planetary information network, a transaction that would have taken days on Barrayar was completed in less than an hour, right from Mayhew's control room. Miles was cannily reluctant to give up the tactical bargaining advantage possession of the toggle box gave them, and Mayhew, after his first astonishment had worn off, became silent and loath to leave.

"Look, kid," he spoke suddenly, about halfway through the complicated transaction. "I appreciate what you're trying to do, but—but it's just too late. You understand, when I get downside, they're not going to just be laughing this off. Security'll be waiting at the docking bay, with a patrol from the Mental Health Board right beside 'em. They'll slap a stun-net over me so fast—you'll see me in a month or two, walking around smiling. You're always smiling, after the M.H.B. gets done . . ." He shook his head helplessly. "It's just too late."

"It's never too late while you're breathing," snapped Miles. He did the free-fall equivalent of pacing the room, shoving off from one wall, turning in midair, and shoving off from the opposite wall, a few dozen turns, thinking.

"I have an idea," he said at last. "I'll wager it would buy time, time enough at least to come up with something better—trouble is, since you're not Barrayaran, you're not going to understand what you're doing, and it's serious stuff."

Mayhew looked thoroughly baffled. "Huh?"

"It's like this." Thump, spin, turn, straighten, thump. "If you were to swear fealty to me as an Armsman simple, taking me for your liege lord—it's the most straightforward of our oath relationships—I *might* be able to include you under my Class III diplomatic immunity. Anyway, I know I could if you were a Barrayaran subject. Of course, you're a Betan citizen. In any case, I'm pretty sure we could tie up a pack of lawyers and several days, trying to figure out which laws take precedence. I would be legally obligated for your bed, board, dress, armament—I suppose this ship could be classed as your armament—your protection, in the event of challenge by any other liegeman—that hardly applies, here on Beta Colony—oh, there's a passel of stuff, about your family, and—do you have a family, by the way?"

Mayhew shook his head.

"That simplifies things." Thump, spin, turn, straighten, thump. "Meanwhile, neither Security nor the M.H.B. could touch you, because legally you'd be like a part of my body."

Mayhew blinked. "That sounds screwy as hell. Where do I sign? How do you register it?"

"All you have to do is kneel, place your hands between mine, and repeat about two sentences. It doesn't even need witnesses, although it's customary to have two."

Mayhew shrugged. "All right. Sure, kid."

Thump, spin, turn, straighten, thump. "All-right-sure-kid. I thought you wouldn't understand it. What I've described is only a tiny part of my half of the bargain, your privileges. It also includes your obligations, and a ream of rights I have over you. For instance—just one for-instance—if you were to refuse to carry out an order of mine in the heat of battle, I would have the right to strike off your head. On the spot."

Mayhew's jaw dropped. "You realize," he said at last, "the Mental Health Board's going to drop a net over you, too. . . ."

Miles grinned sardonically. "They can't. Because if they tried, I could cry havoc to my liege lord for protection. And I'd get it, too. He's pretty touchy about who does what to his subjects. Oh, that's another angle. If you become a liegeman to me, it automatically puts you into a relationship with *my* liege lord, kind of a complicated one."

"And his, and his, and his, I suppose," said Mayhew. "I know all about chains of command."

"Well, no, that's as far as it goes. I'm sworn directly to Gregor Vorbarra, as a vassal secundus." Miles realized he might as well be talking gibberish, for all the meaning his words were conveying.

"Who's this Greg-guy?" asked Mayhew.

"The Emperor. Of Barrayar," Miles added, just to be sure he understood.

"Oh."

Typical Betan, thought Miles, they don't study anybody's history but Earth's and their own. "Think about it, anyway. It's not something you should just jump into."

When the last voice-print had been recorded, Mayhew carefully disconnected the toggle box—Miles held his breath—and the senior pilot officer returned to convey them planetside.

The senior pilot officer addressed Miles with a shade more respect in his voice. "I had no idea you were from such a wealthy family, Lord Vorkosigan. That was a solution to the problem I certainly hadn't anticipated. But perhaps one ship is just a bauble, to a Barrayaran lord."

"Not really," said Miles. "I'm going to have to do some hustling to cover that note. My family used to be well off, I admit, but that was back in the Time of Isolation. Between the economic upheavals at the end of it, and the First Cetagandan War, we were pretty much wiped out, financially." He grinned a little. "You galactics got us coming and going. My great-grandfather on the Vorkosigan side, when the first galactic traders hit us, thought he was going to make a killing in jewels—you know, diamonds, rubies, emeralds—the galactics seemed to be selling them so cheaply. He put all his liquid assets and about half his chattels into them. Well, of course they were synthetics, better than the naturals and cheap as dirt—uh, sand—and the bottom promptly dropped out of the market, taking him with it. I'm told my great-grandmother never forgave him." He waved vaguely at Mayhew who, becoming conditioned, passed over his bottle. Miles offered it to the senior pilot officer, who rejected it with a look of disgust. Miles shrugged, and took a long pull. Amazingly pleasant stuff. His circulatory system, as well as his digestive, now seemed to be glowing with rainbow hues. He felt he could go days without sleep.

"Unfortunately, most of the land he sold was around

Vorkosigan Surleau, which is pretty dry—not by your standards, of course—and the land he kept was around Vorkosigan Vashnoi, which was the better."

"What's unfortunate about that?" asked Mayhew.

"Well, because it was the principal seat of government for the Vorkosigans, and because we owned about every stick and stone in it—it was a pretty important industrial and trade center—and because the Vorkosigans were, uh, prominent in the Resistance, the Cetagandans took the city hostage. It's a long story, but—eventually, they destroyed the place. It's now a big glass hole in the ground. You can still see a faint glow in the sky, on a dark night, twenty kilometers off."

The senior pilot officer brought the little shuttle smoothly into its dock.

"Hey," said Mayhew suddenly. "That land you had around Vorkosigan whatever-you-said—"

"Vashnoi. Have. Hundreds of square kilometers of it, and mostly downwind, yes?"

"Is that the same—" his face was lighting, like the sun coming up after a long, dark night, "is that the same land you mortgaged to—" He began to laugh, delightedly, under his breath; they disembarked. "Is *that* what you pledged to that sand-crawler Calhoun in return for my ship?"

"Caveat emptor," bowed Miles. "He checked the climate plat; he never thought to check the radioactivity plat. He probably doesn't study anybody else's history either."

Mayhew sat down on the docking bay, laughing so hard that he bent his forehead nearly to the floor. His laughter had more than an edge of hysteria—several days without sleep, after all . . . "Kid," he cried, "have a drink on me!"

"I mean to pay him, you understand," explained Miles. "The hectares he chose would make an unaesthetic hole in the map for some descendant of mine, in a few hundred years, when it cools off. But if he gets greedy, or pushy about collecting—well, he'll get what he deserves."

Three groups of people were bearing down upon them. Bothari had escaped customs at last, it appeared, for he led the first group. His collar was undone, and he looked decidedly ruffled. Uh oh, thought Miles, it looks like he's had a strip-search—that's guaranteed to put him in a ferocious mood. He was followed by a new Betan security patrolman, and a limping Betan civilian Miles had never seen before, who was gesticulating and complaining bitterly. The man had a livid bruise on his face, and one eye was swelling shut. Elena trailed, seeming on the verge of tears.

The second group was led by the shuttleport administrator, and included now a number of other officials. The third group was headed by the Betan security woman. She had two burly patrolmen and four medical types in her wake. Mayhew glanced from right to left, and sobered abruptly. The Betan security men had their stunners in hand.

"Oh, lad," he muttered. The security men were fanning out. Mayhew scrambled to his knees. "Oh, kid . . ."

"It's up to you, Arde," said Miles quietly.

"Do it!"

The Botharis arrived. The Sergeant opened his mouth. Miles, dropping his voice, cut across his beginning roar—by God, it *was* an effective trick—"Attention, please, Sergeant. I require your witness. Pilot Officer Mayhew is about to make oath."

The Sergeant's jaw tightened like a vise, but he came to attention.

"Put your hands between mine, Arde—like that—and repeat after me. I, Arde Mayhew—is that your full legal name? use that, then—do testify I am an unsworn freeman, and take service under Lord Miles Naismith Vorkosigan as an Armsman simple—go ahead and say that part—" Mayhew did so, rolling his eyes from left to right. "And will hold him as my liege commander until my death or his releases me."

That repeated, Miles said, rather quickly as the crowd closed in, "I, Miles Naismith Vorkosigan, vassal secundus to Emperor Gregor Vorbarra, do accept your oath, and pledge you the protection of a liege commander; this by my word as Vorkosigan. All done—you can get up now."

One good thing, thought Miles, it's diverted the Sergeant completely from whatever he was about to say. Bothari found his voice at last. "My lord," he hissed, "you can't swear a Betan!"

"I just did," Miles pointed out cheerfully. He bounced a bit, feeling quite unusually pleased with himself. The Sergeant's glance passed across Mayhew's bottle, and narrowed on Miles.

"Why aren't you asleep?" he growled.

The Betan patrolman gestured at Miles. "Is this the man?"

The Betan security officer from the original shuttleport group approached. Mayhew had remained on his knees, as if plotting to crawl off under cover of the fire overhead. "Pilot Officer Mayhew," she cried, "you are under arrest. These are your rights: you have a right to—"

The bruised civilian interrupted, pointing at Elena. "Screw him! This woman assaulted me! There were a dozen witnesses. Damn it, I want her charged. She's vicious."

Elena had her hands over her ears again, lower lip stuck out but trembling slightly. Miles began to get the picture. "Did you hit him?"

She nodded. "But he said the most horrible thing to me. . . ."

"My lord," said Bothari reproachfully, "it was very wrong of you to leave her alone in this place—"

The security woman began again. "Pilot Officer Mayhew, you have a right—"

"I think she cracked the orbit of my eye," moaned the bruised man. "I'm going to sue . . ."

Miles shot Elena a special reassuring smile. "Don't worry, I'll take care of it."

"You have a right—" yelled the security woman.

"I beg your pardon, Officer Brownell," Miles interrupted her smoothly. "Pilot Officer Mayhew is now my liegeman. As his liege commander, any charges against him must be addressed to me. It will then be my duty to determine their validity and issue the orders for the appropriate punishments. He has no rights but the right to accept challenge in single combat for certain categories of slander which are a bit complicated to go into now—" Obsolete, too, since dueling was outlawed by Imperial edict, but these Betans won't know the difference—"So unless you happen to be carrying two pairs of swords and are prepared to, say, offer an insult to Pilot Officer Mayhew's mother, you will simply have to—ah—contain yourself."

Timely advice; the security woman looked as if she were about to explode. Mayhew gave a hopeful nod, smiling weakly. Bothari stirred uneasily, eyes flicking on an inventory of men and weapons in the mob. Gently, thought Miles; let's take it gently. "Get *up*, Arde. . . ."

It took some persuading, but the security officer finally checked with her superiors about Miles's bizarre defense of Pilot Officer Mayhew. At that point, as Miles had hoped and foreseen, proceedings broke down in a morass of untested interplanetary legal hypotheses that threatened to engulf the Barrayaran Embassy and the Betan State Department on ever-ascending levels of personnel.

Elena's case was easier. The outraged Betan was directed to take his case to the Barrayaran Embassy in person. There, Miles knew, it would be swallowed up in an endless möbius loop of files, forms, and reports, kept especially for such occasions by the extremely competent staff. The forms included some particularly creative ones that had to be round-tripped on the six-week journey back to Barrayar itself, and were guaranteed to be sent back several times for minor errors in execution.

"Relax," Miles whispered in an aside to Elena. "They'll bury that guy in files so deep you'll never see him again. It works great with Betans—they're perfectly happy, because all the time they think they're doing something to you. Just don't kill anybody. My diplomatic immunity doesn't go that far."

The exhausted Mayhew was swaying on his feet by the time the Betans gave way. Miles, feeling like an old sea raider after a successful looting spree, bore him off.

"Two hours," muttered Bothari. "We've only been in this bloody place two bloody hours. . . ."

CHAPTER SIX

"Miles, dear," his grandmother greeted him with a peck on the cheek as regulation as a salute. "You're rather late—trouble in customs again? Are you very tired from your trip?"

"Not a bit." He bounced on his heels, missing free fall and its unconstrained motion. He felt like taking a fifty-kilometer run, or going dancing, or something. The Botharis looked weary, though, and Pilot Officer Mayhew was nearly green. The pilot officer, after the briefest introduction, was shipped off to the spare bedroom in Mrs. Naismith's apartment to wash, take his choice of too-small or too-large borrowed pajamas, and fall unconscious across the bed as though slugged with a mallet.

Miles's grandmother fed the survivors dinner, and as Miles had hoped seemed quite taken with Elena. Elena was having an attack of shyness in the presence of the admired Countess Vorkosigan's mother, but Miles was fairly sure the old woman would soon bring her out of it. Elena might even pick up a little of her Betan indifference to Barrayaran class distinctions. Might it ease the oppressive constraint that seemed to have been growing between himself and Elena ever since they had ceased to be children? It was the damn Vor-suit he wore, Miles thought. There were days it felt like armor; archaic, clanking, encrusted and spiked. Uncomfortable to wear, impossible to embrace. Give her a can opener, and let her see what a pale soft miserable slug this gaudy shell encloses—not that that would be any less repellent—his thoughts buried themselves in the dark fall of Elena's hair, and he sighed. He realized his grandmother was speaking to him. "I beg your pardon, ma'am?"

"I said," she repeated patiently between bites, "one of my neighbors—you remember him, Mr. Hathaway, who works at the recycling center—I know you met him when you were here to school—"

"Oh, yeah, sure. Him."

"He has a little problem that we thought you might be able to help with, being Barrayaran. He's sort of been saving it for you, since we knew you were coming. He thought, if you weren't too tired, you might even go with him tonight, since it *is* starting to be rather disturbing. . . ."

"I really can't tell you all that much about him myself," said Hathaway, staring out over the vast domed arena that was his special charge. Miles wondered how long it would take to get used to the smell. "Except that he says he's a Barrayaran. He disappears from time to time, but he always comes back. I've tried to persuade him to go to a Shelter, at least, but he didn't seem to like the idea. Lately, I haven't been able to get near him. You understand, he's never tried to *hurt* anybody or anything, but you never know, what with his being a Barrayaran and all—oh, sorry . . ."

Hathaway, Miles, and Bothari picked their way across the treacherous and uneven footing. Odd-shaped objects in the piles tended to turn unexpectedly, tripping the unwary. All the detritus of high tech, awaiting apotheosis as the next generation of Betan ingenuity, gleamed out amid more banal and universal human rubbish.

"Oh, damn it," cried Hathaway suddenly, "he's gone and lit a fire again." A small curl of grey smoke was rising a hundred meters away. "I hope he's not burning wood this time. I just *cannot* convince him how valuable—well, at least it makes him easy to find. . . ."

A low place in the piles gave an illusion of a sheltered space. A thin, dark-haired man in his late twenties was hunched glumly over a tiny fire, carefully arranged in the bottom of a shallow parabolic antenna dish. A makeshift table that had started life as a computer desk console was evidently now the man's kitchen, for it held some flat pieces of metal and plastic now doing duty as plates and platters. A large carp, its scales gleaming red-gold, lay gutted and ready for cooking upon it.

Dark eyes, black smudges of weariness beneath them, flashed up at the clank of their approach. The man scrambled to his feet, grabbing what appeared to be a homemade knife; Miles couldn't tell what it was made of, but it was clearly a good one, if it had done the job on the fish. Bothari's hand automatically checked his stunner.

"I think he *is* a Barrayaran," muttered Miles to Bothari. "Look at the way he moves."

Bothari nodded agreement. The man held his knife properly, like a soldier, left hand guarding the right, ready to block a snatch or punch an opening for the weapon. He seemed unconscious of his stance.

Hathaway raised his voice. "Hey, Baz! I brought you some visitors, all right?"

"No."

"Uh, look." Hathaway slid down a pile of rubble, closer but not too close. "I haven't bothered you, have I? I let you hang around in my center for days on end, it's all right as long as you don't carry anything out—that's not wood, is it? oh, all right . . . I'll overlook it this time, but I want you to talk to these guys. I figure you owe me. All right? Anyway, they're Barrayarans."

Baz glanced up at them sharply, his expression a strange mixture of hunger and dismay. His lips formed a silent word. Miles read it, Home. I'm silhouetted, thought Miles; let's get down where he can see the light on my face. He picked his way down beside Hathaway.

Baz stared at him. "You're no Barrayaran," he said flatly.

"I'm half Betan," Miles replied, feeling no desire to go into his medical history just then. "But I was raised on Barrayar. It's home."

"Home," whispered the man, barely audibly.

"You're a long way from home." Miles upended a plastic casing from something-or-other—it had some wires hanging out of it, giving it a sad disembowelled air—and seated himself. Bothari took up position above on the rubble within comfortable pouncing distance. "Did you get stuck here or something? Do you, ah—need some help getting home?"

"No." The man glanced away, frowning. His fire had burned down. He placed a metal grill from an air conditioner over it and laid his fish on top.

Hathaway eyed these preparations with fascination. "What are you going to do with that dead goldfish?"

"Eat it."

Hathaway looked revolted. "Look, mister—all you

have to do is report to a Shelter and get Carded, and you can have all the protein slices you want—any flavor, clean and fresh from the vats. Nobody has to eat a dead animal on this planet, really. Where'd you get it, anyway?"

Baz replied uneasily, "Out of a fountain."

Hathaway gasped in horror. "Those displays belong to the Silica Zoo! You can't eat an exhibit!"

"There were lots of them. I didn't think anybody would miss one. It wasn't stealing. I caught it."

Miles rubbed his chin thoughtfully, gave a little upward jerk of his head, and pulled Pilot Officer Mayhew's green bottle, which he had brought along on a last-minute impulse, from under his jacket. Baz started at the movement, then relaxed when he saw it was no weapon. By Barrayaran etiquette, Miles took a swallow first—he made it a small one, this time—wiped the mouthpiece on his sleeve, and offered it to the thin man. "Drink, with dinner? It's good—makes you feel less hungry—dries up your sinuses, too. Tastes like horse-piss and honey."

Baz frowned, but took the bottle. "Thanks." He took a drink, and added in a strangled whisper, "Thanks!"

Baz slipped his dinner onto a cover plate from a tube-car wheel, and sat cross-legged amid the junk to pick out the bones. "Care for any?"

"No, thanks, just had dinner."

"Dear God, I should think not!" cried Hathaway.

"Ah," said Miles. "Changed my mind. Just a taste . . ."

Baz held out a morsel on the point of his knife; Bothari's hands twitched. Miles lipped it off, camp-fashion, and chomped it down with a sardonic smile at Hathaway. Baz waved the bottle at Bothari.

"Would your friend . . . ?"

"He can't," excused Miles. "He's on duty."

"Bodyguard," whispered Baz. He looked again at

Miles with that strange expression, fear, and something else. "What the hell are you?"

"Nothing you need be afraid of. Whatever you're hiding from, it isn't me. You can have my word on that, if you wish."

"Vor," breathed Baz. "You're Vor."

"Well, yes. And what the hell are you?"

"Nobody." He picked rapidly at his fish. Miles wondered how long it had been since his last meal.

"Hard, to be nobody, in a place like this," Miles observed. "Everybody has a number, everybody has a place to be—not many interstices, to be nobody in. It must take a lot of effort and ingenuity."

"You said it," Baz agreed around a mouthful of goldfish. "This is the worst place I've ever been. You've got to keep moving around all the time."

"You do know," said Miles tentatively, "the Barrayaran Embassy will help you get home, if you want. Of course, you have to pay it back later, and they're pretty strict about collecting—they're not in the business of giving free rides to hitchhikers—but if you're really in trouble—"

"No!" It was almost a cry. It echoed faintly across the enormous arena. Baz lowered his voice self-consciously. "No, I don't want to go home. Sooner or later, I'll pick up some kind of job at the shuttleport, and ship off someplace better. There's got to be something turn up soon."

"If you want work," said Hathaway eagerly, "all you have to do is register at—"

"I'll get something my own way," Baz cut him off harshly.

The pieces were falling into place. "Baz doesn't want to register anywhere," Miles explained to Hathaway, coolly didactic. "Up until now, Baz is something I thought impossible on Beta Colony. He's a man who isn't here. He's passed across the information network without a blip. He never arrived—never passed through Customs, and I'll bet that was one hell of a neat trick—as far as the computers are concerned, has not eaten, or slept, or purchased—or Registered, or been Carded—and he would rather starve than do so."

"For pity's sake, why?" asked Hathaway.

"Deserter," commented Bothari laconically from above. "I've seen the look."

Miles nodded. "I think you've hit it, Sergeant."

Baz sprang to his feet. "You're Service Security! You twisty little bastard—"

"Sit down," Miles overrode him, not stirring. "I'm not anybody. I'm just not quite as good at it as you are."

Baz hesitated. Miles studied him seriously, all the pleasure suddenly gone out of the excursion in a wash of cold ambiguity. "I don't suppose—Yeoman?—no. Lieutenant?"

"Yes," growled the man.

"An officer. Yes." Miles chewed his lip, disturbed. "Was it in the heat?"

Baz grimaced reluctantly. "Technically."

"Hm." A deserter. Strange beyond comprehension, for a man to trade the envied splendor of the Service for the worm of fear, riding in his belly like a parasite. Was he running from an act of cowardice? Or another crime? Or an error, some horrible, lethal mistake? Technically, Miles had a duty to help nail the fellow for Service Security. But he had come here tonight to help the man, not destroy him. . . .

"I don't understand," said Hathaway. "Has he committed a crime?"

"Yes. A bloody serious one. Desertion in the heat of battle," said Miles. "If he gets extradited home, the penalty's quartering. Technically."

"That doesn't sound so bad." Hathaway shrugged. "He's been quartered in my recycling center for two months. It could hardly be worse. What's the problem?"

"Quartering," said Miles. "Uh—not domiciled. Cut in four pieces."

Hathaway stared, shocked. "But that would kill him!" He looked around, and wilted under the triple, unified, and exasperated glares of the three Barrayarans.

"Betans," said Baz disgustedly. "I can't stand Betans."

Hathaway muttered something under his breath; Miles caught, "—bloodthirsty barbarians . . ."

"So if you're not Service Security," Baz finished, sitting back down, "you may as well shove off. There's nothing you can do for me."

"I'm going to have to do something," Miles said.

"Why?"

"I'm—I'm afraid I've inadvertently done you a disservice, Mr., Mr.—you may as well tell me your name . . ."

"Jesek."

"Mr. Jesek. You see, I'm, um, under the scrutiny of Security myself. Just by meeting you, I've endangered your cover. I'm sorry."

Jesek paled. "Why is Service Security watching you?"

"Not the S.S. Imperial Security, I'm afraid."

The breath went out of the deserter as from a body blow, and his face drained utterly. He bent over, his head pressed to his knees, as if to counteract a wave of faintness. A muffled whimper—"God . . ." He stared up at Miles. "What did you *do*, boy?"

Miles said sharply, "I haven't asked you that question, Mr. Jesek!"

The deserter mumbled some apology. I can't let him know who I am, thought Miles, or he'll be off like a shot and run straight into my Security so-called safety net—even as it is, Lt. Croye or his minions from the

Barrayaran Embassy Security staff are going to start looking this guy over. They'll go wild when they find he's the invisible man. No later than tomorrow, if they give him the routine check. I've just killed this man—no! "What did you do in the Service, before?" Miles groped for time and thought.

"I was an engineer's assistant."

"Construction? Weapons systems?"

The man's voice steadied. "No, jump ship engines. Some weapons systems. I try to get tech work on private freighters, but most of the equipment I'm trained in is obsolete in this sector. Harmonic impulse engines, Necklin color drive—hard to come by. I've got to get farther out, away from the main economic centers."

A small, high "Hm!" escaped Miles. "Do you know anything about the RG class freighters?"

"Sure. I've worked a couple. Necklin drive. They're all gone now, though."

"Not quite." A discordant excitement shivered through Miles. "I know one. It's going to be making a freight run soon, if it can get a cargo, and crew."

Jesek eyed him suspiciously. "Is it going someplace that doesn't have an extradition treaty with Barrayar?"

"Maybe."

"My lord," Bothari's voice was edged with agitation, "you're not considering *harboring* this deserter?"

"Well . . ." Miles voice was mild. "Technically, I don't know he's a deserter. I've merely heard some allegations."

"He admitted it."

"Bravado, perhaps. Inverted snobbery."

"Are you hankering to be another Lord Vorloupulous?" asked Bothari dryly.

Miles laughed, and sighed; Baz's mouth twisted. Hathaway begged to be let in on the joke.

"It's Barrayaran law again," Miles explained. "Our courts are not kindly disposed to those who maintain the letter of the law and violate its spirit. The classic precedent was the case of Lord Vorloupulous and his 2000 cooks."

"Did he run a chain of restaurants?" asked Hathaway, floundering. "Don't tell me that's illegal on Barrayar too . . ."

"Oh, no. This was at the end of the Time of Isolation, almost a hundred years ago. Emperor Dorca Vorbarra was centralizing the government, and breaking the power of the Counts as separate governing entities—there was a civil war about it. One of the main things he did was eliminate private armies, what they used to call livery and maintenance on old Earth. Each Count was stripped down to twenty armed followers—barely a bodyguard.

"Well, Lord Vorloupulous had a feud going with a few neighbors, for which he found this allotment quite inadequate. So he hired on 2000 'cooks,' so-called, and sent them out to carve up his enemies. He was quite ingenious about arming them, butcher knives instead of short swords and so on. There were plenty of recently unemployed veterans looking for work at the time, who weren't too proud to give it a try. . . ." Miles's eyes glinted amusement.

"The Emperor, naturally, didn't see it his way. Dorca marched his regular army, by then the only one on Barrayar, on Vorloupulous and arrested him for treason, for which the sentence was—still is—public exposure and death by starvation. So the man with 2000 cooks was condemned to waste away in the Great Square of Vorbarr Sultana. And to think they always said Dorca Vorbarra had no sense of humor . . ."

Bothari smiled grimly, and Baz chuckled; Hathaway's laugh was more hollow. "Charming," he muttered.

"But it had a happy ending," Miles went on. Hathaway brightened. "The Cetagandans invaded us about that point, and Lord Vorloupulous was released."

"By the Cetagandans? Lucky," commented Hathaway.

"No, by Emperor Dorca, to fight the Cetagandans. You understand, he wasn't pardoned—the sentence was merely delayed. When the First Cetagandan War was over, he would have been expected to show up to complete it. But he died fighting, in battle, so he had an honorable death after all."

"That's a happy ending?" Hathaway shrugged. "Oh, well."

Baz, Miles noted, had become silent and withdrawn again. Miles smiled at him, experimentally; he smiled back awkwardly, looking younger for it. Miles made his decision.

"Mr. Jesek, I'm going to make you a proposition, which you can take or leave. That ship I mentioned is the RG 132. The jump pilot officer's name is Arde Mayhew. If you can disappear—I mean *really* disappear—for the next couple of days, and then get in touch with him at the Silica shuttleport, he'll see that you get a berth on his ship, outbound."

"Why should you help me at all, Mr.—Lord—"

"Mr. Naismith, for all practical purposes." Miles shrugged. "Call it a fancy for seeing people get second chances. It's something they're not very keen on, at home."

Home, Baz's eyes echoed silently again. "Well—it was good to hear the accent again, for a little time. I might just take you up on that," he remembered to be cagey, "or I might not."

Miles nodded, retrieved his bottle, motioned to Bothari, and withdrew. They threaded their way back across the recycling center with an occasional muted clank. When Miles looked back, Jesek was a shadow, melting toward another exit.

Miles became conscious of a profound frown from Sergeant Bothari. He smiled wryly, and kicked over a control casing from some junked industrial robot, lying skeletally athwart a mound of other rubble. "Would you have had me turn him in?" he asked softly. "But you're Service to the bone, I suppose you would. So would my father, I guess—he's so all-fired stringent about the law, no matter how ghastly the consequences."

Bothari grew still. "Not—always, my lord." He retreated into a suddenly neutral silence.

"Miles," whispered Elena, detaining from a nocturnal trip to the bathroom from the bedroom she was sharing with Mrs. Naismith, "aren't you ever going to bed? It's almost morning."

"Not sleepy." He entered yet another inquiry on his grandmother's comconsole. It was true; he still felt fresh, and preternaturally alert. It was just as well, for he was plugged into a commercial network of enormous complexity. Ninety percent of success seemed to lie in asking the right questions. Tricky, but after several hours' work he seemed to be getting the hang of it. "Besides, with Mayhew in the spare bedroom, I'm doomed to the couch."

"I thought my father had the couch."

"He ceded it to me, with a smile of grim glee. He hates the couch. He slept on it all the time I went to school here. He's blamed every ache, twinge, and lower back pain he's had ever since on it, even after two years. It couldn't possibly be old age creeping up on him, oh, no. . . ."

Elena strangled a giggle. She leaned over his shoulder for a look at the screen. The light from it silvered her profile, and the scent of her hair, falling forward, dizzied him. "Finding anything?" she asked.

Miles entered three wrong directions in a row, swore, and refocused his attention. "Yes, I think so. There were a lot more factors to be taken into account than I realized, at first. But I think I've found something—" He retrieved his fumbled data, and waved his finger through the holoscreen. "*That* is my first cargo."

The screen displayed a lengthy manifest. "Agricultural equipment," she analyzed. "Bound for—whatever is Felice?"

"It's a country on Tau Verde IV, wherever *that* is. It's a four-week run—I've been cost-calculating fuel, and supplies, and the logistics of it in general—everything from spare parts to toilet paper. That's not what's interesting, though. What's interesting is that with that cargo I can pay for the trip *and* clear my debt to Calhoun, well inside the time limit on my note." His voice went small. "I'm afraid I, uh, underestimated the time I'd need for the RG 132 to run enough cargos to cover my note, a little. A lot. Well, quite a lot. Badly. The ship costs more to run than I'd realized, when I finally went to add up all the real numbers." He pointed to a figure. "But that's what they're offering for transport, C.O.D. Felice. And the cargo's ready to go immediately."

Her eyebrows drew down in awed puzzlement. "Pay for the whole ship in one run? But that's wonderful! But . . ."

He grinned. "But?"

"But why hasn't somebody else snapped up this cargo? It seems to have been sitting in the warehouse a long time."

"Clever girl," he crooned encouragingly. "Go on."

"I see they only pay on delivery. But maybe that's normal?"

"Yes . . ." He spread the word out, like butter. "Anything else?"

She pursed her lips. "Something's weird."

"Indeed." His eyes crinkled. "Something is, as you say, weird."

"Do I have to guess? Because if I do, I'm going back to bed. . . ." She stifled a yawn.

"Ah. Well—Tau Verde IV is in a war zone, at the moment. It seems there is a planetary war in progress. One of the sides has the local wormhole exit blocked—not by their own people, it seems to be a somewhat industrially backward place—they've hired a mercenary fleet. And why has this cargo been moldering in a warehouse so long? Because none of the big shipping companies will carry into a war zone—their insurance lapses. That goes for most of the little independents, as well. But since I'm not insured, it does not go for me." He smirked.

Elena looked doubtful. "Is it dangerous, crossing the blockade? If you cooperate on their stop-and-search—"

"In this case, I think so. The cargo happens to be addressed to the other side of the fray."

"Would the mercenaries seize it? I mean, robotic combines or whatever couldn't be classed as contraband—don't they have to abide by interstellar conventions?" Her doubt became wariness.

He stretched, still smiling. "You've almost got it. What is Beta Colony's most noted export?"

"Well, advanced technology, of course. Weapons and weapons systems—" Her wariness became dismay. "Oh, Miles . . ."

"'Agricultural equipment,'" he snickered. "I'll bet! Anyway, there's this Felician who claims to be the agent for the company purchasing the equipment—that's another tip-off, that they should have a man personally shepherding this cargo through—I'm going to go see him first thing in the morning, as soon as the Sergeant wakes up. And Mayhew, I'd better take Mayhew . . ."

CHAPTER SEVEN

Miles reviewed his troops, before pressing the buzzer to the hotel room. Even in civilian dress, there was no mistaking the Sergeant for anything but a soldier. Mayhew—washed, shaved, rested, fed, and dressed in clean new clothes—looked infinitely better than yesterday, but still . . .

"Straighten up, Arde," advised Miles, "and try to look professional. We've just got to get this cargo. I thought Betan medicine was advanced enough to cure any kind of hangover. It's bound to make a bad impression on this guy if you walk around clutching your stomach."

"Grm," muttered Mayhew. But he did return his hands to his sides, and come more-or-less to attention. "You'll find out, kid," he added in a tone of bitter clairvoyance.

"And you're going to have to stop calling me 'kid,'" Miles added. "You're my Armsman now. You're supposed to address me as 'my lord.'"

"You really take that stuff seriously?"

One step at a time. "It's like a salute," Miles explained. "You salute the uniform, not the man. Being Vor is—is like wearing an invisible uniform you can never take off. Look at Sergeant Bothari—he's called me 'my lord' ever since I was born. If he can, you can. You're his brother-in-arms, now."

Mayhew looked up at the Sergeant. Bothari looked back, his face saturnine in the extreme. Miles had the impression that had Bothari been a more expressive man, he would have made a rude noise at the concept of Mayhew as his brother-in-arms. Mayhew evidently received the same impression, for he straightened up a little more, and bit out, "Yes, my lord."

Miles nodded approval, and pressed the buzzer.

The man who answered the door had dark almond eyes, high cheekbones, skin the color of coffee and cream, and bright copper-colored hair, tightly curled as wire, cropped close to his head. His eyes searched the trio anxiously, widening a little at Miles; he had only seen Miles's face that morning, over the viewscreen. "Mr. Naismith? I'm Carle Daum. Come in."

Daum closed the door behind them quickly, and fussed at the lock. Miles deduced they'd just passed through a weapons scan, and the Felician was sneaking a peek at his readout. The man turned back with a look of nervous suspicion, one hand automatically touching his right hip pocket. His gaze did not linger elsewhere in the little hotel room, and Bothari's lips twitched satisfaction at Daum's unconscious revelation of the weapon he must watch for. Legal stunner, most likely, thought Miles, but you never know.

"Won't you sit down?" the Felician invited. His speech had a soft and curious resonance to Miles's ear, neither the flat nasal twang, heavy on the r's, of the Betans, nor the clipped cold gutturals of Barrayar.

Bothari indicated he would prefer to stand, and took up position to Daum's right, uncomfortably far over in the Felician's peripheral vision. Miles and Mayhew sat before a low table. Daum sat across from them, his back to a "window," actually a viewscreen, bright with a panorama of mountains and a lake from some other world. The wind that really howled far overhead would have scoured such trees to sticks in a day. The window silhouetted Daum, while revealing his visitors' expressions in full light; Miles appreciated the choice of views.

"Well, Mr. Naismith," began Daum. "Tell me something about your ship. What is its cargo capacity?"

"It's an RG class freighter. It can easily handle twice the mass of your manifest, assuming those figures you put into the com system are quite correct . . . ?"

Daum did not react to this tiny bait. Instead he said, "I'm not very familiar with jump ships. Is it fast?"

"Pilot Officer Mayhew?" Miles prodded.

"Huh? Oh. Uh, do you mean acceleration? Steady, just steady. We boost a little longer, and get there nearly as fast in the end."

"Is it very maneuverable?"

Mayhew stared. "Mr. Daum, it's a freighter."

Daum's lips compressed with annoyance. "I know that. The question is—"

"The question is," Miles interrupted, "can we either outrun or evade your blockade. The answer is no. You see, I've done my homework."

Frustration darkened Daum's face. "Then we seem to be wasting each other's time. So much time lost . . ." He began to rise.

"The next question is, is there another way to get your cargo to its destination? Yes, I believe," said Miles firmly.

Daum sat back, tense with mistrust and hope. "Go on."

"You've done as much yourself already, in the Betan's comm system. Camouflage. I believe your cargo can be camouflaged well enough to pass a blockade inspection. But we'll have to work together on it, and somewhat more frankly—ah . . ." Miles made a calculation, based on the Felician's age and bearing, "Major Daum?"

The man twitched. Ah ha, thought Miles, nailed him on the first try. He compressed this internal crow to a suave smile.

"If you're a Pelian spy, or an Oseran mercenary, I swear I'll kill you—" Daum began. Bothari's eyelids drooped, in a pose of deceptive calm.

"I'm not," said Miles, "although it would be a great ploy, if I were. Load up you and your weapons, take you halfway, and make you get out and walk—I appreciate your need for caution."

"What weapons?" said Daum, attempting belatedly to regain his cover.

"What weapons?" echoed Mayhew, in a frantic, near-silent whisper to Miles's ear.

"Your plowshares and pruning hooks, then," said Miles tolerantly. "But I suggest we end the game and get to work. I am a professional—" and if you buy that, I have this nice farmland on Barrayar for sale, "and so, obviously, are you, or you wouldn't have gotten this far."

Mayhew's eyes widened. Under the guise of shifting in his seat, Miles kicked him preemptively in the ankle. Make a note, he thought; next time, wake him earlier and brief him better. Although getting the pilot officer functional that morning had been rather like trying to raise the dead. Miles was not sure he could have succeeded, earlier.

"You're a mercenary soldier?" said Daum.

"Ah . . ." said Miles. He had meant to imply, a

professional shipmaster—but might this be even more attractive to the Felician? "What do you think, Major?"

Bothari stopped breathing a moment. Mayhew, however, looked suddenly dismayed. "So that's what you meant yesterday," he murmured. "Recruiting . . ."

Miles, who had meant nothing of a kind in his facetious crack about looking for desperate men, murmured back, "Of course," in a tone of maximum off-handedness. "Surely you realized . . ."

Daum looked doubtfully at Mayhew, but then his gaze fell on Bothari. Bothari maintained parade rest and an expression of remarkable blankness. Belief hardened in Daum's eyes. "By God," he muttered, "if the Pelians can hire galactics, why can't we?" He raised his voice. "How many troops are in your outfit? What ships do you have?"

Oh, hell—now what? Miles extemporized like mad. "Major Daum, I didn't mean to mislead you—" Bothari breathed, gratefully, Miles saw from the corner of his eye. "I'm, uh—detached from my outfit at the moment. They're tied up on another contract. I was just visiting Beta Colony for, uh, medical reasons, so I have only myself and, ah, my immediate staff, and a ship my fleet could spare, here to offer you. But we're expected to operate independently, in my bunch," exhale, Sergeant, please exhale, "so since it will be a little time yet before I can rejoin them, and I find your problem tactically interesting, my services are yours."

Daum nodded slowly, "I see. And by what rank should I address you?"

Miles nearly appointed himself admiral on the spot. Captain? Yeoman? he wondered wildly. "Let's just leave it at Mr. Naismith, for now," he suggested coolly. "A centurion without his hundred men is, after all, a centurion in name only. At the moment, we need to be dealing with realities." Do we ever . . .

"What's the name of your outfit?"

Miles free-associated frantically. "The Dendarii Mercenaries." It fell trippingly from the tongue, at least.

Daum studied him hungrily. "I've been tied down in this damn place for two months, looking for a carrier that would haul me, that I could trust. If I wait much longer, could be delay will destroy the purpose of my mission as certainly as any betrayal. Mr. Naismith, I've waited long enough—too long. I'm going to take a chance on you."

Miles nodded satisfaction, as if he had been concluding such transactions all of a somewhat longer life than he actually possessed. "Then Major Daum, I undertake to get you to Tau Verde IV. My word on it. The first thing I need is more intelligence. Tell me all you know about the Oseran Mercenaries' blockade procedures . . ."

"It was my understanding, my lord," said Bothari severely as they left Daum's hotel for the slidewalk, "that Pilot Officer Mayhew here was to transport your cargo. You didn't tell me anything about going along yourself."

Miles shrugged, elaborately casual. "There are so many variables, so much at stake—I've just got to be on the spot. It's unfair to dump it all on Arde's shoulders. I mean, would you?"

Bothari, apparently caught between his disapproval of his liege lord's get-rich-quick scheme and his low opinion of the pilot officer, gave a noncommittal grunt, which Mayhew chose not to notice.

Miles's eyes glinted. "Besides, it'll put a little excitement in your life, Sergeant. It has to be dull as dirt, following me around all day. I'd be bored to tears."

"I like being bored," said Bothari morosely.

Miles grinned, secretly relieved at not being taken

more strictly to task for his "Dendarii Mercenaries" outbreak. Well, the brief moment of fantasy was probably harmless enough.

The three of them found Elena stalking back and forth across Mrs. Naismith's living room. Two bright spots of color burned in her cheeks, her nostrils flared, and she was muttering under her breath. She transfixed Miles with an angry glare as he entered. "Betans!" she bit out in a voice of loathing.

This only let him half off the hook. "What's the matter?" he inquired cautiously.

She took another turn around the room, stiff-legged, as if trampling bodies underfoot. "That awful holovid," she glowered. "How can they—oh, I can't even describe it."

Ah ha, she found one of the pornography channels, thought Miles. Well, it had to happen eventually. "Holovid?" he said brightly.

"How could they permit such horrible slanders on Admiral Vorkosigan, and Prince Serg, and our forces? I think the producer should be taken out and shot! And the actors—and the scriptwriter—we would at home, by God . . ."

Not the pornography channel, evidently. "Uh, Elena—just what have you been looking at?"

His grandmother was seated, with a fixed nervous smile, in her float chair. "I tried to explain that it's fictionalized—you know, to make the history more dramatic . . ."

Elena gave vent to an ominous rattling hiss; Miles gave his grandmother a pleading look.

"*The Thin Blue Line,*" Mrs. Naismith explained cryptically.

"Oh, I've seen that one," said Mayhew. "It's a rerun."

Miles recalled the docudrama vividly himself; it had first been released two years ago, and had contributed its mite to making his school visit to Beta Colony the sometimes surreal experience it had been. Miles's father, then-Commodore Vorkosigan, had begun the aborted Barrayaran invasion of Beta Colony's ally Escobar nineteen years ago as a Staff officer. He had ended, upon the catastrophic deaths of the co-commanders Admiral Vorrutyer and Crown Prince Serg Vorbarra, as commander of the armada. His brilliant retreat was still cited as exemplary, in the military annals of Barrayar. The Betans naturally took a different view of the affair. The blue in the title of the docudrama referred to the color of the uniform worn by the Betan Expeditionary Force, of which Captain Cordelia Naismith had been a part.

"It's—it's . . ." Elena turned to Miles. "There isn't any truth in it—is there?"

"Well," said Miles, equable from years of practice in coming to terms with the Betan version of history, "some. But my mother says they never wore the blue uniforms until the war was practically over. And she swears up and down, privately, that she didn't murder Admiral Vorrutyer, but she won't say who did. Protests too much, I think. All my father will ever say about Vorrutyer is that he was a brilliant defensive strategist. I've never been quite sure what to make of that, since Vorrutyer was in charge of the offense. All my mother says about him is that he was a bit strange, which doesn't sound too bad, until I reflect that she's a Betan. They've never said a word against Prince Serg, and Father was on his staff and knew him, so I guess the Betan version of him is mainly a crock of war propaganda."

"Our greatest hero," cried Elena. "The Emperor's father—how dare they—"

"Well, even on our side, consensus seems to be that we were overreaching ourselves, to try and take Escobar, on top of Komarr and Sergyar."

Elena turned to her father, as the resident expert. "You served with my lord Count at Escobar, sir! Tell *her*—" a toss of her head indicated Mrs. Naismith, "it isn't so!"

"I don't remember Escobar," replied the Sergeant stonily, in a tone unusually flat and unencouraging even for him. "No point to that—" he jerked one large hand, thumb hooked in his belt, toward the holovid viewer. "It was wrong for you to see that."

The tension in Bothari's shoulders disturbed Miles, and the set look about his eyes. Anger? Over an ephemeral holovid which he had seen before, and ignored as readily as Miles had?

Elena paused, diverted and confused. "Don't remember? But . . ."

Something clicked in Miles's memory—the medical discharge, at last accounted for? "I didn't realize—were you wounded at Escobar, Sergeant?" No wonder he's twitchy about it, then.

Bothari's lips moved about the beginning of the word, wounded. "Yes," he muttered. His eyes shifted away from Miles and Elena.

Miles gnawed his lip. "Head wound?" he inquired in a burst of surmise.

Bothari's gaze shifted back to Miles, quellingly. "Mm."

Miles permitted himself to be quelled, hugging this new prize of information to himself. A head wound would account for much that had long bemused him in his liegeman.

Taking the hint, Miles changed the subject firmly. "Be that as it may," he swept Elena a courtly bow—whatever happened to plumed hats, for men?—"I got my cargo."

Elena's irritation vanished instantly in pleased interest. "Oh, grand! And have you figured out how to get it past the blockade yet?"

"Working on it. Would you care to do some shopping for me? Supplies for the trip. Put the orders in to the ship chandlers—you can do it from here on the comconsole, Grandmother'll show you how. Arde has a standard list. We need everything—food, fuel cells, emergency oxygen, first-aid supplies—and at the best price you can get. This thing is going to wipe out my travel allowance, so anything you can save—eh?" He gave his draftee his most encouraging smile, as if the offer of two full days locked in struggle with the electronic labyrinth of Betan business practices was a high treat.

Elena looked doubtful. "I've never outfitted a ship before."

"It'll be easy," he assured her airily. "Just bang into it—you'll have it figured out in no time. If I can do it, you can do it." He zipped lightly over this argument, giving her no time to reflect on the fact that he had never outfitted a ship either. "Figure for Pilot Officer, Engineer, the Sergeant, me, and Major Daum, for eight weeks, and maybe a little margin, but not too much—remembering the budget. We boost the day after tomorrow."

"All right—when . . . ?" She snapped to full alertness, thunder in the crimp of her black winging eyebrows. "What about me? You're not leaving me behind while you—"

Metaphorically, Miles slunk behind Bothari and waved a white flag. "That's up to your father. And Grandmother, of course."

"She's welcome to stay with me," said Mrs. Naismith faintly. "But Miles—you just got here. . . ."

"Oh, I still mean to make my visit, ma'am," Miles reassured her. "We'll just reschedule our return to Barrayar. It's not like I had to—to get back in time for school or anything."

Elena stared at her father, tight-lipped with silent pleading. Bothari blew out his breath, his gaze turning calculatingly from his daughter to Mrs. Naismith to the holovid viewer, then inward to what thoughts or memories Miles could not guess. Elena barely restrained herself from hopping up and down in agitation. "Miles—my lord—you can order him to—"

Miles flicked a hand palm-out, and gave a tiny shake of his head, signalling, wait.

Mrs. Naismith glanced at Elena's anxiety, and smiled thoughtfully behind her hand. "Actually, dear, it would be lovely having you all to myself for a time. Like having a daughter again. You could meet young people—go to parties—I have some friends over in Quartz who could take you desert-trekking. I'm too old for the sport myself, now, but I'm sure you'd enjoy it. . . ."

Bothari flinched. Quartz, for example, was Beta Colony's principal hermaphrodite community, and although Mrs. Naismith herself typified hermaphrodites as "people who are pathologically incapable of making up their minds," she bristled in patriotic Betan defense of them at Bothari's open Barrayaran revulsion to the sex. And Bothari had personally carried Miles home unconscious from more than one Betan party. As for Miles's nearly disastrous desert-trek . . . Miles shot his grandmother a look of thanks from crinkling eyes. She acknowledged it with a puckish nod, and smiled blandly at Bothari.

Bothari was unamused. Not ironically unamused, befitting the interplay, as his guerilla warfare with Mrs. Naismith on the subject of Miles's cultural mores usually was; but genuinely enraged. An odd knot formed in Miles's stomach. He came to a species of attention, querying his bodyguard with puzzled eyes.

"She goes with us," Bothari growled. Elena nearly

clapped her hands in triumph, although Mrs. Naismith's list of proposed treats had plainly eroded her resolve not to be left sitting in the baggage train when the troops moved out. But Bothari's eyes raked past his daughter unresponsively, lingered for a last frown at the holovid, and met Miles's—belt buckle.

"Excuse me, my lord. I'll—patrol the hall, until you're ready to leave again." He exited stiffly, great hands, all bone and tendon, vein and corded muscle, held half-curled by his sides.

Yes, go, thought Miles, and see if you can patrol up your self-control out there. Overreacting a tad, aren't you? Admittedly, nobody likes having their tail twisted.

"Whew," said Mayhew, as the door closed. "What bit him?"

"Oh, dear," said Mrs. Naismith. "I hope I didn't offend him." But she added under her breath, "The hypocritical old stick . . ."

"He'll come down," Miles promised. "Just leave him alone for a while. Meantime, there's work to do. You heard the man, Elena. Supplies for a crew of two and a supercargo of four."

The next 48 hours were a blur of motion. To prepare an eight-week run for the old ship within that time limit would have been mind-boggling for an ordinary cargo, but crammed atop that were extras needed for the camouflage scheme. These included a partial cargo of hastily purchased items to provide them with a real manifest in which to embed the false, and supplies needed for rearranging the cargo hold bulkheads, flung aboard to wait the actual work to be done en route. Most vital, and correspondingly expensive, were the extremely advanced Betan mass detector jammers, to be run off the ship's artificial gravity and with which, Miles hoped, they would foil the Oseran Mercenaries' cargo check. It had taken all the simulated political weight Miles could muster on the basis of his father's name to convince the Betan company representative that he was a qualified purchaser of the new and still partially classified equipment.

The mass jammers came with an astonishingly lengthy file of instructions. Miles, studying them in bewilderment, began to have qualms over Baz Jesek's qualifications as an engineer. These gave way, as the hours passed, to even more frantic doubts about whether the man was going to show at all. The level of liquid in Mayhew's green bottle, now wholly expropriated by Miles, dropped steadily, and Miles sweated sleeplessly.

The Betan shuttleport authorities, Miles found, were not sympathetic to the suggestion that their stiff usage fees be paid on credit. He was forced to strip himself of his entire travel allowance. It had seemed a wildly generous one, back on Barrayar, but in the suction of these new demands it vanished literally overnight. Growing creative, Miles turned in his first-class return ticket to Barrayar upon one of the better-known commercial spacelines for a third-class one. Then Bothari's. Then Elena's. Then all three were exchanged for tickets on a line Miles had never heard of; then, with a low, guilty mutter of "I'll buy everybody new ones when we get back—or run a cargo to Barrayar on the RG 132," he cashed them in entirely. At the end of two days he found himself teetering atop a dizzying financial structure compounded of truth, lies, credit, cash purchases, advances on advances, shortcuts, a tiny bit of blackmail, false advertising, and yet another mortgage on some more of his glow-in-the-dark farmland.

Supplies were loaded. Daum's cargo, a fascinating array of odd-shaped anonymous plastic crates, was put aboard. Jesek showed. Systems were checked, and Jesek was instantly put to work jury-rigging vital repairs. Luggage, scarcely opened, was stuffed back together and sent back up. Some goodbyes were said; others carefully avoided. Miles had dutifully reported to Bothari that he'd talked to Lieutenant Croye; it wasn't Miles's fault if Bothari neglected to ask what he'd said. At last, they stood in Silica Shuttleport Docking Bay 27, ready to go.

"Waldo handling fee," stated the Betan shuttleport cargo master. "Three-hundred-ten Betan dollars; foreign currencies not accepted." He smiled pleasantly, like a very courteous shark.

Miles cleared his throat nervously, stomach churning. He mentally reviewed his finances. Daum's resources had been stripped in the last two days; indeed, if something Miles had overheard was correct, the man was planning to leave his hotel bill unpaid. Mayhew had already put everything he had into emergency repairs on the ship. Miles had even floated one loan from his grandmother. Courteously, she'd called it her "investment." Just like the *Golden Hind,* she'd said. Some kind of ass, anyway, Miles had reflected in a moment of quavering doubt. He had accepted, rawly embarrassed, but too harried to forgo the offer.

Miles swallowed—perhaps it was pride going down that made that lump—took Sergeant Bothari aside, and lowered his voice. "Uh, Sergeant—I know my father made you a travel allowance . . ."

Bothari's lips twisted thoughtfully, and he gave Miles a penetrating stare. He knows he can kill this scheme right here, Miles realized, and return to his life of boredom—God knows my father'd back him up. He loathed wheedling Bothari, but added, "I could repay you in eight weeks, two for one—for your left pocket? My word on it."

Bothari frowned. "It's not necessary for you to redeem your word to me, my lord. That was prepaid, long ago." He looked down at his liege lord, hesitated a long moment, sighed, then dolefully emptied his pockets into Miles's hands.

"Thanks." Miles smiled awkwardly, turned away, then turned back. "Uh—can we keep this between you and me? I mean, no need to mention it to my father?"

An involuntary smile turned one corner of the Sergeant's mouth. "Not if you pay me back," he murmured blandly.

And so it was done. What a joy, Miles thought, to be a military ship captain—just bill it all to the Emperor. They must feel like a courtesan with a charge card. Not like us poor working girls.

He stood in the Nav and Com room of his own ship and watched Arde Mayhew, far more alert and focused than Miles had ever seen him before, complete the traffic control checklist. In the screen the glimmering ochre crescent of Beta Colony turned beneath them.

"You are cleared to break orbit," came the voice of traffic control. A wave of dizzy excitement swept through Miles. They were really going to bring this off. . . .

"Uh, just a minute, RG 132," the voice added. "You have a communication."

"Pipe it up," said Mayhew, settling under his headset.

This time a frantic face appeared on the viewscreen. Not one Miles wanted to see. He braced himself, quelling guilt.

Lieutenant Croye spoke urgently, tense. "My lord! Is Sergeant Bothari with you?"

"Not just this second. Why?" The Sergeant was below, with Daum, already beginning to tear out bulkheads.

"Who is with you?"

"Just Pilot Officer Mayhew and myself." Miles found he was holding his breath. So close . . .

Croye relaxed just a little. "My lord, you could not have known this, but that engineer you hired is a deserter from Imperial Service. You must shuttle down immediately, and find some pretext for him to accompany you. Make sure the Sergeant is with you—the man must be regarded as dangerous. We'll have a Betan Security patrol waiting at the docking bay. And also," he glanced aside at something, "what the devil did you do to that Tav Calhoun fellow? He's here at the Embassy, howling for the ambassador . . ."

Mayhew's eyes widened in alarm.

"Uh . . ." said Miles. Tachycardia, that's what it was called. Could seventeen-year-olds have heart attacks? "Lieutenant Croye, that transmission was extremely garbled. Could you repeat?" He shot Mayhew an imploring glance. Mayhew gestured at a panel. Croye began his message again, starting to look disturbed. Miles opened the panel and stared at a spidery maze of wires. His head seemed to swim dizzily in panic. So close . . .

"You're still garbled, sir," said Miles brightly. "Here, I'll fix it. Oh, damn." He pulled six tiny wires at random. The screen dissolved in sparkling snow. Croye was cut off in mid-sentence.

"Boost, Arde!" cried Miles. Mayhew needed no urging. Beta Colony wheeled away beneath them.

Quite dizzy. And nauseated. Blast it, this wasn't free fall. He sat abruptly on the deck, weak from the near-disaster. No, it was something more. He had a paranoid flash about alien plagues, then realized what was happening to him.

Mayhew stared, looking first alarmed, then sardonically understanding. "It's about time that stuff caught up with you," he remarked, and keyed the intercom. "Sergeant Bothari? Would you report to Nav and Com, please? Your, uh, lord needs you." He smiled acidly at Miles, who was beginning to seriously repent some of the harsh things he'd said to Mayhew three days ago.

The Sergeant and Elena appeared. Elena was saying, "—everything's so dirty. The medical cabinet doors just came off in my hands, and—" Bothari snapped to alertness at Miles's hunched huddle, and quizzed Mayhew with angry eyes.

"His crème de meth just wore off," Mayhew explained. "Drops you in a hurry, doesn't it, kid?"

Miles mumbled, an inarticulate groan. Bothari growled something exasperatedly under his breath about "deserve," picked him up, and slung him unceremoniously over his shoulder.

"Well, at least he'll stop bouncing off the walls, and give us all a break," said Mayhew cheerfully. "I've never seen anybody overrev on that stuff the way he did."

"Oh, was that liquor of yours a stimulant?" asked Elena. "I wondered why he didn't fall asleep."

"Couldn't you tell?" chuckled Mayhew.

"Not really."

Miles twisted his head to take in Elena's upside-down worried face, and smile in weak reassurance. Sparkly black and purple whirlpools clouded his vision.

Mayhew's laughter faded. "My God," he said hollowly, "you mean he's like that *all the time*?"

CHAPTER EIGHT

Miles extinguished his welding tool, and pushed back his safety goggles. Done. He glanced with pride back up the neat seam that sealed the last false bulkhead into place. If I can't be a soldier, he thought, perhaps I have a future as an engineer's assistant. About time I got some use out of being a shrimp . . . He called back over his shoulder, "You can pull me out now."

Hands grasped his booted ankles, and dragged him out of the crawl space. "Try your black box now, Baz," he suggested, sitting up and stretching cramped muscles. Daum watched anxiously over the engineer's shoulder as he began, once again, to dry-run the check procedure. Jesek walked back and forth beside the bulkhead, scanning. At last, finally, for the first time in seven trials, all the lights on his probe remained green.

A smile lit his tired face. "I think we've done it. According to this, there's nothing behind that wall but the next wall."

Miles grinned at Daum. "I gave you my word I'd get it together in time, did I not?"

Daum grinned back, relieved. "You're lucky you don't own a faster ship."

The intercom buzzed in the cargo hold. "Uh, my lord?" came Mayhew's voice. It had an edge that popped Miles instantly to his feet.

"Trouble, Arde?"

"We're coming up on the jump to Tau Verde in about two hours. There's something out here I think you and the Major ought to have a look at."

"Blockaders? This side of the exit? They'd have no legal authority-"

"No, it's a buoy, of a sort." Mayhew sounded distinctly unhappy. "If you were expecting this, I think you might have told me. . . ."

"Back in a few minutes, Baz," Miles promised, "and we'll help you rearrange the cargo in here more artistically. Maybe we could pile up a bunch against that first seam I welded."

"It's not that bad," Jesek reassured him. "I've seen professional work with more slop."

In Nav and Com Miles and Daum found Mayhew staring, aggrieved, at a screen readout.

"What is it, Arde?" asked Miles.

"Oseran warning buoy. They have to have it, for the regular merchant shipping lanes. It's supposed to prevent accidents, and misunderstandings, in case anybody doesn't know what's going on on the other side—but this time there's a twist. Listen to this." He nipped on the audio.

"Attention. Attention. To all commercial, military, or diplomatic shipping planning to enter Tau Verde local space, warning. You are entering a restricted military area. All entering traffic, without exception, is subject to search and seizure for contraband. Any non-cooperation will be construed as hostile, and the vessel subjected to confiscation or destruction without further warning. Proceed at your own risk.

"Upon emergence into Tau Verde local space, all vessels will be approached and boarded for inspection. All wormhole jump Pilot Officers will be detained at this time, until their vessel completes its contact with Tau Verde IV and returns to the jump point. Pilot Officers will be permitted to rejoin their vessels upon completion of the outbound inspection. . . ."

"Hostages, damn it," groaned Daum. "They're taking hostages now."

"And a very clever choice of hostages," added Miles through his teeth. "Especially for a cul-de-sac like Tau Verde, taking your jump pilot traps you like a bug in a bottle. If you're not a good little tourist there, you just might not be allowed to go home. This is new, you say?"

"They weren't doing it five months ago," said Daum. "I haven't had word from home since I got out. But this means the fighting must still be going on at least." He stared intently into the view-screen, as if he could see through the invisible gateway to his home.

The message went on into technicalities, and ended, "By order of Admiral Yuan Oser, Commanding, Oseran Free Mercenary Fleet, under contract to the legal government of Pelias, Tau Verde IV."

"Legal government!" Daum spat angrily. "Pelians! Damned self-aggrandizing criminals . . ."

Miles whistled soundlessly and stared into the wall. *If I really were a nervous entrepreneur trying to unload that odd-lot of crap down there, what would I do?* he wondered. *I wouldn't be happy about dropping my pilot, but—I sure wouldn't be arguing with a disruptor bell-muzzle. Meek.* "We are going to be meek," said Miles forcefully.

✧ ✧ ✧

They hesitated half a day on the near side of the exit, to put the finishing touches on the arrangement of the cargo, and rehearse their roles. Miles took Mayhew aside for a closed debate, witnessed by Bothari alone. He opened bluntly, studying the pilot's unhappy face.

"Well, Arde, do you want to back out?"

"Can I?" the pilot asked hopefully.

"I'm not going to order you into a hostage situation. If you choose to volunteer, I swear not to abandon you in it. Well, I'm already sworn, as your liege lord, but I don't expect you to know—"

"What happens if I don't volunteer?"

"Once we jump to Tau Verde local space, we'd have no effective way of resisting a demand for your surrender. So I guess we apologize to Daum for wasting his time and money, turn around, and go home." Miles sighed. "If Calhoun was at the Embassy for the reason I think when we left, he's probably started legal proceedings to repossess the ship by now." He tried to lighten his voice. "I expect we'll end up back where we began the day I met you, only more broke. Maybe I can find some way to make up Daum's losses to him . . ." Miles trailed off in penitent thought.

"What if—" began Mayhew. He looked at Miles curiously. "What if they'd wanted, say, Sergeant Bothari instead of me? What would you have done then?"

"Oh, I'd go in," said Miles automatically, then paused. The air hung empty, waiting for explanation. "That's different. The Sergeant is—is my liegeman."

"And I'm not?" asked Mayhew ironically. "The State Department will be relieved."

There was a silence. "I'm your liegelord," replied Miles at last, soberly. "What you are is a question only you can answer."

Mayhew stared into his lap, and rubbed his forehead tiredly, one finger unconsciously caressing a silver circle of his implant contact. He looked up at Miles then, an odd hunger in his eyes that reminded Miles for a disquieting instant of the homesick Baz Jesek. "I don't know what I am anymore," said Mayhew finally. "But I'll make the jump for you. And the rest of the horsing around."

A queasy wavering dizziness—a few seconds' static in the mind—and the wormhole jump to Tau Verde was done. Miles hovered impatiently in Nav and Com, waiting for Mayhew, whose few seconds had been biochemically stretched to subjective hours, to crawl out from under his headset. He wondered again just what it was pilots experienced threading a jump that their passengers did not. And where did they go, the one ship in ten thousand that jumped and was never seen again? "Take a wormhole jump to hell" was an old curse one almost never heard in a pilot's mouth.

Mayhew swung up his headset, stretched, and let out his breath. His face seemed grey and lined, drained from the concentration of the jump. "That was a shit-kicker," he muttered, then straightened, grinned, and met Miles's eye. "That'll never be a popular run, let me tell you, kid. Interesting, though."

Miles did not bother to correct the honorific. Letting Mayhew rest, he slid into the comconsole himself and punched up a view of the outside world. "Well . . ." he muttered after a few moments, "where are they? Don't tell me we got the party ready and the guest of honor's not coming—are we in the right place?" he demanded anxiously of Mayhew.

Mayhew raised his eyebrows. "Kid, at the end of a wormhole jump you're either in the right place or you're a bucket of quarks smeared between Antares and Oz." But he checked anyway. "Seems to be . . ."

It was a full four hours before a blockade ship finally approached them. Miles's nerves stretched taut. Its slow approach seemed freighted with deliberate menace, until voice contact was made. The mercenary communication officer's tone of sleepy boredom then put it in its true light; they were sauntering. Desultorily, a boarding shuttle was launched.

Miles hovered in the shuttle hatch corridor, scenarios of possible disasters flashing through his mind. Daum has been betrayed by a quisling. The war is over, and the side we're expecting to pay us has lost. The mercenaries have turned pirate and are going to steal my ship. Some klutz has dropped and broken their mass detector, and so they're going to physically measure all our interior volumes, and they won't add up. . . . This last notion, once it occurred to him, seemed so likely that he held his breath until he spotted the mercenary technician in charge of the instrument among the boarders.

There were nine of them, all men, all bigger than Miles, and all lethally armed. Bothari, unarmed and unhappy about it, stood behind Miles and inspected them coldly.

There was something motley about them. The grey-and-white uniforms? They weren't particularly old, but some were in disrepair, others dirty. But were they too busy to waste time on nonessentials, or merely too lazy to keep up appearances? At least one man seemed out-of-focus, leaning against a wall. Drunk on duty? Recovering from wounds? They bore an odd variety of weapons, stunners, nerve disrupters, plasma arcs, needlers. Miles tried to add them up and evaluate them the way Bothari would. Hard to tell their working condition from the outside.

"All right," a big man shouldered through the bunch. "Who's in charge of this hulk?"

Miles stepped forward. "I'm Naismith, the owner, sir," he stated, trying to sound very polite. The big man obviously commanded the boarders, and perhaps even the cruiser, judging from his rank insignia.

The mercenary captain's eyes flicked over Miles; a quirk of an eyebrow, a shrug of contemptuous dismissal, clearly categorized Miles as No Threat. That's just what I want, Miles reminded himself firmly. Good.

The mercenary heaved a sigh of ennui. "All right, Shorty, let's get this over with. Is this your whole crew?" He gestured to Mayhew and Daum, flanking Bothari.

Miles lidded his eyes against a flash of anger. "My engineer's at his station, sir," he said, hoping he was achieving the right tone of a timid man anxious to please.

"Search 'em," the big man directed over his shoulder. Bothari stiffened; Miles met his look of annoyance with a quelling shake of his head. Bothari submitted to being pawed over with an obvious ill-grace that was not lost on the mercenary captain. A sour smile slid over the man's face.

The mercenary captain split his crew into three search parties, and gestured Miles and his people ahead of him to Nav and Com. His two soldiers began spot-checking everything that would come apart, even disassembling the padded swivel chairs. Leaving all in disarray, they went on to the cabins, where the search took on the nature of a ransacking. Miles clenched his teeth and smiled meekly as his personal effects were dumped pell-mell on the floor and kicked through.

"These guys have got *nothing* worth having, Captain Auson," muttered one soldier, sounding savagely disappointed. "Wait, here's something . . ."

Miles froze, appalled at his own carelessness. In

collecting and concealing their personal weapons, he had overlooked his grandfather's dagger. He had brought it more as a memento than a weapon, and half-forgotten it at the bottom of a suitcase. It was supposed to date back to Count Selig Vorkosigan himself; the old man had cherished it like a saint's relic. Although clearly not a weapon to tip the balance of the war on Tau Verde IV, it had the Vorkosigan arms inlaid in cloisonne, gold, and jewels on the hilt. Miles prayed the pattern would be meaningless to a non-Barrayaran.

The soldier tossed it to his captain, who withdrew it from its lizard-skin sheath. He turned it in the light, bringing out the strange watermark pattern on the gleaming blade—a blade that had been worth ten times the price of the hilt even in the Time of Isolation, and was now considered priceless for its quality and workmanship, among connoisseurs.

Captain Auson was evidently not a connoisseur, for he merely said, "Huh. Pretty," resheathed it—and jammed it in his belt.

"Hey!" Miles checked himself halfway through a boiling surge forward. Meek. Meek. He tamped his outrage into a form fitting his supposed Betan persona. "I'm not insured for this sort of thing!"

The captain snorted. "Tough luck, Shorty." But he mulled on Miles in a moment of curious doubt.

Backpedal, thought Miles. "Don't I at least get a receipt?" he asked plaintively.

Auson snickered. "A receipt! That's a good one." The soldiers grinned nastily.

Miles controlled his ragged breathing with an effort. "Well . . ." he choked out, "at least don't let it stand wet. It'll rust if it's not properly dried after each use."

"Cheap pot metal," growled the mercenary captain. He ticked it with a fingernail; it rang like a bell. "Maybe

I can get a good stainless blade put on that fancy hilt." Miles went green.

Auson gestured to Bothari. "Open that case there."

Bothari, as usual, glanced at Miles for confirmation. Auson frowned irritably. "Stop looking at Shorty. You take your orders from me."

Bothari straightened, and raised an eyebrow. "Sir?" he inquired dulcetly of Miles.

Meek, damn it, Sergeant, Miles thought, and sent the message by a slight compression of his lips. "Obey this man, Mr. Bothari," he replied, a little too sharply.

Bothari smiled slightly. "Yes, sir." Having established the pecking order in a form more to his taste, he at last unlocked the case, with precise, insulting deliberation. Auson swore under his breath.

The mercenary captain herded them to a final rendezvous, in what the Betans called the rec room and the Barrayarans called the wardroom. "Now," he said, "you will produce all your off-planet currency. Contraband."

"What!" cried Mayhew, outraged. "How can *money* be contraband?"

"Hush, Arde," hissed Miles. "Just do it." Auson might well be telling the truth, Miles realized. Foreign currency was just what Daum's people needed to buy such things as off-planet weaponry and military advisors. Or it might simply be the hold-up it appeared. No matter—judging from the lack of excitement of all hands, Daum's cargo had escaped them, and that was all that counted. Miles secreted triumph in his heart, and emptied his pockets.

"That's *all?*" said Auson disbelievingly, as they placed their final offerings in a little pile on the table before him.

"We're a little shor—broke, at the moment," Miles

explained, "until we get to Tau Verde and make some sales."

"Shit," muttered Auson. His eyes bored exasperatedly into Miles, who shrugged helplessly and produced his most inane smile.

Three more mercenaries entered, pushing Baz and Elena before them.

"Got the engineer?" said the captain tiredly. "I suppose he's bro—short, too." He glanced up and saw Elena. His look of boredom vanished instantly, and he came smoothly to his feet. "Well, *that's* better. I was beginning to think they were all freaks and fright masks here. Business before pleasure, though—you carrying any non-Tau Verdan currency, honey?"

Elena glanced uncertainly at Miles. "I have some," she admitted, looking surprised. "Why?"

"Out with it, then."

"Miles?" she queried.

Miles unclenched his aching jaw. "Give him your money, Elena," he ordered in a low tone.

Auson glowered at Miles. "You're not my frigging secretary, Shorty. I don't need you to transmit my orders. I don't want to hear any more back-chat from you, hear?"

Miles smiled and nodded meekly, and rubbed one sweating palm against his trouser seam where a holster wasn't.

Elena, bewildered, laid five hundred Betan dollars on the table. Bothari's eyebrows drew down in astonishment.

"Where'd you get all that?" whispered Miles as she stepped back.

"Countess—your mother gave it to me," she whispered back. "She said I should have some spending money of my own on Beta Colony. I didn't want to take so much, but she insisted."

Auson counted it, and brightened. "So, you're the banker, eh, honey? That's a bit more reasonable. I was beginning to think you folks were holding out on me." He cocked his head, looking her over and smiling sardonically. "People who hold out on me always come to regret it." The money vanished, along with a meager haul of other small, valuable items.

He checked their cargo manifest. "This right?" he asked the leader of the party who had come in with Elena and Baz.

"All the cases we busted open checked," replied the soldier.

"They made the most awful mess down there," Elena gritted under her breath to Miles.

"Sh. Never mind."

The mercenary captain sighed, and began sorting through their various identification files. At one point he grinned, and glanced up at Bothari, then Elena. Miles sweated. Auson finished the check, and leaned back casually in his seat before the computer console, regarding Mayhew glumly.

"You the pilot officer, eh?" he inquired unenthusiastically.

"Yes, sir," replied Mayhew, well coached in meekness by Miles.

"Betan?"

"Yes, sir."

"Are you—never mind. You're Betan, that answers the question. More frigging weirds per capita than any other . . ." he trailed off. "You ready to go?"

Mayhew glanced at Miles uncertainly.

"Damn it!" cried Auson, "I asked you, not Shorty! Bad enough that I'll have to look at you over the breakfast table for the next few weeks. He'd give me indigestion. Yeah, smile, you little mutant—" this last to Miles, "I bet you'd like to cut my liver out."

Miles smoothed his face, worried. He had been so sure he'd looked meek. Maybe it was Bothari. "No, sir," he said brightly, blinking for a meek effect.

The mercenary captain glared at him a moment, then muttered, "Aw, the hell with it," and rose.

His eye fell on Elena again, and he smiled thoughtfully. Elena frowned back. Auson looked around.

"Tell you what, Shorty," he said, in a benevolent tone. "You can keep your pilot. I've had about all the Betans I can take, lately."

Mayhew sighed relief under his breath. Miles relaxed, secretly delighted.

The mercenary captain waved at Elena. "I'll take her, instead. Go pack your things, honey."

Frozen silence.

Auson smiled at her, invitingly. "You won't be missing a thing by not seeing Tau Verde, believe me. You be a good girl, you might even get your money back."

Elena turned dilated eyes toward Miles. "My lord . . . ?" she said in a small, uncertain voice. It was not a slip of the tongue; she had a right to call for protection from her liege lord. It grieved him that she had not called "Miles," instead. Bothari's stillness was utter, his face blank and hard.

Miles stepped up to the mercenary captain, his meekness slipping badly. "The agreement was you were to hold our pilot officer," he stated in a flat voice.

Auson grinned wolfishly. "I make my own rules. She goes."

"She doesn't want to. If you don't want the pilot officer, choose another."

"Don't worry about it, Shorty. She'll have a good time. You can even have her back on the way out— if she still wants to go with you."

"I said choose another!"

The mercenary captain chuckled and turned away.

Miles's hand closed around his arm. The other mercenaries, watching the show, didn't even bother to draw weapons. Auson's face lit with happiness, and he swung around. *He's been itching for this,* Miles realized. *Well, so have I. . . .*

The contest was brief and unequal. A clutch, a twist, a ringing blow, and Miles was slammed facedown on the deck. The metallic tang of blood filled his mouth. As an afterthought, a deliberately aimed boot to his belly doubled him over where he lay, and assured that he wouldn't be rebounding to his feet in the immediate future.

Miles curled in agony, cheek pressed to the friction matting. *Thank God it wasn't the rib cage,* he thought incoherently through a haze of rage, pain, and nausea. He squinted at the boots, spread aggressively beyond his nose. *Toes must be steel-lined . . .*

The mercenary captain wheeled around, hands on hips. "Well?" he demanded of Miles's crew. Silence and stillness; all looked to Bothari, who might have been stone.

Auson, disappointed, spat disgustedly—either he wasn't aiming at Miles, or he missed—and muttered, "Aw, the hell with it. This tub's not worth confiscating anyway. Lousy fuel efficiency . . ." He raised his voice to his crew. "All right, load up, let's go. Come on, honey," he added to Elena, taking her firmly by the upper arm. The five mercenaries unhinged themselves from their various postures of languid observation, and prepared to follow their captain out the door.

Elena glanced back over her shoulder, to meet Miles's flaming eyes; her lips parted in a little "Ah," of understanding, and she stared at Auson with cold calculation.

"Now, Sergeant!" cried Miles, and launched himself at his chosen mercenary. Still shaken from his encounter with the captain, in an inspiration of rare prudence he picked the one he had seen propping up the wall earlier. The room seemed to explode.

A chair, which no one had seen the Sergeant unfasten from its moorings, flew across the room to smash into the mercenary carrying the nerve disruptor before he even began to draw. Miles, occupied with his own tackle, heard but did not see the Sergeant's second victim go down with a meaty, resonating "Unh!" Daum, too, reacted instantly, disarming his man neatly and tossing the stunner to an astonished Mayhew. Mayhew stared at it a second, woke up and fumbled it right way round, and fired. Unfortunately, it was out of charge.

A needler went off, wildly; its projectile exploded against a far wall. Miles put his elbow with all his strength into his man's stomach, and had his earlier hypothesis confirmed when the man folded, gagging and retching. Unquestionably drunk. Miles dodged emesis, and at last achieved a stranglehold. He put the pressure on full power for the first time in his life. To his surprise, the man jerked but a few times and went still. Is he surrendering? Miles wondered dizzily, and pulled the head back by the hair for a look at the face. The man was unconscious.

A mercenary, bouncing off Bothari, stumbled past Mayhew who at last found a use for the stunner, blackjacking the man to his knees. Mayhew hit him a couple more times, rather experimentally. Bothari, hurtling past, paused to say disgustedly, "Not like that!" grab the stunner, and smash the man flat with one accurately placed blow.

The Sergeant then proceeded to assist Daum with his second, and it was over, but for some yelling by the door accompanying a muffled cracking noise. The mercenary captain, his nose gouting blood, was down on the floor with Elena atop him.

"That's enough, Elena," said Bothari, placing the bell-muzzle of a captured nerve disruptor against the man's temple.

"No, Sergeant!" Miles cried. The yelling stopped abruptly, and Auson rolled fear-whitened eyes toward the gleaming weapon.

"I want to break his legs, too!" cried Elena angrily. "I want to break every bone in his body! I'll Shorty him! When I'm done he's going to be one meter tall!"

"Later," promised Bothari. Daum found a functioning stunner, and the Sergeant put the mercenary captain temporarily out of his misery, then proceeded systematically around the room to make sure of the rest. "We still have three more out there, my lord," he reminded Miles.

"Unh," Miles acknowledged, crawling to his feet. And the eleven or so in the other ship, he thought. "Think you and Daum can ambush and stun 'em?"

"Yes, but . . ." Bothari hefted the nerve disrupter in his hand. "May I suggest, my lord, that it may be preferable to kill soldiers in battle than prisoners after?"

"It may not come to that, Sergeant," said Miles sharply. The full chaotic implications of the situation were just beginning to dawn on him. "Stun 'em. Then we'll—figure out something else."

"Think quickly, my lord," suggested Bothari, and vanished out the door, moving with uncanny silence. Daum chewed his lip worriedly, and followed.

Miles was already starting to think. "Sergeant!" he called after them softly. "Keep one conscious for me!"

"Very good, my lord."

Miles turned back, slipping a little in a spatter of blood from the mercenary captain's nose, and stared at the sudden slaughterhouse. "God," he muttered. "Now what do I do with 'em?"

CHAPTER NINE

Elena and Mayhew stood waiting, looking at him expectantly. Miles suddenly realized he had not seen Baz Jesek in the fight—wait, there he was, pinned against the far wall. His dark eyes were like holes in his milky face, his breathing ragged.

"Are you hurt, Baz?" Miles cried in concern. The engineer shook his head, but did not speak. Their eyes met, and Jesek looked away. Miles knew then why he hadn't noticed him.

We're outnumbered two or three to one, Miles thought frantically. I can't spare a trained fighting man to funk—got to do something *right now*. . . . "Elena, Arde," he spoke, "go out in the corridor and close the door until I call you." They obeyed, looking baffled.

Miles walked up to the engineer. How do I do a heart transplant, he wondered, in the dark, by feel, without anesthetics? He moistened his lips and spoke quietly.

"We've got no choice. We have to capture their ship now. The best shot is to take their shuttle, make them think it's their own people coming back. That can only be done in the next few minutes.

"The only chance of escape for any of us is to take them before they get a squeak out. I'm going to assign the Sergeant and Daum to take their Nav and Com room, and prevent that. The next most vital section is engineering, with all the overrides."

Jesek turned his face away, like a man in pain or grief. Miles went on relentlessly.

"You're clearly the man for that one. So I'm assigning it to you and—" Miles took a breath, "and Elena."

The engineer turned his face back, if possible more drained than before. "Oh, no . . ."

"Mayhew and I will float, stunning anything that moves. Thirty minutes from now it will all be over, one way or another."

Jesek shook his head. "I can't," he whispered.

"Look, you're not the only one who's terrified. I'm scared witless."

Jesek's mouth twisted. "You don't look scared. You didn't even look scared when that mercenary pig decked you. You just looked pissed."

"That's because I've got forward momentum. There's no virtue in it. It's just a balancing act. I don't dare stop."

The engineer shook his head again, helplessly, and spoke through his teeth. "I *can't.* I've *tried.*"

Miles barely kept his lips from curling back in a snarl of frustration. Wild threats cascaded through his mind—no, that wasn't right. Surely the cure for fear was not more fear.

"I'm drafting you," Miles announced abruptly.

"What?"

"I claim you. I'm—I'm confiscating you. I'm seizing

your property—your training, that is—for the war effort. This is totally illegal, but since you're under a death sentence anyway, who cares? Get down on your knees and put your hands between mine."

Jesek's mouth fell open. "You can't—I'm not—nobody but one of the Emperor's designated officers can swear a vassal, and I was already sworn to him when I got my commission—and forsworn when—" he broke off.

"Or a Count or a Count's heir," Miles cut in. "I admit the fact that you're previously sworn to Gregor as an officer puts a wrinkle in it. We'll just have to change the wording around a bit."

"You're not . . ." Jesek stared. "What the hell are you, anyway? Who are you?"

"I don't even want to talk about it. But I really am a vassal secundus to Gregor Vorbarra, and I can take you for a liegeman, and I'm going to right now, because I'm in a hell of a hurry, and we can work out the details later."

"You're a lunatic! What the bloody hell do you think this is going to do?"

Distract you, thought Miles—and it's working already. "Maybe, but I'm a *Vor* lunatic. Down!"

The engineer fell to his knees, staring in disbelief. Miles captured his hands, and began.

"Repeat after me. I, Bazil Jesek, do testify I am, am, am a forsworn military vassal of Gregor Vorbarra, but I take service anyway under—under—" Bothari will be hot as hell if I break security, "under this lunatic in front of me—make that, this Vor lunatic—as an Armsman simple, and will hold him as my liege commander until my death or his releases me."

Jesek, looking hypnotized, repeated the oath verbatim.

Miles began. "I, uh—I better skip that part—I, a

vassal secundus to Emperor Gregor Vorbarra, do accept your oath, and pledge you the protection of a liege-commander; this by my word as—well, by my word. There. You now have the dubious privilege of following my orders to the letter and addressing me as 'my lord,' only you'd better not do it in front of Bothari until I get a chance to break the news to him gently. Oh, and one more thing . . ."

The engineer looked the question, bewildered.

"You're home. For what it's worth."

Jesek shook his head dizzily, and staggered to his feet. "Was that real?"

"Well—it's a little irregular. But from what I've read of our history, I can't help feeling it's closer to the original than the official version."

There was a knock on the door. Daum and Bothari had a prisoner, his hands fastened behind him. He was the pilot officer, by the silver circles on his temples and midforehead. Miles supposed that was why Bothari had picked him—he was bound to know all the recognition codes. The defiant set of the mercenary's head gave Miles a queasy premonition of trouble.

"Baz, take Elena and the major and start hauling these guys to Hold #4, the one with nothing in it. They might wake up and get creative, so weld the door shut on 'em. Then unseal our own weapons cache, get the stunners and plasma arcs, and check out the mercenary shuttle. We'll meet you there in a few minutes."

When Elena dragged out the last unconscious body by the ankles—it was the mercenary captain, and she was noticeably not careful what his head bumped on the way—Miles shut the door and turned to his prisoner, held by Bothari and Mayhew.

"You know," he addressed the man apologetically, "I sure would appreciate it if we could skip all the preliminaries and go straight to your codes. It would save a lot of grief."

The mercenary's lips curled at this, sardonic-sour. "Sure it would—for you. No truth drugs, eh? Too bad, Shorty—you're out of luck."

Bothari tensed, eyes strangely alight; Miles restrained him with a small movement of one finger. "Not yet, Sergeant."

Miles sighed. "You're right," he said to the mercenary, "we have no drugs. I'm sorry. But we still must have your cooperation."

The mercenary snickered. "Stick it, Shorty."

"We don't mean to kill your friends," Miles added hopefully, "just stun them."

The man raised his head proudly. "Time's on my side. Whatever you can dish out, I can take. If you kill me, I can't talk."

Miles motioned Bothari aside. "This is your department, Sergeant," he said in a low voice. "Seems to me he's right. What do you think of trying to board them blind, no codes? Couldn't be any worse than if he gave us a false one. We could skip this—" a nervous wave of his hand indicated the mercenary pilot.

"It would be better with the codes," stated the Sergeant uncompromisingly. "Safer."

"I don't see how we can get them."

"I can get them. You can always break a pilot. If you will give me a free hand, my lord."

The expression on Bothari's face disturbed Miles. The confidence was all right; it was the underlying air of anticipation that put knots in his guts.

"You must decide now, my lord."

He thought of Elena, Mayhew, Daum and Jesek, who had followed him to this place—who wouldn't be here but for him . . . "Go ahead, Sergeant."

"You may wish to wait in the corridor."

Miles shook his head, belly-sick. "No. I ordered it. I'll see it through."

Bothari inclined his head. "As you will. I need the knife." He nodded toward the dagger Miles had retrieved from the unconscious mercenary captain and hung on his belt. Miles, reluctantly, drew it and handed it over. Bothari's face lightened a little at the beauty of the blade, its tensile flexibility and incredible sharpness. "They don't make them like that anymore," he muttered.

What are you planning to do with it, Sergeant? Miles wondered, but did not quite dare ask. If you tell him to drop his trousers, I'm going to stop this session right now, codes or no codes. . . . They returned to their prisoner, who was standing easy, still casually defiant.

Miles tried one more time. "Sir, I beg you to cooperate."

The man grinned. "I just don't buy you, Shorty. I'm not afraid of a little pain."

I am afraid, thought Miles. He stepped aside. "He's yours, Sergeant."

"Hold him still," said Bothari. Miles grasped the prisoner's right arm; Mayhew, looking puzzled, held the left.

The mercenary took in Bothari's face, and his grin slipped. One edge of Bothari's mouth turned upward, in a smile Miles had never seen before and immediately hoped he would never see again. The mercenary swallowed.

Bothari placed the tip of the dagger against the side of the silver button on the man's right temple and wriggled it a little, to slip it beneath the edge. The mercenary's eyes shifted right, gone white-rimmed. "You wouldn't dare. . . ." he whispered. A drop of blood ringed the circle in a quick blink. The mercenary inhaled sharply, and began, "Wait—"

Bothari twisted the knife sideways, grasped the button between the thumb and fingers of his free hand, and yanked. A ululating scream broke from the mercenary's throat. He lunged convulsively from Miles's and Mayhew's grasp and fell to his knees, mouth open, eyes gone huge in shock.

Bothari dangled the implant before the man's eyes. Hair-fine wires hung like broken spider legs from the silver button body. He twirled it, with a glittering gleam and a spatter of blood, thousands of Betan dollars' worth of viral circuitry and microsurgery turned instantly to trash.

Mayhew, watching, went the color of oatmeal at this incredible vandalism. The breath went out of him in a tiny moan. He turned his back and went to lean against the wall in a corner. After a moment, he bent over, stifling vomiting.

I wish he hadn't witnessed that, thought Miles. *I wish I'd kept Daum instead. I wish . . .*

Bothari squatted down to his victim's level, face-to-face. He raised the knife again, and the mercenary pilot recoiled, to bash into the wall and slide into a sitting position, unable to retreat farther. Bothari placed the dagger's point against the button on the man's forehead.

"Pain is not the point," he whispered hoarsely. He paused, then added even more quietly, "Begin."

The man found his tongue abruptly, pouring out betrayal in his terror. There was, thought Miles, no question of clever subterfuge in the information tripping frantically out of his mouth. Miles overcame his own trembling belly to listen intently, carefully, thoroughly, that nothing be lost or missed or wasted. Unbearable, that this sacrifice should be wasted.

When the man began to repeat himself, Bothari pulled him cringing to his feet and frog-marched him to the shuttle hatch corridor. Elena and the others stared uncertainly at the mercenary, a trickle of blood threading down from his gored temple, but asked no questions. At the slightest prodding from Bothari the captured pilot officer, hasty and barely coherent, explained the internal layout of the light cruiser. Bothari pushed him aboard and strapped him in a seat, where he collapsed and burst into shocking sobs. The others looked away from the prisoner uneasily, and chose seats as far from him as possible.

Mayhew sat gingerly before the manual controls of the shuttle, and flexed his fingers.

Miles slid in beside him. "Are you going to be able to fly this thing?"

"Yes, my lord."

Miles took in his shaken profile. "You going to be all right?"

"Yes, my lord." The shuttle's engines whined to life, and they kicked away from the side of the RG 132. "Did you know he was going to do that?" Mayhew demanded suddenly, low-voiced. He glanced back over his shoulder at Bothari and his prisoner.

"Not exactly."

Mayhew's lips tightened. "Crazy bastard."

"Look, Arde, you better keep this straight," murmured Miles. "What Bothari does on my orders is my responsibility, not his."

"The hell you say. I saw the look on his face. He *enjoyed* that. You didn't."

Miles hesitated, then repeated himself with a different emphasis, hoping to make Mayhew understand. "What Bothari does is my responsibility. I've known it for a long time, so I don't excuse myself."

"He *is* psychotic, then," hissed Mayhew.

"He keeps himself together. But understand—if you have a problem about him, you see me."

Mayhew swore under his breath. "You're a pair, all right."

Miles studied the mercenary craft in the forward screens as they approached. It was a swift and powerful small warship, well armed. There was a bravura brilliance to its lines that suggested Illyrican make; it was named, appropriately, the *Ariel.* No question that the lumbering RG 132 would have had no chance of escaping it. He felt a twinge of envy at its deadly beauty, then realized with a start that if things went as planned, he was about to own it, or at least possess it. But the ambiguity of the methods poisoned his pleasure, leaving only a dry cold nervousness.

They came up without challenge or incident on the *Ariel's* shuttle hatch, and Miles floated aft to assist Jesek with locking on. Bothari bound his prisoner more securely to his seat, and loomed up beside Miles. Miles decided not to waste time arguing with him about precedence.

"All right," Miles conceded to his wordless demand. "You first. But I'm next."

"My reaction time will be quicker if my attention is not divided, my lord."

Miles snorted exasperation. "Oh, very well. You, then D—no. Then Baz." The engineer's eyes met his. "Then Daum, me, Elena, and Mayhew."

Bothari approved this schedule with a half-nod. The shuttle hatch sighed open, and Bothari slipped through. Jesek took a breath, and followed.

Miles paused only to whisper, "Elena, keep Baz moving forward as fast as you can. Don't let him stop."

From the ship ahead, he heard an exclamation—"Who the hell—!" and the quiet buzz of Bothari's stunner. Then he was through, into the corridor.

"Only one?" he asked Bothari, taking in the crumpled grey-and-white form on the floor.

"So far," replied the Sergeant. "We seem to have retained surprise."

"Good, let's keep it. Split, and move out."

Bothari and Daum melted down the first cross corridor. Jesek and Elena headed in the opposite direction. Elena cast one look backward; Jesek did not. Excellent, Miles thought. He and Mayhew took the third direction, and stopped before the first closed door. Mayhew stepped forward, in a kind of wobbly aggressiveness.

"Me first, my lord," he said.

God, it's contagious, thought Miles. "Go ahead."

Mayhew swallowed, and raised his plasma arc.

"Uh, wait a second, Arde." Miles pressed the palm lock. The door slid open smoothly. He whispered apologetically, "If it's not locked, you risk welding it shut that way. . . ."

"Oh," said Mayhew. He gathered himself and burst through the aperture with a kind of war whoop, fanning the room with his stunner, then stopped. It was a storage area, and empty but for a few plastic crates strapped into place. No sign of the enemy.

Miles poked his head in for a glance around, and stepped back thoughtfully. "You know," he said as they started back up the corridor, "it might be better if we don't yell, going in. It's startling. It's bound to be a lot easier to hit people if they're not jumping around and ducking behind things."

"They do it that way on the vids," Mayhew offered.

Miles, who had originally been planning his own first rush very much along the lines just demonstrated, and for much the same reason, cleared his throat. "I guess it just doesn't look very heroic to sneak up behind somebody and shoot them in the back. I can't help thinking it would be more efficient, though."

They went up a lift tube, and came to another door.

Miles tried the palm lock, and again the door slid open, revealing a darkened chamber. A dormitory with four bunks, three of them occupied. Miles and Mayhew tiptoed in, and took up can't-miss positions. Miles closed his fist, and they both fired at once. He fired again as the third figure began to lurch up from its bedclothes, reaching for a weapon hung in a holster by its bunk.

"Huh!" said Mayhew. "Women! That captain *was* a pig."

"I don't think they're prisoners," said Miles, switching on the light for a quick confirmation. "Look at the uniforms. They're part of the crew."

They withdrew, Miles very sober. Perhaps Elena had not been in as much danger as the mercenary captain had led them to believe. Too late now . . .

A low voice floated around the corner, growling, "Damn it, I warned that dumb son-of-a-bitch—" The speaker followed at a gallop, scowling and buckling on a holster belt, and ran headlong into them.

The mercenary officer reacted instantly, turning the accidental collision into a tackle. Mayhew received a kick to the abdomen. Miles was slammed into the wall, and found himself in a clutching, scrambling fight for possession of his own arsenal.

"Stun him, Arde!" he cried, muffled by an elbow to his teeth. Mayhew crawled after the stunner, rolled over, and fired. The mercenary slumped, and the nimbus of the bolt took Miles dizzily to his knees.

"Definitely better to catch them asleep," Miles mumbled. "Wonder if there's any more like him—her—"

"It," said Mayhew definitely, rolling the hermaphrodite soldier over to reveal the chiseled features of what could have been either a handsome young man or a strong-faced woman. Tangled brown hair framed the face and fell across the forehead. "Betan, by the accent."

"Makes sense," Miles gasped, and struggled back to his feet. "I think . . ." He clutched the wall, head pounding, queer-colored lights scrambling his vision. Being stunned was not as painless as it looked. "We better keep moving. . . ." He leaned gratefully on Mayhew's supporting arm.

They checked a dozen more chambers, without flushing further quarry. They came eventually to Nav and Com, to find two bodies piled by the door and Bothari and Daum in calm possession.

"Engineering reports secure," Bothari said at once upon seeing them. "They stunned four. That makes seven."

"We got four," said Miles thickly. "Can you get their computers to cough up a roster, and see if that adds up to the total?"

"Already done, my lord," said Bothari, relaxing a little. "They all seem to be accounted for."

"Good." Miles more-or-less fell into a station chair, rubbing his twice-battered mouth.

Bothari's eyes narrowed. "Are you well, my lord?"

"Caught a little stunner flash. I'll be all right." Miles forced himself to focus. What next? "I suppose we'd better get these guys locked up, before they wake up."

Bothari's face became mask-like. "They outnumber us three to one, and are technically trained. Trying to keep them all prisoner is bloody dangerous."

Miles looked up sharply, and held Bothari's eye. "I'll figure something out." He bit out each word emphatically.

Mayhew snorted. "What else can you do? Push 'em out the airlock?" The silence that greeted this joke turned his expression to sick dismay.

Miles shoved to his feet. "As soon as we've got 'em

nailed down we'd better start both ships boosting for the rendezvous. The Oserans are bound to start looking for their missing ship pretty soon, even if they didn't get a distress signal out. Maybe Major Daum's people can take these guys off our hands, eh?"

He nodded to Daum, who gave a "How should I know?" shrug. Miles left on rubbery legs to find Engineering.

The first thing Miles noticed upon entering the engineering section was the empty socket in the wall for the first-aid kit. Fear flashed through him, and he searched the room for Elena. Surely Bothari would have reported casualties—wait, there she was, the bandager, not the bandagee.

Jesek was slumped heavily in a station chair, and Elena was applying something to a burn on his upper arm. The engineer was smiling up at Elena with a quite fatuous, Miles thought, expression of gratitude.

The smile ignited to a grin when he saw Miles. He stood—somewhat to Elena's annoyance, as she was trying to fasten the bandage at the time—and gave Miles a snappy Barrayaran regulation Service salute. "Engineering is secured, my lord," he intoned, and then gulped a giggle. Stifling hysteria, Miles realized. Elena pushed him exasperatedly back into his chair, where another strangled giggle escaped him.

Miles caught Elena's eye. "How did it go, your first combat experience? Ah . . ." He nodded toward Jesek's arm.

"We didn't run into anybody on the way down. Lucky, I guess," she explained. "We caught them by surprise, coming through the door, and stunned two right away. A third one had a plasma arc, and he ducked down behind those conduits over there. Then this woman jumped me—" a wave indicated an unconscious form in grey and white, disposed on the deck, "which probably saved my life, because the one with the plasma arc couldn't fire when we were all tangled up wrestling for my stunner." She smiled at Jesek with enthusiastic admiration. "Baz charged him, and knocked him out. I got a choke on mine, and then Baz stunned her, and it was all over. That took some nerve, charging a plasma arc with a stunner. The mercenary only got one shot off—that's what happened to Baz's arm. I don't think I would have dared, would you?"

Miles walked around the room during this recitation, mentally reconstructing the action. He stirred the inert body of the former plasma arc wielder with the toe of his boot, and thought of his own tally for the day—one tottering drunk and two sleeping women. Jealousy twinged. He cleared his throat thoughtfully and looked up. "No, I'd probably have taken my own plasma arc and tried to burn through the brackets on that overhead light bar, and drop it on him. Then either nail him after he was smashed or else stun him as he jumped out from under."

"Oh," said Elena.

Jesek's grin faded slightly. "I didn't think of that."

Miles kicked himself, mentally. Ass—what kind of commander tries to score points off a man who needs build-up? A damned shortsighted one, obviously. This mess was only beginning. He amended himself immediately. "I might not have either, under fire. It's deceptively easy to second-guess somebody when you're not in the heat yourself. You did extremely well, Mr. Jesek."

Jesek's face sobered. The edge of hysterical glee faded, but left a residue of straightness in his spine. "Thank you, my lord."

Elena went off to examine one of the unconscious mercenaries, and he added to Miles in a low voice,

"How did you know? How did you know I could—hell, I didn't even know myself. I thought I could never face fire again." He stared voraciously at Miles, as though he were some mystic oracle, or talisman.

"I always knew," Miles lied cheerfully. "From the first time I met you. It's in the blood, you know. There's more to being Vor than the right to tack a funny syllable on the front of your name."

"I always thought that was a load of manure," said Jesek frankly. "Now . . ." He shook his head in wonderment.

Miles shrugged, concealing secret agreement. "Well, you carry my shovel now, that's for damn sure. And speaking of work—we're going to stuff all these guys into their own brig, until we decide, uh, how to dispose of them. Is that wound going to incapacitate you, or can you make this ship go pretty soon?"

Jesek stared around. "They've got some pretty advanced systems . . ." he began doubtfully. His eye fell on Miles, standing straight as his limitations would allow before him, and his voice firmed. "Yes, my lord. I can."

Miles, feeling quite maniacally hypocritical, gave the engineer a firm commander's nod copied from observations of his father at Staff conferences and the dinner table. It seemed to work quite well, for Jesek collected himself and began an orienting survey of the systems around him.

Miles paused on the way out the door to repeat the instructions for confining the prisoners to Elena. She cocked her head at him when he finished.

"And how was *your* first combat experience?" she inquired, softly truculent.

He grinned involuntarily. "Educational. Very educational. Ah—did you two happen to yell, charging through the door here?"

She blinked. "Sure. Why?"

"Just a theory I'm working on . . ." He swept her a bow of good-humored mockery, and exited.

The shuttle hatch corridor was lonely and quiet, but for the soft susurrations of air circulation and other life-support systems. Miles ducked through the dim shuttle tube and, free of the artificial gravity field of the larger ship's deck, floated forward. The mercenary pilot officer was still tied where they'd left him, his head and legs lolling in that strange bobbing fashion null-gee gave one. Miles cringed at the thought of having to explain the man's wound.

Miles's calculations about how to keep the man under control on the way to the brig were shattered when he came in view of his face. The mercenary's eyes were rolled back, his jaw slack; his face and forehead were mottled and flushed, and scorchingly hot to Miles's hesitant touch. His hands were waxen and icy, fingernails empurpled, pulse thready and erratic.

Horrified, Miles scrabbled at the knots binding him, then impatiently drew his dagger and cut the cords. Miles patted his face, on the side away from the dried streak of blood, but couldn't rouse him. The mercenary's body stiffened suddenly, and began to jerk and tremble, flailing in free fall. Miles ducked and swore, but his voice squeezed upwards to a squeak, and he clamped his jaw on it. Sickbay, then, get the man to sickbay, find the medtech and try to wake him up, or failing that, get Bothari, most experienced in first aid . . .

Miles wrestled the pilot officer through the shuttle's hatch. When he stepped from free fall into gravity he suddenly found out just how much the man weighed. Miles first tried to maneuver under him for a shoulder carry, to the imminent danger of his own bone structure. He staggered a few steps, then tried dragging him by the shoulders. Then the mercenary began to convulse again. Miles gave up and ran for sickbay and an antigrav stretcher, cursing the whole way, tears of frustration and fear in his voice.

It took time to get there, time to find the stretcher. Time to find Bothari on the ship's intercom and order him in a clipped fierce voice to report to sickbay with the medtech. Time to run back through the empty ship with the lift unit to the shuttle hatch corridor.

When Miles got there, the pilot officer had stopped breathing. His face was as waxy as his hands, his lips purple-blue as his nails, and the dried blood looked like a smear of colored chalk, dark and opaque.

Frantic haste made Miles's fingers seem thick and clumsy as he fitted the unit around the mercenary—he refused to think of it as "the mercenary's body"—and floated him off the floor. Bothari arrived at sickbay as Miles was positioning the mercenary over an examining table and releasing the lift unit.

"What's the matter with him, Sergeant?" asked Miles urgently.

Bothari glanced over the still form. "He's dead," he said flatly, and turned away.

"Not yet, damn it!" cried Miles. "We've got to be able to do something to revive him! Stimulants—heart massage—cryo-stasis—did you find the medtech?"

"Yes, but she was too heavily stunned to rouse."

Miles swore again, and began ransacking drawers for recognizable medications and equipment. They were disorganized, the labels on the outside having, apparently, no relation to the contents.

"It won't do any good, my lord," said Bothari, watching him impassively. "You'd need a surgeon. Stroke."

Miles rocked back on his heels, at last understanding what he had just seen. He pictured the implant wires, ripped through the man's brain, sliding against the rubbery covering of a major artery, slicing a fine groove in the heart-stressed tubule. Then the weakness propagated with every pulse until catastrophic failure filled the tissues with the killing hemorrhage.

Did this little sickbay even have a cryogenic chamber? Miles hastened around the room and into the next, searching. The freezing process would have to be started immediately, or brain death would be too far advanced to be reversed—never mind that he had only the vaguest idea of how patients were prepared for freezing, or how to operate the device, or . . .

There it was! A portable, a gleaming metal chamber on a float pallet looking faintly like some deep-sea probe. Miles's heart seemed to fill his throat. He approached it. Its power pack was empty, its gas canisters read fully discharged, and its control computer was laid open like some crudely dissected biological specimen. Out of order.

Miles slammed his fists against its metal sides, once, leaned his forehead against its coolness, and swore one last heartfelt sibilant. He then stood silent until his breathing steadied, and returned without haste to the other room.

Bothari stood at rest, awaiting orders. "Do you require anything further, my lord? I would feel easier if I could supervise the weapons search of the prisoners myself." He gazed on the corpse with indifferent eyes.

"Yes—no . . ." Miles walked around the examining table at a distance. His eye was drawn to the dark clot on the pilot officer's right temple. "What did you do with his implant nexus?"

Bothari looked mildly surprised, and checked his pockets. "I still have it, my lord."

Miles held out his hand for the crushed silver spider.

It weighed no more than the button it resembled, its smooth surface concealing the complexity of the hundreds of kilometers of viral circuitry packed within.

Bothari frowned a little, watching his face. "One casualty is not bad for an operation of this nature, my lord," he offered. "His life saved many, and not just on our side."

"Ah," said Miles, dry and cold. "I'll keep that in mind, when I come to explain to my father how it was we happened to torture a prisoner to death."

Bothari flinched. After a silence, he reiterated his interest in the ongoing weapons search, and Miles released him with a tired nod. "I'll be along shortly."

Miles puttered nervously around sickbay for a few more minutes, avoiding looking at the examining table. At last, moved by an obscure impulse, he fetched a basin, water, and a cloth, and washed the dried blood from the mercenary's face.

So this is the terror, he thought, that motivates those crazy massacres of witnesses one reads about. I understand them now. I liked it better when I didn't.

He drew his dagger and trimmed the trailing wires from the silver button, and pressed it carefully back into place on the pilot officer's temple. After, until Daum came looking for him with some request for orders, he stood and meditated on the still, waxen features of the thing they'd made. But reason seemed to run backwards, conclusions swallowed in premises, and premises in silence, until in the end only silence and the unanswerable object remained.

CHAPTER TEN

Miles gestured the injured mercenary captain ahead of him into sickbay with a little jab of his nerve disrupter. The deadly weapon seemed unnaturally light and easy in his hand. Something that lethal should have more heft, like a broadsword. Wrong, for murder to be so potentially effortless—one ought to at least have to grunt for it.

He would have felt happier with a stunner, but Bothari had insisted that Miles present a front of maximum authority when moving prisoners about. "Saves argument," he'd said.

The miserable Captain Auson, with two broken arms, nose a swollen blot on his face, did not look very argumentative. But the cat-like tension and calculating flicks of glance of Auson's first officer, the Betan hermaphrodite Lieutenant Thorne, reconciled Miles to Bothari's reasoning.

He found Bothari leaning with deceptive casualness

against a wall within, and the mercenaries' frazzled-looking medtech preparing for her next customers. Miles had deliberately saved Auson for last, and toyed with a pleasantly hostile fantasy of ordering the Captain's arms, when set, immobilized in some anatomically unlikely position.

Thorne was seated to have a cut over one eye sealed, and to receive an injection against stunner-induced migraine. The lieutenant sighed as the medication took effect, and looked at Miles with less squinting curiosity. "Who the hell are you people, anyway?"

Miles arranged his mouth in what he hoped would be taken for a smile of urbane mystery, and said nothing.

"What are you going to do with us?" Thorne persisted.

Good question, he thought. He had returned to Cargo Hold #4 to find their first batch of prisoners well along to having one of the bulkheads apart and escape manufactured. Miles voiced no objection when Bothari prudently had them all stunned again for transport to the *Ariel's* brig. There, Miles found, the chief engineer and her assistants had nearly managed to sabotage the magnetic locks in their cells. Miles rather desperately had them all stunned again.

Bothari was right; it was an intrinsically unstable situation. Miles could hardly keep the whole crew stunned for a week or more, crammed in their little prison, without doing them serious physiological damage. Miles's own people were spread too thinly, manning both ships, guarding the prisoners around the clock—and fatigue would soon multiply error. Bothari's murderous and final solution had a certain logic to it, Miles supposed. But his eye fell on the silent sheeted form of the mercenary pilot officer in the corner of the room, and he shivered inwardly. Not again. He suppressed jittering panic at his abruptly enlarged troubles, and angled for time.

"It would be a favor to Admiral Oser to put you out now and let you walk home," he answered Thorne. "Are they all like you out there?"

Thorne said stonily, "The Oserans are a free coalition of mercenaries. Most captains are Captain-owners."

Miles swore, genuinely surprised. "That's not a chain of command. That's a damned committee."

He stared curiously at Auson. A shot of painkiller was at last unlocking the big man's attention from his own body, and he glowered back. "Is your crew sworn to you, then, or to Admiral Oser?" Miles asked him.

"Sworn? I hold the contracts of everybody on my ship, if that's what you mean," Auson growled. "Everybody." He frowned at Thorne, whose nostrils grew pinched.

"My ship," corrected Miles. Auson's mouth rippled in a silent snarl and he glared at the nerve disrupter but, as Bothari had predicted, did not argue. The medtech laid the deposed captain's arm in a brace, and began working over it with a surgical hand tractor. Auson paled, and became more withdrawn. Miles felt a slight twinge of empathy.

"You are, without a doubt, the sorriest excuse for soldiers I have seen in my career," Miles declaimed, trolling for reactions. One corner of Bothari's mouth twitched, but Miles ignored that one. "It's a wonder you're all still alive. You must choose your foes very carefully." He rubbed his own still-aching stomach, and shrugged. "Well, I know you do."

Auson flushed a dull red, and looked away. "Just trying to stir up a little action. We've been on this damned blockade duty a frigging *year*."

"Stir up action," Thorne muttered disgustedly. "You would."

I have you now. The certainty reverberated like a bell in Miles's mind. His idle dreams of revenge upon the mercenary captain vaporized in the heat of a new and more breathtaking inspiration. His eye nailed Auson, and he rapped out sharply, "How long has it been since your last General Fleet Inspection?"

Auson looked as if it had belatedly occurred to him that he ought to be limiting this conversation to names, ranks, and serial numbers, but Thorne replied, "A year and a half."

Miles swore, with feeling, and raised his chin aggressively. "I don't think I can take any more of this. You're going to have one now."

Bothari maintained an admirable stillness, against the wall, but Miles could feel his eyes boring through his shoulder blades with his sharpest what-the-hell-are-you-doing-now look. Miles did not turn.

"What the hell," said Auson, echoing Bothari's silence, "are you talking about? Who are you? I had you pegged for a smuggler for sure, when you let us shake you down without a squeak, but I'll swear we didn't miss—" He surged to his feet, causing Bothari's disrupter to snap to the aim. His voice edged upward in frustration. "You are a smuggler, damn it! I can't be that wrong. Was it the ship itself? Who'd want it? What the hell are you smuggling?" he cried plaintively.

Miles smiled coldly. "Military advisors."

He fancied he could see the hook of his words set in the mercenary captain and his lieutenant. Now to run in the line.

Miles began inspection, with some relish, in the sickbay itself, since he was fairly sure of his ground there. At disrupter point, the medtech produced her official inventory and began turning out drawers under Miles's intent eye. With a sure instinct Miles focused first on drugs capable of abuse, and immediately turned up some nicely embarrassing discrepancies.

Next was equipment. Miles itched to get to the cryogenic chamber, but his sense of showmanship held it for last. There were enough other breakdowns. Some of his grandfather's more acerbic turns of phrase, suitably edited, had turned the medtech's face to chalk by the time they arrived at the pièce de résistance.

"And just how long has this chamber been out of commission, Medtech?"

"Six months," she muttered. "The repairs engineer kept saying he'd get to it," she added defensively at Miles's frown and raised eyebrows.

"And you never thought to stir him up? Or more properly, ask your superior officers to do so?"

"It seemed like there was plenty of time. We haven't used—"

"And in that six months your captain never once even ran an in-house inspection?"

"No, sir."

Miles swept Auson and Thorne with a gaze like a dash of cold water, then let his eye deliberately linger on the covered form of the dead man. "Time ran out for your pilot officer."

"How did he die?" asked Thorne, sharply, like a sword thrust.

Miles parried with a deliberate misunderstanding. "Bravely. Like a soldier." Horribly, like an animal sacrifice, his thought corrected. Imperative they don't figure that out. But, "I'm sorry," he added impulsively. "He deserved better."

The medtech was looking at Thorne, stricken. Thorne said gently, "The cryo chamber wouldn't have done much good for a disrupter blast to the head anyway, Cela."

"But the next casualty," Miles interposed, "might be

some other injury." Excellent, that the excessively observant lieutenant had evolved a personal theory as to how the pilot officer happened to be dead without a mark on him. Miles was vastly relieved, not least because it freed him of having to dishonorably burden the medtech with a guilt not rightfully hers.

"I will send you the engineering technician later today," Miles went on. "I want every piece of equipment in here operating properly by tomorrow. In the meantime you can start putting this place in an order more like a military sickbay and less like a broom closet, is that understood, Medtech?" He dropped his voice to a whisper, like the hiss of a whip.

The medtech braced to attention, and cried, "Yes, sir!" Auson was flushed; Thorne's lips were parted in an expression very like appreciation. They left her pulling out drawers with trembling hands.

Miles motioned the two mercenaries ahead of him down the corridor, and fell behind for an urgent whispered conference with Bothari.

"You going to leave her unguarded?" Bothari muttered disapprovingly. "Madness."

"She's too busy to bolt. With luck, I may even be able to keep her too busy to run an autopsy on that Pilot Officer. Quick, Sergeant! If I want to fake a General Fleet Inspection, where's the best place to dig up dirt?"

"On this ship? Anywhere."

"No, really! The next stop has got to look bad. I can't fake the technical stuff, have to wait till Baz is ready for a break."

"In that case, try crew's quarters," suggested Bothari. "But why?"

"I want those two to figure we're some sort of mercenary super-outfit. I've got an idea how to keep them from combining to retake their ship."

"They'll never buy it."

"They *will* buy it. They'll love it. They'll eat it up. Don't you see, it saves their pride. We beat them—for now. Which do you think they'd rather believe, that we're great, or that they're a bunch of screw-ups?"

"Isn't it plain?"

"Just watch!" He skipped a silent dance step, composed his face to a mask of sternness, and strode after his prisoners, his boots ringing like iron down the corridor.

The crew's quarters were, from Miles's point of view, a delight. Bothari did the disassembling. His instinct for turning up evidence of slovenly habits and concealed vices was uncanny. Miles supposed he'd seen it all, in his time. When Bothari uncovered the expected bottles of the ethanol addict, Auson and Thorne took it as a matter of course; evidently the man was a known and tolerated borderline functional. The two kavaweed dopers, however, seemed to be a surprise to all. Miles promptly confiscated the lot. He left another soldier's remarkable collection of sexual aids in situ, however, merely inquiring of Auson, with a quirk of an eyebrow, if he were running a cruiser or a cruise ship? Auson fumed, but said nothing. Miles cordially hoped the captain might spend the rest of the day thinking up scathing retorts, too late to use.

Miles studied Auson's and Thorne's own chambers intently, for clues to their owners' personalities. Thorne's, interestingly, came closest to passing inspection. Auson appeared to brace himself for a rampage when they came at last to his own cabin. Miles smiled silkily, and had Bothari put everything away, after inspection, in better order than he'd found it. It was all those years as an officer's batman, perhaps; when they were done the room appeared quite transformed. From the evidence, or lack thereof, Auson himself appeared to have no serious vices beyond a natural indolence exacerbated by boredom into laziness.

The collection of exotic personal weapons picked up during this tour made an impressive pile. Miles had Bothari examine and test each one. He made an elaborate show of noting each substandard item and checking it off against a list of the owners. Exhilarated and inspired, he waxed wonderfully sarcastic; the mercenaries squirmed.

They inspected the arsenal. Miles took a plasma arc from a dusty rack, closing his hand over the control readouts on the grip.

"Do you store your weapons charged or uncharged?"

"Uncharged," muttered Auson, craning his neck slightly.

Miles raised his eyebrows and swung the weapon to point at the mercenary captain, finger tightening on the trigger. Auson went white. At the last instant, Miles flicked his wrist slightly to the left, and sent a bolt of energy sizzling past Auson's ear. The big man recoiled as a molten backsplash of plastic and metal sprayed from the wall behind him.

"Uncharged?" sang Miles. "I see. A wise policy, I'm sure."

Both officers flinched. As they exited, Miles heard Thorne mutter, "Told you so." Auson growled wordlessly.

Miles braced Baz privately before they began in engineering.

"You are now," he told him, "Commander Bazil Jesek of the Dendarii Mercenaries, Chief Engineer. You're rough and tough and you eat slovenly engineering technicians for breakfast, and you're *appalled* at what they've done to this nice ship."

"It's actually not too bad, near as I can tell," said

Baz. "Better than I could do with such an advanced set of systems. But how am I going to make an inspection when they know more than I do? They'll spot me right away!"

"No, they won't. Remember, you're asking the questions, they're answering them. Say 'hm,' and frown a lot. Don't let it start going the other way. Look—didn't you ever have an engineering commander who was a real son-of-a-bitch, that everybody hated—but who was always right?"

Baz looked confusedly reminiscent. "There was Lieutenant Commander Tarski. We used to sit around thinking up ways to poison him. Most of them weren't very practical."

"All right. Imitate him."

"They'll never believe me. I can't—I've never been—I don't even have a cigar!"

Miles thought a second, dashed off, and galloped back moments later with a package of cheroots abstracted from one of the mercenary's' quarters.

"But I don't smoke," worried Baz.

"Just chew on it, then. Probably better if you don't light it, God knows what it might be spiked with."

"Now, there's an idea for poisoning old Tarski that might have worked—"

Miles pushed him along. "All right, you're an air polluting son of a bitch and you don't take 'I don't know' for an answer. If I can do it," he uncorked his argument of desperation, "you can do it."

Baz paused, straightened, bit off the end of the cheroot and spat it bravely on the deck. He eyed it a moment. "I slipped on one of those damned disgusting things once. Nearly broke my neck. Tarski. Right." He clenched the cheroot between his teeth at an aggressive angle, and marched into the main engineering bay.

✧ ✧ ✧

Miles assembled the entire ship's company in their own briefing room, and took center stage. Bothari, Elena, Jesek, and Daum waited in the wings, posted in pairs at each exit, lethally armed.

"My name is Miles Naismith. I represent the Dendarii Free Mercenary Fleet."

"Never heard of it," called a bold heckler from the blur of faces around Miles.

Miles smiled acidly. "If you had, heads would roll in my security department. We do not advertise. Recruitment is by invitation only. Frankly," his gaze swept the crowd, making eye contact, linking each face one by one to its name and personal possessions, "if what I've seen so far represents your general standards, but for our assignment here you'd have gone right on not hearing of us."

Auson, Thorne, and the chief engineer, subdued and weary from fourteen hours of being dragged—raked—over every weld, weapon, tool, data bank, and supply room from one end of the ship to the other, had scarcely a twitch left in them. But Auson looked wistful at the thought.

Miles paced back and forth before his audience, radiating energy like a caged ferret. "We do not normally draft recruits, particularly from such dismal raw material. After yesterday's performance, I personally would have no compunction at disposing of you all by the swiftest means, just to improve the military tone of this ship." He scowled upon them fiercely. They looked nervous, uncertain; was there just the slightest hangdog shuffle there? Onward. "But your lives have been begged for you, upon a point of honor, by a better soldier than most of you can hope to be—" He glanced pointedly at Elena who, prepared, raised her chin and stood in a sort of parade rest, indicating to all the source of this unusual mercy.

Actually, Miles wondered if she wouldn't have personally shoved Auson, at least, out the nearest air lock. But having cast her in the role of "Commander Elena Bothari, my executive officer and unarmed combat instructor," it had occurred to him that he had the perfect setup for a fast round of good guy-bad guy.

"—and so I have agreed to the experiment. To put it in terms you are familiar with—former Captain Auson has yielded your contracts to me."

That stirred them into outraged murmuring. A couple of them rose from their seats, a dangerous precedent. Fortunately, they hesitated, as if uncertain whether to start for Miles's throat first, or Captain Auson's. Before the ripple of motion could become an unstoppable tidal wave, Bothari brought his disrupter to aim with a good loud slap against his other hand. Bothari's lips were drawn back in a canine grimace, and his pale eyes blazed.

The mercenaries lost the moment. The ripple died. Those who had risen sat back down carefully, their hands resting plainly and demurely upon their knees.

Damn, thought Miles enviously, *I wish I could muster that much menace. . . .* The trick of it, alas, was that it was not a trick at all. Bothari's ferocity was palpably sincere.

Elena aimed her nerve disruptor in a white nervous grip, her eyes wide; but then, an obviously nervous person with a lethal weapon has a brand of menace all their own, and more than one mercenary spared a glance from the Sergeant to the other possible source of crossfire. A male mercenary attempted a prudent placating smile, palms out. Elena snarled under her breath, and the smile winked out hastily. Miles raised his voice and overrode the lingering whispers of confusion.

"By Dendarii regulation, you will all start at the same rank—the lowest, recruit-trainee. This is not an insult; every Dendarii, including myself, has started there. Your promotions will be by demonstrated ability—demonstrated to me. Due to your previous experience and the needs of the moment, your promotions will probably be much more rapid than usual. What this means, in effect, is that any one of you could find yourself the brevet captain of this ship within weeks."

The murmur became suddenly thoughtful. What this meant, in effect, thought Miles, was that he had just succeeded in dividing all the lower-ranking echelons from their former seniors. He nearly grinned as ambition visibly lit a scattering of faces. And had he ever lit a fire under those seniors—Thorne and Auson stared at each other in edgy speculation.

"Your new training will begin immediately. Those not assigned to training groups this shift will temporarily re-commence their old duties. Any questions?" He held his breath; his scheme pivoted on the point of a pin. He would know in a minute. . . .

"What's your rank?" asked a mercenary.

Miles decided to stay flexible. "You may address me as Mr. Naismith." There, let them build theories on that.

"Then how do we know who to obey?" asked the original hard-eyed heckler.

Miles bared his teeth in a scimitar smile. "Well, if you disobey one of *my* orders, I'll shoot you on the spot. You figure it out." He drummed his fingers lightly on his holstered nerve disruptor. Some of Bothari's aura seemed to have rubbed off on him, for the heckler wilted.

A mercenary held up her hand, serious as a child at school.

"Yes, Trainee Quinn?"

"When do we get copies of the Dendarii regulations?"

Miles's heart seemed to stop. He hadn't thought of that one. It was such a reasonable request—the sort of commander Miles was trying to pass himself off as should know his regs by heart, or sleep with them under his pillow, or something. He produced a dry-mouthed smile, and croaked boldly, "Tomorrow. I'll have copies distributed to everyone." *Copies of what? I'll figure something out. . . .*

There was a silence. Then another voice from the back popped up. "What kind of insurance package does the, the Dendariis have? Do we get a paid vacation?"

And another: "Do we get any perqs? What's the pay scale?"

And yet another: "Will our pensions carry over from our old contracts? Is there a retirement plan?"

Miles nearly bolted from the room, confounded by this spate of practical questions. He had been prepared for defiance, disbelief, a concerted unarmed rush. . . . He had a sudden maniac vision of Vorthalia the Bold demanding a whole-life policy from his Emperor at sword's point.

He gulped down total confusion, and forged ahead. "I'll distribute a brochure," he promised—he had a vague idea that sort of information came in brochures—"later. As for fringe benefits—" He barely managed to turn a glassy stare into an icy one. "I am permitting you to live. Further privileges will have to be earned."

He surveyed their faces. Confusion, yes, that was what he wanted. Dismay, division, and most of all, distraction. Perfect. Let them, swirled upside-down in this gush of flim-flam, forget that their primary duty was to retake their own ship. Forget it for just a week, keep them too busy to think for just a week, a week was all he needed. After that, they'd be Daum's problem. There was something else in their faces, though; he could not quite put his finger on it. No matter—his next task was to get offstage gracefully, and get them all moving. And get a minute alone with Bothari . . .

"Commander Elena Bothari has a list of your assignments. See her on your way out. Attention!" He put a snap in his voice. They shuffled raggedly to their feet, as if the posture were but dimly remembered. "Dismissed!" Yes, before they came up with any more bizarre questions and his invention failed him.

He caught a snatch of sotto voce conversation as he marched out.

"—homicidal runt lunatic . . ."

"Yes, but with a commander like that, there's a chance I might survive my next battle. . . ."

He recognized the something-else in their faces suddenly—it was that same unnerving hunger he had seen in Mayhew's and Jesek's. It generated an unaccountable coldness in the pit of his belly.

He motioned Sergeant Bothari aside. "Do you still have that old copy of the Barrayaran Imperial Service regs that you used to carry around?" Bothari's bible, it was; Miles had sometimes wondered if the Sergeant had ever read another book.

"Yes, my lord." Bothari gave him a fishy stare, as if to say, Now what?

Miles sighed relief. "Good. I want it."

"What for?"

"Dendarii fleet regulations."

Bothari looked poleaxed. "You'll never—"

"I'll run it through the computer, make a copy—go through and chop out all the cultural references, change the names—it shouldn't take too long."

"My lord—those are the *old* regulations!" The flat

bass voice was almost agitated. "When those gutless slugs get a look at the old discipline parades—"

Miles grinned. "Yeah, if they saw the specs for those lead-lined rubber hoses, they'd probably faint dead away. Don't worry. I'll update them as I go along."

"Your father and the General Staff did that fifteen years ago. It took *them* two years."

"Well, that's what happens with committees."

Bothari shook his head, but told Miles where to find the old data disc among his things.

Elena joined the conference, looking nervous. But impressive, Miles thought; like a thoroughbred horse. "I've got them divided up into groups, by your list," she reported. "Now what?"

"Go ahead and take your group to the gym now and start the phys-ed class. General conditioning, then start teaching them what your father's taught you."

"I've never taught anybody before. . . ."

He smiled up at her, willing confidence into her face, her eyes, her spine. "Look, you can probably kill the first two days just having them demonstrate what they know on each other, while you stand around and say "Um," and "Hm," and "God help us," and things like that. The important thing isn't to teach them anything, but to keep them busy, wear them out, don't give them time to think or plan or combine their forces. It's only for a week. If I can do it," he said manfully, "you can do it."

"I've heard that before somewhere," she muttered.

"And you, Sergeant—take your group and start them on weapons drills. If you run out of Barrayaran drills, the Oseran standard procedures are in the computers, you can filch some of them. Ride them. Baz will be running his people into the ground down in engineering—spring cleaning like they've never had before. And after I've gotten these regs straightened around, we can start quizzing them on those, too. Tire 'em out."

"My lord," said the Sergeant sternly, "there are twenty of them and four of us. At the end of the week, who do you think is going to be tireder?" He slipped into vehemence. "My first responsibility is your hide, damn it!"

"I'm thinking of my hide, believe me! And you can best cover my hide by going out there and making *them* believe I'm a mercenary commander."

"You're not a commander, you're a bloody holovid director," muttered Bothari.

The editing job on the Imperial Regulations proved larger and more grueling than Miles had anticipated. Even the wholesale slaughter of such chapters as those detailing instructions for purely Barrayaran ceremonies such as the Emperor's Birthday Review left an enormous mass of material. Miles slashed into it, gutting almost as fast as he could read.

It was the closest look he had ever given to military regulations, and he meditated on them, deep in the night cycle. Organization seemed to be the key. To get huge masses of properly matched men and material to the right place at the right time in the right order with the swiftness required to even grasp survival—to wrestle an infinitely complex and confusing reality into the abstract shape of victory—organization, it seemed, might even outrank courage as a soldierly virtue.

He recalled a remark of his grandfather's—"More battles have been won or lost by the quartermasters than by any general staff." It had been apropos a classic anecdote about a quartermaster who had issued the young guerilla general's troops the wrong ammunition. "I had him hung by his thumbs for a day," Grandfather had reminisced, "but Prince Xav made me take him down." Miles fingered the dagger at his waist, and removed five screens of regulations about ship-mounted plasma weapons, obsolete for a generation.

His sclera were red and his cheeks hollow and grey with beard stubble at the end of the night cycle, but he had boiled his plagiarization down into a neat, fierce little handbook for getting everybody's weapons pointed in the same direction. He pressed it into Elena's hands to be copied and distributed before staggering off to wash and change clothes, the better to present a front of eagle-eyed, as opposed to pie-eyed, command before his "new troops."

"Done," he murmured to her. "Does this make me a space pirate?"

She groaned.

Miles did his best to be seen everywhere that day cycle. He re-inspected sickbay, and gave it a grudging pass. He observed both Elena's and the Sergeant's "classes," trying to look as if he were noting every mercenary's performance with stern appraisal, and not in truth nearly falling asleep on his feet. He squeezed time for a private conversation with Mayhew, now manning the RG 132 alone, to bring him up to date and bolster his confidence in the new scheme for holding the prisoners. He drew up some superficial written tests of his new "Dendarii Regulations" for Elena and Bothari to administer.

The mercenary pilot officer's funeral was in the afternoon, ship time. Miles made it a pretext for a rigorous inspection of the mercenaries' personal gear and uniforms: a proper parade. For the sake of example and courtesy, he turned himself and the Botharis out in the best clothes they had from his grandfather's funeral. Their somber brilliance artistically complimented the mercenaries' crisp grey-and-whites.

Thorne, pale and silent, observed the sharp turn-out with a strange gratitude. Miles was rather pale and silent himself, and breathed an inward sigh of relief when the pilot officer's body was at last safely cremated, his ashes scattered in space. Miles allowed Auson to conduct the brief ceremonies unhindered; his most soaring thespian hypocrisy, Miles felt, was not up to taking over this function.

He withdrew afterward to the cabin he had appropriated, telling Bothari he wanted to study the Oserans' real regulations and procedures. But his concentration was failing him. Odd flashes of formless movement occurred in his peripheral vision. He lay down but could not rest. He resumed pacing with his uneven stride, notions for fine-tuning his prisoner scheme tumbling through his brain but then escaping him. He was grateful when Elena interrupted him with a status report.

He confided to her, rather randomly, a half dozen of his new ideas, then asked her anxiously, "Do they seem to be buying it? I'm not sure how I'm coming across. Are they going to accept orders from a kid?"

She grinned. "Major Daum seems to have taken care of that angle. Apparently he bought what you told him."

"Daum? What did I tell him?"

"About your rejuvenation treatment."

"My *what?*"

"He seems to think you were on leave from the Dendarii to go to Beta Colony for a rejuvenation treatment. Isn't that what you told him?"

"Hell no!" Miles paced. "I told him I was there for medical treatment, yes—thought it would account for this—" a vague wave of his hand indicating the peculiarities of his body, "combat injuries or something. But—there isn't any such thing as a Betan rejuvenation treatment! That's just a rumor. It's their public health system, and the way they live, and their genetics—"

"You may know it, but a lot of non-Betans don't. Daum seems to think you're not only older but, er, a lot older."

"Well, naturally he believes it, then, if he thought it up himself." Miles paused. "Bel Thorne must know better, though."

"Bel's not contradicting it." She smirked. "I think it has a crush on you."

Miles rubbed his hands through his hair, and over his numb face. "Baz must realize this rejuvenation rumor is nonsense, too. Better caution him not to correct anybody, though, it works to my advantage. I wonder what he thinks I am? I thought he'd have figured it out by now."

"Oh, Baz has his own theory. I—it's my fault, really. Father's always so worried about political kidnappers, I thought I'd better lead Baz astray."

"Good. What kind of fairy tale did you cook up for him?"

"I think you're right about people believing things they make up themselves. I swear I didn't plant any of this, I just didn't contradict it. He knows you're a Count's son, since you swore him in as an Armsman—aren't you going to get in trouble for that?"

Miles shook his head. "I'll worry about that if we live through this. Just so he doesn't figure out which Count's son."

"Well *I* think you did a good thing. It seems to mean a lot to him. Anyway, he thinks you're about his age. Your father, whoever he was, disinherited you, and exiled you from Barrayar to . . ." she faltered, "to get you out of sight," she finished, raising her chin bravely.

"Ah," said Miles. "A reasonable theory." He came to the end of a circuit in his pacing and stood absorbed, apparently, by the bare wall in front of him.

"You mustn't blame him for it—"

"I don't." He smiled a quick reassurance, and paced again.

"You have a younger brother who has usurped your rightful place as heir—"

He grinned in spite of himself. "Baz is a romantic."

"He's an exile himself, isn't he?" she asked quietly. "Father doesn't like him, but he won't say why . . ." She looked at him expectantly.

"I won't either, then. It's—it's not my business."

"But he's your liegeman now."

"All right, so it is my business. I just wish it weren't. But Baz will have to tell you himself."

She smiled at him. "I knew you'd say that." Oddly, the non-answer seemed to content her.

"How did your last combat class go? I hope they all crawled out on their hands and knees."

She smiled tranquilly. "Very nearly. Some of the technical people act like they never expected to do that kind of fighting. Others are awfully good—I've kind of got them working on the klutzy ones."

"That's just right," he approved eagerly. "Conserve your own energy, expend theirs. You've grasped the principle."

She glowed in his praise. "You've got me doing so many things I've never done before, new people, things I'd never dreamed of—"

"Yes . . ." He stumbled. "I'm sorry I got you into this nightmare. I've been demanding so much of you—but I'll get you out. My word on it. Don't be scared."

Her mouth set in indignation. "I'm not scared! Well—some. But I feel more alive than I've ever been. You make anything seem possible."

The longed-for admiration in her eyes perturbed him. It was too much like hunger. "Elena—this whole thing is balanced on a hoax. If those guys out there wake up and realize how badly they have us outnumbered, we'll crash like—" He cut himself off. That wasn't what she needed to hear. He rubbed his eyes, fingertips pressing hard against them, and paced.

"It's not balanced on a hoax," she said earnestly. "You balance it."

"Isn't that what I said?" He laughed, shakily.

She studied him through narrowed eyes. "When was the last time you slept?"

"Oh, I don't know. I've lost track, with the ships on different clocks. That reminds me, got to get them on the same clock. I'll switch the RG 132, that'll be easier. We'll all keep Oseran time. It was before the jump, anyway. A day before the jump."

"Have you had dinner?"

"Dinner?"

"Lunch?"

"Lunch? Was there lunch? I was getting things ready for the funeral, I guess."

She looked exasperated. "Breakfast?"

"I ate some of their field rations, when I was working on the regs last night—look, I'm short, I don't need as much as you overgrown types . . ."

He paced on. Her face grew sober. "Miles," she said, and hesitated. "How did that pilot officer die? He looked, well, not all right, but he was alive in the shuttle. Did he jump you?"

His stomach did a roller-coaster flop. "My God, do you think *I* murdered—" But he had, surely, as surely as if he had held a disrupter to the man's head and fired. He had no desire to detail the events in the RG 132's wardroom to Elena. They looped in his memory, violent images flashing over and over. Bothari's crime, his crime, a seamless whole . . .

"Miles, are you all right?" Her voice was alarmed. He realized he was standing still with his eyes shut. Tears were leaking between the lids.

"Miles, sit down! You're hyper."

"Can't sit down. If I stop I'll . . ." He resumed his circuit, limping mechanically.

She stared at him, her lips parted, then shut her mouth abruptly and slammed out the door.

Now he had frightened her, offended her, perhaps even sabotaged her carefully nurtured confidence. . . . He swore at himself, savage. He was sinking in a black and sucking bog, gluey viscous terror sapping his vital forward momentum. He waded on, blindly.

Elena's voice again. "—bouncing off the walls. I think you'll have to sit on him. I've never seen him this bad. . . ."

Miles looked up into the precious, ugly face of his personal killer. Bothari compressed his lips, and sighed. "Right. I'll take care of it."

Elena, eyes wide with concern but mouth calm with confidence in Bothari, withdrew. Bothari grasped Miles by the back of the collar and belt, frog-marched him over to the bed, and sat him down firmly.

"Drink."

"Oh, hell, Sergeant—you know I can't stand scotch. Tastes like paint thinner."

"I will," said Bothari patiently, "hold your nose and pour it down your throat if I have to."

Miles took in the flinty face and prudently choked down a slug from the flask, which he recognized vaguely as confiscated from mercenary stock. Bothari, with matter-of-fact efficiency, stripped him and slung him into bed.

"Drink again."

"Blech." It burned foully down his throat.

"Now sleep."

"Can't sleep. Too much to do. Got to keep them moving. Wonder if I can fake a brochure? I suppose death-gild is nothing but a primitive form of life insurance, at that. Elena can't possibly be right about Thorne. Hope to God my father never finds out about this—Sergeant, you won't . . . ? I thought of a docking drill with the RG 132 . . ." His protests trailed off to a mumble, and he rolled over and slept dreamlessly for sixteen hours.

CHAPTER ELEVEN

A week later, he was still in command.

Miles took to haunting the mercenary ship's control room as they neared their destination. Daum's rendezvous was a rare metals refinery in the system's asteroid belt. The factory was a mobile of chaotic structures strung together by girdering and powersats, winged by its vast solar collectors, junkyard art. A few lights winked, picking out bright reflections and leaving the rest in charitable dimness.

Too few lights, Miles realized as they approached. The place looked shut down. An off shift? Not likely; it represented too large an investment to let stand idle for the sake of its masters' biology. By rights the smelteries should be operating around the clock to feed the war effort. Tow ships with ore chunks should be jockeying for docking space, outgoing freighters should be wheeling away with their military escorts in a traffic-control minuet. . . .

"Are they still answering your recognition codes correctly?" Miles asked Daum. He barely kept himself from shifting from foot to foot.

"Yes." But Daum looked strained.

He doesn't like the looks of this either, Miles thought. "Shouldn't a strategically important installation like this be more actively guarded? Surely the Pelians and the Oserans have got to be trying to knock it out. Where are your picket ships?"

"I don't know." Daum moistened his lips, and stared into the screen.

"We have a live transmission now, sir," the mercenary communications officer reported.

A Felician colonel appeared in the viewscreen.

"Fehun! Thank God!" cried Daum. The tension melted in his face.

Miles let out his breath. For a horrible moment he'd been crushed by a vision of being unable to unload his prisoners along with Daum's cargo, and then what? He was quite as exhausted by the week as Bothari had predicted, and looked forward with a shiver of relief to its ending.

Lieutenant Thorne, coming on station, smiled and gave Miles a neat salute. Miles pictured the look on Thorne's face when the masquerade and betrayal were at last revealed. His ballooning anticipation turned to lead in his stomach. He returned the salute, and concealed his queasiness by turning to watch Daum's conversation. Maybe he could arrange to be elsewhere when the trap was sprung.

"—made it," Daum was saying. "Where is everybody? This place looks deserted."

There was a flash of static, and the military figure in the screen shrugged. "We drove off an attack by the Pelians a few weeks ago. The solar collectors were damaged. We're awaiting the repair crews now."

"How are things at home? Have we freed Barinth yet?"

Another flash of static. The colonel, seated behind his desk, nodded and said, "The war is going well."

The colonel had a tiny sculpture on his desk, Miles noticed, a mosaic horse cleverly formed of assorted scrap electronic parts soldered together, no doubt by some refinery technician in his off hours. Miles thought of his grandfather, and wondered what kind of horses they had on Felice. Had they ever slipped back enough technologically to have used horse cavalry?

"Great!" Daum chortled, avid upon his fellow Felician's face. "I took so long on Beta, I was afraid—so we're still in business! I'll buy you a drink when we get in, you old snake, and we'll toast the Premier together. How is Miram?"

Static. "The family is well," the colonel said gravely. Static, "Stand by for docking instructions."

Miles stopped breathing. The little horse, which had been on the colonel's right hand, was now on his left.

"Yes," agreed Daum happily, "and we can *carry* on without all this garbage on the channel. Is that you making the white noise?"

There was another blat of static. "Our communications equipment was damaged in an attack by the Pelians a few weeks ago." Now the horse was back on the right. White fuzz on the screen. "Stand by for docking instructions." Now the left. Miles felt like screaming.

Instead he motioned the communications officer to kill the channel.

"It's a trap," Miles said, the instant they were off transmission.

"What?" Daum stared. "Fehun Benar is one of my oldest friends! He wouldn't betray—"

"You haven't been talking to Colonel Benar. You've

been having a synthesized conversation with a computer."

"But his voiceprint—"

"Oh, it really was Benar—prerecorded. Something on his desk was flipping around between those blasts of static. They were being deliberately transmitted to cover the discontinuities—almost. Careless of somebody. They probably recorded his responses in more than one session."

"Pelians," grunted Thorne. "Can't do anything right . . ."

Daum's tan skin greyed. "He wouldn't betray—"

"They probably had a fair amount of time to prepare. There are—" Miles took a breath, "there are lots of ways to break a man. I bet there *was* an attack by the Pelians a few weeks ago—only it wasn't driven off."

It was over, then, surrender inevitable. The RG 132 and its cargo would be confiscated, Daum taken prisoner of war, Miles and his liege-people interned, if they weren't shot outright. Barrayaran security would ransom him eventually, Miles supposed, with all due scandal. Then the Betan, Calhoun, with God-knew-what civil charges, then home at last to explain it all before the ultimate tribunal, his father. Miles wondered, if he waived his Class III diplomatic immunity on Beta Colony, could he be jailed there instead? But no, the Betans didn't jail offenders, they cured them.

Daum's eyes were wide, his mouth taut. "Yes," he hissed, convinced. "What do we do, sir?"

You're asking me? thought Miles wildly. Help, help, help . . . He stared around at the faces in the room, Daum, Elena, Baz, the mercenary technicians, Thorne and Auson. They gazed back with interested confidence, as if he were a goose about to lay a golden egg. Bothari leaned against the wall, his stance for once devoid of suggestions.

"They're asking why our transmission was interrupted," reported the communications officer urgently.

Miles swallowed, and produced his first cockatrice. "Pipe them some gooey music," he ordered, "and put a 'technical difficulties—please stand by' sign on the video."

The communications officer grinned and snapped to obey.

Well, that took care of the next ninety seconds. . . .

Auson, his arms still immobilized, looked as sick as Miles felt. Doubtless he was not looking forward to explaining his humiliating capture to his admiral. Thorne was crackling with suppressed excitement. The lieutenant is about to get revenge for this week, mused Miles miserably, and knows it.

Thorne was standing at attention. "Orders, sir?"

My God, thought Miles, don't they realize they're free? And more wildly, with new rocketing hope—*They followed me home, Dad. Can I keep them?*

Thorne, experienced, knew the ship, soldiers, and equipment intimately, not with facile surface gloss but with true depth; more vital still, Thorne had forward momentum. Miles stood straight as he could and barked, "So, Trainee Thorne, you think you're fit to command a warship, eh?"

Thorne came to a stiffer attention, chin raised eagerly. "Sir!"

"We've been presented with a most interesting little tactical exercise,"—that was the phrase his father had used to describe the conquest of Komarr, Miles recalled—"I'm going to give you the chance at it. We can keep the Pelians on hold for about one more minute. As a commander, how would you handle this?" Miles folded his arms and tilted his head, in the style of a particularly intimidating proctor from his candidacy exams.

"Trojan horse," said Thorne instantly. "Ambush their ambush, and take the station from within—you do want it captured intact, don't you?"

"Ah," said Miles faintly, "that would be fine." He dredged his mind rapidly for some likely sounding military-advisor-type noises. "But they must have some ships concealed around here somewhere. What do you propose to do about them, once you've committed yourself to defending an immobile base? Is the refinery even armed?"

"It can be, in a few hours," Daum put in, "with the maser scramblers we've got in the hold of the RG 132. Cannibalize the powersats—time permitting, even repair the solar collectors, to charge them—"

"Maser scramblers?" muttered Auson. "I thought you said you were smuggling military advisors. . . ."

Miles quickly raised his voice and overrode this. "Remember that personnel are in short supply, and definitely not expendable right now." Particularly Dendarii officers . . . Thorne bore a thoughtful look; Miles was momentarily terrified that he'd overdone his critiquing, causing Thorne to throw the problem back on him. "Convince me, then, Trainee Thorne, that taking a base is not tactically premature," Miles invited hastily.

"Yes, sir. Well, the defending ships we need to worry about are almost certainly Oseran. The Pelian ship-building capacity is way under par—they don't have the biotech for jump ships at all. And we have all the Oseran codes and procedures, but they don't know a thing about our Dendarii ones. I think I—we, can take them."

Our Dendarii? Miles's mind echoed. "Very well, Trainee Thorne. Go ahead," he ordered in a fine loud decisive voice. "I won't interfere unless you get in over your head." He shoved his hands in his pockets by way of emphasis, also to keep from biting his nails.

"Take us into dock, then, without tipping them off," Thorne said. "I'll ready the boarding party. May I have Commander Jesek and Commander Bothari?"

Miles nodded; Sergeant Bothari sucked in his breath, but said nothing, duty-glued to Miles's back. Thorne, dazzled with visions of captaincy, dashed out, followed by the drafted "advisors." Elena's face shone with excitement. Baz rolled a rather soggy cigar stump between his teeth, and strode after her, eyes gleaming unreadably. There was color in his face, Miles noted.

Auson stood downcast, face furrowed with anger, shame, and suspicion. There's a mutiny looking for a place to happen, thought Miles. He lowered his voice for the big man's ear alone.

"May I point out, you're still on the sick list, Trainee Auson."

Auson waggled his arms. "I could've had these off day before yesterday, damn it."

"May I also point out, that while I've promised Trainee Thorne a command, I have not said of what ship. An officer must be able to obey as well as command. To each his own test, to each his own reward. I'll be watching you, too."

"There's only one ship."

"You're full of assumptions. A bad habit."

"You're full of—" Auson shut his mouth with a snap, and gave Miles a long, thoughtful stare.

"Tell them we're ready for docking instructions." Miles nodded to Daum.

Miles itched to be part of the fight, but discovered to his dismay the mercenaries had no space armor small enough to fit him. Bothari grunted frank relief. Miles then thought of going along in a simple pressure suit, if not at the front of the rush, then at least at the rear.

Bothari nearly choked at the suggestion. "I swear I'll knock you down and sit on you if you go near those suits," he snarled.

"Insubordination, Sergeant," Miles hissed back.

Bothari glanced up the line at the mercenaries assembling in the armory to be sure he was not overheard. "I'm not hauling your body back to Barrayar to dump at my lord Count's feet like something the bloody cat caught." The Sergeant traded a driven glare for Miles's irritated frown.

Miles, in dim recognition of a man pushed to his limit, backed down grudgingly. "What if I'd passed my officer's training exams?" he asked. "You couldn't have stopped me from this sort of thing then."

"I'd have retired," Bothari muttered, "while I still had my honor."

Miles grinned involuntarily, and consoled himself with checking equipment and weapons for those who were going. The week of vigorous repair and refurbishment had clearly paid unexpected dividends; the combat group seemed to gleam with wicked efficiency. Now, Miles thought, we shall see if all this beauty is more than skin deep.

He took particular care over Elena's armor. Bothari arranged her comm leads himself before attaching her helmet, unnecessary business concealing most necessary rapid whispered instructions about how to handle herself in the only-half-familiar equipment.

"For God's sake, hang back," Miles told her. "You're supposed to be observing everybody's efficiency and reporting to me anyway, which you can't do if you're—" he swallowed the rest of his sentence, grisly visions of all the ways a beautiful woman could get mangled in combat skidding through his brain, "if you're in front," he substituted. Surely he'd been out of his scattered wits to let Thorne claim her.

Her features were framed in the helmet, hair drawn back and hidden so that the strong structure of her face sprang out, half knight, half nun. Her cheekbones were emphasized by the winged cheekpieces, ivory skin glowing in the tiny colored lights of her helmet readouts. Her lips were parted in exhilaration. They curved at him. "Yes, my lord." Her eyes were bright and fearless. "Thank you."

And more quietly, her gloved hand tightening on his arm for emphasis, "Thank you, Miles—for the honor." She had not quite mastered the touch of the servos, and mashed his flesh to the bone. Miles, who would not have moved to destroy the moment if she'd accidentally torn his arm off, smiled back with no more than a blink of pain. *God, what have I done?* he thought. *She looks like a valkyrie. . . .*

He dropped back for a quick word with Baz.

"Do me a favor, Commander Jesek, would you? Stick close to Elena and make sure she keeps her head down. She's, uh, a little excited."

"Absolutely, my lord." Jesek nodded emphatically. "I'd follow her anywhere."

"Um," said Miles. That hadn't been exactly what he'd meant to convey.

"My lord," Baz added, then hesitated and lowered his voice. "This, ah, commander business—you didn't mean that as a real promotion, did you? It was for show, right?" He jerked his head toward the mercenaries, now being counted off into assault groups by Thorne.

"It's as real as the Dendarii Mercenaries," Miles replied, not quite able to manage an outright lie to his liegeman.

Baz's eyebrows lifted. "And what does that mean?"

"Well . . . My fa—a person I knew once said that meaning is what you bring to things, not what you take from them. He was talking about Vor, as it happened." Miles paused, then added, "Carry on, Commander Jesek."

Baz's eyes glinted amusement. He came to attention and returned Miles an ironic, deliberate salute. "Yes, sir—Admiral Naismith."

Miles, dogged by Bothari, returned to the mercenaries' tactics room to monitor the battle channels alongside Auson and the communications officer. Daum remained posted in the control room with the engineering technician who was substituting for the dead pilot, to guide them into the docking station. Now Miles really did chew his nails. Auson clicked the plastic immobilizers on his arms together in a nervous tattoo, the limit of their motion. They caught each other, looking sideways simultaneously.

"What would you give to be out there, Shorty?"

Miles hadn't realized his anguish was so transparent. He did not even bother to be offended by the nickname. "About fifteen centimeters of height, Captain Auson," he replied, wistfully frank.

The breath of a genuine laugh escaped the mercenary officer, as if against his will. "Yeah." His mouth twisted in agreement. "Oh, yeah . . ."

Miles watched, fascinated, as the communications officer began pulling in telemetry from the assault group's battle armor. The holovid screen, split to display sixteen individuals' readouts at once, was a confetti-like confusion. He framed a cautious remark, hoping to get more information without revealing his own ignorance.

"Very nice. You can see and hear what each of your men are seeing and hearing." Miles wondered which information bits were the key ones. A trained person could tell at a glance, he was sure. "Where was it built? I've, ah—never seen this particular model."

"Illyrica," said Auson proudly. "The system came with the ship. One of the best you can buy."

"Ah . . . Which one is Commander Bothari?"

"What was her suit number?"

"Six."

"She's at the upper right of the screen. See, there's the suit number, keys for visual, audio, their suit-to-suit battle channels, our ship-to-suit battle channels—we can actually control the servos on any suit right from here."

Both Miles and Bothari studied the display intently. "Wouldn't that be a bit confusing for the individual, to be suddenly overridden?" Miles asked.

"Well, you don't do that too often. It's supposed to be for things like operating the suit medkits, pulling back the injured. . . . To tell the truth, I'm not completely sold on that function. The one time I was on this end and tried to pull out a wounded man, his armor was so damaged by the blast that got him, it barely worked at all. I lost most of the telemetry—found out why, when we mopped up. His head had been blown off. I'd spent twenty frigging minutes walking a corpse back through the air locks."

"How often have you used the system?" Miles asked.

Auson cleared his throat. "Well, twice, actually." Bothari snorted; Miles raised an eyebrow. "We were on that damned blockade duty so long," Auson hastened to explain. "Everybody likes a bit of easy work, sure, but . . . Maybe we were on it too long."

"That was my impression, too," Miles agreed blandly. Auson shifted uncomfortably, and returned his attention to his tactics displays.

They were on the verge of docking. The assault

groups were poised, ready. The RG 132 was maneuvering into a parallel bay, lagging behind; the Pelians had cannily instructed the warship to dock first, no doubt planning to pick off the unarmed freighter at their leisure. Miles wished desperately that he'd had some prearranged code by which to warn Mayhew, still manning the freighter alone, what was up. But without scrambled communications channels he risked tipping their hand to the listening Pelians. Hopefully, Thorne's surprise attack would pull whatever troops were waiting away from the RG 132.

The moment's silence seemed to stretch unbearably. Miles finally managed to pick out the medical readouts from the battle armor. Elena's pulse rate was an easy 80 beats a minute. Jesek's, beside her, was running about 110. Miles wondered what his own was. Something astronomical, by the feel of it.

"Does the opposition have anything like this?" asked Miles suddenly, an idea beginning to boil up in his mind. Perhaps he could be more than an impotent observer. . . .

"The Pelians don't. Some of the more advanced ships in our—in the Oseran fleet do. That pocket dreadnought of Captain Tung's, for instance. Betan-built." Auson emitted an envious sigh. "He's got everything."

Miles turned to the communications officer. "Are you picking up anything like that from the other side? Anybody waiting in the docking bay in battle armor?"

"It's scrambled," said the communications officer, "but I'd guess our reception committee to run about thirty individuals." Bothari's jaw tightened at this news.

"Thorne getting this?" asked Miles.

"Of course."

"Are they picking up ours?"

"Only if they're looking for it," said the communications officer. "They shouldn't be. We're tight-beamed and scrambled too."

"Two to one," muttered Auson unhappily. "Nasty odds."

"Let's try and even it up," said Miles. He turned to the communications officer. "Can you break their codes, get into their telemetry? You have the Oseran codes, don't you?"

The communications officer looked suddenly thoughtful. "It doesn't work exactly that way, but . . ." His sentence trailed off in his absorption with his equipment.

Auson's eye lit. "You thinking of taking over their suits? Walking them into walls, having them shoot each other—" The light went out. "Ah, hell—they've all got manual overrides. The second they figure out what's going on, they'll cut us off. It was a nice idea, though."

Miles grinned. "We won't let them figure it out, then. We'll be subtle. You think too much in terms of brute force, Trainee Auson. Now, brute force has never been my strong suit—"

"Got it!" the communications officer cried. The holovid plates threw up a second display beside the first. "There's ten of them over there with full-feedback armor. The rest seem to be Pelians—their armor only has comm links. But there are the ten."

"Ah! Beautiful! Here, Sergeant, take over our monitors." Miles moved to the new station and stretched his fingers, like a concert pianist about to play. "Now, I'll show you what I mean. What we want to do is simulate a lot of little, tiny suit malfunctions. . . ." He zeroed in on one soldier. Medical telemetry—physiological support—there. "Observe."

He pinpointed the reservoir from the man's pilot relief tube, already half full. "Must be a nervous sort of fellow—" He set it to backwash at full power, and checked the audio transmitter. Savage swearing filled the air briefly, overridden by a snarl calling for radio silence. "Now, there is one distracted soldier. And there's not a thing he can do about it until he gets somewhere he can take the suit off."

Auson, beside him, choked with laughter. "You devious-minded little bastard! Yes, yes!" He pounded his feet, in lieu of his hands, and swung about in his own seat. He called up the readings from another soldier, pecking out the commands slowly with his few working fingertips.

"Remember," cautioned Miles, "subtle."

Auson, still cackling, muttered "Right." He bent over his control panel. There. There . . . He sat up, grinning. "Every third servo command now operates on a half-second time lag, and his weapons will fire ten degrees to the right of where he aims them."

"Very good," Miles applauded. "We'd better save the rest until they're in critical positions, not tip our hand with too much too soon."

"Right."

The ship was moving closer, closer to the docking station. The enemy troops were preparing to board through the normal flex tubes.

Suddenly, Thorne's assault groups exploded from the dockside air locks. Magnetic mines were hastily fired onto the station hull, where they flared like sparks burning holes in a rug. Thorne's mercenaries jumped the gap and poured through. The enemy's radio silence burst into shocked chaos.

Miles hummed over his readouts. An enemy officer turned her head to look over her shoulder, calling orders to her platoon; Miles promptly locked the helmet in its position of maximum torsion, and the Oseran's head perforce with it. He picked out another

soldier, in a corridor his own people had not yet reached, and locked his suit's built-in heavy-duty plasma arc into full-on. Fire flared wildly from the man's hand at his surprised reflexive recoil, spraying floor, ceiling, and comrades.

Miles paused to glance over to Elena's readouts. A corridor was flowing past at high speed on the visual. It spun wildly as she used her suit's jets to brake. The artificial gravity was evidently now shut down in the docking station. An automatic air seal had clanged shut, blocking the corridor. She stopped her spin, aimed, and blasted a hole in it with her plasma arc. She flung herself through it as, at the same moment, an enemy soldier on the other side did likewise. They met in a confused scrambling grapple, servos screaming at the overload demands.

Miles searched frantically for the enemy among the ten readouts, but he was a Pelian. Miles had no access to his suit. His heart pounded in his ears. There was another view of the fight between Elena and the Pelian on the screens; Miles had a dizzy sense of being in two places at once, as if his atman had left his body, then realized he was looking at them through another Oseran's suit. The Oseran was raising his weapon to fire—he couldn't miss—

Miles called up the man's medkit and fired every drug in it into the man's veins at once. The audio transmitted a shuddering gasp; the heartbeat readout jumped crazily and then registered fibrillation. Another figure—Baz?—in the *Ariel's* armor rolled through the gash in the air seal, firing as he flew. The plasma washed over the Oseran, interrupting transmission.

"Son-of-a-bitch!" Auson screamed suddenly at Miles's elbow. "Whereinhell did *he* come from?"

Miles thought at first he was referring to the armored soldier, then followed the direction of Auson's

gaze to another screen, showing space opposite the docking station.

Looming up behind them was a large Oseran warship.

CHAPTER TWELVE

Miles swore in frustration. Of course! Oseran full-feedback space armor logically implied an Oseran monitor nearby. He should have realized it instantly. Fool he was, to have simply assumed the enemy was being directed from inside the docking station. He ground his teeth in chagrin. He had totally forgotten, in the overwhelming excitement of the attack, in his particular terror for Elena, the first principle of larger commands: don't get balled up in the little details. It was no consolation that Auson appeared to have forgotten it too.

The communications officer hastily abandoned the game of suit sabotage and returned to his proper post. "They're calling for surrender, sir," he reported.

Miles licked dry lips, and cleared his throat. "Ah—suggestions, Trainee Auson?"

Auson gave him a dirty look. "It's that snob Tung. He's from Earth, and never lets you forget it. He has four times our shielding and firepower, three times our acceleration, three times our crew, and thirty years experience. I don't suppose you'd care to consider surrender?"

"You're right," Miles said after a moment. "I don't care for it."

The assault on the docking station was nearly over. Thorne and company were already moving into adjoining structures for the mopping-up. Victory swallowed so swiftly by defeat? Unbearable. Miles groped vainly in the pit of his inspiration for a better idea.

"It's not very elegant," he said at last, "but we're at such incredibly short range, it's at least possible—we could try to ram them."

Auson mouthed the words: my ship . . . He found his voice. "My ship! The finest technology Illyrica will sell, and you want to use it for a frigging medieval battering ram? Shall we boil some oil and fling it at 'em, while we're at it? Throw a few rocks?" His voice went up an octave, and cracked.

"I bet they wouldn't expect it," offered Miles, a little quelled.

"I'll strangle you with my bare hands—" Auson, trying to raise them, rediscovered the limits of his motion.

"Uh, Sergeant," Miles called, retreating before the rapidly breathing mercenary captain.

Bothari uncoiled from his chair. His narrow eyes mapped Auson coldly, like a coroner planning his first cut.

"It's got to be at least tried," Miles reasoned.

"Not with my ship you don't, you little—" Auson's language sputtered into body language. His balance shifted to free one foot for a karate kick.

"My God! Look!" cried the communications officer.

The RG 132, torpid, massive, was rolling away from

the docking station. Its normal space drives blared at full power, giving it the usual acceleration of an elephant swimming in molasses.

Auson dropped, unheeded, from Miles's attention. "The RG 132, loaded, has four times the mass of that pocket dreadnought," he breathed.

"Which is why it flies like a pig and costs a fortune in fuel to move!" yelled Auson. "That pilot officer of yours is crazy if he thinks he can outrun Tung—"

"Go, Arde!" cried Miles, jumping up and down. "Perfect! You'll pin him right up against that smelting unit—"

"He's not—" began Auson. "Son-of-a-bitch! He is!"

Tung, like Auson, was apparently late in divining the bulk freighter's true intentions. Verniers began to flare, to rotate the warship into position to thrust toward open space. The dreadnought got one shot off, which was absorbed with little visible effect in the freighter's cargo area.

Then, almost in slow motion, with a kind of crazy majesty, the RG 132 lumbered into the warship—and kept going. The dreadnought was nudged into the huge smeltery. Projecting equipment and surface housings snapped and spun off in all directions.

Action calling for reaction, after an aching moment the smeltery heaved back. A wave of motion passed down its adjoining structures, like a giant's game of crack-the-whip. Smashed edges of the dreadnought were caught up on the smeltery, thoroughly entangled. Gaudy chemical fires gouted here and there into the vacuum.

The RG 132 drifted off. Miles stood before the tactics room screen and stared in stunned fascination as half the freighter's outer hull delaminated and peeled into space.

✧ ✧ ✧

The RG 132 was the final detail to be mopped up in the capture of the metals refinery. Thorne's commandos smoked the last of the Oserans out of their crippled ship, and cleared the outlying structures of resisters and refugees. The wounded were sorted from the dead, prisoners taken under guard, booby traps detected and deactivated, atmosphere restored in key areas. Then, at last, the manpower and shuttles could be spared to warp the old freighter into the docking station.

A smudged figure in a pressure suit stumbled out of the flex tube into the loading bay.

"They're *bent!* They're *bent!*" cried Mayhew to Miles, pulling off his helmet. His hair stuck out in all directions, plastered by dried sweat.

Baz and Elena strode up to him, looking, with their helmets off, like a pair of dark knights after the tournament. Elena's hug pulled the pilot off his feet; from Mayhew's suffused look, Miles guessed she was still having a little trouble with her servos. "It was great, Arde!" she laughed.

"Congratulations," added Baz. "That was the most remarkable tactical maneuver I've ever seen. Beautifully calculated trajectory—your impact point was perfect. You hung him up royally, but without structural damage—I've just been over it—with a few repairs, we've captured ourselves a working dreadnought!"

"Beautiful?" said Mayhew. "Calculated? You're as crazy as *he is*—" He pointed at Miles. "As for damage—look at it!" He waved over his shoulder in the direction of the RG 132.

"Baz says they have the equipment to rig some sort of hull repairs at this station," Miles soothed. "It'll delay us here for a few more weeks, which I don't like any more than you do, but it can be done. God help us if anybody asks us to *pay* for it, of course, but with luck I should be able to commandeer—"

"You don't understand!" Mayhew waved his arms in the air. "They're *bent.* The Necklin rods."

The body of the jump drive, as the pilot and his viral control circuitry was its nervous system, was the pair of Necklin field generator rods that ran from one end of the ship to the other. They were manufactured, Miles recalled, to tolerances of better than one part in a million.

"Are you sure?" said Baz. "The housings—"

"You can stand in the housings and look up the rods and see the warp. Actually see it! They look like *skis!*" Mayhew wailed.

Baz let his breath trickle out in a hiss between his teeth.

Miles, although he thought he already knew the answer, turned to the engineer. "Any chance of repairing—?"

Baz and Mayhew both gave Miles much the same look.

"By God, you'd try, wouldn't you?" said Mayhew. "I can see you down there now, with a sledgehammer—"

Jesek shook his head regretfully. "No, my lord. My understanding is the Felicians aren't up to jump ship production on either the biotech or the engineering side. Replacement rods would have to be imported—Beta Colony would be closest—but they don't manufacture this model any more. They would have to be specially made, and shipped, and—well, I estimate it would take a year and cost several times the original value of the RG 132."

"Ah," said Miles. He stared rather blankly through the plexiports at his shattered ship.

"Couldn't we take the *Ariel?*" began Elena. "Break

through the blockade, and—" She stopped, and flushed slightly. "Oh. Sorry."

The murdered pilot's ghost breathed a cold laugh in Miles's ear. "A pilot without a ship," he muttered under his breath, "a ship without a pilot, cargo not delivered, no money, no way home . . ." He turned curiously to Mayhew. "Why did you do it, Arde? You could have just surrendered peaceably. You're Betan, they'd have to have treated you all right. . . ."

Mayhew looked around the docking bay, not meeting Miles's eyes. "Seemed to me that dreadnought was about to blow you all into the next dimension."

"True. So?"

"So—well—it didn't seem to me a, a right and proper Armsman ought to be sitting on his ass while that was going on. The ship itself was the only weapon I had. So I aimed it, and—" He mimed a trigger with his finger, and fired it.

He then inhaled, and added with more heat, "But you never warned me, never briefed—I swear if you ever pull a trick like that again, I'll, I'll—"

A ghostly smiled tinged Bothari's lips. "Welcome to my lord's service—Armsman."

Auson and Thorne appeared at the other end of the docking bay. "Ah, there he is, with the whole Inner Circle," said Auson. They bore down upon Miles.

Thorne saluted. "I have the final totals now, sir."

"Um—yes, go ahead, Trainee Thorne." Miles pulled himself to attentiveness.

"On our side, two dead, five injured. Injuries not too serious but for one bad plasma burn—she'll be needing a pretty complete facial regeneration when we get to proper medical facilities—"

Miles's stomach contracted. "Names?"

"Dead, Deveraux and Kim. The head burn was Elli—uh, Trainee Quinn."

"Go on."

"The enemy's total personnel were 60 from the *Triumph*, Captain Tung's ship—twenty commandos, the rest technical support—and 86 Pelians of whom 40 were military personnel and the rest techs sent to restart the refinery. Twelve dead, 26 injured moderate-to-severe, and a dozen or so minor injuries.

"Equipment losses, two suits of space armor damaged beyond repair, five repairable. And the damages to the RG 132, I guess—" Thorne glanced up through the plexiports; Mayhew sighed mournfully.

"We captured, in addition to the refinery itself and the *Triumph*, two Pelian inner-system personnel carriers, ten station shuttles, eight two-man personal flitters, and those two empty ore tows hanging out beyond the crew's quarters. Uh—one Pelian armed courier appears to have—uh—gotten away." Thorne's litany trailed off; the lieutenant appeared to be watching Miles's face anxiously for his reaction to this last bit of news.

"I see." Miles wondered how much more he could absorb. He was growing numb. "Go on."

"On the bright side—"

There's a bright side? thought Miles.

"—we've found a little help for our personnel shortage problem. We freed 23 Felician prisoners—a few military types, but mostly refinery techs kept working at gunpoint until their Pelian replacements could arrive. A couple of them are a little messed up—"

"How so?" Miles began, then held up a hand. "Later. I'll—I'll be making a complete inspection."

"Yes, sir. The rest are able to help out. Major Daum's pretty happy."

"Has he been able to get in contact with his command yet?"

"No, sir."

Miles rubbed the bridge of his nose between thumb and forefinger, and squeezed his eyes shut, to contain the throbbing in his head.

A patrol of Thorne's weary commandos marched past, moving a batch of prisoners to a more secure location. Miles's eye was drawn to a squat Eurasian of about fifty in torn Oseran grey-and-whites. In spite of his battered and discolored face and painful limp, he maintained a hard-edged alertness. That one looks like he could walk through walls *without* space armor, Miles thought.

The Eurasian stopped abruptly. "Auson!" he cried. "I thought you were dead!" He towed his captors toward Miles's group; Miles gave the anxious guard a nod of permission.

Auson cleared his throat. "Hello, Tung."

"How did they take your ship without—" the prisoner began, and stopped, as he assimilated Thorne's armor, Auson's—in light of his immobilized arms, decorative—sidearm, their lack of guards. His expression of amazement changed to hot disgust. He struggled for words. "I might have known," he choked at last. "I might have known. Oser was right to keep you two clowns as far away from the real combat as possible. Only the comedy team of Auson and Thorne could have captured *themselves.*"

Auson's lips curled back in a snarl. Thorne flashed a thin, razor-edged smile. "Hold your tongue, Tung," it called, and added in an aside to Miles, "If you knew how many years I've been waiting to say that—"

Tung's face flushed a dark bronze-purple, and he shouted back, "Sit on it, Thorne! You're equipped for it—"

They both lunged forward simultaneously. Tung's guards clubbed him to his knees; Auson and Miles grabbed Thorne's arms. Miles was lifted off his feet, but between them they managed to check the Betan hermaphrodite.

Miles intervened. "May I point out, Captain Tung, that the—ah—comedy team has just captured you?"

"If half my commandos hadn't been trapped by that sprung bulkhead—" Tung began hotly.

Auson straightened, and smirked. Thorne stopped flexing on its feet. United at last, thought Miles, by the common enemy . . . Miles breathed a small "Ha!" as he spotted his opportunity to finally put the disbelieving and suspicious Auson in the palm of his hand.

"Who the hell is that little mutant?" Tung muttered to his guard.

Miles stepped forward. "In fact, you have done so well, Trainee Thorne, that I have no hesitation in confirming you in your brevet command. Congratulations, Captain Thorne."

Thorne swelled. Auson wilted, all the old shame and rage crowding in his eyes. Miles turned to him.

"You have also served, Trainee Auson," Miles said, thinking, overlooking that understandable small mutiny in the tactics room. . . . "Even while on the sick list. And for those who also serve, there is also a reward." He gestured grandly out the plexiport where a free-fall crew with cutting torches was just beginning to untangle the *Triumph* from its entrapment. "There is your new command. Sorry about the dents." He dropped his voice. "And perhaps next time you will not be so full of assumptions?"

Auson turned about, waves of bewilderment, astonishment, and delight breaking in his face. Bothari pursed his lips in appreciation of Miles's feudal ploy. Auson in command of his own ship must eventually wake to the fact that it *was* his own ship; Auson subordinate to Thorne must always be a potential focus for disaffection. But Auson in command of a ship held from Miles's hands became, ipso facto, Miles's man. Never mind that Tung's ship in either of their hands was technically grand theft of the most grandiose . . .

Tung took just slightly longer than Auson to understand the drift of the conversation. He began to swear; Miles did not recognize the language, but it was unmistakably invective. Miles had never seen a man actually foam at the lips before.

"See that this prisoner gets a tranquillizer," Miles ordered kindly as Tung was dragged away. An aggressive commander, Miles thought covetously. Thirty years experience—*I wonder if I can do anything with him . . . ?*

Miles looked around and added, "See the medtech and get those things taken off your arms, Captain Auson."

"Yes, sir!" Auson substituted a sharp nod for a curtailed attempt at a salute, and marched off, head held high. Thorne followed, to oversee further intelligence gathering from prisoners and the freed Felicians.

An engineering tech in want of supervision descended upon them instantly, to carry off Jesek. She grinned proudly at Miles. "Would you say we've earned our combat bonus today, sir?"

Combat bonus? Miles wondered blankly. He gazed around the station. Thinly spread but energetic activities of consolidation met his eye wherever he turned. "I should think so, Trainee Mynova."

"Sir." She paused shyly. "Some of us were wondering—just what is our pay schedule going to be? Biweekly or monthly?"

Pay schedule. Of course. His charade must continue—how long? He glanced out at the RG 132. Bent. Bent, and full of undelivered cargo, unpaid for.

He'd have to keep going somehow, until they at least made contact with Felician forces. "Monthly," he said firmly.

"Oh," she said, sounding faintly disappointed. "I'll pass the word along, sir."

"What if we're still here in a month, my lord?" asked Bothari as she left with Jesek. "It could get ugly—mercenaries expect to be paid."

Miles rubbed his hands through his hair, and quavered with desperate assertiveness, "I'll figure something out!"

"Can we get anything to eat around here?" asked Mayhew plaintively. He looked drained.

Thorne popped back up at Miles's elbow. "About the counterattack, sir—"

Miles spun on his heel. "Where?" he demanded, looking around wildly.

Thorne looked slightly taken aback. "Oh, not yet, sir."

Miles slumped, relieved. "Please don't do that to me, Captain Thorne. Counterattack?"

"I'm thinking, sir, there's bound to be one. On account of the escaped courier, if nothing else. Shouldn't we start planning for it?"

"Oh, absolutely. Planning. Yes. You, ah—have an idea to present, do you?" Miles prodded hopefully.

"Several, sir." Thorne began to detail them, with verve; Miles realized he was absorbing about one sentence in three.

"Very good, Captain," Miles interrupted. "We'll, uh, have a senior officer's meeting after—after inspection, and you can present them to everybody."

Thorne nodded contentedly, and dashed off, saying something about setting up a telecom listening post.

Miles's head spun. The jumbled geometries of the refinery, its ups and downs chosen, apparently, at random, did nothing to decrease his sense of disorientation. And it was all his, every rusty bolt, dubious weld, and stopped-up toilet in it . . .

Elena was observing him anxiously. "What's the matter, Miles? You don't look happy. We won!"

A true Vor, Miles told himself severely, does not bury his face in his liegewoman's breasts and cry—even if he is at a convenient height for it.

CHAPTER THIRTEEN

Miles's first tour of his new domain was rapid and exhausting. The *Triumph* was about the only encouraging part of it. Bothari lingered to go over the arrangements for keeping the horde of new prisoners secure with the overworked patrol assigned to that detail. Never had Miles seen a man wish more passionately to be twins; he half-expected Bothari to go into mitosis on the spot. The Sergeant grudgingly left Elena to be Miles's substitute bodyguard. Once out of sight, Miles instead put Elena to work as a real executive officer, taking notes. He did not trust even his own quick memory with the mass of new detail.

A combined sickbay had been set up in the refinery's infirmary, as the largest facility. The air was dry and cold and stale, like all recycled air, sweet with scented antiseptics overlaying a faint tang compounded of sweat, excrement, burnt meat, and fear. All medical personnel were drafted from the new prisoners, to treat their own wounded, requiring yet a couple more of Miles's thinly spread troops as guards. They in turn were sucked in by the needs of the moment as assistant corpsmen. Miles watched Tung's efficient surgeon and staff at work, and let this pass, limiting himself to a quiet reminder to the guards of their primary duty. So long as Tung's medicos stayed busy it was probably safe.

Miles was unnerved by the catatonic Colonel Benar, and the two other Felician military officers who lay listlessly, barely responding to their rescue. Such little wounds, he thought, observing the slight chafing at wrists and ankles, and tiny discolorations under their skins marking hypospray injection points. By such little wounds we kill men . . . The murdered pilot officer's ghost, perched on his shoulder like a pet crow, stirred and ruffled itself in silent witness.

Auson's medtech borrowed Tung's surgeon for the delicate placement of plastiskin that was to serve Elli Quinn for a face until she could be sent—how? when?—to some medical facility with proper regenerative biotech.

"You don't have to watch this," Miles murmured to Elena, as he stood discreetly by to observe the procedure.

Elena shook her head. "I want to."

"Why?"

"Why do you?"

"I've never seen it. Anyway, it was my bill she paid. It's my duty, as her commander."

"Well, then, it's mine, too. I worked with her all week."

The medtech unwrapped the temporary dressings. Skin, nose, ears, lips gone. Subcutaneous fat boiled away. Eyes glazed white and burst, scalp burned off—she tried to speak, a clotted mumble. Miles reminded himself that her pain nerves had been blocked. He turned his back abruptly, hand sneaking to his lips, and swallowed hard.

"I guess we don't have to stay. We're not really contributing anything." He glanced up at Elena's profile, which was pale but steady. "How long are you going to watch?" he whispered. And silently, to himself, for God's sake, it might have been you, Elena . . .

"Until they're done," she murmured back. "Until I don't feel her pain anymore when I look. Until I'm hardened—like *a* real soldier—like my father. If I can block it from a friend, certainly I ought to be able to block it from the enemy—"

Miles shook his head in instinctive negation. "Look, can we continue this in the corridor?"

She frowned, but then took in his face, pursed her lips, and followed him without further argument. In the corridor he leaned against the wall, swallowing saliva and breathing deeply.

"Should I fetch a basin?"

"No. I'll be all right in a minute." I hope. . . . The minute passed without his disgracing himself. "Women shouldn't be in combat," he managed finally.

"Why not?" said Elena. "Why is that," she jerked her head toward the infirmary, "any more horrible for a woman than a man?"

"I don't know," Miles groped. "Your father once said that if a woman puts on a uniform she's asking for it, and you should never hesitate to fire—odd streak of egalitarianism, coming from him. But all my instincts are to throw my cloak across her puddle or something, not blow her head off. It throws me off."

"The honor goes with the risk," argued Elena. "Deny the risk and you deny the honor. I always thought you were the one Barrayaran male I knew who'd allow that a woman might have an honor that wasn't parked between her legs."

Miles floundered. "A soldier's honor is to do his patriotic duty, sure—"

"Or hers!"

"Or hers, all right—but all this isn't serving the Emperor! We're here for Tav Calhoun's ten-percent profit margin. Or anyway, we were . . ."

He gathered himself, to continue his tour, then paused. "What you said in there—about hardening yourself—"

She raised her chin. "Yes?"

"My mother was a real soldier, too. And I don't think she ever failed to feel another's pain. Not even her enemy's."

They were both silent for long after that.

The officers' meeting to plan for the counterattack was not so difficult as Miles had feared. They took over a conference chamber that had belonged to the refinery's senior management; the breathtaking panorama out the plexiports swept the entire installation. Miles growled, and sat with his back to it.

He quickly slid into the role of referee, controlling the flow of ideas while concealing his own dearth of hard factual information. He folded his arms, and said "Um," and "Hm," but only very occasionally "God help us," because it caused Elena to choke. Thorne and Auson, Daum and Jesek, and the three freed Felician junior officers who had not been brain-drained did the rest, although Miles found he had to steer them gently away from ideas too much like those just demonstrated not to work for the Pelians.

"It would help a great deal, Major Daum, if you could reach your command." Miles wound up the session, thinking, How can you have misplaced an entire country, for God's sake? "As a last resort, perhaps a volunteer in one of those station shuttles could sneak on down to the planet and tell them we're here, eh?"

"We'll keep trying, sir," Daum promised.

Some enthusiastic soul had found quarters for Miles in the most luxurious section of the refinery, previously reserved, like the elegant conference chamber, for senior management. Unfortunately, the housekeeping services had been rather interrupted in the past few weeks. Miles picked his way among personal artifacts from the last Pelian to camp in the executive suite, overlaying yet another strata from the Felician he had evicted in his turn. Strewn clothing, empty ration wrappings, data discs, half-empty bottles, all well stirred by the flip-flops in the artificial gravity during the attack. The data discs, when examined, proved all light entertainment. No secret documents, no brilliant intelligence coups.

Miles could have sworn the variegated fuzzy patches growing on the bathroom walls moved, when he was not looking directly at them. Perhaps it was an effect of fatigue. He was careful not to touch them when he showered. He set the lights to maximum UV when he was done, and sealed the door, reminding himself sternly that he had not demanded the Sergeant's nocturnal company on the grounds that there were Things in his closet since he was four. Aching for sleep, he crawled into clean underwear brought with him.

Bed was a null-gee bubble, warmed womb-like by infrared. Null-gee sex, Miles had heard, was one of the high points of space travel. He'd never had a chance to try it, personally. Ten minutes of attempting to relax in the bubble convinced him he never would, either, although when heated the smells and stains that permeated the chamber suggested that a minimum of three people had tried it there before him recently. He crawled out hastily and sat on the floor until his stomach stopped trying to turn itself inside out. So much for the spoils of victory.

There was a splendid view out the plexiports of the RG 132's corrugated, gaping hull. Occasionally stress would release in some tortured flake of metal, and it would snap off spontaneously to stir the smattering of other wrinkled bits, clinging to the ship like dandruff. Miles stared at it for a time, then decided to go see if Sergeant Bothari still had that flask of scotch.

The corridor outside his executive suite ended in an observation deck, a crystal and chrome shell arched by the sweep of hard-edged stars in their powdered millions. Furthermore, it faced away from the refinery. Attracted, Miles wandered toward it.

Elena's voice, raised in a wordless cry, shot him out of somnolence into an adrenaline rush. It came from the observation deck; Miles broke into his uneven run.

He swarmed up the catwalk and spun one-handed around a gleaming upright. The dimmed observation deck was upholstered in royal-blue velvet that glowed in the starlight. Liquid-filled settees and benches in odd curving shapes seemed to invite the indolent recliner. Baz Jesek was spread-eagled backward over one, with Sergeant Bothari atop him.

The Sergeant's knees ground into the engineer's stomach and groin, and the great hands knotted about Baz's neck, twisting. Baz's face was maroon, his frantic words strangled inchoate. Elena, her tunic undone, galloped around the pair, hands clenching and unclenching in despair of daring to physically oppose Bothari. "No, Father! No!" she cried.

Had Bothari caught the engineer trying to attack her? Hot jealous rage shook Miles, dashed immediately by cold reason. Elena, of all women, was capable of defending herself; the Sergeant's paranoias had seen to that. His jealousy went ice green. He could let Bothari kill Baz . . .

Elena saw him. "Miles—my lord! Stop him!"

Miles approached them. "Get off him, Sergeant," he ordered. Bothari, his face yellow with rage, glanced sideways, then back to his victim. His hands did not slacken.

Miles knelt and laid his hand lightly on the corded muscles of Bothari's arm. He had the sick feeling it was the most dangerous thing he had done in his life. He dropped his voice to a whisper. "Must I give my orders twice, Armsman?"

Bothari ignored him.

Miles closed his hands tightly around the Sergeant's wrist.

"You don't have the strength to break my grip," Bothari snarled out of the corner of his mouth.

"I have the strength to break my own fingers trying," Miles murmured back, and threw all his weight into his pull. His fingernails went white. In a moment, his brittle joints would start to snap . . .

The Sergeant's eyes squeezed shut, his breath hissing in and out past his stained teeth. Then, with an oath, he sprang off Baz and shook free of Miles. He turned his back, chest heaving, blind eyes lost in infinity.

Baz writhed off the bench and fell to the carpet with a thump. He gulped air in a hoarse liquid choke, and spat up blood. Elena ran to him and cradled his head in her lap, heedless of the mess.

Miles staggered up and stood, catching his breath. "All right," he said at last, "What's going on here?"

Baz tried to speak, but it came out a gurgling bark. Elena was crying, no help there. "Damn it, Sergeant—"

"Caught her nuzzling that coward," Bothari growled, still with his back to them.

"He is not a coward!" Elena yelled. "He's as good a soldier as you. He saved my life today—" She turned to Miles. "Surely you saw it, my lord, on your monitors. There was an Oseran with a servo-aim locked on me—I thought it was all over—Baz shot him with his plasma arc. Tell him!"

She was talking about the Oseran he had slain with his own medkit, Miles realized. Baz had cooked a corpse, unknowing. *I saved you,* Miles cried inwardly. *It was me, it was me. . . .* "That's right, Sergeant," he heard himself saying. "You owe her life to your brother Armsman."

"That one is no brother to me."

"By my word, I say he is!"

"It's not proper—it's not right—I have to make it right. It has to be perfect—" Bothari swung around, narrow jaw working. In his life, Miles had never seen Bothari more agitated. I've put too much strain on him lately, he thought remorsefully. Too much, too fast, too out-of-control . . .

Baz croaked out words. "No . . . dishonor!" Elena hushed him, and lurched to her feet to face Bothari, fiercely.

"You and your military honor! Well, I've faced fire, and I've killed a man, and it was nothing but butchery. Any robot could have done it. There was nothing to it. It's all a sham, a hoax, a lie, a big put-on. Your uniform doesn't awe me any more, do you hear?"

Bothari's face was dark and rigid. Miles made shushing motions at Elena. He'd no objection to growing independence of spirit, but God in heaven, her timing was terrible. Couldn't she see it? No, she was too tangled up in her own pain and shame, and the new ghost clinging to her shoulder. She had not mentioned that she'd killed a man, earlier; but, Miles knew, there were reasons one might choose not to.

He needed Baz, he needed Bothari, he needed Elena, and he needed them all working together to get them home alive. Not, then, what he ached to cry out of his own anguish and anger, but what they needed to hear.

The first thing Elena and Bothari needed was to be parted until tempers cooled, lest they tear out each other's hearts. As for Baz—"Elena," said Miles, "Help Baz to the infirmary. See that the medtech checks him for internal injuries."

"Yes, my lord," she replied, emphasizing the official nature of the order with his title, for Bothari's benefit, presumably. She levered Baz to his feet, and pulled his arm across her shoulders, with an awkward venomous glower at her father. Bothari's hands twitched, but he said nothing and made no move.

Miles escorted them down the catwalk. Baz's breathing was growing slightly more regular, he saw with relief. "I think I'd better stay with the Sergeant," he murmured to Elena. "You two going to make it all right?"

"Thanks to you," said Elena. "I tried to stop him, but I was afraid. I couldn't do it." She blinked back last tears.

"Better this way. Everybody's edgy, too tired. Him too, you know." He almost asked her for a definition of "nuzzling," but stopped himself. She bore Baz off with tender murmurs that drove Miles wild.

He bit back his frustration and mounted again to the observation deck. Bothari still stood, grievously blank and inward. Miles sighed.

"You still have that scotch, Sergeant?"

Bothari started from his reverie, and felt his hip pocket. He handed the flask silently to Miles, who gestured at the benches. They both sat. The Sergeant's hands dangled between his knees, his head lowered.

Miles took a swallow, and handed the flask over. "Drink."

Bothari shook his head, but then took it and did so. After a time he muttered, "You never called me 'Armsman' before."

"I was trying to get your attention. My apologies."

Silence, and another swig. "It's the right title."

"Why were you trying to kill him? You know how badly we need techs."

A long pause. "He's not a right one. Not for her. Deserter . . ."

"He wasn't trying to rape her." It was a statement.

"No," lowly. "No, I suppose not. You never know."

Miles gazed around the crystal chamber, gorgeous in the sparked darkness. Superb spot for a nuzzle, and more. But those long white hands were down at the infirmary, probably laying cold compresses or something on Baz's brow. While he sat here getting drunk with the ugliest man in the system. What a waste.

The flask went back and forth again. "You never know," Bothari reiterated. "And she must have everything right, and proper. You see that, don't you, my lord? Don't you see it?"

"Of course. But please don't murder my engineer. I need him. All right?"

"Damn techs. Always coddled."

Miles let this pass, as an Old Service reflex complaint. Bothari had always seemed part of his grandfather's generation, somehow, although in fact he was a couple of years younger than Miles's father. Miles relaxed slightly, at this sign of a return to Bothari's normal—well, usual—state of mind. Bothari slipped into a reclining position on the carpet, shoulders against the settee.

"My lord," he added after a time. "You'd see to it, if I were killed—that she was taken care of, right. The dowry. And an officer, a fit officer. And a real go-between, a proper baba, to make the arrangements . . ."

Antique dream, thought Miles hazily. "I'm her liegelord, by right of your service," he pointed out gently. "It would be my duty." If I could only turn that duty to my own dreams.

"Some don't pay much attention to their duty anymore," Bothari muttered. "But a Vorkosigan—Vorkosigans never fail."

"Damn right," Miles mumbled.

"Mm," said Bothari, and slid down a little farther.

After a long silence, Bothari spoke again. "If I were killed, you wouldn't leave me out there, would you, my lord?"

"Huh?" Miles tore his attention from trying to make new constellations. He had just connected the dots into a figure dubbed, mentally, Cavalryman.

"They leave bodies in space sometimes. Cold as hell. . . . God can't find them out there. No one could."

Miles blinked. He had never known the Sergeant concealed a theological streak. "Look, what's all this all of a sudden about getting killed? You're not going to—"

"The Count your father promised me," Bothari raised his voice slightly to override him, "I'd be buried at your lady mother's feet, at Vorkosigan Surleau. He promised. Didn't he tell you?"

"Er . . . The subject never came up."

"His word as Vorkosigan. Your word."

"Uh, right, then." Miles stared out the chamber's transparency. Some saw stars, it seemed, and some saw the spaces between them. Cold . . . "You planning on heaven, Sergeant?"

"As my lady's dog. Blood washes away sin. She swore it to me. . . ." He trailed off, gaze never leaving the depths. Presently, the flask slipped from his fingers, and he began to snore. Miles sat cross-legged, watching over him, a small figure in his underwear against the black immensity, and very far from home.

Fortunately, Baz recovered quickly, and was back on the job the next day with the aid of a neck brace to ease his lacerated cervicals. His behavior to Elena was painfully circumspect whenever Miles was around, offering no further spur to his jealousy; but of course, where Miles was there also was Bothari, which perhaps accounted for it.

Miles began by flinging all their meager resources into getting the *Triumph* operational, overtly to fight the Pelians. Privately, he figured it was the only thing around big enough and fast enough for them to all pile into and successfully run like hell. Tung had two jump pilots; one of them at least might be persuaded to jump them out of Tau Verde local space altogether. Miles contemplated the consequences of turning up back at Beta Colony in a stolen warship with a kidnapped pilot officer, twenty or so unemployed mercenaries, a herd of bewildered refugee technicians, and no money for Tav Calhoun—or even for Betan shuttleport landing fees. The blanket of his Class III diplomatic immunity seemed to shrink to a bare fig leaf.

Miles's attempt to throw himself into the placement and powering up of a selection of weapons from the RG 132's hold alongside the technicians was constantly interrupted by people wanting directions, or orders, or organization, or, most frequently, authorization to seize some piece of refinery equipment or resource or leftover military supplies for the work at hand. Miles blithely authorized anything put in front of him, earning a reputation for brilliant decisiveness. His signature—"Naismith"—was developing into a nicely illegible flourish.

The personnel shortage was not, unfortunately, amenable to like treatment. Double shifts that became triple shifts tended to end in loss of efficiency from exhaustion. Miles took a stab at another approach.

Two bottles of Felician wine, quality unknown. A bottle of Tau Cetan liqueur, pale orange, not green, fortunately. Two nylon and plastic folding camp stools, a small and flimsy plastic table. A half-dozen silvery strip-packs of Felician delicacies—Miles hoped they were delicacies—exact composition mysterious. The last gleanings of non-rotted fresh fruit from the refinery's damaged hydroponics section. It ought to be enough. Miles loaded Bothari's arms with the looted picnic, gathered up the overflow, and marched off toward the prison section.

Mayhew raised an eyebrow as they passed him in a corridor. "Where are you going with all that?"

"Courting, Arde." Miles grinned. "Courting."

The Pelians had left a makeshift brig, a storage area hastily vented, plumbed, and partitioned into a series of tiny, bleak metal boxes. Miles would have felt more guilty about locking human beings in them if it had not been a case of turn-about.

They surprised Captain Tung hanging by one hand from the overhead light fixture and working, as yet vainly, on levering its cover apart with a flattened snap torn from his uniform jacket.

"Good afternoon, Captain," Miles addressed the dangling ankles with sunny good cheer. Tung scowled down upon him, estimation in his eyes; measured Bothari, found the sum of the calculation not in his favor, and dropped to the floor with a grunt. The guard locked the door again behind them.

"What were you going to do with it if you got it apart?" Miles asked curiously, looking up.

Tung swore at him, like a man spitting, then clamped into recalcitrant silence. Bothari set up the table and stools, dumped out the groceries, and leaned against the wall by the door, skeptical. Miles sat down and opened a bottle of wine. Tung remained standing.

"Do join me, Captain," Miles invited cordially. "I know you haven't had supper yet. I was hoping we might have a little chat."

"I am Ky Tung, Captain, Oseran Free Mercenary Fleet. I am a citizen of the People's Democracy of Greater South America, Earth; my social duty number is T275-389-42-1535-1742. This 'chat' is over." Tung's lips flattened together in a granite slit.

"This is not an interrogation," Miles amplified, "which would be far more efficiently conducted by the medical staff anyway. See, I'll even give you some information." He rose, and bowed formally. "Permit me to introduce myself. My name is Miles Naismith." He gestured at the other stool. "Do, please, sit down. I spend enough time with a crick in my neck."

Tung hesitated, but finally sat, compromising by making it on the edge of his seat.

Miles poured wine, and took a sip. He groped for one of his grandfather's wine connoisseur phrases as a conversation opener, but the only one that sprang to his memory was "thin as piss," which didn't seem exactly inviting. He wiped the lip of the plastic cup on his sleeve, instead, and pushed it toward Tung. "Observe. No poison, no drugs."

Tung folded his arms. "The oldest trick in the book. You take the antidote before you come in."

"Oh," said Miles. "Yes, I suppose I could have done that." He shook a packet of rather rubbery protein cubes out between them, and eyed them almost as dubiously as Tung did. "Ah. Meat." He popped one in his mouth and chewed industriously. "Go ahead, ask me anything," he added around a mouthful.

Tung struggled with his resolve, then blurted, "My troops. How are they?"

Miles promptly detailed a list, by full name, of the dead, and of the wounded and their current medical status. "The rest are under lock and key, as you are; excuse me from mapping their exact locations for you—just in case you can do more with that light than I think you can."

Tung sighed sadness and relief, and absently helped himself to a protein cube.

"Sorry things got so messy," Miles apologized. "I realize how it must burn you to have your opponent blunder to victory. I'd have preferred something neater and more tactical myself, like Komarr, but I had to take the situation as I found it."

Tung snorted. "Who wouldn't? Who do you think you are? Lord Vorkosigan?"

Miles inhaled a lungful of wine. Bothari abandoned the wall to pound him, not very helpfully, on the back, and glare suspiciously at Tung. But by the time Miles had regained his breath he had regained his balance. He mopped his lips.

"I see. You mean Admiral Aral Vorkosigan of Barrayar. You, ah, confused me a bit—he's Count Vorkosigan, now."

"Oh, yeah? Still alive, is he?" remarked Tung, interested.

"Very much so."

"Have you ever read his book on Komarr?"

"Book? Oh, the Komarr report. Yes, I'd heard it had been picked up by a couple of military schools, off-planet—off Barrayar, that is."

"I've read it eleven times," Tung said proudly. "Most succinct military memoir I've ever seen. The most complex strategy laid out logically as a wiring diagram—politics, economics, and all—I swear the man's mind must operate in five dimensions. And yet I find most people haven't heard of it. It should be required reading—I test all my junior officers on it."

"Well, I've heard him say that war is the failure of politics—I guess they've always been a part of his strategic thinking."

"Sure, when you get to that level—" Tung's ears pricked. "Heard? I didn't think he'd done any interviews—do you happen to remember where and when you saw it? Can copies be had?"

"Ah . . ." Miles trod a thin line. "It was a personal conversation."

"You've *met* him?"

Miles had the unnerving sensation of suddenly acquiring half a meter of height in Tung's eyes. "Well, yes," he admitted cautiously.

"Do you know—has he written anything like the Komarr Report about the Escobar invasion?" Tung asked eagerly. "I've always felt it should be a companion volume—defensive strategy next to offensive—get the other half of his thinking. Like Sri Simka's two volumes on Walshea and Skya IV."

Miles placed Tung at last; a military history nut. He knew the type very, very well. He suppressed an exhilarated grin.

"I don't think so. Escobar was a defeat, after all. He never talks about it much—I understand. Maybe a touch of vanity there."

"Mm," allowed Tung. "It was an amazing book, though. Everything that seemed so totally chaotic at the time revealed this complete inner skeleton—of course, it always seems chaotic when you're losing."

It was Miles's turn to prick his ears. "At the time? Were you at Komarr?"

"Yes, I was a junior lieutenant in the Selby Fleet, that Komarr hired—what an experience. Twenty-three years ago, now. Seemed like every natural weak point in mercenary-employer relations got blown up in our faces—and that was before the first shot was even fired. Vorkosigan's intelligence pathfinders at work, we learned later."

Miles made encouraging noises, and proceeded to pump this unexpected spring of reminiscence for all it was worth. Pieces of fruit became planets and satellites; variously shaped protein bits became cruisers, couriers, smart bombs and troop carriers. Defeated ships were eaten. The second bottle of wine introduced other well-known mercenary battles. Miles frankly hung on Tung's words, self-consciousness forgotten.

Tung leaned back at last with a contented sigh, full of food and wine and emptied of stories. Miles, knowing his own capacity, had been nursing his own wine to the limits of politeness. He swirled the last of it around in the bottom of his cup, and essayed a cautious probe.

"It seems a great waste for an officer of your experience to sit out a good war like this, locked in a box."

Tung smiled. "I have no intention of staying in this box."

"Ah—yes. But there may be more than one way to get out of it, don't you see. Now, the Dendarii Mercenaries are an expanding organization. There's a lot of room for talent at the top."

Tung's smiled soured. "You took my ship."

"I took Captain Auson's ship, too. Ask him if he's unhappy about it."

"Nice try—ah—Mr. Naismith. But I have a contract. A fact that, unlike some, I remember. A mercenary who can't honor his contract when it's rough as well as when it's smooth is a thug, not a soldier."

Miles fairly swooned with unrequited love. "I cannot fault you for that, sir."

Tung eyed him with amused tolerance. "Now, regardless of what that ass Auson seems to think, I have you pegged as a hotshot junior officer in over his head—and sinking fast. Seems to me it's you, not I, who's going to be looking for a new job soon. You seem to have at least an average grasp of tactics—and you *have* read Vorkosigan on Komarr—but any officer who can get Auson and Thorne hitched together to plow a straight line shows a genius for personnel. If you get out of this alive, come see me—I may be able to find something on the exec side for you."

Miles sat looking at his prisoner in openmouthed appreciation of a chutzpah worthy of his own. Actually, it sounded pretty good. He sighed regret. "You honor me, Captain Tung. But I'm afraid I too have a contract."

"Pigwash."

"Beg pardon?"

"If you have a contract with Felice, it beats me where you got it. I doubt Daum was authorized to make any such agreement. The Felicians are as cheap as their counterparts the Pelians. We could have ended this war six months ago if the Pelians had been willing to pay the piper. But no—they chose to 'economize' and only buy a blockade, and a few installations like this one—and for that, they act like they're doing us a favor. Peh!" Frustration edged his voice with disgust.

"I didn't say my contract was with Felice," said Miles mildly. Tung's eyes narrowed in puzzlement; good. The man's evaluations were entirely too close to the truth for comfort.

"Well, keep your tail down, son," Tung advised. "In the long run more mercenaries have had their asses shot off by their contractors than by their enemies."

Miles took his leave courteously; Tung ushered him out with the panache of a genial host.

"Is there anything else you need?" asked Miles.

"A screwdriver," said Tung promptly.

Miles shook his head and smiled regretfully as the door was closed on the Eurasian. "Damned if I'm not tempted to send him one," said Miles to Bothari. "I'm dying to see what he thinks he can do with that light."

"Just what did all that accomplish?" asked Bothari. "He burned up your time with ancient history and didn't give away anything."

Miles smiled. "Nothing unimportant."

CHAPTER FOURTEEN

The Pelians attacked from the ecliptic, opposite the sun, taking advantage of the scattered masses of the asteroid belt for what cover they provided. They came decelerating, telegraphing their intention to capture, not destroy; and they came alone, without their Oseran employees.

Miles laughed delightedly under his breath as he limped through the scramble of men and equipment in the refinery docking station corridors. The Pelians could scarcely be following his pet scenario more closely if he'd given them their orders himself. There had been some argument when he'd insisted on placing his farthest outlying pickets and his major weapons on the belt and not the planet side of the refinery. But it was inevitable. Barring subterfuge, a tactic currently exhausted, it was the Pelians' only hope of gaining a measure of surprise. A week ago, it would have done them some good.

Miles dodged some of his galloping troops hurrying to their posts. Pray God he would never find himself on foot in a retreat. He might as well volunteer for the rear guard in the first place, and save being trampled by his own side as well as by the enemy.

He dashed through the flex tube into the *Triumph.* The waiting soldier clanged the lock shut behind him, and hastily blew off the tube seals. As he'd guessed, he was the last aboard. He made his way to the tactics room as the ship maneuvered free of the refinery.

The *Triumph's* tactics room was noticeably larger than the *Ariel's,* and quite as sleek. Miles quailed at the number of empty padded swivel chairs. A scant half of Auson's old crew, even augmented by a few volunteer refinery techs, made scarcely a skeleton crew for the new ship.

Holograph displays were up and working in all their bright confusion. Auson looked up from trying to man two stations at once with relief in his eyes.

"Glad you made it, my lord."

Miles slid into a station chair. "Me too. But please—just 'Mr. Naismith.' No 'my lord.'"

Auson looked puzzled. "The others all call you that."

"Yes, but, um—it's not just a courtesy. It denotes a specific legal relationship. You wouldn't call me 'my husband' even if you heard my wife do so, eh? So what have we got out here?"

"Looks like maybe ten little ships—all Pelian local stuff." Auson studied his readouts, worry creasing his broad face. "I don't know where our guys are. This sort of thing should be just their style."

Miles correctly interpreted "our guys" to mean Auson's former comrades, the Oserans. The slip of tongue did not disturb him; Auson was committed, now. Miles glanced sideways at him, and thought he knew exactly why the Pelians hadn't brought their hired guns. For all the Pelians knew to the contrary, an Oseran ship had turned on them. Miles's eyes glittered at the thought of the dismay and distrust that must now be reverberating through the Pelian high command.

Their ship dove in a high arc toward their attackers. Miles keyed Nav and Com.

"You all right, Arde?"

"For flying blind, deaf, dumb, and paralyzed, not bad," Mayhew said. "Manual piloting is a pain. It's like the machine is operating me. It feels awful."

"Keep up the good work," Miles said cheerfully. "Remember, we're more interested in herding them into range of our stationary weapons than in knocking them off ourselves."

Miles sat back and regarded the ever-changing displays. "I don't think they quite realize how much ordnance Daum brought. They're just repeating the same tactics the Felician officers reported they used the last time. Of course, it worked once. . . ."

The lead Pelian ships were just coming into range of the refinery. Miles held his breath as though it could force his people to hold their fire. They were spread lonely, thin, and nervous out there. There were more weapons in place than Miles had personnel to man them, even with computer-controlled fire—especially since control systems had been plagued with bugs during installation that were still not all worked out. Baz had labored to the last instant—was still laboring, for all Miles knew, and Elena alongside him. Miles wished he could have justified keeping her beside himself, instead.

The lead Pelian spewed a glittering string of dandelion bombs, arcing toward the solar collectors. *Not again,* Miles groaned inwardly, seeing two weeks' repairs about to be wasted. The bombs puffed into their thousands of separate needles. Space was suddenly laced with threads of fire as the defense weaponry labored to knock them out. Should have fired an instant sooner. The Pelian ship itself exploded into pelting debris as someone on Miles's side scored a direct, perhaps lucky, hit. A portion of the debris continued on its former track and speed, almost as dangerous in its mindless momentum as the clever guided weapons.

The ships coming up behind it began to peel and swerve, shocked out of their beeline complacency. Auson and Thorne in their respective ships now swung in from either side, like a pair of sheepdogs gone mad and attacking their flock. Miles beat his fist on the panel before him in a paroxysm of joy at the beauty of the formation. If only he'd had a third warship to completely box their flanks, none of the Pelians would make it home to complain. As it was, they were squeezed into a flat layer, carefully precalculated to present its maximum target area to the refinery's defenses.

Auson, beside him, shared his enthusiasm. "Lookatem! Lookatem! Right down the gullet, just like you claimed they would—and Gamad swore you were crazy to strip the solar side—Shorty, you're a frigging genius!"

Miles's thrill was mitigated by the sober reflection of what names he'd have earned by guessing wrong. Relief made him dizzy. He leaned back in the station chair and let out a long, long breath.

A second Pelian ship burst into oblivion, and a third. A numeral buried in a crowded corner of Miles's readouts flipped quietly from a minus to a plus figure. "Ah ha!" Miles pointed. "We've got 'em now! They're starting to accelerate again. They're breaking off the attack."

Their momentum gave the Pelians no choice but to

sweep through the refinery area. But all their attention now was on making it as fast a trip as possible. Thorne and Auson swung in behind to speed them on their way.

A Pelian ship corkscrewed past the installation, and fired—what? Miles's computers could present no interpretation of the—beam? Not plasma, not laser, not driven mass, for which the central factory was able to generate some shielding, the huge solar collectors necessarily being left to fend for themselves. It was not immediately apparent what damage it had done, or even if it were a hit. Strange . . .

Miles closed his hand gently around the Pelian ship's representation in his hologram, as if he could work sympathetic magic. "Captain Auson. Let's try and catch this one."

"Why bother? He's scooting for home with his buddies—"

Miles lowered his voice to a whisper. "That's an order."

Auson braced. "Yes, sir!"

Well, it works sometimes, Miles reflected.

The communications officer achieved a fully scrambled channel to the *Ariel,* and the new objective was transmitted. Auson, growing enthused, chortled at the chance to try his new ship's limits. The ghost imager, confusing the enemy's aim with multiple targets, proved particularly useful; through it they discovered the mystery beam's range limit and odd large time lag between shots. Recharging, perhaps? They bore down rapidly upon the fleeing Pelian.

"What's the script, Mr. Naismith?" Auson inquired. "Stop-or-we-blast-you?"

Miles chewed his lip thoughtfully. "I don't think that would work. I'd guess our problem is more likely to be keeping them from self-destructing when we get close. Threats would fall flat, I'm afraid. They're not mercenaries."

"Hm." Auson cleared his throat, and busied himself with his displays.

Miles suppressed a sardonic smile, for the sake of tact, and turned to his own readouts. The computers presented him with a clairvoyant vision of overtaking the Pelian, then paused, waiting politely on his merely human inspiration. Miles tried to think himself into the Pelian captain's skin. He balanced time lag, range, and the speed with which they could close on the Pelian at maximum red-line boost.

"It's close," he said, watching his holograph. The machine rendered a vivid and chilling display of what might happen if he missed bracketing his timing.

Auson glanced over his shoulder at the miniature fireworks, and muttered something about "—frigging suicidal . . .", which Miles chose to ignore.

"I want all our engineering people suited up and ready to board," Miles said at last. "They know they can't outrun us; my guess is they'll rig some go-to-hell with a time delay, all pile into their lifeboat shuttle, and try to blow the ship up in our faces. But if we don't waste time on the shuttle, and are quick enough getting in the back door as they go out the side, we might disarm it and take—whatever that was—intact."

Auson's lips puckered in worried disapproval at this plan. "Take all my engineers? We could blast the shuttle out of its clamps, when we get close enough to get the accuracy—trap them all aboard—"

"And then try to board a manned warship with four engineers and myself?" Miles interrupted. "No, thanks. Besides, cornering them just might trigger the sort of spectacular suicide move I want to prevent."

"What'll I do if you're not quick enough getting their booby-trap disarmed?"

A black grin stole over Miles's face. "Improvise."

The Pelians, it appeared, were not enough of a suicide squadron to spurn the thin chance of life their shuttle gave them. Into this narrow crack of time Miles and his technicians slipped, blasting their way, crude but quick, through the code-controlled air lock.

Miles cursed the discomfort of his over-large pressure suit. Loose places rubbed and skidded on his skin. Cold sweat, he discovered, was a term with a literal meaning. He glanced up and down the curving corridors of the unfamiliar dark ship. The engineering techs parted at a run, each to their assigned quadrant.

Miles took a fifth and less likely direction, to make a quick check of tactics room, crew's quarters, and bridge for destructive devices and any useful intelligence left lying around. Blasted control panels and melted data stores met him everywhere. He checked the time; barely five minutes, and the Pelian shuttle would be safely beyond the range of, say, radiation from imploded engines.

A triumphant crow pierced his ears over his suit comm link. "I've done it! I've done it!" cried an engineering tech. "They had rigged an implosion! Chain reaction broken—I'm shutting down now."

Cheers echoed over the comm link. Miles sagged into a station chair on the bridge, heart lumping; then it seemed to stop. He keyed his comm link for a general broadcast, overriding and at volume. "I don't think we should assume there was only one booby-trap laid, eh? Keep looking for at least the next ten minutes."

Worried groans acknowledged the order. For the next three minutes the comm links transmitted only ragged breathing. Miles, dashing through the galley in search of the captain's cabin, inhaled sharply. A microwave oven, its control panel ripped out and hastily cross-wired, timer ticking away, had a high-pressure metal oxygen canister jammed into it. The nutrition technician's personal contribution to the war effort, apparently. In two minutes it would have taken out the galley and most of the adjoining chambers. Miles tore it apart and ran on.

A tear-streaked voice hissed over the comm link. "Oh, shit. Oh, shit!"

"Where are you, Kat?"

"Armory. There's too many. I can't get them all! Oh, shit!"

"Keep working! We're on our way." Miles, taking the chance, ordered the rest of his crew to the armory on the double, and ran. A true light guided him as he arrived, overriding the infrared display on the inside of his helmet faceplate. He swung into a storage chamber to find the tech crawling along a row of gleaming ordnance.

"Every dandelion bomb in here is set to go off!" she cried, sparing one glance at him. Her voice shook, but her hands never stopped patting out the reset codes. Miles, lips parted in concentration, watched over her shoulder and then began to repeat her movements on the next row. The great disadvantage to crying in fear in a space suit, Miles discovered, was that you could not wipe either your face or your nose, although the sonic cleaners on the inside of the faceplate saved that valuable informative surface from a sneeze. He sniffed surreptitiously. His stomach sent up a throat-burning, acid belch. His fingers felt like sausages. I could be on Beta Colony right now—I could be home in bed—I could be home *under* my bed. . . .

Another tech joined them, Miles saw out of the

corner of his eye. No one spared attention for social chit-chat. They worked together in silence broken only by the uneven rhythm of hyperventilation. His suit reduced his oxygen flow in stingy disapproval of his state of mind. Bothari would never have let him join the boarding party—maybe he shouldn't have ordered him to duty at the refinery. On to the next bomb—and the next—and the—there was no next. Finished.

Kat rose, and pointed to one bomb in the array. "Three seconds! Three seconds, and—" She burst into unabashed tears, and fell on Miles. He patted her shoulder clumsily.

"There, there—cry all you want. You've earned it—" He killed his comm link broadcast momentarily, and inhaled a powerful sniff.

Miles tottered out of his newly captured ship into the refinery docking station clutching an unexpected prize—a suit of Pelian battle armor nearly small enough to fit him. The plumbing, not surprisingly, was female, but Baz could surely convert it. He spotted Elena among his reception committee, and held it up proudly. "Look what I found!"

She wrinkled her nose in puzzlement. "You captured a whole ship just to get a suit of armor?"

"No, no! The other thing. The—the weapon, whatever it was. This is the ship whose shot penetrated your shielding—did it hit anything? What did it do?"

One of the Felician officers glowered—oddly, at Elena. "It punched a hole—well, not a hole—right through the prison section. It was losing air, and *she* let them all out."

His people, Miles noticed, were moving about in groups of three or more.

"We haven't got them half rounded up yet," the

Felician complained. "They're hiding all over the station."

Elena looked distressed. "I'm sorry, my lord."

Miles rubbed his temples. "Uh. I suppose I'd better have the Sergeant at my back, then, for a while."

"When he wakes up."

"What?"

Elena frowned at her boots. "He was guarding the prison section alone, during the attack—he tried to stop me, from letting them out."

"Tried? And didn't succeed?"

"I shot him with my stunner. I'm afraid he's going to be rather angry—is it all right if I stick with you for a while?"

Miles pursed his lips in an involuntary silent whistle. "Of course. Were any prisoners—no, wait." He raised his voice. "Commander Bothari, I commend your initiative. You did the right thing. We are here to accomplish a specific tactical objective, not perpetrate mindless slaughter." Miles stared down the Felician junior lieutenant, what's his name, Gamad, who shrank under his gaze. He went on more quietly to Elena. "Were any prisoners killed?"

"Two, whose cells were actually penetrated by the electron orbital randomizer—"

"By the what?"

"Baz called it an electron orbital randomizer. And—and eleven asphyxiated that I couldn't get to in time." The pain in her eyes knifed him.

"How many would have died if you hadn't released them?"

"We lost air in the whole section."

"Captain Tung—?"

Elena spread her hands. "He's around here somewhere, I guess. He wasn't among the thirteen. Oh—

one of his jump pilots was, though. And we haven't found the other one yet. Is that important?"

Miles's heart sank into his foaming stomach. He wheeled to the nearest mercenary. "Pass on this order at once. Prisoners are to be re-captured alive, with as little injury as possible." The woman hurried to obey. "If Tung's on the loose, you'd better stick by me," Miles told Elena. "Dear God. Well, I guess I'd better have a look at this hole that isn't a hole, then. Where did Baz come up with that jawbreaking name for it?"

"He said it's a Betan development from a few years back. It never sold very well, because all you have to do to defend from it is re-phase the mass shielding—he told me to tell you he was on it, and should have the shields reprogrammed by tonight."

"Oh." Miles paused, crushed. So much for his fantasy of returning the mystery beam to Barrayar to lay at the Emperor's feet, Captain Illyan agog, his father amazed. He'd pictured it as a splendid offering, proof of his military prowess. More like when the cat drags in a dead horned hopper, to be chased off with brooms. He sighed. At least he had a suit of space armor now.

Miles, Elena, Gamad, and an engineering tech started toward the prison section, several structures down the linked chain of the refinery. Elena fell in beside Miles.

"You look so tired. Hadn't you better, uh, take a shower and get some rest?"

"Ah, yes, the stink of dried terror, well warmed in a pressure suit." He grinned up at her, and tucked his helmet firmly under his arm, like a beheaded ghost. "Wait'll you hear about my day. What does Major Daum say about the defense nexus now? I suppose I'd better get a full battle report from him—he at least seems to have his thinking straight—" Miles eyed the back of the lieutenant in weary distaste.

Lieutenant Gamad, whose hearing was evidently keener than Miles had supposed, glanced back over his shoulder. "Major Daum's killed, sir. He and a tech were switching weapons posts, and their flitter was hit by high-speed debris—nothing left. Didn't they tell you?"

Miles stopped short.

"I'm the ranking officer here, now," the Felician added.

It took three days to ferret out the escaped prisoners from all the corners of the refinery. Tung's commandos were the worst. Miles eventually resorted to closing off sections and filling them with sleep gas. He ignored Bothari's irritated suggestion that vacuum would be more cost-effective. The bulk of the round-up duty fell naturally, if unjustly, to the Sergeant, and he was tight as a drawn bowstring with the tension of it.

When the final head count was made, Tung and seven of his men, including his other Pilot Officer, turned up missing. So did a station shuttle.

Miles moaned under his breath. There was no choice now but to wait for the laggard Felicians to come claim their cargo. He began to doubt whether the shuttle dispatched to try to reach Tau Verde before the counterattack had ever made it through the Oseran-controlled space between. Perhaps they should send another. With a draftee, not a volunteer, this time; Miles had his candidate all picked out.

Lieutenant Gamad, swollen with his newly inherited seniority, was inclined to challenge Miles's authority over the refinery, technically, it was true, Felician property. After Daum's cool, get the-job-done intensity, Miles suffered him ungladly. Gamad was quashed, however, when he overheard one of Miles's mercenaries address him as "Admiral Naismith." Miles was so delighted with the effect of the ersatz title on Gamad that he let it pass unchecked. Unfortunately, it spread; he found himself unable to retrieve the careful neutrality of "Mr. Naismith" thereafter.

Gamad was saved on the eighth day after the counterattack, when a Felician local space cruiser finally appeared on the monitors. Miles's mercenaries, twitchy and suspicious after repeated ambushes, were inclined to obliterate it first and sift the remains for positive ID after. But Miles at last established a measure of trust, and the Felicians came meekly to dock.

Two large, businesslike plastic crates on a float pallet riveted Miles's attention when the Felician officers entered the refinery conference chamber. The crates bore a pleasant resemblance, in size at least, to old sea pirates' treasure chests. Miles lost himself in a brief fantasy of glittering diadems, gold coins, and ropes of pearls. Alas that such gaudy baubles were treasures no more. Crystallized viral microcircuits, data packs, DNA splices, blank drafts on major planetary agricultural and mining futures; such was the tepid wealth men schemed upon in these degenerate days. Of course, there was still artwork. Miles touched the dagger at his belt, and was warmed, as by an old man's handclasp. He decided he would probably settle for a few of those blank drafts.

The pinched and harried Felician paymaster was speaking; "—must have Major Daum's manifest first, and physically check each item for damage in transit."

The Felician cruiser captain nodded wearily. "See my chief engineer, and draft as much help as you need. But make it quick." The captain turned a bloodshot and irritated eye on Gamad, trailing obsequiously. "Haven't you found that manifest yet? Or Daum's personal papers?"

"I'm afraid he may have had them on him when he was hit, sir."

The captain growled, and turned to Miles. "So, you're this mad galactic mutant I've been hearing about."

Miles drew himself up. "I am not a mutant! *Captain*." He drawled the last word out in his father's most sarcastic style, then took hold of his temper. The Felician clearly hadn't slept much the last few days. "I believe you have some business to conduct."

"Yes, mercenaries must have their pay, I suppose," sighed the captain.

"And physically check each item for damage in transit," Miles prodded with a pointed nod at the boxes.

"Take care of him, Paymaster," the captain ordered, and wheeled out. "All right, Gamad, show me this grand strategy of yours . . ."

Baz's eyes smoked. "Excuse me, my lord, but I think I'd better join them."

"I'll go with you," offered Mayhew. He clicked his teeth together gently, as if nibbling for a jugular.

"Go ahead." Miles turned to the paymaster, who sighed and shoved a data cartridge into the tabletop viewer.

"Now—Mr. Naismith? Is that correct? May I see your copy of the contract, please."

Miles frowned uneasily. "Major Daum and I had a verbal agreement. Forty thousand Betan dollars upon safe delivery of his cargo to Felice. This refinery is Felician territory, now."

The paymaster stared, astonished. "A verbal agreement? A verbal agreement is no contract!"

Miles sat up. "A verbal agreement is the most binding of contracts! Your soul is in your breath, and therefore in your voice. Once pledged it must be redeemed."

"Mysticism has no place—"

"It is not mysticism! It's a recognized legal theory!" On Barrayar, Miles realized.

"That's the first I've heard of it."

"Major Daum understood it perfectly well."

"Major Daum was in Intelligence. He specialized in galactics. I'm just Accounting Office—"

"You refuse to redeem your dead comrade's word? But you are real Service, no mercenary—"

The paymaster shook his head. "I have no idea what you're babbling about. But if the cargo is right, you'll be paid. This isn't Jackson's Whole."

Miles relaxed slightly. "Very well." The paymaster was no Vor, nor anything like one. Counting his payment in front of him was not likely to be taken as a mortal insult. "Let's see it."

The paymaster nodded to his assistant, who uncoded the locks. Miles held his breath in happy anticipation of more money than he'd seen in one pile in his life. The lids swung up to reveal stacks and stacks of tightly bundled, particolored pieces of paper. There was a long, long pause.

Miles slid off his leg-swinging perch on the conference table and picked out a bundle. Each contained perhaps a hundred identical, brightly engraved compositions of pictures, numbers, and letters in a strange cursive alphabet. The paper was slick, almost sleazy. He held one piece up to the light.

"What is it?" he asked at last.

The paymaster raised his eyebrows. "Paper currency. It's used commonly for money on most planets—"

"I know that! What currency is it?"

"Felician millifenigs."

"Millifenigs." It sounded faintly like a swear word. "What's it worth in real money? Betan dollars, or, say, Barrayaran Imperial marks."

"Who uses Barrayaran marks?" the paymaster's assistant muttered in puzzlement.

The paymaster cleared his throat. "As of the annual listing, millifenigs were pegged at 150 per Betan dollar on the Betan Exchange," he recited quickly.

"Wasn't that almost a year ago? What are they now?"

The paymaster found something to look at out the plexiports. "The Oseran blockade has prevented us from learning the current rate of exchange."

"Yeah? Well, what was the last figure you had, then?"

The paymaster cleared his throat again; his voice became strangely small. "Because of the blockade, you understand, almost all the information about the war has been sent by the Pelians."

"The rate, please."

"We don't know."

"The last rate," Miles hissed.

The paymaster jumped. "We really don't, sir. Last we heard, Felician currency had been, uh . . ." he was almost inaudible, "dropped from the Exchange."

Miles fingered his dagger. "And just what are these—millifenigs," he would have to experiment, he decided, to find just the right degree of venom to pronounce that word, "backed by?"

The paymaster raised his head proudly. "The government of Felice!"

"The one that's losing this war, right?"

The paymaster muttered something.

"You are losing this war, are you not?"

"Losing the high orbitals was just a setback," the paymaster explained desperately. "We still control our own airspace—"

"Millifenigs," snorted Miles. "Millifenigs . . . Well, I want Betan dollars!" He glared at the paymaster.

The paymaster replied as one goaded in pride and turning at bay. "There are no Betan dollars! Every cent of it, yes, and every flake of other galactic currencies we could round up was sent with Major Daum, to buy that cargo—"

"Which I have risked my life delivering to you—"

"Which he died delivering to us!"

Miles sighed, recognizing an argument he could not win. His most frenetic posturing would not wring Betan dollars from a government that owned none. "Millifenigs," he muttered.

"I have to go," said the paymaster. "I have to initial the inventory—"

Miles flicked a hand at him, tiredly. "Yes, go."

The paymaster and his assistant fled, leaving him alone in the beautiful conference chamber with two crates of money. That the paymaster didn't even bother to set guard, demand receipt, or see it counted merely confirmed its worthlessness.

Miles piled a pyramid of the stuff before him on the conference table, and laid his head on his arms beside it. Millifenigs. He wandered momentarily in a mental calculation of its square area, if laid out in singles. He could certainly paper not only the walls, but the ceiling of his room at home, and most of the rest of Vorkosigan House as well. Mother would probably object.

He idly tested its inflammability, lighting one piece, planning to hold it until it burned down to his fingertips, to see if anything could hurt more than his stomach. But the doorseals clapped shut at the scent of smoke, a raucous alarm went off, and a chemical fire extinguisher protruded from the wall like a red, sardonic tongue. Fire was a real terror in space installations; the next step, he recalled, would be the evacuation of the air from the chamber to smother the flames. He batted the paper out hastily. Millifenigs. He dragged himself across the room to silence the alarm.

He varied his financial structure by building a square fort, with corner towers and an interior keep. The gate lintel had a tendency to collapse with a slight rustle. Perhaps he could pass on Pelian commercial shipping as a mentally retarded mutant, with Elena as his nurse and Bothari as his keeper, being sent to some off-planet hospital—or zoo—by rich relatives. He could take off his boots and socks and bite his toenails during customs inspections . . . But what roles could he find for Mayhew and Jesek? And Elli Quinn—liege-sworn or not, he owed her a face. Worse, he had no credit here—and somehow he doubted the exchange rate between Felician and Pelian currency would be in his favor.

The door sighed open. Miles quickly knocked his fort into a more random-appearing pile, and sat up straight, for the benefit of the mercenary who saluted and entered.

A self-conscious smile was pasted under the man's avid eyes. "Excuse me, sir. I'd heard a rumor that our pay had arrived."

Miles's lips peeled back in an uncontrollable grin. He forced them straight. "As you see."

Who, after all, could say what the exchange rate for millifenigs was—who could contradict any figure he chose to peg them at? As long as his mercenaries were in space, isolated from test markets, no one. Of course, when they did find out, there might not be enough pieces of him to go around, like the Dismemberment of Mad Emperor Yuri.

The mercenary's mouth formed an "o" at the size of the pile. "Shouldn't you set a guard, sir?"

"Just so, Trainee Nout. Good thinking. Ah—why don't you go fetch a float pallet, and secure this payroll in—er—the usual place. Pick two trustworthy comrades to relieve you on guard duty, around the clock."

"Me, sir?" The mercenary's eyes widened. "You'd trust me—"

What could you do? Steal it and go buy a loaf of bread? Miles thought. Aloud, he replied, "Yes, I would. Did you think I haven't been evaluating your performance these past weeks?" He prayed he'd got the man's name right.

"Yes, sir! Right away, sir!" The mercenary rendered him a perfectly unnecessary salute, and danced out as if he had rubber balls in his boots.

Miles buried his face in a pile of millifenigs and giggled helplessly, very close to tears.

He saw the millifenigs bundled back up and trundled safely to cold storage, then lingered in the conference chamber. Bothari should be seeking him out soon, when done turning the last of the prisoners over to Felician control.

The RG 132, floating beyond the plexiports, was getting some attention at last. The hull was taking on the appearance of a half-finished patchwork quilt. Miles wondered if he'd ever get up the nerve to ride in it without a pressure suit on and his helmet at his elbow.

Jesek and Mayhew found him still gazing pensively across the installation. "We set them straight," the engineer declared, planting himself beside Miles. Savage contentment had replaced the burning indignation in his eyes.

"Hm?" Miles broke free of his moody reverie. "Set who straight about what?"

"The Felicians, and that greasy career-builder Gamad."

"About time somebody did that," Miles agreed absently. He wondered what the RG 132 might fetch if sold as an inner-system freighter. Not, preferably, for millifenigs. Or as scrap . . . No, he couldn't do that to Arde.

"Here they come now."

"Hm?"

The Felicians were back, the captain, the paymaster, and what looked like most of the ship's officers, plus some kind of space marine commander Miles had not seen before. From the captain's deference to him in the doorway, Miles guessed he must be the ranking man. A senior colonel, perhaps, or a young general. Gamad was notably absent. Thorne and Auson brought up the rear.

This time the captain came to attention, and saluted. "I believe I owe you an apology, Admiral Naismith. I did not fully understand the situation here."

Miles grasped Baz's arm and stood on tiptoe to his ear, whispering urgently between his teeth. "Baz, what have you been telling these people?"

"Just the truth," Baz began, but there was no time for further reply. The senior officer was stepping forward, extending his hand.

"How do you do, Admiral Naismith. I am General Halify. I have orders from my high command to hold this installation by whatever means necessary."

They shook hands, and were seated. Miles took the head of the table, by way of experiment. The Felician general seated himself earnestly and without demur on Miles's right. There was some interesting jostling for seats farther down the line.

"Since our second ship was lost to the Pelians on our way here, mine is the unenviable task of doing so with 200 men—half my complement," continued Halify.

"I did it with forty," Miles observed automatically. What was the Felician leading up to?

"Mine is also the task of stripping it of Betan ordnance to send back with Captain Sahlin here, to prosecute the war on what has unfortunately become the home front."

"That will make it more complicated for you," Miles agreed.

"Until the Pelians brought in galactics, our two sides were fairly matched. We thought we were on the verge of a negotiated settlement. The Oserans changed that balance."

"So I understand."

"What galactics can do, galactics can surely undo. We wish to hire the Dendarii Mercenaries to break the Oseran blockade and clear local space of all off-planet forces. The Pelians," he sniffed, "we can take care of ourselves."

I'm going to let Bothari finish strangling Baz. . . . "A bold offer, General. I wish I could take you up on it. But as you must know, most of my forces are not here."

The general clasped his hands intensely before him on the table. "I believe we can hold out long enough for you to send for them."

Miles glanced at Auson and Thorne, down the expanse of darkly gleaming plastic. Not, perhaps, the best time to explain just how long a wait that would be . . .

"We would have to run the blockade to do so, and at the moment all my jump ships are disabled."

"Felice has three commercial jump ships left, besides the ones that were trapped outside the blockade when it began. One is very fast. Surely, in combination with your warships, you might get it through."

Miles was about to make a rude reply, when it hit him—here was escape, being offered on a platter. Pile his liege-people into the jump ship, have Thorne and Auson run him through the blockade, and thumb his nose to Tau Verde IV and all its denizens forever. It was risky, but it could be done—was in fact the best idea he'd had all day—he sat up, smiling suavely. "An interesting proposition, General." He must not appear too eager. "Just how do you propose to pay for my services? The Dendarii do not work cheaply."

"I'm authorized to meet whatever terms you ask. Within reason, of course," General Halify added prudently.

"To put it bluntly, General, that's a load of—millifenigs. If Major Daum had no authority to hire outside forces, neither do you."

"They said, by whatever means necessary." The general's jaw set. "They'll back me."

"I'd want a contract in writing, signed by somebody who can properly be shaken down—uh, held responsible, after. Retired generals' incomes are not notoriously vast."

A spark of amusement flared briefly in Halify's eye, and he nodded. "You'll get it."

"We must be paid in Betan dollars. I understood you were fresh out."

"If the blockade is broken, we can get off-planet currencies again. You'll get them."

Miles pressed his lips together firmly. He must not break down into howls of laughter. Yet here he sat, a man with an imaginary battle fleet negotiating for its services with a man with an imaginary budget. Well, the price was certainly right.

The general extended his hand. "Admiral Naismith, you have my personal word on it. May I have yours?"

His humor shattered in a thousand frozen shards, swallowed in a cold vast emptiness that used to be his belly. "My word?"

"I understand it has some meaning to you."

You understand entirely too much. . . . "My word. I

see." He had never yet broken his word. Almost eighteen, and he still preserved that virginity. Well, there was a first time for everything. He accepted the general's handclasp. "General Halify, I'll do my best. My word on it."

CHAPTER FIFTEEN

The three ships dove and wove in an intricate evasion pattern. Around them, twenty more darted, as if hawks hunted in packs. The three ships sparked, blue, red, yellow, then dissolved in a brilliant rainbow glare.

Miles leaned back in his station chair in the *Triumph's* tactics room and rubbed his bleary eyes. "Scratch that idea." He vented a long sigh. If he couldn't be a soldier, perhaps he had a future as a designer of fireworks displays.

Elena drifted in, munching a ration bar. "That looked pretty. What was it?"

Miles held up a didactic finger. "I have just discovered my twenty-third new way to get killed this week." He waved toward the holograph display. "That was it."

Elena glanced across the room to her father, apparently asleep, on the friction matting. "Where is everybody?"

"Catching sleep. I'm just as glad not to have an

audience while I attempt to teach myself first-year tactics. They might begin to doubt my genius."

She gave him an odd look. "Miles—how serious are you about this blockade busting?"

He glanced up to the outside screens, which showed the same boring view of what might be called the backside of the metals refinery they had displayed since the ship had been parked after the counter-attack. The *Triumph* was now being dubbed Miles's flagship. With the arrival of the Felician forces, filling the refinery's crew's quarters, he had decamped, secretly relieved, from the squalid luxury of the executive suite to the more restful austerity of Tung's former quarters.

"I don't know. It's been two weeks since the Felicians promised us that fast courier to leg on out of here, and they haven't produced it yet. We're going to at least have to break through the blockade. . . ." He hastened to erase the worry in her face. "At least it gives me something to do while we wait. This machine is more fun than chess or Strat-O any day."

He hopped up, and gestured her with a courtly bow toward the next station chair. "Look, I'll teach you how to operate it. Show you a game or two. You'll be good."

"Well . . ."

He introduced her to a couple of elementary tactics patterns, demystifying them by calling them "play." "Captain Koudelka and I used to play something like this." She caught on quickly. It had to be some kind of criminal injustice, that Ivan Vorpatril was even now deeply engaged in officer's training for which Elena could not even be considered.

He went through his half of the patterns automatically, while his mind circled again around his real life military dilemma. This was just the sort of thing he would have been taught how to do at the Imperial

Service Academy, he thought with an inward sigh. There was probably a book on it. He wished he had a copy; he was getting mortally tired of having to re-invent the wheel every fifteen minutes. Although it was just barely possible there *was* no way for three small warships and a battered freighter to take out an entire mercenary fleet. The Felicians could offer little assistance, beyond the use of the refinery as a base. Of course, Miles's presence there benefited them at least as much as their support did him, as Pelian-repellant.

He glanced up at Elena, and pushed the importunate strategic hassles from his mind. Her strength and sharpness were blooming these days, in her new challenges. All she'd ever needed was a chance, it seemed. Baz shouldn't have it all his own way. He glanced over to see if Bothari was really asleep, and screwed up his courage. The tactics room with its swivel chairs was not well-arranged for nuzzling, but he would try. He went to her shoulder, and leaned over it, manufacturing some helpful instruction.

"Mr. Naismith?" blatted the intercom. It was Captain Auson, calling from Nav and Com. "Put the outside channels on, I'm coming down."

Miles snapped out of his haze, cursing silently. "What's up?"

"Tung's back."

"Uh, oh. Better scramble everybody."

"I am."

"What's he brought? Can you tell yet?"

"Yes, it's strange. He's standing just out of range in what looks like a Pelian inner-system passenger ship, maybe a little troop-carrier or something, and saying he wants to talk. With you. Probably a trick."

Miles frowned, mystified. "Well, pipe it down, then. But keep scrambling."

In moments the Eurasian's familiar face appeared,

larger than life. Bothari was now up, at his usual post by the door, silent as ever; he and Elena didn't talk much since the incident in the damaged prison section. But then, they never had.

"How do you do, Captain Tung. We meet again, I see." The subtle vibrations of the ship changed, as it powered up and began to move into open space.

"We do indeed." Tung smiled, tight and fierce. "Is that job offer still open, son?"

The two shuttles sandwiched themselves together, belly to belly like a pair of mismatched limpets, in space midway between their mother ships. There the two men met face-to-face in privacy, but for Bothari, tense and discreet just out of earshot, and Tung's pilot, who remained equally discreetly aboard Tung's shuttle.

"My people are loyal to me," said Tung. "I can place them at your service, every one."

"You realize," Miles pointed out mildly, "that if you wished to re-take your ship, that would be an ideal ploy. Load my forces with yours, and strike at will. Can you prove you're not a Trojan Horse?"

Tung sighed agreement. "Only as you proved that memorable lunch was not drugged. In the eating."

"Mm." Miles pulled himself back down into his seat in the gravityless shuttle, as if he could so impose orientation on body and mind. He offered Tung a soft-drink bulb, which Tung accepted without hesitation or comment. They both drank, Miles sparingly; his stomach was already starting to protest null-gee. "You also realize, I cannot give you your ship back. All I have to offer at the moment is a captured Pelian putt-putt, and perhaps the title of Staff Officer."

"Yes, I understand that."

"You'll have to work with both Auson and Thorne, without bringing up, um, past frictions."

Tung looked less than enthusiastic, but he replied, "If I have to, I can even do that." He snapped a squirt of fruit juice out of the air. Practice, thought Miles enviously.

"My payroll, for the moment, is entirely in Felician millifenigs. Do you, ah—know about millifenigs?"

"No, but at a guess from the Felician's strategic situation, I'd suppose they'd make an eye-catching toilet paper."

"That's about right." Miles frowned. "Captain Tung. After going to a great deal of trouble to escape two weeks ago, you have gone to what looks like an equal amount of trouble to return to join what can only be described as the losing side. You know you can't have your ship back, you know your pay is at best problematical—I can't believe it's all for my native charm. Why?"

"It wasn't that much trouble. That delightful young lady—remind me to kiss her hand—let me out," observed Tung.

"That 'delightful young lady' is Commander Bothari to you, sir, and considering what you owe her, you can bloody well confine yourself to saluting her," snapped Miles, surprising himself. He swallowed a squirt of fruit drink to hide his confusion.

Tung raised his eyebrows, and smiled. "I see."

Miles dragged his mind back to the present. "Again. Why?"

Tung's face hardened. "Because you are the only force in local space with a chance of giving Oser a prick in the ass."

"And just when did you acquire this motivation?"

Hard, yes, and inward. "He violated our contract. In the event of losing my ship in combat, he owed me another command."

Miles jerked his chin up, inviting Tung to go on.

Tung's voice lowered. "He had a right to chew me out, yes, for my mistakes—but he had no right to humiliate me before my people . . ." His hands were clenched, ivory-knuckled, on the arms of his seat. His drink bulb floated away, forgotten.

Miles's imagination filled in the picture. Admiral Oser, angry and shocked at this sudden defeat after a year of easy victories, losing his temper, mishandling Tung's hot damaged pride—foolish, that, when it would have been so easy to turn that pride redoubled to his own service—yes, it rang true.

"And so you come to my hand. Ah—with all your officers, you say? Your pilot officer?" Escape, escape in Tung's ship possible again? Escape from the Pelians and Oserans, thought Miles soberly. It's escape from the Dendarii that's beginning to look difficult.

"All. All but my communications officer, of course."

"Why 'of course'?"

"Oh, that's right, you don't know about his double life. He's a military agent, assigned to keep watch on the Oseran fleet for his government. I think he wanted to come—we've gotten to know each other pretty well these past six years—but he had to follow his primary orders." Tung chuckled. "He apologized."

Miles blinked. "Is that sort of thing usual?"

"Oh, there's always a few, scattered through all the mercenary organizations." Tung gave Miles a sharp look. "Haven't you ever had any? Most captains throw them out as soon as they catch on, but I like them. They're generally extremely well trained, and more trustworthy than most, as long as you're not fighting anybody they know. If I'd had occasion to fight the Barrayarans, God forbid, or any of their—well, the Barrayarans are not particularly troubled with allies—I'd have been sure to drop him off somewhere first."

"B—" choked Miles, and swallowed the rest. Ye

gods. Had he been recognized? If the man was one of Captain Illyan's agents, almost certainly. And what the devil had the man made of the recent events, seen from the Oseran point of view? Miles could kiss goodbye any hope of keeping his late adventures secret from his father, then.

His fruit drink seemed to slosh, viscous and nasty, on the roof of his stomach. Damn null-gee. He'd better wind this up. A mercenary admiral didn't need a reputation for space sickness to go with his more obvious disabilities. Miles wondered briefly how many key command decisions in history had been flicked out in the compelling urgency of some like biological necessity.

He stuck out his hand. "Captain Tung, I accept your service."

Tung took it, "Admiral Naismith—it is Admiral Naismith now, I understand?"

Miles grimaced. "So it would appear."

A half-suppressed grin turned one corner of Tung's mouth. "I see. I shall be pleased to serve you, son."

When he had left, Miles sat eyeing his drink bulb for a moment. He gave it a squeeze, and tried to snap it out of the air. Bright red fruit drink marinated his eyebrows, chin, and tunic front. He swore under his breath, and floated off in search of a towel.

The *Ariel* was late. Thorne, accompanied by Arde and Baz, was supposed to be escorting the Betan weapons through to Felician-controlled airspace, and then bringing the fast jump courier back, and they were late. It took two days for Miles to persuade General Halify to relinquish Tung's old crew from their cells; after that, there was nothing to do but watch and wait, and worry.

Five days behind schedule, both ships appeared in the monitors. Miles got Thorne on the com, and demanded, with an edge in his voice, the reason for the delay.

Thorne positively smirked. "It's a surprise. You'll like it. Can you meet us now in the docking bay?"

A surprise. God, now what? Miles was at last beginning to sympathize with Bothari's stated taste for being bored. He stalked to the docking bay, nebulous plans for bracing his laggard subordinates rotating in his brain.

Arde met him, grinning and bouncing on his heels. "Just stand right here, my lord." He raised his voice. "Go ahead, Baz!"

"Hup, hup, hup!" There came a great shuffling thumping from the flex tube. Out of it marched, double-time, a ragged string of men and women. Some wore uniforms, both military and civilian types, others civilian clothes in a wild assortment of various planetary fashions. Mayhew directed them into a standard square formation, where they stood more or less to attention.

There was a group of a dozen or so black-uniformed Kshatryan Imperial mercenaries who formed their own tight little island in the sea of color; on closer look, their uniforms, though clean and mended, were not all complete. Odd buttons, shiny seats and elbows, lop-worn boot heels—they were long, long from their distant home, it seemed. Miles's temporary fascination with them was shattered at the appearance of two dozen Cetagandan ghem-fighters, variously dressed, but all with full formal face paint freshly applied, looking like an array of Chinese temple demons. Bothari swore, and clapped his hand to his plasma arc at the sight of them. Miles motioned him to parade rest.

Freighter and passenger liner tech uniforms, a white-skinned, white-haired man in a feathered g-string—Miles, taking in the polished bandolier and plasma rifle he also bore, was not inclined to smile—a dark-haired woman in her thirties of almost supernatural beauty, engrossed with directing a crew of four techs—she glanced toward him, then frankly stared, a very odd look on her face. He stood a little straighter. *Not a mutant, ma'am,* he thought irritably. When the flex tube emptied at last, perhaps a hundred people stood before him in the docking bay. Miles's head whirled.

Thorne, Baz, and Arde all appeared at his elbow, looking immensely pleased with themselves.

"Baz—" Miles opened his hand in helpless supplication. "What is this?"

Jesek stood to attention. "Dendarii recruits, my lord!"

"Did I ask you to collect recruits?" He had never been that drunk, surely. . . .

"You said we didn't have enough personnel to man our equipment. So I applied a little forward momentum to the problem, and—there you are."

"Where the devil did you get them all?"

"Felice. There must be two thousand galactics trapped there by the blockade. Merchant ship personnel, passengers, businesspeople, techs, a little of everything. Even soldiers. They're not all soldiers, of course. Not yet."

"Ah." Miles cleared his throat. "Hand-picked, are they?"

"Well . . ." Baz scuffed his boot on the deck, and studied it, as if looking for signs of wear. "I gave them some weapons to field-strip and reassemble. If they didn't try to shove the plasma arc power cartridge in the nerve disrupter grip slot, I hired 'em."

Miles wandered up and down the rows, bemused. "I see. Very ingenious. I doubt I could have done better myself." He nodded toward the Kshatryans. "Where were they going?"

"That's an interesting story," put in Mayhew. "They

weren't exactly trapped by the blockade. Seems some local Felician magnate of the, uh, sub-economy, had hired them for bodyguards a few years ago. About six months back they botched the job, rendering themselves unemployed. They'll do about anything for a ride out of here. I found them myself," he added proudly.

"I see. Ah, Baz—Cetagandans?" Bothari had not taken his eyes from their gaudy fierce faces since they had exited the flex tube.

The engineer turned his hands palm-outwards. "They're *trained.*"

"Do they realize that some Dendarii are Barrayaran?"

"They know I am, and with a name like Dendarii, any Cetagandan would have to make the connection. That mountain range made an impression on them during the Great War. But they want a ride out of here too. That was part of the contract, you see, to keep the price down—almost everybody wants to be discharged outside Felician local space."

"I sympathize," muttered Miles. The Felician fast courier floated outside the docking station. He itched for a closer look. "Well—see Captain Tung, and arrange quarters for them all. And, uh, training schedules . . ." Yes, keep them busy, while he—slipped away?

"Captain Tung?" said Thorne.

"Yes, he's a Dendarii now. I've been doing some recruiting too. Should be just like a family reunion for you—ah, Bel," he fixed the Betan with a stern eye, "you are now comrades in arms. As a Dendarii, I expect you to remember it."

"Tung." Thorne sounded more amazed than jealous. "Oser will be foaming."

Miles spent the evening running his new recruits' dossiers into the *Triumph*'s computers, by hand, by himself, and by choice, the better to familiarize himself with his liegemen's human grab-bag. They were in fact well chosen; most had previous military experience, and the rest invariably possessed some arcane and valuable technical specialty.

Some were arcane indeed. He stopped his monitor to study the face of the extraordinarily beautiful woman who had stared at him in the docking bay. What the devil had Baz been about to hire a banking comm link security specialist as a soldier of fortune? To be sure, she might want off-planet badly enough—ah. Never mind. Her resume explained the mystery; she had once held the rank of ensign in the Escobaran military space forces. She'd had an honorable medical discharge after the war with Barrayar nineteen years ago. Medical discharges must have been a fad then, Miles mused, thinking of Bothari's. His amusement drained away, and he felt the hairs on his arms stir.

Great dark eyes, clean square line of jaw—her last name was Visconti, typically Escobaran. Her first name was Elena.

"No," whispered Miles to himself firmly. "Not possible." He weakened. "Anyway, not *likely* . . ."

He read the resume again more carefully. The Escobaran woman had come to Tau Verde IV a year ago to install a comm link system her company had sold to a Felician bank. She must have arrived just days before the war started. She listed herself as unmarried with no dependents. Miles swung around in his chair with his back to the screen, then found himself sneaking another look from the corner of his eye. She had been unusually young to be an officer during the Escobar-Barrayar war—some sort of precocious hotshot, perhaps. Miles caught himself up ironically, wondering when he'd started feeling so middle-aged.

But if she were, just possibly, his Elena's mother, how had she got mixed up with Sergeant Bothari? Bothari had been pushing forty then, and looked much the same as now, judging from vids Miles had seen from his parents' early years of marriage. No accounting for taste, maybe.

A little reunion fantasy blossomed in his imagination, unbidden, galloping ahead of all proof. To present Elena not merely with a grave, but with her longed-for mother in the flesh—to finally feed that secret hunger, sharper than a thorn, that had plagued her all her life, twin to his own clumsy hunger to please his father—that would be a heroism worth stretching for. Better than showering her with the most fabulous material gifts imaginable—he melted at the picture of her delight.

And yet—and yet . . . it was only a hypothesis. Testing it might prove awkward. He had realized the Sergeant was not being strictly truthful when he'd said he couldn't remember Escobar, but it might be partly so. Or this woman might be somebody else altogether. He would make his test in private then, and blind. If he were wrong, no harm done.

Miles held his first full senior officers' meeting the next day, partly to acquaint himself with his new henchmen, but mostly to throw the floor open to ideas for blockade-busting. With all this military and ex-military talent around, there had to be someone who knew what they were doing. More copies of the "Dendarii regulations" were passed out, and Miles retired after to his appropriated cabin on his appropriated flagship, to run the parameters of the Felician courier through the computer one more time.

He had upped the courier's estimated passenger capacity for the two-week run to Beta Colony from a crowded four to a squeezed five by eliminating several sorts of baggage and fudging the life-support back-up figures as much as he dared; surely there had to be something he could do to boost it to seven. He also tried very hard not to think about the mercenaries, waiting eagerly for his return with reinforcements. And waiting. And waiting . . .

They should not linger here any longer. The *Triumph*'s tactics simulator had shown that thinking he could break the Oserans with 200 troops was pure megalomania. Still . . . No. He forced himself to think reasonably.

The logical person to leave behind was Elli Quinn of the slagged face. She was no liegewoman of his, really. Then a toss-up between Baz and Arde. Taking the engineer back to Beta Colony would expose him to arrest and extradition; leaving him here would be for his own good, yessir. Never mind that he had been selflessly busting his tail for weeks to serve Miles's every military whim. Never mind what the Oserans would do to all their deserters and everyone associated with them when they finally caught up with them, as they inevitably must. Never mind that it would also most handily sever Baz's romance with Elena, and wasn't that very possibly the real reason . . . ?

Logic, Miles decided, made his stomach hurt.

Anyway, it was not easy to keep his mind on his work just now. He checked his wrist chronometer. Just a few more minutes. He wondered if it had been silly to lay in that bottle of awful Felician wine, concealed now with four glasses in his cupboard. He need only bring it out if, if, if . . .

He sighed and leaned back, and smiled across the cabin at Elena. She sat on the bed in companionable silence, screening a manual on weapons drills. Sergeant Bothari sat at a small fold-out table, cleaning and recharging their personal weapons. Elena smiled back, and removed her audio bug from her ear.

"Do you have your physical training program figured out for our, uh, new recruits?" he asked her. "Some of them look like it's been a while since they've worked out regularly."

"All set," she assured him. "I'm starting a big group first thing next day-cycle. General Halify is going to lend me the refinery crew's gym." She paused, then added, "Speaking of not working out for a while—don't you think you'd better come too?"

"Uh . . ." said Miles.

"Good idea," said the Sergeant, not looking up from his work.

"My stomach—"

"It would be a good example to your troops," she added, blinking her brown eyes at him in feigned, he was sure, innocence.

"Who's going to warn them not to break me in half?"

Her eyes glinted. "I'll let you pretend you're instructing them."

"Your gym clothes," said the Sergeant, blowing a bit of dust out of the silvered bell-muzzle of a nerve disrupter and nodding to his left, "are in the bottom drawer of that wall compartment."

Miles sighed defeat. "Oh, all right." He checked his chronometer again. Any minute now.

The door of the cabin slid open; it was the Escobaran woman, right on time. "Good day, Technician Visconti," he began cheerfully. His words died on his lips as she raised a needler and held it in both hands to aim.

"Don't anybody move!" she cried.

An unnecessary instruction; Miles, at least, was frozen in shock, mouth open.

"So," she said at last. Hatred, pain, and weariness

trembled her voice. "It is you. I wasn't sure at first. You . . ."

She was addressing Bothari, Miles guessed, for her needler was aimed at his chest. Her hands shook, but the aim never wavered.

The Sergeant had caught up a plasma arc when the door slid open. Now, incredibly, his hand fell to his side, weapon dangling. He straightened slightly by the wall, out of his firing semi-crouch.

Elena sat cross-legged, an awkward position from which to jump. Her hand viewer fell forgotten to the bed. The audio emitted a thin tinny sound, small as an insect, in the silence.

The Escobaran woman's eyes flicked for a moment to Miles, then back to their target. "I think you'd better know, Admiral Naismith, just what you have hired for your bodyguard."

"Uh . . . Why don't you give me your needler, and sit down, and we'll talk about it—" He held out an open hand, experimentally inviting. Hot shivers that began in the pit of his stomach were radiating outward; his hand shook foolishly. This wasn't the way he'd rehearsed this meeting. She hissed, her needler swinging toward him. He recoiled, and her aim jerked back to Bothari.

"That one," she nodded at the Sergeant, "is an ex-Barrayaran soldier. No surprise, I suppose, that he should have drifted into some obscure mercenary fleet. But he was Admiral Vorrutyer's chief torturer, when the Barrayarans tried to invade Escobar. But maybe you knew that—" Her eyes seemed to peel Miles, like flensing knives, for a moment. A moment was quite a long time, at the relativistic speed at which he was now falling.

"I—I—" he stammered. He glanced at Elena; her eyes were huge, her body tense to spring.

"The Admiral never raped his victims himself—he preferred to watch. Vorrutyer was Prince Serg's catamite, perhaps the Prince was jealous. He applied more inventive tortures himself, though. The Prince was waiting, since his particular obsession was pregnant women, which I suppose Vorrutyer's group was obliged to supply—"

Miles's mind screamed through a hundred unwanted connections, no, no, no . . . So, there was such a thing as latent knowledge. How long had he known not to ask questions he didn't want to hear the answers to? Elena's face reflected total outrage and disbelief. God help him to keep it that way. His stunner lay on Bothari's table, across their mutual line of fire; did he stand a chance of leaping for it?

"I was eighteen years old when I fell into their hands. Just graduated, no war lover, but wishing to serve and protect my home—that was no war, out there, that was some personal hell, growing vile in the Barrayaran high command's unchecked power—" She was close to hysteria, as if old cold dormant terrors were erupting in a swarm more overwhelming than even she had anticipated. He had to shut her up somehow—

"And that one," her finger was tight on the trigger of the needler, "was their tool, their best show-maker, their pet. The Barrayarans refused to turn over their war criminals, and my own government bargained away the justice that should have been mine for the sake of the peace settlements. And so he went free, to be my nightmare for the past two decades. But mercenary fleets dispense their own justice. Admiral Naismith, I demand this man's arrest!"

"I don't—it's not—" began Miles. He turned to Bothari, his eyes imploring denial—make it not be true—"Sergeant?"

The explosion of words had spattered over Bothari like acid. His face was furrowed with pain, brow creased with an effort of—memory? His eyes went from his daughter to Miles to the Escobaran, and a sigh went out of him. A man descending forever into hell, vouchsafed one glimpse of paradise, might have such a look on his face. "Lady . . ." he whispered. "You are still beautiful."

Don't goad her, Sergeant! Miles screamed silently.

The Escobaran woman's face contorted with rage and fear. She braced herself. A stream, as of tiny silver raindrops, sang from the shaking weapon. The needles burst against the wall all around Bothari in a whining shower of spinning, razor-sharp shards. The weapon jammed. The woman swore, and scrabbled at it. Bothari, leaning against the wall, murmured, "Rest now," Miles was not sure to whom.

Miles sprang for his stunner as Elena leaped for the Escobaran. Elena struck the needler sliding across the room and had the woman's arms hooked behind her, twisting in their shoulder sockets with the strength of her terror and rage, by the time he'd brought the stunner to aim. But the woman was resistless, spent. Miles saw why as he spun back to the Sergeant.

Bothari fell like a wall toppling, as if in pieces at the joints. His shirt displayed four or five tiny drops of blood only, scarcely a nosebleed's worth. But they were obliterated in a sudden red flood from his mouth as he convulsed, choking. He writhed once on the friction matting, vomiting a second scarlet tide across the first, across Miles's hands, lap, shirt front, as he scrambled on hands and knees to kneel by his bodyguard's head.

"Sergeant?"

Bothari lay still, watchful eyes stopped and open, head twisted, the blood flung from his mouth soaking into the friction matting. He looked like some dead animal, smashed by a vehicle. Miles patted Bothari's chest frantically, but could not even find the pin-hole entrance wounds. Five hits—Bothari's chest cavity, abdomen, organs, must be sliced and stirred to hamburger, within. . . .

"Why didn't he fire?" wailed Elena. She shook the Escobaran woman. "Wasn't it charged?"

Miles glanced at the plasma arc's readouts in the Sergeant's stiffening hand. Freshly charged, Bothari had just done it himself.

Elena took one despairing look at her father's body, and snaked a hand around the Escobaran woman's throat, catching her tunic. Her arm tightened across the woman's windpipe.

Miles rocked back on his heels, his shirt, trousers, hands soaked in blood. "No, Elena! Don't kill her!"

"Why not? Why not?" Tears were swarming down her ravaged face.

"I think she's your mother." Oh, God, he shouldn't have said that. . . .

"You believe those horrible things—" she raged at him. "Unbelievable lies—" But her hold slackened. "Miles—I don't even know what some of those words mean. . . ."

The Escobaran woman coughed, and twisted her head around, to stare in astonishment and dismay over her shoulder. "This is that one's spawn?" she asked Miles.

"His daughter."

Her eyes counted off the features of Elena's face. Miles did too; it seemed to him the secret sources of Elena's hair, eyes, elegant bone structure, stood before him.

"You look like him." Her great brown eyes held a thin crust of distaste over a bog of horror. "I'd heard the Barrayarans had used the fetuses for military research." She eyed Miles in confused speculation. "Are you another? But no, you couldn't be. . . ."

Elena released her, and stood back. Once, at the summer place at Vorkosigan Surleau, Miles had witnessed a horse trapped in a shed burn to death, no one able to get near it for the heat. He had thought no sound could be more heart-piercing than its death screams. Elena's silence was. She was not crying now.

Miles drew himself up in dignity. "No, ma'am. Admiral Vorkosigan saw them all safely delivered to an orphanage, I believe. All but . . ."

Elena's lips formed the word, "lies," but there was no more conviction in her. Her eyes sucked at the Escobaran woman with a hunger that terrified Miles.

The door of the cabin slid open again. Arde Mayhew sauntered in, saying, "My lord, do you want these assignments—God almighty!" He nearly tripped, stopping short. "I'll get the medtech, hang on!" He dashed back out.

Elena Visconti approached Bothari's body with the caution one would use toward a freshly killed poisonous reptile. Her eyes locked with Miles's from opposite sides of the barrier. "Admiral Naismith, I apologize for inconveniencing you. But this was no murder. It was the just execution of a war criminal. It was just," she insisted, her voice edged with passion. "It was." Her voice fell away.

It was no murder, it was a suicide, Miles thought. He could have shot you where you stood at any time, he was that fast. "No . . ."

Her lips thinned in despair. "You call me a liar too? Or are you going to tell me I enjoyed it?"

"No . . ." He looked up at her across a vast gulf, one meter wide. "I don't mock you. But—until I was four, almost five years old, I couldn't walk, only crawl. I spent a lot of time looking at people's knees. But if there was ever a parade, or something to see, I had the best view of anybody because I watched it from on top the Sergeant's shoulder."

For answer, she spat on Bothari's body. A spasm of rage darkened Miles's vision. He was saved from a possibly disastrous action by the return of Mayhew and the medtech.

The medtech ran to him. "Admiral! Where are you hit?"

He stared at her stupidly a moment, then glanced down at himself, realizing the red reason for her concern. "Not me. It's the Sergeant." He brushed ineffectually at the cooling stickiness.

She knelt by Bothari. "What happened? Was it an accident?"

Miles glanced up at Elena where she stood, just stood, arms wrapped around herself as if she were cold. Only her eyes traveled, back and forth from the Sergeant's crumpled form to the harsh straightness of the Escobaran. Back and forth, finding no rest.

His mouth was stiff; he made it move by force of will. "An accident. He was cleaning the weapons. The needler was set on auto rapid-fire." Two true statements out of three.

The Escobaran woman's mouth curled in silent triumph and relief. She thinks I have endorsed her justice, Miles realized. Forgive me . . .

The medtech shook her head, running a hand scanner over Bothari's chest. "Whew. What a mess."

A sudden hope rocketed through Miles. "The cryo chambers—what's their status?"

"All filled, sir, after the counterattack."

"When you triage for them, how—how do you choose?"

"The least messed-up ones have the best hope of

revival. They get first choice. Enemies last, unless Intelligence throws a fit."

"How would you rate this injury?"

"Worse than any I've got on ice now, except two."

"Who are the two?"

"A couple of Captain Tung's people. Do you want me to dump one?"

Miles paused, searching Elena's face. She was staring at Bothari's body as if he were some stranger, wearing her father's face, who had suddenly unmasked. Her dark eyes were like deep caverns; like graves, one for Bothari, one for himself.

"He hated the cold," he muttered at last. "Just—get a morgue pack."

"Yes, sir." She exited, unhurried.

Mayhew wandered up, to stare bemused and bewildered on the face of death. "I'm sorry, my lord. I was just beginning to like him, in a kind of weird way."

"Yes. Thank you. Go away." Miles looked up at the Escobaran woman. "Go away," he whispered.

Elena was turning around and around between the dead and the living, like a creature newly caged discovering that cold iron sears the flesh. "Mother?" she said at last, in a tiny voice not at all like her own.

"You keep away from me," the Escobaran woman snarled at her, low-voiced and pale. "Far away." She gave her a look of loathing, contemptuous as a slap, and stalked out.

"Um," said Arde. "Maybe you should come somewhere and sit down, Elena. I'll get you a, a drink of water or something." He plucked at her anxiously. "Come away now, there's a good girl."

She suffered herself to be led, with one last look over her shoulder. Her face reminded Miles of a bombed-out city.

Miles waited for the medtech, in deathwatch for his

first liegeman, afraid, and growing more so, unaccustomed. He had always had the Sergeant to be afraid for him. He touched Bothari's face; the shaved chin was rough under his fingertips.

"What do I do now, Sergeant?"

CHAPTER SIXTEEN

It was three days before he cried, worried that he could not cry. Then, in bed alone at night, it came as a frightening uncontrollable storm lasting hours. Miles judged it a just catharsis, but it kept repeating on succeeding nights, and then he worried that it would not stop. His stomach hurt all the time now, but especially after meals, which he therefore scarcely touched. His sharp features sharpened further, molding to his bones.

The days were a grey fog. Faces, familiar and unfamiliar, badgered him for directions, to which his reply was an invariable, laconic, "Suit yourself." Elena would not talk to him at all. He was stirred to fear she was finding comfort in Baz's arms. He watched her covertly, anxious. But she seemed not to be finding comfort anywhere.

After a particularly formless and inconclusive Dendarii staff meeting Arde Mayhew took him aside.

Miles had sat silent at the head of the table, seemingly studying his hands, while his officers' voices had croaked on meaningless as frogs.

"God knows," whispered Arde, "I don't know much about being a military officer." He took an angry breath. "But I do know you can't drag two hundred and more people out on a limb with you like this and then go catatonic."

"You're right," Miles snarled back, "you don't know much."

He stamped off, stiff-backed, but shaken inside with the justice of Mayhew's complaint. He slammed into his cabin just in time to throw up in secret for the fourth time that week, the second since Bothari's death, resolve sternly to take up the work at hand immediately and no more nonsense, and fall across his bed to lie immobile for the next six hours.

He was getting dressed. Men who'd done isolated duty all agreed, you had to keep the standards up or things went to hell. Miles had been awake three hours now, and had his trousers on. In the next hour he was either going to try for his socks, or shave, whichever seemed easier. He contemplated the pig-headed masochism of the Barrayaran habit of the daily shave versus, say, the civilized Betan custom of permanently stunning the hair follicles. Perhaps he'd go for the socks.

The cabin buzzer blatted. He ignored it. Then the intercom, Elena's voice: "Miles, let me in."

He lurched to a sitting position, nearly blacking himself out, and called hastily, "Come!" which released the voice-lock.

She picked her way in across strewn clothing, weapons, equipment, disconnected chargers, rations wrappers, and stared around, wrinkling her nose in dismay.

"You know," she said at last, "if you're not going to pick this mess up yourself you ought to at least choose a new batman."

Miles stared around too. "It never occurred to me," he said humbly. "I used to imagine I was a very neat person. Everything just put itself away, or so I thought. You wouldn't mind?"

"Mind what?"

"If I got a new batman."

"Why should I care?"

Miles thought it over. "Maybe Arde. I've got to find something for him to do, sooner or later, now he can't jump anymore."

"Arde?" she repeated dubiously.

"He's not nearly as slovenly as he used to be."

"Mm." She picked up a hand-viewer that was lying upside-down on the floor, and looked for a place to set it. But there was only one level surface in the cabin that held no clutter or dust. "Miles, how long are you going to keep that coffin in here?"

"It might as well be stored here as anywhere. The morgue's cold. He didn't like the cold."

"People are beginning to think you're strange."

"Let 'em think what they like. I gave him my word once that I'd take him back to be buried on Barrayar, if—if anything happened to him out here."

She shrugged angrily. "Why bother keeping your word to a corpse? It'll never know the difference."

"I'm alive," Miles said quietly, "and I'd know."

She stalked around the cabin, lips tight. Face tight, whole body tight—"I've been running your unarmed combat classes for ten days now. You haven't come to a single session."

He wondered if he ought to tell her about throwing up the blood. No, she'd drag him off to the medtech for sure. He didn't want to see the medtech. His age, the secret weakness of his bones—too much would become apparent on a close medical examination.

She went on. "Baz is doing double shifts, reconditioning equipment, Tung and Thorne and Auson are running their tails off organizing the new recruits—but it's all starting to come apart. Everybody's spending all their time arguing with everybody else. Miles, if you spend another week holed up in here, the Dendarii Mercenaries are going to start looking just like this cabin."

"I know. I've been to the staff meetings. Just because I don't say anything doesn't mean I'm not listening."

"Then listen to them when they say they need your leadership."

"I swear to God, Elena, I don't know what for." He ran his hands through his hair, and jerked up his chin. "Baz fixes things, Arde runs them, Tung and Thorne and Auson and their people do the fighting, you keep them all sharp and in condition—I'm the one person who doesn't do anything real at all." He paused. "They say? What do you say?"

"What does it matter what I say?"

"You came . . ."

"They asked me to come. You haven't been letting anyone else in, remember? They've been pestering me for days. They act like a bunch of ancient Christians asking the Virgin Mary to intercede with God."

A ghost of his old grin flitted across his mouth. "No, only with Jesus. God is back on Barrayar."

She choked, then buried her face in her hands. "Damn you for making me laugh!" she said, muffled.

He rose to capture her hands and make her sit beside him. "Why shouldn't you laugh? You deserve laughter, and all good things."

She did not answer, but stared across the room at

the oblong silver box resting in the corner, at the bright scars on the far wall. "You never doubted her accusations," she said at last. "Not even for the first instant."

"I saw a lot more of him than you ever did. He practically lived in my back pocket for seventeen years."

"Yes . . ." Her eyes fell to her hands, now twisting in her lap. "I suppose I never did see more than glimpses. He would come to the village at Vorkosigan Surleau and give Mistress Hysopi her money once a month—he'd hardly ever stay more than an hour. Looking three meters tall in that brown and silver livery of yours. I'd be so excited, I couldn't sleep for a day before or after. Summers were heaven, because when your mother asked me up the lake to the summer place to play with you, I'd see him all day long." Her hands tightened to fists, and her voice broke. "And it was all *lies.* Faking glory, while all the time underneath was this—cesspit."

He made his voice more gentle than he had ever known he could. "I don't think he was lying, Elena. I think he was trying to forge a new truth."

Her teeth were clenched and feral. "The *truth* is, I am a madman's rape-bred bastard, my mother is a murderess who hates the very shape of my shadow—I can't believe I've inherited no more from them than my nose and my eyes—"

There it was, the dark fear, most secret. He started in recognition, and dove after it like a knight pursuing a dragon underground. "No! You're not them. You are you, your own person—totally separate—innocent—"

"Coming from you, I think that's the most hypocritical thing I've ever heard."

"Huh?"

"What are you but the culmination of your generations? The flower of the Vor—"

"Me?" He stared in astonishment. "The culmination of degeneration, maybe. A stunted weed . . ." He paused; her face seemed a mirror of his own astonishment. "They do add up, it's true. My grandfather carried nine generations on his back. My father carried ten. I carry eleven—and I swear that last one weighs more than all the rest put together. It's a wonder I'm not squashed even shorter. I feel like I'm down to about half a meter right now. Soon I'll disappear altogether."

He was babbling, knew he was babbling. Some dam had broken in him. He gave himself over to the flood and boiled on down the sluice.

"Elena, I love you, I've always loved you—" She leaped like a startled deer; he gasped and flung his arms around her. "No, listen! I love you, I don't know what the Sergeant was but I loved him too, and whatever of him is in you I honor with all my heart, I don't know what is truth and I don't give a damn anymore, we'll make our own like he did, he did a bloody good job I think, I can't live without my Bothari, marry me!" He spent the last of his air shouting the last two words, and had to pause for a long inhalation.

"I can't marry you! The genetic risks—"

"I am *not* a mutant! Look, no gills—" he stuck his fingers into the corners of his mouth and spread it wide, "no antlers—" He planted his thumbs on either side of his head and wriggled his fingers.

"I wasn't thinking of your genetic risks. Mine. *His*. Your father must have known what he was—he'll never accept—"

"Look, anybody who can trace a blood relationship with Mad Emperor Yuri through two lines of descent has no room to criticize anybody else's genes."

"Your father is loyal to his class, Miles, like your

grandfather, like Lady Vorpatril—they could never accept me as Lady Vorkosigan."

"Then I'll present them with an alternative. I'll tell them I'm going to marry Bel Thorne. They'll come around so fast they'll trip over themselves."

She sat back helplessly and buried her face in his pillow, shoulders shaking. He had a moment of terror that he'd broken her down into tears. Not break down, build up, and up, and up . . . But, "*Damn* you for making me laugh!" she repeated. "Damn you . . ."

He galloped on, encouraged. "And I wouldn't be so sure about my father's class loyalties. He married a foreign plebe, after all." He dropped into seriousness. "And you cannot doubt my mother. She always longed for a daughter, secretly—never paraded it, so as not to hurt the old man, of course—let her be your mother in truth."

"Oh," she said, as if he had stabbed her. "Oh . . ."

"You'll see, when we get back to Barrayar—"

"I pray to God," she interrupted him, voice intense, "I may never set foot on Barrayar again."

"Oh," he said in turn. After a long pause he said, "We could live somewhere else. Beta Colony. It would have to be pretty quietly, once the exchange rate got done with my income—I could get a job, doing—doing—doing something."

"And on the day the Emperor calls you to take your place on the Council of Counts, to speak for your district and all the poor sods in it, where will you go then?"

He swallowed, struck silent. "Ivan Vorpatril is my heir," he offered at last. "Let him take the Countship."

"Ivan Vorpatril is a jerk."

"Oh, he's not such a bad sort."

"He used to corner me, when my father wasn't around, and try to feel me up."

"What! You never said—"

"I didn't want to start a big flap." She frowned into the past. "I almost wish I could go back in time, just to boot him in the balls."

He glanced sideways at her, considerably startled. "Yes," he said slowly, "you've changed."

"I don't know what I am anymore. Miles, you must believe me—I love you as I love breath—"

His heart rocketed.

"But I can't be your annex."

And crashed. "I don't understand."

"I don't know how to put it plainer. You'd swallow me up the way an ocean swallows a bucket of water. I'd disappear in you. I love you, but I'm terrified of you, and of your future."

His bafflement sought simplicity. "Baz. It's Baz, isn't it?"

"If Baz had never existed, my answer would be the same. But as it happens—I have given him my word."

"You—" the breath went out of him in a "ha,"—"Break it," he ordered.

She merely looked at him, silently. In a moment he reddened, and dropped his eyes in shame.

"You own honor by the ocean," she whispered. "I have only a little bucketful. Unfair to jostle it—my lord."

He fell back across his bed, defeated.

She rose. "Are you coming to the staff meeting?"

"Why bother? It's hopeless."

She stared down at him, lips thinned, and glanced across to the box in the corner. "Isn't it time you learned to walk on your own feet—cripple?"

She ducked out the door just in time to avoid the pillow he threw at her, her lips curving just slightly at this spasmodic display of energy.

"You know me too bloody well," he whispered. "Ought to keep you just for security reasons."

He staggered to his feet and went to shave.

He made it to the staff conference, barely, and sagged into his usual seat at the head of the table. It was a full meeting, held therefore in the roomy refinery conference chamber. General Halify and an aide sat in. Tung and Thorne and Auson, Arde and Baz, and the five men and women picked to officer the new recruits ringed the table. The Cetagandan ghem-captain sat opposite the Kshatryan lieutenant, their growing animosity threatening to equal the three-way rivalry among Tung, Auson, and Thorne. The two united only long enough to snarl at the Felicians, the professional assassin from Jackson's Whole, or the retired Tau Cetan major of commandos, who in turn sniped at the ex-Oserans, making the circle complete.

The alleged agenda for this circus was the preparation of the final Dendarii battle-plan for breaking the Oseran blockade, hence General Halify's keen interest. His keenness had been rather blunted this last week by a growing dismay. The doubt in Halify's eyes was an itch to Miles's spirit; he tried to avoid meeting them. Bargain rates, General, Miles thought sulkily to him. You get what you pay for.

The first half hour was spent knocking down, again, three unworkable pet plans that had been advanced by their owners at previous meetings. Bad odds, requirements of personnel and material beyond their resources, impossibilities of timing, were pointed out with relish by one half of Miles's group to the other, with opinions of the advancers' mentalities thrown in gratis. This rapidly degenerated into a classic slanging match. Tung, who normally suppressed such, was one of the principals this time, so it threatened to escalate indefinitely.

"Look, damn it," shouted the Kshatryan lieutenant, banging his fist on the table for emphasis, "we can't take the wormhole direct and we all know it. Let's concentrate on something we can do. Merchant shipping—we could attack that, a counter-blockade—"

"Attack neutral galactic shipping?" yelped Auson. "Do you want to get us all hung?"

"Hanged," corrected Thorne, earning an ungrateful glare.

"No, see," Auson bulled on, "the Pelians have little bases all over this system we could have a go at. Like guerilla warfare, attacking and fading into the sands—"

"What sands?" snapped Tung. "There's nothing to hide your ass behind out there—the Pelians have our home address. It's a miracle they haven't given up all hope of capturing this refinery and flung a half-c meteor shower through here already. Any plan that doesn't work quickly won't work at all—"

"What about a lightning raid on the Pelian capital?" suggested the Cetagandan captain. "A suicide squadron to drop a nuclear in there—"

"You volunteering?" sneered the Kshatryan. "That might almost be worthwhile."

"The Pelians have a trans-shipping station in orbit around the sixth planet," said the Tau Cetan. "A raid on that would—"

"—take that electron orbital randomizer and—"

"—you're an idiot—"

"—ambush stray ships—"

Miles's intestines writhed like mating snakes. He rubbed his hands wearily over his face, and spoke for the first time; the unexpectedness of it caught their attention momentarily.

"I've known people who play chess like this. They can't think their way to a checkmate, so they spend their time trying to clear the board of the little pieces.

This eventually reduces the game to a simplicity they can grasp, and they're happy. The perfect war is a fool's mate."

He subsided, elbows on the table, face in his hands. After a short silence, expectation falling into disappointment, the Kshatryan renewed the attack on the Cetagandan, and they were off again. Their voices blurred over Miles. General Halify began to push back from the table.

No one noticed Miles's jaw drop, behind his hands, or his eyes widen, then narrow to glints. "Son-of-a-bitch," he whispered. "It's *not* hopeless."

He sat up. "Has it occurred to anyone yet that we're tackling this problem from the wrong end?"

His words were lost in the din. Only Elena, sitting in a corner across the chamber, saw his face. Her own face turned like a sunflower toward him. Her lips moved silently: Miles?

Not a shameful escape in the dark, but a monument. That's what he would make of this war. Yes . . .

He pulled his grandfather's dagger from its sheath and spun it in the air. It came down and stuck point-first in the center of the table with a ringing vibration. He climbed up on the table and marched to retrieve it.

The silence was sudden and complete, but for a mutter from Auson, in front of whom the dagger had landed, "I didn't think that plastic would scratch . . ."

Miles yanked the dagger out, resheathed it, and strode up and down the tabletop. His leg brace had developed an annoying click recently, which he'd meant to have Baz fix; now it was loud in the silence. Locking attention, like a whisper. Good. A click, a club on the head, whatever worked was fine by him. It was time to get their attention.

"It appears to have escaped you gentlemen, ladies, and others, that the Dendarii's appointed task is not to physically destroy the Oserans, but merely to eliminate them as a fighting force in local space. We need not blunt ourselves attacking their strengths."

Their upturned faces followed him like iron filings drawn to a magnet. General Halify sank back in his seat. Baz's face, and Arde's, grew jubilant with hope.

"I direct your attention to the weak link in the chain that binds us—the connection between the Oserans and their employers the Pelians. *There* is where we must apply our leverage. My children," he stood gazing out past the refinery into the depths of space, a seer taken by a vision, "we're going to hit them in the payroll."

The underwear came first, soft, smooth-fitting, absorbent. Then the connections for the plumbing. Then the boots, the piezo-electric pads carefully aligned with points of maximum impact on toes, heels, the ball of the foot. Baz had done a beautiful job adjusting the fit of the space armor. The greaves went on like skin to Miles's uneven legs. Better than skin, an exoskeleton, his brittle bones at last rendered technologically equal to anyone's.

Miles wished Baz were by him at this moment, to take pride in his handiwork, although Arde was doing his best to help Miles ooze into the apparatus. Even more passionately Miles wished himself in Baz's place.

Felician intelligence reported all still quiet on the Pelian home front. Baz and his hand-picked party of techs, starring Elena Visconti, must have penetrated the planetside frontier successfully and be moving into place for their blow. The killing blow of Miles's strategy. The keystone of his arching ambitions. His heart had nearly broken, sending them off alone, but reason ruled. A commando raid, if it could be so called, delicate, technical, invisible, would not benefit from so conspicuous and low-tech a piece of baggage as himself. He was better employed here, with the rest of the grunts.

He glanced up the length of his flagship's armory. The atmosphere seemed a combination of locker room, docking bay, and surgery—he tried not to think about surgeries. His stomach twinged, a probe of pain. Not now, he told it. Later. Be good, and I promise I'll take you to the medtech, later.

The rest of his attack group were arming and armoring themselves as he was. Techs checked out systems to a quiet undercurrent of colored lights and small audio signals as they probed here, there; the quiet undercurrent of voices was serious, attentive, concentrated, almost meditative, like an ancient church before the services began. It was well. He caught Elena's eye, two soldiers down the row from himself, and smiled reassuringly, as if he and not she were the veteran. She did not smile back.

He probed his strategy as the techs did their systems. The Oseran payroll was divided into two parts. The first was an electronic transfer payment of Pelian funds into an Oseran account in the Pelian capital, out of which the Oseran fleet purchased local supplies. Miles's special plan was for that. The second half was in assorted galactic currencies, primarily Betan dollars. This was the cash profit, to be divided among Oser's captain-owners to carry out of Tau Verde local space to their various destinations when their contracts at last expired. It was delivered monthly to Oser's flagship on its blockade station. Miles corrected his thought with a small grin—*had* been delivered monthly.

They had taken the first cash payroll in midspace with devastating ease. Half of Miles's troops were Oserans, after all; several had even done the duty before. Presenting themselves to the Pelian courier as the Oseran pickup had required only the slightest of adjustments in codes and procedures. They were done and far out of range before the real Oserans arrived. The transcript of the subsequent dispatches between the Pelian courier and the Oseran pickup ship was a treasure for Miles. He kept it stored atop Bothari's coffin in his cabin, beside his grandfather's dagger. More to come, Sergeant, he thought. I swear it.

The second operation, two weeks later, had been crude by comparison, a slugging match between the new, more heavily armed Pelian courier and Miles's three warships. Miles had prudently stepped aside and let Tung direct it, confining his comments to an occasional approving "Ah." They gave up maneuvering to board upon the approach of four Oseran ships. The Oserans were taking no chances with this delivery.

The Dendarii had blasted the Pelian and its precious cargo into its component atoms, and fled. The Pelians had fought bravely. Miles burned them a death-offering that night in his cabin, very privately.

Arde connected Miles's left shoulder joint, and began to run through the checklist of rotational movements of all the joints from shoulder to fingertips. His ring finger was running about 20% weak. Arde opened the pressure plate under his left wrist and pinned the tiny power-up control.

His strategy . . . By the third attempted hijacking, it was clear the enemy was learning from experience. Oser sent a convoy practically to the planet's atmosphere for the pickup. Miles's ships, hovering out of range, had been unable to even get near. Miles was forced to use his ace-in-the-hole.

Tung had raised his eyebrows when Miles asked him to send a simple paper message to his former communications officer. "Please cooperate with all Dendarii requests," it read, signed, meaninglessly to the Eurasian, with the Vorkosigan seal concealed in the hilt of Miles's grandfather's dagger. The communications officer had been a fountain of intelligence ever since. Bad, to so endanger one of Captain Illyan's operatives, worse to risk their best eye in the Oseran fleet. If the Oserans ever figured out who had microwaved the money, the man's life was surely forfeit. To date, though, the Oserans held only four packing cases of ashes and a mystery.

Miles felt a slight change in gravity and vibration; they must be moving into attack formation. Time to get his helmet on, and make contact with Tung and Auson in the tactics room. Elena's tech fitted her helmet. She opened her faceplate, spoke to the tech; they collaborated on some minor adjustment.

If Baz was keeping his schedule, this was surely Miles's last chance with her. With the engineer out of the way, there was no one to usurp his hero's role. The next rescue would be his. He pictured himself, blasting menacing Pelians right and left, pulling her out of some tactical hole—the details were vague. She would have to believe he loved her then. His tongue would magically untangle, he'd finally find the right words after so many wrong ones, her snowy skin would warm in the heat of his ardor and bloom again. . . .

Her face, framed by her helmet, was cold, austere in profile, the same blank winter landscape she had exhibited to the world since Bothari's death. Her lack of reaction worried Miles. True, she had had her Dendarii duties to distract her, keep her moving—not like the self-indulgent luxury of his own withdrawal. At least with Elena Visconti gone, she was spared those awkward meetings in the corridors and conference rooms, both women pretending fiercely to cold professionalism.

Elena stretched in her armor, and gazed pensively into the black hole of her plasma arc muzzle built into the right arm of her suit. She slipped on her glove, covering the blue veins like pale rivers of ice in her wrist. Her eyes made Miles think of razors.

He stepped to her shoulder, and waved away her tech. The words he spoke weren't any of the dozens he had rehearsed for the occasion. He lowered his voice to whisper.

"I know all about suicide. Don't think you can fool me."

She started, and flushed. Frowned at him in fierce scorn. Snapped her faceplate shut.

Forgive, whispered his anguished thought to her. It is necessary.

Arde lowered Miles's helmet over his head, connected his control leads, checked the connections. A lacework of fire netted, knotted, and tangled in Miles's gut. Damn, but it was getting hard to ignore.

He checked his comm link with the tactics room. "Commodore Tung? Naismith here. Roll the vids." The inside of his faceplate blurred with color, duplicate readouts of the tactics room telemetry for the field commander. Only communications, no servo links this time. The captured Pelian armor had none, and the old Oseran armor was all safely on manual override. Just in case somebody else out there was learning from experience.

"Last chance to change your mind," Tung said over the comm link, continuing the old argument. "Sure you wouldn't rather attack the Oserans after the transfer, farther from the Pelian bases? Our intelligence on them is so much more detailed. . . ."

"No! We have to capture or destroy the payroll before the delivery. Taking it after is strategically useless."

"Not entirely. We could sure use the money."

And how, Miles reflected glumly. It would soon take scientific notation to register his debt to the Dendarii. A mercenary fleet could hardly burn money faster if the ships ran on steam power and the funds were shoveled directly into their furnaces. Never had one so little owed so much to so many, and it grew worse by the hour. His stomach oozed around his abdominal cavity like a tortured amoeba, throwing out pseudopods of pain and the vacuole of an acid belch. You are a psychosomatic illusion, Miles assured it.

The assault group formed up and marched to the waiting shuttles. Miles moved among them, trying to touch each person, call them by name, give them some personal word; they seemed to like that. He ordered their ranks in his mind, and wondered how many gaps there would be when this day's work was done. Forgive . . . He had run out of clever solutions. This one was to be done the old hard way, head-on.

They moved through the shuttle hatch corridors into the waiting shuttle. This must surely be the worst part, waiting helplessly for Tung to deliver them like cartons of eggs, as fragile, as messy when broken. He took a deep breath, and prepared to cope with the usual effects of zero-gee.

He was totally unprepared for the cramp that doubled him over, snatched his breath away, drained his face to a paper-whiteness. Not like this, it had never come on like this before—. He redoubled into a ball, gasping, lost his grasp on his grip-strap, floated free. Dear God, it was finally happening—the ultimate humiliation—he was going to throw up in a space suit. In moments, everyone would know of his hilarious weakness. Absurd, for a would-be Imperial officer to get space-sick. Absurd, absurd, he had always been absurd. He had barely the presence of mind to hit his ventilator controls to full power with a jerk of his chin, and kill his broadcast—no need to treat his mercenaries to the unedifying sound of their commander retching.

"Admiral Naismith?" came an inquiry from the tactics room. "Your medical readouts look odd—telemetry check requested."

The universe seemed to narrow to his belly. A wrenching rush, gagging and coughing, another, another. The ventilator could not keep up. He'd eaten nothing this day, where was it all coming from?

A mercenary pulled him out of the air, tried to help him straighten his clenched limbs. "Admiral Naismith? Are you all right?"

He opened Miles's faceplate, to Miles's gasp of "No! Not in here—"

"Son-of-a-bitch!" The man jumped back, and raised his voice to a piercing cry. "Medtech!"

You're overreacting, Miles tried to say; I'll clean it up myself. . . . Dark clots, scarlet droplets, shimmering crimson globules, floated past his confused eyes, his secret spilled. It appeared to be pure blood. "No," he whimpered, or tried to. "Not *now* . . ."

Hands grasped him, passed him back to the shuttle hatch he had entered moments before. Gravity pressed him to the corridor deck—who the devil had upped it to three-gee?—hands pulled his helmet off, plucked at his carefully donned carapace. He felt like a lobster supper. His belly wrung itself out again.

Elena's face, nearly as white as his now, circled above him. She knelt, tore off her servo glove and gripped his hand, flesh to flesh at last. "Miles!"

Truth is what you make it . . . "Commander Bothari!" he croaked, as loud as he could. A ring of frightened faces huddled around him. His Dendarii. His people. For them, then. All for them. All. "Take over."

"I can't!" Her face was pale with shock, terrified.

God, Miles thought, I must look just like Bothari, spilling his guts. It's not that bad, he tried to tell her. Silver-black whorls sparkled in his vision, blotting out her face. No! Not yet—

"Liege-lady. You can. You must. I'll be with you." He writhed, gripped by some sadistic giant. "You are true Vor, not I. . . . Must have been changelings, back there in those replicators." He gave her a death's-head grin. "Forward momentum—"

She rose then, determination crowding out the hot terror in her face, the ice that had run like water transmuted to marble.

"Right, my lord," she whispered. And more loudly, "Right! Get back there, let the medtechs do their job—" She drove away his admirers. He was flipped efficiently onto a float pallet.

He watched his booted feet, dark and distant hillocks, waver before him as he was borne aloft. Feet first, it would have to be feet first. He barely felt the prick of the first IV in his arm. He heard Elena's voice, raised tremblingly behind him.

"All right you clowns! No more games. We're going to win this one for Admiral Naismith!"

Heroes. They sprang up around him like weeds. A carrier, he was seemingly unable to catch the disease he spread.

"Damn it," he moaned. "Damn it, damn it, damn it . . ." He repeated this litany like a mantra, until the medtech's second sedative injection parted him from his pain, frustration, and consciousness.

CHAPTER SEVENTEEN

He wandered in and out of reality, like being lost in the Imperial Residence when he was a boy, trying various doors, some leading to treasures, others to broom closets, but none to familiarity. Once he awoke to Tung, sitting beside him, and worried about it; shouldn't the mercenary be in the tactics room?

Tung eyed him with affectionate concern. "You know, son, if you're going to last in this business, you have to learn to pace yourself. We almost lost you there."

It sounded like a good dictum; perhaps he'd have it calligraphied for the wall of his bedroom.

Another time, Elena. How had she come to sickbay? He'd left her in the shuttle. Nothing stayed where you put it . . .

"Damn it," he mumbled apologetically, "things like this never happened to Vorthalia the Bold."

She raised a thoughtful eyebrow. "How do you know? The histories of those times were all written by minstrels and poets. You try and think of a word that rhymes with 'bleeding ulcer.'"

He was still dutifully trying when the greyness swallowed him again.

Once, he woke alone and called over and over for Sergeant Bothari, but the Sergeant didn't come. It's just like the man, he thought petulantly, underfoot all the time and then gone on long leave just when he needed him. The medtech's sedative ended that bout with consciousness, not in Miles's favor.

It was an allergic reaction to the sedative, the surgeon told him later. His grandfather came, and smothered him with a pillow, and tried to hide him under the bed. Bothari, bloody-chested, and the mercenary pilot officer, his implant wires somehow turned inside out and waving about his head like some strange brachiated coral, watched. His mother came at last and shooed away the deadly ghosts like a farm wife clucking to her chickens. "Quick," she advised Miles, "calculate the value of e to the last decimal place, and the spell will be broken. You can do it in your head if you're Betan enough."

Miles waited eagerly all day for his father, in this parade of hallucinatory figures; he had done something extremely clever, although he could not quite remember what, and he ached for a chance at last to impress the Count. But his father never came. Miles wept with disappointment.

Other shadows came and went, the medtech, the surgeon, Elena and Tung, Auson and Thorne, Arde Mayhew, but they were distant, figures reflected on lead glass. After he had cried for a long time, he slept.

When he woke again, the little private room off the sickbay of the *Triumph* was clear and unwavering in outline, but Ivan Vorpatril sat beside his bed.

"Other people," Miles groaned, "get to hallucinate

orgies and giant cicadas and things. What do I get? Relatives. I can see relatives when I'm conscious. It's not fair . . ."

Ivan turned worriedly to Elena, who was perched on the end of the bed. "I thought the surgeon said the antidote would have cleared him out by now."

Elena rose, and bent over Miles in concern, long white fingers across his brow. "Miles? Can you hear me?"

"Of course I can hear you." He suddenly realized the absence of another sensation. "Hey! My stomach doesn't hurt."

"Yes, the surgeon blocked off some nerves during the repair operation. You should be completely healed up inside within a couple of weeks."

"Operation?" He attempted a surreptitious peek down the shapeless garment he seemed to be occupying, looking for he knew not what. His torso seemed to be as smooth, or lumpy, as ever, no important body parts accidently snipped off—"I don't see any dotted lines."

"He didn't cut. It was all shoving things down your gullet, and hand-tractor work, except for installing the biochip on your vagus nerve. A bit grotesque, but very ingenious."

"How long was I out?"

"Three days. You were—"

"Three days! The payroll raid—Baz—" He lunged convulsively upward; Elena pushed him back down firmly.

"We took the payroll. Baz is back, with his whole group. Everything's fine, except for you almost bleeding to death."

"Nobody dies of ulcers. Baz back? Where are we, anyway?"

"Docked at the refinery. I didn't think you could die

of ulcers either, but the surgeon says holes in your body with blood pouring out are the same whether they're on the inside or the outside, so I guess you can. You'll get a full report—" she pushed him back down again, looking exasperated, "but I thought you'd better see Ivan privately first, without all the Dendarii standing around."

"Uh, right." He stared in bewilderment at his big cousin. Ivan was dressed in civilian gear, Barrayaran-style trousers, a Betan shirt, but Barrayaran regulation Service boots.

"Do you want to feel me, to see if I'm real?" Ivan asked cheerfully.

"It wouldn't do any good, you can feel hallucinations, too. Touch them, smell them, hear them . . ." Miles shivered. "I'll take your word for it. But Ivan—what are you doing here?"

"Looking for you."

"Did Father send you?"

"I don't know."

"How can you not know?"

"Well, he didn't talk to me personally—look, are you sure Captain Dimir hasn't arrived yet, or got any messages to you, or anything? He had all the dispatches and secret orders and things."

"Who?"

"Captain Dimir. He's my commanding officer."

"Never heard of him. Or from him."

"I think he works out of Captain Illyan's department," Ivan added helpfully. "Elena thought you might have heard something that you didn't have time to mention, maybe."

"No . . ."

"I don't understand it," sighed Ivan. "They left Beta Colony a day ahead of me in an Imperial fast courier. They should have been here a week ago."

"How was it you travelled separately?"

Ivan cleared his throat. "Well, there was this girl, you see, on Beta Colony. She invited me home—I mean, Miles, a Betan! I met her right there in the shuttleport, practically the first thing. Wearing one of those sporty little sarongs, and nothing else—" Ivan's hands were beginning to wave in dreamy descriptive curves; Miles hastened to cut off what he knew could be a lengthy digression.

"Probably trolling for galactics. Some Betans collect them. Like a Barrayaran getting banners of all the provinces." Ivan had such a collection at home, Miles recalled. "So what happened to this Captain Dimir?"

"They left without me." Ivan looked aggrieved. "And I wasn't even late!"

"How did you get here?"

"Lieutenant Croye reported you'd gone to Tau Verde IV. So I hitched a ride with a merchant vessel bound for one of those neutral countries down there. The captain dropped me off here at this refinery."

Miles's jaw dropped. "Hitched—dropped you off—do you realize the risks—"

Ivan blinked. "She was very nice about it. Er—motherly, you know."

Elena studied the ceiling, coolly disdainful. "That pat on the ass she gave you in the shuttle tube didn't look exactly maternal to me."

Ivan reddened. "Anyway, I got here." He brightened. "And ahead of old Dimir! Maybe I won't be in as much trouble as I thought."

Miles ran his hands through his hair. "Ivan—would it be too much trouble to begin at the beginning? Assuming there is one."

"Oh, yeah, I guess you wouldn't know about the big flap."

"Flap? Ivan, you're the first word we've had from

home since we left Beta Colony. The blockade, you know—although you seem to have passed through it like so much smoke . . ."

"The old bird was clever, I'll give her that. I never knew older women could—"

"The flap," Miles rerouted him urgently.

"Yes. Well. The first report we had at home, from Beta Colony, was that you had been kidnapped by some fellow who was a deserter from the Service—"

"Oh, ye gods! Mother—what did Father—"

"They were pretty worried, I guess, but your mother kept saying that Bothari was with you, and anyway somebody at the Embassy finally thought to talk with your Grandmother Naismith, and she didn't think you'd been kidnapped at all. That calmed your mother down a lot, and she, um, sat on your father—anyway, they decided to wait for further reports."

"Thank God."

"Well, the next reports were from some military agent here in Tau Verde local space. Nobody would tell me what was in them—well, nobody would tell my mother, I guess, which makes sense when you think about it. But Captain Illyan was running in circles between Vorkosigan House and General Headquarters and the Imperial Residence and Vorhartung Castle twenty-six hours a day for while. It didn't help that all the information they got was three weeks out of date, either—"

"Vorhartung Castle?" murmured Miles in surprise. "What does the Council of Counts have to do with this?"

"I couldn't figure it either. But Count Henri Vorvolk was pulled out of class at the Academy three times to attend secret committee sessions at the Counts, so I cornered him—seems there was some fantastic rumor going around that you were in Tau

Verde local space building up your own mercenary fleet, nobody knew why—at least, I thought it was a fantastic rumor—" Ivan stared around at the little sickbay cubicle, at the ship it implied. "Anyway, your father and Captain Illyan finally decided to send a fast courier to investigate."

"Via Beta Colony, I gather. Ah—did you happen to run across a fellow named Tav Calhoun while you were there?"

"Oh, yeah, the crazy Betan. He hangs around the Barrayaran Embassy—he has a warrant for your arrest, which he waves at whoever he can catch going in or out. The guards won't let him in anymore."

"Did you actually talk to him?"

"Briefly. I told him there was a rumor you'd gone to Kshatryia."

"Really?"

"Of course not. But it was the farthest place I could think of. The clan," Ivan said smugly, "should stick together."

"Thanks . . ." Miles mulled this over. "I think." He sighed. "I guess the best thing to do is wait for your Captain Dimir, then. He might at least be able to give us a ride home, which would solve one problem." He looked up at his cousin. "I'll explain it all later, but I have to know some things now—can you keep your mouth shut a while? Nobody here is supposed to know who I really am." A horrid thought shook Miles. "You haven't been going around asking for me by name, have you?"

"No, no, just Miles Naismith," Ivan assured him. "We knew you were travelling with your Betan passport. Anyway, I just got here last night, and practically the first person I met was Elena."

Miles breathed relief, and turned to Elena. "You say Baz is out there? I've got to see him."

She nodded, and withdrew, walking a wide circle around Ivan.

"Sorry to hear about old Bothari," Ivan offered when she'd left. "Who'd have thought he could do himself in cleaning weapons after all these years? Still, there's a bright side—you've finally got a chance to make time with Elena, without him breathing down your neck. So it's not a dead loss."

Miles exhaled carefully, faint with rage and reminded grief. He does not know, he told himself. He cannot know. . . . "Ivan, one of these days somebody is going to pull out a weapon and plug you, and you're going to die in bewilderment, crying, 'What did I say? What did I say?'"

"What did I say?" asked Ivan indignantly.

Before Miles could go into detail, Baz entered, flanked by Tung and Auson, Elena trailing. The chamber was jammed. They all seemed to be grinning like loons. Baz waved some plastic flimsies triumphantly in the air. He was lit like a beacon with pride, scarcely recognizable as the man Miles had found five months ago cowering in a garbage heap.

"The surgeon says we can't stay long, my lord," he said to Miles, "but I thought these might do for a get-well wish."

Ivan started slightly at the honorific, and stared covertly at the engineer.

Miles took the sheets of printing. "Your mission—were you able to complete it?"

"Like clockwork—well, not exactly, there were some bad moments in a train station—you should see the rail system they have on Tau Verde IV. The engineering—magnificent. Barrayar missed something by going from horseback straight to air transport—"

"The *mission*, Baz!"

The engineer beamed. "Take a look. Those are the

transcripts of the latest dispatches between Admiral Oser and the Pelian high command."

Miles began to read. After a time, he began to smile. "Yes . . . I'd understood Admiral Oser had a remarkable command of invective when, er, roused. . . ." Miles's gaze crossed Tung's, blandly. Tung's eyes glinted with satisfaction.

Ivan craned his neck. "What are they? Elena told me about your payroll heists—I take it you managed to mess up their electronic transfer, too. But I don't understand—won't the Pelians just repay, when they find the Oseran fleet wasn't credited?"

Miles's grin became quite wolfish. "Ah, but they *were* credited—eight times over. And now, as I believe a certain Earth general once said, God has delivered them into my hand. After failing four times in a row to deliver their cash payment, the Pelians have demanded the electronic overpayment be returned. And Oser," Miles glanced at the flimsies, "is refusing. Emphatically. That was the trickiest part, calculating just the right amount of overpayment. Too little, and the Pelians might have just let it go. Too much, and even Oser would have felt bound to return it. But just the right amount . . ." He sighed, and cuddled back happily into his pillow. He would have to commit some of Oser's choicest phrases to memory, he decided. They were unique.

"You'll like this, then, Admiral Naismith." Auson, bursting with news, erupted at last. "Four of Oser's independent Captain-owners took their ships and jumped out of Tau Verde local space in the last two days. From the transmissions we intercepted, I don't think they'll be coming back, either."

"Glorious," breathed Miles. "Oh, well done . . ."

He looked to Elena. Pride there, too, strong enough even to nudge out some of the pain in her eyes. "As I thought—intercepting that fourth payroll was vital to the success of the strategy. Well done, Commander Bothari."

She glowed back at him, hesitantly. "We missed you. We—took a lot of casualties."

"I anticipated we would. The Pelians had to be laying for us, by then." He glanced at Tung, who was making a small shushing gesture at Elena. "Was it much worse than we'd calculated?"

Tung shook his head. "There were moments when I was ready to swear she didn't know she was beaten. There are certain situations into which you do not ask mercenaries to follow you—"

"I didn't ask anyone to follow me," said Elena. "They came on their own." She added in a whispered aside to Miles, "I just thought that was what boarding battles were like. I didn't know it wasn't supposed to be that bad."

Tung spoke to Miles's alarmed look. "We would have paid a higher price if she hadn't insisted you'd put her in charge and refused to withdraw when I ordered. Then we would have paid much for nothing—that ratio works out to infinity, I believe." Tung gave Elena a nod of judicious approval, which she returned gravely. Ivan looked rather stunned.

A low-voiced argument penetrated from the corridor; Thorne, and the surgeon. Thorne was saying, "You've got to. This is vital—"

Thorne towed the protesting surgeon into the cubicle. "Admiral Naismith! Commodore Tung! Oser's *here*!"

"What!"

"With his whole fleet—what's left of it—they're just out of range. He's asking permission to dock his flagship."

"That can't be!" said Tung. "Who's guarding the wormhole?"

"Yes, exactly!" cried Thorne. "Who?" They stared at each other in elated, wild surmise.

Miles sprang to his feet, fought off a wave of dizziness, clutched his gown behind him. "Get my clothes," he enunciated.

Hawk-like, Miles decided, was the word for Admiral Oser. Greying hair, a beak of a nose, a bright, penetrating stare, fixed now on Miles. He had mastered the look that makes junior officers search their consciences, Miles thought. He stood up under it, and gave the real mercenary admiral a slow smile, there in the docking bay. The sharp, cold, recycled air was bitter in his nostrils, like a stimulant. You could get high on it, surely.

Oser was flanked by three of his Captain-employees and two of his Captain-owners, and their seconds. Miles trailed the whole Dendarii staff, Elena on his right hand, Baz on his left.

Oser looked him up and down. "Damn," he murmured. "Damn . . ." He did not offer his hand, but stood and spoke; deliberate, rehearsed cadences.

"Since the day you entered Tau Verde local space, I've felt your presence. In the Felicians, in the tactical situation turning under me, in the faces of my own men—" his glance passed over Tung, who smiled sweetly, "even in the Pelians. We have been grappling in the dark, we two, at a distance, long enough."

Miles's eyes widened. My God, is Oser about to challenge me to single combat? Sergeant Bothari, help! He jerked his chin up, and said nothing.

"I don't believe in prolonging agonies," said Oser. "Rather than watch you enspell the rest of my fleet man by man—while I still possess a fleet to offer—I understand the Dendarii Mercenaries are looking for recruits."

It took Miles a moment to realize he had just heard

one of the most stiff-necked surrender speeches in history. *Gracious. We are going to be gracious as hell, oh, yes. . . .* He held out his hand; Oser took it.

"Admiral Oser, your understanding is acute. There's a private chamber, where we can work out the details . . ."

General Halify and some Felician officers were watching at a distance from a balcony overlooking the docking bay. Miles's glance crossed Halify's. *And so my word to you, at least, is redeemed.*

Miles marched across the broad expanse, the whole herd, all Dendarii now, strung out behind him. Let's see, Miles thought, the Pied Piper of Hamlin led all the rats into the river—he looked back—and all the children he led to a mountain of gold. What would he have done if the rats and the children had been inextricably mixed?

CHAPTER EIGHTEEN

Miles reclined on a liquid-filled settee in the refinery's darkside observation chamber, hands behind his head, and stared into the depths of a space no longer empty. The Dendarii fleet glittered and winked, riding at station in the vacuum, a constellation of ships and men.

In his bedroom at the summer place at Vorkosigan Surleau, he had owned a mobile of space warships, classic Barrayaran military craft held in their carefully balanced arrangement by nearly invisible threads of great tensile strength. Invisible threads. He pursed his lips, and blew a puff of breath toward the crystalline windows as if he might set the Dendarii ships circling and dancing.

Nineteen ships of war and over 3000 troops and techs. "Mine," he said experimentally. "All mine." The phrase did not produce a suitable feeling of triumph. He felt more like a target.

In the first place, it was not true. The actual

ownership of those millions of Betan dollars' worth of capital equipment out there was a matter of amazing complexity. It had taken four solid days of negotiations to work out the "details" he had so casually waved his hand over in the docking bay. There were eight independent captain-owners, in addition to Oser's personal possession of eight ships. Almost all had creditors. At least ten percent of "his" fleet turned out to be owned by the First Bank of Jackson's Whole, famous for its numbered accounts and discreet services; for all Miles knew, he was now contributing to the support of gambling rackets, industrial espionage, and the illicit sex trade from one end of the wormhole nexus to the other. It seemed he was not so much the possessor of the Dendarii mercenaries as he was their chief employee.

The ownership of the *Ariel* and the *Triumph* was made particularly complex by Miles's capture of them in battle. Tung had owned his ship outright, but Auson had been deeply in debt to yet another Jackson's Whole lending institution for the *Ariel*. Oser, when still working for the Pelians, had stopped payments after its capture, and left the, what was it called?—Luigi Bharaputra and Sons Household Finance and Holding Company of Jackson's Whole Private Limited—to collect on its insurance, if any. Captain Auson had turned pale upon learning that an inquiry agent from said company would be arriving soon to investigate.

The inventory alone was enough to boggle Miles's mind, and when it came to the assorted personnel contracts—his stomach would hurt if it still could. Before Oser had arrived, the Dendarii had been due for a tidy profit from the Felician contract. Now the profit for 200 must be spread to support 3000.

Or more than 3000. The Dendarii kept ballooning. Another free ship had arrived through the wormhole just yesterday, having heard of them through God-knew-what rumor mill, and excited would-be recruits from Felice managed to turn up with each new ship from the planet. The metals refinery was operating as a refinery again, as control of local space fell into the hands of the Felicians; their forces were even now gobbling up Pelian installations all over the system.

There was talk of re-hiring to Felice, to blockade the wormhole in turn for the former underdogs. The phrase, "Quit while you're winning," popped unbidden into Miles's mind whenever this subject came up; the proposal secretly appalled him. He itched to be gone from here before the whole house of cards collapsed. He should be keeping reality and fantasy separate in his own mind, at least, even while mixing them as much as possible in others'.

Voices whispered from the catwalk, reflected to his ear by some accident of acoustics. Elena's alto captured his attention.

"You don't have to ask him. We're not on Barrayar, we're never going back to Barrayar—"

"But it will be like having a little piece of Barrayar to take with us," Baz's voice, gentle and amused as Miles had never heard it, followed. "A breath of home in airless places. God knows I can't give you much of that 'right and proper' your father wanted for you, but all the pittance I can command shall be yours."

"Mm." Her response was unenthusiastic, almost hostile. All references to Bothari seemed to fall on her like hammer blows to dead flesh these days, a muffled thud that sickened Miles but brought no response from Elena herself.

They emerged from the catwalk, Baz close behind her. He smiled at his liege-lord in shy triumph. Elena smiled too, but not with her eyes.

"Deep meditation?" she inquired lightly. "It looks

more like staring out the window and biting your nails to me."

He struggled upright, causing the settee to slither under him, and responded in kind. "Oh, I just told the guard that to keep the tourists out. I actually came up here for a nap."

Baz grinned at Miles. "My lord. I understand, in the absence of other relations, that Elena's legal guardianship has fallen to you."

"Why—so it has. I haven't had much time to think about it, to tell you the truth." Miles stirred uneasily at this turn in the conversation, not quite sure just what was coming.

"Right. Then as her liege-lord and guardian, I formally request her hand in marriage. Not to mention the rest of her." His silly smile made Miles long to kick him in the teeth. "Oh, and as my liege-commander, I request your permission to marry, uh, 'that my sons may serve you, lord.'" Baz's abbreviated version of the formula was only slightly scrambled.

You're not going to have any sons, because I'm going to chop your balls off, you lamb-stealing, double-crossing, traitorous—he got control of himself before his emotion showed as more than a drawn, lipless grin. "I see. There—there are some difficulties." He marshalled logical argument like a shield-wall, protecting his craven, naked rage from the sting of those two honest pairs of brown eyes.

"Elena is quite young, of course—" He abandoned that line at the ire that lit her eye, as her lips formed the soundless word, You—!

"More to the point, I gave my own word to Sergeant Bothari to perform three services for him in the event of his death. To bury him on Barrayar, to see Elena betrothed with all correct ceremony, and, ah—to see her married to a suitable officer of the

Barrayaran Imperial Service. Would you see me forsworn?"

Baz looked as stunned as if Miles had kicked him. His mouth opened, closed, opened again. "But—aren't I your liege-sworn Armsman? That's certainly the equal of an Imperial officer—hell, the Sergeant was an Armsman himself! Has—has my service been unsatisfactory? Tell me how I have failed you, my lord, that I may correct it!" His astonishment turned to genuine distress.

"You haven't failed me." Miles's conscience jerked the words from his mouth. "Uh . . . But of course, you've only served me for four months, now. Really a very short time, although I know it seems much longer, so much has happened . . ." Miles floundered, feeling more than crippled; legless. Elena's furious glower had chopped him off at the knees. How much shorter could he afford to get in her eyes? He trailed off weakly. "This is all very sudden. . . ."

Elena's voice dropped to a gravelled register of rage. "How dare you—" her voice burst in her indrawn breath like a wave, formed again, "What do you owe—what can anybody owe *that?*" she asked, referring, Miles realized, to the Sergeant. "I was not his chattel and I am not yours, either. Dog in the manger—"

Baz's hand closed anxiously on her arm, stemming the breakers crashing across Miles. "Elena—maybe this isn't the best time to bring it up. Maybe later would be better." He glanced at Miles's stony face, and winced, confusion in his eyes.

"Baz, you're not going to take this seriously—"

"Come away. We'll talk about it."

She forced her voice back to its normal timbre. "I'll meet you at the bottom of the catwalk. In a minute."

Miles nodded a dismissal to Baz for emphasis.

"Well . . ." The engineer left, walking slowly, and looking back over his shoulder in worry.

They waited, by unspoken agreement, until the soft sound of his steps had gone. When she turned, the anger in her eyes had been displaced by pleading.

"Don't you see, Miles? This is my chance to walk away from it all. Start new, fresh and clean, somewhere else. As far away as possible."

He shook his head. He'd have fallen to his knees if he'd thought it would do any good. "How can I give you up? You're the mountains and the lake, the memories—you have them all. When you're with me, I'm at home, wherever I am."

"If Barrayar were my right arm, I'd take a plasma arc and burn it off. Your father and mother knew what he was all the time, and yet they sheltered him. What are they, then?"

"The Sergeant was doing all right—doing well, even, until . . . You were to be his expiation, don't you see it—"

"What, a sacrifice for his sins? Am I to form myself into the pattern of a perfect Barrayaran maiden like trying to work a magic spell for absolution? I could spend my whole life working out that ritual and not come to the end of it, damn it!"

"Not the sacrifice," he tried to tell her. "The altar, perhaps."

"Bah!" She began to pace, leopardess on a short chain. Her emotional wounds seemed to work themselves open and bleed before his eyes. He ached to stanch them.

"Don't you see," he launched himself again, passionate with conviction, "you'd do better with me. Acting or reacting, we carry him in us. You can't walk away from him any more than I can. Whether you travel toward or away, he'll be the compass. He'll be the glass, full of subtle colors and astigmatisms, through which all new things will be viewed. I too have a father who haunts me, and I know."

She was shaken, and shaking. "You make me," she stated, "feel quite ill."

As she stalked away, Ivan Vorpatril emerged from the catwalk. "Ah, there you are, Miles."

Ivan circled warily around Elena as they passed, his hands moving in an unconscious protective gesture toward his crotch. One corner of Elena's mouth turned venomously upward, and she tilted her head in a polite nod. He acknowledged the greeting with a fixed and nervous smile. So much, thought Miles sadly, for his chivalrous plans to protect Elena from Ivan's unwanted attentions.

Ivan settled himself beside Miles with a sigh. "Have you heard anything from Captain Dimir yet?"

"Not a thing. Are you sure they were coming to Tau Verde, and not suddenly ordered somewhere else? I don't see how a fast courier could be two weeks late."

"Oh, God," said Ivan, "do you think that's possible? I'm going to be in so much trouble—"

"I don't know." Miles tried to assuage his alarm. "Your original orders were to find me, and so far you're the only one who seems to have succeeded in carrying them out. Mention that, when you ask Father to get you off the hook."

"Ha," muttered his cousin. "What's the use of living with a system of inherited power if you can't have a little nepotism now and then? Miles, your father doesn't do favors for *anybody.*" He gazed out at the Dendarii fleet, and added elliptically, "That's impressive, y'know?"

Miles was insensibly cheered. "Do you really think

so?" He added facetiously, "Do you want to join? It seems to be the hot new fashion around here."

Ivan chuckled. "No, thanks. I have no desire to diet for the Emperor. Vorloupulous's law, y'know."

Miles's smile died on his lips. Ivan's chuckle drained away like something going down the sink. They stared at each other in stunned silence.

"Oh, *shit* . . ." said Miles at last. "I forgot about Vorloupulous's law. It never even crossed my mind."

"Surely nobody could interpret this as raising a private army," Ivan reassured him feebly. "Not proper livery and maintenance. I mean, they're not liege-sworn to you or anything—are they?"

"Only Baz and Arde," said Miles. "I don't know how Barrayaran law would interpret a mercenary contract. They're not for life, after all—unless you happen to be killed . . ."

"Who is that Baz fellow, anyway?" asked Ivan. "He seems to be your right-hand man."

"I couldn't have done this without him. He was an Imperial Service engineer, before he—" Miles choked himself off, "quit." Miles tried to guess what the laws might be about harboring deserters. He hadn't, after all, originally intended to be caught doing so. Upon reflection, his nebulous plan for returning home with Baz and begging his father to arrange some sort of pardon began to feel more and more like a man falling from an aircraft making plans to land on that soft fluffy cloud rushing up below him. What looked solid at a distance might well turn to fog at closer range.

Miles glanced at Ivan. Then he gazed at Ivan. Then he stared at Ivan. Ivan blinked back in innocent inquiry. There was something about that cheerful, frank face that made Miles hideously uneasy.

"You know," Miles said at last, "the more I think about your being here, the weirder it seems."

"Don't you believe it," said Ivan. "I had to work for my passage. That old bird was the most insatiable—"

"I don't mean your getting here—I mean your being sent in the first place. Since when do they pull first-year cadets out of class and send them on Security missions?"

"I don't know. I assumed they wanted somebody who could identify the body or something."

"Yes, but they've got almost enough medical data on me to build a new one. That idea only makes sense if you don't think about it too hard."

"Look, when a General Staff admiral calls a cadet in the middle of the night and says go, you go. You don't stop to debate with him. He wouldn't appreciate it."

"Well—what did your recorded orders say?"

"Come to think of it, I never saw my recorded orders. I assumed Admiral Hessman must have given them to Captain Dimir personally."

Miles decided his uneasiness stemmed from the number of times the phrase "I assumed" was turning up in this conversation. There was something else—he almost had it. . . . "Hessman? Hessman gave you your orders?"

"In person," Ivan said proudly.

"Hessman doesn't have anything to do with either Intelligence or Security. He's in charge of Procurement. Ivan, this is getting screwier and screwier."

"An admiral is an admiral."

"This admiral is on my father's shit list, though. For one thing, he's Count Vordrozda's pipeline to Imperial Service Headquarters, and Father hates his officers getting involved in party politics. Father also suspects him of peculating Service funds, some kind of sleight-of-hand in shipbuilding contracts. At the time I left home, he was itchy enough to put Captain Illyan on it personally, and you know he wouldn't waste Illyan's talents on anything minor."

"All that's way over my head. I've got enough problems with navigational math."

"It shouldn't be over your head. Oh, as a cadet, sure—but you're also Lord Vorpatril. If anything happened to me, you'd inherit the Countship of our district from my father."

"God forbid," said Ivan. "I want to be an officer, and travel around, and pick up girls. Not chase around through those mountains trying to collect taxes from homicidal illiterates and keep chicken-stealing cases from turning into minor guerilla wars. No insult intended, but your district is the most intractable on Barrayar. Miles, there are people back behind Dendarii Gorge who live in *caves.*" Ivan shuddered. "And they *like* it."

"There are some great caves back there," Miles agreed. "Gorgeous colors when you get the right light on the rock formations." Homesick remembrance twinged through him.

"Well, if I ever inherit a Countship, I'm praying it will be of a city," Ivan concluded.

"You're not in line for any I can think of," grinned Miles. He tried to recapture the thread of their conversation, but Ivan's remarks made lines of inheritance map themselves in his head. He traced his own descent through his Grandmother Vorkosigan to Prince Xav to Emperor Dorca Vorbarra himself. Had the great Emperor ever foreseen what a turn his law, that finally broke the private armies and the private wars of the Counts forever, would give his great-great-grandson?

"Who's your heir, Ivan?" Miles asked idly, staring out at the Dendarii ships, but dreaming of the Dendarii Mountains. "Lord Vortaine, isn't it?"

"Yeah, but I expect to outlive the old boy any

minute. His health wasn't too good, last I heard. Too bad this inheritance thing doesn't work backwards, I'd be in for a bundle."

"Who does get his bundle?"

"His daughter, I guess. His titles go to—let me think—Count Vordrozda, who doesn't even need 'em. From what I've heard of Vordrozda, he'd rather have the money. Don't know if he'd go as far as marrying the daughter to get it, though, she's about fifty years old."

They both gazed into space.

"God," said Ivan after a while, "I hope those orders Dimir got when I ducked out weren't to go home or something. They'll think I've been AWOL for three weeks—there won't be enough room on my record for all the demerits. Thank God they've eliminated the old-style discipline parades."

"You were there when Dimir got his orders? And you didn't stick around to see what they were?" asked Miles, astonished.

"It was like pulling teeth to get that pass out of him. I didn't want to risk it. There was this girl, you see—I wish now I'd taken my beeper."

"You left your comm link?"

"There was this girl—I really did almost really forget it. But he was opening the stuff by then, and I didn't want to go back in and get nabbed."

Miles shook his head hopelessly. "Can you remember anything unusual about the orders? Anything out of the ordinary?"

"Oh, sure. It was the damnedest packet. In the first place, it was delivered by an Imperial Household courier in full livery. Lessee, four data discs, one green for Intelligence, two red for Security, one blue for Operations. And the parchment, of course."

Ivan had the family memory, at least. What would

it be like to have a mind that retained nearly everything, but never bothered to put it in any kind of order? Exactly like living in Ivan's room, Miles decided. "Parchment?" he said. "*Parchment?*"

"Yeah, I thought that was kind of unusual."

"Do you have any idea how bloody—" He surged up, sat back down, squeezed his temples with the heels of his hands in an effort to get his brain into motion. Not only was Ivan an idiot, but he generated a telepathic damping field that turned people nearby into idiots too. He would point this out to Barrayaran Intelligence, who would make of his cousin the newest weapon in their arsenal—if anyone could be found who could remember what they were doing once they closed on him. . . . "Ivan, there are only three kinds of thing written on parchment any more. Imperial edicts, the originals of the official edicts from the Council of Counts and from the Council of Ministers, and certain orders from the Council of Counts to their own members."

"I know that."

"As my father's heir, I am a cadet member of that Council."

"You have my sympathy," said Ivan, his gaze wandering back to the window. "Which of those ships out there is the fastest, d'you think, the Illyrican cruiser or the—"

"Ivan, I'm psychic," Miles announced suddenly. "I'm so psychic, I can tell what color the ribbon was on that parchment without even seeing it."

"I know what color it was," said Ivan irritably. "It was—"

"Black," Miles cut across him. "Black, you idiot! And you never thought to mention it!"

"Look, I have to take that stuff from my mother and your father, I don't have to take it from you, too—" Ivan paused. "How did you know?"

"I know the color because I know the contents." Miles rose to pace uncontrollably back and forth. "You know them too, or you would if you ever stopped to think. I've got a joke for you. What's white, taken from the back of a sheep, tied up with black bows, shipped thousands of light-years, and lost?"

"If that's your idea of a joke, you're weirder than—"

"Death." Miles's voice fell to a whisper, making Ivan jump. "Treason. Civil war. Betrayal, sabotage, almost certainly murder. Evil . . ."

"You haven't had any more of that sedative you're allergic to, have you?" asked Ivan anxiously.

Miles's pacing was becoming frenetic. The urge to pick Ivan up and shake him, in the hope that all that information floating randomly around inside his head would start to polymerize into some chain of reason, was almost overwhelming.

"If Dimir's courier ship's Necklin rods were sabotaged during the stopover at Beta Colony, it would be weeks before the ship was missed. For all the Barrayaran embassy would know, it left on its mission, made the jump—no way for Beta Colony to know if it came out the other side or not. What a *thorough* way to get rid of the evidence." Miles imagined the dismay and terror of the men aboard as the jump began to go wrong, as their bodies began to run and smear like watercolors in the rain—he forced his mind back to abstract reason.

"I don't understand. Where d'you think Dimir is?" asked Ivan.

"Dead. Quite thoroughly dead. You were meant to be quite thoroughly dead too, but you missed the boat." A high, wheeing laugh escaped Miles. He took hold of himself, literally, wrapping his arms around his torso. "I guess they figured if they were going to all that trouble to get rid of that parchment, they'd throw you in at the same time. There's a certain economy in the plot—you might expect it from a mind that ended up in Procurement."

"Back up," demanded Ivan. "What do you figure the parchment was, anyway—and who the devil are 'they'? You're beginning to sound as paranoid as old Bothari."

"The black ribbon. It had to have been a capital charge. An Imperial order for my arrest on a capital charge laid in the Council of Counts. The charge? You said it yourself. Violation of Vorloupulous's law. Treason, Ivan! Now ask yourself—who would benefit by my conviction for treason?"

"Nobody," said Ivan promptly.

"All right." Miles rolled his eyes upward. "Try it this way. Who would suffer by my conviction for treason?"

"Oh, it would destroy your father, of course. I mean, his office overlooks the Great Square. He could stand at his window and watch you starve to death every working day." An embarrassed laugh escaped Ivan. "It would have to about drive him crazy."

Miles paced. "Take his heir, by execution or exile, break his morale, bring him down and his Centrist coalition with him—or—force him to make the false charges real, attempting my rescue. Then bring him down for treason as well. What a demonic fork!" His intellect admired the plot's abstract perfection, even while rage at its cruelty nearly took his breath away.

Ivan shook his head. "How could anything like that get this far and not be quashed by your father? I mean, he may be famous for impartiality, but there are limits even for him."

"You saw the parchment. If Gregor himself had been worked over into a state of suspicion . . ." Miles spoke slowly. "A trial clears as well as convicts. If I showed up voluntarily, it would go a long way toward proving

I had no treasonable intent. That cuts both ways, of course—if I don't show, it's a strong presumption of guilt. But I could hardly show up if I weren't informed it was taking place, could I?"

"The Council of Counts is such a cantankerous body of old relics," argued Ivan. "Your plotters would be taking an awful chance they could swing the vote their way. Nobody would want to get caught voting for the losing side in something like that. Either way, there'd be blood drawn at the end."

"Maybe they were forced. Maybe my father and Illyan finally moved in on Hessman, and he figured the best defense would be a counterattack."

"So what's in it for Vordrozda? Why doesn't he just throw Hessman to the wolves?"

"Ah," said Miles. "There I'm . . . I really wonder if I haven't gone a little paro, but—follow this chain. Count Vordrozda, Lord Vortaine, you, me, my father—who is my father heir to?"

"Your grandfather. He's dead, remember? Miles, you can't convince me that Count Vordrozda would knock off five people to inherit the Dendarii Province. He's the Count of Lorimel, for God's sakes! He's a rich man. Dendarii would drain his purse, not fill it."

"Not my grandfather. We're talking about another title altogether. Ivan, there is a large faction of historically minded people on Barrayar who claim, defensibly, that the Salic bar to Imperial inheritance has no foundation in Barrayaran law or custom. Dorca himself inherited through his mother, after all."

"Yes, and your father would like to ship every one of that faction off to, er, summer camp."

"Who is Gregor's heir?"

"Right now, nobody, which is why everybody is on his back to marry and start swiving—"

"If Salic descent were allowed, who *would* be his heir?"

Ivan refused to be stampeded. "Your father. Everybody knows that. Everybody also knows he wouldn't touch the Imperium with a stick, so what? This is pretty wild, Miles."

"Can you think of another theory that will account for the facts?"

"Sure," said Ivan, happily continuing the role of devil's advocate. "Easy. Maybe that parchment was addressed to someone else. Dimir took it to him, which is why he hasn't shown up here. Have you ever heard of Occam's Razor, Miles?"

"It sounds simpler, until you start to think about it. Ivan, listen. Think back on the exact circumstances of your midnight departure from the Imperial Academy, and that dawn liftoff. Who signed you out? Who saw you go? Who do you know, for certain, who knows where you are right now? Why didn't my father give you any personal messages for me—or my mother or Captain Illyan either, for that matter?" His voice became insistent. "If Admiral Hessman took you off to some quiet, isolated place right now and offered you a glass of wine with his own hands, would you drink it?"

Ivan was silent for a long, thoughtful time, staring out at the Dendarii Free Mercenary Fleet. When he turned back to Miles, his face was painfully somber. "No."

CHAPTER NINETEEN

He tracked them down finally in the crew's mess of the *Triumph*, now parked in Docking Bay 9. It was an off-hour for meals, and the mess was nearly empty but for a few die-hard caffeine addicts swilling an assortment of brews.

They sat, dark heads close, opposite each other. Baz's hand lay open, palm-up, on the small table as he leaned forward. Elena's shoulders were hunched, her hands shredding a napkin in her lap. Neither looked happy.

Miles took a deep breath, carefully adjusted his own expression to one of benevolent good cheer, and sauntered up to them. He no longer bled inside, the surgeon had assured him. Couldn't prove it now. "Hi."

They both started. Elena, still hunched, shot him a look of resentment. Baz answered with a hesitant, dismayed "My lord?" that made Miles feel very small indeed. He suppressed an urge to turn tail and slither out under the door.

"I've been thinking over what you said," Miles began, leaning against an adjoining table in a pose of nonchalance. "Your arguments made a lot of sense, when I came to really examine them. I've changed my opinion. For what it's worth, you're welcome to my blessing."

Baz's face lit with honest delight. Elena's posture opened like a daylily in sudden noon, and as suddenly closed again. The winged brows drew down in puzzlement. She looked at him directly, he felt, for the first time in weeks. "Really?"

He supplied her with a chipper grin. "Really. And we shall satisfy all the forms of etiquette, as well. All it takes is a little ingenuity."

He pulled a colored scarf from his pocket, secreted there for the occasion, and walked around to Baz's side of the table. "We'll start over, on the right foot this time. Picture, if you will, this banal plastic table bolted to the floor before you as a starlit balcony, with a pierced lattice window crawling with those little flowers with the long sharp thorns that make you itch like fire, behind which is, rightly and properly, concealed your heart's desire. Got that? Now—Armsman Jesek, speaking as your liege-lord, I understand you have a request."

Miles's pantomime gestures cued the engineer. Baz leaned back with a grin, and picked up his lead.

"My lord, I ask your permission and aid to wed the first daughter of Armsman Konstantine Bothari, that my sons may serve you."

Miles cocked his head, and smirked. "Ah, good, we've all been watching the same vid dramas, I see. Yes, certainly, Armsman; may they all serve me as well as you do. I shall send the Baba."

He flipped the scarf into a triangle and tied it around his head. Leaning on an imaginary cane, he hobbled arthritically over to Elena's side of the table, muttering in a cracked falsetto. Once there, he removed the scarf and reverted to the role of Elena's liege-lord and guardian, and grilled the Baba as to the suitability of the suitor she represented. The Baba was sent bobbing back twice to Baz's liege-commander, to personally check and guarantee his a) continued employment prospects and b) personal hygiene and absence of head-lice.

Muttering obscene little old lady imprecations, the Baba returned at last to Elena's side of the table to conclude her transaction. Baz by this time was cackling with laughter at assorted Barrayaran in-jokes, and Elena's smile had at last reached her eyes.

When his clowning was over and the last somewhat scrambled formula was completed, Miles hooked a third chair into its floor bolts and fell into it.

"Whew! No wonder the custom is dying out. That's exhausting."

Elena grinned. "I've always had the impression you were trying to be three people. Perhaps you've found your calling."

"What, one-man shows? I've had enough of them lately to last a lifetime." Miles sighed, and grew serious. "You may consider yourselves well and officially betrothed, at any rate. When do you plan to register your marriage?"

"Soon," said Baz, and "I'm not sure," said Elena.

"May I suggest tonight?"

"Why—why . . ." stammered Baz. His eyes sought his lady's. "Elena? Could we?"

"I . . ." She searched Miles's face. "Why, my lord?"

"Because I want to dance at your wedding and fill your bed with buckwheat groats, if I can find any on this benighted space station. You may have to settle for gravel; they've got plenty of that. I'm leaving tomorrow."

Three words should not be so hard to grasp as all that. . . .

"What?" cried Baz.

"Why?" repeated Elena in a shocked whisper.

"I have some obligations to pursue." Miles shrugged. "There's Tav Calhoun to pay off, and—and the Sergeant's burial." And, very possibly, my own . . .

"You don't have to go in person, do you?" protested Elena. "Can't you send Calhoun a draft, and ship the body? Why go back? What is there for you?"

"The Dendarii Mercenaries," said Baz. "How can they function without you?"

"I expect them to function quite well, because I am appointing you, Baz, as their commander, and you, Elena, as his executive officer—and apprentice. Commodore Tung will be your chief of staff. You understand that, Baz? I'm going to charge you and Tung jointly with her training, and I expect it to be the best."

"I—I—" gasped the engineer. "My lord, the honor—I couldn't—"

"You'll find that you can, because you must. And besides, a lady should have a dowry worthy of her. That's what a dowry is for, after all, to provide for the bride's support. Bad form for the bridegroom to squander it, note. And you'll still be working for me, after all."

Baz looked relieved. "Oh—you'll be coming back, then. I thought—never mind. When will you return, my lord?"

"I'll catch up with you sometime," Miles said vaguely. Sometime, never . . . "That's the other thing. I want you to clear out of Tau Verde local space. Pick any direction away from Barrayar, and go. Find employment when you get there, but go soon. The Dendarii Mercenaries have had enough of this Tweedledum-and-Tweedledee war. It's bad for morale when it gets too hard to remember which side you're working for this week. Your next contract should have clearly defined objectives that will weld this motley bunch into a single force, under your command. No more committee warfare. Its weaknesses have been amply demonstrated, I trust—"

Miles went on with instructions and advice until he began to sound like a pint-sized Polonius in his own ears. There was no way he could anticipate every contingency. When the time came to leap in faith, whether you had your eyes open or closed or screamed all the way down or not made no practical difference.

His heart cringed from his next interview even more than from the last, but he forced his feet to carry him to it anyway. He found the comm link technician at work at the electron microscope bench of the *Triumph*'s engineering repairs section. Elena Visconti frowned at his gesture of invitation, but turned the work over to her assistant and came slowly to Miles's side.

"Sir?"

"Trainee Visconti. Ma'am. Can we take a walk?"

"What for?"

"Just to talk."

"If it's what I think, you may as well save your breath. I can't go to her."

"I'm not any more comfortable talking about it than you are, but it's an obligation I cannot honorably evade."

"I've spent eighteen years trying to put what happened at Escobar behind me. Must I be dragged through it again?"

"This is the last time, I promise. I'm leaving tomorrow. The Dendarii fleet will follow soon after. All you short-contract people will be dropped off at Dalton Station, where you can take ship for Tau Ceti or wherever you want. I suppose you'll be going home?"

She fell in reluctantly beside him, and they paced down the corridor. "Yes, my employers will doubtless be astonished at how much backpay they owe me."

"I owe you something myself. Baz says you were outstanding on the mission."

She shrugged. "Straightforward stuff."

"He didn't mean just your technical efforts. Anyway, I didn't want to leave Elena—my Elena—up in the air like this, you see," he began. "She ought to at least have something, to replace what was taken from her. Some little crumb of comfort."

"The only thing she lost was some illusion. And believe me, Admiral Naismith, or whatever you are, the only thing I could give her would be another illusion. Maybe if she didn't look so much like him . . . Anyway, I don't want her following me around, or showing up at my door."

"Whatever Sergeant Bothari was guilty of, she is surely innocent."

Elena Visconti rubbed her forehead wearily with the back of her hand. "I'm not saying you're not right. I'm just saying I *can't.* For me, she radiates nightmares."

Miles chewed his lip gently. They turned out of the *Triumph* into a flex tube and walked across the quiet docking bay. Only a few techs were busy at some small tasks.

"An illusion . . ." he mused. "You could live a long time on an illusion," he offered. "Maybe even a lifetime, if you're lucky. Would it be so difficult, to do a few days—even a few minutes—of acting? I'm going to have to dip into some Dendarii funds anyway to pay for a dead ship, and buy a lady a new face. I could make it worth your time."

He regretted his words immediately at the loathing

that flashed across her face, but the look she finally gave him was ironically thoughtful.

"You really care about that girl, don't you?"

"Yes."

"I thought she was making time with your chief engineer."

"Suits me."

"Pardon my slowness, but that does not compute."

"Association with me could be lethal, where I'm going next. I'd rather she were travelling in the opposite direction."

The next docking bay was busy and noisy with a Felician freighter being loaded with ingots of refined rare metals, vital to the Felician war industries. They avoided it, and searched out another quiet corridor. Miles found himself fingering the bright scarf in his pocket.

"He dreamed of you for eighteen years too, you know," he said suddenly. It wasn't what he'd meant to say. "He had this fantasy. You were his wife, in all honor. He held it so hard, I think it was real to him, at least part of the time. That's how he made it so real for Elena. You can touch hallucinations. Hallucinations can even touch you."

The Escobaran woman, pale, paused to lean against the wall and swallow. Miles pulled the scarf from his pocket and crumpled it anxiously in his hands; he had an absurd impulse to offer it to her, heaven knew what for—a basin?

"I'm sorry," Elena said at last. "But the very thought that he was pawing over me in his twisted imagination all these years makes me ill."

"He was never an easy person . . ." Miles began inanely, then cut himself off. He paced, frustrated, two steps, turn, two steps. He then took a gulp of air, and flung himself to one knee before the Escobaran woman.

"Ma'am. Konstantine Bothari sends me to beg your forgiveness for the wrongs he did you. Keep your revenge, if you will—it is your just right—but be satisfied," he implored her. "At least give me a death-offering to burn for him, some token. I give him aid in this as his go-between by my right as his liege-lord, his friend, and, as he was a father's hand, held over me in protection all my life, as his son."

Elena Visconti was backed up against the wall as though cornered. Miles, still on one knee, shuffled back a step and shrank into himself, as if to crush all hint of pride and coercion to the deck.

"Damned if I'm not starting to think you're as weird—you're no Betan," she muttered. "Oh, do get up. What if somebody comes down this corridor?"

"Not until you give me a death-offering," he said firmly.

"What do you want from me? What's a death-offering?"

"Something of yourself, that you burn, for the peace of the soul of the dead. Sometimes you burn it for friends or relatives, sometimes for the souls of slain enemies, so they don't come back to haunt you. A lock of hair would do." He ran his hand over a short gap in his own crown. "That wedge represents twenty-two dead Pelians last month."

"Some local superstition, is it?"

He shrugged helplessly. "Superstition, custom—I've always thought of myself as an agnostic. It's only lately that I've come to—to need for men to have souls. Please. I won't bother you any more."

She blew out her breath in troubled exasperation. "Well—well . . . Give me that knife in your belt, then. But get up."

He rose, and handed her his grandfather's dagger. She sawed off a short curl. "Is that enough?"

"Yes, that's fine." He took it in his palm, cool and silken like water, and closed his fingers over it. "Thank you."

She shook her head. "Crazy . . ." Wistfulness stole over her face. "It allays ghosts, does it?"

"It is said," replied Miles gently. "I'll make it a proper offering. My word on it." He inhaled shakily. "And as I have given you my word, I'll bother you no more. Excuse me, ma'am. We both have other duties."

"Sir."

They passed through the flex tube to the *Triumph*, turned each away. But the Escobaran woman looked back over her shoulder.

"You are mistaken, little man," she called softly. "I believe you're going to bother me for a long time yet."

Next he searched out Arde Mayhew.

"I'm afraid I never was able to do you the good I intended," Miles apologized. "I have managed to find a Felician shipmaster who will buy the RG 132 for an inner-system freighter. He's offering about a dime on the dollar, but it's cash up front. I thought we could split it."

"At least it's an honorable retirement," sighed Mayhew. "Better than having Calhoun tear it to pieces."

"I'm leaving for home tomorrow, via Beta Colony. I could drop you off, if you want."

Mayhew shrugged. "There's nothing on Beta for me." He looked up more sharply. "What happened to all this liegeman stuff? I thought I was working for you."

"I—don't really think you'd fit in on Barrayar," said Miles carefully. The pilot officer must not follow him home. Betan or no, the deadly bog of Barrayaran politics could suck him down without a bubble, in the vortex of his liege-lord's fall. "But you could certainly have a place with the Dendarii Mercenaries. What rank would you like?"

"I'm no soldier."

"You could re-train, something on the tech side. And they'll certainly need backup pilots, for sub-light, and the shuttles."

Mayhew's forehead wrinkled. "I don't know. Driving a shuttle and so on was always the scut work, something you did so you could jump. I don't know that I want to be so close to ships. It would be like standing outside the bakery hungry, with no credit card to go in and buy." He looked greyly depressed.

"There's one more possibility."

Mayhew's brows lifted in polite inquiry.

"The Dendarii Mercenaries are going to be outward bound, looking for work on the fringes of the wormhole nexus. The RG ships were never all accounted for—it's possible one or two might still be junked out there somewhere. The Felician shipmaster would be willing to lease the RG 132, although for a lot less money. If you could find and salvage a pair of RG Necklin rods—"

Mayhew's back straightened from a slump that had looked to be permanent.

"I don't have time to go hunting all over the galaxy for spare parts," Miles went on. "But if you'd agree to be my agent, I'll authorize Baz to release Dendarii funds to buy them, if you find any, and a ship to bring them back here. A quest, as it were. Just like Vorthalia the Bold and the search for Emperor Xian Vorbarra's lost scepter." Of course, in the legend Vorthalia never actually *found* the scepter. . . .

"Yeah?" Mayhew's face was brightening with hope. "It's a long shot—but I guess it is just barely possible . . ."

"That's the spirit! Forward momentum."

Mayhew snorted. "Your forward momentum is going to lead all your followers over a cliff someday." He paused, beginning to grin. "On the way down, you'll convince 'em all they can fly." He stuck his fists in his armpits, and waggled his elbows. "Lead on, my lord. I'm flapping as hard as I can."

The docking bay, its every second light bar extinguished, provided an illusion of night in the unmarked changeless time of space. Those lights that remained on threw a dull illumination like shimmering puddles of mercury, that gave vision without color. The sounds of the loading, small thumps and clanks, carried in the silence, and voices muted themselves.

The Felician fast courier pilot grimaced as Bothari's coffin was carried past him and vanished into the flex tube. "When we've stripped baggage down to practically a change of underwear each, it seems deuced gaudy to bring that."

"Every parade needs a float," remarked Miles absently, indifferent to the pilot's opinion. The pilot, like his ship, was merely a courtesy loan from General Halify. The general had been reluctant to authorize the expenditure, but Miles had hinted that if his emergency run to Beta Colony failed to bring him to a certain mysterious appointment on time, the Dendarii Mercenaries just might be forced to look for their next contract from the highest bidder here in Tau Verde local space. Halify had reflected only briefly before making all haste to speed him on his way.

Miles shifted from foot to foot, anxious to be gone before the bright activities marking day-cycle began. Ivan Vorpatril appeared, carefully clutching a valise whose mass was most certainly not wasted on clothes. Stripes on the docking bay deck, placed to aid organization in loading and unloading complex cargoes, made pale parallels. Ivan blinked, and walked down one line toward them with dignified precision only slightly spoiled by a list that precessed like an equinox. He hove to by Miles.

"What a wedding party," he sighed happily. "For an impromptu out in the middle of nowhere, your Dendarii came up with quite a spread. Captain Auson is a splendid fellow."

Miles smiled bleakly. "I thought you two would get along well."

"You kind of disappeared about halfway through. We had to start the drinking without you."

"I wanted to join you," said Miles truthfully, "but I had a lot of last-minute things to work out with Commodore Tung."

"Too bad." Ivan smothered a belch, gazed across the docking bay, and muttered, "Now, I can see your wanting to bring a woman along, two weeks in a box and all that, but did you have to pick one that gives me nightmares?"

Miles followed his gaze. Elli Quinn, escorted by Tung's surgeon, was making her slow blind way toward them. Her crisp grey-and-whites outlined the body of an athletic young woman, but above the collar she was a bad dream of an alien race. The hairless uniformity of the bland pink bulb of a head was broken by the black hole of a mouth, two dark slits above it for a nose, and a dot on either side marking the entrances to the ear canals. Only the right one still vented sound into her darkness. Ivan stirred uneasily, and looked away.

Tung's surgeon took Miles aside for last-minute instructions for her care during the journey, and some acerbic advice on Miles's treatment of his own still-healing stomach. Miles patted his hip flask, now filled with medication, and faithfully swore to drink 30 cc's every two hours. He placed the injured mercenary's hand on his arm, and stood on tiptoe to her ear. "We're all set, then. Next stop Beta Colony."

Her other hand patted the air, then found his face for a brief touch. Her damaged tongue tried to form words in her stiff mouth; on the second try Miles correctly interpreted them as "Thank you, Admiral Naismith." Had he been any tireder, he might have wept.

"All right," Miles began, "let's get out of here before the bon voyage committee wakes up and delays us another two hours—" But he was too late. Out of the corner of his eye he saw a willowy form sprinting across the docking bay. Baz followed at a saner pace.

Elena arrived out of breath. "Miles!" she accused. "You were going to leave without saying goodbye!"

He sighed, and twitched a smile at her. "Foiled again." Her cheeks were flushed, and her eyes sparkled from the exertion. Altogether desirable . . . he had hardened his heart for this parting. Why did it hurt worse?

Baz arrived. Miles bowed to each. "Commander Jesek. Commodore Jesek. You know, Baz, perhaps I should have appointed you an admiral. Those names could get confusing over a bad comm link—"

Baz shook his head, smiling. "You have piled enough honors on me, my lord. Honors, and honor, and much more—" His eyes sought Elena. "I once thought it would take a miracle to make a nobody into a somebody once again." His smile broadened. "I was right. And I thank you."

"And I thank you," said Elena quietly, "for a gift I never expected to possess."

Miles obediently cocked his head in an angle of inquiry. Did she mean Baz? Her rank? Escape from Barrayar?

"Myself," she explained.

It seemed to him there was a fallacy in her reasoning somewhere, but there was no time to unravel it. Dendarii were invading the docking bay through several entrances, in twos and threes and then in a steady stream. The lights came up to full day-cycle power. His plans for slipping away quietly were disintegrating rapidly.

"Well," he said desperately, "goodbye, then." He shook Baz's hand hastily. Elena, her eyes swimming, grabbed him in a hug just short of bone-crushing. His toes sought the floor indignantly. Altogether too late . . .

By the time she put him down, the crowd was gathering, hands reaching to shake his hand, to touch him, or just reaching, as if to warm themselves. Bothari would have had a spasm; Miles rendered the Sergeant's spirit an apologetic salute, in his mind.

The docking bay was now a seething sea of people. It rang to babble, and cheers, and cheerful hoots, and foot stamping. These soon picked up rhythm; a chant. "Naismith! Naismith! Naismith . . ."

Miles raised his hands in helpless acquiescence, cursing under his breath. There was always some idiot in a crowd to start these things. Elena and Baz between them hoisted him to their shoulders, and he was cornered. Now he would have to come up with a bloody farewell speech. He lowered his hands; rather to his surprise, they quieted. He flung his hands back up; they roared. He lowered them slowly, like an orchestra director. The silence became absolute. It was terrifying.

"As you can see, I am high because you all have raised me up," he began, pitching his voice to carry to the last and least. A gratified chuckle ran through them. "You have raised me up on your courage, tenacity, obedience, and other soldierly virtues," that was it, stroke them, they were eating it up—although surely he owed as much to their confusion, bad-tempered rivalry, greed, ambition, indolence, and gullibility—pass on, pass on—"I can do no less than to raise you up in return. I hereby revoke your provisional status, and declare you a permanent arm of the Dendarii Mercenaries."

The cheering, whistling, and foot stomping shook the docking bay. Many were Oser's latecomers, curious, along for the ride, but practically all of Auson's original crew were there. He picked out Auson himself, beaming, and Thorne, tears streaming down cheeks.

He raised his arms for silence again, and got it. "I am recalled on urgent affairs for an indefinite period. I request and require that you obey Commodore Jesek as you would me." He glanced down to meet Baz's upturned gaze. "He will not desert you."

He could feel the engineer's shoulder tremble beneath him. Absurd of Baz to look so exalted—Jesek, of them all, knew Miles was a fake. . . . "I thank you all, and bid you farewell."

His feet hit the deck with a thump as he slid down. "And may God have mercy upon me, amen," he muttered under his breath. He backed toward the flex tube, and escape, smiling and waving.

Jesek, blocking the press, spoke to his ear. "My lord. For my curiosity—before you go, may I be permitted to know what house I serve?"

"What, you haven't figured that out yet?" Miles looked to Elena in astonishment.

Bothari's daughter shrugged. "Security."

"Well—I'm not going to shout it out in this crowd, but if you ever go shopping for livery, which doesn't seem too bloody likely—choose brown and silver."

"But—" Baz ground to a halt, there in the crowd, a little knot of personal silence. "But that's—" He paled.

Miles smiled, wickedly gratified. "Break him in gently, Elena."

The silence in the flex tube sucked at him, refuge; the noise in front of him beat on his senses, for the Dendarii had taken up their chant again, Naismith, Naismith, Naismith. The Felician pilot escorted Elli Quinn aboard, Ivan following. The last person Miles saw as he waved and backed into the tube was Elena. Making her way toward her through the crowd, her face drawn and grave and thoughtful, was Elena Visconti.

The Felician pilot bolted the hatch and blew the tube seals, and went ahead of them to Nav and Com.

"Whew," remarked Ivan respectfully. "You sure got them going. You have to be higher than I am now just on psychic waves or something."

"Not really." Miles grimaced.

"Why not? I sure would be." There was an undercurrent of envy in Ivan's voice.

"My name isn't Naismith."

Ivan opened his mouth, closed it, studied him sideways. The screens were up in Nav and Com, showing the refinery and space around them. The ship pulled away from the docking bay. Miles tried to keep that particular slot in the row of docking bays in sight, but soon became confused; fourth or fifth from the left?

"Damn." Ivan thrust his thumbs through his belt, and rocked on his heels. "It still knocks me flat. I mean, here you come into this place with nothing, and in four months you turn their war completely around and end up with all the marbles on top of it."

"I don't want all the marbles," said Miles impatiently. "I don't want any of the marbles. It's death for me to be caught with marbles in my possession, remember?"

"I don't understand you," Ivan complained. "I thought you always wanted to be a soldier. Here you've fought real battles, commanded a whole fleet of ships, wiped the tactical map with fantastically few losses—"

"Is that what you think? That I've been playing soldier? Peh!" Miles began to pace restlessly. He paused, and lowered his head in shame. "Maybe I did. Maybe that was the trouble. Wasting day after day, feeding my ego, while all the time back home Vordrozda's pack of dogs were running my father to ground—staring out the damn *window* for five days while they're *killing* him—"

"Ah," said Ivan. "So that's what's got the hair up you. Never fear," he comforted, "we'll get back all right." He blinked, and added in a much less definite tone, "Miles—assuming you're right about all this—what is it we're going to *do*, once we get back?"

Miles's lips drew back in a mirthless grin. "I'll figure something out."

He turned to watch the screens, thinking silently, But you are mistaken about the losses, Ivan. They were enormous.

The refinery and the ships around it dwindled to a scattered constellation of specks, sparks, water in the eyes, and gone.

CHAPTER TWENTY

The Betan night was hot, even under the force dome that shielded the suburb of Silica. Miles touched the silver circles on his midforehead and temples, praying that his sweat was not loosening their glue. He had passed through Betan customs on the Felician pilot's doctored IDs; it would not do for his supposed implant contact to go sliding down his nose.

Artistically bonsai'd mesquite and acacia trees, picked out with colored spotlights, surrounded the low dome that was the pedestrian entrance to his grandmother's apartment complex. The old building pre-dated the community force shield, and was therefore entirely underground. Miles hooked Elli Quinn's hand over his arm, and patted it.

"We're almost there. Two steps down, here. You'll like my grandmother. She supervises life support equipment maintenance at the Silica University Hospital—she'll know just who to see for the best work. Now here's a door . . ."

Ivan, still clutching the valise, stepped through first. The cooler interior air caressed Miles's face, and relieved him at least of his worries about his fake implant contacts. It had been nerve-racking, crossing Customs with a false ID, but using his real ones would have guaranteed instant entanglement in Betan legal proceedings, entailing God-knew-what delays. Time drummed in his head.

"There's a lift tube there," Miles began to Elli, then choked on an oath, recoiling. Popping out of the Up tube in the foyer was the very man he least wanted to see on his touch-and-go planetary stopover.

Tav Calhoun's eyes started from his head at the sight of Miles. His face turned the color of brick. "You!" he cried. "You—you—you—" He swelled, stuttering, and advanced on Miles.

Miles tried a friendly smile. "Why, good evening, Mr. Calhoun. You're just the man I wanted to see—"

Calhoun's hands clenched on Miles's jacket. "Where is my ship?"

Miles, borne backward to the wall, felt suddenly lonely for Sergeant Bothari. "Well, there was a little problem with the ship," he began placatingly.

Calhoun shook him. "Where is it? What have you goons done with it?"

"It's stuck at Tau Verde, I'm afraid. Damage to the Necklin rods. But I've got your money." He essayed a cheerful nod.

Calhoun's hold did not slacken. "I wouldn't touch your money with a hand-tractor!" he growled. "I've been given the royal run-around, lied to, followed, had my comconsole tapped, had Barrayaran agents questioning my employees, my girlfriend, her wife—I found out about that damned worthless hot land, by the way, you little mutant—I want blood. You're going to *therapy*, because I'm calling Security right now!"

A plaintive mumble came from Elli Quinn, which Miles's practiced ear translated as, "What's happening?"

Calhoun noticed her in the shadows for the first time, jumped, shrugged, then turned on his heel and shot over his shoulder to Miles, "Don't you move! This is a citizen's arrest!" He headed for the public comconsole.

"Grab him, Ivan!" Miles cried.

Calhoun twisted away from Ivan's clutch. His reflexes were quicker than Miles had expected for so beefy a body. Elli Quinn, head cocked to one side, slid into his path in two smooth sideways steps, her ankles and knees flexing. Her hands found his shirt. They whirled for a dizzy instant like a pair of dancers, and suddenly Calhoun was doing spectacular cartwheels. He landed flat on his back on the pavement of the foyer. The air went out of him in a booming whoosh. Elli, sitting, spun around, clamped one leg across his neck, and put his arm in a lock.

Ivan, now that his target was no longer moving, took over and achieved a creditable come-along hold. "How did you do that?" he asked Elli, astonishment and admiration in his voice.

She shrugged. "Used to practice with eyes covered," she mumbled, "to sharpen balance. It works."

"What do we do with him, Miles?" asked Ivan. "Can he really have you arrested, even if you offer to pay him?"

"Assault!" croaked Calhoun. "Battery!"

Miles straightened his jacket. "I'm afraid so. There was some fine print in that contract—look, there's a janitor's closet on the second level. We better take him down there, before somebody comes through here."

"Kidnapping," gurgled Calhoun, as Ivan dragged him to the lift tube.

They found a coil of wire in the roomy janitor's

closet. "Murder!" shrieked Calhoun as they approached him with it. Miles gagged him; his eyes rolled whitely. By the time they finished all the extra loops and knots just in case, the salvage operator began to resemble a bright orange mummy.

"The valise, Ivan," Miles ordered.

His cousin opened it, and they began stuffing Calhoun's shirt and sarong rope with bundles of Betan dollars.

". . . thirty-eight, thirty-nine, forty thousand," Miles counted.

Ivan scratched his head. "Y'know, there's something backwards about this. . . ."

Calhoun was rolling his eyes and moaning urgently. Miles ungagged him for a moment.

"—plus ten percent!" Calhoun panted.

Miles gagged him again, and counted out another four thousand dollars. The valise was much lighter now. They locked the closet behind them.

"Miles!" His grandmother fell on him ecstatically. "Thank God, Captain Dimir found you, then. The Embassy people have been terribly worried. Cordelia says your father didn't think he could get the date for the challenge in the Council of Counts put off a third time—" She broke off as she saw Elli Quinn. "Oh, my."

Miles introduced Ivan, and named Elli hastily as a friend from off-planet with no connections and no place to stay. He quickly outlined his hopes for leaving the injured mercenary in his grandmother's hands. Mrs. Naismith assimilated this at once, merely remarking, "Oh, yes, another of your strays." Miles silently called down blessings upon her.

His grandmother herded them to her living room. Miles sat on the couch with a twinge, remembering Bothari. He wondered if the Sergeant's death would become like a veteran's scar, echoing the old pain with every change of weather.

As if reflecting his thought, Mrs. Naismith said, "Where's the Sergeant, and Elena? Making reports at the Embassy? I'm surprised they let you out even to visit me. Lieutenant Croye gave me the impression they were going to hustle you aboard a fast courier for Barrayar the instant they laid hands on you."

"We haven't been to the Embassy yet," confessed Miles uneasily. "We came straight here."

"Told you we should have reported in first," said Ivan. Miles made a negative gesture.

His grandmother glanced at him with a new penetrating concentration. "What's wrong, Miles? Where is Elena?"

"She's safe," replied Miles, "but not here. The Sergeant was killed two, almost three months ago now. An accident."

"Oh," said Mrs. Naismith. She sat silent a moment, sobered. "I confess I never did understand what your mother saw in the man, but I know he will be sadly missed. Do you want to call Lieutenant Croye from here?" She tilted her head at Miles, and added, "Is that where you've been for the last five months? Training to be a jump pilot? I shouldn't have thought you'd have to do it in secret, surely Cordelia would have supported you—"

Miles touched a silver circle in embarrassment. "This is a fake. I borrowed a jump pilot's ID to get through Customs."

"Miles . . ." Impatience thinned her lips, and worry creased twin verticals between her eyebrows. "What's going on? Is this more to do with those ghastly Barrayaran politics?"

"I'm afraid so. Quickly—what have you heard from home since Dimir left here?"

"According to your mother, you're scheduled to be challenged in the Council of Counts on some sort of trumped-up treason charge, and very soon."

Miles gave Ivan a short I-told-you-so nod; Ivan began nibbling on a thumbnail.

"There's evidently been a lot of behind-the-scenes maneuvering—I didn't understand half of her message discs. I'm convinced only a Barrayaran could figure out how their government works. By all right reason it should have collapsed years ago. Anyway, most of it seemed to revolve around changing the substance of the charge from treason by violation of something called Vorloupulous's law to treason by intent to usurp the Imperial throne."

"What!" Miles shot to his feet. The heat of terror flushed through him. "This is pure insanity! I don't want Gregor's job! Do they think I'm out of my mind? In the first place, I'd need to command the loyalty of the whole Imperial Service, not just some grubby free mercenary fleet—"

"You mean there really *was* a mercenary fleet?" His grandmother's eyes widened. "I thought it was just a wild rumor. What Cordelia said about the charges makes more sense, then."

"What did Mother say?"

"That your father went to a great deal of trouble to goad this Count Vor-what's-his-name—I can never keep all those Vor-people straight—"

"Vordrozda?"

"Yes, that was it."

Miles and Ivan exchanged wild looks.

"To goad Vordrozda to up the charge from the minor to the major, while appearing publicly to want just the opposite. I didn't understand what difference it made, since the penalty's the same."

"Did Father succeed?"

"Apparently. At least as of two weeks ago, when the fast courier that arrived yesterday left Barrayar."

"Ah." Miles began to pace. "Ah. Clever, clever—maybe . . ."

"I don't understand it either," complained Ivan. "Usurpation is a much worse charge!"

"But it happens to be one I'm innocent of. And furthermore, it's a charge of intent. About all I'd have to do is show up to disprove it. Violating Vorloupulous's law is a charge of fact—and in fact, although not in intent, I'm guilty of it. Given that I showed up for my trial, and spoke the truth as I'm sworn to, it'd be a lot harder to wriggle out of."

Ivan finished his second thumbnail. "What makes you think your innocence or guilt is going to have anything to do with the outcome?"

"I beg your pardon?" said Mrs. Naismith.

"That's why I said, maybe," explained Miles. "This thing is so damned political—how many votes d'you suppose Vordrozda will have sewn up in advance, before any evidence or testimony is even presented? He's got to have some, or he'd never have dared to float this in the first place."

"You're asking me?" said Ivan plaintively.

"You . . ." Miles's eye fell on his cousin. "You . . . I am absolutely convinced you are the key to this thing, if only I can figure out how to fit you into the lock."

Ivan looked as if he were trying, and failing, to picture himself as a key to anything. "Why?"

"For one thing, until we report in somewhere, Hessman and Vordrozda will think you're dead."

"What?" said Mrs. Naismith.

Miles explained about the disappearance of Captain Dimir's mission. He touched his forehead, and added to Ivan, "And that's the real reason for this, besides Calhoun, of course."

"Speaking of Calhoun," said his grandmother, "he's been coming around here regularly, looking for you. You'd best be on the lookout for him, if you really mean to stay covert."

"Uh," said Miles, "thanks. Anyway, Ivan, if Dimir's ship was sabotaged, it would have to have taken somebody on the inside to do it. What's to keep whoever doesn't want me to show up for my trial from trying again, if we so-conveniently place ourselves in his hands by popping up at the Embassy?"

"Miles, your mind is crookeder than your bac—I mean—anyway, are you sure you're not catching Bothari's disease?" said Ivan. "You're making me feel like I've got a bull's-eye painted on my back."

Miles grinned, feeling bizarrely exhilarated. "Wakes you up, doesn't it?" It seemed to him he could hear the gates of reason clicking over in his own brain, cascading faster and faster. His voice took on a faraway tone. "You know, if you're trying to take a roomful of people by surprise, it's a lot easier to hit your targets if you don't yell going through the door."

They kept the rest of the visit almost as brief as Miles had hoped. They emptied out the valise onto the living room floor, and Miles counted out piles of Betan dollars to clear his various Betan debts, including his grandmother's original "investment." Rather bemusedly, she agreed to be his agent for the task of distribution.

The largest pile was for Elli Quinn's new face. Miles gulped when his grandmother quoted him the approximate price for the best work. When he was finished, he had one meager wad of bills left in his hand.

Ivan snickered. "By God, Miles, you've made a profit. I think you're the first Vorkosigan to do so in five generations. Must be that bad Betan blood."

Miles weighed the dollars, wryly. "It's getting to be

a kind of family tradition, isn't it? My father gave away 275,000 marks the day before he left the Regency, just so he would have the exact financial balance as the day he took it up sixteen years earlier."

Ivan raised his eyebrows. "I never knew that."

"Why do you think Vorkosigan House didn't get a new roof last year? I think that was the only thing Mother regretted, the roof. Otherwise, it was kind of fun, figuring out where to bury the stuff. The Imperial Service orphanage picked up a packet."

For curiosity, Miles stole a moment and punched up the financial exchange on the comconsole. Felician millifenigs were listed once again. The exchange rate was 1,206 millifenigs to the Betan dollar, but at least they were listed. Last week's rate had been 1,459 to the dollar.

Miles's growing sense of urgency propelled them toward the door.

"If we can have a one-day head start in the Felician fast courier," he told his grandmother, "that should be enough. Then you can call the Embassy and put them out of their misery."

"Yes." She smiled. "Poor Lieutenant Croye was convinced he was going to spend the rest of his career as a private doing guard duty someplace nasty."

Miles paused at the door. "Ah—about Tav Calhoun—"

"Yes?"

"You know that janitor's closet on the second level?"

"Vaguely." She looked at him in unease.

"Please be sure somebody checks it tomorrow morning. But don't go up there before then."

"I wouldn't dream of it," she assured him faintly.

"Come on, Miles," Ivan urged over his shoulder.

"Just a second."

Miles darted back inside to Elli Quinn, still seated

obediently in the living room. He pressed the wad of leftover bills into her palm, and closed her fingers over it.

"Combat bonus," he whispered to her. "For upstairs just now. You earned it."

He kissed her hand and ran after Ivan.

CHAPTER TWENTY-ONE

Miles banked the lightflyer in a gentle, demure turn around Vorhartung Castle, resisting a nervous urge to slam it directly down into the courtyard. The ice had broken on the river winding through the capital city of Vorbarr Sultana, running a chill green now from the snows melting in the Dendarii Mountains far to the south. The ancient building straddled high bluffs; the lightflyer rocked in the updraft puffing from the river.

The modern city spread out for kilometers around was bright and noisy with morning traffic. The parking areas near the castle were jammed with vehicles of all descriptions, and knots of men in half-a-hundred different liveries. Ivan, beside Miles, counted the banners snapping in the cold spring breeze on the battlements.

"It's a full Council session," said Ivan. "I don't think there's a banner missing—there's even Count Vortala's, and I don't think he's been to one in years. Must have been carried in. Ye gods, Miles! There's the Emperor's banner—Gregor must be inside."

"You could figure that from all the fellows on the roof in Imperial livery with the anti-aircraft plasma guns," observed Miles. He flinched inwardly. One such weapon was swivelling to follow their track even now, like a suspicious eye.

Slowly and carefully, he set the lightflyer down in a painted circle outside the castle walls.

"Y'know," said Ivan thoughtfully. "We're going to look a pair of damn fools busting in there if it turns out they're all having a debate on water rights or something."

"That thought has crossed my mind," Miles admitted. "It was a calculated risk, landing in secret. Well, we've both been fools before. There won't be anything new or startling in it."

He checked the time, and paused a moment in the pilot's seat, bent his head down, and breathed carefully.

"You feeling sick?" asked Ivan, alarmed. "You don't look so good."

Miles shook his head, a lie, and begged forgiveness in his heart for all the harsh things he'd once thought about Baz Jesek. So this was the real thing, paralyzing funk. He wasn't braver than Baz after all—he'd just never been as scared. He wished himself back with the Dendarii, doing something simple, like defusing dandelion bombs. "Pray to God this works," he muttered.

Ivan looked even more alarmed. "You've been pushing this surprise-scheme on me for the last two weeks—all right, so you've convinced me. It's *too late* to change your mind!"

"I haven't changed my mind." Miles rubbed the silver circles loose from his forehead, and stared up at the great grey wall of the castle.

"The guards are going to notice us, if we just keep sitting here," Ivan added after a time. "Not to mention the hell that's probably breaking loose back at the shuttleport right now."

"Right," said Miles. He dangled now at the end of a long, long chain of reason, swinging in the winds of doubt. Time to drop to solid ground.

"After you," said Ivan politely.

"Right."

"Any time now," added Ivan.

The vertigo of free fall . . . he popped the doors and clambered to the pavement.

They strode up to a quartet of armed guards in Imperial livery at the castle gate. One's fingers twitched into a devil's horns, down by his side; he had a countryman's face. Miles sighed inwardly. Welcome home. He settled on an incisive nod, by way of greeting.

"Good morning, Armsmen. I am Lord Vorkosigan. I understand the Emperor has commanded me to appear here."

"Damn joker," began a guard, loosening his truncheon. A second guard grasped his arm, staring shocked at Miles.

"No, Dub—it really is!"

They underwent a second search in the vestibule of the great chamber itself. Ivan kept trying to peek around the door, to the annoyance of the guard charged with being the final check against weapons carried into the presence of the Emperor. Voices wafted from the council chamber to Miles's straining ear. He identified Count Vordrozda's, pitched to a carrying nasality, rhythmic in the cadences of formal debate.

"How long has this been going on?" Miles whispered to a guard.

"A week. This was to be the last day. They're doing

the summing up now. You're just in time, my lord." He gave Miles an encouraging nod; the two guard captains finished a sotto voce argument, "—but he's *supposed* to be here!"

"You sure you wouldn't rather be in Betan therapy?" muttered Ivan.

Miles grinned blackly. "Too late now. Won't it be funny if we've arrived just in time for the sentencing?"

"Hysterical. You'll die laughing, no doubt," growled Ivan.

Ivan, approved by the guard, started for the door. Miles grabbed him. "Sh, wait! Listen."

Another identifiable voice; Admiral Hessman.

"What's he doing here?" whispered Ivan. "*I* thought this thing was closed and sealed to the Counts alone."

"Witness, I'll bet, just like you. Sh!"

". . . If our illustrious Prime Minister knew nothing of this plot, then let him produce this 'missing' nephew," Vordrozda's voice was heavy with sarcasm. "He says he cannot. And why not? I submit it is because Lord Vorpatril was dispatched with a secret message. What message? Obviously, some variation of 'Fly for your life—all is revealed!' I ask you—is it reasonable that a plot of this magnitude could have been advanced so far by a son with no knowledge by his father? Where did those missing 275,000 marks, whose fate he so adamantly refuses to disclose, go but to secretly finance the operation? These repeated requests for delays are simply smokescreen. If Lord Vorkosigan is so innocent, why is he not here?" Vordrozda paused dramatically.

Ivan tugged Miles's sleeve. "Come on. You'll never get a better straight line than that if you wait all day."

"You're right. Let's go."

Stained-glass windows high in the east wall splashed the heavy oak flooring of the chamber with colored light. Vordrozda stood in the speaker's circle. Upon the witness bench, behind it, sat Admiral Hessman. The gallery above, with its ornately carved railings, was indeed empty, but the rows of plain wooden benches and desks that ringed the room below were jammed with men.

Formal liveries in a wild assortment of hues peeked out beneath their scarlet and silver robes of office, but for a sprinkling of robe-less men who wore the red and blue parade uniform of active Imperial service. Emperor Gregor, on his raised dais to the left of the room, also wore Imperial service uniform. Miles gulped down a sharp spasm of stage fright. He wished he'd stopped at Vorkosigan House to change; he still wore the plain dark shirt, trousers, and boots he'd stood in when leaving Tau Verde. He estimated the distance to the center of the chamber as about a light-year.

His father sat, looking entirely at home in his red-and-blues, behind his desk in the first row not far from Vordrozda. Count Vorkosigan leaned back, his legs stretched out and crossed at the ankles, arms draped along the backrest, yet looking no more casual than a tiger stalking his prey. His face was sour, murderous, concentrated on Vordrozda; Miles wondered briefly if the old slanderous sobriquet, "the Butcher of Komarr," that had once attached to his father might have some basis in fact after all.

Vordrozda, in the speaker's circle, was the only one directly facing the darkened entrance arch. He was the first to see Miles and Ivan. He had just opened his mouth to continue; it hung there, slack.

"That's just the question I propose to make you answer, Count Vordrozda—and you, Admiral Hessman," Miles called. Two light-years, he thought, and limped forward.

The chamber stirred to murmurs and cries of

astonishment. Of all the men's reactions, Miles searched for only one.

Count Vorkosigan snapped his head around, saw Miles. He inhaled, and his arms and legs drew in. He sat for a moment with his elbows on his desk, face buried in his hands. He rubbed his face, hard; when he raised it again, it was flushed and furrowed, blinking.

When did he grow to look so old? Miles grieved. Was his hair always that grey? Has he changed so much, or is it me? Or both?

Count Vorkosigan's eye fell on Ivan, and his face cleared to stunned exasperation. "Ivan, you idiot! Where have you been?"

Ivan glanced at Miles and rose to the occasion, bowing toward the witness bench. "Admiral Hessman sent me to find Miles, sir. I did. Somehow, I don't think that was what he really had in mind."

Vordrozda turned in the circle to glare furiously at Hessman, who was goggling at Ivan. "You—" Vordrozda hissed at the admiral, voice venomous with rage. He caught himself up almost instantly, straightening his crouch, relaxing his hands from clawed rakes to elegant curves once again.

Miles swept a bow to the encircling assemblage, ending it on one knee in the direction of the dais. "My liege and my lords. I would have been here sooner, but my invitation was lost in the mail. To attest this I wish to call Lord Ivan Vorpatril as my witness."

Gregor's young face stared down at him, stiff, dark eyes troubled and distant. The Emperor's gaze turned in bewilderment to his new advisor, standing in the speaker's circle. His old advisor, Count Vorkosigan, looked wonderfully enlightened; his lips drew back in a tigerish smile.

Miles too glanced at Vordrozda from the corner of his eye. Now, he thought, instantly, is the time to push.

By the time the Lord Guardian of the Circle admits Ivan with all due ceremony, they will have recovered. Give them sixty seconds to confer on the bench, and they will concoct new lies of utmost reasonableness, leaving it their word against ours in the hideous gamble of a stacked Council vote. Hessman, yes, it was Hessman he must put the wind up. Vordrozda was too supple to stampede. Strike now, and cleave the conspiracy in half.

He swallowed, cleared his locked throat, and swung to his feet. "I challenge Admiral Hessman, here before you, lords, on charges of sabotage, murder, and attempted murder. I can prove he ordered the sabotage of Captain Dimir's Imperial fast courier, resulting in the horrible deaths of all aboard her; I can prove his intent that my cousin Ivan have been among them,"

"You are out of order," cried Vordrozda. "These insane charges do not belong in the Council of Counts. You must make them in a military court, if you make them at all, traitor."

"Where Admiral Hessman, most conveniently, must stand them alone, since you, Count Vordrozda, cannot be tried there," said Miles immediately.

Count Vorkosigan was tapping his fist softly on his desk, leaning forward urgently toward Miles; his lips formed a silent litany, yes, go, go . . .

Miles, encouraged, raised his voice. "He will stand alone, and he will die alone, since he has only his own unwitnessed word that his crimes were by your order. They were unwitnessed, were they not, Admiral? Do you really think that Count Vordrozda will be so overcome by emotions of loyalty to a comrade as to endorse that word?"

Hessman was dead white, breathing heavily, stare flicking back and forth between Vordrozda and Ivan. Miles could see the panic blossoming in his eyes.

Vordrozda, straddling the circle, gestured jerkily at Miles. "My lords, this is not a defense. He merely hopes to camouflage his guilt by these wild counteraccusations, and totally out of order at that! My Lord Guardian, I appeal to you to restore order!"

The Lord Guardian of the Circle began to rise, stopped, speared by a penetrating stare from Count Vorkosigan. He sank back weakly to his bench. "This is certainly very irregular . . ." he managed, then ran down. Count Vorkosigan smiled approvingly.

"You haven't answered my question, Vordrozda," called Miles. "Will you speak for Admiral Hessman?"

"Subordinates have committed unauthorized excesses throughout history," began Vordrozda.

He twists, he turns, he's going to torque away—no! I can twist too. "Oh, you admit he is your subordinate, do you now?"

"He is nothing of the sort," snapped Vordrozda. "We have no connection but common interest in the good of the Imperium."

"No connection, Admiral Hessman; do you hear that? How does it feel to be stabbed in the back with such surpassing smoothness? I wager you can scarcely feel the knife going in. It will be like that right up to the end, you know."

Hessman's eyes bulged. He sprang to his feet. "No, it won't," he snarled. "You started this, Vordrozda. If I'm going down I'll take you with me!" He pointed at Vordrozda. "He came to me at Winterfair, wanting me to pass him the latest Imperial Security intelligence about Vorkosigan's son—"

"Shut up!" ground out Vordrozda desperately, fury firing his eyes at being so needlessly taken from behind, "Shut up—" His hand snaked under his scarlet robe, emerged with a glitter. Locked the needler's aim on the babbling admiral. Stopped. Vordrozda stared down at the weapon in his hand as though it were a scorpion.

"Who now is out of order?" mocked Miles softly.

Barrayar's aristocracy still maintained its military tone. Drawing a deadly weapon in the presence of the Emperor struck a deep reflex. Twenty or thirty men started up from their benches.

Only on Barrayar, Miles reflected, would pulling a loaded needler start a stampede *toward* one. Others ran between Vordrozda and the dais. Vordrozda abandoned Hessman and whirled to face his real tormentor, raising the weapon. Miles stood stock-still, transfixed by the needler's tiny dark eye. Fascinating, that the pit of hell should have so narrow an entrance . . .

Vordrozda was buried in an avalanche of tackling bodies, their scarlet robes flapping. Ivan had the honor of the first hit, taking him in the knees.

Miles stood before his Emperor. The chamber had quieted, his late accusers hustled out under arrest. Now he faced his true tribunal.

Gregor sighed uneasily, and motioned the Lord Guardian of the Circle to his side. They conferred briefly.

"The Emperor requests and requires a recess of one hour, to examine the new testimony. For witness, Count Vorvolk, Count Vorhalas."

They all filed into the private chamber behind the dais, Gregor, Count Vorkosigan, Miles and Ivan, and Gregor's curious choice of witnesses. Henri Vorvolk was one of Gregor's few age-mates among the Counts, and a personal friend. Nucleus of a new generation of cronies, Miles supposed. No surprise that Gregor should desire his support. Count Vorhalas . . .

Vorhalas was Miles's father's oldest and most

implacable enemy, since the deaths of his two sons on the wrong side of Vordarian's Pretendership eighteen years before. Miles eyed him queasily. The Count's son and heir had been the man who'd fired the soltoxin gas grenade through the window of Vorkosigan House one night, in a tangled attempt at vengeance for the death of his younger brother. He had been killed in turn as a result of his treason. Had Count Vorhalas seen in Vordrozda's conspiracy an opportunity to complete the job, revenge in perfect symmetry, a son for a son?

Yet Vorhalas was known as a just and honest man—Miles could as easily picture him uniting with his father in disdain of Vordrozda's mushroom upstart plot. The two had been enemies so long, and outlived so many friends and foes, their enmity had almost achieved a kind of harmony. Still, no one would dare accuse Vorhalas of favoritism in witness to the former Regent. Now the two men exchanged nods, like a pair of fencers en garde, and took seats opposite each other.

"So," said Count Vorkosigan, grown serious and intense, "what really happened out there, Miles? I've had Illyan's reports—until lately—but somehow they all seemed to raise more questions than they answered."

Miles was diverted for a moment. "Isn't his agent still sending? I promise you, I didn't interfere with his duties—"

"Captain Illyan is in prison."

"What!"

"Awaiting trial. He was included in your conspiracy charges."

"That's absurd!"

"Not at all. Most logical. Who, moving against me, would not take the precaution first of taking away my eyes and ears, if they could?"

Count Vorhalas nodded a tactician's approval and agreement, as if to say, Just how I'd have done it myself.

Miles's father's eyes narrowed with dry humor. "It's a learning experience for him to be on the other end of the process of justice for a time. No harm done. I admit, he is a trifle annoyed with you at the moment."

"The question," said Gregor distantly, "was whether the Captain served me, or my Prime Minister." Bitter uncertainty still lingered in his eyes.

"All who serve me serve you, through me," Count Vorkosigan stated. "It is the Vor system at work. Streams of experience, all flowing together, combining at last in a river of great power. Yours is the final confluence." It was the closest to flattery Miles had ever heard his father come, a measure of his unease. "You do Simon Illyan an injustice to suspect him. He has served you all your life, and your grandfather before you."

Miles wondered what sort of tributary he now constituted—the Dendarii Mercenaries included some very odd headwaters indeed. "What happened. Well, sir . . ." He paused, groping along the chain of events to some starting point. Truly, it began at a wall not 100 kilometers outside Vobarr Sultana. But he launched his account at his meeting with Arde Mayhew on Beta Colony. He stumbled in fearful hesitation, took a breath, then went on in an exact and honest description of his meeting with Baz Jesek. His father winced at the name. The blockade, the boarding, the battles—self-forgetfulness overcame him during his enthusiastic description of these; at one point he looked up to realize he had the Emperor playing the part of the Oseran fleet, Henri Vorvolk Captain Tung, and his father the Pelian high command. Bothari's death. His father's face grew drawn and inward at this news. "Well," he said after a time, "he is released from a great burden. May he find his ease at last."

Miles glanced at the Emperor, and edited out the Escobaran woman's accusations about Prince Serg. From the sharp and grateful look Count Vorkosigan gave him, Miles gathered that was the correct thing to do. Some truths come in too fierce a flood for some structures to withstand; Miles had no wish to witness another devastation like Elena Bothari's.

By the time he reached the account of how he broke the blockade at last, Gregor's lips were parted in fascination, and Count Vorkosigan's eyes glinted with appreciation. Ivan's arrival, and Miles's deductions from it—he was reminded of the hour, and reached for his hip flask.

"What is that?" asked his father, startled.

"Antacid. Uh—want some?" he offered politely.

"Thank you," said Count Vorkosigan. "Don't mind if I do." He took a grave swig, so straight-faced even Miles was not sure if he was laughing.

Miles gave a brief, bald account of the thinking that led him to return in secret, to attempt to surprise Vordrozda and Hessman. Ivan endorsed all he had been eyewitness to, giving Hessman the lie. Gregor looked disturbed at having his assumptions about his new friends turned so bluntly inside-out. *Wake up, Gregor,* thought Miles. *You of all men cannot afford the luxury of comfortable illusions. No, indeed, I have no desire to trade places with you.*

Gregor was downcast by the time Miles finished. Count Vorkosigan sat at Gregor's right hand, backwards on a plain chair as usual, and gazed at his son with a pensive hunger.

"Why, then?" asked Gregor. "What did you think to make of yourself, when you raised up such force, if not Emperor—if not of Barrayar, perhaps of someplace else?"

"My liege." Miles lowered his voice. "When we played together in the Imperial Residence in the winters, when did I ever demand any part except that of Vorthalia the loyal? You know me—how could you doubt? The Dendarii Mercenaries were an accident. I didn't plan them—they just happened, in the course of scrambling from crisis to crisis. I only wanted to serve Barrayar, as my father before me. When I couldn't serve Barrayar, I wanted—I wanted to serve something. To—" he raised his eyes to his father's, driven to a painful honesty, "to make my life an offering fit to lay at his feet." He shrugged. "Screwed up again."

"Clay, boy." Count Vorkosigan's voice was hoarse but clear. "Only clay. Not fit to receive so golden a sacrifice." His voice cracked.

For a moment, Miles forgot to care about his coming trial. He lidded his eyes, and stored tranquillity away in his heart's most secret recesses, to pleasure him in some lean and desperate future hour. Fatherless Gregor swallowed, and looked away, as if ashamed. Count Vorhalas stared at the floor discomfited, like a man accidentally intruding onto some private and delicate scene.

Gregor's right hand moved hesitantly to touch the shoulder of his first and most loyal protector. "I serve Barrayar," he offered. "Its justice is my duty. I never meant to dispense injustice."

"You were ring-led, boy," Count Vorkosigan muttered, to Gregor's ear alone. "Never mind. But learn from it."

Gregor sighed. "When we played together, Miles, you always beat me at Strat-O. It was because I knew you that I doubted."

Miles knelt, head bowed, and spread his arms. "Your will, my liege."

Gregor shook his head. "May I always endure such treason as that." He raised his voice to his witnesses. "Well, my lords? Are you satisfied that the substance of Vordozda's charge, intent to usurp the Imperium, is false and malicious? And will you so testify to your peers?"

"Absolutely," said Henri Vorvolk with enthusiasm. Miles gauged that the second-year cadet had fallen in love with him about halfway through his account of his adventures with the Dendarii Mercenaries.

Count Vorhalas remained cool and thoughtful. "The usurpation charge does indeed appear false," the old man agreed, "and by my honor I will so testify. But there is another treason here. By his own admission, Lord Vorkosigan was, and indeed remains, in violation of Vorloupulous's law, treason in its own right."

"No such charge," said Count Vorkosigan distantly, "has been laid in the Council of Counts."

Henri Vorvolk grinned. "Who'd dare, after this?"

"A man of proven loyalty to the Imperium, with an academic interest in perfect justice, might so dare," said Count Vorkosigan, still dispassionate. "A man with nothing to lose, might dare—much. Might he not?"

"Beg for it, Vorkosigan," whispered Vorhalas, his coolness slipping. "Beg for mercy, as I did." His eyes shut tight, and he trembled.

Count Vorkosigan gazed at him in silence for a long moment. Then, "As you wish," he said, and rose, and slid to one knee before his enemy. "Let it lay, then, and I will see the boy does not trouble those waters any more."

"Still too stiff-necked."

"If it please you, then."

"Say, 'I beg of you.' "

"I beg of you," repeated Count Vorkosigan obediently. Miles searched for tensions of rage in his father's backbone, found none; this was something old, older than himself, between the two men, labyrinthine; he could scarcely penetrate its inward places. Gregor looked sick, Henri Vorvolk bewildered, Ivan terrified.

Vorhalas's hard stillness seemed edged with a kind of ecstasy. He leaned close to Miles's father's ear. "Shove it, Vorkosigan," he whispered. Count Vorkosigan's head bowed, and his hands clenched.

He sees me, if at all, only as a handle on my father. . . . Time to get his attention. "Count Vorhalas." Miles's voice flexed across the silence like a blade. "Be satisfied. For if you carry this through, at some point you are going to have to look my mother in the eye and repeat that. Dare you?"

Vorhalas wilted slightly. He frowned at Miles. "Can your mother look at you, and not understand desire for vengeance?" He gestured at Miles's stunted and twisted frame.

"Mother," said Miles, "calls it my great gift. Tests are a gift, she says, and great tests are a great gift. Of course," he added thoughtfully, "it's widely agreed my mother is a bit strange . . ." He trapped Vorhalas's gaze direct. "What do you propose to do with your gift, Count Vorhalas?"

"Hell," Vorhalas muttered, after a short, interminable silence, not to Miles but to Count Vorkosigan. "He's got his mother's eyes."

"I've noticed that," Count Vorkosigan murmured back. Vorhalas glared at him in exasperation.

"I am not a bloody saint," Vorhalas declared, to the air generally.

"No one is asking you to be," said Gregor, anxiously soothing. "But you are my sworn servant. And it does not serve me for my servants to be ripping up each other instead of my enemies."

Vorhalas sniffed, and shrugged grudgingly. "True, my liege." His hands unclenched, finger by finger, as if releasing some invisible possession. "Oh, get up," he added impatiently to Count Vorkosigan. The former Regent rose, quite bland again.

Vorhalas glared at Miles. "And just how, Aral, do you propose to keep this gifted young maniac and his accidental army under control?"

Count Vorkosigan measured out his words slowly, drop by drop, as though pursuing some delicate titration. "The Dendarii Mercenaries are a genuine puzzle." He glanced at Gregor. "What is your will, my liege?"

Gregor jerked, startled out of spectatorhood. He looked, rather pleadingly, at Miles. "Organizations do grow and die. Any chance of them just fading away?"

Miles chewed his lip. "That hope has crossed my mind, but—they looked awfully healthy when I left. Growing."

Gregor grimaced. "I can hardly march my army on them and break them up like old Dorca did—it's definitely too long a walk."

"They themselves are innocent of any wrongdoing," Miles hastened to point out. "They never knew who I was—most of them aren't even Barrayaran."

Gregor glanced uncertainly at Count Vorkosigan, who studied his boots, as if to say, You're the one who itched to make your own decisions, boy. But he did add, aloud, "You are just as much Emperor as Dorca ever was, Gregor. Do what you will."

Gregor's gaze returned to Miles for a long moment. "You couldn't break your blockade, within its military context. So you changed the context."

"Yes, sir."

"I cannot change Dorca's law. . . ." said Gregor slowly.

Count Vorkosigan, who had begun to look uneasy, relaxed again. "It saved Barrayar."

The Emperor paused a long time, awash in bafflement. Miles knew just how he felt. Miles let him stew a few moments more, until the silence was stretched taut with expectation, and Gregor was starting to get that desperate glazed look Miles recognized from his candidacy orals, of a man caught without the answer. Now.

"The Emperor's Own Dendarii Mercenaries," Miles said suggestively.

"What?"

"Why not?" Miles straightened, and turned his hands palm-out. "I'd be delighted to give them to you. Declare them a Crown Troop. It's been done."

"With horse cavalry!" said Count Vorkosigan. But his face was suddenly much lighter.

"Whatever he does with them will be a legal fiction anyway, since they are beyond his reach." Miles bowed apologetically to Gregor. "He may as well arrange it to his own maximum convenience."

"Whose maximum convenience?" inquired Count Vorhalas dryly.

"You were thinking of this as a private declaration, I trust," said Count Vorkosigan.

"Well, yes—I'm afraid most of the mercenaries would be, uh, rather disturbed to hear they'd been drafted into the Barrayaran Imperial Service. But why not put them in Captain Illyan's department? Their status would have to remain covert then. Let him figure out something useful to do with 'em. A free mercenary fleet secretly owned by Barrayaran Imperial Security."

Gregor looked suddenly more reconciled; indeed, intrigued. "That might be practical. . . ."

Count Vorkosigan's teeth glinted in a white flash of

a grin, instantly suppressed. "Simon," he murmured, "will be overjoyed."

"Really?" said Gregor dubiously.

"You have my personal guarantee." Count Vorkosigan sketched a bow, sitting.

Vorhalas snorted, and eyed Miles. "You're too bloody clever for your own good, you know, boy?"

"Exactly, sir," said Miles agreeably, in a mild hysteria of relief, feeling lighter by 3000 soldiers and God knew how many tons of equipment. He had done it—the last piece glued back in its place. . . .

". . . dare play the fool with me," muttered Vorhalas. He raised his voice to Count Vorkosigan. "That only answers half my question, Aral."

Count Vorkosigan studied his fingernails, eyes alight. "True, we can't leave him running around loose. I, too, shudder to think what accidents he might commit next. He should doubtless be confined to an institution, where he would be forced to labor all day long under many watchful eyes." He paused thoughtfully. "May I suggest the Imperial Service Academy?"

Miles looked up, mouth open in an idiocy of sudden hope. All his calculations had been concentrated on wriggling out from under Vorloupulous's law. He'd scarcely dared even to dream of life afterwards, let alone such reward as this . . .

His father lowered his voice to him. "Assuming it's not beneath you—Admiral Naismith. I never did get to congratulate you on your promotion."

Miles reddened. "It was all just fakery, sir. You know that."

"All?"

"Well—mostly."

"Ah, you grow subtle, even with me . . . But you have tasted command. Can you go back to subordination?

Demotions are a bitter meat to swallow." An old irony played around his mouth.

"You were demoted, after Komarr, sir. . . ."

"Broken back to captain, yes."

One corner of Miles's mouth twisted up. "I have a bionic stomach now, that can digest anything. I can handle it."

Count Vorhalas raised skeptical brows. "What sort of ensign do you think he will make, Admiral Vorkosigan?"

"I think he will make a terrible ensign," said Count Vorkosigan frankly. "But if he can avoid being strangled by his harried superiors for—er—excessive initiative, I think he might be a fine General Staff officer someday."

Vorhalas nodded reluctant agreement. Miles's eyes blazed up like bonfires, in reflection to his father's.

After two days of testimony and behind-the-scenes maneuvering, the Council vote was unanimous for acquittal. For one thing, Gregor took his place by right as Count Vorbarra and cast a resounding "innocent" as the fourth vote called, instead of the usual abstention customary for the Emperor. The rest swung meekly into line.

Some of Count Vorkosigan's older political opponents looked as if they'd rather spit, but only Count Vorhalas voted an abstention. Then, Vorhalas had never been of Vordrozda's party, and had no taint of association to wash off.

"Ballsy bastard." Count Vorkosigan exchanged a familiar salute across the chamber with his closest enemy. "I wish they all had his backbone, if not his opinions."

Miles sat quietly, absorbing this most mitigated triumph. Elena would have been safe, after all.

But not happy. Hunting hawks do not belong in cages, no matter how much a man covets their grace, no matter how golden the bars. They are far more beautiful soaring free. Heartbreakingly beautiful.

He sighed, and rose to go wrestle with his destiny.

The vineyards garlanding the terraced slopes of the long lake above Vorkosigan Surleau were misted with new green. The surface of the water glittered in a warm breath of air, a spatter of silver coins. It had once been a custom somewhere to put coins on the eyes of the dead, Miles had read, for their journey; it seemed appropriate. He imagined the sun-coins sinking to the bottom of the lake, there to pile up and up until they broke the surface, a new island.

The clods of earth were cold and wet yet, winter lingering beneath the surface of the soil. Heavy. He tossed a shovelful shoulder-high from the hole he dug.

"Your hands are bleeding," observed his mother. "You could do that in five seconds with a plasma arc."

"Blood," said Miles, "washes away sin. The Sergeant said so."

"I see." She made no further demur, but sat in companionable silence, her back against a tree, watching the lake. It was her Betan upbringing, Miles supposed; she never seemed to tire of the delight of water open to the sky.

He finished at last. Countess Vorkosigan gave him a hand up out of the pit. He took up the control lead of the float pallet, and lowered the oblong box, waiting patiently all this time, into its rest. Bothari had always waited patiently for him.

Covering it back up was quicker work. The marker his father had ordered was not yet finished; hand-carved, like the others in this family plot. Miles's grandfather lay not far away, next to the grandmother Miles had never known, dead decades before in Barrayaran civil strife. His eye lingered a moment, uncomfortably, on a double space reserved next to his grandfather, above the slope and perpendicular to the Sergeant's new grave. But that burden was yet to come.

He placed a shallow beaten copper bowl upon a tripod at the foot of the grave. In it he piled juniper twigs from the mountains and a lock of his own hair. He then pulled a colored scarf from his jacket, carefully unfolded it, and placed a curl of finer dark hair among the twigs. His mother added a clipping of short grey hair, and a thick, generous tress of her own red roan, and withdrew to a distance.

Miles, after a pause, laid the scarf beside the hair. "I'm afraid I made a most improper Baba," he whispered in apology. "I never meant to mock you. But Baz loves her, he'll take good care of her . . . My word was too easy to give, too hard to keep. But there. There." He added flakes of aromatic bark. "You shall lie warm here, watching the long lake change its faces, winter to spring, summer to fall. No armies march here, and even the deepest midnights aren't wholly dark. Surely God won't overlook you, in such a spot as this. There will be grace and forgiveness enough, old dog, even for you." He lit the offering. "I pray you will spare me a drink from that cup, when it overflows for you."

EPILOGUE

The emergency docking drill was called in the middle of the night cycle, naturally. He'd probably have timed it that way himself, Miles thought, as he scrambled through the corridors of the orbital weapons platform with his fellow cadets. This four-week stint of orbital and free-fall training was due to end tomorrow for his group, and the instructors hadn't pulled anything nasty for at least four days. Not for him the galloping anticipation of upcoming leave planetside that had formed the bulk of the conversation in the officer's mess last night. He had sat quietly, meditating on all the marvelous possibilities for a grand finale.

He arrived at his assigned shuttle hatch corridor at the same moment as his co-trainee and the instructor. The instructor's face was a mask of neutrality. Cadet Kostolitz looked Miles over sourly.

"Still carrying that obsolete pig-sticker, eh?" said

Kostolitz, with an irritated nod at the dagger at Miles's waist.

"I have permission," said Miles tranquilly.

"D'you sleep with it?"

A small, bland smile. "Yes."

Miles considered the ongoing problem of Kostolitz. The accidents of Barrayaran history guaranteed he would be dealing with class-consciousness in his officers throughout his Imperial Service career, aggressive like Kostolitz's or in more subtle forms. He must learn to handle it not merely well, but creatively, if his officers were ever to give him their best.

He had the uncanny sensation of being able to look through Kostolitz the way a doctor saw through a body with his diagnostic viewers. Every twist and tear and emotional abrasion, every young cancer of resentment growing from them, seemed red-lined in his mind's eye. Patience. The problem displayed itself with ever-increasing clarity. The solution would follow, in time, with opportunity. Kostolitz could teach him much. This docking drill might prove interesting after all. .

Kostolitz had acquired a thin green armband since they had last been paired, Miles saw. He wondered what wit among the instructors had come up with that idea. The armbands were rather like getting a gold star on your paper in reverse; green represented injury in drills, yellow represented death, in the judgment of whatever instructor was umpiring the simulated catastrophe. Very few cadets managed to escape these training cycles without a collection of them. Miles had encountered Ivan Vorpatril yesterday, sporting two greens and a yellow, not as bad as the unfortunate fellow he'd seen at mess last night with five yellows.

Miles's own undecorated sleeve was attracting a bit more attention from the instructors than he really wanted, lately. The notoriety had a pleasant flip side;

some of the more alert among his fellow cadets vied quietly to have Miles in their groups, as armband-repellent. Of course, the very most alert were now avoiding him like a plague, realizing he was beginning to draw fire. Miles grinned to himself, in happy anticipation of something really sneaky and underhanded coming up. Every cell of his body seemed awake and singing.

Kostolitz, with a stifled yawn and a last growl at Miles's upper-class decorative blade, took the starboard side of the shuttle and began working forward with his checklist. Miles took the port side, ditto. The instructor floated between them, watching sharply over their shoulders. He'd got one good thing out of his adventures with the Dendarii Mercenaries, Miles reflected; his free-fall nausea had vanished, an unexpected side-benefit of the work Tung's surgeon had done on his stomach. Small favors.

Kostolitz was working swiftly, Miles saw from the corner of his eye. They were being timed. Kostolitz counted emergency breath masks through the plexiglass of their case and hurried on. Miles almost called a suggestion to him, then clamped his jaw. It wouldn't be appreciated. Patience. Item. Item. Item—first-aid kit, correctly in its wall socket. Automatically suspicious, Miles unlocked it and checked to see that all its contents were indeed intact. Tape, tourniquets, plastic bandage, IV tubing, meds, emergency oxygen—no surprises concealed there. He ran a hand along the bottom of the case, and caught his breath—plastic explosive? No, only a wad of chewing gum. Shucks.

Kostolitz was finished and waiting impatiently as Miles arrived up front. "You're slow, Vorkosigan." Kostolitz jammed his report panel into the read-slot, and slid into the pilot's seat.

Miles eyed an interesting bulge in the instructor's

breast pocket. He patted his own pockets, and essayed a helpless smile. "Oh, sir," he chirped politely to the instructor, "I seem to have misplaced my light-pen. May I borrow yours?"

The instructor disgorged it unwillingly. Miles lidded his eyes. In addition to the light-pen, the instructor's pocket contained three emergency breathmasks, folded. An interesting number, three. Anyone on a space station might carry a breath mask in his pocket as a matter of course, but three? Yet they had a dozen breathmasks ready to hand, Kostolitz had just checked them—no. Kostolitz had just *counted* them.

"Your light-pens are standard issue," said the instructor coldly. "You're supposed to hang onto them. You careless characters are going to bring the Accounting Office down on us all, one of these days."

"Yes, sir. Thank you, sir." Miles signed his name with a flourish, made to pocket the pen, came up with two. "Oh, here's mine. Sorry, sir."

He entered his report, and strapped himself into the co-pilot's chair. With his seat at the limit of its forward adjustment, he could just reach the foot controls. Imperial equipment was not so flexible as the mercenaries' had been. No matter. He schooled himself to strict attention. He was still awkward in his handling of shuttle controls. But a bit more practice, and he would never be at the mercy of a shuttle pilot for transportation again.

It was Kostolitz's turn now, though. Miles was pressed into his padded seat by the acceleration as the shuttle popped free of its clamps and began to boost toward its assigned station. Breath masks. Check lists. Assumptions. The chip on Kostolitz's shoulder. Assumptions . . . Miles's nerves extended themselves, spider-patient, questing. Minutes crept by.

A sharp report, and a hissing, came from the rear

of the cabin. Miles's heart lurched and began to pound violently, in spite of his anticipation. He swung around and took it in at a glance, as when a strobe-flash of lightning betrays the secrets of the dark. Kostolitz swore violently. Miles breathed, "Ha!"

A jagged hole in the paneling on the starboard side of the shuttle was pouring out a thick green gas; a coolant line had snapped, as from a meteor hit. The "meteor" was undoubtedly plastic explosive, since the stuff was streaming into and not out of the cabin. Besides, the instructor was still seated, watching them. Kostolitz leaped for the case of emergency breath masks.

Miles dove instead for the controls. He snapped the atmosphere circuit from recycle to exterior venting, and in one pauseless motion fired the shuttle's attitude verniers at maximum boost. After a groaning moment, the shuttle began to turn, then spin, around an axis through the center of the cabin. Miles, the instructor, and Kostolitz were thrown forward. The coolant gas, heavier than their atmosphere mix, began to pile up against the back wall of the cabin in noxious billows under the influence of this simplest of artificial gravities.

"You crazy bastard!" screamed Kostolitz, scrabbling at a breath mask. "What are you doing?"

The instructor's expression was first an echo of Kostolitz's, then suddenly enlightened. He eased back into the seat he had begun to shoot out of, hanging on tightly and observing, his eyes crinkling with interest.

Miles was too busy to reply. Kostolitz would figure it out shortly, he was sure. Kostolitz donned a breath mask, attempted to inhale. He snatched it off his face and threw it aside, and grabbed up the second of the three he'd brought forward. Miles climbed up the wall toward the first-aid kit.

The second breath mask curved past him. Empty

reservoirs, no doubt. Kostolitz had counted the breath masks without checking their working condition. Miles levered the first-aid kit open and pulled out IV tubing and two Y-connectors. Kostolitz threw aside the third breath mask and began climbing back up the starboard wall toward the case of breath masks. The coolant gas made an acrid, burning stench in Miles's nostrils, but its harmful concentrations remained in the other end of the cabin, for now.

A cry of rage and fear, interrupted by coughing, came from Kostolitz as he began pawing through breath masks, checking their condition readouts at last. Miles's lips drew back in a wicked grin. He pulled his grandfather's dagger from its sheath, cut the IV tubing into four pieces, inserted the Y-connectors, sealed them with blobs of plastic bandage, jammed the hookah-like apparatus into the single outlet of the emergency medical oxygen canister, and skidded back to the instructor.

"Air, sir?" He offered a hissing end of IV tubing to the officer. "I suggest you breathe in through your mouth and out through your nose."

"Thank you, Cadet Vorkosigan," said the instructor in a fascinated tone, taking it. Kostolitz, coughing, eyes rolling desperately, fell back toward them, barely managing not to put his feet through the control panel. Miles blandly handed him a tube. He sucked on it, eyes wide and watering, not, Miles thought, only from the effects of the coolant gas.

Clenching his air-tube between his teeth, Miles began to climb the starboard wall. Kostolitz started after him, then discovered that both he and the instructor had been issued short tethers. Miles uncoiled tubing behind him; yes, it would reach, although just barely. Kostolitz and the instructor could only watch, breathing in yoga-like cadence.

Miles reversed his hold as he passed the midpoint of the cabin and centrifugal force began to pull him toward the pooling green gas slowly filling the shuttle from the back wall. He counted down wall panels, 4a, 4b, 4c—that should be it. He popped it open, and found the manual shutoff valves. That one? No, that one. He turned it. It slipped in his sweating hand.

The panel door on which he rested his weight gave way with a sudden crack, and he swung out over the evilly heaving green gas. The oxygen tube ripped from his mouth and flapped around wildly. He was saved from yelping only by the fact that he was holding his breath. The instructor, forward, lurched futilely, tied to his air supply. But by the time he'd fumbled his pocket open, Miles had swallowed, achieved a more secure grip on the wall, and recovered his tube in a heart-stopping grab. Try again. He turned the valve, hard, and the hissing from the hole in the wall a meter astern of him faded to an elfin moan, then stopped.

The tide of green gas began to recede and thin at last, as the cabin ventilators labored. Miles, shaking only slightly, climbed back to the front end of the shuttle and strapped himself into his copilot's seat without comment. Comment would have been awkward around his oxygen tube anyway.

Cadet Kostolitz, in his role as pilot, returned to his controls. The atmosphere cleared at last. He stopped the spin and aimed the damaged shuttle slowly back toward dock, paying strict and subdued attention to engine temperature readouts. The instructor looked extremely thoughtful, and only a little pale.

The chief instructor himself was waiting in the shuttle hatch corridor of the orbital station when they docked, along with a repairs tech. He smiled cheerily, turning two yellow armbands absently in his hands.

Their own instructor sighed, and shook his head dolefully at the armbands. "No."

"No?" queried the chief instructor. Miles was not sure if it was with amazement or disappointment.

"No."

"This I've got to see." The two instructors ducked into the shuttle, leaving Miles and Kostolitz alone a moment.

Kostolitz cleared his throat. "That, ah—blade of yours came in pretty handy after all."

"Yes, there are times when a plasma arc beam isn't nearly as suitable for cutting," Miles agreed. "Like when you're in a chamber full of inflammable gas."

"Oh, hell." Kostolitz seemed suddenly struck. "That stuff *will* go off, mixed with oxygen. I almost . . ." He cut himself off, cleared his throat again. "You don't miss much, do you?" A sudden suspicion filled his face. "Did you know about this setup in advance?"

"Not exactly. But I figured something must be up when I counted the three breath masks in the instructor's pocket."

"You—" Kostolitz paused, turned. "Did you really lose track of your light-pen?"

"No."

"Hell," Kostolitz muttered again. He scuffed around the corridor a moment, hunched, red, dismally recalcitrant.

Now, thought Miles. "I know a place you can buy good blades, in Vorbarr Sultana," he said with nicely calculated diffidence. "Better than standard-issue stuff. You can get a real bargain there sometimes, if you know what to look for."

Kostolitz stopped. "Oh, yeah?" He began to straighten, as though being relieved of a weight. "You, ah—I don't suppose . . ."

"It's kind of a hole-in-the-wall. I could take you there sometime, during leave, if you're interested."

"Really? You'd—you'd—yes, I'd be interested." Kostolitz feigned a casual air. "Sure." He looked suddenly much more cheerful.

Miles smiled.

The Mountains of Mourning

Miles heard the woman weeping as he was climbing the hill from the long lake. He hadn't dried himself after his swim, as the morning already promised shimmering heat. Lake water trickled cool from his hair onto his naked chest and back, more annoyingly down his legs from his ragged shorts. His leg braces chafed on his damp skin as he pistoned up the faint trail through the scrub, military double-time. His feet squished in his old wet shoes. He slowed curiously as he became conscious of the voices.

The woman's voice grated with grief and exhaustion. "Please, lord, please. All I want is m'justice. . . ."

The front gate guard's voice was irritated and embarrassed. "I'm no lord. C'mon, get *up,* woman. Go back to the village and report it at the district magistrate's office."

"I tell you, I just came from there!" The woman did not move from her knees as Miles emerged from the bushes and paused to take in the tableau across the paved road. "The magistrate's not to return for weeks, weeks. I walked four days to get here. I only have a little money. . . ." A desperate hope rose in her voice, and her spine bent and straightened as she scrabbled in her skirt pocket and held out her cupped hands to the guard. "A mark and twenty pence, it's all I have, but—"

The exasperated guard's eye fell on Miles, and he straightened abruptly, as if afraid Miles might suspect him of being tempted by so pitiful a bribe. "Be off, woman!" he snapped.

Miles quirked an eyebrow, and limped across the road to the main gate. "What's all this about, Corporal?" he inquired easily.

The guard corporal was on loan from Imperial Security, and wore the high-necked dress greens of the Barrayaran Service. He was sweating and uncomfortable in the bright morning light of this southern district, but Miles fancied he'd be boiled before he'd undo his collar on this post. His accent was not local; he was a city man from the capital, where a more-or-less efficient bureaucracy absorbed such problems as the one on her knees before him.

The woman, now, was local and more than local—she had back-country written all over her. She was younger than her strained voice had at first suggested. Tall, fever-red from her weeping, with stringy blond hair hanging down across a ferret-thin face and protuberant grey eyes. If she were cleaned up, fed, rested, happy and confident, she might achieve a near-prettiness, but she was far from that now, despite her remarkable figure. Lean but full-breasted—no, Miles revised himself as he crossed the road and came up to the gate. Her bodice was all blotched with dried milk leaks, though there was no baby in sight. Only temporarily full-breasted. Her worn dress was factory-woven cloth, but hand-sewn, crude and simple. Her feet were bare, thickly callused, cracked and sore.

"No problem," the guard assured Miles. "Go away," he hissed to the woman.

She lurched off her knees and sat stonily.

"I'll call my sergeant," the guard eyed her warily, "and have her removed."

"Wait a moment," said Miles.

She stared up at Miles from her cross-legged position, clearly not knowing whether to identify him as hope or not. His clothing, what there was of it, offered her no clue as to what he might be. The rest of him was all too plainly displayed. He jerked up his chin and smiled thinly. Too-large head, too-short neck, back thickened with its crooked spine, crooked legs with their brittle bones too-often broken, drawing the eye in their gleaming chromium braces. Were the hill woman standing, the top of his head would barely be even with the top of her shoulder. He waited in boredom for her hand to make the backcountry hex sign against evil mutations, but it only jerked and clenched into a fist.

"I must see my lord Count," she said to an uncertain point halfway between Miles and the guard. "It's my right. My daddy, he died in the Service. It's my right."

"Prime Minister Count Vorkosigan," said the guard stiffly, "is on his country estate to rest. If he were working, he'd be back in Vorbarr Sultana." The guard looked as if he wished *he* were back in Vorbarr Sultana.

The woman seized the pause. "You're only a city man. He's *my* count. My right."

"What do you want to see Count Vorkosigan for?" asked Miles patiently.

"Murder," growled the girl/woman. The security guard spasmed slightly. "I want to report a murder."

"Shouldn't you report to your village speaker first?" inquired Miles, with a hand-down gesture to calm the twitching guard.

"I did. He'll do *nothing*." Rage and frustration

cracked her voice. "He says it's over and done. He won't write down my accusation, says it's nonsense. It would only make trouble for everybody, he says. I don't care! I want my justice!"

Miles frowned thoughtfully, looking the woman over. The details checked, corroborated her claimed identity, added up to a solid if subliminal sense of authentic truth which perhaps escaped the professionally paranoid security man. "It's true, Corporal," Miles said. "She has a right to appeal, first to the district magistrate, then to the counts' court. And the district magistrate won't be back for two weeks."

This sector of Count Vorkosigan's native district had only one overworked district magistrate, who rode a circuit that included the lakeside village of Vorkosigan Surleau but one day a month. Since the region of the Prime Minister's country estate was crawling with Imperial Security when the great lord was in residence, and loosely monitored even when he was not, prudent troublemakers took their troubles elsewhere.

"Scan her, and let her in," said Miles. "On my authority."

The guard was one of Imperial Security's best, trained to look for assassins in his own shadow. He now looked scandalized, and lowered his voice to Miles. "Sir, if I let every country lunatic wander the estate at will—"

"I'll take her up. I'm going that way."

The guard shrugged helplessly, but stopped short of saluting; Miles was decidedly not in uniform. The gate guard pulled a scanner from his belt and made a great show of going over the woman. Miles wondered if he'd have been inspired to harass her with a strip-search without Miles's inhibiting presence. When the guard finished demonstrating how alert, conscientious, and loyal he was, he palmed open the gate's lock, entered the transaction, including the woman's retina scan, into the computer monitor, and stood aside in a pose of rather pointed parade rest. Miles grinned at the silent editorial, and steered the bedraggled woman by the elbow through the gates and up the winding drive.

She twitched away from his touch at the earliest opportunity, yet still refrained from superstitious gestures, eyeing him with a strange and hungry curiosity. Time was, such openly repelled fascination with the peculiarities of his body had driven Miles to grind his teeth; now he could take it with a serene amusement only slightly tinged with acid. They would learn, all of them. They would learn.

"Do you serve Count Vorkosigan, little man?" she asked cautiously.

Miles thought about that one a moment. "Yes," he answered finally. The answer was, after all, true on every level of meaning but the one she'd asked it. He quelled the temptation to tell her he was the court jester. From the look of her, this one's troubles were much worse than his own.

She had apparently not quite believed in her own rightful destiny, despite her mulish determination at the gate, for as they climbed unimpeded toward her goal a nascent panic made her face even more drawn and pale, almost ill. "How—how do I talk to him?" she choked. "Should I curtsey . . . ?" She glanced down at herself as if conscious for the first time of her own dirt and sweat and squalor.

Miles suppressed a facetious set-up starting with, *Kneel and knock your forehead three times on the floor before speaking; that's what the General Staff does,* and said instead, "Just stand up straight and speak the truth. Try to be clear. He'll take it from there. He does not, after all," Miles's lip twitched, "lack experience."

She swallowed.

A hundred years ago, the Vorkosigans' summer retreat had been a guard barracks, part of the outlying fortifications of the great castle on the bluff above the village of Vorkosigan Surleau. The castle was now a burnt-out ruin, and the barracks transformed into a comfortable low stone residence, modernized and re-modernized, artistically landscaped and bright with flowers. The arrow slits had been widened into big glass windows overlooking the lake, and comm link antennae bristled from the roof. There was a new guard barracks concealed in the trees downslope, but it had no arrow slits.

A man in the brown-and-silver livery of the Count's personal retainers exited the residence's front door as Miles approached with the strange woman in tow. It was the new man, what was his name? Pym, that was it.

"Where's m'lord Count?" Miles asked him.

"In the upper pavilion, taking breakfast with m'lady." Pym glanced at the woman, waited on Miles in a posture of polite inquiry.

"Ah. Well, this woman has walked four days to lay an appeal before the district magistrate's court. The court's not here, but the Count is, so she now proposes to skip the middlemen and go straight to the top. I like her style. Take her up, will you?"

"During *breakfast?*" said Pym.

Miles cocked his head at the woman. "Have you had breakfast?"

She shook her head mutely.

"I thought not." Miles turned his hands palm-out, dumping her, symbolically, on the retainer. "Now, yes."

"My daddy, he died in the Service," the woman repeated faintly. "It's my right." The phrase seemed as much to convince herself as anyone else, now.

Pym was, if not a hill man, district-born. "So it is."

He sighed, and gestured her to follow him without further ado. Her eyes widened, as she trailed him around the house, and she glanced back nervously over her shoulder at Miles. "Little man . . . ?"

"Just stand straight," he called to her. He watched her round the corner, grinned, and took the steps two at a time into the residence's main entrance.

After a shave and cold shower, Miles dressed in his own room overlooking the long lake. He dressed with great care, as great as he'd expended on the Service Academy ceremonies and Imperial Review two days ago. Clean underwear, long-sleeved cream shirt, dark green trousers with the side piping. High-collared green tunic tailor-cut to his own difficult fit. New pale blue plastic ensign's rectangles aligned precisely on the collar and poking most uncomfortably into his jaw. He dispensed with the leg braces and pulled on mirror-polished boots to the knee, and swiped a bit of dust from them with his pajama pants, ready-to-hand on the floor where he'd dropped them before going swimming.

He straightened and checked himself in the mirror. His dark hair hadn't even begun to recover from that last cut before the graduation ceremonies. A pale, sharp-featured face, not too much dissipated bag under the grey eyes, nor too bloodshot—alas, the limits of his body compelled him to stop celebrating well before he could hurt himself.

Echoes of the late celebration still boiled up silently in his head, crooking his mouth into a grin. He was on his way now, had his hand clamped firmly around the lowest rung of the highest ladder on Barrayar, Imperial Service itself. There were no giveaways in the Service even for sons of the old Vor. You got what you earned. His brother-officers could be relied on to know that, even if outsiders wondered. He was in position at last to prove himself to all doubters. Up and away and never look down, never look back.

One last look back. As carefully as he'd dressed, Miles gathered up the necessary objects for his task. The white cloth rectangles of his former Academy cadet's rank. The hand-calligraphied second copy, purchased for this purpose, of his new officer's commission in the Barrayaran Imperial Service. A copy of his Academy three-year scholastic transcript on paper, with all its commendations (and demerits). No point in anything but honesty in this next transaction. In a cupboard downstairs he found the brass brazier and tripod, wrapped in its polishing cloth, and a plastic bag of very dry juniper bark. Chemical firesticks.

Out the back door and up the hill. The landscaped path split, right going up to the pavilion overlooking it all, left forking sideways to a garden-like area surrounded by a low fieldstone wall. Miles let himself in by the gate. "Good morning, crazy ancestors," he called, then quelled his humor. It might be true, but lacked the respect due the occasion.

He strolled over and around the graves until he came to the one he sought, knelt, and set up the brazier and tripod, humming. The stone was simple, *General Count Piotr Pierre Vorkosigan*, and the dates. If they'd tried to list all the accumulated honors and accomplishments, they'd have had to go to microprint.

He piled in the bark, the very expensive papers, the cloth bits, a clipped mat of dark hair from that last cut. He set it alight and rocked back on his heels to watch it burn. He'd played a hundred versions of this moment over in his head, over the years, ranging from solemn public orations with musicians in the background, to dancing naked on the old man's grave. He'd settled on this private and traditional ceremony, played straight. Just between the two of them.

"So, Grandfather," he purred at last. "And here we are after all. Satisfied now?"

All the chaos of the graduation ceremonies behind, all the mad efforts of the last three years, all the pain, came to this point; but the grave did not speak, did not say, *Well done; you can stop now.* The ashes spelled out no messages, there were no visions to be had in the rising smoke. The brazier burned down all too quickly. Not enough stuff in it, perhaps.

He stood, and dusted his knees, in the silence and the sunlight. So what had he expected? Applause? Why was he here, in the final analysis? Dancing out a dead man's dreams—who did his Service really serve? Grandfather? Himself? Pale Emperor Gregor? Who cared?

"Well, old man," he whispered, then shouted: "ARE YOU SATISFIED YET?" The echoes rang from the stones.

A throat cleared behind him, and Miles whirled like a scalded cat, heart pounding.

"Uh . . . my lord?" said Pym carefully. "Pardon me, I did not mean to interrupt . . . anything. But the Count your father requires you to attend on him in the upper pavilion."

Pym's expression was perfectly bland. Miles swallowed, and waited for the scarlet heat he could feel in his face to recede. "Quite." He shrugged. "The fire's almost out. I'll clean it up later. Don't . . . let anybody else touch it."

He marched past Pym and didn't look back.

The pavilion was a simple structure of weathered silver wood, open on all four sides to catch the breeze, this morning a few faint puffs from the west. Good sailing on the lake this afternoon, maybe. Only ten days precious home leave left, and much Miles wanted to do, including the trip to Vorbarr Sultana with his cousin

Ivan to pick out his new lightflyer. And then his first assignment would be coming through—ship duty, Miles prayed. He'd had to overcome a major temptation, not to ask his father to make sure it was ship duty. He would take whatever assignment fate dealt him, that was the first rule of the game. And win with the hand he was dealt.

The interior of the pavilion was shady and cool after the glare outside. It was furnished with comfortable old chairs and tables, one of which bore the remains of a noble breakfast—Miles mentally marked two lonely-looking oil cakes on a crumb-scattered tray as his own. Miles's mother, lingering over her cup, smiled across the table at him.

Miles's father, casually dressed in an open-throated shirt and shorts, sat in a worn armchair. Aral Vorkosigan was a thick-set, grey-haired man, heavy-jawed, heavy-browed, scarred. A face that lent itself to savage caricature—Miles had seen some, in Opposition press, in the histories of Barrayar's enemies. They had only to draw one lie, to render dull those sharp penetrating eyes, to create everyone's parody of a military dictator.

And how much is he haunted by Grandfather? Miles wondered. He doesn't show it much. But then, he doesn't have to. Admiral Aral Vorkosigan, space master strategist, conqueror of Komarr, hero of Escobar, for sixteen years Imperial Regent and supreme power on Barrayar in all but name. And then he'd capped it, confounded history and all self-sure witnesses and heaped up honor and glory beyond all that had gone before by voluntarily stepping *down* and transferring command smoothly to Emperor Gregor upon his majority. Not that the Prime Ministership hadn't made a dandy retirement from the Regency, and he was showing no signs yet of stepping down from *that*.

And so Admiral Aral's life took General Piotr's like an overpowering hand of cards, and where did that leave Ensign Miles? Holding two deuces and the joker. He must surely either concede or start bluffing like crazy. . . .

The hill woman sat on a hassock, a half-eaten oil cake clutched in her hands, staring openmouthed at Miles in all his power and polish. As he caught and returned her gaze her lips pressed closed and her eyes lit. Her expression was strange—anger? Exhilaration? Embarrassment? Glee? Some bizarre mixture of all? *And what did you think I was, woman?*

Being in uniform (showing off his uniform?), Miles came to attention before his father. "Sir?"

Count Vorkosigan spoke to the woman. "That is my son. If I send him as my Voice, would that satisfy you?"

"Oh," she breathed, her wide mouth drawing back in a weird, fierce grin, the most expression Miles had yet seen on her face, "*yes*, my lord."

"Very well. It will be done."

What will be done? Miles wondered warily. The Count was leaning back in his chair, looking satisfied himself, but with a dangerous tension around his eyes hinting that something had aroused his true anger. Not anger at the woman, clearly they were in some sort of agreement, and—Miles searched his conscience quickly—not at Miles himself. He cleared his throat gently, cocking his head and baring his teeth in an inquiring smile.

The Count steepled his hands and spoke to Miles at last. "A most interesting case. I can see why you sent her up."

"Ah . . ." said Miles. What had he got hold of? He'd only greased the woman's way through Security on a quixotic impulse, for God's sake, and to tweak his father at breakfast. ". . . ah?" he continued noncommittally.

Count Vorkosigan's brows rose. "Did you not know?"

"She spoke of a murder, and a marked lack of cooperation from her local authorities about it. Figured you'd give her a lift on to the district magistrate."

The Count settled back still further, and rubbed his hand thoughtfully across his scarred chin. "It's an infanticide case."

Miles's belly went cold. *I don't want anything to do with this.* Well, that explained why there was no baby to go with the breasts. "Unusual . . . for it to be reported."

"We've fought the old customs for twenty years and more," said the Count. "Promulgated, propagandized . . . In the cities, we've made good progress."

"In the cities," murmured the Countess, "people have access to alternatives."

"But in the backcountry—well—little has changed. We all know what's going on, but without a report, a complaint—and with the family invariably drawing together to protect its own—it's hard to get leverage."

"What," Miles cleared his throat, nodded at the woman, "what was your baby's mutation?"

"The cat's mouth." The woman dabbed at her upper lip to demonstrate. "She had the hole inside her mouth, too, and was a weak sucker, she choked and cried, but she was getting enough, she *was*. . . ."

"Harelip," the Count's off-worlder wife murmured half to herself, translating the Barrayaran term to the galactic standard, "and a cleft palate, sounds like. Harra, that's not even a mutation. They had that back on Old Earth. A . . . a normal birth defect, if that's not a contradiction in terms. Not a punishment for your Barrayaran ancestors' pilgrimage through the Fire. A simple operation could have corrected—" Countess

Vorkosigan cut herself off. The hill woman was looking anguished.

"I'd heard," the woman said. "My lord had made a hospital to be built at Hassadar. I meant to take her there, when I was a little stronger, though I had no money. Her arms and legs were sound, her head was well shaped, anybody could see—surely they would have—" her hands clenched and twisted, her voice went ragged, "but Lem killed her first."

A seven-day walk, Miles calculated, from the deep Dendarii Mountains to the lowland town of Hassadar. Reasonable, that a woman newly risen from childbed might delay that hike a few days. An hour's ride in an aircar . . .

"So one is reported as a murder at last," said Count Vorkosigan, "and we will treat it as exactly that. This is a chance to send a message to the farthest corners of my own district. You, Miles, will be my Voice, to reach where it has not reached before. You will dispense Count's justice upon this man—and not quietly, either. It's time for the practices that brand us as barbarians in galactic eyes to end."

Miles gulped. "Wouldn't the district magistrate be better qualified . . . ?"

The Count smiled slightly. "For this case, I can think of no one better qualified than yourself."

The messenger and the message all in one; *Times have changed.* Indeed. Miles wished himself elsewhere, anywhere—back sweating blood over his final examinations, for instance. He stifled an unworthy wail, *My home leave . . . !*

Miles rubbed the back of his neck. "Who, ah . . . who is it killed your little girl?" *Meaning, who is it I'm expected to drag out, put up against a wall, and shoot?*

"My husband," she said tonelessly, looking at—through—the polished silvery floorboards.

I knew this was going to be messy. . . .

"She cried and cried," the woman went on, "and wouldn't go to sleep, not nursing well—he shouted at me to shut her up—"

"Then?" Miles prompted, sick to his stomach.

"He swore at me, and went to go sleep at his mother's. He said at least a working man could sleep there. I hadn't slept either. . . ."

This guy sounds like a real winner. Miles had an instant picture of him, a bull of a man with a bullying manner—nevertheless, there was something missing in the climax of the woman's story.

The Count had picked up on it too. He was listening with total attention, his strategy-session look, a slit-eyed intensity of thought you could mistake for sleepiness. That would be a grave mistake. "Were you an eyewitness?" he asked in a deceptively mild tone that put Miles on full alert. "Did you actually see him kill her?"

"I found her dead in the midmorning, lord."

"You went into the bedroom—" Count Vorkosigan led her on.

"We've only got one room." She shot him a look as if doubtful for the first time of his total omniscience. "She had slept, slept at last. I went out to get some brillberries, up the ravine a way. And when I came back . . . I should have taken her with me, but I was so glad she slept at last, didn't want to risk waking her—" Tears leaked from the woman's tightly closed eyes. "I let her sleep when I came back, I was glad to eat and rest, but I began to get full," her hand touched a breast, "and I went to wake her . . ."

"What, were there no marks on her? Not a cut throat?" asked the Count. That was the usual method for these backcountry infanticides, quick and clean compared to, say, exposure.

The woman shook her head. "Smothered, I think,

lord. It was cruel, something cruel. The village Speaker said I must have overlain her, and wouldn't take my plea against Lem. I did not, I did not! She had her own cradle, Lem made it with his own hands when she was still in my belly. . . ." She was close to breaking down.

The Count exchanged a glance with his wife, and a small tilt of his head. Countess Vorkosigan rose smoothly.

"Come, Harra, down to the house. You must wash and rest before Miles takes you home."

The hill woman looked taken aback. "Oh, not in your house, lady!"

"Sorry, it's the only one I've got handy. Besides the guard barracks. The guards are good boys, but you'd make 'em uncomfortable . . ." The Countess eased her out.

"It is clear," said Count Vorkosigan as soon as the women were out of earshot, "that you will have to check out the medical facts before, er, popping off. And I trust you will also have noticed the little problem with a positive identification of the accused. This could be the ideal public-demonstration case we want, but not if there's any ambiguity about it. No bloody mysteries."

"I'm not a coroner," Miles pointed out immediately. If he could wriggle off this hook. . . .

"Quite. You will take Dr. Dea with you."

Lieutenant Dea was the Prime Minister's physician's assistant. Miles had seen him around—an ambitious young military doctor, in a constant state of frustration because his superior would never let him touch his most important patient—oh, he was going to be thrilled with this assignment, Miles predicted morosely.

"He can take his osteo kit with him, too," the Count went on, brightening slightly, "in case of accidents."

"How economical," said Miles, rolling his eyes. "Look, uh—suppose her story checks out and we nail this guy. Do I have to, personally . . . ?"

"One of the liveried men will be your bodyguard. And—if the story checks—the executioner."

That was only slightly better. "Couldn't we wait for the district magistrate?"

"Every judgment the district magistrate makes, he makes in my place. Every sentence his office carries out, is carried out in my name. Someday, it will be done in your name. It's time you gained a clear understanding of the process. Historically, the Vor may be a military caste, but a Vor lord's duties were never only military ones."

No escape. Damn, damn, damn. Miles sighed. "Right. Well . . . we could take the aircar, I suppose, and be up there in a couple of hours. Allow some time to find the right hole. Drop out of the sky on 'em, make the message loud and clear . . . be back before bedtime." Get it over with quickly.

The Count had that slit-eyed look again. "No . . ." he said slowly, "not the aircar, I don't think."

"No roads for a groundcar, up that far. Just trails." He added uneasily—surely his father could not be thinking of—"I don't think I'd cut a very impressive figure of central Imperial authority on foot, sir."

His father glanced up at his crisp dress uniform and smiled slightly. "Oh, you don't do so badly."

"But picture this after three or four days of beating through the bushes," Miles protested. "You didn't see us in Basic. Or smell us."

"I've been there," said the Admiral dryly. "But no, you're quite right. Not on foot. I have a better idea."

My own cavalry troop, thought Miles ironically, turning in his saddle, *just like Grandfather.* Actually, he was pretty sure the old man would have had some acerbic comments about the riders now strung out behind Miles on the wooded trail, once he'd got done rolling on the ground laughing at the equitation being displayed. The Vorkosigan stables had shrunk sadly since the old man was no longer around to take an interest, the polo string sold off, the few remaining ancient and ill-tempered ex-cavalry beats put permanently out to pasture. The handful of riding horses left were retained for their sure-footedness and good manners, not their exotic bloodlines, and kept exercised and gentle for the occasional guest by a gaggle of girls from the village.

Miles gathered his reins, tensed one calf, and shifted his weight slightly, and Fat Ninny responded with a neat half turn and two precise back steps. The thickset roan gelding could not have been mistaken by the most ignorant urbanite for a fiery steed, but Miles adored him, for his dark and liquid eye, his wide velvet nose, his phlegmatic disposition equally unappalled by rushing streams or screaming aircars, but most of all for his exquisite dressage-trained responsiveness. Brains before beauty. Just being around him made Miles calmer, the beast was an emotional blotter, like a purring cat. Miles patted Fat Ninny on the neck. "If anybody asks," he murmured, "I'll tell them your name is Chieftain." Fat Ninny waggled one fuzzy ear, and heaved a whooshing, barrel-chested sigh.

Grandfather had a great deal to do with the unlikely parade Miles now led. The great guerilla general had poured out his youth in these mountains, fighting the Cetagandan invaders to a standstill and then reversing their tide. Anti-flyer heatless seeker-strikers smuggled in at bloody cost from off-planet had a lot more to do with the final victory than cavalry horses, which, according to Grandfather, had saved his forces through the worst winter of that campaign mainly by being edible. But through retroactive romance, the horse had become the symbol of that struggle.

Miles thought his father was being overly optimistic, if he thought Miles was going to cash in thusly on the old man's residual glory. The guerilla caches and camps were shapeless lumps of rust and *trees*, dammit, not just weeds and scrub anymore—they had passed some, earlier in today's ride—the men who had fought that war had long since gone to ground for the last time, just like Grandfather. What was he doing here? It was jump ship duty he wanted, taking him high, high above all this. The future, not the past, held his destiny.

Miles's meditations were interrupted by Dr. Dea's horse, which, taking exception to a branch lying across the logging trail, planted all four feet in an abrupt stop and snorted loudly. Dr. Dea toppled off with a faint cry.

"Hang onto the *reins,*" Miles called, and pressed Fat Ninny back down the trail.

Dr. Dea was getting rather better at falling off, he'd landed more or less on his feet this time. He made a lunge at the dangling reins, but his sorrel mare shied away from his grab. Dea jumped back as she swung on her haunches and then, realizing her freedom, bounced back down the trail, tail bannering, horse body-language for *Nyah, nyah, ya can't catch me!* Dr. Dea, red and furious, ran swearing in pursuit. She broke into a canter.

"No, no, don't run after her!" called Miles.

"How the hell am I supposed to catch her if I don't run after her?" snarled Dea. The space surgeon was not a happy man. "My medkit's on that bloody beast!"

"How do you think you can catch her if you do?" asked Miles. "She can run faster than you can."

At the end of the little column, Pym turned his

horse sideways, blocking the trail. "Just wait, Harra," Miles advised the anxious hill woman in passing. "Hold your horse still. Nothing starts a horse running faster than another running horse."

The other two riders were doing rather better. The woman Harra Csurik sat her horse wearily, allowing it to plod along without interference, but at least riding on balance instead of trying to use the reins as a handle like the unfortunate Dea. Pym, bringing up the rear, was competent if not comfortable.

Miles slowed Fat Ninny to a walk, reins loose, and wandered after the mare, radiating an air of calm relaxation. *Who, me? I don't want to catch you. We're just enjoying the scenery, right. That's it, stop for a bite.* The sorrel mare paused to nibble at a weed, but kept a wary eye on Miles's approach.

At a distance just short of starting the mare bolting off again, Miles stopped Fat Ninny and slid off. He made no move toward the mare, but instead stood still and made a great show of fishing in his pockets. Fat Ninny butted his head against Miles eagerly, and Miles cooed and fed him a bit of sugar. The mare cocked her ears with interest. Fat Ninny smacked his lips and nudged for more. The mare snuffled up for her share. She lipped a cube from Miles's palm as he slid his other arm quietly through the loop of her reins.

"Here you go, Dr. Dea. One horse. No running."

"No fair," wheezed Dea, trudging up. "You had sugar in your pockets."

"Of course I had sugar in my pockets. It's called foresight and planning. The trick of handling horses isn't to be faster than the horse, or stronger than the horse. That pits your weakness against his strengths. The trick is to be smarter than the horse. That pits your strength against his weakness, eh?"

Dea took his reins. "It's snickering at me," he said suspiciously.

"That's nickering, not snickering." Miles grinned. He tapped Fat Ninny behind his left foreleg, and the horse obediently grunted down onto one knee. Miles clambered up readily to his conveniently lowered stirrup.

"Does mine do that?" asked Dr. Dea, watching with fascination.

"Sorry, no."

Dea glowered at his horse. "This animal is an idiot. I shall lead it for a while."

As Fat Ninny lurched back to his four feet Miles suppressed a riding-instructorly comment gleaned from his grandfather's store such as, *Be smarter than the horse, Dea.* Though Dr. Dea was officially sworn to Lord Vorkosigan for the duration of this investigation, Space Surgeon Lieutenant Dea certainly outranked Ensign Vorkosigan. To command older men who outranked one called for a certain measure of tact.

The logging road widened out here, and Miles dropped back beside Harra Csurik. Her fierceness and determination of yesterday morning at the gate seemed to be fading even as the trail rose toward her home. Or perhaps it was simply exhaustion catching up with her. She'd said little all morning, been sunk in silence all afternoon. If she was going to drag Miles all the way up to the back of beyond and then wimp out on him . . .

"What, ah, branch of the Service was your father in, Harra?" Miles began conversationally.

She raked her fingers through her hair in a combing gesture more nervousness than vanity. Her eyes looked out at him through the straw-colored wisps like skittish creatures in the protection of a hedge.

"District Militia, m'lord. I don't really remember him, he died when I was real little."

"In combat?"

She nodded. "In the fighting around Vorbarr Sultana, during Vordarian's Pretendership."

Miles refrained from asking which side he had been swept up on—most foot soldiers had had little choice, and the amnesty had included the dead as well as the living.

"Ah . . . do you have any sibs?"

"No, lord. Just me and my mother left."

A little anticipatory tension eased in Miles's neck. If this judgment indeed drove all the way through to an execution, one misstep could trigger a blood feud among the in-laws. *Not* the legacy of justice the Count intended him to leave behind. So the fewer in-laws involved, the better. "What about your husband's family?"

"He's got seven. Four brothers and three sisters."

"Hm." Miles had a mental flash of an entire team of huge, menacing hill hulks. He glanced back at Pym, feeling a trifle understaffed for his task. He had pointed out this factor to the Count, when they'd been planning this expedition last night.

"The village Speaker and his deputies will be your backup," the Count had said, "just as for the district magistrate on court circuit."

"What if they don't want to cooperate?" Miles had asked nervously.

"An officer who expects to command Imperial troops," the Count had glinted, "should be able to figure out how to extract cooperation from a backcountry headman."

In other words, his father had decided this was a test, and wasn't going to give him any more clues. Thanks, Dad.

"You have no sibs, lord?" said Harra, snapping him back to the present.

"No. But surely that's known, even in the back-beyond."

"They *say* a lot of things about you." Harra shrugged.

Miles bit down on the morbid question in his mouth like a wedge of raw lemon. He would not ask it, he would not . . . he couldn't help himself. "Like what?" forced out past his stiff lips.

"Everyone knows the Count's son is a mutant." Her eyes flicked defiant-wide. "Some said it came from the off-worlder woman he married. Some said it was from radiation from the wars, or a disease from, um, corrupt practices in his youth among his brother-officers—"

That last was a new one to Miles. His brow lifted.

"—but most say he was poisoned by his enemies."

"I'm glad most have it right. It was an assassination attempt using soltoxin gas, when my mother was pregnant with me. But it's not—" *a mutation,* his thought hiccoughed through the well-worn grooves—how many times had he explained this?—*it's teratogenic, not genetic, I'm not a mutant, not . . .* What the hell did a fine point of biochemistry matter to this ignorant, bereaved woman? For all practical purposes—for her purposes—he might as well be a mutant. "—important," he finished.

She eyed him sideways, swaying gently in the clop-a-clop rhythm of her mount. "Some said you were born with no legs, and lived all the time in a float chair in Vorkosigan House. Some said you were born with no bones—"

"—and kept in a jar in the basement, no doubt," Miles muttered.

"But Karal said he'd seen you with your grandfather at Hassadar Fair, and you were only sickly and undersized. Some said your father had got you into the

Service, but others said no, you'd gone off-planet to your mother's home and had your brain turned into a computer and your body fed with tubes, floating in a liquid—"

"I knew there'd be a jar turn up in this story somewhere." Miles grimaced. You *knew you'd be sorry you asked, too, but you went and did it anyway.* She was baiting him, Miles realized suddenly. How *dare* she . . . but there was no humor in her, only a sharp-edged watchfulness.

She had gone out, way out on a limb to lay this murder charge, in defiance of family and local authorities alike, in defiance of established custom. And what had her Count given her for a shield and support, going back to face the wrath of all her nearest and dearest? Miles. Could he handle this? She must be wondering indeed. Or would he botch it, cave and cut and run, leaving her to face the whirlwind of rage and revenge alone?

He wished he'd left her weeping at the gate.

The woodland, fruit of many generations of terraforming forestry, opened out suddenly on a vale of brown native scrub. Down the middle of it, through some accident of soil chemistry, ran a half-kilometer-wide swathe of green and pink—feral roses, Miles realized with astonishment as they rode nearer. Earth roses. The track dove into the fragrant mass of them and vanished.

He took turns with Pym, hacking their way through with their Service bush knives. The roses were vigorous and studded with thick thorns, and hacked back with a vicious elastic recoil. Fat Ninny did his part by swinging his big head back and forth and nipping off blooms and chomping them down happily. Miles wasn't sure just how many he ought to let the big roan eat—just because the species wasn't native to Barrayar didn't mean it wasn't poisonous to horses. Miles sucked at his wounds and reflected upon Barrayar's shattered ecological history.

The fifty thousand Firsters from Earth had only meant to be the spearhead of Barrayar's colonization. Then, through a gravitational anomaly, the wormhole jump through which the colonists had come shifted closed, irrevocably and without warning. The terraforming which had begun, so careful and controlled in the beginning, collapsed along with everything else. Imported Earth plant and animal species had escaped everywhere to run wild, as the humans turned their attention to the most urgent problems of survival. Biologists still mourned the mass extinctions of native species that had followed, the erosions and droughts and floods, but really, Miles thought, over the centuries of the Time of Isolation the fittest of both worlds had fought it out to a perfectly good new balance. If it was alive and covered the ground who cared where it came from?

We are all here by accident. Like the roses.

They camped that night high in the hills, and pushed on in the morning to the flanks of the true mountains. They were now out of the region Miles was personally familiar with from his childhood, and he checked Harra's directions frequently on his orbital survey map. They stopped only a few hours short of their goal at sunset of the second day. Harra insisted she could lead them on in the dusk from here, but Miles did not care to arrive after nightfall, unannounced, in a strange place of uncertain welcome.

He bathed the next morning in a stream, and unpacked and dressed carefully in his new officer's Imperial dress greens. Pym wore the Vorkosigan brown-and-silver livery, and pulled the Count's standard on a telescoping aluminum pole from the recesses of his saddlebag and mounted it on his left stirrup. *Dressed to kill,* thought Miles joylessly. Dr. Dea wore ordinary black fatigues and looked uncomfortable. If they constituted a message, Miles was damned if he knew what it was.

They pulled the horses up at midmorning before a two-room cabin set on the edge of a vast grove of sugar maples, planted who-knew-how-many centuries ago but now raggedly marching up the vale by self-seeding. The mountain air was cool and pure and bright. A few chickens stalked and bobbed in the weeds. An algae-choked wooden pipe from the woods dribbled water into a trough, which overflowed into a squishy green streamlet and away.

Harra slid down and smoothed her skirt and climbed the porch. "Karal?" she called. Miles waited high on horseback for the initial contact. Never give up a psychological advantage.

"Harra? Is that you?" came a man's voice from within. He banged open the door and rushed out. "Where have you been, girl? We've been beating the bushes for you! Thought you'd broke your neck in the scrub somewhere—" He stopped short before the three silent men on horseback.

"You wouldn't write down my charges, Karal," said Harra rather breathlessly. Her hands kneaded her skirt. "So I walked to the district magistrate at Vorkosigan Surleau to Speak them myself."

"Oh, girl," Karal breathed regretfully, "that was a *stupid* thing to do. . . ." His head lowered and swayed, as he stared uneasily at the riders. He was a balding man of maybe sixty, leathery and worn, and his left arm ended in a stump. Another veteran.

"Speaker Serg Karal?" began Miles sternly. "I am the Voice of Count Vorkosigan. I am charged to investigate the crime Spoken by Harra Csurik before the Count's court, namely the murder of her infant daughter Raina. As Speaker of Silvy Vale, you are requested and required to assist me in all matters pertaining to the Count's justice."

At this point Miles ran out of prescribed formalities, and was on his own. That hadn't taken long. He waited. Fat Ninny snuffled. The silver-on-brown cloth of the standard made a few soft snapping sounds, lifted by a vagrant breeze.

"The district magistrate wasn't there," put in Harra, "but the Count was."

Karal was grey-faced, staring. He pulled himself together with an effort, came to a species of attention, and essayed a creaking half-bow. "Who—who are you, sir?"

"Lord Miles Vorkosigan."

Karal's lips moved silently. Miles was no lip reader, but he was pretty sure it came to a dismayed variant of *Oh, shit.* "This is my liveried man Sergeant Pym, and my medical examiner, Lieutenant Dea of the Imperial Service."

"You are my lord Count's son?" Karal croaked.

"The one and only." Miles was suddenly sick of the posing. Surely that was a sufficient first impression. He swung down off Ninny, landing lightly on the balls of his feet. Karal's gaze followed him down, and down. *Yeah, so I'm short. But wait'll you see me dance.* "All right if we water our horses in your trough here?" Miles looped Ninny's reins through his arm and stepped toward it.

"Uh, that's for the people, m'lord," said Karal. "Just a minute and I'll fetch a bucket." He hitched up his baggy trousers and trotted off around the side of the cabin. A minute's uncomfortable silence, then Karal's voice floating faintly. "Where'd you put the goat bucket, Zed?"

Another voice, light and young. "Behind the woodstack, Da." The voices fell to a muffled undertone. Karal came trotting back with a battered aluminum bucket, which he placed beside the trough. He knocked out a wooden plug in the side and a bright stream arced out to splash and fill. Fat Ninny flickered his ears and snuffled and rubbed his big head against Miles, smearing his tunic with red and white horsehairs and nearly knocking him off his feet. Karal glanced up and smiled at the horse, though his smile fell away as his gaze passed on to the horse's owner. As Fat Ninny gulped his drink Miles caught a glimpse of the source of the second voice, a boy of around twelve who flitted off into the woods behind the cabin.

Karal fell to, assisting Miles and Harra and Pym in securing the horses. Miles left Pym to unsaddle and feed, and followed Karal into his house. Harra stuck to Miles like glue, and Dr. Dea unpacked his medical kit and trailed along. Miles's boots rang loud and unevenly on the wooden floorboards.

"My wife, she'll be back in the nooning," said Karal, moving uncertainly around the room as Miles and Dea settled themselves on a bench and Harra curled up with her arms around her knees on the floor beside the fieldstone hearth. "I'll . . . I'll make some tea, m'lord." He skittered back out the door to fill a kettle at the trough before Miles could say, *No, thank you.* No, let him ease his nerves in ordinary movements. Then maybe Miles could begin to tease out how much of this static was social nervousness and how much was—perhaps—guilty conscience. By the time Karal had the kettle on the coals he was noticeably better controlled, so Miles began.

"I'd prefer to commence this investigation immediately, Speaker. It need not take long."

"It need not . . . take place at all, m'lord. The baby's

...y Vale ...body has had a Speaking, not for ...ors of tree piracy over the maple ...ot had a blood feud in all that time."

"I have no intention of starting a blood feud, Karal. I just want the facts."

"That's the thing, m'lord. I'm not so in love with fac s as I used to be. Sometimes, they bite." Karal's eyes were urgent.

Really, the man was doing everything but stand on his head and juggle cats—one-handed—to divert Miles. How overt was his obstruction likely to get?

"Silvy Vale cannot be permitted to have its own little Time of Isolation," said Miles warningly. "The Count's justice is for everyone, now. Even if they're small. And weakly. And have something wrong with them. And cannot even speak for themselves—*Speaker*."

Karal flinched, white about the lips—point taken, evidently. He trudged away up the trail, Pym following watchfully, one hand loosening the stunner in his holster.

They drank the tea while they waited, and Miles pottered about the cabin, looking but not touching. The hearth was the sole source of heat for cooking and washwater. There was a beaten metal sink for washi up, filled by hand from a covered bucket but emp ugh a drainpipe under the porch to join the down out of the trough. The se m, with a double bed and c e more pallets; the ly. The place hung death was natural—there were no marks on her. She was weakly, she had the cat's mouth, who knows what else was wrong with her? She died in her sleep, or by some accident."

"It is remarkable," said Miles dryly, "how often such accidents happen in this district. My father the Count himself has . . . remarked on it."

"There was no call to drag you up here." Karal looked in exasperation at Harra. She sat silent, unmoved by his persuasion.

"It was no problem," said Miles blandly.

"Truly, m'lord," Karal lowered his voice, "I believe the child might have been overlain. 'S no wonder, in her grief, that her mind rejected it. Lem Csurik, he's a good boy, a good provider. She really doesn't want to do this, her reason is just temporarily overset by her troubles."

Harra's eyes, looking out from her hair-thatch, were poisonously cold.

"I begin to see," Miles's voice was mild, encouraging.

Karal brightened slightly. "It all could still be all right. If she will just be patient. Get over her sorrow. Talk to poor Lem. I'm sure he didn't kill the babe. Not rush to something she'll regret."

"I begin to see," Miles let his tone go ice cool, "why Harra Csurik found it necessary to walk four days to get an unbiased hearing. 'You think.' 'You believe.' 'Wh knows what?' Not you, it appears. I hear speculation—accusation—innuendo—assertion. I came for fa Speaker Karal. The Count's justice doesn't tu guesses. It doesn't have to. This isn't the Ti Isolation. Not even in the back-beyond.

"My investigation of the facts will begin n judgment will be—rushed into, befo complete. Confirmati

innocence will come from his own mouth, under fast-penta, administered by Dr. Dea before two witnesses—yourself and a deputy of your choice. Simple, clean, and quick." *And maybe I can be on my way out of this benighted hole before sundown.* "I require you, Speaker, to go now and bring Lem Csurik for questioning. Sergeant Pym will assist you."

Karal killed another moment pouring the boiling water into a big brown pot before speaking. "I'm a travelled man, lord. A twenty-year Service man. But most folks here have never been out of Silvy Vale. Interrogation chemistry might as well be magic to them. They might say it was a false confession, got that way."

"Then you and your deputy can say otherwise. This isn't exactly like the good old days, when confessions were extracted under torture. Karal. Besides, if he's as innocent as you *guess*—he'll clear himself, no?"

Reluctantly, Keral went into the adjoining room. He came back shrugging on a faded Imperial Service uniform jacket with a corporal's rank marked on the collar, the buttons of which did not quite meet across his middle anymore. Preserved, evidently, for such official functions. Even as in Barrayaran custom one saluted the uniform, and not the man in it, so might the wrath engendered by an unpopular duty fall on the office and not the individual who carried it out. Miles appreciated the nuance.

Karal paused at the door. Harra still sat wrapped silence by the hearth, rocking slightly.

M'lord," said Karal. "I've been Sp xteen years

They must pick up broadcasts from the station in Hassadar, maybe the high-power government channels from the capital as well.

No other electricity, of course. Powersat receptors were expensive pieces of precision technology. They would come even here, in time; some communities almost as small, but with strong economic co-ops, already had them. Silvy Vale was obviously still stuck in subsistence-level, and must needs wait till there was enough surplus in the district to gift them, if the surplus was not grabbed off first by some competing want. If only the city of Vorkosigan Vashnoi had not been obliterated by Cetagandan atomics, the whole district could be years ahead, economically. . . .

Miles walked out on the porch and leaned on the rail. Karal's son had returned. Down at the end of the cleared yard Fat Ninny was standing tethered, hip-shot, ears aflop, grunting with pleasure as the grinning boy scratched him vigorously under his halter. The boy looked up to catch Miles watching him, and scooted off fearfully to vanish again in the scrub downslope. "Huh," muttered Miles.

Dr. Dea joined him. "They've been gone a long time. About time to break out the fast-penta?"

"No, your autopsy kit, I should say. I fancy that's what we'll be doing next."

Dea glanced at him sharply. "I thought you sent Pym along to enforce the arrest."

"You can't arrest a man who's not there. Are you a wagering man, Doctor? I'll bet you a mark they don't come back with Csurik. No, hold it—maybe I'm wrong. I hope I'm wrong. Here are three coming back. . . ."

Karal, Pym, and another were marching down the trail. The third was a hulking young man, big-handed, heavy-browed, thick-necked, surly. "Harra," Miles called, "is this your husband?" He looked the part, by

God, just what Miles had pictured. And four brothers just like him—only bigger, no doubt . . .

Harra appeared by Miles's shoulder, and let out her breath. "No, m'lord. That's Alex, the Speaker's deputy."

"Oh." Miles's lips compressed in silent frustration. *Well, I had to give it a chance to be simple.*

Karal stopped beneath him and began a wandering explanation of his empty-handed state. Miles cut him off with a lift of his eyebrows. "Pym?"

"Bolted, m'lord," said Pym laconically. "Almost certainly warned."

"I agree." He frowned down at Karal, who prudently stood silent. Facts first. Decisions, such as how much deadly force to pursue the fugitive with, second. "Harra. How far is it to your burying place?"

"Down by the stream, lord, at the bottom of the valley. About two kilometers."

"Get your kit, Doctor, we're taking a walk. Karal, fetch a shovel."

"M'lord, surely it isn't needful to disturb the peace of the dead," began Karal.

"It is entirely needful. There's a place for the autopsy report right in the Procedural I got from the district magistrate's office. Where I will file my completed report upon this case when we return to Vorkosigan Surleau. I have permission from the next-of-kin—do I not, Harra?"

She nodded numbly.

"I have the two requisite witnesses, yourself and your," *gorilla*, "deputy, we have the doctor and the daylight—if you don't stand there arguing till sundown. All we need is the shovel. Unless you're volunteering to dig with your hand, Karal." Miles's voice was flat and grating and getting dangerous.

Karal's balding head bobbed in his distress. "The—

Another voice, light and young. "Behind the woodstack, Da." The voices fell to a muffled undertone. Karal came trotting back with a battered aluminum bucket, which he placed beside the trough. He knocked out a wooden plug in the side and a bright stream arced out to splash and fill. Fat Ninny flickered his ears and snuffled and rubbed his big head against Miles, smearing his tunic with red and white horsehairs and nearly knocking him off his feet. Karal glanced up and smiled at the horse, though his smile fell away as his gaze passed on to the horse's owner. As Fat Ninny gulped his drink Miles caught a glimpse of the source of the second voice, a boy of around twelve who flitted off into the woods behind the cabin.

Karal fell to, assisting Miles and Harra and Pym in securing the horses. Miles left Pym to unsaddle and feed, and followed Karal into his house. Harra stuck to Miles like glue, and Dr. Dea unpacked his medical kit and trailed along. Miles's boots rang loud and unevenly on the wooden floorboards.

"My wife, she'll be back in the nooning," said Karal, moving uncertainly around the room as Miles and Dea settled themselves on a bench and Harra curled up with her arms around her knees on the floor beside the fieldstone hearth. "I'll . . . I'll make some tea, m'lord." He skittered back out the door to fill a kettle at the trough before Miles could say, *No, thank you.* No, let him ease his nerves in ordinary movements. Then maybe Miles could begin to tease out how much of this static was social nervousness and how much was—perhaps—guilty conscience. By the time Karal had the kettle on the coals he was noticeably better controlled, so Miles began.

"I'd prefer to commence this investigation immediately, Speaker. It need not take long."

"It need not . . . take place at all, m'lord. The baby's

death was natural—there were no marks on her. She was weakly, she had the cat's mouth, who knows what else was wrong with her? She died in her sleep, or by some accident."

"It is remarkable," said Miles dryly, "how often such accidents happen in this district. My father the Count himself has . . . remarked on it."

"There was no call to drag you up here." Karal looked in exasperation at Harra. She sat silent, unmoved by his persuasion.

"It was no problem," said Miles blandly.

"Truly, m'lord," Karal lowered his voice, "I believe the child might have been overlain. 'S no wonder, in her grief, that her mind rejected it. Lem Csurik, he's a good boy, a good provider. She really doesn't want to do this, her reason is just temporarily overset by her troubles."

Harra's eyes, looking out from her hair-thatch, were poisonously cold.

"I begin to see," Miles's voice was mild, encouraging.

Karal brightened slightly. "It all could still be all right. If she will just be patient. Get over her sorrow. Talk to poor Lem. I'm sure he didn't kill the babe. Not rush to something she'll regret."

"I begin to see," Miles let his tone go ice cool, "why Harra Csurik found it necessary to walk four days to get an unbiased hearing. 'You think.' 'You believe.' 'Who knows what?' Not you, it appears. I hear speculation—accusation—innuendo—assertion. I came for *facts*, Speaker Karal. The Count's justice doesn't turn on guesses. It doesn't have to. This isn't the Time of Isolation. Not even in the back-beyond.

"My investigation of the facts will begin now. No judgment will be—rushed into, before the facts are complete. Confirmation of Lem Csurik's guilt or innocence will come from his own mouth, under fast-penta, administered by Dr. Dea before two witnesses—yourself and a deputy of your choice. Simple, clean, and quick." *And maybe I can be on my way out of this benighted hole before sundown.* "I require you, Speaker, to go now and bring Lem Csurik for questioning. Sergeant Pym will assist you."

Karal killed another moment pouring the boiling water into a big brown pot before speaking. "I'm a travelled man, lord. A twenty-year Service man. But most folks here have never been out of Silvy Vale. Interrogation chemistry might as well be magic to them. They might say it was a false confession, got that way."

"Then you and your deputy can say otherwise. This isn't exactly like the good old days, when confessions were extracted under torture. Karal. Besides, if he's as innocent as you *guess*—he'll clear himself, no?"

Reluctantly, Keral went into the adjoining room. He came back shrugging on a faded Imperial Service uniform jacket with a corporal's rank marked on the collar, the buttons of which did not quite meet across his middle anymore. Preserved, evidently, for such official functions. Even as in Barrayaran custom one saluted the uniform, and not the man in it, so might the wrath engendered by an unpopular duty fall on the office and not the individual who carried it out. Miles appreciated the nuance.

Karal paused at the door. Harra still sat wrapped in silence by the hearth, rocking slightly.

"M'lord," said Karal. "I've been Speaker of Silvy Vale for sixteen years now. In all that time nobody has had to go to the district magistrate for a Speaking, not for water rights or stolen animals or swiving or even the time Neva accused Bors of tree piracy over the maple [illegible]. We've not had a blood feud in all that time."

"I have no intention of starting a blood feud, Karal. I just want the facts."

"That's the thing, m'lord. I'm not so in love with fac , as I used to be. Sometimes, they bite." Karal's eyes were urgent.

Really, the man was doing everything but stand on his head and juggle cats—one-handed—to divert Miles. How overt was his obstruction likely to get?

"Silvy Vale cannot be permitted to have its own little Time of Isolation," said Miles warningly. "The Count's justice is for everyone, now. Even if they're small. And weakly. And have something wrong with them. And cannot even speak for themselves—*Speaker.*"

Karal flinched, white about the lips—point taken, evidently. He trudged away up the trail, Pym following watchfully, one hand loosening the stunner in his holster.

They drank the tea while they waited, and Miles pottered about the cabin, looking but not touching. The hearth was the sole source of heat for cooking and washwater. There was a beaten metal sink for washing up, filled by hand from a covered bucket but emptied through a drainpipe under the porch to join the streamlet running down out of the trough. The second room was a bedroom, with a double bed and chests for storage. A loft held three more pallets; the boy around back had brothers, apparently. The place was cramped, but swept, things put away and hung up.

On a side table sat a government-issue audio receiver, and a second and older military model, opened up, apparently in the process of getting minor repairs and a new power pack. Exploration revealed a drawer full of old parts, nothing more complex than for simple audio sets, unfortunately. Speaker Karal must double as Silvy Vale's comm link specialist. How appropria

They must pick up broadcasts from the station in Hassadar, maybe the high-power government channels from the capital as well.

No other electricity, of course. Powersat receptors were expensive pieces of precision technology. They would come even here, in time; some communities almost as small, but with strong economic co-ops, already had them. Silvy Vale was obviously still stuck in subsistence-level, and must needs wait till there was enough surplus in the district to gift them, if the surplus was not grabbed off first by some competing want. If only the city of Vorkosigan Vashnoi had not been obliterated by Cetagandan atomics, the whole district could be years ahead, economically. . . .

Miles walked out on the porch and leaned on the rail. Karal's son had returned. Down at the end of the cleared yard Fat Ninny was standing tethered, hip-shot, ears aflop, grunting with pleasure as the grinning boy scratched him vigorously under his halter. The boy looked up to catch Miles watching him, and scooted off fearfully to vanish again in the scrub downslope. "Huh," muttered Miles.

Dr. Dea joined him. "They've been gone a long time. About time to break out the fast-penta?"

"No, your autopsy kit, I should say. I fancy that's what we'll be doing next."

Dea glanced at him sharply. "I thought you sent Pym along to enforce the arrest."

"You can't arrest a man who's not there. Are you a wagering man, Doctor? I'll bet you a mark they don't come back with Csurik. No, hold it—maybe I'm wrong. I hope I'm wrong. Here are three coming back. . . ."

Karal, Pym, and another were marching down the trail. The third was a hulking young man, big-handed, heavy-browed, thick-necked, surly. "Harra," Miles called, "is this your husband?" He looked the part, by

God, just what Miles had pictured. And four brothers just like him—only bigger, no doubt . . .

Harra appeared by Miles's shoulder, and let out her breath. "No, m'lord. That's Alex, the Speaker's deputy."

"Oh." Miles's lips compressed in silent frustration. *Well, I had to give it a chance to be simple.*

Karal stopped beneath him and began a wandering explanation of his empty-handed state. Miles cut him off with a lift of his eyebrows. "Pym?"

"Bolted, m'lord," said Pym laconically. "Almost certainly warned."

"I agree." He frowned down at Karal, who prudently stood silent. Facts first. Decisions, such as how much deadly force to pursue the fugitive with, second. "Harra. How far is it to your burying place?"

"Down by the stream, lord, at the bottom of the valley. About two kilometers."

"Get your kit, Doctor, we're taking a walk. Karal, fetch a shovel."

"M'lord, surely it isn't needful to disturb the peace of the dead," began Karal.

"It is entirely needful. There's a place for the autopsy report right in the Procedural I got from the district magistrate's office. Where I will file my completed report upon this case when we return to Vorkosigan Surleau. I have permission from the next-of-kin—do I not, Harra?"

She nodded numbly.

"I have the two requisite witnesses, yourself and your," *gorilla*, "deputy, we have the doctor and the daylight—if you don't stand there arguing till sundown. All we need is the shovel. Unless you're volunteering to dig with your hand, Karal." Miles's voice was flat and grating and getting dangerous.

Karal's balding head bobbed in his distress. "The—

the father is the legal next-of-kin, while he lives, and you don't have his—"

"Karal," said Miles.

"M'lord?"

"Take care the grave you dig is not your own. You've got one foot in it already."

Karal's hand opened in despair. "I'll . . . get the shovel, m'lord."

The midafternoon was warm, the air golden and summer-sleepy. The shovel bit with a steady *scrunch-scrunch* through the soil at the hands of Karal's deputy. Downslope, a bright stream burbled away over clean rounded stones. Harra hunkered watching, silent and grim.

When big Alex levered out the little crate—so little!—Sergeant Pym went off for a patrol of the wooded perimeter. Miles didn't blame him. He hoped the soil at that depth had been cool, these last eight days. Alex pried open the box, and Dr. Dea waved him away and took over. The deputy too went off to find something to examine at the far end of the graveyard.

Dea looked the cloth-wrapped bundle over carefully, lifted it out and set it on his tarp laid out on the ground in the bright sun. The instruments of his investigation were arrayed upon the plastic in precise order. He unwrapped the brightly patterned cloths in their special folds, and Harra crept up to retrieve them, straighten and fold them ready for reuse, then crept back.

Miles fingered the handkerchief in his pocket, ready to hold over his mouth and nose, and went to watch over Dea's shoulder. Bad, but not too bad. He'd seen and smelled worse. Dea, filter-masked, spoke procedurals into his recorder, hovering in the air by his shoulder, and made his examination first by eye and gloved touch, then by scanner.

"Here, my lord," said Dea, and motioned Miles closer. "Almost certainly the cause of death, though I'll run the toxin tests in a moment. Her neck was broken. See here on the scanner where the spinal cord was severed, then the bones twisted back into alignment."

"Karal, Alex." Miles motioned them up to witness; they came reluctantly.

"Could this have been accidental?" said Miles.

"Very remotely possible. The realignment had to be deliberate, though."

"Would it have taken long?"

"Seconds only. Death was immediate."

"How much physical strength was required? A big man's or . . ."

"Oh, not much at all. Any adult could have done it, easily."

"Any sufficiently motivated adult." Miles's stomach churned at the mental picture Dea's words conjured up. The little fuzzy head would easily fit under a man's hand. The twist, the muffled cartilaginous crack—if there was one thing Miles knew by heart, it was the exact tactile sensation of breaking bone, oh yes.

"Motivation," said Dea, "is not my department." He paused. "I might note, a careful external examination could have found this. Mine did. An experienced layman—" his eye fell cool on Karal, "paying attention to what he was doing, should not have missed it."

Miles too stared at Karal, waiting.

"Overlain," hissed Harra. Her voice was ragged with scorn.

"M'lord," said Karal carefully, "it's true I suspected the possibility-"

Suspected, hell. You knew.

"But I felt—and still feel, strongly," his eye flashed a wary defiance, "that only more grief would come from a fuss. There was nothing I could do to help the baby at that point. My duties are to the living."

"So are mine, Speaker Karal. As, for example, my duty to the next small Imperial subject in mortal danger from those who should be his or her protectors, for the grave fault of being," Miles flashed an edged smile, "physically different. In Count Vorkosigan's view this is not just a case. This is a test case, fulcrum of a thousand cases. Fuss . . ." He hissed the sibilant; Harra rocked to the rhythm of his voice, "you haven't begun to see *fuss* yet."

Karal subsided as if folded.

There followed an hour of messiness yielding mainly negative data; no other bones were broken, the infant's lungs were clear, her gut and bloodstream free of toxins except those of natural decomposition. Her brain held no secret tumors. The defect for which she had died did not extend to spina bifida, Dea reported. Fairly simple plastic surgery would indeed have corrected the cat's mouth, could she somehow have won access to it. Miles wondered what comfort this confirmation was to Harra; cold, at best.

Dea put his puzzle back together, and Harra rewrapped the tiny body in intricate, meaningful folds. Dea cleaned his tools and placed them in their cases and washed his hands and arms and face thoroughly in the stream, for rather a longer time than needed for just hygiene Miles thought, while the gorilla reburied the box.

Harra made a little bowl in the dirt atop the grave and piled in some twigs and bark scraps and a sawed-off strand of her lank hair.

Miles, caught short, felt in his pockets. "I have no offering on me that will burn," he said apologetically.

Harra glanced up, surprised at even the implied offer. "No matter, m'lord." Her little pile of scraps flared briefly and went out, like her infant Raina's life.

But it does matter, thought Miles.

Peace to you, small lady, after our rude invasions. I will give you a better sacrifice, I swear by my word as Vorkosigan. And the smoke of that burning will rise and be seen from one end of these mountains to the other.

Miles charged Karal and Alex straightly with producing Lem Csurik, and gave Harra Csurik a ride home up behind him on Fat Ninny. Pym accompanied them.

They passed a few scattered cabins on the way. At one a couple of grubby children playing in the yard loped alongside the horses, giggling and making hex signs at Miles, egging each other on to bolder displays, until their mother spotted them and ran out and hustled them indoors with a fearful look over her shoulder. In a weird way it was almost relaxing to Miles, the welcome he'd expected, not like Karal's and Alex's strained, self-conscious, careful not-noticing. Raina's life would not have been an easy one.

Harra's cabin was at the head of a long draw, just before it narrowed into a ravine. It seemed very quiet and isolated, in the dappled shade.

"Are you sure you wouldn't rather go stay with your mother?" asked Miles dubiously.

Harra shook her head. She slid down off Ninny, and Miles and Pym dismounted and followed her in.

The cabin was of a standard design, a single room with a field-stone fireplace and a wide roofed front porch. Water apparently came from the rivulet in the ravine. Pym held up a hand and entered first behind Harra, his hand on his stunner. If Lem Csurik had run, might he have run home first? Pym had been making scanner checks of perfectly innocent clumps of bushes all the way here.

The cabin was deserted. Although not long deserted; it did not have the lingering, dusty silence one would expect of eight days' mournful disoccupation. The remains of a few hasty meals sat on the sinkboard. The bed was slept-in, rumpled and unmade. A few man's garments were scattered about. Automatically Harra began to move about the room, straightening it up, reasserting her presence, her worth. If she could not control the events of her life, at least she might control one small room.

The one untouched item was a cradle that sat beside the bed, little blankets neatly folded. Harra had fled for Vorkosigan Surleau just a few hours after the burial.

Miles wandered about the room, checking the view from the windows. "Will you show me where you went to get your brillberries, Harra?"

She led them up the ravine; Miles timed the hike. Pym divided his attention unhappily between the brush and Miles, alert to catch any bone-breaking stumble. After flinching away from about three aborted protective grabs Miles was ready to tell him to go climb a tree. Still, there was a certain understandable self-interest at work here; if Miles broke a leg it would be Pym who'd be stuck with carrying him out.

The brillberry patch was nearly a kilometer up the ravine. Miles plucked a few seedy red berries and ate them absently, looking around, while Harra and Pym waited respectfully. Afternoon sun slanted through green and brown leaves, but the bottom of the ravine was already grey and cool with premature twilight. The brillberry vines clung to the rocks and hung down invitingly, luring one to risk one's neck reaching. Miles resisted their weedy temptations, not being all that fond of brillberries. "If someone called out from your cabin, you couldn't hear them up here, could you?" remarked Miles.

"No, m'lord."

"About how long did you spend picking?"

"About," Harra shrugged, "a basketful."

The woman didn't own a chrono. "An hour, say. And a twenty-minute climb each way. About a two hour time window, that morning. Your cabin was not locked?"

"Just a latch, m'lord."

"Hm."

Method, motive, and opportunity, the district magistrate's Procedural had emphasized. Damn. The method was established, and almost anybody could have used it. The opportunity angle, it appeared, was just as bad. Anyone at all could have walked up to that cabin, done the deed, and departed, unseen and unheard. It was much too late for an aura detector to be of use, tracing the shining ghosts of movements in and out of that room, even if Miles had brought one.

Facts, hah. They were back to motive, the murky workings of men's minds. Anybody's guess.

Miles had, as per the instructions in the district magistrate's Procedural, been striving to keep an open mind about the accused, but it was getting harder and harder to resist Harra's assertions. She'd been proved right about everything so far.

They left Harra re-installed in her little home, going through the motions of order and the normal routine of life as if they could somehow re-create it, like an act of sympathetic magic.

"Are you sure you'll be all right?" Miles asked, gathering Fat Ninny's reins and settling himself in the saddle. "I can't help but think that if your husband's in the area, he could show up here. You say nothing's been taken, so it's unlikely he's been here and gone before we arrived. Do you want someone to stay with you?"

"No, m'lord." She hugged her broom, on the porch. "I'd . . . I'd like to be alone for a while."

"Well . . . all right. I'll, ah, send you a message if anything important happens."

"Thank you, m'lord." Her tone was unpressing; she really did want to be left alone. Miles took the hint.

At a wide place in the trail back to Speaker Karal's, Pym and Miles rode stirrup to stirrup. Pym was still painfully on the alert for boogies in the bushes.

"My lord, may I suggest that your next logical step be to draft all the able-bodied men in the community for a hunt for this Csurik? Beyond doubt, you've established that the infanticide was a murder."

Interesting turn of phrase, Miles thought dryly. *Even Pym doesn't find it redundant. Oh, my poor Barrayar.* "It seems reasonable at first glance, Sergeant Pym, but has it occurred to you that half the able-bodied men in this community are probably relatives of Lem Csurik's?"

"It might have a psychological effect. Create enough disruption, and perhaps someone would turn him in just to get it over with."

"Hm, possibly. Assuming he hasn't already left the area. He could have been halfway to the coast before we were done at the autopsy."

"Only if he had access to transport." Pym glanced at the empty sky.

"For all we know one of his subcousins had a rickety lightflyer in a shed somewhere. But . . . he's never been out of Silvy Vale. I'm not sure he'd know how to run, where to go. Well, if he has left the district it's a problem for Imperial Civil Security, and I'm off the hook." Happy thought. "But—one of the things that bothers me, a lot, are the inconsistencies in the picture I'm getting of our chief suspect. Have you noticed them?"

"Can't say I have, m'lord."

"Hm. Where did Karal take you, by the way, to arrest this guy?"

"To a wild area, rough scrub and gullies. Half a dozen men were out searching for Harra. They'd just called off their search and were on their way back when we met up with them. By which I concluded our arrival was no surprise."

"Had Csurik actually been there, and fled, or was Karal just ring-leading you in a circle?"

"I think he'd actually been there, m'lord. The men claimed not, but as you point out they were relatives, and besides, they did not, ah, lie well. They were tense. Karal may begrudge you his cooperation, but I don't think he'll quite dare disobey your direct orders. He is a twenty-year man, after all."

Like Pym himself, Miles thought. Count Vorkosigan's personal guard was legally limited to a ceremonial twenty men, but given his political position their function included very practical security. Pym was typical of their number, a decorated veteran of the Imperial Service who had retired to this elite private force. It was not Pym's fault that when he had joined he had stepped into a dead man's shoes, replacing the late Sergeant Bothari. Did anyone in the universe besides himself miss the deadly and difficult Bothari? Miles wondered sadly.

"I'd like to question *Karal* under fast-penta," said Miles morosely. "He displays every sign of being a man who knows where the body's buried."

"Why don't you, then?" asked Pym logically.

"I may come to that. There is, however, a certain unavoidable degradation in a fast-penta interrogation.

If the man's loyal it may not be in our best long-range interest to shame him publicly."

"It wouldn't be in public."

"No, but he would remember being turned into a drooling idiot. I need . . . more information."

Pym glanced back over his shoulder. "I thought you had all the information, by now."

"I have facts. Physical facts. A great big pile of—meaningless, useless facts." Miles brooded. "If I have to fast-penta every back-beyonder in Silvy Vale to get to the bottom of this, I will. But it's not an elegant solution."

"It's not an elegant problem, m'lord," said Pym dryly.

They returned to find Speaker Karal's wife back and in full possession of her home. She was running in frantic circles, chopping, beating, kneading, stoking, and flying upstairs to change the bedding on the three pallets, driving her three sons before her to fetch and run and carry. Dr. Dea, bemused, was following her about trying to slow her down, explaining that they had brought their own tent and food, thank you, and that her hospitality was not required. This produced a most indignant response from Ma Karal.

"My lord's own son come to my house, and I to turn him out in the fields like his horse! I'd be ashamed!" And she returned to her work.

"She seems rather distraught," said Dea, looking over his shoulder.

Miles took him by the elbow and propelled him out onto the porch. "Just get out of her way, Doctor. We're doomed to be Entertained. It's an obligation on both sides. The polite thing to do is sort of pretend we're not here till she's ready for us."

Dea lowered his voice. "It might be better, in light

of the circumstances, if we were to eat only our packaged food."

The chatter of a chopping knife, and a scent of herbs and onions, wafted enticingly through the open window. "Oh, I would imagine anything out of the common pot would be all right, wouldn't you?" said Miles. "If anything really worries you, you can whisk it off and check it, I suppose, but—discreetly, eh? We don't want to insult anyone."

They settled themselves in the homemade wooden chairs, and were promptly served tea again by a boy draftee of ten, Karal's youngest. He had apparently already received private instructions in manners from one or the other of his parents, for his response to Miles's deformities was the same flickering covert not-noticing as the adults, not quite as smoothly carried off.

"Will you be sleeping in my bed, m'lord?" he asked. "Ma says we got to sleep on the porch."

"Well, whatever your ma says, goes," said Miles. "Ah . . . do you like sleeping on the porch?"

"Naw. Last time, Zed kicked me and I rolled off in the dark."

"Oh. Well, perhaps, if we're to displace you, you would care to sleep in our tent by way of trade."

The boy's eyes widened. "Really?"

"Certainly. Why not?"

"Wait'll I tell Zed!" He danced down the steps and shot away around the side of the house. "Zed, hey, Zed . . . !"

"I suppose," said Dea, "we can fumigate it, later. . . ."

Miles's lips twitched. "They're no grubbier than you were at the same age, surely. Or than I was. When I was permitted." The late afternoon was warm. Miles took off his green tunic and hung it on the back of his chair, and unbuttoned the round collar of his cream shirt.

Dea's brows rose. "Are we keeping shopman's hours, then, m'lord, on this investigation? Calling it quits for the day?"

"Not exactly." Miles sipped tea thoughtfully, gazing out across the yard. The trees and treetops fell away down to the bottom of this feeder valley. Mixed scrub climbed the other side of the slope. A crested fold, then the long flanks of a backbone mountain, beyond, rose high and harsh to a summit still flecked with dwindling dirty patches of snow.

"There's still a murderer loose out there somewhere," Dea pointed out helpfully.

"You sound like Pym." Pym, Miles noted, had finished with their horses and was taking his scanner for another walk. "I'm waiting."

"What for?"

"Not sure. The piece of information that will make sense of all this. Look, there's only two possibilities. Csurik's either innocent or he's guilty. If he's guilty, he's not going to turn himself in. He'll certainly involve his relations, hiding and helping him. I can call in reinforcements by comm link from Imperial Civil Security in Hassadar, if I want to. Any time. Twenty men, plus equipment, here by aircar in a couple of hours. Create a circus. Brutal, ugly, disruptive, exciting—could be quite popular. A manhunt, with blood at the end.

"Of course, there's also the possibility that Csurik's innocent, but scared. In which case . . ."

"Yes?"

"In which case, there's still a murderer out there." Miles drank more tea. "I merely note, if you want to catch something, running after it isn't always the best way."

Dea cleared his throat, and drank his tea too.

"In the meantime, I have another duty to carry out. I'm here to be seen. If your scientific spirit is yearning for something to do to while away the hours, try keeping count of the number of Vor-watchers that turn up tonight."

Miles's predicted parade began almost immediately. It was mainly women, at first, bearing gifts as to a funeral. In the absence of a comm link system Miles wasn't sure by what telepathy they managed to communicate with each other, but they brought covered dishes of food, flowers, extra bedding, and offers of assistance. They were all introduced to Miles with nervous curtseys, but seldom lingered to chat; apparently a look was all their curiosity desired. Ma Karal was polite, but made it clear that she had the situation well in hand, and set their culinary offerings well back of her own.

Some of the women had children in tow. Most of these were sent to play in the woods in back, but a small party of whispering boys sneaked back around the cabin to peek up over the rim of the porch at Miles. Miles had obligingly remained on the porch with Dea, remarking that it was a better view, without saying for whom. For a few moments, Miles pretended not to notice his audience, restraining Pym with a hand signal from running them off. Yes, *look well, look your fill,* thought Miles. *What you see is what you're going to get, for the rest of your lives or at any rate mine. Get used to it. . . .* Then he caught Zed Karal's whisper, as self-appointed tour guide to his cohort—"That big one's the one that's come to kill Lem Csurik!"

"Zed," said Miles.

There was an abrupt frozen silence from under the edge of the porch. Even the animal rustlings stopped.

"Come here," said Miles.

To a muted background of dismayed whispers and

nervous giggles, Karal's middle boy slouched warily up on to the porch.

"You three—" Miles's pointing finger caught them in mid-flight, "wait there." Pym added his frown for emphasis, and Zed's friends stood paralyzed, eyes wide, heads lined up at the level of the porch floor as if stuck up on some ancient battlement as a warning to kindred malefactors.

"What did you just say to your friends, Zed?" asked Miles quietly. "Repeat it."

Zed licked his lips. "I jus' said you'd come to kill Lem Csurik, lord." Zed was clearly now wondering if Miles's murderous intent included obnoxious and disrespectful boys as well.

"That is not true, Zed. That is a dangerous lie."

Zed looked bewildered. "But Da—said it."

"What is true, is that I've come to catch the person who killed Lem Csurik's baby daughter. That may be Lem. But it may not. Do you understand the difference?"

"But Harra said Lem did it, and she ought to know; he's her husband and all."

"The baby's neck was broken by someone. Harra thinks Lem, but she didn't see it happen. What you and your friends here have to understand is that I won't make a mistake. I *can't* condemn the wrong person. My own truth drugs won't let me. Lem Csurik has only to come here and tell me the truth to clear himself, if he didn't do it.

"But suppose he did. What should I do with a man who would kill a baby, Zed?"

Zed shuffled. "Well, she was only a mutie. . . ." then shut his mouth and reddened, not looking at Miles.

It was, perhaps, a bit much to ask a twelve-year-old boy to take an interest in any baby, let alone a mutie one . . . *no,* dammit. It wasn't too much. But how to get a hook into that prickly defensive surface? And if Miles couldn't even convince one surly twelve-year-old, how was he to magically transmute a whole District of adults? A rush of despair made him suddenly want to rage. These people were so bloody *impossible.* He checked his temper firmly.

"Your Da was a twenty-year man, Zed. Are you proud that he served the Emperor?"

"Yes, lord." Zed's eyes sought escape, trapped by these terrible adults.

Miles forged on. "Well, these practices—mutie-killing—shame the Emperor, when he stands for Barrayar before the galaxy. I've been out there. I know. They call us all savages, for the crimes of a few. It shames the Count my father before his peers, and Silvy Vale before the District. A soldier gets honor by killing an armed enemy, not a baby. This matter touches my honor as a Vorkosigan, Zed. Besides," Miles's lips drew back on a mirthless grin, and he leaned forward intently in his chair—Zed recoiled as much as he dared—"you will all be astonished at what *only a mutie* can do. *That I* have sworn on my grandfather's grave."

Zed looked more suppressed than enlightened, his slouch now almost a crouch. Miles slumped back in his chair and released him with a weary wave of his hand. "Go play, boy."

Zed needed no urging. He and his companions shot away around the house as though released from springs.

Miles drummed his fingers on the chair arm, frowning into the silence that neither Pym nor Dea dared break.

"These hill-folk are ignorant, lord," offered Pym after a moment.

"These hill-folk are *mine,* Pym. Their ignorance is . . . a shame upon my house." Miles brooded. How had this whole mess become his anyway? He hadn't created it. Historically, he'd only just got here himself. "Their continued ignorance, anyway," he amended in fairness. It still made a burden like a mountain. "Is the message so complex? So difficult? 'You don't have to kill your children anymore.' It's not like we're asking them all to learn—5-Space navigational math." That had been the plague of Miles's last Academy semester.

"It's not easy for them," shrugged Dea. "It's easy for the central authorities to make the rules, but these people have to live every minute of the consequences. They have so little, and the new rules force them to give their margin to marginal people who can't pay back. The old ways were wise, in the old days. Even now you have to wonder how many premature reforms we can afford, trying to ape the galactics."

And what's your definition of a marginal person, Dea? "But the margin is growing," Miles said aloud. "Places like this aren't up against famine every winter any more. They're not isolated in their disasters, relief can get from one district to another under the Imperial seal . . . we're all getting more connected, just as fast as we can. Besides," Miles paused, and added rather weakly, "perhaps you underestimate them."

Dea's brows rose ironically. Pym strolled the length of the porch, running his scanner in yet another pass over the surrounding scrubland. Miles, turning in his chair to pursue his cooling teacup, caught a slight movement, a flash of eyes, behind the casement-hung front window swung open to the summer air—Ma Karal, standing frozen, listening. For how long? Since he'd called her boy Zed, Miles guessed, arresting her attention. She raised her chin as his eyes met hers, sniffed, and shook out the cloth she'd been holding with a snap. They exchanged a nod. She turned back to her work before Dea, watching Pym, noticed her.

✧ ✧ ✧

Karal and Alex returned, understandably, around suppertime.

"I have six men out searching," Karal reported cautiously to Miles on the porch, now well on its way to becoming Miles's official HQ. Clearly, Karal had covered ground since midafternoon. His face was sweaty, lined with physical as well as the underlying emotional strain. "But I think Lem's gone into the scrub. It could take days to smoke him out. There's hundreds of places to lie low out there."

Karal ought to know. "You don't think he's gone to some relative's?" asked Miles. "Surely, if he intends to evade us for long, he has to take a chance on resupply, on information. Will they turn him in when he surfaces?"

"It's hard to say." Karal turned his hand palm-out. "It's . . . a hard problem for 'em, m'lord."

"Hm."

How long would Lem Csurik hang around out there in the scrub, anyway? His whole life—his blown-to-bits life—was all here in Silvy Vale. Miles considered the contrast. A few weeks ago, Csurik had been a young man with everything going for him; a home, a wife, a family on the way, happiness; by Silvy Vale standards, comfort and security. His cabin, Miles had not failed to note, though simple, had been kept with love and energy, and so redeemed from the potential squalor of its poverty. Grimmer in the winter, to be sure. Now Csurik was a hunted fugitive, all the little he had torn away in the twinkling of an eye. With nothing to hold him, would he run away and keep running? With nothing to run to, would he linger near the ruins of his life?

The police force available to Miles a few hours away in Hassadar was an itch in his mind. Was it not time to call them in, before he fumbled this into a worse mess? But . . . if he were meant to solve this by a show of force, why hadn't the Count let him come by aircar on the first day? Miles regretted that two-and-a-half-day ride. It had sapped his forward momentum, slowed him down to Silvy Vale's walking pace, tangled him with time to doubt. Had the Count foreseen it? What did he know that Miles didn't? What *could* he know? Dammit, this test didn't need to be made harder by artificial stumbling blocks, it was bad enough all on its own. *He wants me to be clever,* Miles thought morosely. *Worse, he wants me to be seen to be clever, by everyone here.* He prayed he was not about to be spectacularly stupid instead.

"Very well, Speaker Karal. You've done all you can for today. Knock off for the night. Call your men off too. You're not likely to find anything in the dark."

Pym held up his scanner, clearly about to volunteer its use, but Miles waved him down. Pym's brows rose, editorially. Miles shook his head slightly.

Karal needed no further urging. He dispatched Alex to call off the night search with torches. He remained wary of Miles. Perhaps Miles puzzled him as much as he puzzled Miles? Dourly, Miles hoped so.

Miles was not sure at what point the long summer evening segued into a party. After supper the men began to drift in, Karal's cronies, Silvy Vale's elders. Some were apparently regulars who shared the evening government news broadcasts on Karal's audio set. Too many names, and Miles daren't forget a one. A group of amateur musicians arrived with their homemade mountain instruments, rather breathless, obviously the band tapped for all the major weddings and wakes in Silvy Vale; this all seemed more like a funeral to Miles every minute.

The musicians stood in the middle of the yard and played. Miles's porch-HQ now became his aristocratic box seat. It was hard to get involved with the music when the audience was all so intently watching him. Some songs were serious, some—rather carefully at first—funny. Miles's spontaneity was frequently frozen in mid-laugh by a faint sigh of relief from those around him; his stiffening froze them in turn, self-stymied like two people trying to dodge each other in a corridor.

But one song was so hauntingly beautiful—a lament for lost love—that Miles was struck to the heart. *Elena. . . .* In that moment, old pain transformed to melancholy, sweet and distant; a sort of healing, or at least the realization that a healing had taken place, unwatched. He almost had the singers stop there, while they were perfect, but feared they might think him displeased. But he remained quiet and inward for a time afterward, scarcely hearing their next offering in the gathering twilight.

At least the piles of food that had arrived all afternoon were thus accounted for. Miles had been afraid Ma Karal and her cronies had expected him to get around that culinary mountain all by himself.

At one point Miles leaned on the rail and glanced down the yard to see Fat Ninny at tether, making more friends. A whole flock of pubescent girls were clustered around him, petting him, brushing his fetlocks, braiding flowers and ribbons in his mane and tail, feeding him tidbits, or just resting their cheeks against his warm silky side. Ninny's eyes were half-closed in smug content.

God, thought Miles jealously, *if I had half the sex-appeal of that bloody horse I'd have more girlfriends than my cousin Ivan.* Miles considered, very briefly, the pros and cons of making a play for some unattached female. The striding lords of old and all that . . . no. There were some kinds of stupid he didn't have to be, and that was definitely one of them. The service he had already sworn to one small lady of Silvy Vale was surely all he could bear without breaking; he could feel the strain of it all around him now, like a dangerous pressure in his bones.

He turned to find Speaker Karal presenting a woman to him, far from pubescent; she was perhaps fifty, lean and little, work-worn. She was carefully clothed in an aging best-dress, her greying hair combed back and bound at the nape of her neck. She bit at her lips and cheeks in quick tense motions, half-suppressed in her self-consciousness.

"'S Ma Csurik, m'lord. Lem's mother." Speaker Karal ducked his head and backed away, abandoning Miles without aid or mercy—*Come back, you coward!*

"Ma'am," Miles said. His throat was dry. Karal had set him up, dammit, a public play—no, the other guests were retreating out of earshot too, most of them.

"M'lord," said Ma Csurik. She managed a nervous curtsey.

"Uh . . . do sit down." With a ruthless jerk of his chin Miles evicted Dr. Dea from his chair and motioned the hill woman into it. He turned his own chair to face hers. Pym stood behind them, silent as a statue, tight as a wire. Did he imagine the old woman was about to whip a needler-pistol from her skirts? No—it was Pym's job to imagine things like that for Miles, so that Miles might free his whole mind for the problem at hand. Pym was almost as much an object of study as Miles himself. Wisely, he'd been holding himself apart, and would doubtless continue to do so till the dirty work was over.

"M'lord," said Ma Csurik again, and stumbled again to silence. Miles could only wait. He prayed she wasn't about to come unglued and weep on his knees or some damn thing. This was excruciating. *Stay strong, woman,* he urged silently.

"Lem, he . . ." she swallowed, "I'm sure he didn't kill the babe. There's never been any of that in our family, I swear it! He says he didn't, and I believe him."

"Good," said Miles affably. "Let him come say the same thing to me under fast-penta, and I'll believe him too."

"Come away, Ma," urged a lean young man who had accompanied her and now stood waiting by the steps, as if ready to bolt into the dark at a motion. "It's no good, can't you see." He glowered at Miles.

She shot the boy a quelling frown—another of her five sons?—and turned back more urgently to Miles, groping for words. "My Lem. He's only twenty, lord."

"*I'm* only twenty, Ma Csurik," Miles felt compelled to point out. There was another brief impasse.

"Look, I'll say it again," Miles burst out impatiently. "And again, and again, till the message penetrates all the way back to its intended recipient. I *cannot* condemn an innocent person. My truth drugs won't let me. Lem can clear himself. He has only to come in. Tell him, will you? Please?"

She went stony, guarded. "I . . . haven't seen him, m'lord."

"But you might."

She tossed her head. "So? I might not." Her eyes shifted to Pym and away, as if the sight of him burned. The silver Vorkosigan logos embroidered on Pym's collar gleamed in the twilight like animal eyes, moving only with his breathing. Karal was now bringing lighted lamps onto the porch, but keeping his distance still.

"Ma'am," said Miles tightly. "The Count my father has ordered me to investigate the murder of your granddaughter. If your son means so much to you, how can his child mean so little? Was she . . . your first grandchild?"

Her face was sere. "No, lord. Lem's older sister, she has two. *They're* all right," she added with emphasis.

Miles sighed. "If you truly believe your son is innocent of this crime, you must help me prove it. Or—do you doubt?"

She shifted uneasily. There was doubt in her eyes—she didn't know, blast it. Fast-penta would be useless on her, for sure. As Miles's magic wonder drug, much counted-upon, fast-penta seemed to be having wonderfully little utility in this case so far.

"Come away, Ma," the young man urged again. "It's no good. The mutie lord came up here for a killing. They have to have one. It's a show."

Damn straight, thought Miles acidly. He was a perceptive young lunk, that one.

Ma Csurik let herself be persuaded away by her angry and embarrassed son plucking at her arm. She paused on the steps, though, and shot bitterly over her shoulder, "It's all so easy for you, isn't it?"

My head hurts, thought Miles.

There was worse to come before the evening ended.

The new woman's voice was grating, low and angry. "Don't you talk down to me, Serg Karal. I got a right for one good look at this mutie lord."

She was tall and stringy and tough. *Like her daughter,* Miles thought. She had made no attempt to freshen up. A faint reek of summer sweat hung about her working dress. And how far had she walked? Her grey hair hung in a switch down her back, a few strands escaping the tie. If Ma Csurik's bitterness had been a stabbing pain behind the eyes, this one's rage was a wringing knot in the gut.

She shook off Karal's attempted restraint and stalked up to Miles in the lamplight. "So."

"Uh . . . this is Ma Mattulich, m'lord," Karal introduced her. "Harra's mother."

Miles rose to his feet, managed a short formal nod. "How do you do, madam." He was very conscious of being a head shorter. She had once been of a height with Harra, Miles estimated, but her aging bones were beginning to pull her down.

She merely stared. She was a gum-leaf chewer, by the faint blackish stains around her mouth. Her jaw worked now on some small bit, tiny chomps, grinding too hard. She studied him openly, without subterfuge or the least hint of apology, taking in his head, his neck, his back, his short and crooked legs. Miles had the unpleasant illusion that she saw right through to all the healed cracks in his brittle bones as well. Miles's chin jerked up twice in the twitchy, nervous-involuntary tic that he was sure made him look spastic, before he controlled it with an effort.

"All right," said Karal roughly, "you've seen. Now come away, for God's sake, Mara." His hand opened in apology to Miles. "Mara, she's been pretty distraught over all this, m'lord. Forgive her."

"Your only grandchild," said Miles to her, in an effort to be kind, though her peculiar anguish repelled kindness with a scraped and bleeding scorn. "I understand your distress, ma'am. But there will be justice for little Raina. That I have sworn."

"How can there be justice *now?*" she raged, thick and low. "It's too late—a world too late—for justice, mutie lordling. What use do I have for your damned justice *now?*"

"Enough, Mara!" Karal insisted. His brows drew down and his lips thinned, and he forced her away and escorted her firmly off his porch.

The last lingering remnant of visitors parted for her with an air of respectful mercy, except for two lean teenagers hanging on the fringes who drew away as if avoiding poison. Miles was forced to revise his mental image of the Brothers Csurik. If those two were another sample, there was no team of huge menacing hill hulks after all. They were a team of little skinny menacing hill squirts instead. Not really an improvement, they looked like they could move as fast as striking ferrets if they had to. Miles's lips curled in frustration.

The evening's entertainments ended finally, thank God, close to midnight. Karal's last cronies marched off into the woods by lantern light. The repaired and re-powered audio set was carried off by its owner with many thanks to Karal. Fortunately it had been a mature and sober crowd, even somber, no drunken brawls or anything. Pym got the Karal boys settled in the tent, took a last patrol around the cabin, and joined Miles and Dea in the loft. The pallets' stuffing had been spiked with fresh scented native herbs, to which Miles hoped devoutly he was not allergic. Ma Karal had wanted to turn her own bedroom over to Miles's exclusive lordly use, exiling herself and her husband to the porch too, but fortunately Pym had been able to persuade her that putting Miles in the loft, flanked by Dea and himself, was to be preferred from a security standpoint.

Dea and Pym were soon snoring, but sleep eluded Miles. He tossed on his pallet as he turned his ploys of the day, such as they had been, over and over in his mind. Was he being too slow, too careful, too conservative? This wasn't exactly good assault tactics, surprise with a superior force. The view he'd gained of the terrain from Karal's porch tonight had been ambiguous at best.

On the other hand, it did no good to charge off across a swamp, as his fellow cadet and cousin Ivan Vorpatril had demonstrated so memorably once on summer maneuvers. It had taken a heavy hovercab with a crane to crank the six big, strong, healthy, fully field-equipped young men of Ivan's patrol out of the chest-high gooey black mud. Ivan had got his revenge simultaneously, though, when the cadet "sniper" they had been attacking fell out of his tree and broke his arm while laughing hysterically as they sank slowly and beautifully into the ooze. Ooze that a little guy, with his laser rifle wrapped in his loincloth, could swim across like a frog. The war games umpire had ruled it a draw. Miles rubbed his forearm and grinned in memory, and faded out at last.

Miles awoke abruptly and without transition deep in the night with a sense of something wrong. A faint orange glow shimmered in the blue darkness of the loft. Quietly, so as not to disturb his sleeping companions, he rose on his pallet and peered over the edge into the main room. The glow was coming through the front window.

Miles swung onto the ladder and padded downstairs for a look outdoors. "Pym," he called softly.

Pym shot awake with a snort. "M'lord?" he said, alarmed.

"Come down here. Quietly. Bring your stunner."

Pym was by his side in seconds. He slept in his trousers with his stunner holster and boots by his pillow. "What the hell—?" Pym muttered, looking out too.

The glow was from fire. A pitchy torch, flung to the top of Miles's tent set up in the yard, was burning quietly. Pym lurched toward the door, then controlled his movements as the same realization came to him as had to Miles. Theirs was a Service-issue tent, and its combat-rated synthetic fabric would neither melt nor burn.

Miles wondered if the person who'd heaved the torch had known that. Was this some arcane warning, or a singularly inept attack? If the tent had been ordinary fabric, and Miles in it, the intended result might not have been trivial. Worse with Karal's boys in it—a bursting blossom of flame—Miles shuddered.

Pym loosened his stunner in his holster and stood poised by the front door. "How long?"

"I'm not sure. Could have been burning like that for ten minutes before it woke me."

Pym shook his head, took a slight breath, raised his scanner, and vaulted into the fire-gilded darkness.

"Trouble, m'lord?" Speaker Karal's anxious voice came from his bedroom door.

"Maybe. Wait—" Miles halted him as he plunged for the door. "Pym's running a patrol with a scanner and a stunner. Wait'll he calls the all-clear, I think. Your boys may be safer inside the tent."

Karal came up to the window, caught his breath, and swore.

Pym returned in a few minutes. "There's no one within a kilometer, now," he reported shortly. He helped Karal take the goat bucket and douse the torch. The boys, who had slept through the fire, woke at its quenching.

"I think maybe it was a bad idea to lend them my tent," said Miles from the porch in a choked voice. "I am profoundly sorry, Speaker Karal. I didn't think."

"This should never . . ." Karal was spluttering with anger and delayed fright, "this should *never* have happened, m'lord. I apologize for . . . for Silvy Vale." He turned helplessly, peering into the darkness. The night sky, star-flecked, lovely, was threatening now.

The boys, once the facts penetrated their sleepiness, thought it was all just great, and wanted to return to the tent and lie in wait for the next assassin. Ma Karal, shrill and firm, herded them indoors instead and made them bed down in the main room. It was an hour before they stopped complaining at the injustice of it and went back to sleep.

Miles, keyed up nearly to the point of gibbering, did not sleep at all. He lay stiffly on his pallet, listening to Dea, who slept breathing heavily, and Pym, feigning sleep for courtesy and scarcely seeming to breathe at all.

Miles was about to suggest to Pym that they give up and go out on the porch for the rest of the night when the silence was shattered by a shrill squeal, enormously loud, pain-edged, from outside.

"The horses!" Miles spasmed to his feet, heart racing, and beat Pym to the ladder. Pym cut ahead of him by dropping straight over the side of the loft into an elastic crouch, and beat him to the door. There, Pym's trained bodyguard's reflexes compelled him to try to thrust Miles back inside. Miles almost bit him. "Go, dammit! I've got a weapon!"

Pym, good intentions frustrated, swung out the cabin door with Miles on his heels. Halfway down the yard they split to each side as a massive snorting shape loomed out of the darkness and nearly ran them down; the sorrel mare, loose again. Another squeal pierced the night from the lines where the horses were tethered.

"Ninny?" Miles called, panicked. It was Ninny's voice making those noises, the like of which Miles had not heard since the night a shed had burned down at Vorkosigan Surleau with a horse trapped inside. "Ninny!"

Another grunting squeal, and a thunk like someone splitting a watermelon with a mallet. Pym staggered back, inhaling with difficulty, a resonant deep stutter, and tripped to the ground where he lay curled up around himself. Not killed outright, apparently, because between gasps he was managing to swear lividly. Miles dropped to the ground beside him, checked his skull—no, thank God it had been Pym's chest Ninny's hoof had hit with that alarming sound. The bodyguard only had the wind knocked out of him, maybe a cracked rib. Miles more sensibly ran around to the *front* of the horse lines. "Ninny!"

Fat Ninny was jerking his head against his rope, attempting to rear. He squealed again, his white-rimmed eyes gleaming in the darkness. Miles ran to his head. "Ninny, boy! What is it?" His left hand slid up the rope to Ninny's halter, his right stretched to stroke Ninny's shoulder soothingly. Fat Ninny flinched, but stopped trying to rear, and stood trembling. The horse shook his head. Miles's face and chest were suddenly spattered with something hot and dark and sticky.

"Dea!" Miles yelled. "*Dea!*"

Nobody slept through this uproar. Six people tumbled off the porch and down the yard, and not one of them thought to bring a light . . . no, the brilliant flare of a cold light sprang from between Dr. Dea's fingers, and Ma Karal was struggling even now to light a lantern. "Dea, get that damn light over here!" Miles demanded, and stopped to choke his voice back down an octave to its usual carefully cultivated deeper register.

Dea galloped up and thrust the light toward Miles, then gasped, his face draining. "My lord! Are you shot?" In the flare the dark liquid soaking Miles's shirt glowed suddenly scarlet.

"Not me," Miles said, looking down at his chest in horror. A flash of memory turned his stomach over, cold at the vision of another blood-soaked death, that of the late Sergeant Bothari whom Pym had replaced. Would never replace.

Dea spun. "Pym?"

"He's all right," said Miles. A long inhaling wheeze rose from the grass a few meters off, the exhalation punctuated with obscenities. "But he got kicked by the horse. Get your medkit!" Miles peeled Dea's fingers off the cold light, and Dea dashed back to the cabin.

Miles held the light up to Ninny, and swore in a sick whisper. A huge cut, a third of a meter long and of unknown depth, scored Ninny's glossy neck. Blood soaked his coat and runneled down his foreleg. Miles's fingers touched the wound fearfully; his hands spread on either side, trying to push it closed, but the horse's skin was elastic and it pulled apart and bled profusely as Fat Ninny shook his head in pain. Miles grabbed the horse's nose—"Hold still, boy!" Somebody had been going for Ninny's jugular. And had almost made it; Ninny—tame, petted, friendly, trusting Ninny—would not have moved from the touch until the knife bit deep.

Karal was helping Pym to his feet as Dr. Dea returned. Miles waited while Dea checked Pym over, then called, "Here, Dea!"

Zed, looking quite as horrified as Miles, helped to hold Ninny's head as Dea made inspection of the cut. "I took tests," Dea complained *sotto voce* as he worked. "I beat out twenty-six other applicants, for the honor of becoming the Prime Minister's personal physician. I have practiced the procedures of seventy separate possible medical emergencies, from coronary thrombosis to attempted assassination. Nobody—*nobody*—told me my duties would include sewing up a damned horse's neck in the middle of the night in the middle of a howling wilderness. . . ." But he kept working as he complained, so Miles didn't quash him, but kept gently petting Ninny's nose, and hypnotically rubbing the hidden pattern of his muscles, to soothe and still him. At last Ninny relaxed enough to rest his slobbery chin on Miles's Shoulder.

"Do horses get anesthetics?" asked Dea plaintively, holding his medical stunner as if not sure just what to do with it.

"This one does," said Miles stoutly. "You treat him just like a person, Dea. This is the last animal that the Count my grandfather personally trained. He named him. I watched him get born. We trained him together. Grandfather had me pick him up and hold him every day for a week after he was foaled, till he got too big. Horses are creatures of habit, Grandfather said, and take first impressions to heart. Forever after Ninny thought I was bigger than he was."

Dea sighed and made busy with anesthetic stun, cleansing solution, antibiotics, muscle relaxants, and biotic glue. With a surgeon's touch, he shaved the edges of the cut and placed the reinforcing net. Zed held the light anxiously.

"The cut is clean," said Dea, "but it will undergo a lot of flexing—I don't suppose it can very well be immobilized, in this position? No, hardly. This should do. If he were a human, I'd tell him to rest at this point."

"He'll be rested," Miles promised firmly. "Will he be all right now?"

"I suppose so. How the devil should I know?" Dea looked highly aggrieved, but his hand sneaked out to recheck his repairs.

"General Piotr," Miles assured him, "would have been very pleased with your work." Miles could hear him in his head now, snorting, *Damned technocrats. Nothing but horse doctors with a more expensive set of toys.* Grandfather would have loved being proved right. "You, ah . . . never met my grandfather, did you?"

"Before my time, my lord," said Dea. "I've studied his life and campaigns, of course."

"Of course."

Pym had a hand-light now, and was limping with Karal in a slow spiral around the horse lines, inspecting the ground. Karal's eldest boy had recaptured the sorrel mare and brought her back and re-tethered her. Her tether had been torn loose, not cut; had the mysterious attacker's choice of equine victim been random, or calculated? How calculated? Was Ninny attacked as a mere symbol of his master, or had the person known how passionately Miles loved the animal? Was this vandalism, a political statement, or an act of precisely directed, subtle cruelty?

What have I ever done to you? Miles's thought howled silently to the surrounding darkness.

"They got away, whoever it was," Pym reported. "Out of scanner range before I could breathe again. My apologies, m'lord. They don't seem to have dropped anything on the ground."

There had to have been a knife, at least. A knife, its haft gory with horse blood in a pattern of perfect fingerprints, would have been extremely convenient just now. Miles sighed.

Ma Karal drifted up and eyed Dea's medkit, as he cleaned and repacked it. "All that," she muttered under her breath, "for a horse. . . ."

Miles refrained, barely, from leaping to a hot defense of the value of this particular horse. How many people in Silvy Vale had Ma Karal seen suffer and die, in her lifetime, for lack of no more medical technology than what Dea was carrying under his arm just now?

Guarding his horse, Miles watched from the porch as dawn crept over the landscape. He had changed his shirt and washed off. Pym was inside getting his ribs taped. Miles sat with his back to the wall and a stunner on his lap as the night mists slowly grew grey. The valley was a blur, fog-shrouded, the hills darker rolls of fog beyond. Directly overhead, grey thinned to a paling blue. The day would be fine and hot once the fog burned away.

It was surely time now to call out the troops from Hassadar. This was getting just too weird. His bodyguard was half out of commission—true, it was Miles's horse that had rendered him so, not the mystery attacker. But just because the attacks hadn't been fatal didn't mean they hadn't been intended so. Perhaps a third attack would be brought off more expertly. Practice makes perfect.

Miles felt unstrung with nervous exhaustion. How had he let a mere horse become such a handle on his emotions? Bad, that, almost unbalanced—yet Ninny's was surely one of the truly innocent pure souls Miles had ever known. Miles remembered the other innocent in the case then, and shivered in the damp. *It was cruel, lord, something cruel. . . .* Pym was right, the bushes could be crawling with Csurik assassins right now.

Dammit, the bushes *were* crawling—over there, a movement, a damping wave of branch lashing in recoil from—what? Miles's heart lurched in his chest. He adjusted his stunner to full power, slipped silently off the porch, and began his stalk, crouching low, taking advantage of cover wherever the long grasses of the yard had not been trampled flat by the activities of the last day, and night. Miles froze like a predatory cat as a shape seemed to coalesce out of the mist.

A lean young man, not too tall, dressed in the baggy trousers that seemed to be standard here, stood wearily by the horse lines, staring up the yard at Karal's cabin. He stood so for a full two minutes without moving. Miles held a bead on him with his stunner. If he dared make one move toward Ninny . . .

The young man walked back and forth uncertainly, then crouched on his heels, still gazing up the yard. He pulled something from the pocket of his loose jacket—Miles's finger tightened on the trigger—but he only put it to his mouth and bit. An apple. The crunch carried clearly in the damp air, and the faint perfume of its juices. He ate about half, then stopped, seeming to have trouble swallowing. Miles checked the knife at his belt, made sure it was loose in its sheath. Ninny's nostrils widened, and he nickered hopefully, drawing the young man's attention. He rose and walked over to the horse.

The blood pulsed in Miles's ears, louder than any other sound. His grip on the stunner was damp and white-knuckled. The young man fed Ninny his apple. The horse chomped it down, big jaw rippling under his skin, then cocked his hip, dangled one hind hoof, and sighed hugely. If he hadn't seen the man eat off the fruit first Miles might have shot him on the spot. It couldn't be poisoned. . . . The man made to pet Ninny's neck, then his hand drew back in startlement as he encountered Dea's dressing. Ninny shook his head uneasily. Miles rose slowly and stood waiting. The man scratched Ninny's ears instead, looked up one last time at the cabin, took a deep breath, stepped forward, saw Miles, and stood stock-still.

"Lem Csurik?" said Miles.

A pause, a frozen nod. "Lord Vorkosigan?" said the young man. Miles nodded in turn.

Csurik swallowed. "Vor lord," he quavered, "do you keep your word?"

What a bizarre opening. Miles's brows climbed. Hell, go with it. "Yes. Are you coming in?"

"Yes and no, m'lord."

"Which?"

"A bargain, lord. I must have a bargain, and your word on it."

"If you killed Raina . . ."

"No, lord. I swear it. I didn't."

"Then you have nothing to fear from me."

Lem Csurik's lips thinned. What the devil could this hill man find ironic? How dare he find irony in Miles's confusion? Irony, but no amusement.

"Oh, lord," breathed Csurik, "I wish that were so. But I have to prove it to Harra. Harra must believe me—you have to make her believe me, lord!"

"You have to make me believe you first. Fortunately, that isn't hard. You come up to the cabin and make that same statement under fast-penta, and I will rule you cleared."

Csurik was shaking his head.

"Why not?" said Miles patiently. That Csurik had turned up at all was strong circumstantial indication of his innocence. Unless he somehow imagined he could beat the drug. Miles would be patient for, oh, three or four seconds at least. Then, by God, he'd stun him, drag him inside, tie him up till he came round, and get to the bottom of this before breakfast.

"The drug—they say you can't hold anything back."

"It would be pretty useless if you could."

Csurik stood silent a moment.

"Are you trying to conceal some lesser crime on your conscience? Is that the bargain you wish to strike? An amnesty? It . . . might be possible. If it's short of another murder, that is."

"No, lord. I've never killed anybody!"

"Then maybe we can deal. Because if you're innocent, I need to know as soon as possible. Because it means my work isn't finished here."

"That's . . . that's the trouble, m'lord." Csurik shuffled, then seemed to come to some internal decision and stood sturdily. "I'll come in and risk your drug. And I'll answer anything about me you want to ask. But you have to promise—swear!—you won't ask me about . . . about anything else. Anybody else."

"Do you know who killed your daughter?"

"Not for sure." Csurik threw his head back defiantly. "I didn't see it. I have guesses."

"I have guesses too."

"That's as may be, lord. Just so's they don't come from my mouth. That's all I ask."

Miles bolstered his stunner, and rubbed his chin. "Hm." A very slight smile turned one corner of his lip. "I admit, it would be more—elegant—to solve this case by reason and deduction than brute force. Even so tender a force as fast-penta."

Csurik's head lowered. "I don't know elegant, lord. But I don't want it to be from my mouth."

Decision bubbled up in Miles, straightening his spine. Yes. He *knew,* now. He had only to run through the proofs, step by chained step. Just like 5-Space math. "Very well. I swear by my word as Vorkosigan, I shall confine my questions to the facts to which you were an eyewitness. I will not ask you for conjectures about persons or events for which you were not present. There, will that do?"

Csurik bit his lip. "Yes, lord. If you keep your word."

"Try me," suggested Miles. His lips wrinkled back on a vulpine smile, absorbing the implied insult without comment.

Csurik climbed the yard beside Miles as if to an executioner's block. Their entrance created a tableau of astonishment among Karal and his family, clustered around their wooden table where Dea was treating Pym. Pym and Dea looked rather blanker, till Miles made introduction: "Dr. Dea, get out your fast-penta. Here's Lem Csurik come to talk with us."

Miles steered Lem to a chair. The hill man sat with his hands clenched. Pym, a red and purpling bruise showing at the edges of the white tape circling his chest, took up his stunner and stepped back.

Dr. Dea muttered under his breath to Miles as he got out the hypospray. "How'd you *do* that?"

Miles's hand brushed his pocket. He pulled out a sugar cube and held it up, and grinned through the C of his thumb and finger. Dea snorted, but pursed his lips with reluctant respect.

Lem flinched as the hypospray hissed on his arm, as if he expected it to hurt.

"Count backwards from ten," Dea instructed. By the time Lem reached three, he had relaxed; at zero, he giggled.

"Karal, Ma Karal, Pym, gather round," said Miles. "You are my witnesses. Boys, stay back and stay quiet. No interruptions, please."

Miles ran through the preliminaries, half a dozen questions designed to set up a rhythm and kill time while the fast-penta took full effect. Lem Csurik grinned foolishly, lolling in his chair, and answered them all with sunny goodwill. Fast-penta interrogation had been part of Miles's military intelligence course at the Service Academy. The drug seemed to be working exactly as advertised, oddly enough.

"Did you return to your cabin that morning, after you spent the night at your parents?"

"Yes, m'lord." Lem smiled.

"About what time?"

"Midmorning."

Nobody here had a chrono, that was probably as precise an answer as Miles was likely to get. "What did you do when you got there?"

"Called for Harra. She was gone, though. It frightened me that she was gone. Thought she might've run out on me." Lem hiccoughed. "I want my Harra."

"Later. Was the baby asleep?"

"She was. She woke up when I called for Harra. Started crying again. It goes right up your spine."

"What did you do then?"

Lem's eyes widened. "I got no milk. She wanted Harra. There's nothing I could do for her."

"Did you pick her up?"

"No, lord, I let her lay. There was nothing I could do for her. Harra, she'd hardly let me touch her, she was that nervous about her. Told me I'd drop her or something."

"You didn't shake her, to stop her screaming?"

"No, lord, I let her lay. I left to look down the path for Harra."

"Then where did you go?"

Lem blinked. "My sister's. I'd promised to help haul wood for a new cabin. Bella—m'other sister—is getting married, y'see, and—"

He was beginning to wander, as was normal for this drug. "Stop," said Miles. Lem fell silent obediently, swaying slightly in his chair. Miles considered his next question carefully. He was approaching the fine line, here. "Did you meet anyone on the path? Answer yes or no."

"Yes."

Dea was getting excited. "Who? Ask him who!"

Miles held up his hand. "You can administer the antagonist now, Dr. Dea."

"Aren't you going to ask him? It could be vital!"

"I can't. I gave my word. Administer the antagonist now, Doctor!"

Fortunately, the confusion of two interrogators stopped Lem's mumbled willing reply to Dea's question.

Dea, bewildered, pressed his hypospray against Lem's arm. Lem's eyes, half-closed, snapped open within seconds. He sat up straight and rubbed his arm, and his face.

"Who did you meet on the path?" Dea asked him directly.

Lem's lips pressed tight; he looked for rescue to Miles.

Dea looked too. "Why won't you ask him?"

"Because I don't need to," said Miles. "I know precisely who Lem met on the path, and why he went on and not back. It was Raina's murderer. As I shall shortly prove. And—witness this, Karal, Ma Karal—that information did not come from Lem's mouth. Confirm!"

Karal nodded slowly. "I . . . see, m'lord. That was . . . very good of you."

Miles gave him a direct stare, his mouth set in a tight smile. "And when is a mystery no mystery at all?"

Karal reddened, not replying for a moment. Then he said, "You may as well keep on like you're going, m'lord. There's no stopping you now, I suppose."

"No."

Miles sent runners to collect the witnesses, Ma Karal in one direction, Zed in a second, Speaker Karal and his eldest in a third. He had Lem wait with Pym, Dea, and himself. Having the shortest distance to cover, Ma Karal arrived back first, with Ma Csurik and two of her sons in tow.

His mother fell on Lem, embracing him and then looking fearfully over her shoulder at Miles. The younger brothers hung back, but Pym had already moved between them and the door.

"It's all right, Ma." Lem patted her on the back. "Or . . . anyway, I'm all right. I'm clear. Lord Vorkosigan believes me."

She glowered at Miles, still holding Lem's arm. "You didn't let the mutie lord give you that poison drug, did you?"

"Not poison," Miles denied. "In fact, the drug may have saved his life. That damn near makes it a medicine, I'd say. However," he turned toward Lem's two younger brothers, and folded his arms sternly. "I would like to know which of you young morons threw the torch on my tent last night?"

The younger one whitened; the elder, hotly indignant, noticed his brother's expression and cut his denial off in midsyllable. "You didn't!" he hissed in horror.

"Nobody," said the white one. "Nobody did."

Miles raised his eyebrows. There followed a short, choked silence.

"Well, *nobody* can make his apologies to Speaker and Ma Karal, then," said Miles, "since it was their sons who were sleeping in the tent last night. I and my men were in the loft."

The boy's mouth opened in dismay. The youngest Karal stared at the pale Csurik brother, his age-mate, and whispered importantly, "You, Dono! You idiot, didn't ya know that tent wouldn't burn? It's real Imperial Service issue!"

Miles clasped his hands behind his back, and fixed the Csuriks with a cold eye. "Rather more to the point, it was attempted assassination upon your Count's heir, which carries the same capital charge of treason as an attempt upon the Count himself. Or perhaps Dono didn't think of that?"

Dono was thrown into flummoxed confusion. No need for fast-penta here, the kid couldn't carry off a lie worth a damn. Ma Csurik now had hold of Dono's arm too, without letting go of Lem's; she looked as frantic as a hen with too many chicks, trying to shelter them from a storm.

"I wasn't trying to kill you, lord!" cried Dono.

"What were you trying to do, then?"

"You'd come to kill Lem. I wanted to . . . make you go away. Frighten you away. I didn't think anyone would really get hurt—I mean, it was only a tent!"

"You've never seen anything burn down, I take it. Have you, Ma Csurik?"

Lem's mother nodded, lips tight, clearly torn between a desire to protect her son from Miles, and a desire to beat Dono till he bled for his potentially lethal stupidity.

"Well, but for a chance, you could have killed or horribly injured three of your friends. Think on that, please. In the meantime, in view of your youth and ah, apparent mental defectiveness, I shall hold the treason charge. In return, Speaker Karal and your parents shall be responsible for your good behavior in future, and decide what punishment is appropriate."

Ma Csurik melted with relief and gratitude. Dono looked like he'd rather have been shot. His brother poked him, and whispered, "Mental defective!" Ma Csurik slapped the taunter on the side of his head, suppressing him effectively.

"What about your horse, m'lord?" asked Pym.

"I . . . do not suspect them of the business with the horse," Miles replied slowly. "The attempt to fire the tent was plain stupidity. The other was . . . a different order of calculation altogether."

Zed, who had been permitted to take Pym's horse, returned then with Harra up behind him. Harra entered Speaker Karal's cabin, saw Lem, and stopped with a bitter glare. Lem stood openhanded, his eyes wounded, before her.

"So, lord," Harra said. "You caught him." Her jaw was clenched in joyless triumph.

"Not exactly," said Miles. "He came here and turned

himself in. He's made his statement under fast-penta, and cleared himself. Lem did not kill Raina."

Harra turned from side to side. "But I saw he'd been there! He'd left his jacket, and took his good saw and wood planer away with him. I knew he'd been back while I was out! There must be something wrong with your drug!"

Miles shook his head. "The drug worked fine. Your deduction was correct as far as it went, Lem did visit the cabin while you were out. But when he left, Raina was still alive, crying vigorously. It wasn't Lem."

She swayed. "Who, then?"

"I think you know. I think you've been working very hard to deny that knowledge, hence your excessive focus on Lem. As long as you were sure it was Lem, you didn't have to think about the other possibilities."

"But who else would care?" Harra cried. "Who else would bother?"

"Who, indeed?" sighed Miles. He walked to the front window and glanced down the yard. The fog was clearing in the full light of morning. The horses were moving uneasily. "Dr. Dea, would you please get a second dose of fast-penta ready?" Miles turned, paced back to stand before the fireplace, its coals still banked for the night. The faint heat was pleasant on his back.

Dea was staring around, the hypospray in his hand, clearly wondering to whom to administer it. "My lord?" he queried, brows lowering in demand for explanation.

"Isn't it obvious to you, Doctor?" Miles asked lightly.

"*No*, my lord." His tone was slightly indignant.

"Nor to you, Pym?"

"Not . . . entirely, m'lord." Pym's glance, and stunner aim, wavered uncertainly to Harra.

"I suppose it's because neither of you ever met my grandfather," Miles decided. "He died just about a year before you entered my father's service, Pym. He was born at the very end of the Time of Isolation, and lived through every wrenching change this century has dealt to Barrayar. He was called the last of the Old Vor, but really, he was the first of the new. He changed with the times, from the tactics of horse cavalry to that of flyer squadrons, from swords to atomics, and he changed *successfully.* Our present freedom from the Cetagandan occupation is a measure of how fiercely he could adapt, then throw it all away and adapt again. At the end of his life he was called a conservative, only because so much of Barrayar had streamed past him in the direction he had led, prodded, pushed, and pointed all his life.

"He changed, and adapted, and bent with the wind of the times. Then, in his age—for my father was his youngest and sole surviving son, and did not himself marry till middle-age—in his age, he was hit with me. And he had to change again. And he couldn't.

"He begged for my mother to have an abortion, after they knew more or less what the fetal damage would be. He and my parents were estranged for five years after I was born. They didn't see each other or speak or communicate. Everyone thought my father moved us to the Imperial Residence when he became Regent because he was angling for the throne, but in fact it was because the Count my grandfather denied him the use of Vorkosigan House. Aren't family squabbles jolly fun? Bleeding ulcers run in my family, we give them to each other." Miles strolled back to the window and looked out. Ah, yes. Here it came.

"The reconciliation was gradual, when it became quite clear there would be no other son," Miles went on. "No dramatic denouement. It helped when the medics got me walking. It was essential that I tested out bright. Most important of all, I never let him see me give up."

Nobody had dared interrupt this lordly monologue, but it was clear from several expressions that the point of it was escaping them. Since half the point was to kill time, Miles was not greatly disturbed by their failure to track. Footsteps sounded on the wooden porch outside. Pym moved quietly to cover the door with an unobscured angle of fire.

"Dr. Dea," said Miles, sighting through the window, "would you be so kind as to administer that fast-penta to the first person through the door, as they step in?"

"You're not waiting for a volunteer, my lord?"

"Not this time."

The door swung inward, and Dea stepped forward, raising his hand. The hypospray hissed. Ma Mattulich wheeled to face Dea, the skirts of her work dress swirling around her veined calves, hissing in return—"You dare!" Her arm drew back as if to strike him, but slowed in mid-swing and failed to connect as Dea ducked out of her way. This unbalanced her, and she staggered. Speaker Karal, coming in behind, caught her by the arm and steadied her. "You dare!" she wailed again, then turned to see not only Dea but all the other witnesses waiting; Ma Csurik, Ma Karal, Lem, Harra, Pym. Her shoulders sagged, and then the drug cut in and she just stood, a silly smile fighting with anguish for possession of her harsh face.

The smile made Miles ill, but it was the smile he needed. "Sit her down, Dea, Speaker Karal."

They guided her to the chair lately vacated by Lem Csurik. She was fighting the drug desperately, flashes of resistance melting into flaccid docility. Gradually the docility became ascendant, and she sat draped in the chair, grinning helplessly. Miles sneaked a peek at Harra. She stood white and silent, utterly closed.

For several years after the reconciliation Miles had never been left with his grandfather without his personal bodyguard. Sergeant Bothari had worn the Count's livery, but been loyal to Miles alone, the one man dangerous enough—some said, crazy enough—to stand up to the great General himself. There was no need, Miles decided, to spell out to these fascinated people just what interrupted incident had made his parents think Sergeant Bothari a necessary precaution. Let General Piotr's untarnished reputation serve—Miles, now. As *he* willed. Miles's eyes glinted.

Lem lowered his head. "If I had known—if I had guessed—I wouldn't have left them alone together, m'lord. I thought—Harra's mother would take care of her. I couldn't have—I didn't know *how*—"

Harra did not look at him. Harra did not look at anything.

"Let us conclude this." Miles sighed. Again, he requested formal witness from the crowd in the room, and cautioned against interruptions, which tended to unduly confuse a drugged subject. He moistened his lips and turned to Ma Mattulich.

Again, he began with the standard neutral questions, name, birth-date, parents' names, checkable biographical facts. Ma Mattulich was harder to lull than the cooperative Lem had been, her responses scattered and staccato. Miles controlled his impatience with difficulty. For all its deceptive ease, fast-penta interrogation required skill, skill and patience. He'd got too far to risk a stumble now. He worked his questions up gradually to the first critical ones.

"Were you there, when Raina was born?"

Her voice was low and drifting, dreamy. "The birth came in the night. Lem, he went for Jean the midwife. The midwife's son was supposed to go for me but he fell back to sleep. I didn't get there till morning, and then it was too late. They'd all seen."

"Seen what?"

"The cat's mouth, the dirty mutation. Monsters in us. Cut them out. Ugly little man." This last, Miles realized, was an aside upon himself. Her attention had hung up on him, hypnotically. "Muties make more muties, they breed faster, overrun . . . I saw you watching the girls. You want to make mutie babies on clean women, poison us all. . . ."

Time to steer her back to the main issue. "Were you ever alone with the baby after that?"

"No, Jean she hung around. Jean knows me, she knew what I wanted. None of her damn business. And Harra was always there. Harra must not know. Harra must not . . . why should she get off so soft? The poison must be in her. Must have come from her Da, I lay only with her Da and they were all wrong but the one."

Miles blinked. "What were all wrong?" Across the room Miles saw Speaker Karal's mouth tighten. The headman caught Miles's glance and stared down at his own feet, absenting himself from the proceedings. Lem, his lips parted in absorption, and the rest of the boys were listening with alarm. Harra hadn't moved.

"All my babies," Ma Mattulich said.

Harra looked up sharply at that, her eyes widening.

"Was Harra not your only child?" Miles asked. It was an effort to keep his voice cool, calm; he wanted to shout. He wanted to be gone from here. . . .

"No, of course not. She was my only clean child, I thought. I thought, but the poison must have been hidden in her. I fell on my knees and thanked God when she was born clean, a clean one at last, after so many, so much pain. . . . I thought I had finally been punished enough. She was such a pretty baby, I thought it was over at last. But she must have been mutie after all, hidden, tricksy, sly. . . ."

"How many," Miles choked, "babies did you have?"

"Four, besides Harra my last."

"And you killed all four of them?" Speaker Karal, Miles saw, gave a slow nod to his feet.

"No!" said Ma Mattulich. Indignation broke through the fast-penta wooze briefly. "Two were born dead already, the first one, and the twisted-up one. The one with too many fingers and toes, and the one with the bulgy head, those I cut. Cut out. My mother, she watched over me to see I did it right. Harra, I made it soft for Harra. I did it for her."

"So you have in fact murdered not one infant, but three?" said Miles frozenly. The younger witnesses in the room, Karal's boys and the Csurik brothers, looked horrified. The older ones, Ma Mattulich's contemporaries, who must have lived through the events with her, looked mortified, sharing her shame. Yes, they all must have known.

"Murdered?" said Ma Mattulich. "No! I cut them out. I had to. I had to do the right thing." Her chin lifted proudly, then drooped. "Killed my babies, to please, to please . . . I don't know who. And now you call me a murderer? Damn you! What use is your justice to me *now?* I needed it then—where were you then?" Suddenly, shockingly, she burst into tears, which wavered almost instantly into rage. "If mine must die then so must hers! Why should she get off so soft? Spoiled her . . . I tried my best, I did my best, it's not fair. . . ."

The fast-penta was not keeping up with this . . . no, it was working, Miles decided, but her emotions were too overwhelming. Upping the dose might level her emotional surges, at some risk of respiratory arrest, but it would not elicit any more complete a confession. Miles's belly was trembling, a reaction he trusted he concealed. It had to be completed now.

"Why did you break Raina's neck, instead of cutting her throat?"

"Harra, she must not know," said Ma Mattulich. "Poor baby. It would look like she just died. . . ."

Miles eyed Lem, Speaker Karal. "It seems a number of others shared your opinion that Harra should not know."

"I didn't want it to be from my mouth," repeated Lem sturdily.

"I wanted to save her double grief, m'lord," said Karal. "She'd had so much. . . ."

Miles met Harra's eyes at that. "I think you all underestimate her. Your excessive tenderness insults both her intelligence and will. She comes from a tough line, that one."

Harra inhaled, controlling her own trembling. She gave Miles a short nod, as if to say *Thank you, little man.* He returned her a slight inclination of the head, *Yes, I understand.*

"I'm not sure yet where justice lies in this case," said Miles, "but this I swear to you, the days of cooperative concealment are over. No more secret crimes in the night. Daylight's here. And speaking of crimes in the night," he turned back to Ma Mattulich, "*was* it you who tried to cut my horse's throat last night?"

"I tried," said Ma Mattulich, calmer now in a wave of fast-penta mellowness, "but it kept rearing up on me."

"Why my *horse?*" Miles could not keep exasperation from his voice, though a calm, even tone was enjoined upon fast-penta interrogators by the training manual.

"I couldn't get at you," said Ma Mattulich simply.

Miles rubbed his forehead. "Retroactive infanticide by proxy?" he muttered.

"You," said Ma Mattulich, and her loathing came through even the nauseating fast-penta cheer, "*you* are the worst. All I went through, all I did, all the grief, and you come along at the end. A mutie made lord over us all, and all the rules changed, betrayed at the end by an off-worlder woman's weakness. You make it all for *nothing*. Hate you. Dirty mutie . . ." Her voice trailed off in a drugged mumble.

Miles took a deep breath, and looked around the room. The stillness was profound, and no one dared break it.

"I believe," he said, "that concludes my investigation into the facts of this case."

The mystery of Raina's death was solved.

The problem of justice, unfortunately, remained.

Miles took a walk.

The graveyard, though little more than a crude clearing in the woodland, was a place of peace and beauty in the morning light. The stream burbled endlessly, shifting green shadows and blinding brilliant reflections. The faint breeze that had shredded away the last of the night fog whispered in the trees, and the tiny short-lived creatures that everyone on Barrayar but biologists called bugs sang and twittered in the patches of native scrub.

"Well, Raina," Miles sighed, "and what do I do now?" Pym lingered by the borders of the clearing, giving Miles room. "It's all right," Miles assured the tiny grave. "Pym's caught me talking to dead people before. He may think I'm crazy, but he's far too well trained to say so."

Pym in fact did not look happy, nor altogether well. Miles felt rather guilty for dragging him out; by rights the man should be resting in bed, but Miles had desperately needed this time alone. Pym wasn't just suffering the residual effect of having been kicked by Ninny. He had been silent ever since Miles had extracted the confession from Ma Mattulich. Miles was unsurprised. Pym had steeled himself to play executioner to their imagined hill bully; the substitution of a mad grandmother as his victim had clearly given him pause. He would obey whatever order Miles gave him, though, Miles had no doubt of that.

Miles considered the peculiarities of Barrayaran law, as he wandered about the clearing, watching the stream and the light, turning over an occasional rock with the toe of his boot. The fundamental principle was clear; the spirit was to be preferred over the letter, truth over technicalities. Precedent was held subordinate to the judgment of the man on the spot. Alas, the man on the spot was himself. There was no refuge for him in automated rules, no hiding behind *the law says* as if the law were some living overlord with a real Voice. The only voice here was his own.

And who would be served by the death of that half-crazed old woman? Harra? The relationship between mother and daughter had been wounded unto death by this, Miles had seen that in their eyes, yet still Harra had no stomach for matricide. Miles rather preferred it that way, having her standing by his ear crying for bloody revenge would have been enormously distracting just now. The obvious justice made a damn poor reward for Harra's courage in reporting the crime. Raina? Ah. That was more difficult.

"I'd like to lay the old gargoyle right there at your feet, small lady," Miles muttered to her. "Is it your desire? Does it serve you? What *would* serve you?" Was this the great burning he had promised her?

What judgment would reverberate along the entire Dendarii mountain range? Should he indeed sacrifice these people to some larger political statement, regardless of their wants? Or should he forget all that, make his judgment serve only those directly involved? He scooped up a stone and flung it full force into the stream. It vanished invisibly in the rocky bed.

He turned to find Speaker Karal waiting by the edge of the graveyard. Karal ducked his head in greeting and approached cautiously.

"So, m'lord," said Karal.

"Just so," said Miles.

"Have you come to any conclusion?"

"Not really." Miles gazed around. "Anything less than Ma Mattulich's death seems . . . inadequate justice, and yet . . . I cannot see who her death would serve."

"Neither could I. That's why I took the position I did in the first place."

"No . . ." said Miles slowly, "no, you were wrong in that. For one thing, it very nearly got Lem Csurik killed. I was getting ready to pursue him with deadly force at one point. It almost destroyed him with Harra. Truth is better. Slightly better. At least it isn't a fatal error. Surely I can do . . . something with it."

"I didn't know what to expect of you, at first," admitted Karal.

Miles shook his head. "I meant to make changes. A difference. Now . . . I don't know."

Speaker Karal's balding forehead wrinkled. "But we are changing."

"Not enough. Not fast enough."

"You're young yet, that's why you don't see how much, how fast. Look at the difference between Harra and her mother. God—look at the difference between Ma Mattulich and *her* mother. *There* was a harridan." Speaker Karal shuddered. "I remember her, all right. And yet, she was not so unusual, in her day. So far from having to make change, I don't think you could stop it if you tried. The minute we finally get a powersat receptor up here, and get on the comm net, the past will be done and over. As soon as the kids see the future—their future—they'll be mad after it. They're already lost to the old ones like Ma Mattulich. The old ones know it, too, don't believe they don't know it. Why d'you think we haven't been able to get at least a small unit up here yet? Not just the cost. The old ones are fighting it. They call it off-planet corruption, but it's really the future they fear."

"There's so much still to be done."

"Oh, yes. We are a desperate people, no lie. But we have hope. I don't think you realize how much you've done, just by coming up here."

"I've done nothing," said Miles bitterly. "Sat around, mostly. And now, I swear, I'm going to end up doing more nothing. And then go home. Hell!"

Speaker Karal pursed his lips, looked at his feet, at the high hills. "You are doing something for us every minute. Mutie lord. Do you think you are invisible?"

Miles grinned wolfishly. "Oh, Karal, I'm a one-man band, I am. I'm a parade."

"As you say, just so. Ordinary people need extraordinary examples. So they can say to themselves, well, if he can do *that,* I can surely do *this.* No excuses."

"No quarter, yes, I know that game. Been playing it all my life."

"I think," said Karal, "Barrayar needs you. To go on being just what you are."

"Barrayar will eat me, if it can."

"Yes," said Karal, his eyes on the horizon, "so it will." His gaze fell to the graves at his feet. "But it swallows us all in the end, doesn't it? You will outlive the old ones."

"Or in the beginning." Miles pointed down. "Don't tell *me* who I'm going to outlive. Tell Raina."

Karal's shoulders slumped. "True. S'truth. Make your judgment, lord. I'll back you."

✧ ✧ ✧

Miles assembled them all in Karal's yard for his Speaking, the porch now having become his podium. The interior of the cabin would have been impossibly hot and close for this crowd, suffocating with the afternoon sun beating on the roof, though outdoors the light made them squint. They were all here, everyone they could round up, Speaker Karal, Ma Karal, their boys, all the Csuriks, most of the cronies who had attended last night's funereal festivities, men, women, and children. Harra sat apart. Lem kept trying to hold her hand, though from the way she flinched it was clear she didn't want to be touched. Ma Mattulich sat displayed by Miles's side, silent and surly, flanked by Pym and an uncomfortable-looking Deputy Alex.

Miles jerked up his chin, settling his head on the high collar of his dress greens, as polished and formal as Pym's batman's expertise could make him. The Imperial Service uniform that Miles had earned. Did these people know he had earned it, or did they all imagine it a mere gift from his father, nepotism at work? Damn what they thought. He knew. He stood before his people, and gripped the porch rail.

"I have concluded the investigation of the charges laid before the Count's Court by Harra Csurik of the murder of her daughter Raina. By evidence, witness, and her own admission, I find Mara Mattulich guilty of this murder, she having twisted the infant's neck until it broke, and then attempted to conceal that crime. Even when that concealment placed her son-in-law Lem Csurik in mortal danger from false charges. In light of the helplessness of the victim, the cruelty of the method, and the cowardly selfishness of the attempted concealment, I can find no mitigating excuse for the crime.

"In addition, Mara Mattulich by her own admission testifies to two previous infanticides, some twenty years ago, of her own children. These facts shall be announced by Speaker Karal in every corner of Silvy Vale, until every subject has been informed."

He could feel Ma Mattulich's glare boring into his back. Yes, *go on and hate me, old woman. I will bury you yet, and you know it,* He swallowed, and continued, the formality of the language a sort of shield before him.

"For this unmitigated crime, the only proper sentence is death. And I so sentence Mara Mattulich. But in light of her age and close relation to the next-most-injured party in the case, Harra Csurik, I choose to hold the actual execution of that sentence. Indefinitely." Out of the corner of his eye Miles saw Pym let out, very carefully and covertly, a sigh of relief. Harra combed at her straw-colored bangs with her fingers and listened intently.

"But she shall be as dead before the law. All her property, even to the clothes on her back, now belongs to her daughter Harra, to dispose of as she wills. Mara Mattulich may not own property, enter contracts, sue for injuries, nor exert her will after death in any testament. She shall not leave Silvy Vale without Harra's permission. Harra shall be given power over her as a parent over a child, or as in senility. In Harra's absence Speaker Karal will be her deputy. Mara Mattulich shall be watched to see she harms no other child.

"Further. She shall die without sacrifice. No one, not Harra nor any other, shall make a burning for her when she goes into the ground at last. As she murdered her future, so her future shall return only death to her spirit. She will die as the childless do, without remembrance."

A low sigh swept the older members of the crowd before Miles. For the first time, Mara Mattulich bent her stiff neck.

Some, Miles knew, would find this only spiritually symbolic. Others would see it as literally lethal, according to the strength of their beliefs. The literal-minded, such as those who saw mutation as a sin to be violently expiated. But even the less superstitious, Miles saw in their faces, found the meaning clear. So.

Miles turned to Ma Mattulich, and lowered his voice. "Every breath you take from this moment on is by my mercy. Every bite of food you eat, by Harra's charity. By charity and mercy—such as you did not give—you shall live. Dead woman."

"Some mercy. Mutie lord." Her growl was low, weary, beaten.

"You get the point," he said through his teeth. He swept her a bow, infinitely ironic, and turned his back on her. "I am the Voice of Count Vorkosigan. This concludes my Speaking."

Miles met Harra and Lem afterward, in Speaker Karal's cabin.

"I have a proposition for you." Miles controlled his nervous pacing and stood before them. "You're free to turn it down, or think about it for a while. I know you're very tired right now." As *are we all.* Had he really been in Silvy Vale only a day and a half? It seemed like a century. His head ached with fatigue. Harra was red-eyed too. "First of all, you can read and write?"

"Some," Harra admitted. "Speaker Karal taught us some, and Ma Lannier."

"Well, good enough. You wouldn't be starting completely blind. Look. A few years back Hassadar started a teacher's college. It's not very big yet, but it's begun. There are some scholarships. I can swing one your way, if you will agree to live in Hassadar for three years of intense study."

"Me!" said Harra. "I couldn't go to a college! I barely know . . . any of that stuff."

"Knowledge is what you're supposed to have coming out, not going in. Look, they know what they're dealing with in this district. They have a lot of remedial courses. It's true, you'd have to work harder, to catch up with the town-bred and the lowlanders. But I know you have courage, and I know you have will. The rest is just picking yourself up and ramming into the wall again and again until it falls down. You get a bloody forehead, so what? You can do it, I swear you can."

Lem, sitting beside her, looked worried. He captured her hand again. "Three years?" he said in a small voice. "Gone away?"

"The school stipend isn't that much," said Miles. "But Lem, I understand you have carpenter's skills. There's a building boom going on in Hassadar right now. Hassadar's going to be the next Vorkosigan Vashnoi, I think. I'm certain you could get a job. Between you, you could live."

Lem looked at first relieved, then extremely worried. "But they all use power tools—computers—robots. . . ."

"By no means. And they weren't all born knowing how to use that stuff either. If they can learn it, you can. Besides, the rich pay well for hand-work, unique one-off items, if the quality's good. I can see you get a start, which is usually the toughest moment. After that you should be able to figure it out all right."

"To leave Silvy Vale . . ." said Harra in a dismayed tone.

"Only in order to return. That's the other half of the bargain. I can send a comm unit up here, a small one with a portable power pack that lasts a year. Somebody'd have to hump down to Vorkosigan Surleau to replace it annually, no big problem. The whole setup wouldn't cost much more than oh, a new lightflyer." Such as the shiny red one Miles had coveted in a dealer's showroom in Vorbarr Sultana, very suitable for a graduation present, he had pointed out to his parents. The credit chit was sitting in the top drawer of his dresser in the lake house at Vorkosigan Surleau right now. "It's not a massive project like installing a powersat receptor for the whole of Silvy Vale or anything. The holovid would pick up the educational satellite broadcasts from the capital; set it up in some central cabin, add a couple of dozen lap-links for the kids, and you've got an instant school. All the children would be required to attend, with Speaker Karal to enforce it, though once they'd discovered the holovid you'd probably have to beat them to make them go home. I, ah," Miles cleared his throat, "thought you might name it the Raina Csurik Primary School."

"Oh," said Harra, and began to cry for the first time that grueling day. Lem patted her clumsily. She returned the grip of his hand at last.

"I can send a lowlander up here to teach," said Miles. "I'll get one to take a short-term contract, till you're ready to come back. But he or she won't understand Silvy Vale like you do. Wouldn't understand *why*. You—you already know. You know what they can't teach in any lowland college."

Harra scrubbed her eyes, and looked up—not very far up—at him. "You went to the Imperial Academy."

"I did." His chin jerked up.

"Then I," she said shakily, "can manage . . . Hassadar Teacher's College." The name was awkward in her mouth. At first. "At any rate—I'll try, m'lord."

"I'll bet on you," Miles agreed. "Both of you. Just, ah," a smile sped across his mouth and vanished, "stand up straight and speak the truth, eh?"

Harra blinked understanding. An answering half-smile lit her tired face, equally briefly. "I will. Little man."

Fat Ninny rode home by air the next morning, in a horse van, along with Pym. Dr. Dea went along with his two patients, and his nemesis the sorrel mare. A replacement bodyguard had been sent with the groom who flew the van from Vorkosigan Surleau, and stayed with Miles to help him ride the remaining two horses back down. Well, Miles thought, he'd been considering a camping trip in the mountains with his cousin Ivan as part of his home leave anyway. The liveried man was the laconic veteran Esterhazy, whom Miles had known most of his life; excellent company for a man who didn't want to talk about it, unlike Ivan you could almost forget he was there. Miles wondered if Esterhazy's assignment had been random chance, or a mercy of the Count's. Esterhazy was good with horses.

They camped overnight by the river of roses. Miles walked up the vale in the evening light, desultorily looking for the spring of it; indeed, the floral barrier did seem to peter out a couple of kilometers upstream, merging into slightly less impassable scrub. Miles plucked a rose, checked to make sure that Esterhazy was nowhere in sight, and bit into it curiously. Clearly, he was not a horse. A cut bunch would probably not survive the trip back as a treat for Ninny. Ninny could settle for oats.

Miles watched the evening shadows flowing up along the backbone of the Dendarii range, high and massive in the distance. How small those mountains looked from space! Little wrinkles on the skin of a globe he could cover with his hand, all their crushing mass made invisible. Which was illusory, distance or nearness?

Distance, Miles decided. Distance was a damned lie. Had his father known this? Miles suspected so.

He contemplated his urge to throw all his money, not just a lightflyer's worth, at those mountains; to quit it all and go teach children to read and write, to set up a free clinic, a powersat net, or all of these at once. But Silvy Vale was only one of hundreds of such communities buried in these mountains, one of thousands across the whole of Barrayar. Taxes squeezed from this very district helped maintain the very elite military school he'd just spent—how much of their resources in? How much would he have to give back just to make it even, now? He was himself a planetary resource, his training had made him so, and his feet were set on their path.

What God means you to do, Miles's theist mother claimed, could be deduced from the talents He gave you. The academic honors, Miles had amassed by sheer brute work. But the war games, outwitting his opponents, staying one step ahead—a necessity, true, he had no margin for error—the war games had been an unholy joy. War had been no game here once, not so long ago. It might be so again. What you did best, that was what was wanted from you. God seemed to be lined up with the Emperor on that point, at least, if no other.

Miles had sworn his officer's oath to the Emperor less than two weeks ago, puffed with pride at his achievement. In his secret mind he had imagined himself keeping that oath through blazing battle, enemy torture, what-have-you, even while sharing cynical cracks afterwards with Ivan about archaic dress swords and the sort of people who insisted on wearing them.

But in the dark of subtler temptations, those which hurt without heroism for consolation, he foresaw, the

Emperor would no longer be the symbol of Barrayar in his heart.

Peace to you, small lady, he thought to Raina. *You've won a twisted poor modern knight, to wear your favor on his sleeve. But it's a twisted poor world we were both born into, that rejects us without mercy and ejects us without consultation. At least I won't just tilt at windmills for you. I'll send in sappers to mine the twirling suckers, and blast them into the sky. . . .*

He knew who he served now. And why he could not quit. And why he must not fail.

The Vor Game

For Mom.

And with thanks to
Charles Marshall
for firsthand accounts
of arctic engineering, and
William Melgaard
for comments on war and
wargames

CHAPTER ONE

"Ship duty!" chortled the ensign four ahead of Miles in line. Glee lit his face as his eyes sped down his orders, the plastic flimsy rattling slightly in his hands. "I'm to be junior weaponry officer on the Imperial Cruiser *Commodore Vorhalas.* Reporting at once to Tanery Base Shuttleport for orbital transfer." At a pointed prod he removed himself with an unmilitary skip from the way of the next man in line, still hissing delight under his breath.

"Ensign Plause." The aging sergeant manning the desk managed to look bored and superior at the same time, holding the next packet up with deliberation between thumb and forefinger. How long had he been holding down this post at the Imperial Military Academy? Miles wondered. How many hundreds—thousands—of young officers had passed under his bland eye at this first supreme moment of their careers? Did they all start to look alike after a few years? The same fresh green uniforms. The same shiny blue plastic rectangles of shiny new-won rank armoring the high collars. The same hungry eyes, the go-to-hell graduates of the Imperial Services' most elite school with visions of military destiny dancing in their heads. *We don't just march on the future, we charge it.*

Plause stepped aside, touched his thumbprint to the lock-pad, and unzipped his envelope in turn.

"Well?" said Ivan Vorpatril, just ahead of Miles in line. "Don't keep us in suspense."

"Language school," said Plause, still reading.

Plause spoke all four of Barrayar's native languages perfectly already. "As student or instructor?" Miles inquired.

"Student."

"Ah, ha. It'll be galactic languages, then. Intelligence will be wanting you, after. You're bound off-planet for sure," said Miles.

"Not necessarily," said Plause. "They could just sit me in a concrete box somewhere, programming translating computers till I go blind." But hope gleamed in his eyes.

Miles charitably did not point out the major drawback of Intelligence, the fact that you ended up working for Chief of Imperial Security Simon Illyan, the man who remembered *everything*. But perhaps on Plause's level he would not encounter the acerb Illyan.

"Ensign Lubachik."

Lubachik was the second most painfully earnest man Miles had ever met; Miles was therefore unsurprised when Lubachik zipped open his envelope and choked, "ImpSec. The advanced course in Security and Counter-assassination."

"Ah, palace guard school," said Ivan with interest, kibbitzing over Lubachik's shoulder.

"That's quite an honor," Miles observed. "Illyan

usually pulls his students from the twenty-year men with rows of medals."

"Maybe Emperor Gregor asked Illyan for someone nearer his own age," suggested Ivan, "to brighten the landscape. Those prune-faced fossils Illyan usually surrounds him with would give *me* depressive fits. Don't let on you have a sense of humor, Lubachik, I think it's an automatic disqualification."

Lubachik was in no danger of losing the posting if that were so, Miles reflected.

"Will I really meet the Emperor?" Lubachik asked. He turned nervous eyes on Miles and Ivan.

"You'll probably get to watch him eat breakfast every day," said Ivan. "Poor sod." Did he mean Lubachik, or Gregor? Gregor, definitely.

"You Vorish types know him—what's he like?"

Miles cut in before the glint in Ivan's eye could materialize into some practical joke. "He's very straightforward. You'll get along fine."

Lubachik moved off, looking faintly reassured, rereading his flimsy.

"Ensign Vorpatril," intoned the sergeant. "Ensign Vorkosigan."

Tall Ivan collected his packet and Miles his, and they moved out of the way with their two comrades.

Ivan unzipped his envelope. "Ha. Imperial HQ in Vorbarr Sultana for me. I am to be, I'll have you know, aide-de-camp to Commodore Jollif, Operations." He bowed and turned the flimsy over. "Starting tomorrow, in fact."

"Ooh," said the ensign who'd drawn ship duty, still bouncing slightly. "Ivan gets to be a *secretary*. Just watch out if General Lamitz asks you to sit on his lap, I hear he—"

Ivan flipped him an amiable rude gesture. "Envy, sheer envy. I'll get to live like a civilian. Work seven to five, have my own apartment in town—no girls on that ship of yours up there, I might point out." Ivan's voice was even and cheerful, only his eyes failing to totally conceal his disappointment. Ivan had wanted ship duty too. They all did.

Miles did. *Ship duty. Eventually, command, like my father, his father, his, his . . .* A wish, a prayer, a dream . . . He hesitated for self-discipline, for fear, for a last lingering moment of high hope. He thumbed the lock-pad and unzipped the envelope with deliberate precision. A single plastic flimsy, a handful of travel passes. . . . His deliberation lasted only for the brief moment it took him to absorb the short paragraph before his eyes. He stood frozen in disbelief, began reading again from the top.

"So what's up, coz?" Ivan glanced down over Miles's shoulder.

"Ivan," said Miles in a choked voice, "have I got a touch of amnesia, or did we indeed never have a meteorology course on our sciences track?"

"Five-space math, yes. Xenobotany, yes." Ivan absently scratched a remembered itch. "Geology and terrain evaluation, yes. Well, there was aviation weather, back in our first year."

"Yes, but . . ."

"So what have they done to you this time?" asked Plause, clearly prepared to offer congratulations or sympathy as indicated.

"I'm assigned as Chief Meteorology Officer, Lazkowski Base. Where the hell is Lazkowski Base? I've never even heard of it!"

The sergeant at the desk looked up with a sudden evil grin. "I have, sir," he offered. "It's on a place called Kyril Island, up near the arctic circle. Winter training base for infantry. The grubs call it Camp Permafrost."

"*Infantry?*" said Miles.

Ivan's brows rose, and he frowned down at Miles. "Infantry? You? That doesn't seem right."

"No, it doesn't," said Miles faintly. Cold consciousness of his physical handicaps washed over him.

Years of arcane medical tortures had almost managed to correct the severe deformities from which Miles had nearly died at birth. Almost. Curled like a frog in infancy, he now stood almost straight. Chalk-stick bones, friable as talc, now were almost strong. Wizened as an infant homunculus, he now stood almost four-foot-nine. It had been a trade-off, toward the end, between the length of his bones and their strength, and his doctor still opined that the last six inches of height had been a mistake. Miles had finally broken his legs enough times to agree with him, but by then it was too late. But not a mutant, not . . . it scarcely mattered any more. If only they would let him place his strengths in the Emperor's service, he would make them forget his weaknesses. The deal was understood.

There had to be a thousand jobs in the Service to which his strange appearance and hidden fragility would make not one whit of difference. Like aide-de-camp, or Intelligence translator. Or even a ship's weaponry officer, monitoring his computers. It had been understood, surely it had been understood. But infantry? Someone was not playing fair. Or a mistake had been made. That wouldn't be a first. He hesitated a long moment, his fist tightening on the flimsy, then headed toward the door.

"Where are you going?" asked Ivan.

"To see Major Cecil."

Ivan exhaled through pursed lips. "Oh? Good luck."

Did the desk sergeant hide a small smile, bending his head to sort through the next stack of packets? "Ensign Draut," he called. The line moved up one more.

✧ ✧ ✧

Major Cecil was leaning with one hip on his clerk's desk, consulting about something on the vid, as Miles entered his office and saluted.

Major Cecil glanced up at Miles and then at his chrono. "Ah, less than ten minutes. I win the bet." The major returned Miles's salute as the clerk, smiling sourly, pulled a small wad of currency from his pocket, peeled off a one-mark note, and handed it across wordlessly to his superior. The major's face was only amused on the surface; he nodded toward the door, and the clerk tore off the plastic flimsy his machine had just produced and exited the room.

Major Cecil was a man of about fifty, lean, even-tempered, watchful. Very watchful. Though he was not the titular head of Personnel, that administrative job belonging to a higher-ranking officer, Miles had spotted Cecil long ago as the final-decision man. Through Cecil's hands passed at the last every assignment for every Academy graduate. Miles had always found him an accessible man, the teacher and scholar in him ascendant over the officer. His wit was dry and rare, his dedication to his duty intense. Miles had always trusted him. Till now.

"Sir," he began. He held out his orders in a frustrated gesture. "What *is* this?"

Cecil's eyes were still bright with his private amusement as he pocketed the mark-note. "Are you asking me to read them to you, Vorkosigan?"

"Sir, I question—" Miles stopped, bit his tongue, began again. "I have a few questions about my assignment."

"Meteorology Officer, Lazkowski Base," Major Cecil recited.

"It's . . . not a mistake, then? I got the right packet?"

"If that's what that says, you did."

"Are . . . you aware the only meteorology course I had was aviation weather?"

"I am." The major wasn't giving away a thing.

Miles paused. Cecil's sending his clerk out was a clear signal that this discussion was to be frank. "Is this some kind of punishment?" *What have I ever done to you?*

"Why, Ensign," Cecil's voice was smooth, "it's a perfectly normal assignment. Were you expecting an extraordinary one? My job is to match personnel requests with available candidates. Every request must be filled by someone."

"Any tech school grad could have filled this one." With an effort, Miles kept the snarl out of his voice, uncurled his fingers. "Better. It doesn't require an Academy cadet."

"That's right," agreed the major.

"Why, then?" Miles burst out. His voice came out louder than he'd meant it to.

Cecil sighed, straightened. "Because I have noticed, Vorkosigan, watching you—and you know very well you were the most closely watched cadet ever to pass through these halls barring Emperor Gregor himself—"

Miles nodded shortly.

"That despite your demonstrated brilliance in some areas, you have also demonstrated some chronic weaknesses. And I'm not referring to your physical problems, which everybody but me thought were going to take you out before your first year was up—you've been surprisingly sensible about those—"

Miles shrugged. "Pain hurts, sir. I don't court it."

"Very good. But your most insidious chronic problem is in the area of . . . how shall I put this precisely . . . subordination. You argue too much."

"No, I don't," Miles began indignantly, then shut his mouth.

Cecil flashed a grin. "Quite. Plus your rather irritating habit of treating your superior officers as your, ah . . ." Cecil paused, apparently groping again for just the right word.

"Equals?" Miles hazarded.

"Cattle," Cecil corrected judiciously. "To be driven to your will. You're a manipulator *par excellence,* Vorkosigan. I've been studying you for three years now, and your group dynamics are fascinating. Whether you were in charge or not, somehow it was always your idea that ended up getting carried out."

"Have I been . . . that disrespectful, sir?" Miles's stomach felt cold.

"On the contrary. Given your background, the marvel is that you conceal that, ah, little arrogant streak so well. But Vorkosigan," Cecil dropped at last into perfect seriousness, "the Imperial Academy is not the whole of the Imperial Service. You've made your comrades here appreciate you because here, brains are held at a premium. You were picked first for any strategic team for the same reason you were picked last for any purely physical contest—these young hotshots wanted to win. All the time. Whatever it took."

"I can't be ordinary and survive, sir!"

Cecil tilted his head. "I agree. And yet, sometime, you must also learn how to command ordinary men. And be commanded by them!

"This isn't a punishment, Vorkosigan, and it isn't my idea of a joke. Upon my choices may depend not only our fledgling officers' lives, but also those of the innocents I inflict 'em on. If I seriously miscalculate, overmatch or mismatch a man with a job, I not only risk him, but also those around him. Now, in six months (plus unscheduled overruns), the Imperial Orbital Shipyard is going to finish commissioning the *Prince Serg.*"

Miles's breath caught.

"You've got it." Cecil nodded. "The newest, fastest, deadliest thing His Imperial Majesty has ever put into space. And with the longest range. It will go out, and stay out, for longer periods than anything we've ever had before. It follows that everyone on board will be in each other's hair for longer unbroken periods than ever before. High Command is actually paying some attention to the psych profiles on this one. For a change.

"Listen, now," Cecil leaned forward. So did Miles, reflexively. "If you can keep your nose clean for just six months on an isolated downside post—bluntly, if you prove you can handle Camp Permafrost, I'll allow as how you can handle anything the Service might throw at you. And I'll support your request for a transfer to the *Prince.* But if you screw up, there will be nothing I or anybody else can do for you. Sink or swim, Ensign."

Fly, thought Miles. *I want to fly.* "Sir . . . just how much of a pit is this place?"

"I wouldn't want to prejudice you, Ensign Vorkosigan," said Cecil piously.

And I love you too, sir. "But . . . infantry? My physical limits . . . won't prevent my serving if they're taken into account, but I can't pretend they're not there. Or I might as well jump off a wall, destroy myself immediately, and save everybody time." *Dammit, why did they let me occupy some of Barrayar's most expensive classroom space for three years if they meant to kill me outright?* "I'd always assumed they were going to be taken into account."

"Meteorology Officer is a technical specialty, Ensign," the major reassured him. "Nobody's going to try and drop a full field pack on you and smash you flat. I doubt there's an officer in the Service who would choose to explain your dead body to the admiral." His voice cooled slightly. "Your saving grace. Mutant."

Cecil was without prejudice, merely testing. Always testing. Miles ducked his head. "As I may be, for the mutants who come after me."

"You've figured that out, have you?" Cecil's eye was suddenly speculative, faintly approving.

"Years ago, sir."

"Hm." Cecil smiled slightly, pushed himself off the desk, came forward and extended his hand. "Good luck, then. Lord Vorkosigan."

Miles shook it. "Thank you, sir." He shuffled through the stack of travel passes, ordering them.

"What's your first stop?" asked Cecil.

Testing again. Must be a bloody reflex. Miles answered unexpectedly, "The Academy archives."

"Ah!"

"For a downloading of the Service meteorology manual. And supplementary material."

"Very good. By the way, your predecessor in the post will be staying on a few weeks to complete your orientation."

"I'm extremely glad to hear that, sir," said Miles sincerely.

"We're not trying to make it impossible, Ensign."

Merely very difficult. "I'm glad to know that too. Sir." Miles's parting salute was almost subordinate.

Miles rode the last leg to Kyril Island in a big automated airfreight shuttle with a bored backup pilot and eighty tons of supplies. He spent most of the solitary journey frantically swotting up on weather. Since the flight schedule went rapidly awry due to hours-long delays at the last two loading stops, he found himself reassuringly further along in his studies than

he'd expected by the time the air-shuttle rumbled to a halt at Lazkowski Base.

The cargo bay doors opened to let in watery light from a sun skulking along near the horizon. The high-summer breeze was about five degrees above freezing. The first soldiers Miles saw were a crew of black-coveralled men with loaders under the direction of a tired-looking corporal, who met the shuttle. No one appeared to be specially detailed to meet a new weather officer. Miles shrugged on his parka and approached them.

A couple of the black-clad men, watching him as he hopped down from the ramp, made remarks to each other in Barrayaran Greek, a minority dialect of Earth origin, thoroughly debased in the centuries of the Time of Isolation. Miles, weary from his journey and cued by the all-too-familiar expressions on their faces, made a snap decision to ignore whatever they had to say by simply pretending not to understand their language. Plause had told him often enough that his accent in Greek was execrable anyway.

"Look at that, will you? Is it a kid?"

"I knew they were sending us baby officers, but this is a new low."

"Hey, that's no kid. It's a damn dwarf of some sort. The midwife sure missed her stroke on that one. Look at it, it's a mutant!"

With an effort, Miles kept his eyes from turning toward the commentators. Increasingly confident of their privacy, their voices rose from whispers to ordinary tones.

"So *what's it doing in uniform, ha?"*

"Maybe it's our new mascot."

The old genetic fears were so subtly ingrained, so pervasive even now, you could get beaten to death by people who didn't even know quite why they hated you but simply got carried away in the excitement of a group feedback loop. Miles knew very well he had always been protected by his father's rank, but ugly things could happen to less socially fortunate odd ones. There had been a ghastly incident in the Old Town section of Vorbarr Sultana just two years ago, a destitute crippled man found castrated with a broken wine bottle by a gang of drunks. It was considered Progress that it was a scandal, and not simply taken for granted. A recent infanticide in the Vorkosigans' own district had cut even closer to the bone. Yes, rank, social or military, had its uses. Miles meant to acquire all he could before he was done.

Miles twitched his parka back so that his officer's collar tabs showed clearly. "Hello, Corporal. I have orders to report in to a Lieutenant Ahn, the base Meteorology Officer. Where can I find him?"

Miles waited a beat for his proper salute. It was slow in coming; the corporal was still goggling down at him. It dawned on him at last that Miles might really be an officer.

Belatedly, he saluted. "Excuse me, uh, what did you say, sir?"

Miles returned the salute blandly and repeated himself in level tones.

"Uh, Lieutenant Ahn, right. He usually hides out—that is, he's usually in his office. In the main administration building." The corporal swung his arm around to point toward a two-story pre-fab sticking up beyond a rank of half-buried warehouses at the edge of the tarmac, maybe a kilometer off. "You can't miss it, it's the tallest building on the base."

Also, Miles noted, well marked by the assortment of comm equipment sticking out of the roof. Very good.

Now, should he turn his pack over to these goons and pray that it would follow him to his eventual destination, whatever it was? Or interrupt their work and commandeer a loader for transport? He had a brief vision of himself stuck up on the prow of the thing like a sailing ship's figurehead, being trundled toward his meeting with destiny along with half a ton of Underwear, Thermal, Long, 2 doz per unit crate, Style #6774932. He decided to shoulder his duffle and walk.

"Thank you, Corporal." He marched off in the indicated direction, too conscious of his limp and the leg-braces concealed beneath his trouser legs taking up their share of the extra weight. The distance turned out to be farther than it looked, but he was careful not to pause or falter till he'd turned out of sight beyond the first warehouse-unit.

The base seemed nearly deserted. Of course. The bulk of its population was the infantry trainees who came and went in two batches per winter. Only the permanent crew was here now, and Miles bet most of them took their long leaves during this brief summer breathing space. Miles wheezed to a halt inside the Admin building without having passed another man.

The Directory and Map Display, according to a hand-lettered sign taped across its vid plate, was down. Miles wandered up the first and only hallway to his right, searching for an occupied office, any occupied office. Most doors were closed, but not locked, lights out. An office labeled Gen. Accounting held a man in black fatigues with red lieutenant's tabs on the collar, totally absorbed in his holovid, which was displaying long columns of data. He was swearing under his breath.

"Meteorology Office. Where?" Miles called in the door.

"Two." The lieutenant pointed upward without turning around, crouched more tightly, and resumed swearing. Miles tiptoed away without disturbing him further.

He found it at last on the second floor, a closed door labeled in faded letters. He paused outside, set down his duffle, and folded his parka atop it. He checked himself over. Fourteen hours' travel had rumpled his initial crispness. Still, he'd managed to keep his green undress uniform and half-boots free of food stains, mud, and other unbecoming accretions. He flattened his cap and positioned it precisely in his belt. He'd crossed half a planet, half a lifetime, to achieve this moment. Three years training to a fever pitch of readiness lay behind him. Yet the Academy years had always had a faint air of pretense, We-are-only-practicing; now, at last, he was face-to-face with the real thing, his first real commanding officer. First impressions could be vital, especially in his case. He took a breath and knocked.

A gravelly muffled voice came through the door, words unrecognizable. Invitation? Miles opened it and strode in.

He had a glimpse of computer interfaces and vid displays gleaming and glowing along one wall. He rocked back at the heat that hit his face. The air within was blood-temperature. Except for the vid displays, the room was dim. At a movement to his left, Miles turned and saluted. "Ensign Miles Vorkosigan, reporting for duty as ordered, sir," he snapped out, looked up, and saw no one.

The movement had come from lower down. An unshaven man of about forty dressed only in his skivvies sat on the floor, his back against the comconsole desk. He smiled up at Miles, raised a bottle half-full of amber liquid, mumbled, "Salu', boy. Love ya," and fell slowly over.

Miles gazed down on him for a long, long, thoughtful moment.

The man began to snore.

⟡ ⟡ ⟡

After turning down the heat, shedding his tunic, and tossing a blanket over Lieutenant Ahn (for such he was), Miles took a contemplative half hour and thoroughly examined his new domain. There was no doubt, he was going to require instruction in the office's operations. Besides the satellite real-time images, automated data seemed to be coming in from a dozen micro-climate survey rigs spotted around the island. If procedural manuals had ever existed, they weren't around now, not even on the computers. After an honorable hesitation, bemusedly studying the snoring, twitching form on the floor, Miles also took the opportunity to go through Ahn's desk and comconsole files.

Discovery of a few pertinent facts helped put the human spectacle before Miles into a more understandable perspective. Lieutenant Ahn, it seemed, was a twenty-year man within weeks of retirement. It had been a very, very long time since his last promotion. It had been an even longer time since his last transfer; he'd been Kyril Island's only weather officer for the last fifteen years.

This poor sod has been stuck on this iceberg since I was six years old, Miles calculated, and shuddered inwardly. Hard to tell, at this late date, if Ahn's drinking problem were cause or effect. Well, if he sobered up enough within the next day to show Miles how to go on, well and good. If he didn't, Miles could think of half a dozen ways, ranging from the cruel to the unusual, to bring him around whether he wanted to be conscious or not. If Ann could just be made to disgorge a technical orientation, he could return to his coma till they came to roll him onto outgoing transport, for all Miles cared.

Ahn's fate decided, Miles donned his tunic, stowed his gear behind the desk, and went exploring.

Somewhere in the chain of command there must be a conscious, sober and sane human being who was actually doing his job, or the place couldn't even function on this level. Or maybe it was run by corporals, who knew? In that case, Miles supposed, his next task must be to find and take control of the most effective corporal available.

In the downstairs foyer a human form approached Miles, silhouetted at first against the light from the front doors. Jogging in precise double time, the shape resolved into a tall, hard-bodied man in sweat pants, T-shirt, and running shoes. He had clearly just come in off some condition-maintaining five-kilometer run, with maybe a few hundred push-ups thrown in for dessert. Iron-grey hair, iron-hard eyes; he might have been a particularly dyspeptic drill sergeant. He stopped short to stare down at Miles, startlement compressing to a thin-lipped frown.

Miles stood with his legs slightly apart, threw back his head, and stared up with equal force. The man seemed totally oblivious to Miles's collar tabs. Exasperated, Miles snapped, "Are all the keepers on vacation, or is anybody actually running this bloody zoo?"

The man's eyes sparked, as if their iron had struck flint; they ignited a little warning light in Miles's brain, one mouthy moment too late. *Hi, there, sir!* cried the hysterical commenter in the back of Miles's mind, with a skip, bow, and flourish. *I'm your newest exhibit!* Miles suppressed the voice ruthlessly. There wasn't a trace of humor in any line of that seamed countenance looming over him.

With a cold flare of his carved nostril, the Base Commander glared down at Miles and growled, "*I* run it, Ensign."

✧ ✧ ✧

Dense fog was rolling in off the distant, muttering sea by the time Miles finally found his way to his new quarters. The officers' barracks and all around it were plunged into a grey, frost-scummed obscurity. Miles decided it was an omen.

Oh, God, it was going to be a long winter.

CHAPTER TWO

Rather to Miles's surprise, when he arrived at Ahn's office next morning at an hour he guessed might represent beginning-of-shift, he found the lieutenant awake, sober, and in uniform. Not that the man looked precisely well; pasty-faced, breathing stertorously, he sat huddled, staring slit-eyed at a computer-colorized weather vid. The holo zoomed and shifted dizzyingly at signals from the remote controller he clutched in one damp and trembling palm.

"Good morning, sir." Miles softened his voice out of mercy, and closed the door behind himself without slamming it.

"Ha?" Ahn looked up, and returned his salute automatically. "What the devil are you, ah . . . Ensign?"

"I'm your replacement, sir. Didn't anyone tell you I was coming?"

"Oh, yes!" Ahn brightened right up. "Very good, come in." Miles, already in, smiled briefly instead. "I meant to meet you on the shuttlepad," Ahn went on. "You're early. But you seem to have found your way all right."

"I came in yesterday, sir."

"Oh. You should have reported in."

"I did, sir."

"Oh." Ahn squinted at Miles in worry. "You did?"

"You promised you'd give me a complete technical orientation to the office this morning, sir," Miles added, seizing the opportunity.

"Oh." Ahn blinked. "Good." The worried look faded slightly. "Well, ah . . ." Ahn rubbed his face, looking around. He confined his reaction to Miles's physical appearance to one covert glance, and, perhaps deciding they must have gotten the social duties of introduction out of the way yesterday, plunged at once into a description of the equipment lining the wall, in order from left to right.

Literally an introduction; all the computers had women's names. Except for a tendency to talk about his machines as though they were human, Ahn seemed coherent enough as he detailed his job, only drifting into randomness, then hungover silence, when he accidentally strayed from the topic. Miles steered him gently back to weather with pertinent questions, and took notes. After a bewildered Brownian trip around the room Ahn rediscovered his office procedural disks at last, stuck to the undersides of their respective pieces of equipment. He made fresh coffee on a non-regulation brewer—named "Georgette"—parked discreetly in a corner cupboard, then took Miles up to the roof of the building to show him the data-collection center there.

Ahn went over the assorted meters, collectors, and samplers rather perfunctorily. His headache seemed to be growing worse with the morning's exertions. He leaned heavily on the corrosion-proof railing surrounding the automated station and squinted out at the distant horizon. Miles followed him around dutifully as he appeared to meditate deeply for a few minutes on each of the cardinal compass points. Or maybe that introspective look just meant he was getting ready to throw up.

It was pale and clear this morning, the sun up—the sun had been up since two hours after midnight, Miles reminded himself. They were just past the shortest nights of the year for this latitude. From this rare high vantage point, Miles gazed out with interest at Lazkowski Base and the flat landscape beyond.

Kyril Island was an egg-shaped lump about seventy kilometers wide and 160 kilometers long, and over five hundred kilometers from the next land of any description. *Lumpy and brown* described most of it, both base and island. The majority of the nearby buildings, including Miles's officers' barracks, were dug in, topped with native turf. Nobody had bothered with agricultural terraforming here. The island retained its original Barrayaran ecology, scarred by use and abuse. Long fat rolls of turf covered the barracks for the winter infantry trainees, now empty and silent. Muddy water-filled ruts fanned out to deserted marksmanship ranges, obstacle courses, and pocked live-ammo practice areas.

To the near-south, the leaden sea heaved, muting the sun's best efforts at sparkle. To the far north a grey line marked the border of the tundra at a chain of dead volcanic mountains.

Miles had taken his own officers' short course in winter maneuvers in the Black Escarpment, mountain country deep in Barrayar's second continent; plenty of snow, to be sure, and murderous terrain, but the air had been dry and crisp and stimulating. Even today, at high summer, the sea dampness seemed to creep up under his loose parka and gnaw his bones at every old break. Miles shrugged against it, without effect.

Ahn, still draped over the railing, glanced sideways at Miles at this movement. "So tell me, ah, Ensign, are you any relation to *the* Vorkosigan? I wondered, when I saw the name on the orders the other day."

"My father," said Miles shortly.

"Good God." Ahn blinked and straightened, then sagged selfconsciously back onto his elbows as before. "Good God," he repeated. He chewed his lip in fascination, dulled eyes briefly alight with honest curiosity. "What's he really like?"

What an impossible question, Miles thought in exasperation. Admiral Count Aral Vorkosigan. The colossus of Barrayaran history in this half-century. Conqueror of Komarr, hero of the ghastly retreat from Escobar. For sixteen years Lord Regent of Barrayar during Emperor Gregor's troubled minority; the Emperor's trusted Prime Minister in the four years since. Destroyer of Vordarian's Pretendership, engineer of the peculiar victory of the third Cetagandan war, unshaken tiger-rider of Barrayar's murderous internecine politics for the past two decades. *The* Vorkosigan.

I have seen him laugh in pure delight, standing on the dock at Vorkosigan Surleau and yelling instructions over the water, the morning I first sailed, dumped, and righted the skimmer by myself. I have seen him weep till his nose ran, more dead drunk than you were yesterday, Ahn, the night we got the word Major Duvallier was executed for espionage. I have seen him rage, so brick-red we feared for his heart, when the reports came in fully detailing the stupidities that led to the last riots in Solstice. I have seen him wandering around Vorkosigan House at dawn in his underwear, yawning and prodding my sleepy mother into helping him find two matching socks. He's not like *anything, Ahn. He's the original.*

"He cares about Barrayar," Miles said aloud at last, as the silence grew awkward. "He's . . . a hard act to follow." *And, oh yes, his only child is a deformed mutant. That, too.*

"I should think so." Ahn blew out his breath in sympathy, or maybe it was nausea.

Miles decided he could tolerate Ahn's sympathy. There seemed no hint in it of the damned patronizing pity, nor, interestingly, of the more common repugnance. *It's because I'm his replacement here,* Miles decided. *I could have two heads and he'd still be overjoyed to meet me.*

"That what you're doing, following in the old man's footsteps?" said Ahn equably. And more dubiously, looking around, "Here?"

"I'm Vor," said Miles impatiently. "I serve. Or at any rate, I try to. Wherever I'm put. That was the deal."

Ahn shrugged bafflement, whether at Miles or at the vagaries of the Service that had sent him to Kyril Island, Miles could not tell. "Well." He pushed himself up off the rail with a grunt. "No wah-wah warnings today."

"No what warnings?"

Ahn yawned, and tapped an array of figures—pulled out of thin air, as far as Miles could tell—into his report panel representing hour-by-hour predictions for today's weather. "Wah-wah. Didn't anybody tell you about the wah-wah?"

"No . . ."

"They should have, first thing. Bloody dangerous, the wah-wah."

Miles began to wonder if Ahn was trying to diddle his head. Practical jokes could be a subtle enough form of victimization to penetrate even the defenses of rank, Miles had found. The honest hatred of a beating inflicted only physical pain.

Ahn leaned across the railing again to point. "You notice all those ropes, strung from door to door between buildings? That's for when the wah-wah comes up. You hang onto 'em to keep from being blown away. If you lose your grip, don't fling out your arms to try and stop yourself. I've seen more guys break their wrists that way. Go into a ball and roll."

"What the hell's a wah-wah? Sir."

"Big wind. Sudden. I've seen it go from dead calm to 160 kilometers, with a temperature drop from ten degrees cee above freezing to twenty below, in seven minutes. It can last from ten minutes to two days. They almost always blow up from the northwest, here, when conditions are right. The remote station on the coast gives us about a twenty-minute warning. We blow a siren. That means you must never let yourself get caught without your cold gear, or more than fifteen minutes away from a bunker. There's bunkers all around the grubs' practice fields out there." Ahn waved his arm in that direction. He seemed quite serious, even earnest. "You hear that siren, you run like hell for cover. The size you are, if you ever got picked up and blown into the sea, they'd never find you again."

"All right," said Miles, silently resolving to check out these alleged facts in the base's weather records at the first opportunity. He craned his neck for a look at Ahn's report panel. "Where did you read off those numbers from, that you just entered on there?"

Ahn stared at his report panel in surprise. "Well—they're the right figures."

"I wasn't questioning their accuracy," said Miles patiently. "I want to know how you came up with them.

So I can do it tomorrow, while you're still here to correct me."

Ahn waved his free hand in an abortive, frustrated gesture. "Well . . ."

"You're not just making them up, are you?" said Miles in suspicion.

"No!" said Ahn. "I hadn't thought about it, but . . . it's the way the day smells, I guess." He inhaled deeply, by way of demonstration.

Miles wrinkled his nose and sniffed experimentally. Cold, sea salt, shore slime, damp and mildew. Hot circuits in some of the blinking, twirling array of instruments beside him. The mean temperature, barometric pressure, and humidity of the present moment, let alone that of eighteen hours into the future, was not to be found in the olfactory information pressing on *his* nostrils. He jerked his thumb at the meteorological array. "Does this thing have any sort of a smell-o-meter to duplicate whatever it is you're doing?"

Ahn looked genuinely nonplussed, as if his internal system, whatever it was, had been dislocated by his sudden self-consciousness of it. "Sorry, Ensign Vorkosigan. We have the standard computerized projections, of course, but to tell you the truth I haven't used 'em in years. They're not accurate enough."

Miles stared at Ahn, and came to a horrid realization. Ahn wasn't lying, joking, or making this up. It was the fifteen years' experience, gone subliminal, that was carrying out these subtle functions. A backlog of experience Miles could not duplicate. *Nor would I wish to,* he admitted to himself.

Later in the day, while explaining with perfect truth that he was orienting himself to the systems, Miles covertly checked out all of Ahn's startling assertions in the base meteorological archives. Ahn hadn't been kidding about the wah-wah. Worse, he hadn't been kidding about the computerized projections. The automated system produced local predictions of 86% accuracy, dropping to 73% at a week's long-range forecast. Ahn and his magical nose ran an accuracy of 96%, dropping to 94% at a week's range. *When Ahn leaves, this island is going to experience an 11 to 21% drop in forecast accuracy. They're going to notice.*

Weather Officer, Camp Permafrost, was clearly a more responsible position than Miles had at first realized. The weather here could be deadly.

And this guy is going to leave me alone on this island with six thousand armed men, and tell me to go sniff for wah-wahs?

On the fifth day, when Miles had just about decided that his first impression had been too harsh, Ahn relapsed. Miles waited an hour for Arm and his nose to show up at the weather office to begin the day's duties. At last he pulled the routine readings from the substandard computerized system, entered them anyway, and went hunting.

He ran Ahn down at last still in his bunk, in his quarters in the officers' barracks, sodden and snoring, stinking of stale . . . fruit brandy? Miles shuddered. Shaking, prodding, and yelling in Ahn's ear failed to rouse him. He only burrowed deeper into his bedclothes and noxious miasma, moaning. Miles regretfully set aside visions of violence, and prepared to carry on by himself. He'd be on his own soon enough anyway.

He limp-marched off to the motor pool. Yesterday Ahn had taken him on a scheduled maintenance patrol of the five remote-sensor weather stations nearest the base. The outlying six had been planned for today. Routine travel around Kyril Island was accomplished in an all-terrain vehicle called a scat-cat, which had turned out to be almost as much fun to drive as an antigrav sled. Scat-cats were ground-hugging iridescent teardrops that tore up the tundra, but were guaranteed not to blow away in the wah-wah winds. Base personnel, Miles had been given to understand, had grown extremely tired of picking lost antigrav sleds out of the frigid sea.

The motor pool was another half-buried bunker like most of the rest of Lazkowski Base, only bigger. Miles routed out the corporal, what's his name, Olney, who'd signed Ahn and himself out the previous day. The tech who assisted him, driving the scat-cat up from the underground storage to the entrance, also looked faintly familiar. Tall, black fatigues, dark hair—that described eighty percent of the men on the base—it wasn't until he spoke that his heavy accent cued Miles. He was one of the sotto voce commenters Miles had overheard on the shuttlepad. Miles schooled himself not to react.

Miles went over the vehicle's supply checklist carefully before signing for it, as Ahn had taught him. All scat-cats were required to carry a complete cold-survival kit at all times. Corporal Olney watched with faint contempt as Miles fumbled around finding everything. *All right, so I'm slow,* Miles thought irritably. *New and green. This is the only way I'm gonna get less new and green. Step by step.* He controlled his self-consciousness with an effort. Previous painful experience had taught him it was a most dangerous frame of mind. *Concentrate on the task, not the bloody audience. You've always had an audience. Probably always will.*

Miles spread out the map flimsy across the scat-cat's shell, and pointed out his projected itinerary to the corporal. Such a briefing was also safety SOP, according to Ahn. Olney grunted acknowledgment with a finely tuned look of long-suffering boredom, palpable but just short of something Miles would be forced to notice.

The black-clad tech, Pattas, watching over Miles's

uneven shoulder, pursed his lips and spoke. "Oh, Ensign *sir*." Again, the emphasis fell just short of irony. "You going up to Station Nine?"

"Yes?"

"You might want to be sure and park your scat-cat, uh, out of the wind, in that hollow just below the station." A thick finger touched the map flimsy on an area marked in blue. "You'll see it. That way your scat-cat'll be sure of re-starting."

"The power pack in these engines is rated for space," said Miles. "How could it not re-start?"

Olney's eye lit, then went suddenly very neutral. "Yes, but in case of a sudden wah-wah, you wouldn't want it to blow away."

I'd blow away before it would. "I thought these scat-cats were heavy enough not to."

"Well, not *away*, but they have been known to blow *over*," murmured Pattas.

"Oh. Well, thank you."

Corporal Olney coughed. Pattas waved cheerfully as Miles drove out.

Miles's chin jerked up in the old nervous tic. He took a deep breath and let his hackles settle, as he turned the scat-cat away from the base and headed cross-country. He powered up to a more satisfying speed, lashing through the brown bracken-like growth. He had been what, a year and a half? two years? at the Imperial Academy proving and re-proving his competence to every bloody man he crossed every time he did anything. The third year had perhaps spoiled him, he was out of practice. Was it going to be like this every time he took up a new post? Probably, he reflected bitterly, and powered up a bit more. But he'd known that would be part of the game when he'd demanded to play.

The weather was almost warm today, the pale sun

almost bright, and Miles almost cheerful by the time he reached Station Six, on the eastern shore of the island. It was a pleasure to be alone for a change, just him and his job. No audience. Time to take his time and get it right. He worked carefully, checking power packs, emptying samplers, looking for signs of corrosion, damage, or loose connections in the equipment. And if he dropped a tool, there was no one around to make comments about spastic mutants. With the fading tension, he made fewer fumbles, and the tic vanished. He finished, stretched, and inhaled the damp air benignly, reveling in the unaccustomed luxury of solitude. He even took a few minutes to walk along the shoreline, and notice the intricacies of the small sea life washed up there.

One of the samplers in Station Eight was damaged, a humidity-meter shattered. By the time he'd replaced it he realized his itinerary timetable had been overly optimistic. The sun was slanting down toward green twilight as he left Station Eight. By the time he reached Station Nine, in an area of mixed tundra and rocky outcrops near the northern shore, it was almost dark.

Station Ten, Miles reconfirmed by checking his map flimsy by pen-light, was up in the volcanic mountains among the glaciers. Best not try to go hunting it in the dark. He would wait out the brief four hours till dawn. He reported his change-of-plan via comm link to the base, 160 kilometers to the south. The man on duty did not sound terribly interested. Good.

With no watchers, Miles happily seized the opportunity to try out all that fascinating gear packed in the back of the scat-cat. Far better to practice now, when conditions were good, than in the middle of some later blizzard. The little two-man bubble shelter, when set up, seemed almost palatial for Miles's short and lonely splendor. In winter it was meant to be insulated with packed snow. He positioned it downwind of the scat-cat, parked in the recommended low spot a few hundred meters from the weather station, which was perched on a rocky outcrop.

Miles reflected on the relative weight of the shelter versus the scat-cat. A vid that Ahn had shown him of a typical wah-wah remained vivid in his mind. The portable latrine traveling sideways in the air at a hundred kilometers an hour had been particularly impressive. Ahn hadn't been able to tell him if there'd been anyone in it at the time the vid was shot. Miles took the added precaution of attaching the shelter to the scat-cat with a short chain. Satisfied, he crawled inside.

The equipment was first-rate. He hung a heat-tube from the roof and touched it on, and basked in its glow, sitting cross-legged. Rations were of the better grade. A pull tab heated a compartmentalized tray of stew with vegetables and rice. He mixed an acceptable fruit drink from the powder supplied. After eating and stowing the remains, he settled on a comfortable pad, shoved a book-disk into his viewer, and prepared to read away the short night.

He had been rather tense these last few weeks. These last few years. The book-disk, a Betan novel of manners which the Countess had recommended to him, had nothing whatsoever to do with Barrayar, military maneuvers, mutation, politics, or the weather. He didn't even notice what time he dozed off.

He woke with a start, blinking in the thick darkness gilded only with the faint copper light from the heat-tube. He felt he had slept long, yet the transparent sectors of the bubble-shelter were pitchy black. An unreasoning panic clogged his throat. Dammit, it didn't matter if he overslept, it wasn't like he would be late for an exam, here. He glanced at the glowing readout on his wrist chrono.

It ought to be broad daylight.

The flexible walls of the shelter were pressing inward. Not one-third of the original volume remained, and the floor was wrinkled. Miles shoved one finger against the thin cold plastic. It yielded slowly, like soft butter, and retained the dented impression. What the *hell* . . . ?

His head was pounding, his throat constricted; the air was stuffy and wet. It felt just like . . . like oxygen depletion and CO_2 excess in a space emergency. Here? The vertigo of his disorientation seemed to tilt the floor.

The floor *was* tilted, he realized indignantly, pulled deeply downward on one side, pinching one of his legs. He convulsed from its grip. Fighting the CO_2-induced panic, he lay back, trying to breathe slower and think faster.

I'm underground. Sunk in some kind of quicksand. Quick-mud. Had those two bloody bastards at the motor-pool set him up for this? He'd fallen for it, fallen right in it.

Slow-mud, maybe. The scat-cat hadn't settled noticeably in the time it had taken him to set up this shelter. Or he would have twigged to the trap. Of course, it had been dark. But if he'd been settling for hours, asleep . . .

Relax, he told himself frantically. The tundra surface, the free air, might be a mere ten centimeters overhead. Or ten meters . . . *relax!* He felt about the shelter for something to use as a probe. There'd been a long, telescoping, knife-bitted tube for sampling glacier ice. Packed in the scat-cat. Along with the comm link. Now located, Miles gauged by the angle of the floor, about two-and-a-half meters down and to the west of his present location. It was the scat-cat that was dragging him down. The bubble-shelter alone might well have floated in the tundra-camouflaged mud-pond. If he could detach the chain, might it rise? Not fast enough. His chest felt stuffed with cotton. He had to break through to air soon, or asphyxiate. Womb, tomb. Would his parents be there to watch, when he was found at last, when this grave was opened, scat-cat and shelter winched out of the bog by heavy hovercab . . . his body frozen rictus-mouthed in this hideous parody of an amniotic sac . . . *relax.*

He stood, and shoved upward against the heavy roof. His feet sank in the pulpy floor, but he was able to jerk loose one of the bubble's interior ribs, now bent in an overstrained curve. He almost passed out from the effort, in the thick air. He found the top edge of the shelter's opening, and slid his finger down the burr-catch just a few centimeters. Just enough for the pole to pass through. He'd feared the black mud would pour in, drowning him at once, but it only crept in extrusive blobs, to fall with oozing plops. The comparison was obvious and repulsive. *God, and I thought I'd been in deep shit before.*

He shoved the rib upward. It resisted, slipping in his sweating palms. Not ten centimeters. Not twenty. A meter, a meter and a third, and he was running short on probe. He paused, took a new grip, shoved again. Was the resistance lessening? Had he broken through to the surface? He heaved it back and forth, but the sucking slime sealed it still.

Maybe, maybe a little less than his own height between the top of the shelter and breath. Breath, death. How long to claw through it? How fast did a hole in this stuff close? His vision was darkening, and it wasn't because the light was going dim. He turned the heat tube off and stuck it in the front pocket of his jacket. The uncanny dark shook him with horror. Or perhaps it was the CO_2. Now or never.

On an impulse, he bent and loosened his boot-catches and belt buckle, then zipped open the burr by feel. He began to dig like a dog, heaving big globs of mud down into the little space left in the bubble. He squeezed through the opening, braced himself, took his last breath, and pressed upward.

His chest was pulsing, his vision a red blur, when his head broke the surface. Air! He spat black muck and bracken bits, and blinked, trying with little success to clear his eyes and nose. He fought one hand up, then the other, and tried to pull himself up horizontal, flat like a frog. The cold confounded him. He could feel the muck closing around his legs, numbing like a witch's embrace. His toes pressed at full extension on the shelter's roof. It sank and he rose a centimeter. The last of the leverage he could get by pushing. Now he must pull. His hands closed over bracken. It gave. More. More. He was making a little progress, the cold air raking his grateful throat. The witch's grip tightened. He wriggled his legs, futilely, one last time. All right, now. Heave!

His legs slid out of his boots and pants, his hips sucked free, and he rolled away. He lay spread-eagled for maximum support on the treacherous surface, faceup to the grey swirling sky. His uniform jacket and long underwear were soaked with slime, and he'd lost one thermal sock, as well as both boots and his trousers. It was sleeting.

They found him hours later, curled around the dimming heat-tube, crammed into an eviscerated equipment bay in the automated weather station. His eye-sockets were hollow in his black-streaked face, his toes and ears white. His numb purple fingers jerked two wires across each other in a steady, hypnotic tattoo, the Service emergency code. To be read out in bursts of static in the barometric pressure meter in base's weather room. If and when anybody bothered to look at the suddenly defective reading from this station, or noticed the pattern in the white noise.

His fingers kept twitching in this rhythm for minutes after they pulled him free of his little box. Ice cracked off the back of his uniform jacket as they tried to straighten his body. For a long time they could get no words from him at all, only a shivering hiss. Only his eyes burned.

CHAPTER THREE

Floating in the heat tank in the base infirmary, Miles considered crucifixion for the two saboteurs from the motor pool from several angles. Such as upside down. Dangling over the sea at low altitude from an antigrav sled. Better still, staked out faceup in a bog in a blizzard. . . . But by the time his body had warmed up, and the corpsman had pulled him out of the tank to dry, be reexamined, and eat a supervised meal, his head had cooled.

It hadn't been an assassination attempt. And therefore, not a matter he was compelled to turn over to Simon Illyan, dread Chief of Imperial Security and Miles's father's left-hand man. The vision of the sinister officers from ImpSec coming to take those two jokers away, far away, was lovely, but impractical, like shooting mice with a maser cannon. Anyway, where could ImpSec possibly send them that was worse than here?

They'd meant his scat-cat to bog, to be sure, while he serviced the weather station, and for Miles to have the embarrassment of calling the base for heavy equipment to pull it out. Embarrassing, not lethal. They could not have—no one could have—foreseen Miles's inspired safety-conscious precaution with the chain, which was in the final analysis what had almost killed him. At most it was a matter for Service Security, bad enough, or for normal discipline.

He dangled his toes over the side of his bed, one of a row in the empty infirmary, and pushed the last of his food around on his tray. The corpsman wandered in, and glanced at the remains.

"You feeling all right now, sir?"

"Fine," said Miles morosely.

"You, uh, didn't finish your tray."

"I often don't. They always give me too much."

"Yeah, I guess you are pretty, um . . ." The corpsman made a note on his report panel, leaned over to examine Miles's ears, and bent to inspect his toes, rolling them between practiced fingers. "It doesn't look like you're going to lose any pieces, here. Lucky."

"Do you treat a lot of frostbite?" *Or am I the only idiot?* Present evidence would suggest it.

"Oh, once the grubs arrive, this place'll be crammed. Frostbite, pneumonia, broken bones, contusions, concussions . . . gets real lively, come winter. Wall-to-wall moro—unlucky trainees. And a few unlucky instructors, that they take down with 'em." The corpsman stood, and tapped a few more entries on his panel. "I'm afraid I have to mark you as recovered now, sir."

"Afraid?" Miles raised his brows inquiringly.

The corpsman straightened, in the unconscious posture of a man transmitting official bad news. That old they-told-me-to-say-this-it's-not-my-fault look. "You are ordered to report to the base commander's office as soon as I release you, sir."

Miles considered an immediate relapse. No. Better to get the messy parts over with. "Tell me, corpsman, has anyone else ever sunk a scat-cat?"

"Oh, sure. The grubs lose about five or six a season. Plus minor bog-downs. The engineers get real pissed about it. The commandant promised them next time he'd . . . ahem!" The corpsman lost his voice.

Wonderful, thought Miles. Just great. He could see it coming. It wasn't like he couldn't see it coming.

Miles dashed back to his quarters for a quick change of clothing, guessing a hospital robe might be inappropriate for the coming interview. He immediately found he had a minor quandary. His black fatigues seemed too relaxed, his dress greens too formal for office wear anywhere outside Imperial HQ at Vorbarr Sultana. His undress greens' trousers and half-boots were still at the bottom of the bog. He had only brought one of each uniform style with him; his spares, supposedly in transit, had not yet arrived.

He was hardly in a position to borrow from a neighbor. His uniforms were privately made to his own fit, at approximately four times the cost of Imperial issue. Part of that cost was for the effort of making them indistinguishable on the surface from the machine cut, while at the same time partially masking the oddities of his body through subtleties of hand-tailoring. He cursed under his breath, and shucked on his dress greens, complete with mirror-polished boots to the knees. At least the boots obviated the leg braces.

General Stanis Metzov, read the sign on the door, *Base Commander.* Miles had been assiduously avoiding the base commander ever since their first unfortunate encounter. This had not been hard to do in

Ahn's company, despite the pared population of Kyril Island this month; Ahn avoided everybody. Miles now wished he'd tried harder to strike up conversations with brother officers in mess. Permitting himself to stay isolated, even to concentrate on his new tasks, had been a mistake. In five days of even the most random conversation, someone must surely have mentioned Kyril Island's voracious killer mud.

A corporal manning the comconsole in an antechamber ushered Miles through to the inner office. He must now try to work himself back round to Metzov's good side, assuming the general had one. Miles needed allies. General Metzov looked across his desk unsmiling as Miles saluted and stood waiting.

Today, the general was aggressively dressed in black fatigues. At Metzov's altitude in the hierarchy, this stylistic choice usually indicated a deliberate identification with The Fighting Man. The only concession to his rank was their pressed neatness. His decorations were stripped down to a mere modest three, all high-combat commendations. Pseudo-modest; pruned of the surrounding foliage, they leapt to the eye. Mentally, Miles applauded, even envied, the effect. Metzov looked his part, the combat commander, absolutely, unconsciously natural.

A fifty-fifty chance with the uniform, and I had to guess wrong, Miles fumed as Metzov's eye traveled sarcastically down, and back up, the subdued glitter of his dress greens. All right, so Metzov's eyebrows signaled, Miles now looked like some kind of Vorish headquarters twit. Not that that wasn't another familiar type. Miles decided to decline the roasting and cut Metzov's inspection short by forcing the opening. "Yes, sir?"

Metzov leaned back in his chair, lips twisting. "I see you found some pants, Ensign Vorkosigan. And, ah . . . riding boots, too. You know, there are no horses on this island."

None at Imperial Headquarters, either, Miles thought irritably. *I didn't design the damn boots.* His father had once suggested his staff officers must need them for riding hobbyhorses, high horses, and nightmares. Unable to think of a useful reply to the general's sally, Miles stood in dignified silence, chin lifted, parade rest. "Sir."

Metzov leaned forward, clasping his hands, abandoning his heavy humor, eyes gone hard again. "You lost a valuable, fully equipped scat-cat as a result of leaving it parked in an area clearly marked as a Permafrost Inversion Zone. Don't they teach map-reading at the Imperial Academy anymore, or is it to be all diplomacy in the New Service—how to drink tea with the ladies?"

Miles called up the map in his mind. He could see it clearly. "The blue areas were labelled P.I.Z. Those initials were not defined. Not in the key or anywhere."

"Then I take it you also failed to read your manual."

He'd been buried in manuals ever since he'd arrived. Weather office procedural, equipment tech-specs . . . "Which one, sir?"

"Lazkowski Base Regulations."

Miles tried frantically to remember if he'd ever seen such a disk. "I . . . think Lieutenant Ahn may have given me a copy . . . night before last." Ahn had in fact dumped an entire carton of disks out on Miles's bed in officers' quarters. He was doing some preliminary packing, he'd said, and was willing Miles his library. Miles had read two weather disks before going to sleep that night. Ahn, clearly, had returned to his own cubicle to do a little preliminary celebrating. The next morning Miles had taken the scat-cat out. . . .

"And you haven't read it yet?"

"No, sir."

"Why not?"

I was set up, Miles's thought wailed. He could feel the highly interested presence of Metzov's clerk, undismissed, standing witness by the door behind him. Making this a public, not a private, dressing-down. And if only he'd read the damn manual, would those two bastards from the motor pool even have been able to set him up? Will or nill, he was going to get down-checked for this one. "No excuse, sir."

"Well, Ensign, in Chapter Three of Lazkowski Base Regulations you will find a complete description of all the permafrost zones, together with the rules for avoiding them. You might look into it, when you can spare a little leisure from . . . drinking tea."

"Yes, sir." Miles's face was set like glass. The general had a right to skin him with a vibra-knife, if he chose—in private. The authority lent Miles by his uniform barely balanced the deformities that made him a target of Barrayar's historically grounded, intense genetic prejudices. A public humiliation that sapped that authority before men he must also command came very close to an act of sabotage. Deliberate, or unconscious?

The general was only warming up. "The Service may still provide warehousing for excess Vor lordlings at Imperial Headquarters, but out here in the real world, where there's fighting to be done, we have no use for drones. Now, I fought my way up through the ranks. I saw casualties in Vordarian's Pretendership before you were born—"

I was *a casualty in Vordarian's Pretendership before I was born,* thought Miles, his irritation growing wilder. The soltoxin gas that had almost killed his pregnant mother and made Miles what he was, had been a purely military poison.

"—and I fought the Komarr Revolt. You infants who've come up in the past decade and more have no concept of combat. These long periods of unbroken peace weaken the Service. If they go on much longer, when a crisis comes there'll be no one left who's had any real practice in a crunch."

Miles's eyes crossed slightly, from internal pressure. *Then should His Imperial Majesty provide a war every five years, as a convenience for the advancement of his officers' careers?* His mind boggled slightly over the concept of "real practice." Had Miles maybe acquired his first clue why this superb-looking officer had washed up on Kyril Island?

Metzov was still expanding, self-stimulated. "In a real combat situation, a soldier's equipment is vital. It can be the difference between victory and defeat. A man who loses his equipment loses his effectiveness as a soldier. A man disarmed in a technological war might as well be a woman, useless! And you disarmed yourself!"

Miles wondered sourly if the general would then agree that a woman armed in a technological war might as well be a man . . . no, probably not. Not a Barrayaran of his generation.

Metzov's voice descended again, dropping from military philosophy to the immediately practical. Miles was relieved. "The usual punishment for a man bogging a scat-cat is to dig it out himself. By hand. I understand that won't be feasible, since the depth to which you sank yours is a new camp record. Nevertheless, you will report at 1400 to Lieutenant Bonn of Engineering, to assist him as he sees fit."

Well, that was certainly fair. And would probably be educational, too. Miles prayed this interview was winding down. *Dismissed, now?* But the general fell silent, squinty-eyed and thoughtful.

"For the damage you did to the weather station," Metzov began slowly, then sat up more decisively—his eyes, Miles could almost swear, lighting with a faint red glow, the corner of that seamed mouth twitching upward, "you will supervise basic-labor detail for one week. Four hours a day. That's in addition to your other duties. Report to Sergeant Neuve, in Maintenance, at 0500 daily."

A slight choked inhalation sounded from the corporal still standing behind Miles, which Miles could not interpret. Laughter? Horror?

But . . . *unjust!* And he would lose a significant fraction of the precious time remaining to decant technical expertise from Ahn. . . . "The damage I did to the weather station was not a stupid accident like the scatcat, sir! It was necessary to my survival."

General Metzov fixed him with a very cold eye. "Make that six hours a day, Ensign Vorkosigan."

Miles spoke through his teeth, words jerked out as though by pliers. "Would you have preferred the interview you'd be having right now if I'd permitted myself to freeze, sir?"

Silence fell, very dead. Swelling, like a road-killed animal in the summer sun.

"You are dismissed, Ensign," General Metzov hissed at last. His eyes were glittering slits.

Miles saluted, about-faced, and marched, stiff as any ancient ramrod. Or board. Or corpse. His blood beat in his ears; his chin jerked upward. Past the corporal, who was standing at attention doing a fair imitation of a waxwork. Out the door, out the outer door. Alone at last in the Administration Building's lower corridor.

Miles cursed himself silently, then out loud. He really had to try to cultivate a more normal attitude toward senior officers. It was his bloody upbringing that lay at the root of the problem, he was sure. Too many years of tripping over herds of generals, admirals, and senior staff at Vorkosigan House, at lunch, dinner, all hours. Too much time sitting quiet as a mouse, cultivating invisibility, permitted to listen to their extremely blunt argument and debate on a hundred topics. He saw them as they saw each other, maybe. When a normal ensign looked at his commander, he ought to see a godlike being, not a, a . . . future subordinate. New ensigns were supposed to be a subhuman species anyway.

And yet . . . *What is it about this guy Metzov?* He'd met others of the type before, of assorted political stripes. Many of them were cheerful and effective soldiers, as long as they stayed out of politics. As a party, the military conservatives had been eclipsed ever since the bloody fall of the cabal of officers responsible for the disastrous Escobar invasion, over two decades ago. But the danger of revolution from the far right, some would-be junta assembling to save the Emperor from his own government, remained quite real in Miles's father's mind, he knew.

So, was it some subtle political odor emanating from Metzov that had raised the hairs on the back of Miles's neck? Surely not. A man of real political subtlety would seek to use Miles, not abuse him. *Or are you just pissed because he stuck you on some humiliating garbage detail?* A man didn't have to be politically extreme to take a certain sadistic joy in sticking it to a representative of the Vor class. Could be Metzov had been diddled in the past himself by some arrogant Vor lord. Political, social, genetic . . . the possibilities were endless.

Miles shook the static from his head, and limped off to change to his black fatigues and locate Base Engineering. No help for it now, he was sunk deeper than his scat-cat. He'd simply have to avoid Metzov as much as possible for the next six months. Anything Ahn could do so well, Miles could surely do too.

Lieutenant Bonn prepared to probe for the scat-cat. The engineering lieutenant was a slight man, maybe twenty-eight or thirty years old, with a craggy face surfaced with pocked sallow skin, reddened by the climate. Calculating brown eyes, competent-looking hands, and a sardonic air which, Miles sensed, might be permanent and not merely directed at himself. Bonn and Miles squished about atop the bog, while two engineering techs in black insulated coveralls sat perched on their heavy hovercab, safely parked on a nearby rocky outcrop. The sun was pale, the endless wind cold and damp.

"Try about there, sir," Miles suggested, pointing, trying to estimate angles and distances in a place he had only seen at dusk. "I think you'll have to go down at least two meters."

Lieutenant Bonn gave him a joyless look, raised his long metal probe to the vertical, and shoved it into the bog. It jammed almost immediately. Miles frowned puzzlement. Surely the scat-cat couldn't have floated upward. . . .

Bonn, looking unexcited, leaned his weight into the rod and twisted. It began to grind downward.

"What did you run into?" Miles asked.

"Ice," Bonn grunted. "'Bout three centimeters thick right now. We're standing on a layer of ice, underneath this surface crud, just like a frozen lake except it's frozen mud."

Miles stamped experimentally. Wet, but solid. Much as it had felt when he had camped on it.

Bonn, watching him, added, "The ice thickness varies with the weather. From a few centimeters to solid-to-the-bottom. Midwinter, you could park a freight shuttle on this bog. Come summer, it thins out. It can thaw from seeming-solid to liquid in a few hours, when the temperature is just right, and back again."

"I . . . think I found that out."

"Lean," ordered Bonn laconically, and Miles wrapped his hands around the rod and helped shove. He could feel the scrunch as it scraped past the ice layer. And if the temperature had dropped a little more, the night he'd sunk himself, and the mud re-frozen, would he have been able to punch up through the icy seal? He shuddered inwardly, and zipped his parka half-up, over his black fatigues.

"Cold?" said Bonn.

"Thinking."

"Good. Make it a habit." Bonn touched a control, and the rod's sonic probe beeped at a teeth-aching frequency. The readout displayed a bright teardrop shape a few meters over. "There it is." Bonn eyed the numbers on the readout. "It's really down in there, isn't it? I'd let you dig it out with a teaspoon, Ensign, but I suppose winter would set in before you were done." He sighed, and stared down at Miles as though picturing the scene.

Miles could picture it too. "Yes, sir," he said carefully.

They pulled the probe back out. Cold mud slicked the surface under their gloved hands. Bonn marked the spot and waved to his techs. "Here, boys!" They waved back, hopped down off the hovercab, and swung within. Bonn and Miles scrambled well out of the way, onto the rocks toward the weather station.

The hovercab whined into the air and positioned itself over the bog. Its heavy-duty space-rated tractor beam punched downward. Mud, plant matter, and ice geysered out in all directions with a roar. In a couple of minutes, the beam had created an oozing crater, with a glimmering pearl at the bottom. The crater's sides began to slump inward at once, but the hovercab operator narrowed and reversed his beam, and the scat-cat rose, noisily sucking free from its matrix. The limp bubble shelter dangled repellently from its chain. The hovercab set its load down delicately in the rocky area, and landed beside it.

Bonn and Miles trooped over to view the sodden remains. "You weren't in that bubble-shelter, were you, Ensign?" said Bonn, prodding it with his toe.

"Yes, sir, I was. Waiting for daylight. I . . . fell asleep."

"But you got out before it sank."

"Well, no. When I woke up, it was all the way under."

Bonn's crooked eyebrows rose. "How far?"

Miles's flat hand found the level of his chin.

Bonn looked startled. "How'd you get out of the suction?"

"With difficulty. And adrenaline, I think. I slipped out of my boots and pants. Which reminds me, may I take a minute and look for my boots, sir?"

Bonn waved a hand, and Miles trudged back out onto the bog, circling the ring of muck spewed from the tractor beam, keeping a safe distance from the now water-filling crater. He found one mud-coated boot, but not the other. Should he save it, on the off-chance he might have one leg amputated someday? It would probably be the wrong leg. He sighed, and climbed back up to Bonn.

Bonn frowned down at the ruined boot dangling from Miles's hand. "You could have been killed," he said in a tone of realization.

"Three times over. Smothered in the bubble shelter, trapped in the bog, or frozen waiting for rescue."

Bonn gave him a penetrating stare. "Really." He walked away from the deflated shelter, idly, as if seeking a wider view. Miles followed. When they were out of earshot of the techs, Bonn stopped and scanned the bog. Conversationally, he remarked, "I heard—unofficially—that a certain motor-pool tech named Pattas was bragging to one of his mates that he'd set you up for this. And you were too stupid to even realize you'd been had. That bragging could have been . . . not too bright, if you'd been killed."

"If I'd been killed, it wouldn't have mattered if he'd bragged or not." Miles shrugged. "What a Service investigation missed, I flat guarantee the Imperial Security investigation would have found."

"You knew you'd been set up?" Bonn studied the horizon.

"Yes."

"I'm surprised you didn't call Imperial Security in, then."

"Oh? Think about it, sir."

Bonn's gaze returned to Miles, as if taking inventory of his distasteful deformities. "You don't add up for me, Vorkosigan. Why did they let you in the Service?"

"Why d'you think?"

"Vor privilege."

"Got it in one."

"Then why are you here? Vor privilege gets sent to HQ."

"Vorbarr Sultana is lovely this time of year," said Miles agreeably. And how was his cousin Ivan enjoying it right now? "But I want ship duty."

"And you couldn't arrange it?" said Bonn skeptically.

"I was told to earn it. That's why I'm here. To prove I can handle the Service. Or . . . not. Calling in a wolf pack from ImpSec within a week of my arrival to turn the base and everyone on it inside out looking for assassination conspiracies—where, I judge, none exist—

would not advance me toward my goal. No matter how entertaining it might be." Messy charges, his word against their two words—even if Miles had pushed it to a formal investigation, with fast-penta to prove him right, the ruckus could hurt him far more in the long run than his two tormentors. No. No revenge was worth the *Prince Serg*.

"The motor pool is in Engineering's chain of command. If Imperial Security fell on it, they'd also fall on me." Bonn's brown eyes glinted.

"You're welcome to fall on anyone you please, sir. But if you have unofficial ways of receiving information, it follows you must have unofficial ways of sending it, too. And after all, you've only my word for what happened." Miles hefted his useless single boot, and heaved it back into the bog.

Thoughtfully, Bonn watched it arc and splash down in a pool of brown meltwater. "A Vor lord's word?"

"Means nothing, in these degenerate days." Miles bared his teeth in a smile of sorts. "Ask anyone."

"Huh." Bonn shook his head, and started back toward the hovercab.

Next morning Miles reported to the maintenance shed for the second half of the scat-cat retrieval job, cleaning all the mud-caked equipment. The sun was bright today, and had been up for hours, but Miles's body knew it was only 0500. An hour into his task he'd begun to warm up, feel better, and get into the rhythm of the thing.

At 0630, the deadpan Lieutenant Bonn arrived, and delivered two helpers unto Miles.

"Why, Corporal Olney. Tech Pattas. We meet again." Miles smiled with acid cheer. The pair exchanged an uneasy look. Miles kept his demeanor absolutely even.

He then kept everyone, starting with himself, moving

briskly. The conversation seemed to automatically limit itself to brief, wary technicalities. By the time Miles had to knock off and go report to Lieutenant Ahn, the scat-cat and most of the gear had been restored to better condition than Miles had received it.

He wished his two helpers, now driven to near-twitchiness by uncertainty, an earnest good-day. Well, if they hadn't figured it out by now, they were hopeless. Miles wondered bitterly why he seemed to have so much better luck establishing rapport with bright men like Bonn. Cecil had been right, if Miles couldn't figure out how to command the dull as well, he'd never make it as a Service officer. Not at Camp Permafrost, anyway.

The following morning, the third of his official punishment seven, Miles presented himself to Sergeant Neuve. The sergeant in turn presented Miles with a scat-cat full of equipment, a disk of the related equipment manuals, and the schedule for drain and culvert maintenance for Lazkowski Base. Clearly, it was to be another learning experience. Miles wondered if General Metzov had selected this task personally. He rather thought so.

On the bright side, he had his two helpers back again. This particular civil engineering task had apparently never fallen on Olney or Pattas before either, so they had no edge of superior knowledge with which to trip Miles. They had to stop and read the manuals first too. Miles swotted procedures and directed operations with a good cheer that edged toward manic as his helpers became glummer.

There was, after all, a certain fascination to the clever drain-cleaning devices. And excitement. Flushing pipes with high pressure could produce some surprising effects. There were chemical compounds that had some quite military properties, such as the ability to dissolve anything instantly, including human flesh. In the following three days Miles learned more about the infrastructure of Lazkowski Base than he'd ever imagined wanting to know. He'd even calculated the point where one well-placed charge could bring the entire system down, if he ever decided he wanted to destroy the place.

On the sixth day, Miles and his team were sent to clear a blocked culvert out by the grubs' practice fields. It was easy to spot. A silver sheet of water lapped the raised roadway on one side; on the other only a feeble trickle emerged to creep away down the bottom of a deep ditch.

Miles took a long telescoping pole from the back of their scat-cat, and probed down into the water's opaque surface. Nothing seemed to be blocking the flooded end of the culvert. Whatever it was must be jammed farther in. Joy. He handed the pole back to Pattas and wandered over to the other side of the road, and stared down into the ditch. The culvert, he noted, was something over half a meter in diameter. "Give me a light," he said to Olney.

He shucked his parka and tossed it into the scat-cat, and scrambled down into the ditch. He aimed his light into the aperture. The culvert evidently curved slightly; he couldn't see a damned thing. He sighed, considering the relative width of Olney's shoulders, Pattas's, and his own.

Could there be anything further from ship duty than this? The closest he'd come to anything of the sort was spelunking in the Dendarii Mountains. Earth and water, versus fire and air. He seemed to be building up a helluva supply of yin, the balancing yang to come had better be stupendous.

He gripped the light tighter, dropped to hands and knees, and shinnied into the drain.

The icy water soaked the trouser knees of his black fatigues. The effect was numbing. Water leaked around the top of one of his gloves. It felt like a knife blade on his wrist.

Miles meditated briefly on Olney and Pattas. They had developed a cool, reasonably efficient working relationship over the last few days, based, Miles had no illusions, on a fear of God instilled in the two men by Miles's good angel Lieutenant Bonn. How did Bonn accomplish that quiet authority, anyway? He had to figure that one out. Bonn was good at his job, for starters, but what else?

Miles scraped round the curve, shone his light on the clot, and recoiled, swearing. He paused a moment to regain control of his breath, examined the blockage more closely, and backed out.

He stood up in the bottom of the ditch, straightening his spine vertebra by creaking vertebra. Corporal Olney stuck his head over the road's railing, above. "What's in there, Ensign?"

Miles grinned up at him, still catching his breath. "Pair of boots."

"That's all?" said Olney.

"Their owner is still wearing 'em."

CHAPTER FOUR

Miles called the base surgeon on the scat-cat's comm link, urgently requesting his presence with forensic kit, body bag, and medical transport. Miles and his crew then blocked the upper end of the drain with a plastic signboard forcibly borrowed from the empty practice field beyond. Now so thoroughly wet and cold that it made no difference, Miles crawled back into the culvert to attach a rope to the anonymous booted ankles. When he emerged, the surgeon and his corpsman had arrived.

The surgeon, a big, balding man, peered dubiously into the drainpipe. "What could you see in there, Ensign? What happened?"

"I can't see anything from this end but legs, sir," Miles reported. "He's got himself wedged in there but good. Drain crud up above him, I'd guess. We'll have to see what spills out with him."

"What the hell was he doing in there?" The surgeon scratched his freckled scalp.

Miles spread his hands. "Seems a peculiar way to commit suicide. Slow and chancy, as far as drowning yourself goes."

The surgeon raised his eyebrows in agreement. Miles and the surgeon had to lend their weight on the rope to Olney, Pattas, and the corpsman before the stiff form wedged in the culvert began to scrape free.

"He's *stuck,*" observed the corpsman, grunting. The body jerked out at last with a gush of dirty water. Pattas and Olney stared from a distance; Miles glued himself to the surgeon's shoulder. The corpse, dressed in sodden black fatigues, was waxy and blue. His collar tabs and the contents of his pockets identified him as a private from Supply. His body bore no obvious wounds, but for bruised shoulders and scraped hands.

The surgeon spoke clipped, negative preliminaries into his recorder. No broken bones, no nerve disruptor blisters. Preliminary hypothesis, death from drowning or hypothermia or both, within the last twelve hours. He flipped off his recorder and added over his shoulder, "I'll be able to tell for sure when we get him laid out back at the infirmary."

"Does this sort of thing happen often around here?" Miles inquired mildly.

The surgeon shot him a sour look. "I slab a few idiots every year. What d'you expect, when you put five thousand kids between the ages of eighteen and twenty together on an island and tell 'em to go play war? I admit, this one seems to have discovered a completely new method of slabbing himself. I guess you never see it all."

"You think he did it to himself, then?" True, it would be real tricky to kill a man and *then* stuff him in there.

The surgeon wandered over to the culvert and squatted, and stared into it. "So it would seem. Ah, would you take one more look in there, Ensign, just in case?"

"Very well, sir." Miles hoped it was the last trip. He'd never have guessed drain cleaning would turn out to be so . . . thrilling. He slithered all the way under the road to the leaky board, checking every centimeter, but found only the dead man's dropped hand light. So. The private had evidently entered the pipe on purpose. With intent. What intent? Why go culvert-crawling in the middle of the night in the middle of a heavy rainstorm? Miles skinned back out and turned the light over to the surgeon.

Miles helped the corpsman and surgeon bag and load the body, then had Olney and Pattas raise the blocking board and return it to its original location. Brown water gushed, roaring, from the bottom end of the culvert and roiled away down the ditch. The surgeon paused with Miles, leaning on the road railing and watching the water level drop in the little lake.

"Think there might be another one at the bottom?" Miles inquired morbidly.

"This guy was the only one listed as missing on the morning report," the surgeon replied, "so probably not." He didn't look like he was willing to bet on it, though.

The only thing that did turn up, as the water level fell, was the private's soggy parka. He'd clearly tossed it over the railing before entering the culvert, from which it had fallen or blown into the water. The surgeon took it away with him.

"You're pretty cool about that," Pattas noted, as Miles turned away from the back of the medical transport and the surgeon and corpsman drove off.

Pattas was not that much older than Miles himself. "Haven't you ever had to handle a corpse?"

"No. You?"

"Yes."

"Where?"

Miles hesitated. Events of three years ago flickered through his memory. The brief months he'd been caught in desperate combat far from home, having accidently fallen in with a space mercenary force, was not a secret to be mentioned or even hinted at here. Regular Imperial troops despised mercenaries anyway, alive or dead. But the Tau Verde campaign had surely taught him the difference between "practice" and "real," between war and war games, and that death had subtler vectors than direct touch. "Before," said Miles dampingly. "Couple of times."

Pattas shrugged, veering off. "Well," he allowed grudgingly over his shoulder, "at least you're not afraid to get your hands dirty. Sir."

Miles's brows crooked, bemused. *No. That's not what I'm afraid of.*

Miles marked the drain "cleared" on his report panel, turned the scat-cat, their equipment, and a very subdued Olney and Pattas back in to Sergeant Neuve in Maintenance, and headed for the officers' barracks. He'd never wanted a hot shower more in his entire life.

He was squelching down the corridor toward his quarters when another officer stuck his head out a door. "Ah, Ensign Vorkosigan?"

"Yes?"

"You got a vid call a while ago. I encoded the return for you."

"Call?" Miles stopped. "Where from?"

"Vorbarr Sultana."

Miles felt a chill in his belly. Some emergency at home? "Thanks." He reversed direction, and beelined for the end of the corridor and the vidconsole booth that the officers on this level shared.

He slid damply into the seat and punched up the message. The number was not one he recognized. He entered it, and his charge code, and waited. It chimed several times, then the vidplate hissed to life. His cousin Ivan's handsome face materialized over it, and grinned at him.

"Ah, Miles. There you are."

"Ivan! Where the devil are you? What is this?"

"Oh, I'm at home. And that doesn't mean my mother's. I thought you might like to see my new flat."

Miles had the vague, disoriented sensation that he'd somehow tapped a line into some parallel universe, or alternate astral plane. Vorbarr Sultana, yes. He'd lived in the capital himself, in a previous incarnation. Eons ago.

Ivan lifted his vid pick-up, and aimed it around, dizzyingly. "It's fully furnished. I took over the lease from an Ops captain who was being transferred to Komarr. A real bargain. I just got moved in yesterday. Can you see the balcony?"

Miles could see the balcony, drenched in late-afternoon sunlight the color of warm honey. The Vorbarr Sultana skyline rose like a fairy-tale city, swimming in the summer haze beyond. Scarlet flowers swarmed over the railing, so red in the level light they almost hurt his eyes. Miles felt like drooling into his shirt pocket, or bursting into tears. "Nice flowers," he choked.

"Yeah, m'girlfriend brought 'em."

"Girlfriend?" Ah yes, human beings had come in two sexes, once upon a time. One smelled much better than the other. Much. "Which one?"

"Tatya."

"Have I met her?" Miles struggled to remember.

"Naw, she's new."

Ivan stopped waving the vid pick-up around, and reappeared over the vid-plate. Miles's exacerbated senses settled slightly. "So how's the weather up there?" Ivan peered at him more closely. "Are you wet? What have you been doing?"

"Forensic . . . plumbing," Miles offered after a pause.

"What?" Ivan's brow wrinkled.

"Never mind." Miles sneezed. "Look, I'm glad to see a familiar face and all that," he was, actually—a painful, strange gladness, "but I'm in the middle of my duty day, here."

"I got off-shift a couple of hours ago," Ivan remarked. "I'm taking Tatya out for dinner in a bit. You just caught me. So just tell me quick, how's life in the infantry?"

"Oh, great. Lazkowski Base is the real thing, y'know." Miles did not define what real thing. "Not a . . . warehouse for excess Vor lordlings like Imperial Headquarters."

"I do my job!" said Ivan, sounding slightly stung. "Actually, you'd like my job. We process information. It's amazing, all the stuff Ops accesses in a day's time. It's like being on top of the world. It would be just your speed."

"Funny. I've thought that Lazkowski Base would be just yours, Ivan. Suppose they could have got our orders reversed?"

Ivan tapped the side of his nose and sniggered. "I wouldn't tell." His humor sobered in a glint of real concern. "You, ah, take care of yourself up there, eh? You really don't look so good."

"I've had an unusual morning. If you'd sod off, I could go get a shower."

"Oh, right. Well, take care."

"Enjoy your dinner."

"Right-oh. 'Bye."

Voices from another universe. At that, Vorbarr Sultana was only a couple of hours away by sub-orbital flight. In theory. Miles was obscurely comforted, to be reminded that the whole planet hadn't shrunk to the lead-grey horizons of Kyril Island, even if his part of it seemed to have.

Miles found it difficult to concentrate on the weather, the rest of that day. Fortunately his superior didn't much notice. Since the scat-cat sinking Ahn had tended to maintain a guilty, nervous silence around Miles except when directly prodded for specific information. When his duty-day ended Miles headed straight for the infirmary.

The surgeon was still working, or at least sitting, at his desk console when Miles poked his head around the door frame. "Good evening, sir."

The surgeon glanced up. "Yes, Ensign? What is it?"

Miles took this as sufficient invitation despite the unencouraging tone of voice, and slipped within. "I was wondering what you'd found out about that fellow we pulled from the culvert this morning."

The surgeon shrugged. "Not that much to find out. His ID checked. He died of drowning. All the physical and metabolic evidence—stress, hypothermia, the hematomas—are consistent with his being stuck in there for a bit less than half an hour before death. I've ruled it death by misadventure."

"Yes, but why?"

"Why?" The surgeon's eyebrows rose. "He slabbed himself, you'll have to ask him, eh?"

"Don't you want to find out?"

"To what purpose?"

"Well . . . to know, I guess. To be sure you're right."

The surgeon gave him a dry stare.

"I'm not questioning your medical findings, sir," Miles added hastily. "But it was just so damn weird. Aren't you curious?"

"Not anymore," said the surgeon. "I'm satisfied it wasn't suicide or foul play, so whatever the details, it comes down to death from stupidity in the end, doesn't it?"

Miles wondered if that would have been the surgeon's final epitaph on him, if he'd sunk himself with the scat-cat. "I suppose so, sir."

Standing outside the infirmary afterward in the damp wind, Miles hesitated. The corpse, after all, was not Miles's personal property. Not a case of finders-keepers. He'd turned the situation over to the proper authority. It was out of his hands now. And yet . . .

There were still several hours of daylight left. Miles was having trouble sleeping anyway, in these almost-endless days. He returned to his quarters, pulled on sweat pants and shirt and running shoes, and went jogging.

The road was lonely, out by the empty practice fields. The sun crawled crabwise toward the horizon. Miles broke from a jog back to a walk, then to a slower walk. His leg-braces chafed, beneath his pants. One of these days very soon he would take the time to get the brittle long bones in his legs replaced with synthetics. At that, elective surgery might be a quasi-legitimate way to lever himself off Kyril Island, if things got too desperate before his six months were up. It seemed like cheating, though.

He looked around, trying to imagine his present surroundings in the dark and heavy rain. If he had been the private, slogging along this road about midnight, what would he have seen? What could possibly have attracted the man's attention to the ditch? Why the hell had he come out here in the middle of the night in the first place? This road wasn't on the way to anything but an obstacle course and a firing range.

There was the ditch . . . no, his ditch was the next one, a little farther on. Four culverts pierced the raised roadway along this half-kilometer straight stretch. Miles found the correct ditch and leaned on the railing, staring down at the now-sluggish trickle of drain water. There was nothing attractive about it now, that was certain. Why, why, why . . . ?

Miles sloped along up the high side of the road, examining the road surface, the railing, the sodden brown bracken beyond. He came to the curve and turned back, studying the opposite side. He arrived back at the first ditch, on the baseward end of the straight stretch, without discovering any view of charm or interest.

Miles perched on the railing and meditated. All right, time to try a little logic. What overwhelming emotion had led the private to wedge himself in the drain, despite the obvious danger? Rage? What had he been pursuing? Fear? What could have been pursuing him? Error? Miles knew all about error. What if the man had picked the wrong culvert . . . ?

Impulsively, Miles slithered down into the first ditch. Either the man had been methodically working his way through all the culverts—if so, had he been working from the base out, or from the practice fields back?—or else he had missed his intended target in the dark and rain and got into the wrong one. Miles would give them all a crawl-through if he had to, but he preferred to be right the first time. Even if there wasn't anybody watching. This culvert was slightly wider in diameter than the second, lethal one. Miles pulled his hand light from his belt, ducked within, and began examining it centimeter by centimeter.

"Ah," he breathed in satisfaction, midway beneath the road. There was his prize, stuck to the upper side of the culvert's arc with sagging tape. A package, wrapped in waterproof plastic. How *interesting.* He slithered out and sat in the mouth of the culvert, careless of the damp but carefully out of view from the road above.

He placed the packet on his lap and studied it with pleasurable anticipation, as if it had been a birthday present. Could it be drugs, contraband, classified documents, criminal cash? Personally, Miles hoped for classified documents, though it was hard to imagine anyone classifying anything on Kyril Island except maybe the efficiency reports. Drugs would be all right, but a spy ring would be just wonderful. He'd be a Security hero—his mind raced ahead, already plotting the next move in his covert investigation. Following the dead man's trail through subtle clues to some ring-leader, who knew how high up? The dramatic arrests, maybe a commendation from Simon Illyan himself. . . . The package was lumpy, but crackled slightly—plastic flimsies?

Heart hammering, he eased it open—and slumped in stunned disappointment. A pained breath, half-laugh, half-moan, puffed from his lips.

Pastries. A couple of dozen lisettes, a kind of miniature popover glazed and stuffed with candied fruit, made, traditionally, for the midsummer day celebration. Month and a half old stale pastries. What a cause to die for. . . .

Miles's imagination, fueled by knowledge of barracks life, sketched in the rest readily enough. The private had received this package from some sweetheart/mother/sister, and sought to protect it from his ravenous mates, who would have wolfed it all down in seconds. Perhaps the man, starved for home, had been rationing them out to himself morsel by morsel in a lingering masochistic ritual, pleasure and pain mixed with each bite. Or maybe he'd just been saving them for some special occasion.

Then came the two days of unusual heavy rain, and the man had begun to fear for his secret treasure's, ah, liquidity margin. He'd come out to rescue his cache, missed the first ditch in the dark, gone at the second in desperate determination as the waters rose, realized his mistake too late. . . .

Sad. A little sickening. But not *useful.* Miles sighed, and bundled the lisettes back up, and trotted off with the package under his arm, back to the base to turn it over to the surgeon.

The surgeon's only comment, when Miles caught up with him and explained his findings, was "Yep. Death from stupidity, all right." Absently, he bit into a lisette and sniffed.

Miles's time on maintenance detail ended the next day without his finding anything in the sewers of greater interest than the drowned man. It was probably just as well. The following day Ahn's office corporal arrived back from his long leave. Miles discovered that the corporal, who'd been working the weather office for some two years, was a ready reservoir of the greater part of the information Miles had spent the last two weeks busting his brains to learn. He didn't have Ahn's nose, though.

Ahn actually left Camp Permafrost sober, walking up the transport's ramp under his own power. Miles went to the shuttle pad to see him off, not certain if he was glad or sorry to see the weatherman go. Ahn looked happy, though, his lugubrious face almost illuminated.

"So where are you headed, once you turn in your uniforms?" Miles asked him.

"The equator."

"Ah? Where on the equator?"

"*Anywhere* on the equator," Ahn replied with fervor.

Miles trusted he'd at least pick a spot with a suitable land mass under it.

Ahn hesitated on the ramp, looking down at Miles. "Watch out for Metzov," he advised at last.

This warning seemed remarkably late, not to mention maddeningly vague. Miles gave Ahn an exasperated look, up from under his raised eyebrows. "I doubt I'll be much featured on his social calendar."

Ahn shifted uncomfortably. "That's not what I meant."

"What do you mean?"

"Well . . . I don't know. I once saw . . ."

"What?"

Ahn shook his head. "Nothing. It was a long time ago. A lot of crazy things were happening, at the height of the Komarr revolt. But it's better that you should stay out of his way."

"I've had to deal with old martinets before."

"Oh, he's not exactly a martinet. But he's got a streak of . . . he can be a funny kind of dangerous. Don't ever really threaten him, huh?"

"Me, threaten Metzov?" Miles's face screwed up in bafflement. Maybe Ahn wasn't as sober as he smelled after all. "Come on, he can't be that bad, or they'd never put him in charge of trainees."

"He doesn't command the grubs. They have their own hierarchy comes in with 'em—the instructors report to their own commander. Metzov's just in charge of the base's permanent physical plant. You're a pushy little sod, Vorkosigan. Just don't . . . ever push him to the edge, or you'll be sorry. And that's all I'm going to say." Ahn shut his mouth determinedly, and headed up the ramp.

I'm already sorry, Miles thought of calling after him. Well, his punishment week was over now. Perhaps Metzov had meant the labor detail to humiliate Miles, but actually it had been quite interesting. Sinking his scat-cat, now, that had been humiliating. *That* he had done to himself. Miles waved one last time to Ahn as he disappeared into the transport shuttle, shrugged, and headed back across the tarmac toward the now-familiar admin building.

It took a full couple of minutes, after Miles's corporal had left the weather office for lunch, for Miles to yield to the temptation to scratch the itch Ahn had planted in his mind, and punch up Metzov's public record on the comconsole. The mere listing of the base commander's dates, assignments, and promotions was not terribly informative, though a little knowledge of history filled in between the lines.

Metzov had entered the Service some thirty-five years ago. His most rapid promotions had occurred, not surprisingly, during the conquest of the planet Komarr about twenty-five years ago. The wormhole-rich Komarr system was Barrayar's sole gate to the greater galactic wormhole route nexus. Komarr had proved its immense strategic importance to Barrayar earlier in the century, when its ruling oligarchy had accepted a bribe to let a Cetagandan invasion fleet pass through its wormholes and descend on Barrayar. Throwing the Cetagandans back out again had consumed a Barrayaran generation. Barrayar had turned its bloody lesson around in Miles's father's day. As an unavoidable side effect of securing Komarr's gates, Barrayar had been transformed from backwater cul-de-sac to a minor but significant galactic power, and was still wrestling with the consequences.

Metzov had somehow managed to end up on the correct side during Vordarian's Pretendership, a purely

Barrayaran attempt to wrest power from then-five-year-old Emperor Gregor and his Regent, two decades past—picking the wrong side in that civil affray would have been Miles's first guess why such an apparently competent officer had ended up marking out his later years on ice on Kyril Island. But the dead halt to Metzov's career seemed to come during the Komarr Revolt, some sixteen years ago now. No hint in this file as to why, but for a cross-reference to another file. An Imperial Security code, Miles recognized. Dead end there.

Or maybe not. Lips compressed thoughtfully, Miles punched through another code on his comconsole.

"Operations, Commodore Jollif's office," Ivan began formally as his face materialized over the comconsole vid plate, then, "Oh, hello, Miles. What's up?"

"I'm doing a little research. Thought you might help me out."

"I should have known you wouldn't call me at HQ just to be sociable. So what d'you want?"

"Ah . . . do you have the office to yourself, just at present?"

"Yeah, the old man's stuck in committee. Nice little flap—a Barrayaran-registered freighter got itself impounded in the Hegen Hub—at Vervain Station—for suspicion of espionage."

"Can we get at it? Threaten rescue?"

"Not past Pol. No Barrayaran military vessels may jump through their wormholes, period."

"I thought we were sort of friends with Pol."

"Sort of. But the Vervani have been threatening to break off diplomatic relations with Pol, so the Polians are being extra cautious. Funny thing about it, the freighter in question isn't even one of our real agents. Seems to be a completely manufactured accusation."

Wormhole route politics. Jump ship tactics. Just the

sort of challenge his Imperial Academy courses had trained Miles to meet. Furthermore, it was probably warm on those spaceships and space stations. Miles sighed envy.

Ivan's eyes narrowed in belated suspicion. "Why do you ask if I'm alone?"

"I want you to pull a file for me. Ancient history, not current events," Miles reassured him, and reeled off the code-string.

"Ah." Ivan's hand started to tap it out, then stopped. "Are you crazy? That's an Imperial Security file. No can do!"

"Of course you can, you're right there, aren't you?"

Ivan shook his head smugly. "Not any more. The whole ImpSec file system's been made super-secure. You can't transfer data out of it except through a coded filter-cable, which you must physically attach. Which I would have to sign for. Which I would have to explain why I wanted it and produce authorization. You got an authorization for this? Ha. I thought not."

Miles frowned frustration. "Surely you can call it up on the internal system."

"On the internal system, yes. What I can't do is connect the internal system to any external system for a data dump. So you're out of luck."

"You got an internal system comconsole in that office?"

"Sure."

"So," said Miles impatiently, "call up the file, turn your desk around, and let the two vids talk to each other. You can do that, can't you?"

Ivan scratched his head. "Would that work?"

"Try it!" Miles drummed his fingers while Ivan dragged his desk around and fiddled with focus. The signal was degraded but readable. "There, I thought so. Scroll it up for me, would you?"

Fascinating, utterly fascinating. The file was a collection of secret reports from an ImpSec investigation into the mysterious death of a prisoner in Metzov's charge, a Komarran rebel who had killed his guard and himself been killed while attempting to escape. When ImpSec had demanded the Komarran's body for an autopsy, Metzov had turned over cremated ashes and an apology; if only he had been told a few hours earlier the body was wanted, etc. The investigating officer hinted at charges of illegal torture—perhaps in revenge for the death of the guard?—but was unable to amass enough evidence to obtain authorization to fast-penta the Barrayaran witnesses, including a certain Tech-ensign Ahn. The investigating officer had lodged a formal protest of his superior officer's decision to close the case, and there it ended. Apparently. If there was any more to the story it existed only in Simon Illyan's remarkable head, a secret file Miles was not about to attempt to access. And yet Metzov's career had stopped, literally, cold.

"Miles," Ivan interrupted for the fourth time, "I really don't think we should be doing this. This is slit-your-throat-before-reading stuff, here."

"If we shouldn't do it, we shouldn't be *able* to do it. You'd still have to have the cable for flash-downloading. No real spy would be dumb enough to sit there inside Imperial HQ by the hour and scroll stuff through by hand, waiting to be caught and shot."

"That does it." Ivan killed the Security file with a swat of his hand. The vid image wavered wildly as Ivan dragged his desk back around, followed by scrubbing noises as he frantically rubbed out the tracks in his carpet with his boot. "I didn't do this, you hear?"

"I didn't mean you. *We're* not spies." Miles subsided glumly. "Still . . . I suppose somebody ought to tell Illyan about the little hole they overlooked in his Security arrangements."

"Not me!"

"Why not you? Put it in as a brilliant theoretical suggestion. Maybe you'll earn a commendation. Don't tell 'em we actually did it, of course. Or maybe we were just testing your theory, eh?"

"You," said Ivan severely, "are career-poison. Never darken my vid-plate again. Except at home, of course."

Miles grinned, and permitted his cousin to escape. He sat awhile in the office, watching the colorful weather holos flicker and change, and thinking about his base commander, and the kinds of accidents that could happen to defiant prisoners.

Well, it had all been very long ago. Metzov himself would probably be retiring in another five years, with his status as a double-twenty-years-man and a pension, to merge into the population of unpleasant old men. Not so much a problem to be solved as to be outlived, at least by Miles. His ultimate purpose at Lazkowski Base, Miles reminded himself, was to escape Lazkowski Base, silently as smoke. Metzov would be left behind in time.

In the next weeks Miles settled into a tolerable routine. For one thing, the grubs arrived. All five thousand of them. Miles's status rose on their shoulders, to that of almost-human. Lazkowski Base suffered its first real snow of the season, as the days shortened, plus a mild wah-wah lasting half a day, both of which Miles managed to predict accurately in advance.

Even more happily, Miles was completely displaced as the most famous idiot on the island (an unwelcome notoriety earned by the scat-cat sinking) by a group of grubs who managed one night to set their barracks on fire while lighting fart-flares. Miles's strategic suggestion at the officers' fire-safety meeting next day that they tackle the problem with a logistical assault on the enemy's fuel supply, i.e., eliminate red-bean stew from the menu, was shot down with one icy glower from General Metzov. Though in the hallway later, an earnest captain from Ordnance stopped Miles to thank him for trying.

So much for the glamour of the Imperial Service. Miles took to spending long hours alone in the weather office, studying chaos theory, his readouts, and the walls. Three months down, three to go. It was getting darker.

CHAPTER FIVE

Miles was out of bed and half dressed before it penetrated his sleep-stunned brain that the galvanizing klaxon was not the wah-wah warning. He paused with a boot in his hand. Not fire or enemy attack, either. Not his department, then, whatever it was. The rhythmic blatting stopped. They were right, silence was golden.

He checked the glowing digital clock. It claimed midevening. He'd only been asleep about two hours, having fallen into bed exhausted after a long trip up-island in a snowstorm to repair wind damage to Weather Station Eleven. The comm link by his bed was not blinking its red call light to inform him of any surprise duties he must carry out. He could go back to bed.

Silence was *baffling.*

He pulled on the second boot and stuck his head out his door. A couple of other officers had done the same, and were speculating to each other on the cause of the alarm. Lieutenant Bonn emerged from his quarters and strode down the hall, jerking on his parka. His face looked strained, half-worry, half-annoyance.

Miles grabbed his own parka and galloped after him. "You need a hand, Lieutenant?"

Bonn glanced down at him, and pursed his lips. "I might," he allowed.

Miles fell in beside him, secretly pleased by Bonn's implicit judgment that he might in fact be useful. "So what's up?"

"Some sort of accident in a toxic stores bunker. If it's the one I think, we could have a real problem."

They exited the double-doored heat-retaining vestibule from the officers' quarters into a night gone crystal cold. Fine snow squeaked under Miles's boots and swept along the ground in a faint east wind. The brightest stars overhead held their own against the base's lights. The two men slid into Bonn's scat-cat, their breath smoking until the canopy-defrost cut in. Bonn headed west out of the base at high acceleration.

A few kilometers past the last practice fields, a row of turf-topped barrows hunched in the snow. A cluster of vehicles was parked at the end of one bunker—a couple of scat-cats, including the one belonging to the base fire marshall, and medical transport. Hand lights moved among them. Bonn slewed in and pulled up, and popped his door. Miles followed him, crunching rapidly across the packed ice.

The surgeon was directing a pair of corpsmen, who were loading a foil-blanketed shape and a second coverall-clad soldier who shivered and coughed onto the med transport. "All of you, put everything you're wearing into the destruct bin when you hit the door," he called after them. "Blankets, bedding, splints, everything. Full decontamination showers for you all before you even start to worry about that broken leg of his. The painkiller will hold him through it, and if it doesn't, ignore him and keep scrubbing. I'll be right behind you." The surgeon shuddered, turning away, whistling dismay through his teeth.

Bonn headed for the bunker door. "Don't open that!" the surgeon and the fire marshall called together. "There's nobody left inside," the surgeon added. "All evacuated now."

"What exactly happened?" Bonn scrubbed with a gloved hand at the frosted window set in the door, in an effort to see inside.

"Couple of guys were moving stores, to make room for a new shipment coming in tomorrow," the fire marshall, a lieutenant named Yaski, filled him in rapidly. "They dumped their loader over, one got pinned underneath with a broken leg."

"That . . . took ingenuity," said Bonn, obviously picturing the mechanics of the loader in his mind.

"They had to have been horsing around," said the surgeon impatiently. "But that's not the worst of it. They took several barrels of fetaine over with them. And at least two broke open. The stuff's all over the place in there. We've sealed the bunker as best we could. Cleanup," the surgeon exhaled, "is your problem. I'm gone." He looked like he wanted to crawl out of his own skin, as well as his clothes. He waved, making quickly for his scat-cat to follow his corpsmen and their patients through medical decontamination.

"Fetaine!" Miles exclaimed in startlement. Bonn had retreated hastily from the door. Fetaine was a mutagenic poison invented as a terror weapon but never, so far as Miles knew, used in combat. "I thought that stuff was obsolete. Off the menu." His academy course in Chemicals and Biologicals had barely mentioned it.

"It is obsolete," said Bonn grimly. "They haven't made any in twenty years. For all I know this is the last stockpile on Barrayar. Dammit, those storage barrels shouldn't have broken open even if you'd dropped 'em out a shuttle."

"Those storage barrels are at least twenty years old, then," the marshall pointed out. "Corrosion?"

"In that case," Bonn craned his neck, "what about the rest of them?"

"Exactly," nodded Yaski.

"Isn't fetaine destroyed by heat?" Miles asked nervously, checking to make sure they were standing around discussing this upwind of the bunker. "Chemically dissociated into harmless components, I heard."

"Well, not exactly harmless," said Lieutenant Yaski. "But at least they don't unravel all the DNA in your balls."

"Are there any explosives stored in there, Lieutenant Bonn?" Miles asked.

"No, only the fetaine."

"If you tossed a couple of plasma mines through the door, would the fetaine all be chemically cracked before the roof melted in?"

"You wouldn't want the roof to melt in. Or the floor. If that stuff ever got loose in the permafrost . . . But if you set the mines on slow heat release, and threw a few kilos of neutral plas-seal in with 'em, the bunker might be self-sealing." Bonn's lips moved in silent calculation. ". . . Yeah, that'd work. In fact, that could be the safest way to deal with that crap. Particularly if the rest of the barrels are starting to lose integrity too."

"Depending on which way the wind is blowing," put in Lieutenant Yaski, looking back toward the base and then at Miles.

"We're expecting a light east wind with dropping

temperatures till about 0700 tomorrow morning," Miles answered his look. "Then it'll shift around to the north and blow harder. Potential wah-wah conditions starting around 1800 tomorrow night."

"If we're going to do it that way, we'd better do it tonight, then," said Yaski.

"All right," said Bonn decisively. "I'll round up my crew, you round up yours. I'll pull the plans for the bunker, calculate the charges' release-rate, and meet you and the ordnance chief in Admin in an hour."

Bonn posted the fire marshall's sergeant as guard to keep everyone well away from the bunker. An unenviable duty, but not unbearable in present conditions, and the guard could retreat inside his scat-cat when the temperature dropped, toward midnight. Miles rode back with Bonn to the base Administration building to double-check his promises about wind direction at the weather office.

Miles ran the latest data through the weather computers, that he might present Bonn with the most refined possible update on predicted wind vectors over the next 26.7-hour Barrayaran day. But before he had the printout in his hand, he saw Bonn and Yaski out the window, down below, hurrying away from the Admin building into the dark. Perhaps they were meeting with the ordnance chief elsewhere? Miles considered chasing after them, but the new prediction was not significantly different from the older one. Did he really need to go watch them cauterize the poison dump? It could be interesting—educational—on the other hand, he had no real function there now. As his parents' only child—as the father, perhaps, of some future Count Vorkosigan—it was arguable if he even had the right to expose himself to such a vile mutagenic hazard for mere curiosity. There seemed no immediate danger to the base, till the wind shifted anyway.

Or was cowardice masquerading as logic? Prudence was a virtue, he had heard.

Now thoroughly awake, and too rattled to even imagine recapturing sleep, he pottered around the weather office, and caught up on all the routine files he had set aside that morning in favor of the repairs junket. An hour of steady plugging finished off everything that even remotely looked like work. When he found himself compulsively dusting equipment and shelves, he decided it was time to go back to bed, sleep or no sleep. But a shifting light from the window caught his eye, a scat-cat pulling up out front.

Ah, Bonn and Yaski, back. Already? That had been fast, or hadn't they started yet? Miles tore off the plastic flimsy with the new wind readout and headed downstairs to the Base Engineering office at the end of the corridor.

Bonn's office was dark. But light spilled into the corridor from the Base Commander's office. Light, and angry voices rising and falling. Clutching the flimsy, Miles approached.

The door was open to the inner office. Metzov sat at his desk console, one clenched fist resting on the flickering colored surface. Bonn and Yaski stood tensely before him. Miles rattled the flimsy cautiously to announce his presence.

Yaski's head swivelled around, and his gaze caught Miles. "Send Vorkosigan, he's a mutant already, isn't he?"

Miles gave a vaguely directed salute and said immediately, "Pardon me, sir, but no, I'm not. My last encounter with a military poison did teratogenic damage, not genetic. My future children should be as healthy as the next man's. Ah, send me where, sir?"

Metzov glowered across at Miles, but did not pursue Yaski's unsettling suggestion. Miles handed the flimsy wordlessly to Bonn, who glanced at it, grimaced, and stuffed it savagely into his trouser pocket.

"Of course I intended them to wear protective gear," continued Metzov to Bonn in irritation. "I'm not mad."

"I understood that, sir. But the men refuse to enter the bunker even with contamination gear," Bonn reported in a flat, steady voice. "I can't blame them. The standard precautions are inadequate for fetaine, in my estimation. The stuff has an incredibly high penetration value, for its molecular weight. Goes right through permeables."

"You can't *blame* them?" repeated Metzov in astonishment. "Lieutenant, you gave an order. Or you were supposed to."

"I did, sir, but—"

"But—you let them sense your own indecision. Your weakness. Dammit, when you give an order you have to give it, not dance around it."

"Why do we have to save this stuff?" said Yaski plaintively.

"We've been over that. It's our charge," Metzov grunted at him. "Our orders. You can't ask a man to give an obedience you don't give yourself."

What, blind? "Surely Research still has the recipe," Miles put in, feeling he was at last getting the alarming drift of this argument. "They can mix up more if they really want it. Fresh."

"Shut up, Vorkosigan," Bonn growled desperately out of the corner of his mouth, as General Metzov snapped, "Open your lip tonight with one more sample of your humor, Ensign, and I'll put you on charges."

Miles's lips closed over his teeth in a tight glassy smile. Subordination. The *Prince Serg*, he reminded himself. Metzov could go drink the fetaine, for all Miles cared, and it would be no skin off his nose. His clean nose, remember?

"Have you never heard of the fine old battlefield practice of shooting the man who disobeys your order, Lieutenant?" Metzov went on to Bonn.

"I . . . don't think I can make that threat, sir," said Bonn stiffly.

And besides, thought Miles, *we're not on a battle-field. Are we?*

"Techs!" said Metzov in a tone of disgust. "I didn't say threaten, I said shoot. Make one example, the rest will fall in line."

Miles decided he didn't much care for Metzov's brand of humor, either. Or was the general speaking literally?

"Sir, fetaine is a violent mutagen," said Bonn doggedly. "I'm not at all sure the rest would fall into line, no matter what the threat. It's a pretty unreasonable topic. I'm . . . a little unreasonable about it myself."

"So I see." Metzov stared at him coldly. His glare passed on to Yaski, who swallowed and stood straighter, his spine offering no concession. Miles tried to cultivate invisibility.

"If you're going to go on pretending to be military officers, you techs need a lesson in how to extract obedience from your men," Metzov decided. "Both of you go and assemble your crew in front of Admin in twenty minutes. We're going to have a little old-fashioned discipline parade."

"You're not—seriously thinking of shooting anyone, are you?" said Lieutenant Yaski in alarm.

Metzov smiled sourly. "I doubt I'll have to." He regarded Miles. "What's the outside temperature right now, Weather Officer?"

"Five degrees of frost, sir," replied Miles, careful now to speak only when spoken to.

"And the wind?"

"Winds from the east at nine kilometers per hour, sir."

"Very good." Metzov's eye gleamed wolfishly. "Dismissed, *gentlemen.* See if you can carry out your orders, this time."

General Metzov stood, heavily gloved and parka-bundled, beside the empty metal bannerpole in front of Admin, and stared down the half-lit road. Looking for what? Miles wondered. It was pushing midnight now. Yaski and Bonn were lining up their tech crews in parade array, some fifteen thermal-coveralled and parka-clad men.

Miles shivered, and not just from the cold. Metzov's seamed face looked angry. And tired. And old. And scary. He reminded Miles a bit of his grandfather on a bad day. Though Metzov was in fact younger than Miles's father; Miles had been a child of his father's middle age, some generational skew there. His grandfather, the old General Count Piotr himself, had sometimes seemed a refugee from another century. Now, the really old-fashioned discipline parades had involved lead-lined rubber hoses. How far back in Barrayaran history was Metzov's mind rooted?

Metzov smiled, a gloss over rage, and turned his head at a movement down the road. In a horribly cordial voice he confided to Miles, "You know, Ensign, there was a secret behind that carefully cultivated interservice rivalry they had back on Old Earth. In the event of a mutiny you could always persuade the army to shoot the navy, or vice versa, when they could no longer discipline themselves. A hidden disadvantage to a combined Service like ours."

"Mutiny!" said Miles, startled out of his resolve to speak only when spoken to. "I thought the issue was poison exposure."

"It *was.* Unfortunately, due to Bonn's mishandling, it's now a matter of principle." A muscle jumped in Metzov's jaw. "It had to happen sometime, in the New Service. The Soft Service."

Typical Old Service talk, that, old men bullshitting each other about how tough they'd had it in the old days. "Principle, sir, what principle? It's *waste disposal,*" Miles choked.

"It's a mass refusal to obey a direct order, Ensign. Mutiny by any barracks-lawyer's definition. Fortunately, this sort of thing is easy to dislocate, if you move quickly, while it's still small and confused."

The motion down the road resolved itself into a platoon of grubs in their winter-white camouflage gear, marching under the direction of a Base sergeant. Miles recognized the sergeant as part of Metzov's personal power-net, an old veteran who'd served under Metzov as far back as the Komarr Revolt, and who had moved on with his master.

The grubs, Miles saw, had been armed with lethal nerve-disruptors, which were purely anti-personnel hand weapons. For all the time they spent learning about such things, the opportunity for even advanced trainees such as these to lay hands on fully powered deadly weapons was rare, and Miles could sense their nervous excitement from here.

The sergeant lined the grubs up in a cross-fire array around the stiff-standing techs, and barked an order. They presented their weapons, and aimed them, the silver bell-muzzles gleaming in the scattered light from the Admin building. A twitchy ripple ran through Bonn's men. Bonn's face was ghastly white, his eyes glittering like jet.

"Strip," Metzov ordered through set teeth.

Disbelief, confusion; only one or two of the techs grasped what was being demanded, and began to undress. The others, with many uncertain glances around, belatedly followed suit.

"When you are again ready to obey your orders," Metzov continued in a parade-pitched voice that carried to every man, "you may dress and go to work. It's up to you." He stepped back, nodded to his sergeant, and took up a pose of parade rest. "That'll cool 'em off," he muttered to himself, barely loud enough for Miles to catch. Metzov looked like he fully expected to be out there no more than five minutes; he looked like he was already thinking of warm quarters and a hot drink.

Olney and Pattas were among the techs, Miles noted, along with most of the rest of the Greek-speaking cadre who had plagued Miles early on. Others Miles had seen around, or talked to during his private investigation into the background of the drowned man, or barely knew. Fifteen naked men starting to shiver violently as the dry snow whispered around their ankles. Fifteen bewildered faces beginning to look terrified. Eyes shifted toward the nerve-disruptors trained on them. *Give in,* Miles urged silently. *It's not worth it.* But more than one pair of eyes flickered at him, and squeezed shut in resolution.

Miles silently cursed the anonymous clever boffin who'd invented fetaine as a terror weapon, not for his chemistry, but for his insight into the Barraryaran psyche. Fetaine could surely never have been used, could never be used. Any faction trying to do so must rise up against itself and tear apart in moral convulsions.

Yaski, standing back from his men, looked thoroughly horrified. Bonn, his expression black and brittle as obsidian, began to strip off his gloves and parka.

No, no, no! Miles screamed inside his head. *If you join them they'll never back down. They'll know they're right.* Bad mistake, bad . . . Bonn dropped the rest of his clothes in a pile, marched forward, joined the line, wheeled, and locked eyes with Metzov. Metzov's eyes narrowed with new fury. "So," he hissed, "you convict yourself. Freeze, then."

How had things gone so bad, so fast? Now would be a good time to remember a duty in the weather office, and get the hell out of here. If only those shivering bastards would back down, Miles could get through this night without a ripple in his record. He had no duty, no function here. . . .

Metzov's eye fell on Miles. "Vorkosigan, you can either take up a weapon and be useful, or consider yourself dismissed."

He could leave. Could he leave? When he made no move, the sergeant walked over and thrust a nerve disruptor into Miles's hand. Miles took it up, still struggling to think with brains gone suddenly porridge. He did retain the wit to make sure the safety was "on" before pointing the disruptor vaguely in the direction of the freezing men.

This isn't going to be a mutiny. It's going to be a massacre.

One of the armed grubs giggled nervously. What had they been told they were doing? What did they *believe* they were doing? Eighteen-, nineteen-year-olds—could they even recognize a criminal order? Or know what to do about it if they did?

Could Miles?

The situation was ambiguous, that was the problem. It didn't quite fit. Miles knew about criminal orders, every academy man did. His father came down personally and gave a one-day seminar on the topic to the seniors at midyear. He'd made it a requirement to graduate, by Imperial fiat back when he'd been Regent. What exactly constituted a criminal order, when and how to disobey it. With vid evidence from various historical test cases and bad examples, including the politically disastrous Solstice Massacre, that had taken place under the admiral's own command. Invariably one or more cadets had to leave the room to throw up during that part.

The other instructors hated Vorkosigan's Day. Their classes were subtly disrupted for weeks afterward. One reason Admiral Vorkosigan didn't wait till any later in the year; he almost always had to make a return trip a few weeks after, to talk some disturbed cadet out of dropping out at almost the finale of his schooling. Only the academy cadets got this live lecture, as far as Miles knew, though his father talked of canning it on holovid and making it a part of basic training Service-wide. Parts of the seminar had been a revelation even to Miles.

But this . . . If the techs had been civilians, Metzov would clearly be in the wrong. If this had been in wartime, while being harried by some enemy, Metzov might be within his rights, even duty. This was somewhere between. Soldiers disobeying, but passively. Not an enemy in sight. Not even a physical situation threatening, necessarily, lives on the base (except theirs), though when the wind shifted that could change. *I'm not ready for this, not yet, not so soon.* What was right?

My career . . . Claustrophobic panic rose in Miles's chest, like a man with his head caught in a drain. The nerve disrupter wavered just slightly in his hand. Over the parabolic reflector he could see Bonn standing dumbly, too congealed now even to argue anymore. Ears were turning white out there, and fingers and feet. One man crumpled into a shuddering ball, but made no move to surrender. Was there any softening of doubt yet, in Metzov's rigid neck?

For a lunatic moment Miles envisioned thumbing

off the safety and shooting Metzov. And then what, shoot the grubs? He couldn't possibly get them all before they got him.

I could be the only soldier here under thirty who's ever killed an enemy before, in battle or out of it. The grubs might fire out of ignorance, or sheer curiosity. They didn't know enough *not* to. *What we do in the next half hour will replay in our heads as long as we breathe.*

He could try doing nothing. Only follow orders. How much trouble could he get into, only following orders? Every commander he'd ever had agreed, he needed to follow orders better. *Think you'll enjoy your ship duty, then, Ensign Vorkosigan, you and your pack of frozen ghosts? At least you'd never be lonely. . . .*

Miles, still holding up the nerve disruptor, faded backward, out of the grubs' line-of-sight, out of the corner of Metzov's eye. Tears stung and blurred his vision. From the cold, no doubt.

He sat on the ground. Pulled off his gloves and boots. Let his parka fall, and his shirts. Trousers and thermal underwear atop the pile, and the nerve-disruptor nested carefully on them. He stepped forward. His leg braces felt like icicles against his calves.

I hate passive resistance. I really, really hate it.

"What the hell do you think you're doing, Ensign?" Metzov snarled as Miles limped past him.

"Breaking this up, sir," Miles replied steadily. Even now some of the shivering techs flinched away from him, as if his deformities might be contagious. Pattas didn't draw away, though. Nor Bonn.

"Bonn tried that bluff. He's now regretting it. It won't work for you either, Vorkosigan." Metzov's voice shook too, though not from the cold.

You should have said "Ensign." What's in a name? Miles could see the ripple of dismay run through the grubs, that time. No, this hadn't worked for Bonn. Miles might be the only man here for whom this sort of individual intervention could work. Depending on how far gone Mad Metzov was by now.

Miles spoke now for both Metzov's benefit and the grubs'. "It's possible—barely—that Service Security wouldn't investigate the deaths of Lieutenant Bonn and his men, if you diddled the record, claimed some accident. I guarantee Imperial Security will investigate mine."

Metzov grinned strangely. "Suppose no witnesses survive to complain?"

Metzov's sergeant looked as rigid as his master. Miles thought of Ahn, drunken Ahn, silent Ahn. What had Aim seen, once long ago, when crazy things were happening on Komarr? What kind of surviving witness had he been? A guilty one, perhaps? "S-s-sorry, sir, but I see at least ten witnesses, behind those nerve disrupters." Silver parabolas—they looked enormous, like serving dishes, from this new angle. The change in point of view was amazingly clarifying. No ambiguities now.

Miles continued, "Or do you propose to execute your firing squad and then shoot yourself? Imperial Security will fast-penta everyone in sight. You can't silence me. Living or dead, through my mouth or yours—or theirs—I will testify." Shivers racked Miles's body. Astonishing, the effect of just that little bit of east wind, at this temperature. He fought to keep the shakes out of his voice, lest cold be mistaken for fear.

"Small consolation, if you—ah—permit yourself to freeze, I'd say, Ensign." Metzov's heavy sarcasm grated on Miles's nerves. The man still thought he was winning. Insane.

Miles's bare feet felt strangely warm now. His eyelashes were crunchy with ice. He was catching up fast to the others, in terms of freezing to death, no doubt because of his smaller mass. His body was turning a blotchy purple-blue.

The snow-blanketed base was so silent. He could almost hear the individual snow grains skitter across the sheet ice. He could hear the vibrating bones of each man around him, pick out the hollow frightened breathing of the grubs. Time stretched.

He could threaten Metzov, break up his complacency with dark hints about Komarr, *the truth will out*. . . . He could call on his father's rank and position. He could . . . dammit, Metzov must realize he was overextended, no matter how mad he was. His discipline parade bluff hadn't worked and now he was stuck with it, stonily defending his authority unto death. *He can be a funny kind of dangerous, if you really threaten him*. . . . It was hard, to see through the sadism to the underlying fear. But it had to be there, underneath. . . . Pushing wasn't working. Metzov was practically petrified with resistance. What about pulling . . . ?

"But consider, sir," Miles's words stuttered out persuasively, "the advantages to yourself of stopping now. You now have clear evidence of a mutinous, er, conspiracy. You can arrest us all, throw us in the stockade. It's a better revenge, 'cause you get it all and lose nothing. I lose my career, get a dishonorable discharge or maybe prison—do you think I wouldn't rather die? Service Security punishes the rest of us for you. You get it all."

Miles's words had hooked him; Miles could see it, in the red glow fading from the narrowed eyes, in the slight bending of that stiff, stiff neck. Miles had only to let the line out, refrain from jerking on it and renewing Metzov's fighting frenzy, *wait*. . . .

Metzov stepped nearer, bulking in the half-light;

haloed by his freezing breath. His voice dropped, pitched to Miles's ear alone. "A typical soft Vorkosigan answer. Your father was soft on Komarran scum. Cost us lives. A court-martial for the admiral's little boy—that might bring down that holier-than-thou buggerer, eh?"

Miles swallowed icy spit. *Those who do not know their history,* his thought careened, *are doomed to keep stepping in it.* Alas, so were those who did, it seemed. "Thermo the damned fetaine spill," he whispered hoarsely, "and see."

"You're all under arrest," Metzov bellowed out suddenly, his shoulders hunching. "Get dressed."

The others looked stunned with relief then. After a last uncertain glance at the nerve disrupters they dove for their clothes, donning them with frantic cold-clumsy hands. But Miles had seen it complete in Metzov's eyes sixty seconds earlier. It reminded him of that definition of his father's. A *weapon is a device for making your enemy change his mind.* The mind was the first and final battleground, the stuff in between was just noise.

Lieutenant Yaski had taken the opportunity afforded by Miles's attention-arresting nude arrival on center stage to quietly disappear into the Admin building and make several frantic calls. As a result the trainee's commander, the base surgeon, and Metzov's second-in-command arrived, primed to persuade or perhaps sedate and confine Metzov. But by that time Miles, Bonn, and the techs were already dressed and being marched, stumbling, toward the stockade bunker under the argus-eyes of the nerve disrupters.

"Am I s-supposed to th-thank you for this?" Bonn asked Miles through chattering teeth. Their hands and feet swung like paralyzed lumps; he leaned on Miles, Miles hung on him, hobbling down the road together.

"We got what we wanted, eh? He's going to plasma the fetaine on-site before the wind shifts in the morning. Nobody dies. Nobody gets their nuts curdled. We win. I think." Miles emitted a deathly cackle through numb lips.

"I never thought," wheezed Bonn, "that I'd ever meet anybody crazier than Metzov."

"I didn't do anything you didn't," protested Miles. "Except I made it work. Sort of. It'll all look different in the morning, anyway."

"Yeah. Worse," Bonn predicted glumly.

Miles jerked up out of an uneasy doze on his cell cot when the door hissed open. They were bringing Bonn back.

Miles rubbed his unshaven face. "What time is it out there, Lieutenant?"

"Dawn." Bonn looked as pale, stubbled, and criminally low as Miles felt. He eased himself down on his cot with a pained grunt.

"What's happening?"

"Service Security's all over the place. They flew in a captain from the mainland, just arrived, who seems to be in charge. Metzov's been filling his ear, I think. They're just taking depositions, so far."

"They get the fetaine taken care of?"

"Yep." Bonn vented a grim snicker. "They just had me out to check it, and sign the job off. The bunker made a neat little oven, all right."

"Ensign Vorkosigan, you're wanted," said the security guard who'd delivered Bonn. "Come with me now."

Miles creaked to his feet and limped toward the cell door. "See you later, Lieutenant."

"Right. If you spot anybody out there with breakfast, why don't you use your political influence to send 'em my way, eh?"

Miles grinned bleakly. "I'll try."

Miles followed the guard up the stockade's short corridor. Lazkowski Base's stockade was not exactly what one would call a high-security facility, being scarcely more than a living quarters bunker with doors that only locked from the outside and no windows. The weather usually made a better guard than any force screen, not to mention the 500-kilometer-wide ice-water moat surrounding the island.

The Base security office was busy this morning. Two grim strangers stood waiting by the door, a lieutenant and a big sergeant with the Horus-eye insignia of Imperial Security on their sleek uniforms. *Imperial* Security, not Service Security. Miles's very own Security, who had guarded his family all his father's political life. Miles regarded them with possessive delight.

The Base security clerk looked harried, his desk console lit up and blinking. "Ensign Vorkosigan, sir, I need your palm print on this."

"All right. What am I signing?"

"Just the travel orders, sir."

"What? Ah . . ." Miles paused, holding up his plastic-mitted hands. "Which one?"

"The right, I guess would do, sir."

With difficulty, Miles peeled off the right mitten with his awkward left. His hand glistened with the medical gel that was supposed to be healing the frostbite. His hand was swollen, red-blotched and mangled-looking, but the stuff must be working. All his fingers now wriggled. It took three tries, pressing down on the ID pad, before the computer recognized him.

"Now yours, sir," the clerk nodded to the Imperial Security lieutenant. The ImpSec man laid his hand on the pad and the computer bleeped approval. He lifted it and glanced dubiously at the sticky sheen, looked around futilely for some towel, and wiped it surreptitiously on his trouser seam just behind his stunner holster. The clerk dabbed nervously at the pad with his uniform sleeve, and touched his intercom.

"Am I glad to see you fellows," Miles told the ImpSec officer. "Wish you'd been here last night."

The lieutenant did not smile in return. "I'm just a courier, Ensign. I'm not supposed to discuss your case."

General Metzov ducked through the door from the inner office, a sheaf of plastic flimsies in one hand and a Service Security captain at his elbow, who nodded warily to his counterpart on the Imperial side.

The general was almost smiling. "Good morning, Ensign Vorkosigan." His glance took in Imperial Security without dismay. Dammit, ImpSec should be making that near-murderer shake in his combat boots. "It seems there's a wrinkle in this case even I hadn't realized. When a Vor lord involves himself in a military mutiny, a charge of high treason follows automatically."

"What?" Miles swallowed, to bring his voice back down. "Lieutenant, I'm not under arrest by *Imperial* Security, am I?"

The lieutenant produced a set of handcuffs and proceeded to attach Miles to the big sergeant. *Overholt,* read the name on the man's badge, which Miles mentally redubbed Overkill. He had only to lift his arm to dangle Miles like a kitten.

"You are being detained, pending further investigation," said the lieutenant formally.

"How long?"

"Indefinitely."

The lieutenant headed for the door, the sergeant and perforce Miles following. "Where?" Miles asked frantically.

"Imperial Security Headquarters."

Vorbarr Sultana! "I need to get my things—"

"Your quarters have already been cleared."

"Will I be coming back here?"

"I don't know, Ensign."

Late dawn was streaking Camp Permafrost with grey and yellow when the scat-cat deposited them at the shuttlepad. The Imperial Security sub-orbital courier shuttle sat on the icy concrete like a bird of prey accidentally placed in a pigeon cote. Slick and black and deadly, it seemed to break the sound barrier just resting there. Its pilot was at the ready, engines primed for takeoff.

Miles shuffled awkwardly up the ramp after Sergeant Overkill, the handcuff jerking coldly on his wrist. Tiny ice crystals danced in the northeasterly wind. The temperature would be stabilizing this morning, he could tell by the particular dry bite of the relative humidity in his sinuses. Dear God, it was past time to get off this island.

Miles took one last sharp breath, then the shuttle door sealed behind them with a snaky hiss. Within was a thick, upholstered silence that even the howl of the engines scarcely penetrated.

At least it was warm.

CHAPTER SIX

Autumn in the city of Vorbarr Sultana was a beautiful time of year, and today was exemplary. The air was high and blue, the temperature cool and perfect, and even the tang of industrial haze smelled good. The autumn flowers were not yet frosted off, but the Earth-import trees had turned their colors. As he was hustled out of the Security lift van and into a back entrance to the big blocky building that was Imperial Security Headquarters, Miles glimpsed one such tree. An Earth maple, with carnelian leaves and a silver-grey trunk, across the street. Then the door closed. Miles held that tree before his mind's eye, trying to memorize it, just in case he never saw it again.

The Security lieutenant produced passes that sped Miles and Overholt through the door guards, and led them into a maze of corridors to a pair of lift tubes. They entered the up tube, not the down one. So, Miles was not being taken directly to the ultra-secure cell block beneath the building. He woke to what this meant, and wished wistfully for the down tube.

They were ushered into an office on an upper level, past a Security captain, then into an inner office. A man, slight, bland, civilian-clothed, with brown hair greying at the temples, sat at his very large comconsole desk, studying a vid. He glanced up at Miles's escort. "Thank you, Lieutenant, Sergeant. You may go."

Overholt detached Miles from his wrist as the lieutenant asked, "Uh, will you be safe, sir?"

"I expect so," said the man dryly.

Yeah, but what about me? Miles wailed inwardly. The two soldiers exited, and left Miles alone, standing literally on the carpet. Unwashed, unshaven, still wearing the faintly reeking black fatigues he'd flung on—only last night? Face weather-raked, with his swollen hands and feet still encased in their plastic medical mittens—his toes now wriggled in their squishy matrix. No boots. He had dozed, in a jerky intermittent exhaustion, on the two-hour shuttle flight, without being noticeably refreshed. His throat was raw, his sinuses felt stuffed with packing fiber, and his chest hurt when he breathed.

Simon Illyan, Chief of Barrayaran Imperial Security, crossed his arms and looked Miles over slowly, from head to toe and back again. It gave Miles a skewed sense of *déja vù.*

Practically everyone on Barrayar feared this man's name, though few knew his face. This effect was carefully cultivated by Illyan, building in part—but only in part—on the legacy of his formidable predecessor, the legendary Security Chief Negri. Illyan and his department, in turn, had provided security for Miles's father for the twenty years of his political career, and had slipped up only once, during the night of the infamous soltoxin attack. Offhand, Miles knew of no one Illyan feared except Miles's mother. He'd once asked his father if this was guilt, about the soltoxin, but Count Vorkosigan had replied, No, it was only the lasting effect of vivid first impressions. Miles had called Illyan "Uncle Simon" all his life until he'd entered the Service, "Sir" after that.

Looking at Illyan's face now, Miles thought he finally grasped the distinction between exasperation, and utter exasperation.

Illyan finished his inspection, shook his head, and groaned, "Wonderful. Just wonderful."

Miles cleared his throat. "Am I . . . really under arrest, sir?"

"That is what this interview will determine," Illyan sighed, leaning back in his chair. "I have been up since two hours after midnight over this escapade. Rumors are flying all over the Service, as fast as the vid net can carry them. The facts appear to be mutating every forty minutes, like bacteria. I don't suppose you could have picked some more public way to self-destruct? Attempted to assassinate the Emperor with your pocket-knife during the Birthday Review, say, or raped a sheep in the Great Square during rush hour?" The sarcasm melted to genuine pain. "He had so much hope of you. How could you betray him so?"

No need to ask who "he" was. *The* Vorkosigan. "I . . . don't think I did, sir. I don't know."

A light blinked on Illyan's comconsole. He exhaled, with a sharp glance at Miles, and touched a control. The second door to his office, camouflaged in the wall to the right of his desk, slid open, and two men in dress greens ducked through.

Prime Minister Admiral Count Aral Vorkosigan wore the uniform as naturally as an animal wears its fur. He was a man of no more than middle height, stocky, grey-haired, heavy-jawed, scarred, almost a thug's body and yet with the most penetrating grey eyes Miles had ever encountered. He was flanked by his aide, a tall blond lieutenant named Jole. Miles had met Jole on his last home leave. Now, there was a perfect officer, brave and brilliant—he'd served in space, been decorated for some courage and quick thinking during a horrendous on-board accident, been rotated through HQ while recovering from his injuries, and promptly been snabbled up as his military secretary by the Prime Minister, who had a sharp eye for hot new talent. Jaw-dropping gorgeous, to boot, he ought to be making recruiting vids. Miles sighed in hopeless jealousy every time he ran across him. Jole was even worse than Ivan, who while darkly handsome had never been accused of brilliance.

"Thanks, Jole," Count Vorkosigan murmured to his aide, as his eye found Miles. "I'll see you back at the office."

"Yes, sir." So dismissed, Jole ducked back out, glancing back at Miles and his superior with worried eyes, and the door hissed closed again.

Illyan still had his hand pressed to a control on his desk. "Are you officially here?" he asked Count Vorkosigan.

"No."

Illyan keyed something off—recording equipment, Miles realized. "Very well," he said, editorial doubt injected into his tone.

Miles saluted his father. His father ignored the salute and embraced him gravely, wordlessly, sat in the room's only other chair, crossed his arms and booted ankles, and said, "Continue, Simon."

Illyan, who had been cut off in the middle of what had been shaping up, in Miles's estimation, to a really classic reaming, chewed his lip in frustration. "Rumors aside," Illyan said to Miles, "what really happened last night out on that damned island?"

In the most neutral and succinct terms he could muster, Miles described the previous night's events, starting with the fetaine spill and ending with his arrest/detainment/to-be-determined by Imperial Security. His father said nothing during the whole recitation, but he had a light-pen in his hand which he kept turning absently around and over, *tap* against his knee, around and over.

Silence fell when Miles finished. The light-pen was driving Miles to distraction. He wished his father would put the damned thing away, or drop it, or anything.

His father slipped the light-pen back into his breast pocket, thank God, leaned back, and steepled his fingers, frowning. "Let me get this straight. You say Metzov hopscotched the command chain and dragooned *trainees* for his firing squad?"

"Ten of them. I don't know if they were volunteers or not, I wasn't there for that part."

"Trainees." Count Vorkosigan's face was dark. "Boys."

"He was babbling something about it being like the army versus the navy, back on Old Earth."

"Huh?" said Illyan.

"I don't think Metzov was any too stable when he was exiled to Kyril Island after his troubles in the Komarr Revolt, and fifteen years of brooding about it didn't improve his grip." Miles hesitated. "Will . . . General Metzov be questioned about his actions at all, sir?"

"General Metzov, by your account," said Admiral Vorkosigan, "dragged a platoon of eighteen-year-olds into what came within a hair of being a mass torture-murder."

Miles nodded in memory. His body still twinged with assorted agonies.

"For that sin, there is no hole deep enough to hide him from my wrath. Metzov will be taken care of, all right." Count Vorkosigan was terrifyingly grim.

"What about Miles and the mutineers?" asked Illyan.

"Necessarily, I fear we will have to treat that as a separate matter."

"Or two separate matters," said Illyan suggestively.

"Mm. So, Miles, tell me about the men on the other end of the guns."

"Techs, sir, mostly. A lot of greekies."

Illyan winced. "Good God, had the man no political sense at all?"

"None that I ever saw. I thought it would be a problem." Well, later he'd thought of it, lying awake on his cell cot after the med squad left. The other political ramifications had spun through his mind. Over half the slowly freezing techs had been of the Greek-speaking minority. The language separatists would have been rioting in the streets, had it become a massacre, sure to claim the general had ordered the greekies into the cleanup as racial sabotage. More deaths, chaos reverberating down the timeline like the consequences of the Solstice Massacre? "It . . . occurred to me, that if I died with them, at least it would be crystal clear that it hadn't been some plot of your government or the Vor oligarchy. So that if I lived, I won, and if I died, I won too. Or at least served. Strategy, of sorts."

Barrayar's greatest strategist of this century rubbed his temples, as if they ached. "Well . . . of sorts, yes."

"So," Miles swallowed, "what happens now, sirs? Will I be charged with high treason?"

"For the second time in four years?" said Illyan. "Hell, no. I'm not going through that again. I will simply disappear you, until this blows over. Where to, I haven't quite figured yet. Kyril Island is out."

"Glad to hear it." Miles's eyes narrowed. "What about the others?"

"The trainees?" said Illyan.

"The techs. My . . . fellow mutineers."

Illyan twitched at the term.

"It would be seriously unjust if I were to slither up some Vor-privileged line and leave them standing charges alone," Miles added.

"The public scandal of your trial would damage your father's Centrist coalition. Your moral scruples may be admirable, Miles, but I'm not sure I can afford them."

Miles stared steadily at Prime Minister Count Vorkosigan. "Sir?"

Count Vorkosigan sucked thoughtfully on his lower lip. "Yes, I could have the charges against them quashed, by Imperial fiat. That would involve another price, though." He leaned forward intently, eyes peeling Miles. "You could never serve again. Rumors will travel even without a trial. No commander would have you, after. None could trust you, trust you to be a real officer, not an artifact protected by special privilege. I can't ask anyone to command you with his head cranked over his shoulder all the time."

Miles exhaled, a long breath. "In a weird sense, they were my men. Do it. Kill the charges."

"Will you resign your commission, then?" demanded Illyan. He looked sick.

Miles felt sick, nauseous and cold. "I will." His voice was thin.

Illyan looked up suddenly from a blank brooding stare at his comconsole. "Miles, how did you know about General Metzov's questionable actions during the Komarr Revolt? That case was Security-classified."

"Ah . . . didn't Ivan tell you about the little leak in the ImpSec files, sir?"

"*What?*"

Damn Ivan. "May I sit down, sir?" said Miles faintly. The room was wavering, his head thumping. Without waiting for permission, he sat cross-legged on the carpet, blinking. His father made a worried movement toward him, then restrained himself. "I'd been checking upon Metzov's background because of something Lieutenant Ahn said. By the way, when you go after Metzov, I strongly suggest you fast-penta Ahn first. He knows more than he's told. You'll find him somewhere on the equator, I expect."

"*My files,* Miles."

"Uh, yes, well, it turns out that if you face a secured console to an outgoing console, you can read off Security files from anywhere in the vid net. Of course, you have to have somebody inside HQ who can and will aim the consoles and call up the files for you. And you can't flash-download. But I, uh, thought you should know, sir."

"Perfect security," said Count Vorkosigan in a choked voice. Chortling, Miles realized in startlement.

Illyan looked like a man sucking on a lemon. "How did you," Illyan began, stopped to glare at the Count, started again, "how did you figure this out?"

"It was obvious."

"Airtight security, you said," murmured Count Vorkosigan, unsuccessfully suppressing a wheezing laugh. "The most expensive yet devised. Proof against the cleverest viruses, the most sophisticated eavesdropping equipment. And two ensigns waft right through it?"

Goaded, Illyan snapped, "I didn't promise it was idiot-proof!"

Count Vorkosigan wiped his eyes and sighed. "Ah, the human factor. We will correct the defect, Miles. Thank you."

"You're a bloody loose cannon, boy, firing in all

directions," Illyan growled to Miles, craning his neck to see over his desk to where Miles sat in a slumping heap. "This, on top of your earlier escapade with those damned mercenaries, on top of it all—house arrest isn't enough. I won't sleep through the night till I have you locked in a cell with your hands tied behind your back."

Miles, who thought he might kill for a decent hour's sleep right now, could only shrug. Maybe Illyan could be persuaded to let him go to that nice quiet cell soon.

Count Vorkosigan had fallen silent, a strange thoughtful glow starting in his eye. Illyan noticed the expression too, and paused.

"Simon," said Count Vorkosigan, "there's no doubt ImpSec will have to go on watching Miles. For his sake, as well as mine."

"And the Emperor's," put in Illyan dourly. "And Barrayar's. And the innocent bystanders'."

"But what better, more direct and efficient way for security to watch him than if he is assigned *to* Imperial Security?"

"What?" said Illyan and Miles together, in the same sharp horrified tone. "You're not serious," Illyan went on, as Miles added, "Security was never on my top-ten list of assignment choices."

"Not choice. Aptitude. Major Cecil discussed it with me at one time, as I recall. But as Miles says, he didn't put it on his list."

He hadn't put Arctic Weatherman on his list either, Miles recalled.

"You had it right the first time," said Illyan. "No commander in the Service will want him now. Not excepting myself."

"None that I could, in honor, lean on to take him. Excepting yourself. I have always," Count Vorkosigan flashed a peculiar grin, "leaned on you, Simon."

Illyan looked faintly stunned, as a top tactician beginning to see himself outmaneuvered.

"It works on several levels," Count Vorkosigan went on in that same mild persuasive voice. "We can put it about that it's an unofficial internal exile, demotion in disgrace. It will buy off my political enemies, who would otherwise try to stir profit from this mess. It will tone down the appearance of our condoning a mutiny, which no military service can afford."

"True exile," said Miles. "Even if unofficial and internal."

"Oh yes," Count Vorkosigan agreed softly. "But, ah—not true disgrace."

"Can he be trusted?" said Illyan doubtfully.

"Apparently." The count's smile was like the gleam off a knife blade. "Security can use his talents. Security more than any other department needs his talents."

"To see the obvious?"

"And the less obvious. Many officers may be trusted with the Emperor's life. Rather fewer with his honor."

Illyan, reluctantly, made a vague acquiescent gesture. Count Vorkosigan, perhaps prudently, did not troll for greater enthusiasm from his Security chief at this time, but turned to Miles and said, "You look like you need an infirmary."

"I need a bed."

"How about a bed in an infirmary?"

Miles coughed, and blinked blearily. "Yeah, that'd do."

"Come on, we'll find one."

He stood, and staggered out on his father's arm, his feet squishing in their plastic bags.

"Other than that, how was Kyril Island, Ensign Vorkosigan?" inquired the Count. "You didn't vid home much, your mother noticed."

"I was busy. Lessee. The climate was ferocious, the

terrain was lethal, a third of the population including my immediate superior was dead drunk most of the time. The average IQ equalled the mean temperature in degrees cee, there wasn't a woman for five hundred kilometers in any direction, and the base commander was a homicidal psychotic. Other than that, it was lovely."

"Doesn't sound like it's changed in the smallest detail in twenty-five years."

"You've been there?" Miles squinted. "And yet you let *me* get sent there?"

"I commanded Lazkowski Base for five months, once, while waiting for my captaincy of the cruiser *General Vorkraft*. During the period my career was, so to speak, in political eclipse."

So to speak. "How'd you like it?"

"I can't remember much. I was drunk most of the time. Everybody finds their own way of dealing with Camp Permafrost. I might say, you did rather better than I."

"I find your subsequent survival . . . encouraging, sir."

"I thought you might. That's why I mentioned it. It's not otherwise an experience I'd hold up as an example."

Miles looked up at his father. "Did . . . I do the right thing, sir? Last night?"

"Yes," said the count simply. "A right thing. Perhaps not the best of all possible right things. Three days from now you may think of a cleverer tactic, but you were the man on the ground at the time. I try not to second-guess my field commanders."

Miles's heart rose in his aching chest for the first time since he'd left Kyril Island.

Miles thought his father might take him to the great and familiar Imperial Military Hospital complex, a few kilometers away across town, but they found an infirmary closer than that, three floors down in ImpSec HQ. The facility was small but complete, with a couple of examining rooms, private rooms, cells for treating prisoners and guarded witnesses, a surgery, and a closed door labelled, chillingly, *Interrogation Chemistry Laboratory.* Illyan must have called down in advance, for a corpsman was hovering in attendance waiting to receive them. A Security surgeon arrived shortly, a little out of breath. He straightened his uniform and saluted Count Vorkosigan punctiliously before turning to Miles.

Miles fancied the surgeon was more used to making people nervous than being made nervous by them, and was awkward about the role reversal. Was it some aura of old violence, clinging to his father still after all these years? The power, the history? Some personal charisma, that made erstwhile forceful men flatten out like cowed dogs? Miles could sense that radiating heat perfectly clearly, and yet it didn't seem to affect him the same way.

Acclimatization, perhaps. The former Lord Regent was the man who used to take a two-hour lunch every day, regardless of any crisis short of war, and disappear into his Residence. Only Miles knew the interior view of those hours, how the big man in the green uniform would bolt a sandwich in five minutes and then spend the next hour and a half down on the floor with his son who could not walk, playing, talking, reading aloud. Sometimes, when Miles was locked in hysterical resistance to some painful new physical therapy, daunting his mother and even Sergeant Bothari, his father had been the only one with the firmness to *insist* on those ten extra agonizing leg stretches, the polite submission to the hypospray, to another round of surgery, to the icy chemicals searing his veins. "You are Vor. You must not frighten your liege people with this show of uncontrol, Lord Miles." The pungent smell of this infirmary, the tense doctor, brought back a flood of memories. No wonder, Miles reflected, he had failed to be afraid enough of Metzov. When Count Vorkosigan left, the infirmary seemed altogether empty.

There did not appear to be much going on in ImpSec HQ this week. The infirmary was numbingly quiet, except for a trickle of headquarters staff coming down to cadge headache or cold remedies or hangover-killers from the pliant corpsman. A couple of techs spent three hours rattling around the lab one evening on a rush job, and rushed off. The doctor arrested Miles's incipient pneumonia just before it turned into galloping pneumonia. Miles brooded, and waited for the six-day antibiotic therapy to run its course, and plotted details of a home leave in Vorbarr Sultana that must surely be forthcoming when the medics released him.

"Why can't I go home?" Miles complained to his mother on her next visit. "Nobody's telling me anything. If I'm not under arrest, why can't I take home leave? If I am under arrest, why aren't the doors locked? I feel like I'm in limbo."

Countess Cordelia Vorkosigan vented an unladylike snort. "You are in limbo, kiddo." Her flat Betan accent fell warmly on Miles's ears, despite her sardonic tone. She tossed her head—she wore her red-roan hair pinned back from her face and waving loose down her back today, gleaming against a rich autumn brown jacket picked out with silver embroidery, and the swinging skirts of a Vor-class woman. Grey-eyed, striking, her pale face seemed so alive with flickering thought one scarcely noticed she was not beautiful. For twenty-one years she'd passed as a Vor matron in the wake of her Great Man, yet still seemed as unimpressed by Barrayaran hierarchies as ever—though not, Miles thought, unmoved by Barrayaran wounds.

So why do I never think of my ambition as ship command like my mother *before me?* Captain Cordelia Naismith, Betan Astronomical Survey, had been in the risky business of expanding the wormhole nexus jump by blind jump, for humanity, for pure knowledge, for Beta Colony's economic advancement, for—what *had* driven her? She'd commanded a sixty-person survey vessel, far from home and help—there were certain enviable aspects to her former career, to be sure. Chain-of-command, for example, would have been a legal fiction out in the farbeyond, the wishes of Betan HQ a matter for speculation and side bets.

She moved now so wavelessly through Barrayaran society, only her most intimate observers realized how detached she was from it, fearing no one, not even the dread Illyan, controlled by no one, not even the Admiral himself. It was the casual fearlessness, Miles decided, that made his mother so unsettling. The Admiral's Captain. Following in her footsteps would be like firewalking.

"What's going on out there?" Miles asked. "This place is almost as much fun as solitary confinement, y'know? Have they decided I'm a mutineer after all?"

"I don't think so," said the Countess. "They're discharging the others—your Lieutenant Bonn and the rest—not precisely dishonorably, but without benefits or pensions or that Imperial Liegeman status that seems to mean so much to Barrayaran men—"

"Think of it as a funny sort of Reservist," Miles advised. "What about Metzov and the grubs?"

"He's being discharged the same way. He lost the most, I think."

"They're just turning him loose?" Miles frowned.

Countess Vorkosigan shrugged. "Because there were no deaths, Aral was persuaded he couldn't make a court-martial with any harsher punishment stick. They decided not to involve the trainees with any charges."

"Hm. I'm glad, I think. And, ah . . . me?"

"You remain officially listed as detained by Imperial Security. Indefinitely."

"Limbo is supposed to be an indefinite sort of place." His hand picked at his sheet. His knuckles were still swollen. "How long?"

"However long it takes to have its calculated psychological effect."

"What, to drive me crazy? Another three days ought to do it."

Her lip quirked. "Long enough to convince the Barrayaran militarists that you are being properly punished for your, uh, crime. As long as you are confined in this rather sinister building, they can be encouraged to imagine you undergoing—whatever they imagine goes on in here. If you're allowed to run around town partying, it will be much harder to maintain the illusion that you've been hung upside down on the basement wall."

"It all seems so . . . unreal." He hunched back into his pillow. "I only wanted to serve."

A brief smile flicked her wide mouth up, and vanished. "Ready to reconsider another line of work, love?"

"Being Vor is more than just a job."

"Yes, it's a pathology. Obsessional delusion. It's a big galaxy out there, Miles. There are other ways to serve, larger . . . constituencies."

"So why do you stay here?" he shot back.

"Ah." She smiled bleakly at the touché. "Some people's needs are more compelling than guns."

"Speaking of Dad, is he coming back?"

"Hm. No. I'm to tell you, he's going to distance himself for a time. So as not to give the appearance of endorsing your mutiny, while in fact shuffling you out from under the avalanche. He's decided to be publicly angry with you."

"And is he?"

"Of course not. Yet . . . he was beginning to have some long-range plans for you, in his socio-political reform schemes, based on your completing a solid military career . . . he saw ways of making even your congenital injuries serve Barrayar."

"Yeah, I know."

"Well, don't worry. He'll doubtless think of some way to use this, too."

Miles sighed glumly. "I want something to *do.* I want my *clothes* back."

His mother pursed her lips, and shook her head.

He tried calling Ivan that evening. "Where are you?" Ivan demanded suspiciously.

"Stuck in limbo."

"Well, I don't want any of it stuck to me," said Ivan roughly, and punched off-line.

CHAPTER SEVEN

The next morning Miles was moved to new quarters. His guide led him just one floor down, dashing Miles's hopes of seeing the sky again. The officer keyed open a door to one of the secured apartments usually used by protected witnesses. And, Miles reflected, certain political nonpersons. Was it possible life in limbo was having a chameleon effect, rendering him translucent?

"How long will I be staying here?" Miles asked the officer.

"I don't know, Ensign," the man replied, and left him.

His duffle, jammed with his clothes, and a hastily packed box sat in the middle of the apartment's floor. All his worldly goods from Kyril Island, smelling moldy, a cold breath of arctic damp. Miles poked through them—everything seemed to be there, including his weather library—and prowled his new quarters. It was a one-room efficiency, shabbily furnished in the style of twenty years back, with a few comfortable chairs, a bed, a simple kitchenette, empty cupboards and shelves and closets. No abandoned garments or objects or leftovers to hint at the identity of any previous occupant.

There had to be bugs. Any shiny surface could conceal a vid pickup, and the ears were probably not even within the room. But were they switched on? Or, almost more of an insult, maybe Illyan wasn't even bothering to run them?

There was a guard in the outer corridor, and remote monitors, but Miles did not appear to have neighbors at present. He discovered he could leave the corridor, and walk about the few non-top-secured areas of the building, but the guards at the outside doors, briefed as to who he was, turned him back politely but firmly. He pictured himself attempting escape by rappelling down from the roof—he'd probably get himself shot, and ruin some poor guard's career.

A Security officer found him wandering aimlessly, conducted him back to his apartment, gave him a handful of chits for the building's cafeteria, and hinted strongly that it would be appreciated if he would stay in his quarters between meals. After he left Miles morbidly counted the chits, trying to guess the expected duration of his stay. There were an even hundred. Miles shuddered.

He unpacked his box and bag, ran everything that would go through the sonic laundry to eliminate the last lingering odor of Camp Permafrost, hung up his uniforms, cleaned his boots, arranged his possessions neatly on a few shelves, showered, and changed to fresh undress greens.

One hour down. How many to go?

He attempted to read, but could not concentrate, and ended sitting in the most comfortable chair with his eyes closed, pretending this windowless, hermetically sealed chamber was a cabin aboard a spaceship. Outbound.

He was sitting in the same chair two nights later, digesting a leaden cafeteria dinner, when the door chimed.

Startled, Miles clambered up and limped to answer it personally. It was probably not a firing squad, though you never knew.

He almost changed his assumptions about the firing squad at the sight of the hard-faced Imperial Security officers in dress greens who stood waiting. "Excuse me, Ensign Vorkosigan," one muttered perfunctorily, and brushed past him to start running a scan over Miles's quarters. Miles blinked, then saw who stood behind them in the corridor, and breathed an "Ah" of understanding. At a mere look from the scanner man, Miles obediently held out his arms and turned to be scanned.

"Clear, sir," the scanner man reported, and Miles was sure it was. These fellows never, ever cut corners, not even in the heart of ImpSec itself.

"Thank you. Leave us, please. You may wait out here," said the third man. The ImpSec men nodded and took up parade rest flanking Miles's door.

Since they were both wearing officer's undress greens, Miles exchanged salutes with the third man, although the visitor's uniform bore neither rank nor department insignia. He was thin, of middle height, with dark hair and intense hazel eyes. A crooked smile winked in a serious young face that lacked laugh lines.

"Sire," Miles said formally.

Emperor Gregor Vorbarra jerked his head, and Miles keyed his door closed on the Security duo. The thin young man relaxed slightly. "Hi, Miles."

"Hello yourself. Uh . . ." Miles motioned toward the armchairs. "Welcome to my humble abode. Are the bugs running?"

"I asked not, but I wouldn't be surprised if Illyan disobeys me, for my own good." Gregor grimaced, and followed Miles. He swung a plastic bag from his left hand, from which came a muted clank. He flung himself into the larger chair, the one Miles had just vacated, leaned back, hooked a leg over one chair arm, and sighed wearily, as if all the air were being let out of him. He held out the bag. "Here. Elegant anesthesia."

Miles took it and peered in. Two bottles of wine, by God, already chilled. "Bless you, my son. I've been wishing I could get drunk for days, now. How did you guess? For that matter, how did you get in here? I thought I was in solitary confinement." Miles put the second bottle into the refrigerator, found two glasses, and blew the dust out of them.

Gregor shrugged. "They could scarcely keep me out. I'm getting better at insisting, you know. Though Illyan made sure my private visit was really private, you can wager. And I can only stay till 2500." Gregor's shoulders slumped, compressed by the minute-by-minute box of his schedule. "Besides, your mother's religion grants some kind of good karma for visiting the sick and prisoners, and I hear you've been the two in one."

Ah, so Mother had put Gregor up to this. He should have guessed by the Vorkosigan private label on the wine—heavens, she'd sent the *good* stuff. He stopped swinging the bottle by its neck and carried it with greater respect. Miles was lonely enough by now to be more grateful for than embarrassed by this maternal intervention. He opened the wine and poured, and by Barrayaran etiquette took the first sip. Ambrosia. He slung himself into another chair in a posture similar to Gregor's. "Glad to see you, anyway."

Miles contemplated his old playmate. If they'd been even a little closer in age, he and Gregor, they might have fallen more into the role of foster-brothers; Count and Countess Vorkosigan had been Gregor's official guardians ever since the chaos and bloodshed of Vordarian's Pretendership. The child-cohort had been thrown together anyway as "safe" companions, Miles and Ivan and Elena near-agemates, Gregor, solemn even then, tolerating games a little younger than he might have preferred.

Gregor picked up his wine and sipped. "Sorry things didn't work out for you," he said gruffly.

Miles tilted his head. "A short soldier, a short career." He took a bigger gulp. "I'd hoped to get off-planet. Ship duty."

Gregor had graduated from the Imperial Academy two years before Miles entered it. His brows rose in agreement. "Don't we all."

"You had a year on active space duty," Miles pointed out.

"Mostly in orbit. Pretend patrols, surrounded by Security shuttles. It got to be painful after a while, all the pretending. Pretending I was an officer, pretending I was doing a job instead of making everyone else's job harder just by being there . . . you at least were permitted real risk."

"Most of it was unplanned, I assure you."

"I'm increasingly convinced that's the trick of it," Gregor went on. "Your father, mine, both our grandfathers—all survived real military situations. That's how they became real officers, not this . . . study." His free hand made a downward chopping motion.

"Flung into situations," Miles disagreed. "My father's military career officially began the day Mad Yuri's death squad broke in and blew up most of his family—I think he was eleven, or something. I'd just as soon pass on that sort of initiation, thanks. It's not something anybody in their right mind would choose."

"Mm." Gregor subsided glumly. As oppressed tonight, Miles guessed, by his legendary father Prince Serg as Miles was by his live one Count Vorkosigan. Miles reflected briefly on what he had come to think of as "The Two Sergs." One—maybe the only version Gregor knew?—was the dead hero, bravely sacrificed on the field of battle or at least cleanly disintegrated in orbit. The other, the Suppressed Serg: the hysteric commander and sadistic sodomite whose early death in the ill-fated Escobar invasion might have been the greatest stroke of political good fortune ever to befall Barrayar . . . had even a hint of this multi-faceted personality ever been permitted to filter back to Gregor? Nobody who knew Serg talked about him, Count Vorkosigan least of all. Miles had once met one of Serg's victims. Miles hoped Gregor never would.

Miles decided to change the subject. "So we all know what happened to me, what have you been up to for the last three months? I was sorry to miss your last birthday party. Up at Kyril Island they celebrated it by getting drunk, which made it virtually indistinguishable from any other day."

Gregor grinned, then sighed. "Too many ceremonies. Too much time standing up—I think I could be replaced at half my functions by a life-sized plastic model, and no one would notice. A lot of time spent ducking the broad marital hints of my assorted counsellors."

"Actually, they have a point," Miles had to allow. "If you got . . . run over by a teacart tomorrow, the succession question goes up for grabs in a big way. I can think offhand of at least six candidates with arguable stakes in the Imperium, and more would come out of the woodwork. Some without personal ambition would nevertheless kill to see that some of the others didn't get it, which is precisely why you still don't have a named heir."

Gregor cocked his head. "You're in that crowd yourself, you know."

"With this body?" Miles snorted. "They'd have to . . . really hate somebody, to tag me. At that point it really would be time to run away from home. Far and fast. Do me a favor. Get married, settle down, and have six little Vorbarras real quick."

Gregor looked even more depressed. "Now there's an idea. Running away from home. I wonder how far I'd get, before Illyan caught up with me?"

They both glanced involuntarily upward, though in fact Miles was still not certain where the room's bugs were located. "Better hope Illyan caught up with you before anybody else did." God, this conversation was getting morbid.

"I don't know, wasn't there an emperor of China who ended up pushing a broom somewhere? And a thousand lesser emigrees—countesses running restaurants—escape *is* possible."

"From being Vor? More like . . . trying to run away from your own shadow." There would be moments, in the dark, when success would seem achieved, but then—Miles shook his head, and checked out the still-lumpy bag. "Ah! You brought a tacti-go set." He didn't in the least want to play tacti-go, it had bored him by age fourteen, but anything was better than this. He pulled it out and set it up between them with determined good cheer. "Brings back old times." Hideous thought.

Gregor bestirred himself, and made an opening move. Pretending to be interested to amuse Miles, who was simulating interest to cheer Gregor, who was feigning . . . Miles, distracted, beat Gregor too fast on the first round, and began to pay more attention. On the next round he kept it closer, and was rewarded by a spark of genuine interest—blessed self-forgetfulness—on Gregor's part. They opened the second bottle of wine. At that point Miles began to feel the effects, going tongue-thick and sleepy and stupid; it took hardly any effort to let Gregor almost win the next round.

"I don't think I've beaten you at this since you were fourteen," sighed Gregor, concealing secret satisfaction at the low point-spread of that last round. "You should be an officer, dammit."

"This isn't a good war game, Dad says," commented Miles. "Not enough random factors and uncontrolled surprises to simulate reality. I like it that way." It was almost soothing, a mindless routine of logic, check and counter, multiple chained moves with, always, perfectly objective options.

"You should know." Gregor glanced up. "I still don't understand why they sent you to Kyril Island. You've already commanded a real space fleet. Even if they were only a pack of grubby mercenaries."

"Shh. That episode is officially nonexistent, in my military files. Fortunately. It wouldn't charm my superiors. I'd commanded, I hadn't obeyed. Anyway, I didn't so much command the Dendarii Mercenaries as hypnotize 'em. Without Captain Tung, who decided to prop up my pretensions for his own purposes, it would have all ended very unpleasantly. And much sooner."

"I always thought Illyan would do more with them, after," said Gregor. "However inadvertently, you brought a whole military organization secretly into the service of Barrayar."

"Yes, without them even knowing it themselves. Now, *that's* secret. Come on. Assigning them to Illyan's section was a legal fiction, everybody knew it." And would his own assignment to Illyan's section turn out to be a legal fiction too? "Illyan's too careful to get drawn into intergalactic military adventuring as a hobby. I'm afraid his main interest in the Dendarii Mercenaries is to keep them as far away from Barrayar as possible. Mercenaries thrive on other people's chaos.

"Plus, they're a funny size—less than a dozen ships, three or four thousand personnel—not your basic invisible six-man covert ops team, though they can field such, and yet they're too little to take on planetary situations. Space-based, not ground troops. Wormhole blockades were their specialty. Safe, easy on the equipment, mostly bullying unarmed civilians—which is how I first ran into them, when our freighter was stopped by their blockade, and the bullying went too far. I cringe to think of the risks I ran. Though I've often wondered if, knowing what I know now, I could have. . . ." Miles stopped, shook his head. "Or maybe it's like heights. Better not to look down. You freeze, and then you fall." Miles was not fond of heights.

"As a military experience, how did it compare with Lazkowski Base?" asked Gregor bemusedly.

"Oh, there were certain parallels," Miles admitted. "Both were jobs I wasn't trained for, both were potentially lethal, I got out of both by my skin—lost some skin. The Dendarii episode was . . . worse. I lost Sergeant Bothari. In a sense, I lost Elena. At least at Camp Permafrost I managed not to lose anyone."

"Maybe you're getting better," Gregor suggested.

Miles shook his head, and drank. He should have put on some music. The thick silence of this room was oppressive, when the conversation faltered. The ceiling was probably not hydraulically arranged to descend and crush him in his sleep; Security had far less messy ways of dealing with recalcitrant prisoners. It only seemed to lower at him. *Well, I'm short. Maybe it'd miss me.*

"I suppose it would be . . . improper," Miles began hesitantly, "to ask you to try and get me out of here. It's always seemed rather embarrassing, to ask for Imperial favors. Like cheating, or something."

"What, are you asking one prisoner of ImpSec to rescue another?" Gregor's hazel eyes were ironic under black brows. "It's a little embarrassing to me to come up against the limits of my absolute Imperial Rule. Your father and Illyan, like two parentheses around me." His cupped hands closed in a squeezing motion.

It was a subliminal effect of this room, Miles decided. Gregor was feeling it too.

"I would if I could," Gregor added more apologetically. "But Illyan's made it crystal clear he wants you kept out of sight. For a time, anyway."

"Time." Miles swallowed the last of his wine, and decided he'd better not pour himself any more. Alcohol was a depressant, it was said. "How much time? Dammit, if I don't get something to do soon, I'm going to be the first case of human spontaneous combustion recorded on vid." He jerked a rude finger at the ceiling. "I don't need to—don't even have to leave the building, but at least they could give me some *work*. Clerical, janitorial—I do terrific drains—anything. Dad talked with Illyan about assigning me to Security—as the only Section left that would take me—he must have had something more in mind than a m-, m-, mascot." He poured and drank again, to stop the spate of words. He'd said too much. Damn the wine. Damn the whine.

Gregor, who had built a little tower of tacti-go chips, toppled it with one finger. "Oh, being a mascot isn't bad work, if you can get it." He stirred the pile slowly. "I'll see what I can do. No promises."

✧ ✧ ✧

Miles didn't know if it was the Emperor, the bugs, or wheels already in motion (grinding slowly), but two days afterwards he found himself assigned to the job of administrative assistant to the guard commander for the building. It was comconsole work; scheduling, payroll, updating computer files. The job was interesting for a week, while he was learning it, mind-numbing after that. By the end of a month, the boredom and banality were beginning to prey on his nerves. Was he loyal, or merely stupid? Guards, Miles now realized, had to stay in prison all day long too. Indeed, as a guard, one of his jobs was now to keep himself in. Damn clever of Illyan; nobody else could have held him, if he'd been determined on escape. He did find a window once, and looked out. It was sleeting.

Was he going to get out of this bloody box before Winterfair? How long did it take the world to forget him, anyway? If he committed suicide, could he be officially listed as shot by a guard while escaping? Was Illyan trying to drive him out of his mind, or just out of his Section?

Another month slipped by. As a spiritual exercise, he decided to fill his off-duty hours by watching every training vid in the military library, in strict alphabetical order. The assortment was truly astonishing. He was particularly bemused by the thirty-minute vid (under "H: Hygiene") explaining how to take a shower—well, yes, there probably were backcountry recruits who really needed the instruction. After some weeks he had worked his way down to "L: Laser-rifle Model D-67; power-pack circuitry, maintenance, and repair," when he was interrupted by a call ordering him to report to Illyan's office.

Illyan's office was almost unchanged from Miles's last excruciating visit—same spartan windowless inner chamber occupied mainly by a comconsole desk that looked as if it could be used to pilot a jump ship—but now there were two chairs. One was promisingly empty. Maybe Miles wouldn't end up so literally on the carpet this round? The other was occupied by a man in undress, greens with captain's tabs and the Horus-eye insignia of Imperial Security on the collar.

Interesting fellow, that captain. Miles summed him out of the corner of his eye as he exchanged formal salutes with Illyan. Maybe thirty-five years old, he had something of Illyan's unmemorable bland look about the face, but was more heavily built. Pale. He might easily pass for some minor bureaucrat, a sedentary indoorsman. But that particular look could also be acquired by spending a great deal of time cooped up on spaceships.

"Ensign Vorkosigan, this is Captain Ungari. Captain Ungari is one of my galactic operatives. He has ten years' experience gathering information for this department. His specialty is military evaluation."

Ungari favored Miles with a polite nod by way of acknowledging the introduction. His level gaze summed Miles right back. Miles wondered what the spy's evaluation of the dwarfish soldier standing before him might be, and tried to stand straighter. There was nothing obvious about Ungari's reaction to Miles.

Illyan leaned back in his swivel chair. "So tell me, Ensign, what have you heard lately from the Dendarii Mercenaries?"

"Sir?" Miles rocked back. *Not* the curve he was expecting . . . "I . . . lately, nothing. I had a message about a year ago from Elena Bothari—Bothari-Jesek, that is. But it was only private, uh, birthday greetings."

"That one I have," Illyan nodded.

Do you, you bastard.

"—Nothing since?"

"No, sir."

"Hm." Illyan waved a hand at the spare chair. "Sit down, Miles." His voice grew quicker and more businesslike. Meat at last? "Let's go over a little astrography. Geography is the mother of strategy, they say." Illyan fiddled with a control on his comconsole.

A wormhole nexus route map formed in three bright dimensions over the holovid plate. It looked rather like a ball-and-stick model of some weird organic molecule done in colored light, balls representing local-space crossings, sticks the wormhole-space jumps between; schematic, compressing information, rather than to scale. Illyan zoomed in on a portion, red and blue sparks in the center of an otherwise empty ball, with four sticks leading out at crazy angles to more complex balls like some skewed Celtic cross. "Look familiar?"

"That in the center is the Hegen Hub, isn't it, sir?"

"Good." Illyan handed him his controller. "Give me a strategic summation of the Hegen Hub, Ensign."

Miles cleared his throat. "It's a double star system with no habitable planets, a few stations and powersats, and very little reason to linger in. Like many nexus connections, it's more route than place, taking its value by what's around it. In this case, four adjoining regions of local space with settled planets." Miles brightened each part of the image as he spoke, for emphasis.

"Aslund. Aslund is a cul-de-sac like Barrayar; the Hegen Hub is its sole gate to the greater galactic web. The Hegen Hub is as vital to Aslund as our gateway Komarr is to us.

"Jackson's Whole. The Hegen Hub is just one of five gates from Jacksonian local space; beyond Jackson's Whole lies half the explored galaxy.

"Vervain. Vervain has two exits; one to the Hub, the other into the nexus sectors controlled by the Cetagandan Empire.

"And fourth, of course, our, ah, good neighbor the Planet and Republic of Pol. Which in turn connects to our own multinexus Komarr. Also from Komarr is our one straight jump to the Cetagandan sector, which route has been either tightly controlled or outright barred to Cetagandan traffic ever since we conquered it." Miles glanced at Illyan for approval, hoping he was on the right track. Illyan glanced at Ungari, who allowed his brows to rise fractionally. Meaning what?

"Wormhole strategy. The devil's cat's cradle," Illyan muttered editorially. He squinted at his glowing schematic. "Four players, one game-board. It ought to be simple. . . .

"Anyway," Illyan stretched out his hand for the controller, and sat back with a sigh, "the Hegen Hub is more than a potential choke-point for the four adjoining systems. Twenty-five percent of our own commercial traffic passes through it, via Pol. And although Vervain is closed to Cetagandan military vessels just as Pol is closed to ours, the Cetas ship significant civilian exchange through the same slot and out past Jackson's Whole. Anything—like a war—that blocks the Hegen Hub would seem almost as damaging to Cetaganda as to us.

"And yet, after years of cooperative disinterest and dull neutrality, this empty region is suddenly alive with what I can only call an arms race. All four neighbors seem to be creating military interests. Pol has been beefing up the armament on all six of its jump point stations strung toward the Hub—even pulling forces from the side toward us, which I find a little startling, since Pol has been extremely wary of us ever since we took Komarr. The Jackson's Whole consortium is doing the same on its side. Vervain has hired a mercenary fleet called Randall's Rangers.

"All this activity is causing low-grade panic on

Aslund, whose interest in the Hegen Hub is for obvious reasons most critical. They're throwing half this year's military budget into a major jump-point station—hell, a floating fortress—and to cover the gap while they prepare, they too have hired guns. You may be familiar with them. They used to be called the Dendarii Free Mercenary Fleet." Illyan paused, and raised an eyebrow, watching for Miles's reaction.

Connections at last—or were there? Miles blew out his breath. "They were blockade specialists, at one time. Makes sense, I guess. Ah . . . used to be called the Dendarii? Have they changed lately?"

"They've recently reverted to their original title of Oseran Mercenaries, it seems."

"Strange. Why?"

"Why, indeed?" Illyan's lips compressed. "One of many questions, though hardly the most urgent. But it's the Cetagandan connection—or lack of it—that bothers me. General chaos in the region would be as damaging to Cetaganda as to us. But if, after the chaos passes, Cetaganda could somehow end up in control of the Hegen Hub—ah! Then they could block or control Barrayaran traffic as we do theirs through Komarr. Indeed, if you look at the other side of the Komarr-Cetaganda jump as being under their control, that would put them across two out of our four major galactic routes. Something labyrinthine, indirect—it smells of Cetaganda's methods. Or would, if I could spot their sticky hands pulling any of the strings. They must be there, even if I can't see them yet. . . ." Brooding, Illyan shook his head. "If the Jackson's Whole jump were cut, everyone would have to reroute through the Cetagandan Empire . . . profit, there. . . ."

"Or through us," Miles pointed out. "Why should Cetaganda do us that favor?"

"I have thought of one possibility. Actually, I've

thought of nine, but this one's for you, Miles. What's the best way to capture a jump point?"

"From both ends at once," Miles recited automatically.

"Which is one reason Pol has been careful never to let us amass any military presence in the Hegen Hub. But let us suppose someone on Pol stumbles across that nasty rumor I had so much trouble scotching that the Dendarii Mercenaries are the private army of a certain Barrayaran Vor lordling? What will they think?"

"They'll think we're getting ready to jump them," said Miles. "They might go paranoid—panic—even seek a temporary alliance, with, say, Cetaganda?"

"Very good," nodded Illyan.

Captain Ungari, who had been listening with the attentive patience of a man who'd been over it all before, glanced at Miles as if faintly encouraged, and approved this hypothesis with a nod of his head.

"But even if perceived as an independent force," Illyan went on, "the Dendarii are one more destabilizing influence in the region. The whole situation is disturbing—growing tenser by the day, for no apparent reason. Only a little more force—one mistake, one lethal incident—could trigger turbulence, classic chaos, the real thing, unstoppable. Reasons, Miles! I want information."

Illyan, generally, wanted information with the same passion that a strung-out juba freak craved a spike. He turned now to Ungari. "So what do you think, Captain? Will he do?"

Ungari was slow to reply. "He's . . . more physically conspicuous than I'd realized."

"As camouflage, that's not necessarily a disadvantage. In his company you ought to be nearly invisible. The stalking goat and the hunter."

"Perhaps. But can he carry the load? I'm not going

to have much time for babysitting." Ungari's voice was an urban baritone, evidently one of the modern educated officers, though he did not wear an Academy pin. "The Admiral seems to think so. Am I to argue?"

Ungari glanced at Miles. "Are you sure the Admiral's judgment is not swayed by . . . personal hopes?"

You mean wishful thinking, Miles mentally translated that delicate hesitancy.

"If so, it's for the first time." Illyan shrugged. *And there's a first time for everything,* hung unspoken in the air. Illyan turned now to pin Miles with a gaze of grim intensity. "Miles, do you think you would—if required—be capable of playing the part of Admiral Naismith again, for a short time?"

He'd seen it coming, but the words spoken out loud were still a strange cold thrill. To activate that suppressed persona again. . . . *It wasn't just a part, Illyan.* "I could play Naismith again, sure. It's *stopping* playing Naismith that scares me."

Illyan allowed himself a wintry smile, taking this for a joke. Miles's smile was a little sicker. *You don't know, you don't know what it was like.* . . . Three parts fakery and flim-flam, and one part . . . something else. Zen, gestalt, delusion? Uncontrollable moments of alpha-state exaltation. . . . Could he do it again? Maybe he knew too much now. *First you freeze, and then you fall.* Perhaps it *would* only be playacting, this time.

Illyan leaned back, held up his hands palm to palm, and let them fall in a releasing gesture. "Very well, Captain Ungari. He's all yours. Use him as you see fit. Your mission, then, is to gather information on the current crisis in the Hegen Hub; secondly, if possible, to use Ensign Vorkosigan to remove the Dendarii Mercenaries from the stage. If you decide to use a bogus contract to pull them out of the Hub, you can draw on the covert ops account for a convincing down-payment. You know the results I want. I'm sorry I can't make my orders more specific in advance of the intelligence you yourself must obtain."

"I don't mind, sir," said Ungari, smiling slightly.

"Hm. Enjoy your independence while it lasts. It ends with your first mistake." Illyan's tone was sardonic, but his eyes were confident, until he turned them toward Miles. "Miles, you'll be travelling as 'Admiral Naismith,' himself travelling incognito, returning, possibly, to the Dendarii fleet. Should Captain Ungari decide for you to activate the Naismith role, he'll pose as your bodyguard, so as to be always in position to control the situation. It's a little too much to ask Ungari to be responsible for his mission and also your safety, so you'll also have a real bodyguard. This setup will give Captain Ungari unusual freedom of movement, because it will account for your possession of a personal ship—we have a jump pilot and a fast courier we obtained from—never mind where, but it has no connection with Barrayar. It's under Jacksonian registration at present, which fits in nicely with Admiral Naismith's mysterious background. It's so obviously bogus, no one will look for a second layer of, er, bogusity." Illyan paused. "You will, of course, obey Captain Ungari's orders. *That* goes without saying." Illyan's direct stare was chill as a Kyril Island midnight.

Miles smiled dutifully, to show he took the hint. *I'll be good, sir—let me off-planet!* From ghost to goat—was this a promotion?

CHAPTER EIGHT

Victor Rotha, Procurement Agent. Sounded like a pimp. Dubiously, Miles regarded his new persona twinned over the vid plate in his cabin. What was wrong with a simple spartan mirror, anyway? *Where* had Illyan gotten this *ship?* Of Betan manufacture, it was stuffed with Betan gimmickry of a luxurious order. Miles entertained himself with a gruesome vision of what could happen if the programming on the elaborate sonic tooth-cleaner ever went awry.

"Rotha" was vaguely dressed, with respect to his supposed point-of-origin. Miles had drawn the line at a Betan sarong, Pol Station Six was not nearly warm enough for it. He did wear his loose green trousers held up with a Betan sarong rope, though, and Betan-style sandals. The green shirt was a cheap synthetic silk from Escobar, the baggy cream jacket an expensive one of like style. The eclectic wardrobe of someone originally from Beta Colony, who'd been knocking around the galaxy for a while, sometimes up, sometimes down. Good. He muttered to himself aloud, warming up his disused Betan accent, as he pottered about the elaborate Owner's Cabin.

They had docked here at Pol Six a day ago without incident. The whole three-week trip from Barrayar had passed without incident. Ungari seemed to like it that way. The ImpSec captain had spent most of the journey counting things, taking pictures and counting; ships, troops, security guards both civil and military. They'd managed excuses to stop over at four of the six jump point stations on the route between Pol and the Hegen Hub, with Ungari counting, measuring, sectioning, computer-stuffing, and calculating the whole way. Now they had arrived at Pol's last (or first, depending on your direction of travel) outpost, its toehold in the Hegen Hub itself.

At one time, Pol Six had merely marked the jump point, no more than an emergency stop and communications transfer link. No one had yet solved the problem of getting messages through a wormhole jump except by physically transporting them on a jump ship. In the most developed regions of the nexus, comm ships jumped hourly or even more often, to emit a tight-beam burst that travelled at the speed of light to the next jump point in that region of local space, where messages were picked up and relayed out in turn, the fastest possible flow of information. In the less developed regions, one simply had to wait, sometimes for weeks or months, for a ship to happen by, and hope they'd remember to drop off your mail.

Now Pol Six didn't just mark, it frankly guarded. Ungari had clicked his tongue in excitement, identifying and adding up Pol Navy ships clustered in the area around the new construction. They'd managed a spiral flight path into dock that revealed every side of the station, and all ships both moored and moving.

"Your main job here," Ungari had told Miles, "will be to give anyone watching us something more interesting to watch than me. Circulate. I doubt you'll need to expend any special effort to be conspicuous. Develop your cover identity—with luck, you may even pick up a contact or two who'll be worthy of further study. Though I doubt you'll run across anything of great value immediately, it doesn't work that way."

Now, Miles laid his samples case open on his bed and rechecked it. *Just a traveling salesman, that's me.* A dozen hand weapons, power-packs removed, gleamed wickedly back at him. A row of vid-disks described larger and more interesting weapons systems. An even more interesting—you might even say, "arresting"—collection of tiny disks nestled concealed in Miles's jacket. *Death. I can get it for you wholesale.*

Miles's bodyguard met him at the docking hatch. Why, oh God, had Illyan assigned Sergeant Overkill to this mission? Same reason he'd sent him to Kyril Island, because he was trusted, no doubt, but it embarrassed Miles to be working with a man who'd once arrested him. What did Overholt make of Miles, by now? Happily, the big man was the silent type.

Overholt was dressed as informally and eclectically as Miles himself, though with safety boots in place of sandals. He looked exactly like somebody's bodyguard trying to look like a tourist. Much the sort of man small-time arms dealer Victor Rotha would logically employ. *Both functional and decorative, he slices, dices, and chops. . . .* By themselves, either Miles or Overholt would be memorable. Together, well . . . Ungari was right. They needn't worry about being overlooked.

Miles led the way through the docking tube and into Pol Six. This docking spoke funneled into a Customs area, where Miles's sample case and person were carefully examined, and Overholt had to produce registration for his stunner. From there they had free run of the transfer station facilities, but for certain guarded corridors leading into the, as it were, militarized zones. Those areas, Ungari had made clear, were his business, not Miles's.

Miles, in good time for his first appointment, strolled slowly, enjoying the sensation of being on a space station. The place wasn't as free-wheeling as Beta Colony, but without question he moved in the midst of mainstream galactic technoculture. Not like poor half-backwards Barrayar. The brittle artificial environment emitted its own whiff of danger, a whiff that could balloon instantly into claustrophobic terror in the event of a sudden depressurization emergency. A concourse lined with shops, hostels, and eating facilities made a central meeting area.

A curious trio idled just across the busy concourse from Miles. A big man dressed in loose clothing ideal for concealing weapons scanned the area uneasily. A professional counterpart of Sergeant Overkill's, no doubt. He and Overholt spotted each other and exchanged grim glances, carefully ignored each other after that. The bland man he guarded faded into near-invisibility beside his woman.

She was short, but astonishingly intense, slight figure and white-blond hair cropped close to her head giving her an odd elfin look. Her black jumpsuit seemed shot with electric sparks, flowing over her skin like water, evening-wear in the day-cycle. Thin-heeled black shoes boosted her a few futile centimeters. Her lips were colored blood-carmine to match the shimmering scarf that looped across alabaster collarbones to cascade from each shoulder, framing the bare white skin of her back. She looked . . . expensive.

Her eye caught Miles's fascinated stare. Her chin lifted, and she stared back coldly.

"Victor Rotha?" The voice at Miles's elbow made him jump.

"Ah . . . Mr. Liga?" Miles, wheeling, hazarded in return. Rabbitlike pale features, protruding lip, black hair; this was the man who claimed he wished to improve the armament of his security guards at his asteroid mining facility. Sure. How—and where—had Ungari scraped Liga up? Miles was not sure he wanted to know.

"I've arranged a private room for us to talk." Liga smiled, tilting his head toward a nearby hostel entrance. "Eh," Liga added, "looks like everybody's doing business this morning." He nodded toward the trio across the concourse, who were now a quartet and moving off. The scarves snapped along like banners, floating in the quick-stepping blonde's wake.

"Who was that woman?" asked Miles.

"I don't know," said Liga. "But the man they're following is your main competition here. The agent of House Fell, the Jacksonian armaments specialists."

He looked more like a middle-aged businessman type, at least from the back. "Pol lets the Jacksonians operate here?" Miles asked. "I thought tensions were high."

"Between Pol, Aslund, and Vervain, yes," said Liga. "The Jacksonian consortium is loudly claiming neutrality. They hope to profit from all sides. But this isn't the best place to talk politics. Let's go, eh?"

As Miles expected, Liga settled them in what was obviously an otherwise-unoccupied hostel room, rented for the purpose. Miles began his memorized pitch, working through the hand-weapons, bafflegabbing about available inventory and delivery dates.

"I'd hoped," said Liga, "for something a little more . . . authoritative."

"I have another selection of samples aboard my ship," Miles explained. "I didn't want to trouble Pol customs with them. But I can give you an overview by vid."

Miles trotted out the heavy weapons manuals. "This vid is for educational purposes only, of course, as these weapons are of a grade illegal for a private person to own in Pol local space."

"In Pol space, yes," Liga agreed. "But Pol's law doesn't run in the Hegen Hub. Yet. All you have to do is cast off from Pol Six and take a little run out beyond the ten-thousand-kilometer traffic control limit to conduct any sort of business you want, perfectly legally. The problem comes in delivering the cargo back *in* to Pol local space."

"Difficult deliveries are one of my specialties," Miles assured him. "For a small surcharge, of course."

"Eh. Good . . ." Liga flicked fast-forward through the vid catalogue. "These heavy-duty plasma arcs, now . . . how do they compare with the cannon-grade nerve disrupters?"

Miles shrugged. "Depends entirely upon whether you want to blow away people alone, or people and property both. I can make you a very good price on the nerve disrupters." He named a figure in Pol credits.

"I got a better quote than that, on a device of the same kilowattage, lately," Liga mentioned disinterestedly.

"I'll bet you did." Miles grinned. "Poison, one credit. Antidote, one hundred credits."

"What's that supposed to mean, eh?" asked Liga suspiciously.

Miles unrolled his lapel and ran his thumb down the underside, and pulled out a tiny vid tab. "Take a look at this." He inserted it into the vid viewer. A figure sprang to life, and pirouetted. It was dressed from head to toe- and fingertips in what appeared to be glittering skintight netting.

"A bit drafty for long underwear, eh?" said Liga skeptically.

Miles flashed him a pained smile. "What you're looking at is what every armed force in the galaxy would like to get their hands on. The perfected single-person nerve disrupter shield net. Beta Colony's latest technological card."

Liga's eyes widened. "First I'd heard they were on the market."

"The open market, no. These are, as it were, private advance sales." Beta Colony only advertised its second or third latest advantages; staying several steps ahead of everybody else in R&D had been the harsh world's stock-in-trade for a couple of generations. In time, Beta Colony would be marketing its new device galaxy-wide. In the meantime . . .

Liga licked his pouty lower lip. "We use nerve disrupters a lot."

For security guards? Right, sure. "I have a limited supply of shield nets. First come, first served."

"The price?"

Miles named a figure in Betan dollars.

"Outrageous!" Liga rocked back in his float chair.

Miles shrugged. "Think about it. It could put your . . . organization at a considerable disadvantage not to be the first to upgrade its defenses. I'm sure you can imagine."

"I'll . . . have to check it out. Eh . . . can I have that disk to show my, eh, supervisor?"

Miles pursed his lips. "Don't get caught with it."

"No way." Liga spun the demo vid through its paces one more time, staring in fascination at the sparkling soldier-figure, before pocketing the disk.

There. The hook was baited, and cast upon dark

waters. It was going to be very interesting to see what nibbled, whether minnows or monstrous leviathans. Liga was a fish of the ramora underclass, Miles judged. Well, he had to start somewhere.

Back out on the concourse, Miles muttered worriedly to Overholt, "Did I do all right?"

"Very smooth, sir," Overholt reassured him.

Well, maybe. It had felt good, running by plan. He could almost feel himself submerging into the smarmy personality of Victor Rotha.

For lunch, Miles led Overholt to a cafeteria with seating open to the concourse, the better for anyone not-watching Ungari to observe them. He munched a sandwich of vat-produced protein, and let his tight nerves unwind a little. This act could be all right. Not nearly as overstimulating as—

"Admiral Naismith!"

Miles nearly choked on a half-chewed bite, his head swivelling frantically to identify the source of the surprised voice. Overholt jerked to full-alert, though he managed to keep his hand from flying prematurely to his concealed stunner.

Two men had paused beside his table. One Miles did not recognize. The other . . . damn! He knew that face. Square-jawed, brown-skinned, too neat and fit for his age to pass as anything but a soldier despite his Polian civilian clothes. The name, the name . . . ! One of Tung's commandos, a combat-drop-shuttle squad commander. The last time Miles had seen him they'd been suiting up together in the *Triumph's* armory, preparing for a boarding battle. Clive Chodak, that was his name.

"I'm sorry, you're mistaken," Miles's denial was pure spinal reflex. "My name is Victor Rotha."

Chodak blinked. "What? Oh! Sorry. That is—you look a lot like somebody I used to know." He took in

Overholt. His eyes queried Miles urgently. "Uh, can we join you?"

"No!" said Miles sharply, panicked. No, wait. He shouldn't throw away a possible contact. This was a complication for which he should have been prepared. But to activate Naismith prematurely, without Ungari's orders . . . "Anyway, not here," he amended hastily.

"I . . . see, sir." With a short nod, Chodak immediately withdrew, drawing his reluctant companion with him. He managed to glance back over his shoulder only once. Miles restrained the impulse to bite his napkin in half. The two men faded into the concourse. By their urgent gestures, they appeared to be arguing.

"Was that smooth?" Miles asked plaintively.

Overholt looked mildly dismayed. "Not very." He frowned down the concourse in the direction the two men had disappeared.

It didn't take Chodak more than an hour to track Miles down aboard his Betan ship in dock. Ungari was still out.

"He says he wants to talk to you," said Overholt. He and Miles studied the vid monitor of the hatchway, where Chodak shifted impatiently from foot to foot. "What do you think he really wants?"

"Probably, to talk to me," said Miles. "Damn me if I don't want to talk to him, too."

"How well did you know him?" asked Overholt suspiciously, staring at Chodak's image.

"Not well," Miles admitted. "He seemed a competent non-com. Knew his equipment, kept his people moving, stood his ground under fire." In truth, thinking back, Miles's actual contacts with the man had been brief, all in the course of business . . . but some of those minutes had been critical, in the wild uncertainty of shipboard combat. Was Miles's gut-feel really adequate security clearance for a man he hadn't seen for almost four years? "Scan him, sure. But let's let him in and see what he has to say."

"If you so order it, sir," said Overholt neutrally.

"I do."

Chodak did not seem to resent being scanned. He carried only a registered stunner. Though he had also been an expert at hand-to-hand combat, Miles recalled, a weapon no one could confiscate. Overholt escorted him to the small ship's wardroom/mess—the Betans would have called it the rec room.

"Mr. Rotha." Chodak nodded. "I, uh . . . hoped we could talk here privately." He looked doubtfully at Overholt. "Or have you replaced Sergeant Bothari?"

"Never." Miles motioned Overholt to follow him into the corridor, didn't speak till the doors sighed shut. "I think you are an inhibiting presence, Sergeant. Would you mind waiting outside?" Miles didn't specify whom Overholt inhibited. "You can monitor, of course."

"Bad idea." Overholt frowned. "Suppose he jumps you?"

Miles's fingers tapped nervously on his trouser seam. "It's a possibility. But we're heading for Aslund next, where the Dendarii are stationed, Ungari says. He may bear useful information."

"If he tells the truth."

"Even lies can be revealing." With this doubtful argument Miles squeezed back into the wardroom, shedding Overholt.

He nodded to his visitor, now seated at a table. "Corporal Chodak."

Chodak brightened. "You do remember."

"Oh, yes. And, ah . . . are you still with the Dendarii?"

"Yes, sir. It's Sergeant Chodak, now."

"Very good. I'm not surprised."

"And, um . . . the Oseran Mercenaries."

"So I understand. Whether it's good or not remains to be seen."

"What are you posing as, sir?"

"Victor Rotha is an arms dealer."

"That's a good cover." Chodak nodded, judiciously.

Miles tried to put a casual mask on his next words by punching up two coffees. "So what are you doing on Pol Six? I thought the Den—the fleet was hired out on Aslund."

"At Aslund Station, here in the Hub," Chodak corrected. "It's just a couple days' flight across-system. What there is of it, so far. Government contractors." He shook his head.

"Behind schedule and over cost?"

"You got it." He accepted the coffee without hesitation, holding it between lean hands, and took a preliminary slurp. "I can't stay long." He turned the cup, set it on the table. "Sir, I think I may have accidentally done you a bad turn. I was so startled to see you there. . . . Anyway, I wanted to . . . to warn you, I guess. Are you on the way back to the fleet?"

"I'm afraid I can't discuss my plans. Not even with you."

Chodak gave him a penetrating stare from black almond eyes. "You always were tricky."

"As an experienced combat soldier, do you prefer frontal assaults?"

"No, sir!" Chodak smiled slightly.

"Suppose you tell me. I take it you are—or are one—of the fleet intelligence agents scattered around the Hub. There had better be more than one of you, or the organization's fallen apart sadly in my absence." In fact, half the inhabitants of Pol Six at the moment were probably spies of some stripe, considering the number of potential players in this game. Not to mention double agents—ought they to be counted twice?

"Why have you been gone so *long,* sir?" Chodak's tone was almost accusatory.

"It wasn't my intention," Miles temporized. "For a portion of the time I was a prisoner in a . . . place I'd rather not describe. I only escaped about three months back." Well, that was one way of describing Kyril Island.

"You, sir! We could have rescued—"

"No, you couldn't have," Miles said sharply. "The situation was one of extreme delicacy. It was resolved to my satisfaction. But I was then faced with . . . considerable clean-up in areas of my operations other than the Dendarii fleet. Far-flung areas. Sorry, but you people are not my only concern. Nevertheless, I'm worried. I should have heard more from Commodore Jesek." Indeed, he should have.

"Commodore Jesek no longer commands. There was a financial reorganization and command restructuring, about a year ago, through the committee of captain-owners and Admiral Oser. Spearheaded by Admiral Oser."

"Where is Jesek?"

"He was demoted to fleet engineer."

Disturbing, but Miles could see it. "Not necessarily a bad thing. Jesek was never as aggressive as, say, Tung. And Tung?"

Chodak shook his head. "He was demoted from chief-of-staff to personnel officer. A nothing-job."

"That seems . . . wasteful."

"Oser doesn't trust Tung. And Tung doesn't love Oser, either. Oser's been trying to force him out for a year, but he hangs on, despite the humiliation of . . . um. It's not easy to get rid of him. Oser can't afford—yet—to decimate his staff, and too many key people are personally loyal to Tung."

Miles's eyebrow rose. "Including yourself?"

Chodak said distantly, "He got things done. I considered him a superior officer."

"So did I."

Chodak nodded shortly. "Sir . . . the thing is . . . the man who was with me in the cafeteria is my senior here. And he's one of Oser's. I can't think of any way short of killing him to stop him reporting our encounter."

"I have no desire to start a civil war in my own command structure," said Miles mildly. *Yet.* "*I* think it's more important that he not suspect you spoke to me privately. Let him report. I've struck deals with Admiral Oser before, to our mutual benefit."

"I'm not sure Oser thinks so, sir. I think he thinks he was screwed."

Miles barked a realistic laugh. "What, I doubled the size of the fleet during the Tau Verde war. Even as third officer, he ended up commanding more than he had before, a smaller slice of a bigger pie."

"But the side he originally contracted us to lost."

"Not so. Both sides gained from that truce we forced. It was a win-win result, except for a little lost face. What, can't Oser feel he's won unless somebody else loses?"

Chodak looked grim. "I think that may be the case, sir. He says—I've heard him say—you ran a scam on us. You were never an admiral, never an officer of any kind. If Tung hadn't double-crossed him, he'd have kicked your ass to hell." Chodak's gaze on Miles was broodingly thoughtful. "What were you really?"

Miles smiled gently. "I was the winner. Remember?"

Chodak snorted, half-amused. "Yee-ah."

"Don't let poor Oser's revisionist history fog your mind. You were there."

Chodak shook his head ruefully. "You didn't really need my warning, did you." He moved to stand up.

"Never assume anything. And, ah . . . take care of yourself. That means, cover your ass. I'll remember you, later."

"Sir." Chodak nodded. Overholt, waiting in the corridor in a quasi-Imperial Guardsman pose, escorted him firmly to the shuttle hatch.

Miles sat in the wardroom, and nibbled gently on the rim of his coffee cup, considering certain surprising parallels between command restructuring in a free mercenary fleet and the internecine wars of the Barrayaran Vor. Might the mercenaries be thought of as a miniature, simplified, or laboratory version of the real thing? *Oser should have been around during the Vordarian's Pretendership, and seen how the big boys operate.* Still, Miles had best not underestimate the potential dangers and complexities of the situation. His death in a miniature conflict would be just as absolute as his death in a large one.

Hell, what death? What had he to do with the Dendarii, or the Oserans, after all? Oser was right, it had been a scam, and the only wonder was how long it had taken the man to wake to the fact. Miles could see no immediate need to reinvolve himself with the Dendarii at all. In fact, he could be well rid of a dangerous political embarrassment. Let Oser have them, they'd been his in the first place anyway.

I have three sworn liege-people in that fleet. My own personal body politic.

How *easy* it had been to slip back into being Naismith. . . .

Anyway, activating Naismith wasn't Miles's decision. It was Captain Ungari's.

Ungari was the first to point this out, when he returned later and Overholt briefed him. A controlled man, his fury showed by subtle signs, a sharpening of the voice, deeper lines of tension around the eyes and mouth. "You violated your cover. You *never* break cover. It's the first rule of survival in this business."

"Sir, may I respectfully submit, I didn't blow it," Miles replied steadily. "Chodak did. He seemed to realize it, too, he's not stupid. He apologized as best he could." Chodak indeed might be subtler than first glance would indicate, for at this point, he had an in with both sides in the putative Dendarii command schism, whoever came out on top. Calculation or chance? Chodak was either smart or lucky, in either case he could be a useful addition to Miles's side. . . . *What side, huh? Ungari isn't going to let me near the Dendarii after this.*

Ungari frowned at the vid-plate, which had just replayed the recording of Miles's interview with the mercenary. "It sounds more and more like the Naismith cover may be too dangerous to activate at all. If your Oser's little palace coup is anything like what this fellow indicates, Illyan's fantasy of you simply ordering the Dendarii to get lost is straight out the air lock. I thought it sounded too easy." Ungari paced the wardroom, tapping his right fist into his left palm. "Well, we may still get some use out of Victor Rotha. Much as I'd like to confine you to quarters—"

Strange, how many of his superiors said that.

"—Liga wants to see Rotha again this evening. Maybe to place an order for some of our fictitious cargo. String it out—I want you to get past him to the next level of his organization. His boss, or his boss's boss."

"Who owns Liga, do you suspect?"

Ungari stopped pacing, and turned his hands palm-out. "The Cetagandans? Jackson's Whole? Any one of half a dozen others? ImpSec is spread thin out here.

But if it were proved Liga's criminal organization are Cetagandan puppets, it could be worth sending a full-time agent to penetrate their ranks. So find out! Hint at more goodies in your bag. Take bribes. Blend in. And move it along. I'm almost finished here, and Illyan particularly wants to know when Aslund Station will be fully operational as a defensive base."

Miles punched the door chime of the hostel room. His chin tic'd up. He cleared his throat and straightened his shoulders. Overholt glanced up and down the empty corridor.

The door hissed open. Miles blinked in astonishment.

"Ah, Mr. Rotha." The light cool voice belonged to the brief blonde he'd seen in the concourse that morning. Her jumpsuit was now skin-fitting red silk with a downcurving neckline, a glittering red ruff rising from the back of the neck to frame her sculptured head, and high-heeled red suede boots. She favored him with a high-voltage smile.

"I'm sorry," said Miles automatically. "I must be in the wrong place."

"Not at all." A slim hand opened in an expansive, welcoming gesture. "You're right on time."

"I had an appointment with a Mr. Liga, here."

"Yes, and I've taken over the appointment. Do come in. My name is Livia Nu."

Well, she couldn't possibly be carrying any concealed weapons. Miles stepped within, and was unsurprised to see her bodyguard, idling in one corner of the hostel room. The man nodded to Overholt, who nodded back, both wary as two cats. And where was the third man? Not here, evidently.

She drifted to a liquid-filled settee, and arranged herself upon it.

"Are you, uh, Mr. Liga's supervisor?" Miles asked. No, Liga had denied knowing who she was. . . .

She hesitated fractionally. "In a sense, yes."

One of them was lying—no, not necessarily. If she were indeed high in Liga's organization, he would not have identified her to Rotha. Damn.

"—but you may think of me as a procurement agent."

God. Pol Six really was hip-deep in spies. "For whom?"

"Ah," she smiled. "One of the advantages of dealing with small suppliers is always their no-questions-asked policy. One of the few advantages."

"No-questions-asked is House Fell's slogan, I believe. They have the advantage of a fixed and secure base. I've learned to be cautious about selling arms to people who might be shooting at me in the near future."

Her blue eyes widened. "Who would want to shoot at you?"

"Misguided folk," Miles tossed off. Ye gods. He was not in control of this conversation. He exchanged a harried look with Overholt, who was being out-blanded by his counterpart.

"We must chat." She patted the cushion beside her invitingly. "Do sit down, Victor. Ah," she nodded to her bodyguard, "why don't you wait outside."

Miles seated himself on the edge of the settee, trying to guess the woman's age. Her complexion was smooth and white. Only the skin of her eyelids was soft and faintly puckered. Miles thought of Ungari's orders—take bribes, blend in. . . . "Perhaps you should wait outside also," he said to Overholt.

Overholt looked torn, but of the two, he clearly wanted more to keep an eye on the large armed man. He nodded, apparently in acquiescence, actually in approval, and followed her man out.

Miles smiled in what he hoped was a friendly way. She looked positively seductive. Miles eased cautiously back in the cushions, and tried to look seduceable. A veritable espionage fantasy encounter, of the sort Ungari had told him never happened. Maybe they just never happened to Ungari, eh? *My, what sharp teeth you have, miss.*

Her hand went to her cleavage—a riveting gesture—and withdrew a tiny, familiar vid disk. She leaned over to insert it in the vid player on the low table before them, and it took Miles a moment to shift his attention to the vid. The little glittering soldier-figure went through its stylized gestures once again. Ha. So, she really was Liga's supervisor. Very good, he was getting somewhere now.

"This is really remarkable, Victor. How did you come by it?"

"A happy accident."

"How many can you supply?"

"A strictly limited number. Say, fifty. I'm not a manufacturer. Liga did mention the price?"

"I thought it high."

"If you can find another supplier who offers these for less, I will be happy to match his price and knock off ten percent." Miles managed to bow sitting down.

She made a faint amused sound, down in her throat. "The volume offered is too low."

"There are several ways you could profit from even a small number of these, if you got into the trade early enough. Such as selling working models to interested governments. I mean to have a share of that profit, before the market is saturated and the price drops. You could too."

"Why don't you? Sell them directly to governments, that is."

"What makes you think I haven't?" Miles smiled.

"But—consider my routes out of this area. I came in past Barrayar and Pol. I must exit via either Jackson's Whole or the Cetagandan Empire. Unfortunately, through either route I run a high risk of being relieved of this particular cargo without any compensation whatsoever." For that matter, where had Barrayar obtained its working model of the shield-suit? Was there a real Victor Rotha, and where was he now? Where *had* Illyan gotten their ship?

"So, you carry them with you?"

"I didn't say that."

"Hm." She smiled. "Can you deliver one tonight?"

"What size?"

"Small." One long-nailed finger traced a line down her body, from breast to thigh, to indicate exactly how small.

Miles sighed mournfully. "Unfortunately, these were sized for the average-to-large combat soldier. Cutting one down is a considerable technical challenge—one which I am in fact still working on myself."

"How thoughtless of the manufacturer."

"I entirely agree, Citizen Nu."

She looked at him more carefully. Did her smile grow slightly more genuine?

"Anyway, I prefer to sell them in wholesale lots. If your organization isn't financially up to it—"

"An arrangement might yet be made."

"Promptly, I trust. I'll be moving on soon."

She murmured absently, "Perhaps not . . ." then looked up with a quick frown. "What's your next stop?"

Ungari had to file a public flight plan anyway. "Aslund."

"Hm . . . yes, we must come to some arrangement. Absolutely."

Were those blue flickers what were called bedroom eyes? The effect was lulling, almost hypnotic. *I finally meet a woman who's barely taller than I am, and I don't even know which side she's on.* He of all men ought not to mistake short for weak or helpless.

"Can I meet your boss?"

"Who?" Her brows lowered.

"The man I saw you both with this morning."

". . . oh. So, you've already seen him."

"Set me up a meeting. Let's do serious business. Betan dollars, remember."

"Pleasure before business, surely." Her breath puffed against his ear, a faint spicy fog.

Was she trying to soften him up? What *for?* Ungari had said, don't break cover. Surely it would be in character for Victor Rotha to take all he could get. Plus ten percent. "You don't have to do this," he managed to choke out. His heart was beating entirely too fast.

"I don't do *everything* for business reasons," she purred.

Why, indeed, should she bother to seduce a sleazy little gun runner? What pleasure was in it for her? What was in it *besides* pleasure for her? *Maybe she likes me.* Miles winced, picturing himself offering that explanation to Ungari. Her arm circled his neck. His hand, unwilled, rose to stroke the fine pelt of her hair. A highly aesthetic tactile experience, just as he'd imagined . . .

Her hand tightened. In pure nervous reflex, Miles leapt to his feet.

And stood there feeling like an idiot. It had been a caress, not incipient strangulation. The angle was all wrong for attack leverage.

She flung herself back in the seat, slim arm stretching along the top of the cushions. "Victor!" Her voice was amused, her brow arched. "I wasn't going to bite your neck."

His face was hot. "I-have-to-go-now." He cleared his

throat to bring his voice back down to its lower register. His hand swooped to pluck the vid disk from the player. Her hand leapt toward it, then fell back languidly, pretending disinterest. Miles hit the door comm.

Overholt was there at once, in the sliding door aperture. Miles's gut eased. If his bodyguard had been gone, Miles would have known this at once for some kind of setup. Too late, of course.

"Maybe later," Miles gabbled. "After you've taken delivery. We could get together." Delivery of a nonexistent cargo? What was he saying?

She shook her head in disbelief. Her laugh followed him down the corridor. It had a brittle edge.

Miles lurched awake when the lights snapped on in his cabin. Ungari, fully dressed, was in the doorway. Behind him their jump pilot, wearing only his underwear and a sleep-stunned expression, jittered uncertainly.

"Dress later," Ungari snarled to the pilot. "Just get us free of the dock and run us out beyond the ten-thousand-kilometer limit. I'll be up to help set course in a few minutes." He added half to himself, "As soon as I know where the devil we're going. *Move.*"

The pilot fled. Ungari strode to Miles's bedside. "Vorkosigan, what the hell happened in that hostel room?"

Miles squeezed his eyes against the glares of both the lights and Ungari, and suppressed an impulse to hide under the covers from both. "Ha?" His mouth was dry with sleep.

"I've just gotten an advance warning—bare minutes' advance warning—of an arrest order being put out by Pol Six civil security for Victor Rotha."

"But I never touched the lady!" Miles protested, dizzied.

"Liga's body was found murdered in your meeting room."

"What!"

"The security lab has just finished timing it—to about when you met. Were to meet. The arrest order will be on the net in minutes, and we'll be locked in here."

"But I didn't. I never even saw Liga, only his boss, Livia Nu. I mean—if I'd done any such thing, I'd have reported it to you immediately, sir!"

"Thank you," said Ungari dryly. "I'm glad to know that." His voice harshened. "You're being framed, of course."

"Who—" Yes. There could have been another, grimmer way for Livia Nu to have relieved Liga of that top secret vid disk. But if she wasn't Liga's superior, or even a member of his Polian criminal organization at all, who was she? "We need to know more, sir! This could be the start of something."

"This could be the *end* of our mission. Damn! And now we can't retreat back through Pol to Barrayar. Cut off. Where next?" Ungari paced, evidently thinking aloud. "I want to go to Aslund. Its extradition treaty with Pol has broken down at present, but . . . then there are your mercenary complications. Now that they've connected Rotha to Naismith. Thanks to your carelessness."

"From what Chodak said, I don't think Admiral Naismith would exactly be welcomed back with open arms," Miles agreed reluctantly.

"Jackson's Whole's consortium station has no extradition treaty with anyone. This cover's gone completely sour. Rotha and Naismith, both useless. It has to be the Consortium. I'll ditch this ship there, go underground, and double back to Aslund on my own."

"What about me, sir?"

"You and Overholt will have to split off and take the long way home."

Home. Home in disgrace. "Sir . . . running away looks bad. Suppose we sat tight, and cleared Rotha of the charges? We wouldn't be cut off anymore, and Rotha would still be a viable cover. It's possible we're being hustled into doing just this, cutting and running."

"I don't see how anyone could have anticipated my information source in Polian civil security. I think we're meant to be locked up here in dock." Ungari tapped his right fist into his palm once, a gesture of decision this time. "The Consortium it is." He wheeled and exited, boots tromping down the deck. A change of vibration and air pressure, and a few muted clanks, told Miles their ship was now breaking from Pol Six.

Miles said aloud to the empty cabin, "But what if they have plans for both contingencies? *I* would." He shook his head doubtfully, and rose to dress and follow Ungari.

CHAPTER NINE

The Jacksonian Consortium's jump point station, Miles decided, differed from Pol's mainly in the assortment of things its merchants offered for sale. He stood before the book-disk dispenser in a concourse very like Pol Six's and flicked the vid fast-forward through a huge catalogue of pornography. Well, mostly fast-forward; his search was punctuated by a few pauses, from bemused to stunned. Nobly resisting curiosity, he reached the military history section only to find a disappointingly thin collection of titles.

He inserted his credit card and the machine dispensed three wafers. Not that he was all that interested in *The Adumbration of Trigonial Strategy in the Wars of Minos IV*, but it was going to be a long, dull ride home, and Sergeant Overholt did not promise to be the most sparkling of traveling companions. Miles pocketed the disks and sighed. What a waste of time, effort, and anticipation this mission had been.

Ungari had arranged for the "sale" of Victor Rotha's ship, pilot, and engineer to a front man who would deliver it, eventually, back to Barrayaran Imperial Security. Miles's pleading suggestions to his superior on how to make more use of Rotha, Naismith, or even Ensign Vorkosigan had then been interrupted by an ultra-coded message from ImpSec HQ, for Ungari's eyes only. Ungari had withdrawn to decode it, and emerged half an hour later, dead-white around the lips.

He had then moved his timetable up and departed within the hour on a commercial ship to Aslund Station. Alone. Refusing to impart the contents of the message to Miles, or even to Sergeant Overholt. Refusing to take Miles along. Refusing Miles permission to at least continue military observations independently on the Consortium.

Ungari left Overholt to Miles, or vice versa. It was a little hard to tell who had been left in charge of whom. Overholt seemed to be acting less like a subordinate and more like a nanny all the time, discouraging Miles's attempted explorations of the Consortium, insisting he keep safely to his hostel room. They waited now to board an Escobaran commercial liner slated for a nonstop run to Escobar, where they would report to the Barrayaran Embassy, which would no doubt ship them home. Home, and with nothing to show for it.

Miles checked his chrono. Another twenty minutes to kill before boarding. They might as well go sit. With an irritable glance at his shadow Overholt, Miles trudged wearily down the concourse. Overholt followed, frowning general disapproval.

Miles brooded on Livia Nu. In fleeing from her erotic invitation he'd surely missed the adventure of his short lifetime. Yet that hadn't been the look of love on her face. Anyway, he'd worry about a woman who could fall madly in love at first sight with Victor Rotha.

The light in her eyes had been more on the order of a gourmet contemplating an unusual hors d'oeuvre just presented by the waiter. He'd felt like he'd had parsley sticking out of his ears.

She might have been dressed like a courtesan, moved like a courtesan, but there'd been none of the courtesan's eagerness to please about her, nothing servile. The gestures of power in the garments of powerlessness. Unsettling.

So beautiful.

Courtesan, criminal, spy, what was she? Above all, who did she belong to? Was she Liga's boss, or Liga's opponent? Or Liga's fate? Had she killed the rabbity man herself? Whatever else she was, Miles was increasingly convinced, she was a key piece in the puzzle of the Hegen Hub. They should have followed her up, not fled from her. Sex wasn't the only opportunity he'd missed. The meeting with Livia Nu was going to bother him for a long time.

Miles looked up to find his way blocked by a pair of Consortium goons—civil security officers, he corrected his thought ironically. He stood, feet planted, and lifted his chin. What now? "Yes, gentlemen?"

The big one looked to the enormous one, who cleared his throat. "Mr. Victor Rotha?"

"If I am, then what?"

"An arrest order has been purchased for you. It charges you with the murder of one Sydney Liga. Do you wish to outbid?"

"Probably." Miles's lip curled in exasperation. What a development. "Who's bidding for my arrest?"

"The name is Cavilo."

Miles shook his head. "Don't even know him. Is he with Polian Civil Security, by chance?"

The officer checked his report panel. "No." He added chattily, "The Polians almost never do business with us. They think we ought to trade them criminals for free. As if we wanted any back!"

"Huh. That's supply and demand for you." Miles blew out his breath. Illyan was not going to be thrilled about *this* charge on his expense account. "How much did this Cavilo offer for me?"

The officer checked his panel again. His brows rose. "Twenty thousand Betan dollars. He must want you a lot."

Miles made a small leaky noise. "I don't have that much *on* me."

The officer pulled out his come-along stick. "Well, then."

"I'll have to make arrangements."

"You'll have to make arrangements from Detention, sir."

"But I'll miss my ship!"

"That's probably the idea," the officer agreed. "Considering the timing and all."

"Suppose—if that's all this Cavilo wants—he then withdraws his bid?"

"He'll lose a substantial deposit."

Jacksonian justice was truly blind. They'd sell it to anyone. "Uh, may I have a word with my assistant?"

The officer pursed his lips, and studied Overholt suspiciously. "Make it fast."

"What d'you think, Sergeant?" Miles turned to Overholt and asked lowly. "They don't seem to have an order for you. . . ."

Overholt looked tense, tight mouth annoyed and eyes almost panicked. "If we could make it to the ship . . ."

The rest hung unspoken. The Escobarans shared the Polian disapproval of Jacksonian Consortium "law." Once aboard the liner, Miles would be on Escobaran "soil"; the captain would not voluntarily yield him up. Could, would, this Cavilo be able to bid enough to intern the whole Escobaran liner? The sum involved would be astronomical. "Try."

Miles turned back toward the Consortium officers, smiling, wrists held out in surrender. Overholt exploded into action.

The sergeant's first kick sent the enormous goon's come-along stick flying. Overholt's momentum flowed into a whirl that brought his double hands up against the second goon's head with great force. Miles was already in motion. He dodged a wild grab, and sprinted as best he could up the concourse. At this point he spotted the third goon, in plainclothes. Miles could tell who he was by the glitter of the tangle-field he tossed in front of Miles's pistoning legs. The man snorted with laughter as Miles pitched forward, trying to roll and save his brittle bones. Miles hit the concourse floor with a whump that knocked the air from his lungs. He inhaled through clenched teeth, not crying out, as the pain in his chest competed with the burn of the tangle-net around his ankles. He wrenched himself around on the floor, looking back the way he had come.

The less enormous goon was standing bent over, hands to his head, dizzied. The other was retrieving his come-along stick from where it had skittered to a stop. By elimination, the stunned heap on the pavement must be Sergeant Overholt.

The goon with the stick stared at Overholt and shook his head, and stepped over him toward Miles. The dizzied goon pulled out his own stick and gave the downed man a shock to the head, and followed without a backward glance. Nobody, apparently, wanted to buy Overholt.

"There will be a ten-percent surcharge for resisting arrest," the spokesman-goon remarked coldly down to Miles. Miles squinted up the shiny columns of his boots. The shock-stick came down like a club.

On the third blazing blow he began screaming. On the seventh, he passed out.

He came to consciousness altogether too soon, while still being dragged along between the two uniformed men. He was shivering uncontrollably. His breathing was messed up somehow, irregular shallow gasps that didn't give him enough air. Waves of pins-and-needles pulsed through his nervous system. He had a kaleidoscopic impression of lift tubes and corridors, and more bare functional corridors. They jerked to a halt at last. When the goons let his arms go he fell to hands and knees, then the cold floor.

Another civil security officer peered over a comconsole desk at him. A hand grasped Miles's head by the hair, and yanked it back; the red flicker of a retinal scan blinded him momentarily. His eyes seemed extraordinarily sensitive to light. His shaking hands were pressed hard against some sort of identification pad; released, he fell back into his huddle. His pockets were stripped out, stunner, IDs, tickets, cash, all dumped pell-mell into a plastic bag. Miles emitted a muffled squeak of dismay as they bundled the white jacket, with all its useful secrets, into the bag as well. The lock was keyed closed with his thumbprint, pinched against it.

The Detention officer craned his neck. "Does he want to outbid?"

"Unh . . ." Miles managed to respond, when his head was pulled back again.

"He said he did," the arresting goon said helpfully.

The Detention officer shook his head. "We're going to have to wait till the shock wears off. You guys overdid it, I think. He's only a little runt."

"Yeah, but he had a big guy with him who gave us trouble. The little mutant seemed to be in charge, so we let him take payment for both."

"That's fair," the Detention officer conceded. "Well, it'll be a while. Throw him in the cooler till he stops shaking enough to talk."

"Sure that's a good idea? Funny-looking as he is, the boy-ohs might want to play games. He might still ransom himself."

"Mm." The Detention officer looked Miles over judiciously. "Throw him in the waiting room with Marda's techies, then. They're a quiet bunch, they'll leave him alone. And they'll be gone soon."

Miles was dragged again—his legs didn't respond at all to his will, only jerking spasmodically. The leg braces seemed to have had some amplifying effect on the shocks administered there, or maybe it was the combination with the tangle-field. A long room like a barracks, with a row of cots down each wall, swam past his vision. The goons heaved him, not unkindly, onto an empty cot in the less populated end of the room. The senior one made a dim sort of effort to straighten him out, tossed a light blanket across his still uncontrollably twitching form, and they left him.

A little time passed, with nothing to distract him from the full enjoyment and appreciation of his new array of physical sensations. He'd thought he'd sampled every sort of agony in the catalogue, but the goons' shock-sticks had found out nerves and synapses and ganglial knots he'd never known he possessed. Nothing like pain, to concentrate the attention upon the self. Practically solipsistic, it was. But it seemed to be easing—if only his body would stop these quasi-epileptic seizures, which were exhausting him. . . .

A face wavered into view. A familiar face.

"Gregor! Am I glad to see you," Miles burbled inanely. He felt his burning eyes widen. His hands shot out to clench Gregor's shirt, a pale blue prisoner's smock. "*What the hell are you doing here?*"

"It's a long story."

"Ah! Ah!" Miles struggled up onto his elbow and stared around wildly for assassins, hallucinations, he knew not what. "God! Where's—"

Gregor pushed him back down with a hand on his chest. "Calm down." And under his breath, "And shut up! . . . You better rest a bit. You don't look very good right now."

Actually, Gregor didn't look so good himself, sitting on the edge of Miles's cot. His face was pale and tired, peppered with beard stubble. His normally military-cut and combed black hair was a tangle. His hazel eyes looked nervous. Miles choked back panic.

"My name is Greg Bleakman," the emperor informed Miles urgently.

"I can't remember what my name is right now," Miles stuttered. "Oh—yeah. Victor Rotha. I think. But how did you get from—"

Gregor looked around vaguely. "The walls have ears, I think?"

"Yes, maybe." Miles subsided slightly. The man on the next cot shook his head with a God-save-me-from-these-assholes look, turned over and put his pillow over his head. "But, uh . . . did you get here, like, under your own power?"

"Unfortunately, all my own doing. You remember that time we were joking about running away from home?"

"Yeah?"

"Well," Gregor took a breath, "it turned out to be a really bad idea."

"Couldn't you have figured that out in advance?"

"I—" Gregor broke off, to stare up the long room as a guard stuck his head in the door to bawl, "Five minutes!"

"Oh, hell."

"What? What?"

"They're coming for us."

"Who's coming for who, what the hell is going on, *Gregor*—Greg-"

"I had a berth on a freighter, I thought, but they dumped me off here. Without pay," Gregor explained rapidly. "Stiffed me. I didn't have so much as a half-mark on me. I tried to get something on an outbound ship, but before I could, I got arrested for vagrancy. Jacksonian law is insane," he added reflectively.

"I know. Then what?"

"They were apparently making a deliberate sweep, press-gang style. Seems some entrepreneur is selling tech-trained work gangs to the Aslunders, to work on their Hub station, which is running behind schedule."

Miles blinked. "Slave labor?"

"Of a sort. The carrot is, when the sentence is up, we're to be discharged on Aslund Station. Most of these techs don't seem to mind too much. No pay, but we—they—will be fed and housed, and escape Jacksonian security, so in the end they'll be no worse off than when they started, broke and unemployed. Most of them seem to think they'll find berths outbound from Aslund eventually. Being without funds is not such a heinous crime, there."

Miles's head pounded. "They're taking you away?"

Tension pooled in Gregor's eyes, contained, not permitted to seep over into the rest of his stiff face. "Right now, I think."

"God! I can't let—"

"But how did you find me here—" Gregor began in turn, then looked in frustration up the room, where blue-smocked men and women were grumbling to their feet. "Are you here to—"

Miles stared around frantically. The blue-clad man

on the cot next to his now lay on his side, watching them with a bored glower. He wasn't overtall. . . .

"You!" Miles scrambled overboard, and crouched at the man's side. "You want to get out of this trip?"

The man looked slightly less bored. "How?"

"Trade clothes. Trade IDs. You take my place, I take yours."

The man looked suspicious. "What's the catch?"

"No catch. I got a lot of credit. I was going to buy my way out of here in a while." Miles paused. "There's going to be a surcharge for my resisting arrest, though."

"Ah." A catch identified, the man looked slightly more interested.

"Please! I have to go with—with my friend. Right now." The babble was rising, as the techs assembled in the room's far end by the exit. Gregor wandered around behind the man's cot.

The man pursed his lips. "Naw," he decided. "If whatever you're in for is worse than this, I don't want anything to do with it." He swung to a sitting position, preparing to rise and join the line.

Miles, still crouched on the floor, raised his hands in supplication. "Please—"

Gregor, perfectly placed, pounced. He grabbed the man around the neck in a neat choke and flipped him over the side of his cot, out of sight. Thank God the Barrayaran aristocracy still insisted on military training for its scions. Miles staggered to his feet, the better to obscure the view from up the room. Some small thumping noises came from the floor. In a few moments, a prisoner's blue smock skidded under the cot to fetch up at Miles's sandaled feet. Miles squatted and pulled it on over his green silks—fortunately, it was a bit oversized—then struggled into the loose trousers that followed. Some shoving sounds, as the man's unconscious body was pushed out of sight under the cot, and Gregor stood, panting slightly, very white.

"I can't get these damn belt strings," Miles said. They skittered from his trembling hands.

Gregor tied up Miles's pants, and rolled up his overlong trouser legs. "You need his ID, or you can't get food or register your work-credits," Gregor hissed out of the corner of his mouth, and leaned artistically against the end of the cot in an idle pose.

Miles checked his pocket and found the standard computer card. "All right." He stood next to Gregor, teeth bared in a weird grin. "I'm about to pass out."

Gregor's hand locked his elbow. "Don't. It'll draw attention."

They walked up the room and slipped into the end of the shuffling, complaining, blue-clad line. A sleepy-looking guard at the door checked them out, running a scanner over the IDs.

". . . twenty-three, twenty-four, twenty-five. That's it. Take 'em away."

They were turned over to another set of guards, not in the uniform of the Consortium but some minor Jacksonian House livery, gold and black. Miles kept his face down as they were herded out of Detention. Only Gregor's hand kept him on his feet. They passed through a corridor, another corridor, down a lift tube—Miles nearly threw up during the drop—another corridor. *What if this damned ID has a locator?* Miles thought suddenly. At the next drop tube he shed it; the little card twinkled away into the dim distance, silent and unnoticed. A docking bay, a hatchway, the brief weightlessness of the flexible docking tube, and they boarded a ship. *Sergeant Overholt, where are you now?*

It was clearly an intra-system carrier, not a jump ship, and not very large. The men were separated from the women and directed down opposite ends of a corridor lined with cabin doors leading to four-bunk cubicles. The prisoners spread out, selecting their quarters without apparent interference from the guards.

Miles made a quick count and multiplication. "We can get one to ourselves, if we try," he whispered urgently to Gregor. He ducked into the nearest, and they hit the door control quickly. Another prisoner made to follow them in, to be met with a united snarl of "Back off!" He withdrew hastily. The door did not slide open again.

The cabin was dirty, and lacked such amenities as bedding for the mattresses, but the plumbing worked. As Miles got a drink of lukewarm water he heard and felt the hatch close, and the ship undock. They were safe for the moment. How long?

"When do you think that guy you choked is going to wake up?" Miles asked Gregor, who sat on the edge of one bunk.

"I'm not sure. I've never choked a man before." Gregor looked sick. "I . . . felt something strange, under my hand. I'm afraid I might have broken his neck."

"He was still breathing," Miles said. He walked to the opposite lower bunk and prodded it. No sign of vermin. He seated himself gingerly. The severe shakes were passing off, leaving only a tremula, but he still felt weak in the knees. "When he wakes up—as soon as they find him, whether he wakes up or not—it's not going to take them long to figure out where I went. I should have just waited, and followed you, and bought you back. Assuming I could bid myself free. This was a *stupid* idea. Why didn't you stop me?"

Gregor stared. "I thought you knew what you were doing. Isn't Illyan right behind you?"

"Not as far as I know."

"I thought you were in Illyan's department now. I thought you were sent to find me. This . . . isn't some kind of bizarre rescue?"

"No!" Miles shook his head, and immediately regretted the motion. "Maybe you'd better begin at the beginning."

"I'd been on Komarr for a week. Under the domes. High-level talks on wormhole route treaties—we're still trying to get the Escobarans to permit passage of our military vessels. There's some idea of letting their inspection teams seal our weapons during passage. Our general staff thinks it's too much, theirs thinks it's too little. I signed a couple of agreements—whatever the Council of Ministers shoved in front of me—"

"Dad makes you *read* them, surely."

"Oh, yes. Anyway, there was a military review that afternoon. And a state dinner in the evening, which broke up early, a couple of the negotiators had to catch ships. I went back to my quarters, some oligarch's old town house. Big place at the edge of the dome, near the shuttleport. My suite was high in this building. I went out on the balcony—it didn't help much. Still felt claustrophobic, under the dome."

"Komarrans don't like open air, either," Miles noted in fairness. "I knew one who had breathing problems—like asthma—whenever he had to go outside. Strictly psychosomatic."

Gregor shrugged, gazing at his shoes. "Anyway, I noticed . . . there were no guards in sight. For a change. I don't know why the hole, there'd been a man there earlier. They thought I was asleep, I guess. It was after midnight. I couldn't sleep. I was leaning over the balcony, and thinking, if I toppled off . . ." Gregor hesitated.

"It would be quick," Miles supplied dryly. He knew that state of mind, oh yes.

Gregor glanced up at him, and smiled ironically. "Yes. I was a little drunk."

You were a lot drunk.

"Quick, yes. Smash my skull. It would hurt a lot, but not for long. Maybe even not a lot. Maybe just a flash of heat."

Miles shuddered, concealed in his shock-stick tremula.

"I went over—I caught these plants. Then I realized, I could climb down as easily as up. More easily. I felt free, as if I *had* died. I started walking. Nobody stopped me. All the time, I expected someone to stop me.

"I ended up in the freightyard end of the shuttleport. At a bar. I told this fellow, this free trader, I was a norm-space navigator. I'd done that, on my ship duty. I'd lost my ID, and was afraid Barrayaran Security would rough me up. He believed me—or believed something. Anyway, he gave me a berth. We probably broke orbit before my batman went in to wake me that morning."

Miles chewed his knuckles. "So from ImpSec's point of view, you evaporated from a fully guarded room. No note, no trace—and on *Komarr.*"

"The ship made a straight run through to Pol—I stayed aboard—and then nonstop to the Consortium. I didn't get along too well at first, on the freighter. I thought I was doing better. Guess not. But I thought, Illyan was probably right behind me anyway."

"Komarr." Miles rubbed his temples. "Do you realize what has to be happening back there? Illyan will be convinced it's some sort of political kidnapping. I bet he's got every Security operative and half the army tearing those domes apart bolt by bolt, looking for you. You're way out ahead of them. They won't look beyond Komarr till . . ." Miles counted out days on his fingers.

"Still, Illyan should have alerted all his outlying agents . . . almost a week ago. Ha! I bet that was the message that put Ungari up in the air, just before he left in such a hurry. Sent to Ungari, not to me." *Not to me. Nobody's even counting me.* "But it should have been all over the news—"

"It was, sort of," Gregor offered. "There was a sententious announcement that I'd been ill and retired to rest in seclusion at Vorkosigan Surleau. They're suppressing."

Miles could just picture it. "Gregor, how could you do this! They'll be going insane back home!"

"I'm sorry," said Gregor stiffly. "I knew it was a mistake . . . almost immediately. Even before the hangover cut in."

"Why didn't you get off at Pol, then, and go to the Barrayaran embassy?"

"I thought I might still . . . dammit," he broke off, "why should these people *own* me?"

"Childish, stunt," Miles gritted through his teeth.

Gregor's head jerked up in anger, but he said nothing.

The full realization of his position was just beginning to sink in to Miles, like lead in his belly. *I'm the only man in the universe who knows where the Emperor of Barrayar is right now. If anything happens to Gregor, I could be his heir. In fact, if anything happens to Gregor, quite a lot of people will think I . . .*

And if the Hegen Hub found out who Gregor really was, a free-for-all of epic proportions could follow. The Jacksonians would take him for simple ransom. Aslund, Pol, Vervain, any or all might seek some power play. The Cetagandans most of all—if they could gain possession of Gregor in secret, who knew what subtle psychological programming they might attempt; if openly, what threats? And Miles and Gregor were both trapped on a ship they didn't control—Miles might be snatched away at any moment by Consortium goons or worse—

Miles was an ImpSec officer, now, however junior or disgraced. And ImpSec's sworn duty was the Emperor's safety. The Emperor, Barrayar's unifying icon. Gregor, unwilling flesh pressed into that mold. Icon, flesh, which claimed Miles's allegiance? *Both. He's mine. A prisoner, on the run, trailed by God-knows-what enemies, suicidally depressed, and all mine.*

Miles choked down a lunatic cackle.

CHAPTER TEN

With a little reflection, possible now that the shock-stick reverberations were wearing off, Miles realized that he needed to hide. Gregor, by his place as a contract slave, would be warm, fed, and safe all the way to Aslund Station if Miles did not endanger him. Maybe. Miles added it to his life's lessons list. Call it Rule 27B. Never make key tactical decisions while having electro-convulsive seizures.

Miles began by examining the bunk cubicle. The vessel was not a prison ship; the cabin had originally been designed as cheap transport, not a secured cell. Empty storage cupboards beneath the two bunk-stacks were too large and obvious. A floor panel lifted for access to between-decks control, coolant and power lines, and the grav grid—long, narrow, flat. . . . Rough voices in the corridor propelled Miles's decision. He squeezed himself into the slice of space, face up, arms tight to his sides, and exhaled.

"You always were good at hide-and-seek," said Gregor admiringly, and pressed the panel down.

"I was smaller then," Miles mumbled through squashed cheeks. Pipes and circuit boxes sank into his back and buttocks. Gregor refastened the catches, and all was dark and silent for a few minutes. Like a coffin. Like a pressed flower. Some kind of biological specimen, anyway. Canned ensign.

The door hissed open; footsteps passed over Miles's body, compressing him still further. Would they notice the muffled echo from this strip of floor?

"On your feet, Techie." A guard's voice, directed to Gregor. Thumpings and hangings, as the mattresses were flipped and the cupboard doors flung open. Yes, he'd figured the cupboards for useless.

"Where is he, Techie?" From the directions of the shufflings, Miles placed Gregor as now near the wall, probably with an arm twisted up behind his back.

"Where is who?" said Gregor in a smeary tone. Face against the wall, all right.

"Your little mutant buddy."

"The weird little guy who followed me in? He's no buddy of mine. He left."

More shuffling—"Ow!" The Emperor's arm had just been lifted another five centimeters, Miles gauged.

"Where'd he go?"

"I don't know! He didn't look so good. Somebody'd worked him over with a shock-stick. Recently. I wasn't about to get involved. He took off again a few minutes before we undocked."

Good Gregor; depressed maybe, stupid no. Miles's lips drew back. His head was turned, with one cheek against the floor above and the other pressing against something that resembled a cheese grater.

More thumps. "All right! He left! Don't hit me!"

Unintelligible guard growls, the crackle of a shock-stick, a sharp intake of breath, a thump as of a body curling up on a lower bunk.

A second guard's voice, edged with uncertainty, "He must have doubled back onto the Consortium before we cast off."

"Their problem, good. But we'd better search the whole ship to be sure. Detention sounded ready to chew ass on this one."

"Chew or be chewed?"

"Hah. *I'm* taking no bets."

The booted feet—four of them, Miles estimated—stalked toward the cabin door. The door hissed closed. Silence.

He was going to have a truly remarkable collection of bruises on his backside, Miles decided, by the time Gregor got around to popping the lid. He could get about half a breath with each pulse of his lungs. He needed to pee. Come on, Gregor. . . .

He must certainly free Gregor from his slave labor contract as soon as possible after their arrival at Aslund Station. Contract laborers of this order were bound to be stuck with the dirtiest and most dangerous jobs, the most exposure to radiation, to dubious life-support systems, to long, exhausting, accident-prone hours. Though—true—it was also an incognito no enemy would quickly penetrate. Once free to move they must find Ungari, the man with the credit cards and the contacts; after that—well, after that Gregor would be Ungari's problem, eh? Yes, all simple, right and tight. No need to panic at all.

Had they taken Gregor away? Dare he release himself, and risk—

Shuffling footsteps; a widening line of light, as his lid was raised. "They're gone," Gregor whispered. Miles unmolded himself, centimeter by painful centimeter, and climbed onto the floor, a suitable staging area. He would attempt to stand up very soon now.

Gregor had one hand pressed to a red mark on his cheek. Selfconsciously, he lowered his hand to his side. "They tapped me with a shock-stick. It . . . wasn't as bad as I'd imagined." If anything, he looked faintly proud of himself.

"They were using low power," Miles growled up at him. Gregor's face grew more masked. He offered Miles a hand up. Miles took it and grunted to his feet, and sat heavily on a bunk. He told Gregor about his plans for finding Ungari.

Gregor shrugged, dully acquiescent. "Very well. It will be quicker than my plan."

"Your plan?"

"I was going to contact the Barrayaran Consul on Aslund."

"Oh. Good." Miles subsided. "Guess you . . . didn't really need my rescue, at that."

"I could have made it on my own. I got this far. But . . . then there was my other plan."

"Oh?"

"*Not* to contact the Barrayaran Consul . . . Maybe it's just as well you came along when you did." Gregor lay back on his bunk, staring blindly upward. "One thing is certain, an opportunity like this will never come again."

"To escape? And just how many would die, back home, to buy your freedom?"

Gregor pursed his lips, "Taking Vordarian's Pretendership as a benchmark for palace coups—say, seven or eight thousand."

"You're not counting in Komarr."

"Ah. Yes. Adding in Komarr would inflate the figure," Gregor conceded. His mouth twitched in an irony altogether devoid of humor. "Don't worry, I'm not serious. I just . . . wanted to know. I could have made it on my own, don't you think?"

"Of course! That's not the question."

"It was for me."

"Gregor." Miles's fingers tapped in frustration, against his knee. "You're doing this to yourself. You *have* real power. Dad fought through the whole Regency to preserve it. Just be more assertive!"

"And, Ensign, if I, your supreme commander, ordered you to leave this ship at Aslund Station and forget you ever saw me, would you?"

Miles swallowed. "Major Cecil said I had a problem with subordination."

Gregor almost grinned. "Good old Cecil. I remember him." His grin faded to nothing. He rolled up onto one elbow. "But if I can't even control one rather short ensign, how much less an army or a government? Power isn't the question. I've had all your dad's lectures on power, its illusions and uses. It will come to me in time, whether I want it or not. But do I have the strength to handle it? Think about the bad showing I made during Vordrozda and Hessman's plot, four years ago."

"Will you make that mistake again? Trust a flatterer?"

"Not that one, no."

"Well, then."

"But I must do better, or I might be as bad for Barrayar as no Emperor at all."

Just how unintentional had that topple off the balcony been? Miles gritted his teeth. "I didn't answer your question—about orders—as an ensign. I answered it as Lord Vorkosigan. And as a friend."

"Ah."

"Look, you don't need my rescue. Such as it is. Illyan's maybe, not mine. But it makes *me* feel better."

"It's always nice to feel useful," Gregor agreed. They mirrored edged smiles. Gregor's smile lost its bitter bite. "And . . . it's nice to have company."

Miles nodded. "That, truly."

Miles spent quite a lot of time over the next two days squashed under the deck or crouched in the cupboards, but their cabin was searched only once and that very early on. Twice other prisoners wandered in to chat with Gregor, and once, on Miles's suggestion, Gregor returned the visit. Gregor really was doing quite well, Miles thought. Gregor divided his rations with Miles automatically, without complaint or even comment, and would not accept a larger portion although Miles urged it on him.

Gregor was herded out with the rest of the labor crew soon after the ship docked at Aslund Station. Miles waited nervously, trying to give as long as possible for the ship to quiet down, for the crew to go off-guard, yet not so long as to risk the ship undocking and thrusting off with him still aboard.

The corridor, when Miles cautiously poked his head out, was dark and deserted. The docking hatch was unguarded, on this side. Miles still wore the blue smock and pants over his other clothes, on the calculated risk the work gangs were treated as trustees, with the run of the station, and he would at least blend in at a distance.

He stepped out firmly, and nearly panicked when he found a man in the gold and black House livery idling around the hatch's exit. His stunner was holstered; his hands cradled a steaming plastic cup. His squinting red eyes regarded Miles incuriously. Miles favored him with a brief smile, not breaking stride. The guard returned a sour grimace. Evidently his charge was to prevent strange people from entering, not leaving, the ship.

The station-side loading bay beyond the hatch proved to contain half a dozen coveralled maintenance personnel, working quietly down on one end. Miles took a deep breath, and walked casually across the bay without looking around, as if he knew just where he was going. Just an errand boy. No one hailed him.

Reassured, Miles marched off purposefully at random. A wide ramp led to a great chamber, raucous with new construction and busy work crews in all sorts of dress—a fighter-shuttle refueling and repairs bay, judging by the half-assembled equipment. Just the sort of thing to interest Ungari. Miles didn't suppose he'd be so lucky as to . . . no. No sign of Ungari camouflaged among these crews. There were a number of men and women in dark blue Aslunder military uniforms, but they appeared to be overworked and absorbed engineer-types, not suspicious guards. Miles kept walking briskly nonetheless, out another corridor.

He found a portal, its transparent plexi bellied out to offer passersby a wide-angle view. He put one foot on the lower edge and leaned out—casually—and bit back a few choice swear words. Glittering a few kilometers off was the commercial transfer station. A tiny glint of a ship was docking even now. The military station was apparently being designed as a separate facility, or at least not connected yet. No wonder blue-smocks could wander at will. Miles stared across the gap in mild frustration. Well, he'd search this place first for Ungari, the other later. Somehow. He turned and started—

"Hey, you! Little techie!"

Miles froze, controlling a reflexive urge to sprint—that tactic hadn't worked last time—and turned, trying for an expression of polite inquiry. The man who'd hailed him was big but unarmed, wearing tan supervisor's coveralls. He looked harried. "Yes, sir?" said Miles.

"You're just what I need." The man's hand fell heavily on Miles's shoulder. "Come with me."

Miles perforce followed, trying to stay calm, maybe project a little bored annoyance.

"What's your specialization?" the man asked.

"Drains," Miles intoned.

"Perfect!"

Dismayed, Miles followed the man to where two half-finished corridors intersected. An archway gaped raw and uncapped by molding, though the molding lay ready to install.

The super pointed to a narrow space between walls. "See this pipe?"

Sewage, by the grey color-coding, air and grav pumped. It disappeared in darkness. "Yeah?"

"There's a leak somewhere behind this corridor wall. Crawl in and find it, so's we don't have to tear out all the damn paneling we just put up."

"Got a light?"

The man fished in his pocketed coverall and produced a hand light.

"Right," sighed Miles. "Is it hooked up yet?"

"About to be. Damn thing failed the final pressure test."

Only air would be spewing out. Miles brightened slightly. Maybe his luck was changing.

He slid in and inched along the smooth round surface, listening and feeling. About seven meters in he found it, a rush of cool air from a crack under his hands, quite marked. He shook his head, attempted to turn in the constricted space, and put his foot through the paneling.

He stuck his head out the hole in astonishment, and glanced up and down the corridor. He wriggled a chunk of paneling from the edge and stared at it, turning it in his hands.

Two men putting up light fixtures, their tools sparking, turned to stare. "What the hell are you doing?" said the one in tan coveralls, sounding outraged.

"Quality control inspection," said Miles glibly, "and boy, do you have a problem."

Miles considered kicking the hole wider and just walking back to his starting point, but turned and inched instead. He emerged by the anxiously waiting super.

"Your leak's in section six," Miles reported. He handed the man his panel chunk. "If those corridor panels are supposed to be made of flammable fiberboard instead of spun silica on a military installation planned to withstand enemy fire, somebody's hired a real poor designer. If they're not—I suggest you take a couple of those big goons with the shock-sticks and go pay a visit to your supplier."

The super swore. Lips compressed, he grasped the nearest panel edge fronting the wall and twisted hard. A fist-sized segment cracked and tore off. "Bitchen. How much of this stuff's been installed already?"

"Lots," Miles suggested cheerfully. He turned to escape before the super, worrying off fragments and muttering under his breath, thought of another chore. Flushed and sweating, Miles skittered off and didn't relax till he'd rounded the second corner.

He passed a pair of armed men in grey-and-white uniforms. One turned to stare. Miles kept walking, teeth clenching his lower lip, and did not look back.

Dendarii! or, Oserans! Here, aboard this station—how many, where? Those two were the first he'd seen. Shouldn't they be out on patrol somewhere? He wished he were back in the walls, like a rat in the wainscotting.

But if most of the mercenaries here were a danger to him, there was one—Dendarii truly, not Oseran—who might be a help. If he could make contact. If he dared make contact. Elena . . . he could seek out Elena. . . . His imagination outraced him.

Miles had left Elena four years ago as Baz Jesek's wife, as Tung's military apprentice, as much protection as he could get her at the time. But he hadn't had any messages from Baz since Oser's command coup—could Oser be intercepting them? Now Baz was demoted, Tung apparently disgraced—what position in the mercenary fleet did Elena hold now?

What position in his heart? He paused in grave doubt. He'd loved her passionately, once. Once, she'd known him better than any other human being. Yet her daily hold on his mind had passed, like his grief for her dead father Sergeant Bothari, fading in the rush of his new life. But for an occasional twinge, like an old bonebreak. He wanted/did not want to see her again. To talk to her again. To touch her again . . .

But more to the practical point, she would recognize Gregor; they'd all been playmates in their youth. A second line of defense for the Emperor? Reopening contact with Elena might be emotionally awkward—all right, emotionally searing. But it was better than this ineffectual and dangerous wandering around. Now that he'd scouted the layout, he must somehow get into position to bring his resources to bear. How much human credit did Admiral Naismith still have? Interesting question.

He needed to find a place to watch without being seen. There were all sorts of ways to be invisible while in plain sight, as his blue smock was presently demonstrating. But his unusual height—well, shortness—made him reluctant to rely on clothes alone. He needed—ha!—tools, such as the case a tan-coveralled man had just set down in the corridor while he ducked into a lavatory. Miles had the case in hand and was around the corner in a blink.

A couple of levels away he found a corridor leading to a cafeteria. Hm. Everyone must eat; therefore, everyone must pass this way in time. The food smells excited his stomach, which protested half-rations or less for the past three days by gurgling. He ignored it. He pulled a panel off the wall, donned a pair of protective goggles from the tool case by way of a modest facial disguise, climbed into the wall to half-conceal his height, and began pretending to work on a control box and some pipes, diagnostic scanners placed decoratively to hand. His view up the corridor was excellent.

From the wafting odors, he judged they were serving an unusually good grade of vat-grown beef in there, though they were also doing something nasty to vegetables. He tried not to salivate into the beam of the tiny laser-solderer he manipulated while he studied passers-by. Very few were civilian-clothed, Rotha's wear would clearly have been more conspicuous than the blue smock. Lots of color-coded coveralls, blue smocks, some similar green smocks; not a few Aslunder military blues, mostly lower ranks. Did the Dendarii—Oserans—mercenaries—aboard eat elsewhere? He was considering abandoning his outpost—he'd about repaired the control boxes to death by now—when a duo of grey-and-whites passed. Not faces he knew, he let them go by unhailed.

He contemplated the odds reluctantly. Of all the couple thousand mercenaries now present around the Aslunders' wormhole jump, he might know a few hundred by sight, fewer by name. Only some of the mercenary fleet's ships were now docked at this half-built military station. And of the portion of a portion, how many people could he trust absolutely? Five? He let another quartet of grey-and-whites pass, though he was certain that older blond woman was an engineering tech from the *Triumph,* once loyal to Tung. Once. He was getting ravenous.

But the leather-colored face topping the next set of grey-and-whites to pass down the corridor made Miles forget his stomach. It was Sergeant Chodak. His luck had turned—maybe. For himself, he'd take the chance, but to risk Gregor . . . ? Too late to waffle now, Chodak had spotted Miles in turn. The sergeant's eyes widened in astonishment before his face grew swiftly blank.

"Oh, Sergeant," Miles caroled, tapping a control box, "would you take a look at this, please?"

"I'll be along in a minute." Chodak waved on his companion, a man in the uniform of an Aslunder ranker.

When their heads were together and their backs to the corridor, Chodak hissed, "Are you insane? What are you *doing* here?" It was a mark of his agitation that he omitted his habitual "sir."

"It's a long story. For now, I need your help."

"But how did you get in here? Admiral Oser has guards all over the transfer station, on the lookout for you. You couldn't smuggle in a sand flea."

Miles smirked convincingly. "I have my methods." And his next plan had been to scheme his way across to that very transfer station . . . Truly, God protected fools and madmen. "For now, I need to make contact with Commander Elena Bothari-Jesek. Urgently. Or, failing her, Engineering Commodore Jesek. Is she here?"

"She should be. The *Triumph's* in dock. Commodore Jesek is out with the repairs tender, I know."

"Well, if not Elena, Tung. Or Arde Mayhew. Or Lieutenant Elli Quinn. But I prefer Elena. Tell her—but no one else—that I have our old friend Greg with me. Tell her to meet me in an hour in the contract-laborers quarters, Greg Bleakman's cubicle. Can do?"

"Can do, sir." Chodak hurried off, looking worried. Miles patched up his poor battered wall, replaced the panel, picked up his tool box, and marched casually away, trying not to feel as if he had a flashing red light atop his head. He kept his goggles on and his face down, and chose the least populated corridors he could find. His stomach growled. *Elena will feed you,* he told it firmly. *Later.* A rising population of blue and green smocks told Miles he was nearing the contract laborer's quarters.

There was a directory. He hesitated, then punched up "Bleakman, G." Module B, Cubicle 8. He found the module, checked his chrono—Gregor should be off-shift by now—and knocked. The door sighed open and Miles slipped within. Gregor was there, sitting up sleepily on his bunk. It was a one-man cubicle, offering privacy, though barely room to turn around. Privacy was a greater psychological luxury than space. Even slave-techs must be kept minimally happy, they had too much power for potential sabotage to risk driving them over the edge.

"We're saved," Miles announced. "I've just made contact with Elena." He sat down heavily on the end of the bunk, weak with the sudden release of tension in this safe pocket.

"Elena's here?" Gregor scrubbed a hand through his hair. "I thought you wanted your Captain Ungari."

"Elena's the first step to Ungari. Or, failing Ungari, to smuggling us out of here. If Ungari hadn't been so damn insistent on the left hand not knowing what the right was doing, it would be a lot easier. But this will do." He studied Gregor in worry. "Have you been all right?"

"A few hours putting up light fixtures isn't going to break my health, I assure you," said Gregor dryly.

"Is that what they had you doing? Not what I'd pictured, somehow . . ."

Gregor seemed all right, anyway. Indeed, the Emperor was acting almost cheerful about his stint as a slave laborer, as Gregor's morose standards of cheer went. *Maybe we ought to send him to the salt mines for two weeks every year, to keep him happy and content with his regular job.* Miles relaxed a little.

"It's hard to imagine Elena Bothari as a mercenary," Gregor added reflectively.

"Don't underestimate her." Miles concealed a moment of raw doubt. Almost four years. He knew how much he had changed in four years. What of Elena? Her years could have been hardly less hectic. *Times change. People change with them. . . .* No. As well doubt himself as Elena.

The half-hour wait for his chrono to creep to the appointed moment was a bad interval, enough to loosen Miles's driving tension and wash him in weariness but not enough to rest or refresh him. He was miserably conscious of losing his edge, of a crying need for alertness when alertness and straight-thinking escaped like sand between his fingers. He rechecked his chrono. *An hour* had been too vague. He should have named the minute. But who knew what difficulties or delays Elena must overcome from her end?

Miles blinked hard, realizing from his wavering and disconnected thoughts that he was falling asleep sitting up. The door hissed open without Gregor's having released the lock.

"Here he is, men!"

A half-squad of grey-and-white-clad mercenaries filled the aperture and the corridor beyond. It hardly needed the stunners and shock-sticks in their hands, the purposive descent on his person, to tell Miles this hairy crew was not Elena's. The surge of adrenaline scarcely cleared the fatigue-fog from his head. *And what do I pretend to be now? A moving target?* He sagged against the wall, not even bothering, though Gregor lurched to his feet and made a valiant try in the constricted space, an accurate karate-kick sending a stunner flying from the hand of a closing mercenary. Two men smashed Gregor against the wall for his effort. Miles winced.

Then Miles himself was jerked from the bunk to be coiled, triple-coiled, in a tangle-net. The field burned against him. They were using enough power to immobilize a plunging horse. *What do you think I am, boys?*

The excited squad leader cried into his wrist comm, "I got him, sir!"

Miles raised an ironic brow. The squad leader flushed and straightened, his hand twitching in the effort not to salute. Miles smiled slightly. The squad leader's lips tightened. *Ha. Almost got you going, didn't I?*

"Take them away," ordered the squad leader.

Miles was carried out the door between two men, his bound feet dangling ridiculous inches from the floor. A groaning Gregor was dragged in his wake. As they passed a cross-corridor, Miles saw Chodak's strained face from the corner of his eye, floating in the shadows.

He damned his own judgment then. *You thought you could read people. Your one demonstrable talent. Right, Sure. Should have, should have, should have,* mocked his mind, like the caw of some vile scavenging bird surprised at a carcass.

When they were dragged across a large docking bay and through a small personnel hatch, Miles knew at once where he was. The *Triumph*, the pocket dreadnought that had occasionally served as the fleet's flagship, was doing that duty again now. Tung of the dubious current status had been captain-owner of the

Triumph, once, before Tau Verde. Oser had used to favor his own *Peregrine* as flag—was this some deliberate political statement? The corridors of the ship had a strange, painful, powerful familiarity. The odors of men, metal, and machinery. That crooked archway, legacy of the lunatic ramming that had captured her on Miles's first encounter, still not properly straightened out . . . *I thought I had forgotten more.*

They were hustled along swiftly and secretly, a pair of squadmen going ahead to clear the corridor of witnesses before them. This was going to be a very private chat, then. Fine, that suited Miles. He would have preferred to avoid Oser altogether, but if they must meet again, he would simply have to find some way of turning it to use. He ordered his persona as if adjusting his cuffs—Miles Naismith, space mercenary and mystery entrepreneur, come to the Hegen Hub for . . . what? And his glum if faithful sidekick Greg, of course—he would have to think of some particularly benign explanation for Gregor.

They clattered down the corridor past the tactics room, the *Triumph's* combat nerve center, and fetched up at the smaller of the two briefing rooms across from it. The holovid plate in the center of the gleaming conference table was dark and silent. Admiral Oser sat equally dark and silent at the table's head, flanked by a pale blond man Miles presumed to be a loyal lieutenant; not anyone Miles knew from before. Miles and Gregor were forcibly seated in two chairs pulled back and distanced from the table, that their hands and feet might be unconcealed. Oser dismissed all but one guard to the corridor outside.

Oser's appearance hadn't changed much in four years, Miles decided. Still lean and hawk-faced, dark hair maybe a little greyer at the temples. Miles had remembered him as taller, but he was actually shorter than Metzov. Oser reminded Miles somehow of the general. Was it the age, the build? The hostile glower, the murderous pinpricks of red light in the eye?

"Miles," Gregor muttered out of the corner of his mouth, "what did you do to piss this guy off?"

"Nothing!" Miles protested back, sotto voce. "Nothing on purpose, anyway."

Gregor looked less than reassured.

Oser placed his palms flat on the table before him and leaned forward, staring at Miles with predatory intensity. If Oser'd had a tail, Miles fancied, its end would be flicking back and forth. "What are you doing here?" Oser opened bluntly, without preamble.

You brought me, don't you know? Not the time to get cute, no. Miles was highly conscious of the fact that he did not precisely look his best. But Admiral Naismith wouldn't care, he was too goal-directed; Naismith would carry on painted blue, if he had to. He answered equally bluntly. "I was hired to do a military evaluation of the Hegen Hub for an interested noncombatant who ships through here." There, the truth up front, where it was sure to be disbelieved. "Since they don't care for mounting rescue expeditions, they wanted enough warning to clear the Hub of their citizens before hostilities break out. I'm doing a little arms dealing on the side. A cover that pays for itself."

Oser's eyes narrowed. "Not Barrayar . . ."

"Barrayar has its own operatives."

"So does Cetaganda . . . Aslund fears Cetagandan ambitions."

"As well they should."

"Barrayar is equidistant."

"In my professional opinion," fighting the tangle-field, Miles favored Oser with a small bow, sitting down—Oser almost nodded back, but caught himself—

"Barrayar is no threat to Aslund in this generation. To control the Hegen Hub, Barrayar must control Pol. With the terraforming of their own second continent plus the opening of the planet Sergyar, Barrayar is rather oversupplied with frontiers at present. And then there is the problem of holding restive Komarr. A military adventure toward Pol would be a serious overextension of Barrayar's human resources just now. Cheaper to be friends, or at least neutral."

"Aslund also fears Pol."

"They are unlikely to fight unless attacked first. Keeping peace with Pol is cheap and easy. Just do nothing."

"And Vervain?"

"I haven't evaluated Vervain yet. It's next on my list."

"Is it?" Oser leaned back in his chair, crossing his arms. It was not a relaxed gesture. "As a spy, I could have you executed."

"But I'm not an *enemy* spy," Miles answered, simulating easiness. "A friendly neutral or—who knows?—potential ally."

"And what is your interest in my fleet?"

"My interest in the Denda—in the mercenaries is purely academic, I assure you. You are simply part of the picture. Tell me, what's your contract with Aslund like?" Miles cocked his head, talking shop.

Oser almost answered, then his lips thinned in annoyance. If Miles had been a ticking bomb he could not have more thoroughly commanded the mercenary's attention.

"Oh, come on," Miles scoffed in the lengthening silence. "What could I do, by myself with one man?"

"I remember the last time. You entered Tau Verde local space with a staff of four. Four months later you were dictating terms. So what are you planning now?"

"You overestimate my impact. I merely helped

people along in the direction they wished to go. An expediter, so to speak."

"Not for me. I spent three years recovering the ground I lost. In my own fleet!"

"It's hard to please everyone." Miles intercepted Gregor's look of mute horror, and toned himself down. Come to think, Gregor had never met Admiral Naismith, had he? "Even you were not seriously damaged."

Oser's jaw compressed further. "And who's he?" He jerked a thumb at Gregor.

"Greg? He's just my batman," Miles cut across Gregor's opening mouth.

"He doesn't look like a batman. He looks like an officer."

Gregor looked insensibly cheered at this unbiased encomium.

"You can't go by looks. Commodore Tung looks like a wrestler."

Oser's eyes were suddenly freezing. "Indeed. And how long have you been in correspondence with *Captain* Tung?"

By the sick lurch in his belly, Miles realized mentioning Tung had been a major mistake. He tried to keep his features coolly ironic, not reflecting his unease. "If I'd been in correspondence with Tung, I should not have been troubled with making this personal evaluation of Aslund Station."

Oser, elbows on table, hands clasped, studied Miles in silence for a full minute. At last one hand fell open, to point at the guard, who straightened attentively. "Space them," Oser ordered.

"What?!" yelped Miles.

"You," the pointing finger collected Oser's silent lieutenant, "go with them. See that it's done. Use the portside access lock, it's closest. If *he,*" pointing to

Miles, "starts to talk, stop his tongue. It's his most dangerous organ."

The guard released the tangle-field from Miles's legs and pulled him to his feet.

"Aren't you even going to have me chemically interrogated?" asked Miles, dizzied by this sudden downturn.

"And contaminate my interrogators? The last thing I want is to give you rein to talk, to anyone. I can think of nothing more fatal than for the rot of disloyalty to start in my own Intelligence section. Whatever your planned speech, removing your air will neutralize it. You nearly convince *me.*" Oser almost shuddered.

We were getting on so well, yes. . . . "But I—" They were hoisting Gregor to his feet too. "But you don't need to—"

Two waiting members of the half-squad fell in as they were bundled out the door, frog-marching Miles and Gregor rapidly down the corridor. "But—!" The conference room door hissed closed.

"This is not going well, Miles," Gregor observed, his pale face a weird compound of detachment, exasperation, and dismay. "Any more bright ideas?"

"You're the man who was experimenting with wingless flight. Is this any worse than, say, plummeting?"

"At my own hand," Gregor began to drag his feet, to struggle, as the air lock chamber heaved into view, "not at the whim of a bunch of . . ." it took three guards to wrestle him now, "bloody *peasants!*"

Miles was getting seriously frantic. Screw the damn cover. "You know," he called out loudly, "you fellows are about to throw a fortune in ransom out the air lock!"

Two guards kept wrestling with Gregor, but the third paused. "How big a fortune?"

"Huge," Miles promised. "Buy your own fleet."

The lieutenant abandoned Gregor and closed on Miles, drawing a vibra-knife. The lieutenant was interpreting his orders with horrific literality, Miles realized when the man went for a grip on his tongue. He almost got it—the evil insect whine of the knife dopplered centimeters from Miles's nose—Miles bit the thick thrusting fingers, and twisted against the grip of the guard holding him. The tangle-field binding Miles's arms to his torso whined and crackled, unbreakable. Miles jammed backward against the crotch of the man behind, who yipped at the field's bite. His grip slipped and Miles dropped, rolling and banging into the lieutenant's knees. It wasn't exactly a judo throw; the lieutenant more or less tripped over him.

Gregor's two opponents were distracted, as much by the bloody barbaric promise of the vibra-knife show as by Miles's ultimately futile struggles. They did not see the leather-faced man step out from a cross-corridor, aim his stunner, and spray. They arched convulsively as the buzzing charges struck their backs, and dropped heap-fashion to the deck. The man who'd been holding Miles, and was now trying to grab him again as he flopped around evasively as a fish, whirled just in time to intersect a beam square in the face.

Miles flung himself across the blond lieutenant's head, pinning him—only momentarily, alas—to the deck. Miles wriggled, to press the tangle-field into the man's face, then was heaved off with a curse. The lieutenant had one knee under himself, preparing to launch an attack and wobbling around in search of his target, when Gregor hopped over and kicked him in the jaw. A stunner charge hit the lieutenant in the back of the head and he went down.

"Damn fine soldiering," Miles panted to Sergeant Chodak in the sudden silence. "I don't think they even saw what hit them." So, *I called him straight the first time. Haven't lost my touch after all. Bless you, Sergeant.*

"You two aren't so bad yourselves, for men with both hands tied behind their backs." Chodak shook his head in harried amusement, and trod forward to release the tangle-fields.

"What a team," said Miles.

CHAPTER ELEVEN

A quick ring of boots from further up the corridor drew Miles's eye. He exhaled, a long-held breath, and stood. *Elena.*

She wore a mercenary officer's undress uniform, grey-and-white pocketed jacket, trousers, ankle-topping boots gleaming on her long, long legs. Still tall, still slim, still with pale pure skin, ember-brown eyes, arched aristocratic nose and long sculptured jaw. *She's cut her hair,* Miles thought, stupid-stunned. Gone was the straight-shining black cascade to her waist. Now it was clipped out over her ears, only little dark points grace-noting her high cheekbones and forehead, a similar point echoed at the nape of her neck; severe, practical, very smart. Soldierly.

She strode up, eyes taking in Miles, Gregor, the four Oserans. "Good work, Chodak." She dropped to one knee beside the nearest body and probed its neck for a pulse. "Are they dead?"

"No, just stunned," Miles explained.

She regarded the open inner air lock door with some regret. "I don't suppose we can space them."

"They were going to space us, but no. But we probably ought to get them out of sight while we run," said Miles.

"Right." She rose and nodded to Chodak, who began helping Gregor drag the stunned bodies into the air lock. She frowned at the blond lieutenant, going past feet-first. "Not that spacing wouldn't *improve* some personalities."

"Can you give us a bolt-hole?"

"That's what we came for." She turned to the three soldiers who had followed her cautiously into view. A fourth stood guard at the nearest cross-corridor. "It seems we just got lucky," she told them. "Scout ahead and clear the aisles on our escape route—subtly. Then disappear. You weren't here and didn't see this."

They nodded and withdrew. Miles heard a retreating mutter, "Was that *him?*" "Yeah . . ."

Miles, Gregor, and Elena, with the bodies, piled cozily into the lock and closed the inner door temporarily. Chodak stood guard outside. Elena helped Gregor pull the boots from the Oseran nearest his size while Miles stripped off his blue prisoner's outfit and stood, revealing Victor Rotha's wrinkled clothing, much the worse for four days' wear, sleep, and sweat. Miles wished for boots to replace the vulnerable sandals, but none here came close to his size.

Gregor and Elena exchanged looks, each warily amazed at the other, as Gregor yanked on grey-and-whites and plunged his feet into the boots.

"It's really you." Elena shook her head in dismay. "What are you doing here?"

"It was by mistake," said Gregor.

"No lie. Whose?"

"Mine, I'm afraid," said Miles. Somewhat to his annoyance, Gregor did not gainsay this.

A peculiar smile, her first, quirked Elena's lips. Miles decided not to ask her to explain it. This hurried practical exchange did not in the least resemble any of the dozens of conversations he had rehearsed in his head for this first, poignant meeting with her.

"The search will be up in minutes, when these guys don't report back," Miles jittered. He collected two stunners, the tangle-field, and the vibra-knife, and stuck them in his waistband. On second thought, he swiftly relieved the four Oserans of credit cards, pass chits, IDs, and odd cash, stuffing his pockets and Gregor's, and made sure Gregor ditched his prisoner's traceable ID. To his secret delight, he also found a half-eaten ration bar, and bit into it there and then. He chewed as Elena led the way back out the lock. He conscientiously offered a bite to Gregor, who shook his head. Gregor'd probably had dinner in that cafeteria.

Chodak hastily straightened Gregor's uniform, and they all marched off, Miles to the center, half-concealed, half-guarded. Before he could go half-paranoid at his conspicuousness they took to a drop-tube, emerged several decks down, and found themselves at a large cargo-lock, engaged to a shuttle. One of Elena's scout squad, leaning as if idle against the wall, nodded. With a half-salute to Elena, Chodak split off and they hurried away. Miles and Gregor followed Elena across the flex-seal of the shuttle hatch and into the empty cargo hold of one of the *Triumph's* shuttles, stepping from the artificial gravity field of the mother ship abruptly into the vertigo of free fall. They floated forward to the pilot's compartment. Elena sealed the compartment hatch behind them, and anxiously gestured Gregor to the vacant seat at the engineering/ comm station.

The pilot's and co-pilot's seats were filled. Arde Mayhew grinned cheerfully over his shoulder at Miles, and waved/saluted hello. Miles recognized the shaved bullet-head of the second man even before he turned.

"Hello, son." Ky Tung's smile was far more ironic than cheerful. "Welcome back. You took your sweet time." Tung, arms folded, did not salute.

"Hello, Ky." Miles nodded to the Eurasian. Tung had not changed, anyway. Still looked any age between forty and sixty. Still built like an ancient tank. Still seemed to see more than he spoke, most uncomfortable for the guilty of conscience.

Mayhew the pilot spoke into his comm. "Traffic control, I've traced that red light on my panel now. Defective pressure reading. All fixed. We're ready to break away."

"About time, C-2," a disembodied voice returned. "You're clear."

The pilot's swift hands activated hatch seal controls, aimed attitude jets. Some hissing and clanks, and the shuttle popped away from its mothership and started on its trajectory. Mayhew killed the comm and breathed a long sigh of relief. "Safe. For now."

Elena wedged herself across the aisle behind Miles, long legs locking. Miles hooked an arm around a handhold to anchor against Mayhew's current mild accelerations. "I hope you're right," said Miles, "but what makes you think so?"

"He means, safe to talk," said Elena. "Not safe in any cosmic sense. This is a routine scheduled run, except for us unlisted passengers. We know you haven't been missed yet, or traffic control would have stopped us. Oser will search the *Triumph* and the military station for you first. We may even be able to slip you back aboard the *Triumph* after the search has passed to wider areas."

"This is Plan B," Tung explained, swivelling around to half-face Miles. "Or maybe Plan C. Plan A, on the assumption that your rescue was going to be a lot noisier, was to flee at once to the *Ariel,* now on picket-station, and declare the revolution. I'm grateful for the chance to bring things off a little, er, less spontaneously."

Miles choked. "God! That would have been worse than the first time." Pitched into an interlocking chain of events he did not control, drafted gonfalonier to some mercenary military mutiny, thrust to the lead of its parade with all the free will of a head on a pike . . . "No. No spontaneity, thanks. Definitely not."

"So," Tung steepled his thick fingers, "what *is* your plan?"

"My what?"

"Plan," Tung pronounced the word with sardonic care. "In other words, why are you here?"

"Oser asked me that same question," sighed Miles. "Would you believe, I'm here by accident? Oser wouldn't. You wouldn't happen to know *why* he wouldn't, would you?"

Tung pursed his lips. "Accident? Maybe . . . Your 'accidents,' I once noticed, have ways of entangling your enemies that are the green envy of mature and careful strategists. Far too consistent for chance, I concluded it had to be unconscious will. If only you'd stuck with me, son, between us we could've . . . or maybe you are simply a supreme opportunist. In which case I direct your attention to the opportunity now before you to retake the Dendarii Mercenaries."

"You didn't answer my question," Miles noted.

"You didn't answer mine," Tung countered.

"I don't want the Dendarii Mercenaries."

"I do."

"Oh." Miles paused. "Why don't you split off with

the personnel who are loyal to you and start your own, then? It's been done."

"Shall we swim through space?" Tung imitated fish fins with his waving fingers, and puffed his cheeks. "Oser controls the equipment. Including my ship. The *Triumph* is everything I've accumulated in a thirty-year career. Which I lost through your machinations. Somebody owes me another. If not Oser, then . . ." Tung glowered significantly at Miles.

"I tried to give you a fleet in trade," said Miles, harried. "How'd you lose control of it—old strategist?"

Tung tapped a finger to his left breast, to indicate a touché. "Things went well at first, for a year, year and a half after we departed Tau Verde. Got two sweet little contracts in a row out toward the Eastnet—small-scale commando operations, sure things. Well, not too sure—kept us on our toes. But we brought them off."

Miles glanced at Elena. "I'd heard about those, yes."

"On the third, we got into troubles. Baz Jesek had gotten more and more involved with equipment and maintenance—he is a good engineer, I'll give him that—I was tactical commander, and Oser—I thought by default, but now I think design—took up the administrative slack. Could have been good, each doing what he did best, if Oser'd been working with and not against us. In the same situation, I'd have sent assassins. Oser employed guerilla accountants.

"We took a bit of a beating on that third contract. Baz was up to his ears in engineering and repairs, and by the time I got out of sickbay, Oser'd lined up one of his no-combat specials—worm-hole guard duty work. Long-term contract. Seemed like a good idea at the time. But it gave him a wedge. With no actual combat going on, I . . ." Tung cleared his throat, "got bored, didn't pay attention. Oser'd outflanked me before I realized there was a war on. He sprang the financial reorganization on us—"

"I told you not to trust him, six months before that," Elena put in with a frown, "after he tried to seduce me."

Tung shrugged uncomfortably. "It seemed like an understandable temptation."

"To bang his commander's wife?" Elena's eyes sparked. "Anyone's wife? I knew then he wasn't level. If my oaths meant nothing to him, how little did his own?"

"He did take no for an answer, you said," Tung excused himself. "If he'd kept leaning on you, I'd have been willing to step in. I thought you ought to be flattered, ignore it, and go on."

"Overtures of that sort contain a judgment of my character that I find anything but flattering, thank you," Elena snapped.

Miles bit his knuckles, hard and secretly, remembering his own longings. "It might just have been an early move in his power-play," he put in. "Probing for weaknesses in his enemies' defenses. And in this case, not finding them."

"Hm." Elena seemed faintly comforted by this view. "Anyway, Ky was no help, and I got tired of playing Cassandra. Naturally, I couldn't tell Baz. But Oser's double-dealing didn't come as a complete surprise to *all* of us."

Tung frowned, frustrated. "Given the nucleus of his own surviving ships, all he had to do was swing the votes of half the other captain-owners. Auson voted with him. I could have strangled the bastard."

"You lost Auson yourself, with your moaning about the *Triumph*," Elena put in, still acerb. "He thought you threatened his captaincy of it."

Tung shrugged. "As long as I was Chief-of-Staff/Tactical, in charge during actual combat, I didn't think he could really hurt my ship. I was content to let the *Triumph* ride along as if owned by the fleet corporation. I could wait—till *you* got back," his dark eyes glinted at Miles, "and we found out what was going on. And then you never came back."

"The king will return, eh?" murmured Gregor, who had been listening with fascination. He raised an eyebrow at Miles.

"Let it be a lesson to you," Miles murmured back through set teeth. Gregor subsided, less humorous.

Miles turned to Tung. "Surely Elena disabused you of any such immediate expectation."

"I tried," muttered Elena. "Although . . . I suppose, I couldn't help hoping a bit myself. Maybe you'd . . . quit your other project, come back to us."

If I flunked out of the Academy, eh? "It wasn't a project I could quit, short of death."

"I know that now."

"In five minutes, max," put in Arde Mayhew, "I've either got to lock into the transfer station traffic control for docking, or else cut for the *Ariel.* Which is it going to be, folks?"

"I can put over a hundred loyal officers and noncoms at your back at a word," said Tung to Miles. "Four ships."

"Why not at your own back?"

"If I could, I would have already. But I'm not going to tear the fleet apart unless I can be certain of putting it back together again. All of it. But with you as leader, with your reputation—which has grown in the retelling—"

"Leader? Or figurehead?" The image of that pike bobbed in Miles's mind's eye again.

Tung's hands opened noncommittally. "As you wish.

The bulk of the officer cadre will go for the winning side. That means we must appear to be winning quickly, if we move at all. Oser has about another hundred personally loyal to himself, who we're going to have to physically overpower if he insists on holding out—which suggests to my mind that a well-timed assassination could save a lot of lives."

"Jolly. I think you and Oser have been working together too long, Ky. You're starting to think alike. Again. I did not come here to seize command of a mercenary fleet. I have other priorities." He schooled himself not to glance at Gregor.

"What higher priorities?"

"How about, preventing a planetary civil war? Maybe an interstellar one?"

"I have no professional interest in that." It almost succeeded in being a joke.

Indeed, what were Barrayar's agonies to Tung? "You do if you're on the doomed side. You only get paid for winning, and only get to spend your pay if you live, mercenary."

Tung's narrow eyes narrowed further. "What do you know that I don't? *Are* we on the doomed side?"

I am, if I don't get Gregor back. Miles shook his head. "Sorry. I can't talk about that. I've got to get to—" Pol closed to him, the Consortium station blocked, and now Aslund become even more dangerous, "Vervain." He glanced at Elena. "Get us both to Vervain."

"You working for the Vervani?" Tung asked.

"No."

"Who, then?" Tung's hands twitched, so tense with his curiosity they seemed to want to squeeze out information by main force.

Elena noticed the unconscious gesture too. "Ky, back off," she said sharply. "If Miles wants Vervain, Vervain he shall have."

Tung looked at Elena, at Mayhew. "Do you back him, or me?"

Elena's chin lifted. "We're both oath-sworn to Miles. Baz too."

"And you have to ask why I need you?" said Tung in exasperation to Miles, gesturing at the pair. "What is this larger game, that you all seem to know all about, and I, nothing?"

"I don't know anything," chirped Mayhew. "I'm just going by Elena."

"Is this a chain of command, or a chain of credulity?"

"There's a difference?" Miles grinned.

"You've exposed us, by coming here," Tung argued. "Think! We help you, you leave, we're left naked to Oser's wrath. There's too many witnesses already. There might be safety in victory, none in half-measures."

Miles looked with anguish at Elena, picturing her, quite vividly in light of his recent experiences, being shoved out an air lock by evil, witless goons. Tung noted with satisfaction the effect of his plea on Miles and sat smugly back. Elena glared at Tung.

Gregor stirred uneasily. "I think . . . should you become refugees on Our behalf," (Elena, Miles saw, heard that official capital O too, as Tung and Mayhew of course could not) "We can see that you do not suffer. Financially, at least."

Elena nodded understanding and acceptance. Tung leaned toward Elena, jerking his thumb at Gregor. "All right, who is this guy?" Elena shook her head mutely.

Tung vented a small hiss. "You've no means of support visible to me, son. What if we become corpses on your behalf?"

Elena remarked, "We've risked becoming corpses for much less."

"Less than what?" snapped Tung.

Mayhew, his eyes going briefly distant, touched the communications plug in his ear. "Decision time, folks."

"Can this ship go across-system?" asked Miles.

"No. Not fueled up for it." Mayhew shrugged apology.

"Not fast enough or armored for it, either," said Tung.

"You'll have to smuggle us out on commercial transport, past Aslunder security," Miles said unhappily.

Tung stared around at his recalcitrant little committee, and sighed. "Security's tighter for incoming than outgoing. I think it can be done. Take us in, Arde."

After Mayhew had docked the cargo shuttle at its assigned loading niche at the Aslunders' transfer station, Miles, Gregor, and Elena lay low, locked in the pilot's compartment. Tung and Mayhew went off "to see what we can do," as Tung put it, rather airily to Miles's mind. Miles sat and nibbled his knuckles nervously, and tried not to jump with each thump, clink, or hiss of the robotic loaders placing supplies for the mercenaries on the other side of the bulkhead. Elena's steady profile did not twitch at every little noise, Miles noticed enviously. *I loved her once. Who is she now?*

Could one choose *not* to fall in love all over again with this new person? A chance to choose. She seemed tougher, more willing to speak her mind—this was good—yet her thoughts had a bitter tang. Not good. That bitterness made him ache.

"Have you been all right?" he asked her hesitantly. "Apart from this command structure mess, that is. Tung treating you right? He was supposed to be your mentor. On-the-job, for you, the training I was getting in the classroom . . ."

"Oh, he's a good mentor. He stuffs me with military information, tactics, history. . . . I can run every phase of a combat drop patrol now, logistics, mapping, assault, withdrawal, even emergency shuttle take-offs and landings, if you don't mind a few bumps. I'm almost up to really handling my fictional rank, at least on fleet equipment. He likes teaching."

"It seemed to me you were a little . . . tense, with him."

She tossed her head. "Everything is tense, just now. It's not possible to be 'apart from' this command structure mess, thank you. Although . . . I suppose I haven't quite forgiven Tung for not being infallible about it. I thought he was, at first."

"Yeah, well, there's a lot of fallibility going around these days," Miles said uncomfortably. "Uh . . . how's Baz?" *Is your husband treating you right?* he wanted to demand, but didn't.

"He's well," she replied, not looking happy, "but discouraged. This power struggle was alien to him, repugnant, I think. He's a tech at heart, he sees a job that needs doing, he does it . . . Tung hints that if Baz hadn't buried himself in Engineering he might have foreseen—prevented—fought the takeover, but I think it was the other way around. He couldn't lower himself to fight on Oser's back-stabbing level, so he withdrew to where he could keep his own standards of honesty . . . for a little while longer. This schism's affected morale all up and down the line."

"I'm sorry," said Miles.

"You should be." Her voice cracked, steadied, harshened. "Baz felt he'd failed you, but you failed us first, when you never came back. You couldn't expect us to keep up the illusion forever."

"Illusion?" said Miles. "I knew . . . it would be difficult, but I thought you might . . . grow into your roles. Make the mercenaries your own."

"The mercenaries may be enough for Tung. I

thought they might be for me, too, till we came to the killing. . . . I hate Barrayar, but better to serve Barrayar than nothing, or your own ego."

"What does Oser serve?" Gregor asked curiously, brows raised at this mixed declamation about their homeworld.

"Oser serves Oser. 'The fleet,' he says, but the fleet serves Oser, so it's just a short circuit," said Elena. "The fleet is no home-country. No building, no children . . . sterile. I don't mind helping out the Aslunders, though; they need it. A poor planet, and scared."

"You and Baz—and Arde—could have left, gone off on your own," began Miles.

"How?" said Elena. "You gave us the Dendarii in *charge.* Baz was a deserter once. Never again."

All my fault, right, thought Miles. *Great.*

Elena turned to Gregor, who had acquired a strange guarded expression on his face while listening to her charges of abandonment. "You still haven't said what you're doing here in the first place, besides putting your feet in things. Was this supposed to be some sort of secret diplomatic mission?"

"You explain it," said Miles to Gregor, trying not to grit his teeth. *Tell her about the balcony, eh?*

Gregor shrugged, eyes sliding aside from Elena's level look. "Like Baz, I deserted. Like Baz, I found it was not the improvement I'd hoped for."

"You can see why it's urgent to get Gregor back home as quickly as possible," Miles put in. "They think he's missing. Maybe kidnapped." Miles gave Elena a quick edited version of their chance meeting in Consortium Detention.

"God." Elena's lips pursed. "I see why it's urgent to you to get him off your hands, anyway. If anything happened to him in your company, fifteen factions would cry 'Treason plot!'"

"That thought has occurred to me, yes," growled Miles.

"Your father's Centrist coalition government would be the first thing to fall," Elena continued. "The military right would get behind Count Vorinnis, I suppose, and square off with the anti-centralization liberals. The French speakers would want Vorville, the Russian Vortugalov—or has he died yet?"

"The far-right blow-up-the-wormhole isolationist loonie faction would field Count Vortrifrani against the anti-Vor pro-galactic faction who want a written constitution," put in Miles glumly. "And I do mean field."

"Count Vortrifrani scares me," Elena shivered. "I've heard him speak."

"It's the suave way he mops the foam from his lips," said Miles. "The Greek minorists would seize the moment to attempt secession—"

"Stop it!" Gregor, who had propped his forehead on his hands, said from behind the barrier of his arms.

"I thought that was *your* job," said Elena tartly. At his bleak look, raising his head, she softened, her mouth twisting up. "Too bad I can't offer you a job with the fleet. We can always use formally trained officers, to train the rest if nothing else."

"A mercenary?" said Gregor. "There's a thought. . . ."

"Oh, sure. A lot of our people are former regular military folk. Some are even legitimately discharged."

Fantasy lit Gregor's eye with brief amusement. He sighted down his grey-and-white jacket sleeve. "If only you were in charge here, aye, Miles?"

"No!" Miles cried in a suffused voice.

The light died. "It was a joke."

"Not funny." Miles breathed carefully, praying it would not occur to Gregor to make that an *order*. . . . "Anyway, we're now trying to make it to the Barrayaran Consul on Vervain Station. It's still there,

I hope. I haven't heard news for days—what's going on with the Vervani?"

"As far as I know, it's business as usual, except for the heightened paranoia," said Elena. "Vervain's putting its resources into ships, not stations—"

"Makes sense, when you've got more than one wormhole to guard," Miles conceded.

"But it makes Aslund perceive the Vervani as potential aggressors. There's an Aslunder faction that's actually urging a first strike before the new Vervani fleet comes on-line. Fortunately, the defensive strategists have prevailed so far. Oser has set the price for a strike by us prohibitively high. He's not stupid. He knows the Aslunders couldn't back us up. Vervain hired a mercenary fleet as a stopgap too—in fact, that's what gave the Aslunders the idea to hire us. They're called Randall's Rangers, though I understand Randall is no more."

"We shall avoid them," Miles asserted fervently.

"I hear their new second officer is a Barrayaran. You might be able to swing some help, there."

Gregor's brows rose in speculation. "One of Illyan's plants? Sounds like his work."

Was that where Ungari had gone? "Approach with caution, anyway," Miles allowed.

"About time," Gregor commented under his breath.

"The Rangers' commander's name is Cavilo—"

"What?" yelped Miles.

Elena's winged brows rose. "Just Cavilo. Nobody seems to know if it's the given or surname—"

"Cavilo is the person who tried to buy me—or Victor Rotha—at the Consortium Station. For twenty thousand Betan dollars."

Elena's brows stayed up. "Why?"

"I don't know why." Miles rethought their goal. Pol, the Consortium, Aslund . . . no, it still came up Vervain.

"But we definitely avoid the Vervani's mercs. We step off the ship and go straight to the Consul, go to ground, and don't even squeak till Illyan's men arrive to take us home, Momma. Right."

Gregor sighed. "Right."

No more playing secret agent. His best efforts had only served to get Gregor nearly murdered. It was time to try less hard, Miles decided.

"Strange," said Gregor, looking at Elena—at the new Elena, Miles guessed—"to think you've had more combat experience than either of us."

"Than both of you," Elena corrected dryly. "Yes, well . . . actual combat . . . is a lot stupider than I'd imagined. If two groups can cooperate to the incredible extent it takes to meet in battle, why not put in a tenth that effort to talk? That's not true of guerilla wars, though," Elena went on thoughtfully. "A guerilla is an enemy who won't play the game. Makes more sense to me. If you're going to be vile, why not be totally vile? That third contract—if I ever get involved in another guerilla war, I want to be on the side of the guerillas."

"Harder to make peace, between totally vile enemies," Miles reflected. "War is not its own end, except in some catastrophic slide into absolute damnation. It's peace that's wanted. Some better peace than the one you started with."

"Whoever can be the most vile longest, wins?" Gregor posited.

"Not . . . historically true, I don't think. If what you do during the war so degrades you that the next peace is worse . . ." Human noises from the cargo bay froze Miles in midsentence, but it was Tung and Mayhew returning.

"Come on," Tung urged. "If Arde doesn't keep to schedule, he'll draw attention."

They filed into the cargo hold, where Mayhew held the control leash of a float pallet with a couple of plastic packing crates attached. "Your friend can pass as a fleet soldier," Tung told Miles. "For you, I found a box. It would have been classier to roll you up in a carpet, but since the freighter captain is male, I'm afraid the historical reference would be wasted."

Dubiously, Miles regarded the box. It seemed to lack air holes. "Where are you taking me?"

"We have a regular irregular arrangement, for getting fleet intelligence officers in and out quietly. Got this inner-system freighter captain, an independent owner—he's Vervani, but he's been on the payroll three times before. He'll take you across, get you through Vervani customs. After that you're on your own."

"How much danger is this arrangement to you all?" Miles worried.

"Not a lot," said Tung, "all things considered. He'll think he's delivering more mercenary agents, for a price, and naturally keep his mouth shut. It'll be days before he gets back to even be questioned. I arranged it all myself, Elena and Arde didn't appear, so he can't give them away."

"Thank you," Miles said quietly.

Tung nodded, and sighed. "If only you'd stayed on with us. What a soldier I could've made of you, these last three years."

"If you do find yourselves out of a job as a consequence of helping us," Gregor added, "Elena will know how to put you in touch."

Tung grimaced. "In touch with what, eh?"

"Better not to know," said Elena, helping Miles position himself in the packing crate.

"All right," grumbled Tung, "but . . . all right."

Miles found himself face-to-face with Elena, for the last time till—when? She hugged him, but then gave

Gregor an identical, sisterly embrace. "Give my love to your mother," she told Miles. "I often think of her."

"Right. Uh . . . give my best to Baz. Tell him, it's all right. Your personal safety comes first, yours and his. The Dendarii are, are, were . . ." He could not quite bring himself to say, *not important,* or, a *naive dream,* or, *an illusion,* though that last came closest. "A good try," he finished lamely.

The look she gave him was cool, edged, indecipherable—no, readily decodable, he feared. *Idiot,* or stronger words to that effect. He sat down, his head to his knees, and let Mayhew affix the lid, feeling like a zoological specimen being crated for shipment to the lab.

The transfer went smoothly. Miles and Gregor found themselves installed in a small but decent cabin designed for the freighter's occasional supercargo. The ship undocked, free of Aslund Station and danger of discovery, some three hours after they boarded. No Oseran search parties, no uproars . . . Tung, Miles had to admit, still did good work.

Miles was intensely grateful for a wash, a chance to clean his remaining clothes, a real meal, and sleep in safety. The ship's tiny crew seemed allergic to their corridor; he and Gregor were left strictly alone. Safe for three days, as he chugged across the Hegen Hub yet again, in yet another identity. Next stop, the Barrayaran consulate on Vervain Station.

Oh, God, he was going to have to write a report on all this when they got there. True confessions, in the approved ImpSec official style (dry as dust, judging from samples he'd read). Ungari, now, given the same tour, would have produced columns of concrete, objective data, all ready to be reanalyzed six different ways. What had Miles counted? *Nothing, I was in a box*. He had little to offer but gut feel based on a limited view snatched while dodging what seemed like every security goon in the system. Maybe he should center his report on the security forces, eh? One ensign's opinion. The general staff would be so impressed.

So what was his opinion, by now? Well, Pol didn't seem to be the source of the troubles in the Hegen Hub; they were reacting, not acting. The Consortium seemed supremely uninterested in military adventures; the only party weak enough for the eclectic Jacksonians to take on and beat was Aslund, and there would be little profit in conquering Aslund, a barely terraformed agricultural world. Aslund was paranoid enough to be dangerous, but only half-prepared, and shielded by a mercenary force waiting only the right spark to itself split into warring factions. No sustained threat there. The action, the energy for this destabilization, by elimination must be coming from or via Vervain. How could one find out . . . no. He'd sworn off secret agenting. Vervain was somebody else's problem.

Miles wondered wanly if he could persuade Gregor to give him an Imperial pardon from writing a report, and if Illyan would accept it. Probably not.

Gregor was very quiet. Miles, stretched out on his bunk, tucked his hands behind his head and smiled to conceal worry, as Gregor—somewhat regretfully, it seemed to Miles—put aside his stolen Dendarii uniform and donned civilian clothes contributed by Arde Mayhew. The shabby trousers, shirt, and jacket hung a little short and loose on Gregor's spare frame; so dressed he seemed a down-on-his-luck drifter, with hollow eyes. Miles secretly resolved to keep him away from high places.

Gregor regarded him back. "You were weird, as

Admiral Naismith, you know? Almost like a different person."

Miles shrugged himself up onto one elbow. "I guess Naismith is me with no brakes. No constraints. He doesn't have to be a good little Vor, or any kind of a Vor. He doesn't have a problem with subordination, he isn't subordinate to anyone."

"I noticed." Gregor ordered the Dendarii uniform in Barrayaran regulation folds. "Do you regret having to duck out on the Dendarii?"

"Yes . . . no . . . I don't know." *Deeply.* The chain of command, it seemed, pulled both ways on a middle link. Pull hard enough, and that link must twist and snap. . . . "I trust you don't regret escaping contract slavery."

"No . . . it wasn't what I'd pictured. It was peculiar, that fight at the air lock, though. Total strangers wanting to kill me without even knowing who I was. Total strangers trying to kill the Emperor of Barrayar, I can understand. This . . . I'm going to have to think about this one."

Miles allowed himself a brief crooked grin. "Like being loved for yourself, only different."

Gregor gave him a sharp glance. "It was strange to see Elena again, too. Bothari's dutiful daughter . . . she's changed."

"I'd meant her to," Miles avowed.

"She seems quite attached to her deserter husband."

"Yes," Miles said shortly.

"Had you meant that too?"

"Not mine to choose. It . . . follows logically, from the integrity of her character. I might have foreseen it. Since her convictions about loyalty just saved both our lives, I can hardly . . . hardly regret them, eh?"

Gregor's brow rose, an oblique gloss.

Miles bit down irritation. "Anyway, I hope she'll be

all right. Oser's proved himself dangerous. She and Baz seem to be protected only by Tung's admittedly eroding power base."

"I'm surprised you didn't take up Tung's offer." Gregor grinned as briefly as Miles had. "Instant admiralty. Skip all those tedious Barrayaran intervening steps."

"Tung's offer?" Miles snorted. "Didn't you hear him? I thought you said Dad made you read all those treaties. Tung didn't offer command, he offered a fight, at five to one odds against. He sought an ally, frontman, or cannon-fodder, not a boss."

"Oh. Hm." Gregor settled back on his bunk. "That's so. Yet I still wonder if you'd have chosen something other than this prudent retreat if I hadn't been along." His lids were hooded over a sharp glance.

Miles choked on visions. A sufficiently liberal interpretation of Illyan's vague "use Ensign Vorkosigan to clear the Dendarii Mercenaries from the Hub" might be stretched to include . . . no. "No. If I hadn't run into you, I'd be on my way to Escobar with Sergeant-nanny Overholt. You, I suppose, would still be installing lights." Depending, of course, on what the mysterious Cavilo—Commander Cavilo?—had planned for Miles once he'd caught up with him in Consortium Detention.

So where was Overholt, by now? Had he reported to HQ, tried to contact Ungari, been picked off by Cavilo? Or followed Miles? Too bad Miles couldn't have followed Overholt to Ungari—no, that was circular reasoning. It was all very weird, and they were well out of it.

"We're well out of it," Miles opined to Gregor.

Gregor rubbed the pale grey mark on his face, fading shadow of his shock-stick encounter. "Yeah, probably. I was getting good at the lights, though."

✧ ✧ ✧

Almost over, Miles thought as he and Gregor followed the freighter captain through the hatch tube into the Vervain Station docking bay. Well, maybe not quite. The Vervani captain was nervous, obsequious, clearly tense. Still, if the man had managed this spy transfer three times before, he should know what he was doing by now.

The docking bay with its harsh lighting was the usual chilly echoing cavern, arranged to the rigid grid-pattern taste of robots, not human curves. It was in fact empty of humans, its machinery silent. Their path had been cleared before them, Miles supposed, though if he'd been doing it he'd have picked the busiest chaotic period of loading or unloading to slip something past.

The captain's eyes darted from corner to corner. Miles could not help following his glance. They stopped near a deserted control booth.

"We wait here," the freighter captain said. "There are some men coming who will take you the rest of the way." He leaned against the booth wall and kicked it gently with one heel in an idle compulsive rhythm for several minutes. Then he stopped kicking and straightened, head turning.

Footsteps. Half a dozen men emerged from a nearby corridor. Miles stiffened. Uniformed men, with an officer, judging by their posture, but they weren't wearing the garb of either Vervani civil or military security. Unfamiliar short-sleeved tan fatigues with black tabs and trim, and short black boots. They carried stunners, drawn and ready. *But if it walks like an arrest squad, and talks like an arrest squad, and quacks like an arrest squad . . .*

"Miles," muttered Gregor doubtfully, taking in the same cues, "is this in the script?" The stunners were pointed their way, now.

"He's pulled this off three times," Miles offered in unfelt reassurance. "Why not a fourth?"

The freighter captain smiled thinly, and stepped away from the wall, out of the line of fire. "I pulled it off twice," he informed them. "The third time, I got caught."

Miles's hands twitched. He held them carefully away from his sides, biting back swear words. Slowly, Gregor raised his hands as well, face wonderfully blank. Score one for Gregor's self-control, as always, the one virtue his constrained life had surely inculcated.

Tung had set this up. All by himself. Had Tung known? Sold by *Tung? No . . . !* "Tung said you were reliable," Miles grated to the freighter captain.

"What's Tung to me?" the man snarled back. "I have a family, mister."

Under the stunners' aim, two—God, goons again!—soldiers stepped forward to lean Miles and Gregor, hands to the wall, and shake them down, relieving them of all their hard-won Oseran weapons, equipment, and multiple IDs. The officer examined the cache. "Yeah, these are Oser's men, all right." He spoke into his wrist comm. "We have them."

"Carry on," a thin voice returned. "We'll be right down. Cavilo out."

Randall's Rangers, evidently, hence the unfamiliar uniforms. But why no Vervani in sight? "Pardon me," Miles said mildly to the officer, "but are you people acting under the misapprehension we are Aslunder agents?"

The officer stared down at him and snorted.

"I wonder if it might not be time to establish our real identity," Gregor murmured tentatively to Miles.

"Interesting dilemma," Miles returned out of the corner of his mouth. "We'd better find out if they shoot spies."

A brisk tapping of boots heralded a new arrival. The squad braced as the sound rounded the corner. Gregor came to attention too, in automatic military courtesy, his straightness looking very strange hung about with Arde Mayhew's clothes. Miles no doubt looked least military of all, with his mouth gaping open in shock. He closed it before something flew in, such as his foot.

Five feet tall and a bit added by black boots with higher-than-regulation heels. Cropped blond hair like a dandelion aureole on that sculptured head. Crisp tan-and-black rank-gilded uniform that fit her body language in perfect complement. *Livia Nu.*

The officer saluted. "Commander Cavilo, ma'am."

"Very good, Lieutenant. . . ." Her blue eyes, falling on Miles, widened in unfeigned surprise, instantly covered. "Why, *Victor,* darling," her voice went syrupy with exaggerated amusement and delight, "*fancy* meeting you here. Still selling miracle suits to the unwitting?"

Miles spread his empty hands. "This is the totality of my luggage, ma'am. You should have bought when you could."

"I wonder." Her smile was tight and speculative. Miles found the glitter in her eyes disturbing. Gregor, silent, looked frantically bewildered.

So, *your name wasn't Livia Nu, and you weren't a procurement agent.* So why the devil was the commandant of Vervain's mercenary force meeting incognito on Pol Station with a representative of the most powerful House of the Jacksonian Consortium? *That was no mere arms deal, darling.*

Cavilo/Livia Nu raised her wrist comm to her lips. "Sickbay, *Kurin's Hand.* Cavilo here. I'm sending you up a couple of prisoners for questioning. I may sit in on this one myself." She keyed off.

The freighter captain stepped forward, half-fearful,

half-pugnacious. "My wife and son. Now you prove they're safe."

Judiciously, she looked him over. "You may be good for another run. All right." She gestured to a soldier. "Take this man to the *Kurin's* brig and let him have a look on the monitors. Then bring him back to me. You're a fortunate traitor, Captain. I have another job for you by which you may earn them—"

"Their freedom?" the freighter captain demanded.

She frowned slightly at the interruption. "Why should I inflate your salary? Another week of life."

He trailed off after the soldier, hands clenched angrily, teeth clenched prudently.

What the hell? Miles thought. He didn't know much about Vervain, but he was pretty sure not even their martial law made provisions for holding innocent relatives hostage against the good behavior of unconvicted traitors.

The freighter captain gone, Cavilo keyed her wrist comm again. "*Kurin's Hand* Security? Ah, good. I'm sending you my pet double agent. Run the recording we made last week of Cell Six for his motivation, ai? Don't let him know it's not real-time . . . right. Cavilo out."

So, was the man's family free? Already dead? Being held elsewhere? What were they getting into here?

More boots rounded the corner, a heavy regulation tread. Cavilo smiled sourly, but smoothed the expression into something sweeter as she turned to greet the newcomer.

"Stanis, darling. Look what we netted this time. It's that little renegade Betan who was trying to deal stolen arms on Pol Station. It appears he isn't an independent after all."

The tan and black Rangers' uniform looked just fine on General Metzov, too, Miles noted crazily. Now would be a wonderful time to roll up his eyes and pass out, if only he had the trick of it.

General Metzov stood equally riveted, his iron-grey eyes ablaze with sudden unholy joy. "He's no Betan, Cavie."

CHAPTER TWELVE

"He's a Barrayaran. And not just any Barrayaran. We've got to get him out of sight, quickly," Metzov went on.

"Who sent him, then?" Cavilo stared anew at Miles, her lip in a dubious curl.

"God," Metzov avowed fervently. "God has delivered him into my hand." Metzov, that cheerful, was an unusual and alarming sight. Even Cavilo raised her brow.

Metzov glanced at Gregor for the first time. "We'll take him and his—bodyguard, I suppose . . ." Metzov slowed.

The pictures on the mark-notes didn't look much like Gregor, being several years out of date, but the Emperor had appeared in enough vid-casts—not dressed like this, of course. . . . Miles could almost see Metzov thinking, *The face is familiar, I just can't place the name*. . . . Maybe he wouldn't recognize Gregor. Maybe he wouldn't *believe* it.

Gregor, drawn up in a dignity concealing dismay, spoke for the first time. "Is this yet another of your old friends, Miles?"

It was the measured, cultured voice that triggered the connection. Metzov's face, reddened with excitement, drained white. He looked around involuntarily—for Illyan, Miles guessed.

"Uh, this is General Stanis Metzov," Miles explained.

"The Kyril Island Metzov?"

"Yeah."

"Oh." Gregor maintained his closed reserve, nearly expressionless.

"Where is your security, sir?" Metzov demanded of Gregor, his voice harsh with unacknowledged fear.

You're looking at it, Miles mourned.

"Not far behind, I imagine," Gregor essayed, cool. "Let Us go Our way, and they will not trouble you."

"Who is this fellow?" Cavilo tapped a boot impatiently.

"What," Miles couldn't help asking Metzov, "what are you doing here?"

Metzov went grim. "How shall a man my age, stripped of his Imperial Pension—his life savings—live? Did you hope I would sit down and quietly starve? Not I."

Inopportune, to remind Metzov of his grudge, Miles realized. "This . . . looks like an improvement over Kyril Island," Miles suggested hopefully. His mind still boggled. Metzov, working under a woman? The internal dynamics of this command chain must be fascinating. Stanis *darling?*

Metzov did not look amused.

"*Who are they?*" Cavilo demanded again.

"Power. Money. Strategic leverage. More than you can imagine," Metzov answered.

"Trouble," Miles put in. "More than you can imagine."

"You are a separate matter, mutant," Metzov said.

"I beg to differ, General," said Gregor in his best Imperial tones. Feeling for footing in this floating conversation, though concealing his confusion well.

"We must take them to the *Kurin's Hand* at once. Out of sight," said Metzov to Cavilo. He glanced at the arrest squad. "Out of hearing. We'll continue this in private."

They marched off, escorted by the patrol. Metzov's gaze felt like a knife blade in Miles's back, prodding and probing. They passed through several deserted docking bays till they arrived at a major one actively servicing a ship. The command ship, judging by the number and formality of duty guards.

"Take them to Medical for questioning," Cavilo ordered the squad as they were saluted through a personnel hatch by the officer in charge.

"Hold on that," said Metzov. He stared around the cross-corridors, almost jittering. "Do you have a guard who's deaf and mute?"

"Hardly!" Cavilo stared indignantly at her mysteriously agitated subordinate. "To the brig, then."

"No," said Metzov sharply. Hesitating to throw the Emperor into a cell, Miles realized. Metzov turned to Gregor and said with perfect seriousness, "May I have your parole, sire—sir?"

"What?" cried Cavilo. "Have you stripped a gear, Stanis?"

"A parole," Gregor noted gravely, "is a promise given between honorable enemies. Your honor I am willing to assume. But are you thus declaring yourself Our enemy?"

Excellent bit of weaseling, Miles approved.

Metzov's eye fell on Miles. His lips thinned. "Perhaps not yours. But you have a poor choice of favorites. Not to mention advisors."

Gregor was now very hard to read. "Some acquaintances are imposed on me. Also some advisors."

"To my cabin," Metzov held up his hand as Cavilo opened her mouth to object, "for now. For our initial conversation. Without witnesses, or Security recordings. After that, we decide, Cavie."

Cavilo, eyes narrowing, closed her mouth. "All right, Stanis. Lead off." Her hand curved open ironically, and gestured them onward.

Metzov posted two guards outside his cabin door, and dismissed the rest. When the door had sealed behind them, he tied Miles with a tangle-cord and sat him on the floor. With helplessly ingrained deference, he then seated Gregor in the padded station chair at his comconsole desk, the best the spartan chamber had to offer.

Cavilo, seated cross-legged on the bed watching the play, objected to the logic of this. "Why tie up the little one and leave the big one loose?"

"Keep your stunner drawn, then, if he worries you," Metzov advised. Breathing heavily, he stood hands on hips and studied Gregor. He shook his head, as if still not believing his eyes.

"Why not your stunner?"

"I have not yet decided whether to draw a weapon in his presence."

"We're *alone* now, Stanis," Cavilo said in a sarcastic lilt. "Would you kindly explain this insanity? And it had better be good."

"Oh yes. That—" he pointed to Miles, "is Lord Miles Vorkosigan, the son of the Prime Minister of Barrayar. Admiral Aral Vorkosigan—I trust you've heard of *him*."

Cavilo's brows lowered. "What was he doing on Pol Six in the guise of a Betan gunrunner, then?"

"I'm not sure. The last I'd heard he was under arrest

by Imperial Security, though of course no one believed they were serious about it."

"Detainment," Miles corrected. "Technically."

"And he—" Metzov swung to point to Gregor, "is the Emperor of Barrayar. Gregor Vorbarra. What *he's* doing here, I cannot imagine."

"Are you sure?" Even Cavilo was taken aback. At Metzov's stern nod, her eye lit with speculation. She looked at Gregor as if for the first time. "*Really.* How *interesting.*"

"But where is his security? We must tread very cautiously, Cavie."

"What's he worth to them? Or for that matter, to the highest bidder?"

Gregor smiled at her. "I'm Vor, ma'am. In a sense, *the* Vor. Risk in service is the Vorish trade. I wouldn't assume my value was infinite, if I were you."

Gregor's complaint had some truth to it, Miles thought; when he wasn't being emperor he seemed hardly anyone at all. But he sure did the *role* well.

"An opportunity, yes," said Metzov, "but if we create an enemy we can't handle—"

"If we hold *him* hostage, we ought to be able to handle them with ease," Cavilo commented thoughtfully.

"An alternate and more prudent course," Miles interjected, "would be to help us swiftly and safely on our way, and collect a lucrative and honorable thank-you. A, as it were, win-win strategy."

"Honorable?" Metzov's eyes burned. He fell into a brooding silence, then muttered. "But what are they doing here? And where's the snake Illyan? I want the mutant, in any case. Damn! It must be played boldly, or not at all." He stared malignantly at Miles. "Vorkosigan . . . so. And what is Barrayar to me now, a Service that stabbed me in the back after thirty-five years. . . ." He straightened decisively, but still did not, Miles noticed, draw a weapon in the Emperor's presence. "Yes, take them to the brig, Cavie."

"Not so fast," said Cavilo, looking newly pensive. "Send the little one to the brig, if you like. He's nothing, you say?"

The only son of the most powerful military leader on Barrayar kept his mouth shut for a change. If, if, if . . .

"By comparison," Metzov temporized, looking suddenly fearful of being cheated of his prey.

"Very well." Cavilo slid her stunner, which she had stopped aiming and started playing with some time back, soundlessly into her holster. She moved to unseal the door and beckon to the guards. "Put him," she gestured to Gregor, "in Cabin Nine, G Deck. Cut the outgoing comm, lock the door, and post a guard with a stunner. But supply him with any reasonable comfort he may request." She added aside to Gregor, "It's the most comfortable visiting officer's quarters the *Kurin's Hand* can supply, ah—"

"Call me Greg." Gregor sighed.

"Greg. Nice name. Cabin Nine is next to my own. We will continue this conversation shortly, after you, ah, freshen up. Perhaps over dinner. Oversee his arrival there, will you, Stanis?" She favored both men with an impartial, glittering smile, and wafted out, a neat trick in boots. She stuck her head back in and indicated Miles. "Bring *him* along to the brig."

Miles was removed by the second guard with a wave of a stunner and the prod of a blessedly inactivated shock-stick, to follow in her wake.

The *Kurin's Hand*, judging from his passing glimpses, was a much larger command ship than the *Triumph*, able to field bigger and punchier combat drop or boarding forces, but correspondingly sluggish in maneuver. Its brig was larger too, Miles discovered shortly, and more formidably secured. A single entrance opened onto an elaborate guard monitor station, from which led two deadend cell bays.

The freighter captain was just leaving the guard station, under the watchful eye of the squadman detailed to escort him. He exchanged a hostile look with Cavilo.

"As you see, they remain in good health," Cavilo said to him. "My half of the bargain, Captain. See that you continue to complete your own part."

Let's see what happens. . . . "You saw a recording," Miles piped up. "Demand to see 'em in the flesh."

Cavilo's white teeth clenched rigidly, but her annoyed grimace melted seamlessly into a vulpine smile as the freighter captain jerked around. "What? You . . ." He planted himself mulishly. "All right, which of you is lying?"

"Captain, that's all the guarantee you get," said Cavilo, gesturing to the monitors. "You chose to gamble, gamble you shall."

"Then that—" he pointed to Miles, "is the last result you get."

A subtle hand motion down by her trouser seam brought the guards to the alert, stunners drawn. "Take him out," she ordered.

"No!"

"Very well," her eyes widened in exasperation, "take him to Cell Six. And lock him in."

As the freighter captain turned, torn between resistance and eagerness, Cavilo motioned the guard to open distance from his prisoner. He fell away, brows rising in question. Cavilo glanced at Miles and smiled very sourly, as if to say, *All right, Smartass, watch me.* In a cold smooth motion Cavilo flipped open her left side holster seal, brought up a nerve disrupter, took careful aim, and fried the back of the captain's head. He convulsed once and dropped, dead before he hit the deck.

She walked over and pensively prodded the body with the pointed toe of her boot, then glanced up at Miles, whose jaw was gaping open. "You *will* keep your mouth shut next time, won't you, little man?"

Miles's mouth shut with a snap. *You had to experiment.* . . . At least now he knew who'd killed Liga. The rabbity Polian's reported death seemed suddenly real and vivid. The exalted look flashing over Cavilo's face as she blew the freighter captain away fascinated even as it horrified Miles. *Who did you really see in your gunsights, darling?* "Yes, ma'am," he choked, trying to conceal his shakes, delayed reaction to this shocking turn. *Damn* his tongue. . . .

She stepped down to the security monitoring station and spoke to the tech at—frozen at—her post. "Unload the recording of General Metzov's cabin that includes the last half-hour, and give it to me. Start a fresh one. No, don't play it back!" She placed the disk in a breast pocket and carefully sealed the flap. "Put this one in Cell Fourteen." She nodded toward Miles. "Or, ah—if it's empty, make that Cell Thirteen." Her teeth bared briefly.

The guards re-searched Miles, and took ID scans. Cavilo blandly informed them that his name should be entered as Victor Rotha.

As he was pulled to his feet, two men with medical insignia arrived with a float-pallet to remove the body. Cavilo, watching without expression now, remarked tiredly to Miles, "You chose to damage my double-agent's utility. A vandal's prank. He had better uses than as an object-lesson for a fool. I do not warehouse non-useful items. I suggest you start thinking of how you can make yourself more useful to me than as merely General Metzov's catnip toy." She smiled faintly into some invisible distance. "Though he does jump for you, doesn't he? I shall have to explore that motivation."

"What is the use of Stanis-darling to you?" Miles dared, pigheaded-defiant in his wash of angry guilt. Metzov as her paramour? Revolting thought.

"He's an experienced ground combat commander."

"What's a fleet on all-space wormhole guard duty want with a ground commander?"

"Well, then," she smiled sweetly, "he amuses me."

That was supposed to have been the first answer. "No accounting for taste," Miles muttered inanely, careful not to be heard. Should he warn her about Metzov? On second thought, should he warn Metzov about *her*?

His head was still spinning with this new dilemma when the blank door of his solitary cell sealed him in.

It didn't take long for Miles to exhaust the novelties of his new quarters, a space a little larger than two by two meters, furnished only with two padded benches and a fold-out lavatory. No library viewer, no relief from the wheel of his thoughts mired in the quag of his self-recriminations.

A Ranger field-ration bar, inserted some time later through a force-shielded aperture in the door, proved even more repellent than the Barrayaran Imperial version, resembling a rawhide dog chew. Wetted with spit, it softened slightly, enough to tear off gummy shreds if your teeth were in good health. More than a temporary distraction, it promised to last till the next issue. Probably nutritious as hell. Miles wondered what Cavilo was serving Gregor for dinner. Was it as scientifically vitamin-balanced?

They'd been so close to their goal. Even now, the Barrayaran consulate was only a few locks and levels away, less than a kilometer. If only he could get there from here. If a chance came . . . On the other hand, how long would Cavilo hesitate to disregard diplomatic custom and violate the consulate, if she saw some utility in it? About as long as she'd hesitated to shoot the freighter captain in the back, Miles gauged. She would surely have ordered the consulate, and all known Barrayaran agents on Vervain Station, watched by now. Miles unstuck his teeth from a fragment of ration-leather, and hissed.

A beeping from the code-lock warned Miles he was about to have a visitor. Interrogation, so soon? He'd expected Cavilo to wine, dine, and evaluate Gregor first, then get back to him. Or was he to be a mere project for underlings? He swallowed, throat tight on a ration blob, and sat up, trying to look stern and not scared.

The door slid back to reveal General Metzov, still looking highly military and efficient in the tan and black Ranger fatigues.

"Sure you don't need me, sir?" the guard at his elbow asked as Metzov shouldered through the opening.

Metzov glanced contemptuously at Miles, looking low and unmilitary in Victor Rotha's now limp and grimy green silk shirt, baggy trousers, and bare feet—the processing guards had taken his sandals. "Hardly. *He's* not going to jump me."

Damn straight, Miles agreed with regret.

Metzov tapped his wrist comm. "I'll call you when I'm done."

"Very well, sir." The door sighed closed. The cell seemed suddenly very tiny indeed. Miles drew his legs up, sitting in a small defensive ball on his pallet. Metzov stood at ease, contemplating Miles for a long, satisfied moment, then settled himself comfortably on the bench opposite.

"Well, well," said Metzov, his mouth twisting. "What a turn of fate."

"I thought you'd be dining with the Emperor," said Miles.

"Commander Cavilo, being female, can get a little scattered under stress. When she calms down again, she'll see the need for my expertise in Barrayaran matters," said Metzov in measured tones.

In other words, you weren't invited. "You left the Emperor *alone* with her?" *Gregor, watch your step!*

"Gregor's no threat. I fear his upbringing has made him altogether weak."

Miles choked.

Metzov sat back, allowed his fingers to tap gently on his knee. "So tell me, Ensign Vorkosigan—if it is still Ensign Vorkosigan. There being no justice in the world, I suppose you've retained your rank and pay. What are you doing here? With *him?*"

Miles was tempted to confine himself to name, rank, and serial number, except Metzov knew all those already. Was Metzov an enemy, exactly? Of Barrayar, that is, not of Miles personally. Did Metzov divide the two in his own mind? "The Emperor became separated from his security. We hoped to regain contact with them via the Barrayaran consulate here." There, nothing in that that wasn't perfectly obvious.

"And where did you come from?"

"Aslund."

"Don't bother playing the idiot, Vorkosigan. I know Aslund. Who sent you there in the first place? And don't bother lying, I can cross-question the freighter captain."

"No, you can't. Cavilo killed him."

"Oh?" A flicker of surprise, suppressed. "Clever of her. He was the only witness to know where you went."

Had that been part of Cavilo's calculation, when

she'd raised her nerve disrupter? Probably. And yet . . . the freighter captain was also the only corroborating witness who knew where they'd come *from.* Maybe Cavilo was not so formidable as she seemed at first glance.

"Again," Metzov said patiently—Miles could see he felt he had all the time in the world—"how did you come to be in the Emperor's company?"

"How do you think?" Miles countered, buying time.

"Some plot, of course." Metzov shrugged.

Miles groaned. "Oh, of course!" He uncurled in his indignation. "And what sane—or insane, for that matter—chain of conspiracy do you imagine accounts for our arrival here, alone, from Aslund? I mean, I know what it really was, I lived it, but what does it look like?" *To a professional paranoid, that is.* "I'd just love to hear it."

"Well . . ." Metzov was drawn out in spite of himself. "You have somehow separated the Emperor from his security. You must either be setting up an elaborate assassination, or planning to implement some form of personality-control."

"That's what just *springs* to mind, huh?" Miles thumped his back against the wall with a frustrated growl, and slumped.

"Or perhaps you're on some secret—and therefore dishonorable—diplomatic mission. Some sellout."

"If so, where's Gregor's security?" Miles sang. "Better watch out."

"So, my first hypothesis is proved."

"In that case, where's *my* security?" Miles snarled. Where, indeed?

"A Vorkosigan plot—no, perhaps not the Admiral's. He controls Gregor at home—"

"Thank you, I was about to point that out."

"A twisted plot from a twisted mind. Do you

dream of making yourself emperor of Barrayar, mutant?"

"A nightmare, I assure you. Ask Gregor."

"It scarcely matters. The medical staff will squeeze out your secrets as soon as Cavilo gives the go-ahead. In a way, it's a shame fast-penta was ever invented. I'd enjoy breaking every bone in your body till you talked. Or screamed. You won't be able to hide behind your father's," he grinned briefly, "skirts, out here, Vorkosigan." He grew thoughtful. "Maybe I will anyway. One bone a day, for as long as they last."

206 *bones in the human body.* 206 *days. Illyan ought to be able to catch up with us in* 206 *days.* Miles smiled bleakly.

Metzov looked too comfortable to arise and initiate this plan immediately, though. This speculative conversation scarcely constituted a serious interrogation. But if not for interrogation, nor revenge-tortures, why was the man here?

His lover threw him out, he felt lonely and strange and wanted someone familiar to talk to. Even a familiar enemy. It was weirdly understandable. But for the Komarr invasion, Metzov had probably never set foot off Barrayar in his life. A life spent mostly in the constrained, ordered, predictable world-within-a-world of the Imperial military. Now the rigid man was adrift, and faced with more free-will choices than he'd ever imagined. *God. The maniac's homesick.* Chilling insight.

"I'm beginning to think I may have accidentally done you a good turn," Miles began. If Metzov was in a talking mood, why not encourage him? "Cavilo's certainly better-looking than your last commander."

"She is that."

"Is the pay higher?"

"Everyone pays more than the Imperial Service," Metzov snorted.

"Not boring, either. On Kyril Island, every day was like every other day. Here, you don't know what's going to happen next. Or does she confide in you?"

"I'm essential to her plans." Metzov practically smirked.

"As a bedroom warrior? Thought you were infantry. Switching specialties, at your age?"

Metzov merely smiled. "Now you're getting obvious, Vorkosigan."

Miles shrugged. *If so, I'm the only obvious thing here.* "As I recall, you didn't think much of women soldiers. Cavilo seems to have made you change your tune."

"Not at all." Metzov sat back smugly. "I expect to be in command of Randall's Rangers in six months."

"Isn't this cell monitored?" Miles asked, startled. Not that he cared how much trouble Metzov's mouth bought him, but still. . . .

"Not at present."

"Cavilo planning to retire, is she?"

"There are a number of ways her retirement might be expedited. The fatal accident Cavilo arranged for Randall might easily be repeated. Or I might even work out a way to charge her with it, since she was stupid enough to brag about murder in bed."

That was no boast, that was a warning, dunderhead. Miles's eyes nearly crossed, imagining pillow-talk between Metzov and Cavilo. "You two must have a lot in common. No wonder you get on so well."

Metzov's amusement thinned. "I have nothing in common with that mercenary slut. I was an Imperial officer." Metzov glowered. "Thirty-five years. And they wasted me. Well, they'll discover their mistake."

Metzov glanced at his chrono. "I still don't understand your presence here. Are you sure there isn't something else you want to say to me now, privately, before you say everything tomorrow to Cavilo under fast-penta?"

Cavilo and Metzov, Miles decided, had set up the old interrogation game of good-guy-bad-guy. Except they'd gotten their signals mixed, and both accidentally taken the part of bad-guy. "If you really want to be helpful, get Gregor to the Barrayaran Consul. Or even just get out a message that he's here."

"In good time, we may. Given suitable terms." Metzov's eyes were narrowed, studying Miles. As puzzled by Miles as Miles by him? After a stretched silence, Metzov called the guard on his wrist comm, and withdrew, with no more violent parting threat than "See you tomorrow, Vorkosigan." Sinister enough.

I don't understand your presence here either, Miles thought as the door hissed closed and the lock beeped. Clearly, some kind of planetary ground-attack was in the planning stage. Were Randall's Rangers to spearhead a Vervani invasion force? Cavilo had met secretly with a high-ranking Jackson's Consortium representative. Why? To guarantee Consortium neutrality during the coming attack? That made excellent sense, but why hadn't the Vervani dealt directly? So they could disavow Cavilo's arrangements if the balloon went up too early?

And who, or what, was the target? Not the Consortium Station, obviously, nor its distant parent Jackson's Whole. That left Aslund and Pol. Aslund, a cul-de-sac, was not strategically tempting. Better to take Pol first, cut Aslund off from the Hub (with Consortium cooperation) and mop up the weak planet at leisure. But Pol had Barrayar behind it, who would like nothing better than an alliance with its nervous neighbor that would give the Imperium a toehold in the Hegen Hub. An open attack must drive Pol into Barrayar's waiting arms. That left Aslund, but . . .

This makes no sense. It was almost more disturbing than the thought of Gregor supping unguarded with Cavilo, or the fear of the promised chemical interrogation. *I'm not seeing something. This makes no sense.*

The Hegen Hub turned in his head, in all its strategic complexity, all the light-dimmed night cycle. The Hub, and pictures of Gregor. Was Cavilo feeding him mind-altering drugs? Doggie chews, like Miles's? Steak and champagne? Was Gregor being tortured? Being seduced? Visions of Cavilo/Livia Nu's dramatic red evening-wear undulated in Miles's mind's eye. Was Gregor having a wonderful time? Miles thought Gregor'd had little more experience with women than he had, but he'd been out of touch with the Emperor these last few years; for all he knew Gregor was keeping a harem now. No, that couldn't be, or Ivan would have picked up the scent, and commented. At length. How susceptible was Gregor to a very old-fashioned form of mind-control?

The day-cycle crept by with Miles anticipating every moment being taken out for his very first experience of fast-penta interrogation from the wrong end of the hypospray. What would Cavilo and Metzov make of the bizarre truth of his and Gregor's odyssey? Three ration-chews arrived at interminable intervals, and the lights dimmed again, marking another ship-night. Three meals, and no interrogation. What was keeping them out there? No noises or subtle gravitic vibrations suggested the ship had left dock; they were still locked to Vervain Station. Miles tried to exercise himself weary, pacing, two steps, turn, two steps, turn, two steps . . . but merely succeeded in increasing his personal stink and making himself dizzy.

Another day writhed by, and another light-dimmed "night." Another breakfast chew fell through onto the floor. Were they artificially stretching or compressing time, confusing his biological clock to soften him up for interrogation? Why bother?

He bit his fingernails. He bit his toenails. He pulled tiny green threads from his shirt and tried flossing his teeth. Then he tried making little green designs with tiny, tiny knots. Then he hit on the idea of weaving messages. Could he macramé "Help, I am a prisoner . . ." and plant it on the back of someone's jacket by static charge? If someone ever came back, that is? He got as far as a delicate gossamer H, E, L, caught the thread on a hangnail while rubbing his stubbled chin, and reduced his plea to an illegible green wad. He pulled another thread and started over.

The lock twinkled and beeped. Miles snapped alert, realizing only then that he had fallen into an almost hypnotic fugue in his mumbling isolation. How much time had passed?

His visitor was Cavilo, crisp and businesslike in her Ranger's fatigues. A guard took up station just outside the cell door, which closed behind her. Another private chat, it seemed. Miles struggled to pull his thoughts together, to remember what he was about.

Cavilo settled herself opposite Miles in the same spot Metzov had chosen, in somewhat the same leisurely posture, leaning forward, hands clasped loosely on her knees, attentive, assured. Miles sat cross-legged, back to the wall, feeling distinctly at the disadvantage.

"Lord Vorkosigan, ah . . ." she cocked her head, interrupting herself aside, "you don't look at all well."

"Solitary confinement doesn't suit me." His disused voice came out raspy, and he had to stop and clear his throat. "Perhaps a library viewer," his brain grated into gear, "—or better, an exercise period." Which would get him out of this cell, and in contact with subornable humans. "My medical problems compel me to a self-disciplined lifestyle, if they're not to flare up and impede me. I definitely need an exercise period, or I'm going to get really sick."

"Hm. We'll see." She ran a hand through her short hair, and refocused. "So, Lord Vorkosigan. Tell me about your mother."

"Huh?" A most dizzying sharp left turn, for a military interrogation. "Why?"

She smiled ingratiatingly. "Greg's tales have interested me."

Greg's tales? Had the Emperor been fast-penta'd? "What . . . do you want to know?"

"Well . . . I understand Countess Vorkosigan is an off-worlder, a Betan who married into your aristocracy."

"The Vor are a military caste, but yes."

"How was she received, by the power-class—whatever they choose to call themselves? I'd thought Barrayarans were totally provincial, prejudiced against off-worlders."

"We are," Miles admitted cheerfully. "The first contact most Barrayarans—of all classes—had with off-worlders, after the end of the Time of Isolation when Barrayar was rediscovered, was with the Cetagandan invasion forces. They left a bad impression that lingers even now, three, four generations after we threw them off."

"Yet no one questioned your father's choice?"

Miles jerked up his chin in bafflement. "He was in his forties. And . . . and he was *Lord Vorkosigan.*" *So am I, now. Why doesn't it work for me like that?*

"Her background made no difference?"

"She was Betan. Is Betan. In the Astronomical Survey first, but then a combat officer. Beta Colony had just helped beat us soundly in that stupid attempt we made to invade Escobar."

"So despite being an enemy, her military background actually helped gain her respect and acceptance among the Vor?"

"I guess so. Plus, she established quite a local military reputation in the fighting of Vordarian's Pretendership, the year I was born, twice. Led loyal troops, oh, several times, when my father couldn't be two places at once." And had been personally responsible for the five-year-old emperor-in-hiding's safety. More successfully than her son was doing so far for the twenty-five-year-old Gregor. *Total screw-up* was the phrase that sprang to mind, actually. "Nobody's messed with her since."

"Hm." Cavilo sat back, murmuring half to herself, "So, it has been done. Therefore, it can be done."

What, what can be done? Miles rubbed a hand over his face, trying to wake up and concentrate. "How is Gregor?"

"Quite amusing."

Gregor the Lugubrious, amusing? But then, if it matched the rest of her personality, Cavilo's sense of humor was probably vile. "I meant his health."

"Rather better than yours, from the look of you."

"I trust he's been better fed."

"What, a taste of real military life too strong for you, Lord Vorkosigan? You've been fed the same as my troops."

"Can't be." Miles held up a ragged half-gnawed breakfast chew. "They'd have mutinied by now."

"Oh, dear." She regarded the repellent morsel with a sympathetic frown. "Those. I thought they'd been condemned. How did they end up here? Someone must be economizing. Shall I order you a regular menu?"

"Yes, thank you," said Miles immediately, and paused. She had neatly misdirected his attention from Gregor to himself. He must keep his mind on the Emperor.

How much *useful* information had Gregor spilled, by now?

"You realize," Miles said carefully, "you are creating a massive interplanetary incident between Vervain and Barrayar."

"Not at all," said Cavilo reasonably. "I'm Greg's friend. I've rescued him from falling into the hands of the Vervani secret police. He's now under my protection, until the opportunity arises to restore him to his rightful place."

Miles blinked. "Do the Vervani have a secret police, as such?"

"Close enough." Cavilo shrugged. "Barrayar, of course, definitely does. Stanis seems quite worried about them. They must be very embarrassed, back in ImpSec, to have so thoroughly mislaid their charge. I fear their reputation is exaggerated."

Not quite. I'm ImpSec, and I know where Gregor is. So technically, ImpSec is right on top of the situation. Miles wasn't sure whether to laugh or cry. *Or right under it.*

"If we're all such good friends," said Miles, "why am I locked in this cell?"

"For your protection too, of course. After all, General Metzov has openly threatened to, ah—what was it—break every bone in your body." She sighed. "I'm afraid dear Stanis is about to lose his utility."

Miles blanched, remembering what else Metzov had said in that conversation. "For . . . disloyalty?"

"Not at all. Disloyalty can be very useful at times, under proper management. But the overall strategic situation may be about to change drastically. Unimaginably. And after all the time I wasted cultivating him, too. I hope all Barrayarans are not so tedious as Stanis." She smiled briefly. "I very much hope it."

She leaned forward, growing more intent. "Is it true that Gregor, ah, ran away from home to evade pressure from his advisors to marry a woman he loathed?"

"He hadn't mentioned it to me," said Miles, startled. Wait—what was Gregor about, out there? He'd better be careful not to step on his lines. "Though there is . . . concern. If he were to die without an heir any time soon, many fear a factional struggle would follow."

"He has no heir?"

"The factions can't agree. Except on Gregor."

"So his advisors would be glad to see him marry."

"Overjoyed, I expect. Uh . . ." Miles's unease at this turn of the conversation bloomed into sudden light, like the flash before the shock-wave. "Commander Cavilo—you're *not* imagining you could make yourself Empress of Barrayar, are you?"

Her smile grew sharp. "Of course I couldn't. But Greg could." She straightened, evidently annoyed by Miles's stunned expression. "Why not? I'm the right sex. And, apparently, of the right military background."

"How old are you?"

"Lord Vorkosigan, really, what a rude question." Her blue eyes glinted. "If we were on the same side, we could work together."

"Commander Cavilo, I don't think you understand Barrayar. Or Barrayarans." Actually, there'd been eras in Barrayaran history where Cavilo's command style would have fit right in. Mad Emperor Yuri's reign of terror, for example. But they'd spent the last twenty years trying to get *away* from all that.

"I need your cooperation," Cavilo said. "Or at any rate, it could be very useful. To both of us. Your neutrality would be . . . tolerable. Your active opposition, however, would be a problem. For you. But we should avoid getting caught in negative attitude traps at this early stage, I think?"

"Whatever did happen to that freighter captain's wife and child? Widow and orphan, rather?" Miles inquired through his teeth.

Cavilo hesitated fractionally. "The man was a traitor. Of the worst sort. Sold out his planet for money. He was caught in an act of espionage. There is no moral difference between ordering an execution, and carrying it out."

"I agree. So do a lot of legal codes. How about a difference between execution and murder? Vervain is not at war. His actions may have been illegal, warranting arrest, trial, jail, or sociopath therapy—where did the trial part drop out?"

"A Barrayaran, arguing legalities? How strange."

"And what happened to his family?"

She'd had a moment to think, blast it. "The tedious Vervani demanded their release. Naturally, I didn't want him to know they were out of my hands, or I'd lose my only hold on his actions at a distance."

Lie or truth? No way to tell. *But she backpedals from her mistake. She let establishing her dominance through terror rule her reactions, before she was sure of her ground. Because she was unsure of her ground. I know the look that was on her face. Homicidal paranoids are as familiar as breakfast, I had one for a bodyguard for seventeen years.* Cavilo, for a brief instant, seemed homey and routine, if no less dangerous. But he should strive to appear convinced, nonthreatening, even if it made him gag.

"It's true," he conceded, "it's rank cowardice to give an order you're not willing to carry out yourself. And you're no coward, Commander, I'll grant you that." There, that was the right tone, persuadable but not changing his stance too suspiciously fast.

Her brow rose sardonically, as if to say, *Who are you to judge?* But her tension eased slightly. She glanced at her chrono and rose. "I'll leave you now, to think about the advantages of cooperation. You're theoretically familiar with the mathematics of the Prisoner's Dilemma, I hope. It will be an interesting test of your wits, to see if you can connect theory with practice."

Miles managed a weird return smile. Her beauty, her energy, even her flaring ego, did exert a real fascination. Had Gregor indeed been . . . activated, by Cavilo? Gregor, after all, hadn't watched her raise her nerve disrupter and . . . What weapon was a good ImpSec man to use, in the face of this personal assault on Gregor? Try to seduce her back? To sacrifice himself for the Emperor by flinging himself on Cavilo had about as much appeal as belly-smothering a live sonic grenade.

Besides, he doubted he could work it. The door slid closed, eclipsing her scimitar smile. Too late, he raised a hand to remind her of her promise to change his rations.

But she remembered anyway. Lunch arrived on a trolley, with an experienced, if expressionless, batman to serve it in five elegant courses with two wines and espresso coffee for an antidote. Miles didn't think Cavilo's troops ate like this, either. He envisioned a platoon of smiling, replete, obese gourmets strolling happily into battle . . . the dog chews would be much more effective for raising aggression levels.

A chance remark to his waiter brought a package along with the next meal-trolley, which proved to contain clean underwear, a set of insignialess Ranger fatigues cut down to his fit, and a pair of soft felt slippers; also a tube of depilatory and assorted toiletries. Miles was inspired to wash, by sections, in the fold-out lavatory basin, and shave before dressing. He felt almost human. Ah, the virtues of cooperation. Cavilo was not exactly subtle.

God, where had she come from? A mercenary veteran, she had to have been around for a while to have risen this far, even with shortcuts. Tung might know. *I think she must have lost bad at least once.* He wished Tung were here now. Hell, he wished *Illyan* were here now.

Her flamboyance, Miles increasingly felt, was an effective act, meant to be viewed at a distance like stage makeup, to dazzle her troops. At the right range, it might work rather well, like the popular Barrayaran general of his grandfather's generation who'd gained visibility by carrying a plasma rifle like a swagger stick. Usually uncharged, Miles had heard privately—the man wasn't stupid. Or a Vorish ensign who wore a certain antique dagger at every opportunity. A trademark, a banner. A calculated bit of mass psychology. Cavilo's public persona pushed the envelope of that strategy, surely. Was she scared inside, knowing herself for overextended? *You wish.*

Alas, after a dose of Cavilo, one thought of Cavilo, fogging one's tactical calculations. Focus, Ensign. Had she forgotten Victor Rotha? Had Gregor concocted some bullshit explanation to account for their Pol Station encounter? Gregor seemed to be feeding Cavilo skewed facts—or were they? Maybe there really was a loathed proposed bride, and Gregor had not trusted Miles enough to mention it. Miles began to regret being quite so acerbic to Gregor.

His thoughts were still running like a hyped-up rat on an exercise wheel, spinning to nowhere, when the door code-lock beeped again. Yes, he would fake cooperation, promise anything, if only she'd give him a chance to check on Gregor.

Cavilo appeared with a soldier in tow. The man looked vaguely familiar—one of the arresting goons? No . . .

The man ducked his head through the cell door, stared at Miles a moment in bemusement, and turned to Cavilo.

"Yeah, that's him, all right. Admiral Naismith, of the Tau Verde Ring war. I'd recognize the little runt anywhere." He added aside to Miles, "What are you doing here, sir?"

Miles mentally transmuted the man's tan-and-blacks to grey and white. Yeah. There'd been several thousand mercenaries involved in the Tau Verde war. They all had to have gone somewhere.

"Thank you, that will be all, Sergeant." Cavilo took the man by the arm and firmly pulled him away. The non-com's fading advice drifted back down the cell bay, "You ought to try and hire him, ma'am, he's a military genius. . . ."

Cavilo reappeared after a moment, to stand in the aperture with her hands on her hips and her chin outthrust in exasperated disbelief. "How many people *are* you, anyway?"

Miles opened his hands and smiled weakly. Just as he'd been about to talk his way out of this hole . . .

"Huh." She spun on her heel, the closing door cutting off her sputter.

Now what? He'd slam his fist into the wall in frustration, but the wall was sure to slam back with greater devastation.

CHAPTER THIRTEEN

However, all three of his identities were granted an exercise period that afternoon. A small onboard gymnasium was cleared for his exclusive use. He studied the setup sharply for the hour as he tried out various pieces of equipment, checking distances and trajectories to guarded exits. He could see a couple of ways Ivan might succeed in jumping a guard and making a break for it. Not fragile, short-legged Miles. For a moment, he found himself actually wishing he had Ivan along.

On the way back to Cell 13 with his escort, Miles passed another prisoner being checked in at the guard station. He was a shambling, wild-eyed man, his blond hair damped to brown with sweat. Miles's shock of recognition was the greater for the changes it had to encompass. *Oser's lieutenant.* The bland-faced killer was transformed.

He wore only grey trousers, his torso was bare. Livid shock-stick marks dappled his skin. Recent hypospray injection points marched like little pink paw prints up his arm. He mumbled continuously through wet lips, shivered and giggled. Just coming back from interrogation, it seemed.

Miles was so startled he reached over to grasp the man's left hand, to check—yes, there were his own scabbed-over teeth marks across the knuckles, souvenir of last week's fight at the *Triumph's* air lock, across the system. The silent lieutenant wasn't silent anymore.

Miles's guards motioned him sternly along. Miles almost tripped, staring back over his shoulder till the door of Cell 13 sighed shut, imprisoning him once more.

What are you doing here? That had to be the most-asked, least-answered question in the Hegen Hub, Miles decided. Though he bet the Oseran lieutenant had answered it—Cavilo must command one of the sharpest counter-intelligence departments in the Hub. How fast had the Oseran mercenary traced Miles and Gregor here? How soon had Cavilo's people spotted him and picked him up? The marks on his body were not over a day old. . . .

Most important question of all, had the Oseran come to Vervain Station as part of a general, systematic sweep, or had he followed specific clues—was Tung compromised? Elena arrested? Miles shuddered, and paced frenetically, helplessly. *Have I just killed my friends?*

So, what Oser knew, Cavilo now knew, the whole silly mix of truth, lies, rumors and mistakes. So the identification of Miles as "Admiral Naismith" hadn't necessarily come from Gregor as Miles had first assumed. (The Tau Verde veteran had clearly been scrounged up as an unbiased cross-check.) If Gregor was systematically withholding information from her, Cavilo would now realize it. If he was withholding anything. Maybe he was in love by now. Miles's head throbbed, feeling on the verge of exploding.

The guards came for him in the middle of the night-cycle, and made him dress. Interrogation at last, eh? He thought of the drooling Oseran, and cringed. He insisted on washing up, and adjusted every burr-seam and cuff of his Ranger fatigues with slow deliberation, till the guards began to shift impatiently and tap fingers suggestively on shock-sticks. He too would shortly be a drooling fool. On the other hand, what could he possibly say under fast-penta at this point that could make things worse? Cavilo had it all, as far as he could tell. He shrugged off the guards' grasps, and marched out of the brig between them with all the forlorn dignity he could muster.

They led him through the night-dimmed ship and exited a lift-tube at something marked "G-Deck." Miles snapped alert. Gregor was supposed to be around here somewhere. . . . They arrived at an otherwise-blank cabin door marked 10A, where the guards beeped the code-lock for permission to enter. The door slid aside.

Cavilo sat at a comconsole desk, a pool of light in the somber room making her blond-white hair gleam and glow. They had arrived at the commander's personal office, apparently, adjoining her quarters. Miles strained his eyes and ears for signs of the Emperor. Cavilo was fully dressed in her neat fatigues. At least Miles wasn't the only one going short on sleep these days; he fancied optimistically that she looked a little tired. She placed a stunner out on her desk, ominously ready to her right hand, and dismissed the guards. Miles craned his neck, looking for the hypospray. She stretched, and sat back. The scent of her perfume, a greener, sharper, less musky scent than she'd worn as

Livia Nu, sublimated from her white skin and tickled Miles's nose. He swallowed.

"Sit down, Lord Vorkosigan."

He took the indicated chair, and waited. She watched him with calculating eyes. The insides of his nostrils began to itch abominably. He kept his hands down, and still. The first question of this interview would not catch him with his fingers shoved up his nose.

"Your Emperor is in terrible trouble, little Vor lord. To save him, you must return to the Oseran Mercenaries, and retake them. When you are back in command, we will communicate further instructions."

Miles boggled. "Danger from what?" he choked. "You?"

"Not at all! Greg is my best friend. The love of my life, at last. I'd do anything for him. I'd even give up my career." She smirked piously. Miles's lip curled in repelled response; she grinned. "If any other course of action occurs to you besides following your instructions to the letter, well . . . it could land Greg in unimaginable troubles. At the hands of worse enemies."

Worse than you? Not possible . . . is it? "Why do you want me in charge of the Dendarii Mercenaries?"

"I can't tell you." Her eyes widened, positively sparkling at her private, ironic joke. "It's a surprise."

"What would you give me to support this enterprise?"

"Transportation to Aslund Station."

"What else? Troops, guns, ships, money?"

"I'm told you could do it with your wits alone. This I wish to see."

"Oser will kill me. He's already tried once."

"That's a chance I must take."

I really like that "I," lady. "You mean me to be killed," Miles deduced. "What if I succeed instead?"

His eyes were starting to water; he sniffed. He would have to rub his madly itching nose soon.

"The key of strategy, little Vor," she explained kindly, "is not to choose *a* path to victory, but to choose so that *all* paths lead to a victory. Ideally. Your death has one use; your success, another. I will emphasize that any premature attempt to contact Barrayar could be very counterproductive. Very."

A nice aphorism on strategy; he'd have to remember that one. "Let me hear my marching orders from my own supreme commander, then. Let me talk to Gregor."

"Ah. *That* will be your reward for success."

"The last guy who bought that line got shot in the back of his head for his credulity. What say we save steps, and you just shoot me now?" He blinked and sniffed, tears now running down the inside of his nose.

"*I* don't wish to shoot you." She actually batted her eyelashes at him, then straightened, frowning. "Really, Lord Vorkosigan, I hardly expected you to dissolve into tears."

He inhaled; his hands made a helpless pleading gesture. Startled, she tossed him a handkerchief from her breast pocket. A green-scented handkerchief. Without other recourse, he pressed it to his face.

"Stop crying, you cowar—" Her sharp order was interrupted by his first, mighty sneeze, followed by a rapid volley of repeats.

"I'm not crying, you bitch, I'm allergic to your goddamn perfume!" Miles managed to choke out between paroxysms.

She held her hand to her forehead and broke into giggles; real ones, not mannered ploys for a change. The real, spontaneous Cavilo at last; he'd been right, her sense of humor was vile. "Oh, dear," she gasped.

"This gives me the most marvelous idea for a gas grenade. A pity I'll never . . . ah, well."

His sinuses throbbed like kettle drums. She shook her head helplessly, and tapped out something on her comconsole.

"I think I had best speed you on your way, before you explode," she told him.

Bent over in his seat wheezing, his water-clouded gaze fell on his brown felt slippers. "Can I at least have a pair of boots for this trip?"

She pursed her lips in a moment of thought. " . . . No," she decided. "It will be more interesting to see you carry on just as you are."

"In this uniform, on Aslund, I'll be like a cat in a dog suit," he protested. "Shot on sight by mistake."

"By mistake . . . on purpose . . . goodness, you're going to have an exciting time." She keyed the door lock open.

He was still sneezing and gasping as the guards came in to take him away. Cavilo was still laughing.

The effects of her poisonous perfume took half an hour to wear off, by which time he was locked in a tiny cabin aboard an inner-system ship. They had boarded via a lock on the *Kurin's Hand;* he hadn't even set foot on Vervain Station again. Not a chance of a break for it.

He checked out the cabin. Its bed and lavatory arrangements were highly reminiscent of his last cell. Space duty, hah. The vast vistas of the wide universe, hah. The glory of the Imperial Service—un-hah. He'd lost Gregor. . . . *I may be small, but I screw up big because I'm standing on the shoulders of GIANTS.* He tried pounding on the door and screaming into the intercom. No one came.

It's a surprise.

He could surprise them all by hanging himself, a briefly attractive notion. But there was nothing up high to hook his belt on.

All right. This courier-type ship was swifter than the lumbering freighter in which he and Gregor had taken three days to cross the system last time, but it wasn't instantaneous. He had at least a day and a half to do some serious thinking, he and Admiral Naismith.

It's a surprise. God.

An officer and a guard came for him, very close to the time Miles estimated they would arrive back at Aslund Station's defense perimeter. *But we haven't docked yet. This seems premature.* His nervous exhaustion still responded to a shot of adrenaline; he inhaled, trying to clear his frenzy-fogged brain back to alertness again. Much more of this, though, and no amount of adrenaline would do him any good. The officer led him through the short corridors of the little ship to Nav and Com.

The Ranger captain was present, leaning over the communication console manned by his second officer. The pilot and flight engineer were busy at their stations.

"If they board, they'll arrest him, and he'll be automatically delivered as ordered," the second officer was saying.

"If they arrest him, they could arrest us too. She said to plant him, and she didn't care if it was head or feet first. She didn't order us to get ourselves interned," said the captain.

A voice from the comm; "This is the picket ship *Ariel*, Aslund Navy Contract Auxiliary, calling the *C6-WG* out of Vervain Hubside Station. Cease accelerating, and clear your portside lock for boarding for pre-docking inspection. Aslund Station reserves the right to deny you docking privileges if you fail to cooperate in pre-docking inspection." The voice took on a cheery tone, "I reserve the right to open fire if you don't stand and deliver in one minute. That's enough stalling, boys." The voice, once gone ironic, was suddenly intensely familiar. *Bel?*

"Cease accelerating," the captain ordered, and motioned the second to close the comm channel. "Hey you, Rotha," he called to Miles. "Come over here."

So *I'm "Rotha" again.* Miles mustered a smarmy smile, and sidled closer. He eyed the viewer, striving to conceal his hungry interest. The *Ariel?* Yes, there it was in the vid display, the sleek Illyrican-built cruiser . . . did Bel Thorne still command her? *How can I get myself onto that ship?*

"Don't throw me out there!" Miles protested urgently. "The Oserans are after my hide. I swear, I didn't know the plasma arcs were defective!"

"What plasma arcs?" asked the captain.

"I'm an arms dealer. I sold them some plasma arcs. Cheap. Turns out they had a tendency to lock on overload and blow their user's hand off. I didn't know, I got them wholesale."

The Ranger captain's right hand opened and closed in sympathetic identification. He rubbed his palm unconsciously on his trousers, back of his plasma arc holster. He studied Miles, frowning sourly. "Head first it is," he said after a moment. "Lieutenant, you and the corporal take this little mutant to the portside personnel lock, pack him in a bod-pod, and eject him. We're going home."

"No," said Miles weakly, as they each took an arm. *Yes!* He dragged his feet, careful not to offer enough resistance to risk his bones. "You're not going to space me . . . !" The *Ariel,* my God . . .

"Oh, the Aslunder merc'll pick you up," said the captain. "Maybe. If they don't decide you're a bomb, and try to set you off in space with plasma fire from their ship or something." Smiling slightly at this vision, he turned back to the comm, and intoned in a bored traffic-control sing-song, "*Ariel,* ah, this is the *C6-WG.* We chose to, ah, change our filed flight plan and return to Vervain Station. We therefore have no need for pre-docking inspection. We are going to leave you a, ah, small parting gift, though. Quite small. What you choose to do with it is your problem. . . ."

The door to Nav and Com closed behind them. A few meters of corridor and a sharp turn brought Miles and his handlers to a personnel hatch. The corporal held Miles, who struggled; the lieutenant opened a locker and shook out a bod-pod.

The bod-pod was a cheap inflatable life-support unit designed to be entered in seconds by endangered passengers, suitable either for pressurization emergencies or abandoning ship. They were also dubbed idiot-balloons. They required no knowledge to operate because they had no controls, merely a few hours of recycleable air and a locator-beeper. Passive, foolproof, and not recommended for claustrophobes, they were very cost-effective in saving lives—when adequate pick-up ships arrived in time.

Miles emitted a realistic wail as he was stuffed into the bod-pod's dank, plastic-smelling interior. A jerk of the rip cord, and it sealed and inflated automatically. He had a brief, horrible flashback to the mud-sunken bubble-shelter on Kyril Island, and choked back a real scream. He was tumbled as his captors rolled the pod into the air lock. A whoosh, a thump, a lurch, and he was free-falling in pitch darkness.

The spherical pod was little more than a meter in diameter. Miles, half-doubled-up, felt around, his stomach and inner ear protesting the spin imparted by the ejecting kick outward, till his shaking fingers found what he hoped was a cold-light tube. He squeezed it, and was rewarded with a nauseous greenish glow.

The silence was profound, broken only by the tiny hiss of the air recycler and his ragged breathing. *Well . . . it's better than the last time somebody tried to shove me out an air lock.* He had several minutes in which to imagine all the possible courses of action the *Ariel* might take instead of picking him up. He had just discarded skin-crawling anticipation of the ship opening fire on him in favor of abandonment to cold dark asphyxiation, when he and his pod were wrenched by a tractor beam.

The tractor beam's operator, clearly, had ham hands and palsy, but after a few minutes of juggling, the return of gravity and outside sound reassured Miles he'd been safely stowed in a working air lock. The swish of the inner door, garbled human voices. Another moment, and the idiot balloon began to roll. He yelped loudly, and curled up into a protective ball to roll with the flow till the motion stopped. He sat up, and took a deep breath, and tried to straighten his uniform.

Muffled thumps against the bod-pod's fabric. "Somebody in there?"

"Yeah!" Miles called back.

"Just a minute . . ."

Squeaks, clinks., and a rending grind, as the seals were broken. The bod-pod began to collapse as the air sighed out. Miles fought his way clear of its folds, and stood, shakily, with all the gracelessness and indignity of a newly hatched chick.

He was in a small cargo bay. Three grey-and-white-uniformed soldiers stood in a circle around him, aiming stunners and nerve-disruptors at his head. A slim officer with captain's insignia leaned with one foot on a canister, watching Miles emerge.

The officer's neat uniform and soft brown hair gave no clue whether one was looking at a delicate man or an unusually determined woman. This ambiguity was deliberately cultivated; Bel Thorne was a Betan hermaphrodite, minority descendant of a century-past social/genetic experiment that had not caught on. Thorne's expression melted from skepticism to astonishment as Miles rose into view.

Miles grinned back. "Hello, Pandora. The gods send you a gift. But there's a catch."

"Isn't there always?" Face lighting with delight, Thorne strode forward to grasp Miles's waist with bubbling enthusiasm. "Miles!" Thorne held Miles away again, and gazed avidly down into his face. "What are you doing here?"

"Somehow, I figured that might be your first question," Miles sighed.

"—and what are you doing in the Ranger-suit?"

"*Goodness,* I'm glad you're not of the shoot-first-and-ask-questions-later school." Miles kicked his slippered feet clear of the deflated bod-pod. The soldiers, somewhat uncertainly, held their aim. "Ah—" Miles gestured toward them.

"Stand down, men," Thorne ordered. "It's all right."

"I wish that were true," Miles said. "Bel, we've got to talk."

Thorne's cabin aboard the *Ariel* was the same wrenching mix of familiarity and change Miles had encountered in all the mercenary matters. The shapes, the sounds, the smells of the *Ariel's* interior triggered cascades of memory. The captain's cabin was now overlaid with Bel's personal possessions; vid library, weapons, campaign souvenirs including a half-melted space-armor helmet that had been slagged saving Thorne's life, now made into a lamp; a small cage housing an exotic pet from Earth Thorne called a *hamster*.

Between sips of a cup of Thorne's private stock of non-synthetic tea, Miles gave Thorne the Admiral Naismith version of reality, closely related to the one he'd given Oser and Tung; the Hub evaluation assignment, the mystery employer, etc. Gregor, of course, was edited out, together with any mention of Barrayar; Miles Naismith spoke with a pure Betan accent. Otherwise Miles stuck as close as he could to the facts of his sojourn with Randall's Rangers.

"So Lieutenant Lake's been captured by our competitors," Thorne mused upon Miles's description of the blond lieutenant he'd passed in the *Kurin's Hand's* brig. "Couldn't happen to a nicer fellow, but—we'd better change our codes again."

"Quite." Miles set down his cup, and leaned forward. "I was authorized by my employer not only to observe but to prevent war in the Hegen Hub, if possible." Well, sort of. "I'm afraid it may no longer be possible. What does it look like from your end?"

Thorne frowned. "We were last in-dock five days ago. That's when the Aslunders concocted this pre-docking inspection routine. All the smaller ships were pressed into round-the-clock service on it. With their military station nearing completion, our employers are getting jumpier about sabotage—bombs, biologicals . . ."

"I won't argue with that. What about, ah, Fleet internal matters?"

"You mean rumors of your death, life, and/or resurrection? They're all over, fourteen garbled versions. I'd have discounted 'em—you've been sighted before, y'know—but then suddenly Oser arrested Tung."

"What?" Miles bit his lip. "Only Tung? Not Elena, Mayhew, Chodak?"

"Only Tung."

"That makes no sense. If he'd arrested Tung, he'd have fast-penta'd him, and he'd have to have spilled on Elena. Unless she's been left free as bait."

"Things got real tense, when Tung was taken. Ready to explode. I think if Oser'd moved on Elena and Baz it would have sparked the war right then. Yet he hasn't backed down and reinstated Tung. Very unstable. Oser's taking care to keep the old inner circle separated, that's why I've been out here for nearly a bloody week. But last time I saw Baz he was damn near edgy enough to commit to fight. And that was the last thing he'd wanted to do."

Miles exhaled slowly. "A fight . . . is exactly what Commander Cavilo wants. It's why she shipped me back gift-wrapped in that . . . undignified package. The Bod-pod of Discord. She doesn't care if I win or lose, as long as her enemy's forces are thrown into chaos just as she springs her *surprise.*"

"Have you figured out what her surprise is, yet?"

"No. The Rangers were setting up for some sort of ground-attack, at one point. Sending me here suggests they're aiming for Aslund, against all strategic logic. Or something else? The woman's mind is incredibly twisted. Gah!" He slapped his fist gently into his palm in nervous rhythm. "I've got to talk to Oser. And he's got to listen this time. I've thought it over. Cooperation between us may be the one and only course of action Cavilo doesn't expect, doesn't have a half-sawn-through branch of her strategy-tree ready and waiting for me. . . . Are you willing to put it all on the line for me, Bel?"

Thorne pursed lips judiciously. "From here, yeah. The *Ariel's* the fleet's fastest ship. I can outrun retribution if I have to." Thorne grinned.

Should we run to Barrayar? No—Cavilo still held

Gregor. Better appear to be following instructions. For a time yet.

Miles took a long breath, and settled himself firmly in the station chair in the *Ariel's* Nav and Com room. He'd cleaned up, and borrowed a mercenary's grey and white uniform from the smallest woman on the ship. The rolled-up pant cuffs were stuffed neatly out of sight down boots that almost fit. A belt covered the fastener gaping open at the too-narrow waistband. The loose jacket looked all right, sitting down. Permanent alterations later. He nodded to Thorne. "All right. Open your channel."

A buzz, a glitter, and Admiral Oser's hawk face materialized over the vid plate. "Yes, what is it—you!" His teeth shut with a beak's snap; his hand, a vague unfocused blur to the side, tapped on intercom keys and vid controls.

He can't throw me out the air lock this time, but he can cut me off. Time to talk fast.

Miles leaned forward and smiled. "Hello, Admiral Oser. I've completed my evaluation of Vervani forces in the Hegan Hub. And my conclusion is, you are in deep trouble."

"How did you get on this secured channel?" snarled Oser. "Tight-beam, double-encode—comm officer, trace this!"

"How, you will be able to determine in a few minutes. You'll have to keep me on-line till you do," said Miles. "But your enemy is at Vervain Station, not here. Not Pol, not Jackson's Whole. And most certainly not me. Note I said Vervain Station, not Vervain. You know Cavilo? Your opposite number, across-system?"

"I've encountered her once or twice." Oser's face was guarded now, waiting for his scrambling tech team to report.

"Face like an angel, mind like a rabid mongoose?"

Oser's lips twitched very slightly. "You've met her."

Oh, yes. She and I had several heart-to-heart talks. They were . . . educational. Information is the most valuable trade-good in the Hub right now. At any rate, mine is. I want to deal."

Oser held up his hand for a pause, and keyed off-line briefly. When his face returned, its expression was black. "Captain Thorne, this is mutiny!"

Thorne leaned into the range of the vid pick-up, and said brightly, "No, sir, it's not. We are trying to save your ungrateful neck, if you will permit it. Listen to the man. He has lines we don't."

"He has lines, all right," and under his breath, "Damn Betans, sticking together. . . ."

"Whether you fight me, or I fight you, Admiral Oser, we both lose," said Miles rapidly.

"You can't win," said Oser. "You cannot take my fleet. Not with the *Ariel*."

"The *Ariel's* just a starter-set, if it comes to that. But no, I probably can't win. What I can do is make an unholy mess. Divide your forces—screw you with your employer—every weapon-charge you expend, every piece of equipment that's damaged, every soldier hurt or killed is *pure loss* in an in-fight like this. Nobody wins but Cavilo, who expends nothing. Which is precisely what she sent me back here for. How much profit do you foresee in doing precisely what your enemy wishes you to, eh?"

Miles waited, breathless. Oser's jaw worked, chewing over this impassioned argument. "What's your profit?" he asked at last.

"Ah. I'm afraid I'm the dangerous variable in that calculation, Admiral. I'm not in it for profit." Miles grinned. "So I don't care what I wreck."

"Any information you had from Cavilo is worth shit," said Oser.

He begins to barter—he's hooked, he's hooked. . . . Miles tamped down exultation, cultivated a serious expression. "Anything Cavilo says must certainly be sifted with great care. But, ah . . . beauty is as beauty does. And I've found her vulnerable side."

"Cavilo has no vulnerable side."

"Yes, she does. Her passion for utility. Her self-interest."

"I fail to see how that makes her vulnerable."

"Precisely why you need to add *me* to your staff at once. You need my vision."

"Hire you!" Oser recoiled in astonishment.

Well, he'd achieved surprise, anyway. A military objective of sorts. "I understand the post of Chief-of-Staff/Tactical is now empty."

Oser's expression flowed from astonished to stunned to a kind of amused fury. "You're insane."

"No, just in a tearing hurry. Admiral, there's nothing irrevocable gone wrong between us. Yet. You attacked me—not the other way around—and now you expect me to attack you back. But I'm not on holiday, and I don't have time to waste on personal amusements like revenge."

Oser's eyes narrowed. "What about Tung?"

Miles shrugged. "Keep him locked up, for now, if you insist. Unharmed, of course." *Just don't tell him I said so.*

"Suppose I hang him."

"Ah . . . *that* would be irrevocable." Miles paused. "I will point out, jailing Tung is like cutting off your right hand before heading into battle."

"What battle? With whom?"

"It's a surprise. Cavilo's surprise. Though I've

developed an idea or two on the problem, that I'd be willing to share."

"Would you?" Oser had that same man-sucking-a-lemon expression Miles had now and then surprised on Illyan's face. It seemed almost homey.

Miles continued, "As an alternative to my becoming your employee, I'm willing to become your employer. I'm authorized to offer a bona fide contract, all the usual perqs, equipment replacement, insurance, from my . . . sponsor." *Illyan, hear my plea.* "Not in conflict with Aslund's interests. You can collect twice for the same fight, and you don't even have to switch sides. A mercenary's dream."

"What guarantees can you offer up front?"

"It seems to me that I'm the one who's owed a guarantee, sir. Let us begin with small steps. I won't start a mutiny; you stop trying to thrust me out air locks. I will join you openly—everyone to know I've arrived—I will make my information available to you." How thin his "information" seemed, in the breeze of these airy promises. No numbers, no troop movements; all *intentions,* shifting mental topographies of loyalty, ambition, and betrayal. "We will confer. You may even have an angle I lack. Then we go on from there."

Oser thinned his lips, bemused, half-persuaded, deeply suspicious.

"The risk, I would point out," said Miles, "the personal risk, is more mine than yours."

"I think—"

Miles hung suspended on the mercenary's words.

"I think I'm going to regret this." Oser sighed.

The detailed negotiations just to bring the *Ariel* into dock took another half day. As the initial excitement wore off, Thorne became more thoughtful. As the *Ariel* actually maneuvered into its clamps, Thorne grew positively meditative.

"I'm still not exactly sure what's supposed to keep Oser from bringing us in, stunning us, and hanging us at leisure," Thorne said, buckling on a sidearm. Thorne kept the complaint to an undertone, in care for the tender ears of the escort squad kitting up nearby in the *Ariel's* shuttle hatch corridor.

"Curiosity," said Miles firmly.

"All right, stun, fast-penta, and hang, then."

"If he fast-penta's me, I'll tell him exactly the facts I was going to tell him anyway." *And a few more besides, alas.* "And he'll have fewer doubts. So much the better."

Miles was rescued from further hollow flummery by the clank and hiss of the flex tube's sealing. Thorne's sergeant undogged the hatch without hesitation, though he was also careful not to stand silhouetted in the aperture, Miles noted.

"Squad, form up!" the sergeant ordered. His six people checked their stunners. Thorne and the sergeant in addition bore nerve disrupters, a nicely calculated mix of weapons; stunners to allow for human error, the nerve disrupters to encourage the other side not to risk mistakes. Miles went unarmed. With a mental salute to Cavilo—well, a rude gesture, actually—he'd put his felt slippers back on. Thorne at his side, he took the lead of the little procession and marched through the flex tube into one of the Aslunder military station's almost-finished docking bays.

True to his word, Oser had a party of witnesses lined up and waiting. The squad of twenty or so bore a mix of weapons almost identical to the *Ariel's* group. "We're outnumbered," muttered Thorne.

"It's all in the mind," Miles muttered in return. "March like you had an empire at your back." *And don't look over your shoulder, they may be gaining on us. They'd better be gaining on us.* "The more people who see me, the better."

Oser himself stood waiting in parade rest, looking highly dyspeptic. Elena—*Elena!*—stood at his side, unarmed, face frozen. Her tight-lipped stare at Miles was tense with suspicion, not of his motives, perhaps, but certainly of his methods. *Now what foolishness?* her eyes asked. Miles gave her the briefest of ironic nods before saluting Oser.

Reluctantly, Oser returned the military courtesy. "Now—'Admiral'—let us return to the *Triumph* and get down to business," he grated.

"Indeed, yes. But let's have a little tour of this Station on the way, eh? The non-top-secured areas, of course. My last view was so . . . rudely cut short, after all. After you, Admiral?"

Oser gritted his teeth. "Oh, after you, Admiral."

It became a parade. Miles led them around for a good forty-five minutes, including a march through the cafeteria during the dinner rush with several noisy stops to greet by name the few old Dendarii he recognized, and favor the others with blinding smiles. He left babble in his wake, those in the dark demanding explanation from those in the know.

An Aslunder work crew was busy tearing out fiberboard paneling, and he paused to compliment them on their labors. Elena seized an opportunity of Oser's distraction to bend down and breathe fiercely in Miles's ear, "*Where's Gregor?*"

"Thereby hangs—me, if I fail to get him back," Miles whispered. "Too complicated, tell you later."

"Oh, God." She rolled her eyes.

When he had, judging from the admiral's darkening complexion, just about reached the limits of Oser's strained tolerance, Miles suffered himself to be led

Triumph-ward again. There. Obedient to Cavilo's orders, Miles had made no attempt to contact Barrayar. But if Ungari couldn't find him after this, it was time to fire the man. A prairie bird thrumming out a mad mating dance could scarcely have put on a more conspicuous display.

Finishing touches on construction were still in progress around the *Triumph's* docking bay as Miles marched his parade across it. A few Aslunder workers in tan, light blue, and green leaned over to goggle down from catwalks. Military techs in their dark blue uniforms paused in mid-installation to stare, then had to re-sort connections and realign bolts. Miles refrained from smiling and waving, lest Oser's set jaw crack. No more baiting, time to get serious. The thirty or so mercenaries could change from honor guard to prison guard with his next roll of the dice.

Thorne's tall sergeant, marching beside Miles, gazed around the bay, noting new construction. "The robotic loaders should be fully automated by this time tomorrow," he noted. "That'll be an improvement—*crap!*" His hand descended abruptly on Miles's head, shoving him downward. The sergeant half-spun, clawed hand arcing toward his holster, when the crackling blue bolt of a nerve disrupter charge struck him square in the chest at the level Miles's head had been. He spasmed, his breath stopping. The smell of ozone, hot plastic, and blistered meat slapped Miles's nose. Miles kept on diving, hitting the deck, rolling. A second bolt splattered on the deck, its outwashing field stinging like twenty wasps up Miles's outstretched arm. He jerked his hand back.

As the sergeant's corpse collapsed, Miles grabbed at the man's jacket and jerked himself underneath, burrowing his head and spine under where the meat was thickest, the sergeant's torso. He drew his arms and legs in as tight as he could. Another bolt crackled into the deck nearby, then two struck the body in close succession. Even with the absorbing mass between it was worse than the blow of a shock-stick on high power.

Miles's ringing ears heard screaming, thumping, yelling, running, chaos. The chirping buzz of stunner fire. A voice. "He's up there! Go get him!", and another voice, high and hoarse. "You spotted him—he's yours. *You* go get him!" Another bolt hit the decking.

The weight of the big man, the stench of his fatal injury, pressed into Miles's face. He wished the fellow'd massed another fifty kilos. No wonder Cavilo had been willing to front twenty thousand Betan dollars toward a line on a shield-suit. Of all the loathsome weapons Miles had ever faced, this had to be the most personally terrifying. A head injury that didn't quite kill him, but stole his humanity and left him animal or vegetable was the worst nightmare. His intellect was surely his sole justification for existence. Without it . . .

The crackle of a nerve disrupter *not* aimed his way penetrated his hearing. Miles turned his head to scream, cloth- and meat-muffled, "Stunners! Stunners! We want him alive for questioning!" *He's yours, you go get him.* . . . He should shove out from under this body and join the fight. But if he was the assassin's special target, and why else pump charges into a corpse . . . perhaps he ought to stay right here. He squirmed, trying to draw his hands and legs in tighter.

The shouting died down; the firing stopped. Someone kneeling beside him tried to roll the sergeant's body off Miles. It took Miles a moment to realize he had to unclutch the dead man's uniform jacket before he could be rescued. He straightened his fingers with difficulty.

Thorne's face wavered over him, white and breathing open-mouthed, urgent. "Are you all right, Admiral?"

"I think," Miles panted.

"He was aiming at you," Thorne reported. "Only."

"I noticed," Miles stuttered. "I'm only lightly fried." Thorne helped him sit up. He was shaking as badly as after the shock-stick beating. He regarded his spasming hands, lowered one to touch the corpse beside him in morbid wonder. *Every day of the rest of my life will be your gift. And I don't even know your name.* "Your sergeant—what was his name?"

"Collins."

"Collins. Thanks."

"Good man."

"I saw."

Oser came up, looking strained. "Admiral Naismith, this was *not* my doing."

"Oh?" Miles blinked. "Help me up, Bel. . . ." That might have been a mistake; Thorne then had to help him keep standing as his muscles twitched. He felt weak, washed-out as a sick man. *Elena—where? She had no weapon. . . .*

There she was, with another female mercenary. They were dragging a man in the dark blue uniform of an Aslunder ranker toward Miles and Oser. Each woman held a booted foot; the man's arms trailed nervelessly across the deck. Stunned? Dead? They dropped the feet with a thump beside Miles, with the matter-of-fact air of lionesses delivering prey to their cubs. Miles stared down at a very familiar face indeed. *General Metzov. What are you doing here?*

"Do you recognize this man?" Oser asked an Aslunder officer who had hurried up to join them. "Is he one of yours?"

"I don't know him—" The Aslunder knelt to check for IDs. "He has a valid pass. . . ."

"He could have had me, and gotten away," said Elena to Miles, "but he kept firing at you. You were bright to stay put."

A triumph of wit, or a failure of nerve? "Yes. Quite." Miles made another attempt to stand on his own, gave up, and leaned on Thorne. "I hope you didn't kill him."

"Just stunned," said Elena, holding up the weapon as evidence. Some intelligent person must have tossed it to her when the melee began. "He probably has a broken wrist."

"Who *is* he?" asked Oser. Quite sincerely, Miles judged.

"Why, Admiral," Miles bared his teeth, "I told you I was going to deliver you more intelligence data than your Section could collect in a month. May I present," rather like an entree at that—he made a gesture designed to evoke a waiter lifting a domed cover from a silver platter, but which probably looked like another muscle spasm, "General Stanis Metzov. Second-in-command, Randall's Rangers."

"Since when do senior staff officers undertake field assassinations?"

"Excuse me, second-in-command as of three days ago. That may have changed. He was up to his stringy neck in Cavilo's schemes. You, I, and he have an appointment with a hypospray."

Oser stared. "You planned this?"

"Why do you think I spent the last hour flitting around the Station, if not to smoke him out?" Miles said brightly. *He must have been stalking me this whole time. I think I'm going to throw up. Have I just claimed to be brilliant, or incredibly stupid?* Oser looked like he was trying to figure out the answer to that same question.

Miles stared down at Metzov's unconscious form, trying to think. Had Metzov been sent by Cavilo, or was this murder attempt entirely on his own time? If sent by Cavilo—had she planned him to fall alive into her enemies' hands? If not, was there a back-up assassin around here somewhere, and if so was his target Metzov, if Metzov succeeded, or Miles, if Metzov failed? Or both? *I need to sit down and draw a flowchart.*

Medical squads had arrived. "Yes, sickbay," said Miles faintly. "Till my old friend here wakes up."

"I'll agree to that," said Oser, shaking his head in something akin to dismay.

"Better put a protective as well as holding guard on our prisoner. I'm not sure if he was meant to survive capture."

"Right," Oser agreed bemusedly.

Thorne supporting one arm and Elena the other, Miles staggered home into the *Triumph's* hatchway.

CHAPTER FOURTEEN

Miles sat trembling on a bench in a glassed-in cubicle normally used for bio-isolation in the *Triumph's* sickbay, and watched Elena tie General Metzov to a chair with a tangle-cord. It would have given Miles a smug sense of turn-about, if the interrogation upon which they were about to embark was not so fraught with dangerous complications. Elena was disarmed again. Two stunner-armed men stood guard beyond the soundproof transparent door, glancing in occasionally. It had taken all Miles's eloquence to keep the audience for this initial questioning limited to himself, Oser, and Elena.

"How hot can this man's information be?" Oser had inquired irritably. "They let him go out in the field."

"Hot enough that I think you should have a chance to think about it before broadcasting it to a committee," Miles had argued. "You'll still have the recording."

Metzov looked sick and silent, tight-mouthed and unresponsive. His right wrist was neatly bandaged.

Awakening from stun accounted for the sick; the silence was futile, and everyone knew it. It was a kind of strange courtesy, not to badger him with questions before the fast-penta cut in.

Now Oser frowned at Miles. "Are you up to this yet?"

Miles glanced down at his still-shaking hands. "As long as no one asks me to do brain surgery, yes. Proceed. I have reason to suspect that time is of the essence."

Oser nodded to Elena, who held up a hypospray to calibrate the dose, and pressed it to Metzov's neck. Metzov's eyes shut briefly in despair. After a moment his clenched hands relaxed. The muscles of his face unlocked to sag into a loose, idiotic smile. The transformation was most unpleasant to watch. Without the tension his face looked aged.

Elena checked Metzov's pulse and pupils. "All right. He's all yours, gentlemen." She stepped back to lean against the door frame with folded arms, her expression almost as closed as Metzov's had been.

Miles opened his hand. "After you, Admiral."

Oser's mouth twisted. "Thank you. Admiral." He walked over to stare speculatively into Metzov's face. "General Metzov. Is your name Stanis Metzov?"

Metzov grinned. "Yeah, that's me."

"Presently second-in-command, Randall's Rangers?"

"Yeah."

"Who sent you to assassinate Admiral Naismith?"

Metzov's face took on an expression of sunny bewilderment. "Who?"

"Call me Miles," Miles suggested. "He knows me under a . . . pseudonym." His chance of getting through this interview with his identity undisclosed equalled that of a snowball surviving a worm-hole jump to the center of a sun, but why rush the complications?

"Who sent you to kill Miles?"

"Cavie did. Of course. He escaped, you see. I was the only one she could trust . . . trust . . . the bitch. . . ."

Miles's brow twitched. "In fact, Cavilo shipped me back here herself," he informed Oser. "General Metzov was therefore set up. But to what end? My turn, now, I think."

Oser made the after-you gesture and stepped back. Miles tottered off his bench and into Metzov's line-of-sight. Metzov breathed rage even through the fast-penta euphoria, then grinned vilely.

Miles decided to start with the question that had driven him most nuts the longest. "Who—what target—was your ground-attack planned to be upon?"

"Vervain," said Metzov.

Even Oser's jaw dropped. The blood thudded in Miles's ears in the stunned silence.

"Vervain is your *employer*," Oser choked.

"God—God!—finally it adds up!" Miles almost capered; it came out a stagger, which Elena lurched away from the wall to catch. "Yes, yes, *yes* . . ."

"It's *insane*," said Oser. "So that's Cavilo's surprise."

"That's not the end of it, I'll bet. Cavilo's drop forces are bigger than ours by far, but no way are they big enough to take on a fully settled planet like Vervain on the ground. They can only raid and run."

"Raid and run, right," smiled Metzov equably.

"What was your particular target, then?" asked Miles urgently.

"Banks . . . art museums . . . gene banks . . . hostages . . ."

"That's a *pirate* raid," said Oser. "What the hell were you going to do with the loot?"

"Drop it off on Jackson's Whole, on the way out; they fence it."

"How did you figure to escape the irate Vervani Navy, then?" asked Miles.

"Hit them just before the new fleet comes on-line. Cetagandan invasion fleet'll catch 'em in orbital dock. Sitting targets. Easy."

The silence this time was utter.

"*That's* Cavilo's surprise," Miles whispered at last. "Yeah. That one's *worthy* of her."

"Cetagandan . . . invasion?" Oser unconsciously began to chew a fingernail.

"God, it fits, it fits." Miles began to pace the cubicle with uneven steps. "What's the only way to take a wormhole jump? From both sides at once. The Vervani aren't Cavilo's employers—the *Cetagandans* are." He turned to point at the slack-lipped, nodding general. "And now I see Metzov's place, clear as day."

"Pirate," shrugged Oser.

"No—goat."

"What?"

"This man—you apparently don't know—was cashiered from the Barrayaran Imperial Service for brutality."

Oser blinked. "From the Barrayaran Service? That must have taken some doing."

Miles bit down a twinge of irritation. "Well, yes. He, ah . . . took on the wrong victim. But anyway, don't you see it? The Cetagandan invasion fleet jumps through into Vervani local space on Cavilo's invitation—probably on Cavilo's signal. The Rangers raid, do a fast trash of Vervain. The Cetagandans, out of the kindness of their hearts, 'rescue' the planet from the treacherous mercenaries. The Rangers run. Metzov is left behind as goat—just like throwing the guy out of the troika to the wolves," oops, that wasn't a very Betan metaphor, "to be publicly hung by the Cetagandans to demonstrate their 'good faith.' See, this evil Barrayaran harmed you, you need our Imperial protection from the Barrayaran Imperial threat, and here we are.

"And Cavilo gets paid *three* times. Once by the Vervani, once by the Cetagandans, and the third time by Jackson's Whole when she fences her loot on the way out. Everybody profits. Except the Vervani, of course." He paused to catch his breath.

Oser was beginning to look convinced, and worried. "Do you think the Cetagandans plan to punch through into the Hub? Or will they stop at Vervain?"

"Of course they'll punch through. The Hub is the strategic target; Vervain is just a stepping stone to it. Hence the 'bad mercenary' setup. The Cetagandans want to expend as little energy as possible pacifying Vervain. They'll probably label them an 'allied satrapy,' hold the space routes, and barely touch down on the planet. Absorb them economically over a generation. The question is, will the Cetagandans stop at Pol? Will they try to take it on this one move, or leave it as a buffer between them and Barrayar? Conquest or wooing? If they can bait the Barrayarans into attacking through Pol without permission, it might even drive the Polians into a Cetagandan alliance—agh!" He paced again.

Oser looked as if he'd bitten into something nasty. With half a worm in it. "I wasn't hired to take on the Cetagandan Empire. I expected to be fighting the Vervani's mercenaries, at most, if the whole thing didn't just fizzle out. If the Cetagandans arrive here, in force in the Hub, we'll be . . . trapped. Penned up with a cul-de-sac at our backs." And in a trailing mutter, "Maybe we ought to think about getting out while the getting's good. . . ."

"But Admiral Oser, don't you realize," Miles pointed to Metzov, "*she'd* never have let him out of her sight with all this in his head if it was still an active plan.

She may have meant him to die trying to kill me, but there was always the chance he might not—that just this sort of interrogation might result. All this is the *old* plan. There must be a *new* plan." *And I think I know what it is.* "There is . . . another factor. A new X in the equation." *Gregor.* "Unless I miss my guess, the Cetagandan invasion is now a considerable embarrassment to Cavilo."

"Admiral Naismith, I would believe that Cavilo would double-cross anyone you care to name—except the Cetagandans. They'd spend a generation, pursuing their revenge. She couldn't run far enough. She wouldn't live to spend her profits. Incidentally, what conceivable profit outweighs triple pay?"

But if she expects to have the Barrayaran Empire to defend her from retribution—all our Security resources . . . "I see one way she could expect to get away with it," said Miles. "If it works out like she wants, she'll have all the protection she wants. And all the profits."

It could work, it really could. If Gregor were indeed under her spell. And if two embarrassingly hostile character witnesses, Miles and General Metzov, conveniently killed each other. Abandoning her fleet, she could take Gregor and flee before the oncoming Cetagandans, presenting herself to Barrayar as Gregor's "rescuer" at great personal cost; if in addition a smitten Gregor urged her as his fiancee, worthy mother to a future scion of the military caste—the romantic appeal of the drama could swing popular support enough to overwhelm cooler advisors' judgments. God knew Miles's own mother had laid the groundwork for that scenario. *She could really bring this off. Empress Cavilo of Barrayar. It even scans.* And she could cap her career by betraying absolutely *everybody*, even her own forces. . . .

"Miles, the look on your face . . ." said Elena in worry.

"When?" said Oser. "When will the Cetagandans attack?" He got Metzov's wandering attention, and repeated the question.

"Only Cavie knows." Metzov snickered. "Cavie knows everything."

"It has to be imminent," Miles argued. "It may even be starting now. Guessing from Cavilo's timing of my return here. She meant the De—the Fleet to be paralyzed with our infighting right now."

"If that's true," murmured Oser, "what to do . . . ?"

"We're too far away. A day and a half from the action. Which will be at the Vervain Station wormhole. And beyond, in Vervani local space. We have to get closer. We have to move the Fleet across-system—pin Cavilo up against the Cetagandans. Blockade her—"

"Whoa! I'm not mounting a headlong attack against the Cetagandan Empire!" interrupted Oser sharply.

"You must. You'll have to fight them sooner or later. You pick the time, or they will. The only chance of stopping them is at the wormhole. Once they're through, it will be impossible."

"If I moved my fleet away from Aslund, the Vervani would think we were attacking them."

"And mobilize, go on the alert. Good. But in the wrong direction—not good. We would end up being a feint for Cavilo. Damn! No doubt another branch of her strategy-tree."

"Suppose—if the Cetagandans are now such an embarrassment to Cavilo as you claim—she doesn't send her code?"

"Oh, she still needs them. But for a different purpose. She needs them to flee from. And to mass-murder her witnesses for her. But she doesn't need them to succeed. In fact, she now needs their invasion to bog down. If she's really thinking as long-term as she should be, in her new plan."

Oser shook his head, as if to clear it. "Why?"

"Our only hope—Aslund's only hope—is to capture Cavilo, and fight the Cetagandans to a standstill at the Vervain Station worm-hole. No, wait—we have to hold both sides of the Hub-Vervain jump. Until reinforcements arrive."

"What reinforcements?"

"Aslund, Pol—once the Cetagandans actually materialize in force, they'll see their threat. And if Pol comes in on Barrayar's side instead of Cetaganda's, Barrayar can pour forces through via them. The Cetagandans can be stopped, if everything occurs in the right order." But could Gregor be rescued alive? Not a path to victory, but all paths . . .

"Would the Barrayarans come in?"

"Oh, I think so. Your counter-intelligence must keep track of these things—haven't they noticed a sudden increase in Barrayaran Intelligence activity here in the Hub the last few days?"

"Now that you mention it, yes. Their coded traffic has quadrupled."

Thank God. Maybe relief was closer than he'd dared hope. "Have you broken any of their codes?" Miles asked brightly, while he was at it.

"Only the least sensitive one, so far."

"Ah. Good. That is, too bad."

Oser stood with his arms folded, gnawing at his lip, intensely inward for a full minute. It reminded Miles uncomfortably of the meditative expression the admiral'd had just before ordering him shoved out the nearest air lock, barely more than a week back. "No," Oser said at last. "Thanks for the information. In return, I suppose I will spare your life. But we're pulling out. It's not a fight we can possibly win. Only some propaganda-blinded planetary force, with a planet's resources behind it, can afford that sort of insane self-sacrifice. I designed my fleet to be a fine tactical tool, not a, a damn doorstop made of dead bodies. I'm not a—as you say—goat."

"Not a goat, a spearhead."

"Your 'spearhead' has no spear behind it. No."

"Is that your last word, sir?" asked Miles in a thin voice.

"Yes." Oser reached to key his wrist comm, to call in the waiting guards. "Corporal, this party's going to the brig. Call down and notify them."

The guard saluted through the glass as Oser keyed off.

"But sir," Elena approached him, her arms raised in pleading. With a snake-strike sideways flick of her wrist, she jabbed the hypospray against the side of Oser's neck. His eyes widened, his pulse beat once, twice, three times, as his lips drew back in rage. He tensed to strike her. His blow sagged in mid-arc.

The guards beyond the glass snapped alert at Oser's sudden movement, drawing their stunners. Elena caught Oser's hand and kissed it, smiling gratefully. The guards relaxed; one nudged the other and said something pretty nasty, judging from their grins, but Miles's wits were too momentarily scattered to try to read lips.

Oser swayed and panted, fighting the drug. Elena sidled up the captured arm and slipped a hand cozily around his waist, half-turning him so they stood with their backs to the door. The stereotypical stupid fast-penta smile slipped across and receded from Oser's face, then fixed itself at last.

"He acted like I was unarmed." Elena shook her head in exasperation, and slipped the hypospray into her jacket pocket.

"Now what?" Miles hissed frantically as the guard-corporal bent over the door's code-lock.

"We all go to the brig, I guess. Tung's there," said Elena.

"Ah . . ." Oh-hell-we'll-never-bring-this-off. Had to try. Miles smiled cheerily at the entering guards, and helped them release Metzov, largely getting in their way and keeping their attention off the peculiarly happy-looking Oser. At a moment when their eyes were elsewhere, he tripped Metzov, who staggered.

"You'd better each take one of his arms, he's not too steady," Miles told the guards. He was none too steady himself, but he managed to block the doorway so the guards and Metzov led the way, himself second, and Elena, arm-in-arm with Oser, followed last. "Come, love, come," he heard Elena intone behind him, like a woman coaxing a cat to her lap.

It was the longest short walk he'd ever taken. He dropped back to growl out of the corner of his mouth to Elena, "All right, we get to the brig, it will be stocked with Oser's finest. What then?"

She bit her lip. "Don't know."

"That's what I was afraid of. Turn right here." They swung around the next corner.

A guard looked back over his shoulder. "Sir?"

"Carry on, boys," Miles called. "When you've got that spy locked up, report back to us at the admiral's cabin."

"Very good, sir."

"Keep walking," breathed Miles. "Keep smiling. . . ."

The guards' footsteps faded. "Where now?" asked Elena. Oser stumbled. "This is untenable."

"Admiral's cabin, why not?" Miles decided. His grin was fixed and fey. Elena's inspired mutinous gesture had given him the best break of the day. He had the momentum now. He wouldn't stop till he was brought down bodily. His head spun with the unutterable relief of at last getting the shifting, writhing, cluttering *might-be-might-be-might-be* nailed to a fixed *is. The time is now. The word is go.*

Maybe. If.

They passed a few Oseran techs. Oser was sort of nodding, Miles hoped it would pass as casual acknowledgment of their salutes. Nobody turned and cried Hey! anyway. Two levels and another turn brought them to the well-remembered corridors of officer's country. They passed the captain's cabin (God, he'd have to deal with Auson, and soon); Oser's palm, pressed by Elena against the lock, admitted them to the quarters Oser had made his flag office. When the door slipped shut behind them Miles realized he'd been holding his breath.

"We're in it now," said Elena, sagging for a moment with her back to the door. "You going to run out on us again?"

"Not this time," Miles replied grimly. "You may have noticed one item I didn't bring up for discussion, down in sickbay."

"Gregor."

"Just so. Cavilo holds him hostage aboard her flagship right now."

Elena's neck bent in dismay. "She means to sell him to the Cetagandans for a bonus, then?"

"No. Weirder than that. She means to marry him."

Elena's lip curled in astonishment. "What? Miles, there's no way she could have got such an impossible notion in her head, unless—"

"Unless Gregor planted it. Which, I believe, he did. Watered and fertilized it, too. What I don't know is whether he was serious, or playing for time. She was very careful to keep us separated. You knew Gregor almost as well as I do. What do you think?"

"It's hard to imagine Gregor love-struck to idiocy.

He was always . . . rather quiet. Almost, well, undersexed. Compared to, say, Ivan."

"I'm not sure that's a fair comparison."

"No, you're right. Well, compared to you, then."

Miles wondered just how to take that. "Gregor never had much in the way of opportunities, when we were younger. I mean, no privacy. Security always in his back pocket. That . . . that can inhibit a man, unless he's a bit of an exhibitionist."

Her hand turned, as if measuring out Gregor's smooth gripless surface. "He was not that."

"Certainly Cavilo must be taking care to present only her most attractive side."

Elena licked her lips in thought. "Is she pretty?"

"Yeah, if you happen to like blond power-mad homicidal maniacs, I suppose she could be quite overwhelming." His hand closed, the texture of Cavilo's pelted hair remembered like an itch on his palm. He rubbed it on his trouser seam.

Elena brightened slightly. "Ah. You don't like her."

Miles gazed up at Elena's Valkyrie face. "She's too short for my taste."

Elena grinned. "That, I believe." She guided the shambling Oser to a chair and sat him down. "We're going to have to tie him up soon. Or something."

The comm buzzed. Miles went to Oser's desk console to answer it. "Yes?" he said in his calmest bored voice.

"Corporal Meddis here, sir. We've put the Vervani agent in Cell Nine."

"Thank you, Corporal. Ah . . ." It was worth a try. "We still have some fast-penta left. Would you two please bring Captain Tung up here for questioning?"

Beyond range of the vid pick-up, Elena's dark brows rose in hope.

"Tung, sir?" The guard's voice was doubtful. "Uh,

may I add a couple of reinforcements to my squad, then?"

"Sure . . . see if Sergeant Chodak's around, he may have some people up for extra duties. In fact, isn't he on the extra-duty roster himself?" He glanced up to see Elena hold up her thumb and forefinger in an O.

"I think so, sir."

"Fine, whatever. Carry on. Naismith out." He keyed off the comm and stared at it, as if it had transmuted into Aladdin's lamp. "I don't think I'm destined to die today. I must be being saved for day after tomorrow."

"You think?"

"Oh, yes. I'll have a much bigger, more public and spectacular chance to blow it all away then. Be able to take thousands more lives down with me."

"Don't you fall into one of your stupid funks now, you haven't got time for it." She rapped the hypospray smartly across his knuckles. "You've got to think us out of this hole."

"Yes, ma'am," Miles said meekly, rubbing his hand. *Whatever happened to "my lord" ? No respect, none. . . .* But he was strangely comforted. "By the way, when Oser arrested Tung for arranging my getaway, why didn't he go on to take you and Arde and Chodak, and the rest of your cadre?"

"He didn't arrest Tung for that. At least, I don't think so. He was baiting Tung, which is his habit, they were both on the bridge at the same time—that was unusual—and Tung finally lost his temper and tried to deck him. Did deck him, I heard, and was part way to strangling him when security pulled him off."

"It had nothing to do with us, then?" That was a relief.

"I'm . . . not sure. I wasn't there. It might have been an emergency diversion, to get Oser's attention away from making just that connection." Elena nodded to the still-blandly-smiling Oser. "And now?"

"Leave him loose, till Tung is delivered. We're all just happy allies here." Miles grimaced. "But for the love of God don't let anybody try to talk to him."

The door comm buzzed. Elena went to stand behind Oser's chair with one hand on his shoulder, trying to look as allied as possible. Miles went to the door and keyed the lock. The door slid open.

Six nervous squadmen surrounded a hostile-looking Ky Tung. Tung wore prisoner's bright yellow pajamas, and radiated malice like a small pre-nova sun. His teeth clenched in utter confusion when he saw Miles.

"Ah, thank you, Corporal," said Miles. "We will be having a little informal staff conference after this interrogation. I'd appreciate it if you and your squad would stand guard out here. And in case Captain Tung gets violent again, we'd better have—oh, Sergeant Chodak and a couple of your people inside." He emphasized the *your* with no change of voice, but only a direct look into Chodak's eyes.

Chodak made the catch. "Yes, sir. You, Private, come with me."

I'm promoting you to lieutenant, Miles thought, and stood aside to let the sergeant and his chosen man guide Tung within. Oser, looking cheerful, was quite clearly visible to the squad for a moment before the door hissed closed again.

Oser was clearly visible to Tung, too. Tung shrugged off his guards and stalked toward the admiral. "What now, you son-of-a-bitch, do you think you—" Tung paused, as Oser continued to smile dimly up at him. "What's wrong with him?"

"Nothing," shrugged Elena. "I think that dose of fast-penta made a real improvement in his personality. Too bad it's only temporary."

Tung threw back his head and barked a laugh, and whirled to shake Miles by the shoulders. "You did it, you little—you came back! We're in business!"

Chodak's man twitched, as if uncertain which way, or whom, to jump. Chodak caught him by the arm, shook his head silently, and indicated the wall by the door. Chodak holstered his stunner and leaned against the door frame with his arms folded; after a startled moment, his man followed suit, flanking the other side. "Fly on the wall," Chodak grinned out of the corner of his mouth to him. "Consider it a gift."

"It wasn't exactly voluntary," said Miles through his teeth to Tung, only in part to keep from biting his tongue in the blast of the Eurasian's enthusiasm. "And we're not in business yet." *Sorry, Ky. I can't be your front man this time. You've got to follow me.* Miles kept his face stern, and removed Tung's hands from his shoulders with icy deliberation. "That Vervani freighter captain you found delivered me straight to Commander Cavilo. And I've been wondering ever since if it was an accident."

"Ah!" Tung fell back, looking as if Miles had just hit him in the stomach.

Miles felt as if he had. No, Tung was no traitor. But Miles dared not give up the only edge he had. "Betrayal, or botchery, Ky?" *And have you stopped beating your wife?*

"Botchery," whispered Tung, gone sallow-pale. "Dammit, I'm going to kill the triple-crossing—"

"That's already been done," said Miles coldly. Tung's brows rose in surprised respect.

"I came to the Hegen Hub on a contract," continued Miles, "which is now in disarray almost beyond repair. I haven't come back here to put you in operational combat command of the Dendarii—" a beat, as Tung's worried features attempted to settle on an expression, "unless you are prepared to serve *my* ends. Priorities and targets are to be my choice. Only the *how* is yours." And just who was going to put whom in command of the Dendarii? As long as that question didn't occur to Tung.

"As my ally," began Tung.

"Not ally. Your commander. Or nothing," said Miles.

Tung stood stockily, his brows struggling to find their level. In a mild tone he finally said, "Daddy Ky's little boy is growing up, it seems."

"That's not the half of it. Are you in, or out?"

"The other half of this is something I've got to hear." Tung sucked on his lower lip. "In."

Miles stuck out his hand. "Done."

Tung took it. "Done." His grip was determined.

Miles let out a long breath. "All right. I gave you some half-truths, last time. Here's what's really going on." He began to pace, his shaking not all from the nerve disrupter nimbus. "I do have a contract with an interested outsider, but it wasn't for 'military evaluation,' which is the smoke screen I gave Oser. The part I told you about preventing a planetary civil war was not smoke. I was hired by the Barrayarans."

"They don't normally hire mercenaries," said Tung.

"I'm not a normal mercenary. I'm being paid by Barrayaran Imperial Security," God, at least one whole-truth, "to find and rescue a hostage. On the side I hope to stop a now-imminent Cetagandan invasion fleet from taking over the Hub. Our second strategic priority will be to hold both sides of the Vervain wormhole jump and as much else as we can till Barrayaran reinforcements arrive."

Tung cleared his throat. "Second priority? What if they don't arrive? There's Pol to cross. . . . And, ah, hostage-rescue does not normally take precedence over fleetwide strat-tac ops, eh?"

"Given the identity of this hostage, I guarantee their arrival. The Barrayaran emperor, Gregor Vorbarra, was kidnapped. I found him, lost him, and now I've got to get him back. As you can imagine, I expect the reward for his safe return to be substantial."

Tung's face was a study in appalled enlightenment. "That skinny neurasthenic git you had in tow before—that wasn't *him,* was it?"

"Yes, it was. And between us, you and I managed to deliver him straight to Commander Cavilo."

"Oh. Shit." Tung rubbed his burr-haired skull. "She'll sell him straight to the Cetagandans."

"No. She means to collect her reward from Barrayar."

Tung opened his mouth, closed it, held up a finger. "Wait a minute. . . ."

"It's *complicated,*" Miles conceded helplessly. "That's why I'm going to delegate the simple part, holding the wormhole, to you. The hostage-rescue part will be my responsibility."

"Simple. The Dendarii mercenaries. All five thousand of us. Singlehanded. Against the Cetagandan Empire. Have you forgotten how to count in the last four years?"

"Think of the glory. Think of your reputation. Think how great it'll look on your next resume."

"On my cenotaph, you mean. Nobody will be able to collect enough of my scattered atoms to bury. You going to cover my funeral expenses, son?"

"Splendidly. Banners, dancing girls, and enough beer to float your coffin to Valhalla."

Tung sighed. "Make it plum wine to float the boat, eh? Drink the beer. Well." He stood silent a moment, rubbing his lips. "The first step is to put the fleet on one-hour-alert status instead of twenty-four."

"They're not already?" Miles frowned.

"We were defensive. We figured we had at least thirty-six hours to study anything coming at us across the Hub. Or so Oser figured it. It'll take about six hours to bring us up to one-hour readiness."

"Right . . . that's the second step, then. Your first step will be to kiss and make up with Captain Auson."

"Kiss my ass!" cried Tung. "That vacuumhead—"

"Is needed to command the *Triumph* while you run Fleet Tac. You can't do both. I can't reorganize the fleet this close to the action. If I had a week to weed out—well, I don't. Oser's people must be persuaded to stay on their jobs. If I have Auson," Miles's upheld hand closed cage-like, "I can run the rest. One way or another."

Tung growled frustrated acquiescence. "All right." His glower faded to a slow grin. "I'd pay money to watch you make him kiss Thorne, though."

"One miracle at a time."

Captain Auson, a big man four years ago, had put on a little more weight but seemed otherwise unchanged. He stepped into Oser's cabin, took in the stunners aimed his way, and stood, hands clenching. When he saw Miles, sitting on the edge of Oser's comconsole desk (a psychological ploy to put his head level with everyone else's; in the station chair Miles feared he looked like a child in need of a booster seat at the dinner table), Auson's expression melted from anger to horror. "Oh, hell! Not you again!"

"But of course," shrugged Miles. The stunner-armed flies on the wall, Chodak and his man, suppressed grins of happy anticipation. "The action's about to start."

"You can't take this—" Auson broke off to peer at Oser. "What did you do to him?"

"Let's just say, we adjusted his attitude. As for the fleet, it's already mine." Well, he was working on it, anyway. "The question is, will you choose to be on the winning side? Pocket a combat bonus? Or shall I give command of the *Triumph* to—"

Auson bared his teeth to Tung in a silent snarl.

"—Bel Thorne?"

"What?" Auson yelped. Tung flinched, wincing. "You can't—"

Miles cut over him, "Do you happen to recall how you graduated from command of the *Ariel* to command of the *Triumph?* Yes?"

Auson pointed to Tung. "What about him?"

"My contractor will contribute value equal to the *Triumph,* which will become Tung's vested share in the fleet corporation. In return Commodore Tung will relinquish all claim on the ship itself. I will confirm Tung's rank as Chief of Staff/Tactical, and yours as captain of the flagship *Triumph.* Your original contribution, equal to the value of the *Ariel* less liens, will be confirmed as your vested share in the fleet corporation. Both ships will be listed as owned by the fleet."

"Do you go along with this?" Auson demanded of Tung.

Miles prodded Tung with a steely look. "Yeah," said Tung grudgingly.

Auson frowned over this. "It isn't just the money . . ." He paused, brow wrinkling. "What combat bonus? What combat?"

He who hesitates, is had. "Are you in or out?"

Auson's moon face took on a cunning look. "I'm in—if he apologizes."

"What? This meatmind thinks—"

"Apologize to the man, Tung dear," Miles sang through his teeth, "and let's get on. Or the *Triumph* gets a captain who can be its own first mate. Who, among other manifold virtues, doesn't *argue* with me."

"Of course not, the little Betan flipsider's in love,"

snapped Auson. "I've never been able to figure out if it wants to get screwed or bugger you—"

Miles smiled and held up a restraining hand. "Now, now." He nodded toward Elena, who had bolstered her stunner in favor of a nerve disrupter. Pointed steadily at Auson's head.

Her smile reminded Miles unsettlingly of one of Sergeant Bothari's. Or worse, of Cavilo's. "Have I ever mentioned, Auson, how much the sound of your voice *irritates* me?" she inquired.

"You wouldn't fire," said Auson uncertainly.

"I wouldn't stop her," Miles lied. "I need your ship. It would be convenient—but not necessary—if you would command her for me." His gaze flicked like a knife toward his putative Chief of Staff/Tac. "*Tung?*"

With ill-grace, Tung mouthed a nobly worded, if vague, apology to Auson for past slurs on his character, intelligence, ancestry, appearance—as Auson's face darkened Miles stopped Tung's catalogue in mid-list and made him start over. "Keep it simpler."

Tung took a breath. "Auson, you can be a real shithead sometimes, but dammit, you can fight when you have to. I've seen you. In the tight and the bad and the crazy, I'll take you at my back before any other captain in the fleet."

One side of Auson's mouth curled up. "Now, *that's* sincere. Thank you so much. I really appreciate your concern for my safety. How tight and bad and crazy do you think this is going to get?"

Tung, Miles decided, had a most unsavory chuckle.

The captain-owners were brought in one by one, to be persuaded, bribed, blackmailed and bedazzled till Miles's mouth was dry, throat raw, voice hoarse. Only the *Peregrine's* captain tried to physically fight. He was stunned and bound, and his second-in-command given the immediate choice between brevet promotion and a long walk out a short air lock. He chose promotion, though his eyes said, *Another day.* As long as that other day came after the Cetagandans, Miles was satisfied.

They moved to the larger conference chamber across from the Tactics Room for the strangest Staff conference Miles had ever attended. Oser was fortified with a booster shot of fast-penta and propped up at the head of the table like a stuffed and smiling corpse. At least two others were tied to their chairs gagged. Tung traded his yellow pajamas for undress greys, commodore's insignia pinned hastily over his captain's tags. The reaction of the audience to Tung's initial tactical presentation ranged from dubious to appalled, overcome (almost) by the pelting headlong pace of the actions demanded of them. Tung's most compelling argument was the sinister suggestion that if they didn't set themselves up as the wormhole's defenders, they might be required to attack through it later against a prepared Cetagandan defense, a vision that generated shudders all around the table. *It could be worse* was always an unassailable assertion.

Partway through, Miles massaged his temples and leaned over to whisper to Elena, "Was it always this bad, or have I just forgotten?"

She pursed her lips thoughtfully and murmured back, "No, the insults were better in the old days."

Miles muffled a grin.

Miles made a hundred unauthorized claims and unsupported promises, and at last things broke up, each to their duty stations. Oser and the *Peregrine's* captain were marched away under guard to the brig. Tung paused only to frown down at the brown felt slippers. "If you're going to command my outfit, son, would you please do an old soldier a favor and get a pair of regulation boots?" At last only Elena remained.

"I want you to re-interrogate General Metzov," Miles told her. "Pull out all the Ranger tactical disposition data you can—codes, ships on-line, off-line, last known positions, personnel oddities, plus whatever he may know about the Vervani. Edit out any unfortunate references he may make to my real identity, and pass it on to Ops, with the warning that not everything Metzov thinks is true, necessarily is. It may help."

"Right."

Miles sighed, slumping wearily on his elbows at the empty conference table. "You know, the planetary patriots like the Barrayarans—us Barrayarans—have it wrong. Our officer cadre thinks that mercenaries have no honor, because they can be bought and sold. But honor is a luxury only a free man can afford. A good Imperial officer like me isn't honor-bound, he's just *bound.* How many of these honest people have I just lied to their deaths? It's a strange game."

"Would you change anything, today?"

"Everything. Nothing. I'd have lied twice as fast if I'd had to."

"You do talk faster in your Betan accent," she allowed.

"You understand. Am I doing the right thing? If I can bring it off. Failure being automatically wrong." *Not a path to disaster, but all paths. . . .*

Her brows rose. "Certainly."

His lips twisted up. "So you," *whom I love,* "my Barrayaran lady who hates Barrayar, are the only person in the Hub I can honestly sacrifice."

She tilted her head in consideration of this. "Thank you, my lord." She touched her hand to the top of his head, passing out of the chamber.

Miles shivered.

CHAPTER FIFTEEN

Miles returned to Oser's cabin for a fast perusal of the admiral's comconsole files, trying to get a handle on all the changes in equipment and personnel that had occurred since he'd last commanded, and to assimilate the Dendarii/Aslunder intelligence picture of events in the Hub. Somebody brought him a sandwich and coffee, which he consumed without tasting. The coffee was no longer working to keep him alert, though he was still keyed to an almost unbearable tension.

As *soon as we undock, I'll crash in Oser's bed.* He'd better spend at least some of the thirty-six hours transit time sleeping, or he'd be more liability than asset upon arrival. When he would have to deal with Cavilo, who made him feel like the proverbial unarmed man in the battle of wits even when he was at his best.

Not to mention the Cetagandans. Miles considered the historical three-legged-race between weapons development and tactics.

Projectile weapons for ship-to-ship combat in space had early been made obsolete by mass shielding and laser weapons. Mass shielding, designed to protect moving ships from space debris encountered at normal-space speeds up to half-cee, shrugged off missiles without even trying. Laser weapons in turn had been rendered useless by the arrival of the Sword-swallower, a Betan-developed defense that actually used the enemy fire as its own power source; a similar principle in the plasma mirror, developed in Miles's parents' generation, promised to do the same to the shorter-range plasma weapons. Another decade might see plasma all phased out.

The up-and-coming weapon for ship-to-ship fighting in the last couple of years seemed to be the gravitic imploder lance, a modification of tractor-beam technology; variously designed artificial-gravity shields were still lagging behind in protection from it. The imploder beam made ugly twisty wreckage where it hit mass. What it did to a human body was a horror.

But the energy-sucking imploder lance's range was insanely short, in terms of space speeds and distances, barely a dozen kilometers. Now, ships had to cooperate to grapple, to slow and close up and maneuver. Given also the small scale of wormhole volumes, fighting looked like it might suddenly become tight and intimate once again, except that too-tight formations invited "sun wall" attacks of massed nuclears. Round and round. It was hinted that ramming and boarding could actually become practical popular tactics once again. Till the next surprise arrived from the devil's workshops, anyway. Miles longed briefly for the good old days of his grandfather's generation, when people could kill each other from a clean fifty thousand kilometers. Just bright sparks.

The effect of the new imploders on concentration

of firepower promised to be curious, especially where a wormhole was involved. It was now possible that a small force in a small area could apply as much power per cubic whatever as a large force, which could not squeeze its largeness down to the effective range; although the difference in reserves still held good, of course. A large force willing to make sacrifices could keep beating away till sheer numbers overcame the smaller concentration. The Cetagandan ghem-lords were not allergic to sacrifice, though generally preferring to start with subordinates, or better still, allies. Miles rubbed his knotted neck muscles.

The cabin buzzer blatted; Miles reached across the comconsole desk to key the door open.

A lean, dark-haired man in his early thirties wearing mercenary grey-and-whites with tech insignia stood uncertainly in the aperture. "My lord?" he said in a soft voice.

Baz Jesek, Fleet Engineering Officer. Once, Barrayaran Imperial Service deserter on the run; subsequently liege-sworn as a private Armsman to Miles in his identity as Lord Vorkosigan. And finally, husband to the woman Miles loved. Once loved. Still loved. Baz. Damn. Miles cleared his throat uncomfortably. "Come in, Commodore Jesek."

Baz trod soundlessly across the deck matting, looking defensive and guilty. "I just got in off the repairs tender, and heard the word that you were back." His Barrayaran accent was polished thin and smooth by his years of galactic exile, significantly less pronounced than four years ago.

"Temporarily, anyway."

"I'm . . . sorry you didn't find things as you'd left them, my lord. I feel like I've squandered Elena's dowry that you bestowed. I didn't realize the implications of Oser's economic maneuvers until . . . well . . . no excuses."

"The man finessed Tung, too," Miles pointed out. He cringed inwardly, to hear Baz apologize to him. "I gather it wasn't exactly a fair fight."

"It wasn't a fight at all, my lord," Baz said slowly. "That was the problem." Baz stood to parade rest. "I've come to offer you my resignation, my lord."

"Offer rejected," said Miles promptly. "In the first place, liege-sworn Armsmen can't resign, in the second place, where am I going to get a competent fleet engineer on," he glanced at his chrono, "two hours' notice, and in the third place, in the third place . . . I need a witness to clear my name if things go wrong. Wronger. You've got to fill me in on Fleet equipment capabilities, then help get it all in motion. And I've got to fill you in on what's really going on. You're the only one besides Elena I can trust with the secret half of this."

With difficulty, Miles persuaded the hesitant engineer to sit down. Miles poured out a speed-edited precis of his adventures in the Hegen Hub, leaving out only mention of Gregor's half-hearted suicide attempt; that was Gregor's private shame. Miles was not altogether surprised to learn Elena had not confided his earlier, brief and ignominious return, rescue, and departure from the Dendarii; Baz seemed to think the presence of the incognito Emperor obvious and sufficient reason for her silence. By the time Miles finished, Baz's inner guilt was quite thoroughly displaced by outer alarm.

"If the Emperor is killed—if he doesn't return—the mess at home could go on for years," Baz said. "Maybe you should let Cavilo rescue him, rather than risk—"

"Up to a point, that's just what I intend to do," said

Miles. "If only I knew Gregor's *mind.*" He paused. "If we lose both Gregor and the wormhole battle, the Cetagandans will arrive on our doorstep just at the point we will be in maximum internal disarray. What a temptation to them—what a lure—they've always wanted Komarr—we could be looking down the throat of the second Cetagandan invasion, almost as much a surprise to them as to us. They may prefer deep-laid plans, but they're not above a little opportunism—not an opportunity this overwhelming—"

Determinedly, driven by this vision, they turned to the tech specs, Miles reminding himself about the ancient saying about the want of a nail. They had nearly completed an overview when the comm officer on duty paged Miles through his comconsole.

"Admiral Naismith, sir?" The comm officer stared with interest at Miles's face, then went on, "There's a man in the docking bay who wants to see you. He claims to have important information."

Miles bethought himself of the theorized backup assassin. "What's his ID?"

"He says to tell you his name's Ungari. That's all he'll say."

Miles caught his breath. The cavalry at last! Or a clever ploy to gain admittance. "Can you give me a look at him, without letting him know he's being scanned?"

"Right, sir." The comm officer's face was replaced on the vid by a view of the *Triumph's* docking bay. The vid zoomed down to focus on a pair of men in Aslunder tech coveralls. Miles melted with relief. Captain Ungari. And blessed Sergeant Overholt.

"Thank you, comm officer. Have a squad escort the two men to my cabin." He glanced at Baz. "In, uh, about ten minutes." He keyed off and explained, "It's my ImpSec boss. Thank God! But—I'm not sure I'd be able to explain to him the peculiar status of your desertion charges. I mean, he's ImpSec, not Service Security, and I don't imagine your old arrest order is exactly at the top of his list of concerns right now, but it might be . . . simpler, if you avoid him, eh?"

"Mm." Baz grimaced in agreement. "I believe I have duties to attend to?"

"No lie. Baz . . ." For a wild moment he longed to tell Baz to take Elena and run, safe away from the coming danger. "It's going to get real crazy soon."

"With Mad Miles back in charge, how could it be otherwise?" Baz shrugged, smiling. He started for the door.

"I'm not as crazy as Tung—Good God, nobody calls me that, do they?"

"Ah—it's an old joke. Only among a few old Dendarii." Baz's step quickened.

And there are very few old Dendarii. That, unfortunately, was not a funny joke. The door hissed closed behind the engineer.

Ungari. Ungari. Somebody in charge at last. *If only I had Gregor with me, I could be done right now. But at least I can find out what Our Side has been up to all this time.* Exhausted, he laid his head down on his arms on Oser's comconsole desk, and smiled. Help. Finally.

Some wriggling dream was fogging his mind; he snatched himself back from too-long-delayed sleep as the cabin buzzer blatted again. He rubbed his numb face and hit the lock control on the desk. "Enter." He glanced at the chrono; he'd lost only four minutes, on that downward slide of consciousness. It was definitely time for a break.

Chodak and two Dendarii guards escorted Captain Ungari and Sergeant Overholt into the room. Ungari and Overholt were both dressed in tan Aslunder supervisor's coveralls, no doubt with IDs and passes to match. Miles smiled happily at them.

"Sergeant Chodak, you and your men wait outside." Chodak looked sadly disappointed at this exclusion. "And if she's finished with her current task, ask Commander Elena Bothari-Jesek to attend on us here. Thanks."

Ungari waited impatiently till the door had hissed closed behind Chodak to stride forward. Miles stood up and saluted him smartly. "Glad to see y—"

To Miles's surprise, Ungari did not return the salute; instead his hands clenched on Miles's uniform jacket and lifted. Miles sensed that it was only with the greatest restraint that Ungari's grip had closed on his lapels and not his neck. "Vorkosigan, you idiot! What the hell kind of game have you been up to?"

"I found Gregor, sir. I—" don't say *lost him.* "I'm mounting an expedition to recover him right now. I'm so glad you made contact with me, another hour and you'd have missed the boat. If we pool our information and resources—"

Ungari's clutch did not loosen, nor did his peeled-back lips relax. "We know you found the Emperor, we traced you both here from Consortium Detention. Then you both vanished utterly."

"Didn't you ask Elena? I thought you would—look sir, sit down, please," *and put me down, dammit—* Ungari seemed not to notice that Miles's toes were stretched to the floor, "and tell me what all this looked like from your point of view. It's very important."

Ungari, breathing heavily, released Miles and sat in the indicated station chair, or at least on its edge. At a hand signal, Overholt took up a pose of parade rest at his shoulder. Miles gazed with some relief at Overholt, whom he'd last seen face-down unconscious on the Consortium Station concourse; the sergeant appeared fully recovered, if tired and strained.

Ungari said, "When he finally woke up, Sergeant Overholt followed you to Consortium Detention, but by then you'd disappeared. He thought *they'd* done it, they thought *he'd* done it. He spent bribe-money like water, finally got the story from the contract-slave you'd beaten up—a day later, when the man could finally talk—"

"He lived, then," said Miles. "Good, Gre—we were worried about that."

"Yes, but Overholt didn't recognize the Emperor at first, in the contract-slave records—the sergeant hadn't been on the need-to-know list about his disappearance."

A faint irate look passed over the sergeant's face, as if in memory of great injustices.

"—it wasn't until he'd made contact with me here, we dead-ended, and we retraced all the steps in hopes of finding some clue about you we'd overlooked, that I identified the missing contract-slave as Emperor Gregor. *Days* lost."

"I was sure you'd make contact with Elena Bothari-Jesek, sir. She knew where we'd gone. You knew she was my sworn liege-woman, it's in my files."

Ungari shot him a flat-lipped glare, but did not otherwise offer explanation for this gaffe. "When the first wave of Barrayaran agents hit the Hub, we finally had enough reinforcements to mount a serious search—"

"Good! So they know Gregor's in the Hub, back home. I was afraid Illyan would still be squandering all his resources on Komarr, or worse, towards Escobar."

Ungari's fingers clenched again. "Vorkosigan, *what did you do with the Emperor?*"

"He's safe, but in great danger." Miles thought that

one over a second. "That is, he's all right for the moment, I think, but that will change with the tactical—"

"We know *where* he is, he was spotted three days ago by an agent in Randall's Rangers."

"Must have been just after I left," Miles calculated. "Not that he could have spotted me, I was in the brig—what are we doing about it?"

"Rescue forces are being scrambled; I don't know how large a fleet."

"What about permission to cross Pol?"

"I doubt they'll wait for it."

"We've got to alert them, not to offend Pol! The—"

"Ensign, Vervain holds the Emperor!" Ungari snarled in exasperation. "I'm not going to tell the—"

"Vervain doesn't hold Gregor, Commander Cavilo does," Miles interrupted urgently. "It's strictly non-political, a plot for her personal gain. I think—in fact, I'm dead certain—the Vervani government doesn't know the first thing about her 'guest.' Our rescue forces must be warned to commit no hostile act until the Cetagandan invasion shows up."

"The what?"

Miles faltered, and said in a smaller voice, "You mean you don't know anything about the Cetagandan invasion?" He paused. "Well, just because you don't have the word yet, doesn't mean Illyan hasn't figured it out. Even if we haven't spotted where they're massing, inside the Empire, as soon as ImpSec adds up how many Cetagandan warships have disappeared from their home bases, they'll realize something must be up. Somebody must still be keeping track of such things, even in the current flap over Gregor." Ungari was still sitting there looking stunned, so Miles kept explaining. "I expect a Cetagandan force to invade Vervani local space and continue on to secure the Hegen Hub, with Commander Cavilo's connivance. Very shortly. I plan to take the Dendarii fleet across-system and fight them at the Vervani wormhole, hold it till Gregor's rescue fleet arrives. I hope they're sending more than a diplomatic negotiation team. . . . By the way, do you still have that blank mercenary contract credit chit Illyan gave you? I need it."

"You, mister," Ungari began when he had mastered his voice again, "are going *nowhere* but to our safe house on Aslund Station. Where you will wait quietly—very quietly—until Illyan's reinforcements arrive to take you *off my hands.*"

Miles politely ignored this impractical outburst. "You have to have been collecting data for your report to Illyan. Got anything I can use?"

"I have a complete report on Aslund Station, its naval and mercenary dispositions and strengths, but—"

"*I* have all that, now." Miles tapped his fingers impatiently on Oser's comconsole. "Damn. I wish you'd spent the last two weeks on Vervain Station instead."

Ungari gritted, "Vorkosigan, you will stand up now, and come with Sergeant Overholt and me. Or so help me I will have Overholt carry you bodily."

Overholt was eyeing him with cool calculation, Miles realized. "That could be a serious mistake, sir. Worse than your failure to contact Elena. If you will just let me explain the over-all strategic situation—"

Goaded beyond endurance, Ungari snapped, "Overholt, grab him."

Miles hit the alarm on his comconsole desk as Overholt swooped down on him. He dodged around his station chair, knocking it loose from its clamps, as Overholt missed his first grab. The cabin door hissed open. Chodak and his two guards pelted through, followed by Elena. Overholt, chasing Miles around the end of the comconsole desk, skidded straight into Chodak's stunner fire. Overholt dropped with a massive thud; Miles winced. Ungari lurched to his feet and stopped, bracketed by the aim of four Dendarii stunners. Miles felt like bursting into tears, or possibly cackles. Neither would be useful. He got control of his breath and voice.

"Sergeant Chodak, take these two men to the *Triumph's* brig. Put them . . . put them next to Metzov and Oser, I guess."

"Yes, Admiral."

Ungari went bravely silent, as befit a captured spy, and suffered himself to be led out, though the veins in his neck pulsed with suppressed fury as he glared back at Miles.

And I can't even fast-penta him, Miles thought mournfully. An agent on Ungari's level was certain to have been implanted with an induced allergic reaction to fast-penta; not euphoria, but anaphylactic shock and death, would result from such a dose. In a moment two more Dendarii appeared with a float pallet and removed the inert Overholt.

As the door closed behind them, Elena asked, "All right, what was all that about?"

Miles sighed deeply. "That, unfortunately, was my ImpSec superior, Captain Ungari. He was not in a listening mood."

Elena's eye lit with a skewed enthusiasm. "Dear God, Miles. Metzov—Oser—Ungari—all in a row—you sure are hard on your commanding officers. What are you going to do when the time comes to let them all out?"

Miles shook his head mutely. "I don't know."

The fleet disengaged from Aslund Station within the hour, maintaining strict comm silence; the Aslunders, naturally, were thrown into a panic. Miles sat in the

Triumph's comm center and monitored their frantic queries, resolved not to interfere with the natural course of events unless the Aslunders opened fire. Until he again laid hands on Gregor, he must at all costs present the correct profile to Cavilo. Let her think she was getting what she wanted, or at least what she'd asked for.

In fact, the natural course of events promised to deliver more of the results Miles wanted than he could have gained through planning and persuasion. The Aslunders had three main theories, Miles deduced from their comm chatter; the mercenaries were fleeing from the Hub altogether at secret word of some impending attack, the mercenaries were off to join one or more of Aslund's enemies, or worst of all, the mercenaries were opening an unprovoked attack on said enemies, with subsequent retribution to recoil on the Aslunders' heads. Aslunder forces went to maximum alert status. Reinforcements were called for, mobile forces shifted into the Hub, reserves brought on-line as the sudden departure of their faithless mercenaries stripped them of assumed defenses.

Miles breathed relief as the last of the Dendarii fleet cleared the Aslunders' region and headed into open space. Delayed by the confusion, no Aslunder naval pursuit force could catch them now till they decelerated near the Vervain wormhole. Where, with the arrival of the Cetagandans, it should not be hard to persuade the Aslunders to reclassify themselves as Dendarii reserves.

Timing was, if not everything, a lot. Suppose Cavilo hadn't already transmitted her go-code to the Cetagandans. The sudden movement of the Dendarii fleet might well spook her into aborting the plot. Fine, Miles decided. In that case he would have stopped the Cetagandan invasion without a shot being fired. A perfect war of maneuver, by Admiral Aral Vorkosigan's own definition. *Of course, I'll have political egg on my face and a lynch mob after me from three sides, but Dad will understand. I hope.* That would leave staying alive and rescuing Gregor as his only tactical goals, which in present contrast seemed absurdly, delightfully simple. Unless, of course, Gregor didn't want to be rescued . . .

Further, finer branches of the strategy-tree must await events, Miles decided blearily. He staggered off to Oser's cabin to fall into bed and sleep for twelve solid, sodden hours.

The *Triumph*'s comm officer woke Miles, paging him on the vid. Miles, in his underwear, padded across to the comconsole and slung himself into the station chair. "Yes?"

"You asked to be apprised of messages from Vervain Station, sir."

"Yes, thank you." Miles rubbed amber grains of sleep from his eyes, and checked the time. Twelve hours flight-time left till their arrival at target. "Any signs of abnormal activity levels at Vervain Station or their wormhole yet?"

"Not yet, sir."

"All right. Continue to monitor, record, and track any outbound traffic. What's the transmission time lag from us to them at present?"

"Thirty-six minutes, sir."

"Mm. Very well. Pipe the message down here." Yawning, he leaned his elbows on Oser's comconsole and studied the vid. A high-ranking Vervani officer appeared over the plate, and demanded explanation for the Oseran/Dendarii Fleet's movements. He sounded a lot like the Aslunders. No sign of Cavilo. Miles keyed the comm officer. "Transmit back that their important message was hopelessly garbled by static and a malfunction in our de-scrambler. Urgently request a repeat, with amplification."

"Yes, sir."

In the ensuing seventy minutes Miles took a leisurely shower, dressed in a properly fitting uniform (and boots) that had been provided while he slept, and ate a balanced breakfast. He strolled into the *Triumph's* Nav and Com just in time for the second transmission. This time, Commander Cavilo stood, arms crossed, at the Vervani officer's shoulder. The Vervani repeated himself, literally with amplification, his voice was louder and sharper this time around. Cavilo added, "Explain yourselves at once, or we will regard you as a hostile force and respond accordingly."

That was the amplification he'd wanted. Miles settled himself in the comm station chair and adjusted his Dendarii uniform as neatly as possible. He made sure the admiral's rank insignia was clearly visible in the vid. "Ready to transmit," he nodded to the comm officer. He smoothed his features into as straight-faced and dead-serious an expression as he could manage.

"Admiral Miles Naismith, Commanding, Dendarii Free Mercenary Fleet, speaking. To Commander Cavilo, Randall's Rangers, eyes only. Ma'am. I have accomplished my mission precisely as you ordered. I remind you of the reward you promised me for my success. What are your next instructions? Naismith out."

The comm officer logged the recording into the tight-beam scrambler. "Sir," she said uncertainly, "if that's for Commander Cavilo's eyes only, should we be sending it on the Vervain command channel? The Vervani will have to de-process it before sending it on. It will be seen by a lot of eyes besides hers."

"Just so, Lieutenant," said Miles. "Go ahead and transmit."

"Oh. And when—if—they respond, what do you want me to do?"

Miles checked his chrono. "By the time of their next response, our line of travel should take us behind the twin suns' interference corona. We should be out of communications for a good, oh, three hours."

"I can boost the gain, sir, and cut through—"

"No, no, Lieutenant. The interference is going to be something terrible. In fact, if you can stretch that to four hours, so much the better. But make it look real. Until we're in range for a tight-beam conference between myself and Cavilo in near-real-time, I want you to think of yourself as a noncommunications officer."

"Yes, sir." She grinned. "Now I understand."

"Carry on. Remember, I want maximum inefficiency, incompetence, and error. On the Vervani channels, that is. You've worked with trainees, surely. Be creative."

"Yes, *sir.*"

Miles went off to find Tung.

He and Tung were deeply engrossed in the tactical computer display in the *Triumph's* tactics room, running projected wormhole scenarios, when the comm officer paged again.

"Changes at Vervain Station, sir. All outgoing commercial ship traffic has been halted. Incoming are being denied permission to dock. Encoded transmissions on all military channels have just about tripled. And four large warships just jumped."

"Into the Hub, or out to Vervain?"

"Out to Vervain, sir."

Tung leaned forward. "Dump data into the tactics display as you confirm it, Lieutenant."

"Yes, sir."

"Thank you," said Miles. "Continue to keep us advised. And monitor civilian clear-code messages, too, any you can pick up. I want to keep tabs on the rumors as they start to fly."

"Right, sir. Out."

Tung keyed up what was laughingly called the "real-time" tactics display, a colorful schematic, as the comm officer shunted the new data. He studied the identity of the four departing warships. "It's starting," he said grimly. "You called it."

"You don't think it's something we're causing?"

"Not those four ships. They wouldn't have moved off-station if they weren't badly wanted elsewhere. Better get your ass over to—that is, transfer your flag to the *Ariel,* son."

Miles rubbed his lips nervously, and eyed what he'd mentally dubbed his "Little Fleet" in the schematic display in the *Ariel's* tactics room. The equipment was now displaying the *Ariel* itself plus the two next-fastest ships in the Dendarii forces. His own personal attack-group; fast, maneuverable, amenable to violent course-changes, requiring less turning-room than any other possible combination. Admittedly, they were low in firepower. But if things went as Miles projected, firing was not going to be a desirable option anyway.

The *Ariel's* tac room was manned now by a mere skeleton crew; Miles, Elena as his personal communications officer, Arde Mayhew for all other systems. Inner Circle all, in anticipation of this next most-private conversation. If it came to actual combat, he'd turn the chamber over to Thorne, presently exiled to Nav and Com. And then, perhaps, retire to his cabin and slit his belly open.

"Let's see Vervain Station now," he told Elena in her comm station chair. The main holovid display in the center of the room whirled dizzyingly at her touch on the controls. The schematic representation of their target area seemed to boil with shifting lines and colors, representing ship movements, power shunts to various weapons systems and shieldings, and communications transmissions. The Dendarii were now barely a million kilometers out, a little more than three light-seconds. The rate of closure was slowing as the Little Fleet, fully two hours ahead of the slower ships of the main Dendarii fleet, decelerated.

"They're sure stirred up now," Elena commented. Her hand went to her ear-bug. "They're reiterating their demands that we communicate."

"But still not launching a counter-attack," Miles observed, studying the schematic. "I'm glad they realize where the true danger lies. All right. Tell them that we've got our comm problems straightened out—finally—but say again that I will speak first only to Commander Cavilo."

"They—ah—I think they're finally putting her through. I've got a tight-beam coming in on the dedicated channel."

"Trace it." Miles hung over her shoulder as she coaxed this information from the comm net.

"The source is moving. . . ."

Miles closed his eyes in prayer, snapped them open again at Elena's triumphant, "Got it! There. That little ship."

"Give me its course and energy profile. Is she heading toward the wormhole?"

"No, away."

"Ha!"

"It's a fast ship—small—it's a *Falcon-class* courier," Elena reported. "If her goal is Pol—and Barrayar—she must intersect our triangle."

Miles exhaled. "Right. Right. She waited to speak on a line her Vervani bosses couldn't monitor. I thought she might. Wonder what lies she's told them? She's past the point of no return, does she know it?" He opened his arms to the new short vector line in the schematic. "Come, love. Come to me."

Elena raised her brow sardonically at him. "Coming through. Your sweetheart is about to appear on Monitor Three."

Miles swung into the indicated Station chair, settling himself before the holovid plate, which began to sparkle. Now was the time to muster every bit of self-control he'd ever owned. He smoothed his face to an expression of cool ironic interest, as Cavilo's fine features formed before him. Out of range of the vid pick-up, he rubbed his sweating palms on his trouser knees.

Cavilo's blue eyes were alight with triumph, constrained by her tight mouth and tense brows as if in echo of Miles's ships constraining her flight-path. "Lord Vorkosigan. What are you doing here?"

"Following your orders, ma'am. You told me to go get the Dendarii. And I've transmitted nothing to Barrayar."

A six-second time lag, as the tight-beam flew from ship to ship and returned her answer. Alas that it gave her as much time to think as it did him.

"I didn't order you to cross the Hub."

Miles wrinkled his brow in puzzlement. "But where else would you need my fleet except at the point of action? I'm not dense."

Cavilo's pause this time was longer than accounted for by the transmission lag. "You mean you didn't get Metzov's message?" she asked.

Damn near. What a fabulous array of double meanings there. "Why, did you send him as a courier?"

Lag. "Yes!"

A palpable lie for a palpable lie. "I never saw him. Maybe he deserted. He must have realized he'd lost your love to another. Perhaps he's holed up in some spaceport bar right now, drowning his sorrows." Miles sighed deeply at this sad scenario.

Cavilo's concerned attentive expression melted to rage when this one arrived. "Idiot! I know you took him prisoner!"

"Yes, and I've been wondering ever since why you allowed that to happen. If that accident was undesired, you should have taken precautions against it."

Cavilo's eyes narrowed; she shifted her ground. "I feared Stanis's emotions made him unreliable. I wanted to give him one more chance to prove himself. I gave my backup man orders to kill him if he tried to kill you, but when Metzov missed, the dolt waited."

Substitute *as soon as/succeeded* for that *if/tried,* and the statement was probably near-truth. Miles wished he had a recording of that Ranger agent's field report, and Cavilo's blistering reply. "There, you see? You *do* want subordinates who can think for themselves. Like me."

Cavilo's head jerked back. "You, for a subordinate? I'd sooner sleep with a snake!"

Interesting image, that. "You'd better get used to me. You're seeking entry into a world strange to you, familiar to me. The Vorkosigans are an integral part of Barrayar's power-class. You could use a native guide."

Lag. "Exactly. I'm trying—I must—get your emperor to safety. You're blocking his flight path. Out of my way!"

Miles spared a glance for the tactics display. Yes, just so. *Good, come to me.* "Commander Cavilo, I feel certain you are missing an important datum in your calculations about me."

Lag. "Let me clarify my position, little Barrayaran. I hold your emperor. I control him absolutely."

"Fine, let me hear those orders from him, then."

Lag . . . fractionally briefer, yes. "I can have his throat cut before your eyes. Let me pass!"

"Go ahead." Miles shrugged. "It'll make an awful mess on your deck, though."

She grinned sourly, after the lag. "You bluff badly."

"I bluff not at all. Gregor is far more valuable alive to you than to me. You can do nothing, where you're going, except through him. He's your meal ticket. But has anyone mentioned to you yet that if Gregor dies, I could become the next emperor of Barrayar?" Well, arguably, but this was hardly time to go into the finer details of the six competing Barrayaran succession theories.

Cavilo's face froze. "He said . . . he had no heir. You said so too."

"None *named.* Because my father refuses to be named, not because he lacks the bloodlines. But ignoring the bloodlines doesn't erase them. And I am my father's only child. And he can't live forever. Ergo . . . So, resist my boarding parties, by all means. Threaten away. Carry out your threats. Give me the Imperium. I shall thank you prettily, before I have you summarily executed. Emperor Miles the First. How does it sound? As good as Empress Cavilo?" Miles gave it an intense beat. "*Or,* we could work together. The Vorkosigans have traditionally felt that the substance was better than the name. The power behind the throne, as my father before me—who has held just that power, as Gregor has doubtless told you, for far too long—you're not going to dislodge *him* by batting your eyelashes. He's immune to women. But I know his every weakness. I've thought it through. This could be my big chance, one way or another. By the way—milady—do you care which emperor you wed?"

The time lag allowed him to fully savor her changes

of expression, as his plausible calumnies thudded home. Alarm; revulsion; finally, reluctant respect.

"I underestimated you, it seems. Very well . . . Your ships may escort us to safety. Where—clearly—we must confer further."

"I will *transport* you to safety, aboard the *Ariel.* Where we will confer immediately."

Cavilo straightened, nostrils flaring. "No way."

"All right, let's compromise. I will abide by Gregor's orders, and Gregor's orders only. As I said, milady, you'd better get used to this. No Barrayaran will take orders from you directly at first, till you've established yourself. If that's the game you're choosing to play, you'd better start practicing. It only gets more complicated after this. Or, you can choose to resist, in which case I get it all." *Play for time, Cavilo! Bite!*

"I'll get Gregor." The vid went to the grey haze of a holding signal.

Miles flung himself back in his station chair, rubbed his neck and rolled his head, trying to relieve his screaming nerves. He was shaking. Mayhew was staring at him in alarm.

"Damn," said Elena in a hushed voice. "If I didn't know you, I'd think you were Mad Yuri's understudy. The look on your face . . . am I reading too much into all that innuendo, or did you in fact just connive to assassinate Gregor in one breath, offer to cuckold him in the next, accuse your father of homosexuality, suggest a patricidal plot against him, and league yourself with Cavilo—what are you going to do for an encore?"

"Depends on the straight lines. I can hardly wait to find out," Miles panted. "Was I convincing?"

"You were *scary.*"

"Good." He wiped his palms on his trousers again. "It's mind-to-mind, between Cavilo and me, before it ever becomes ship-to-ship. . . . She's a compulsive plotter. If I can smoke her, wind her in with words, with what-ifs, with all the bifurcations of her strategy-tree, just long enough to get her eye off the one real *now* . . ."

"Signal," Elena warned.

Miles straightened, waited. The next face to form over the vid plate was Gregor's. Gregor, alive and well. Gregor's eyes widened, then his face went very still.

Cavilo hovered behind his shoulder, just slightly out of focus. "Tell him what we want, love."

Miles bowed sitting down, as profoundly as physically possible. "Sire. I present you with the Emperor's Own Dendarii Free Mercenary Fleet. Do with us as You will."

Gregor glanced aside, evidently at some tactical readout analogous to the *Ariel's* own. "By God, you've even got them *with* you. Miles, you are supernatural." The flash of humor was instantly muffled in sere formality. "Thank you, Lord Vorkosigan. I accept your vassal-offering of troops."

"If you would care to step aboard the *Ariel,* sire, you can take personal command of your forces."

Cavilo leaned forward, interrupting. "And *now* his treachery is made plain. Let me play a portion of his last words for you, Greg." Cavilo reached past Gregor to touch a control, and Miles was treated to an instant replay of his breathless sedition, beginning with—naturally—the flim-flam about the named heir, and ending with his offer of himself as a substitute Imperial groom. Very nicely selected, clearly unedited.

Gregor listened with his head in a thoughtful tilt, his face perfectly controlled, as the Miles-image stammered to its damning conclusion. "But does this surprise you, Cavie?" asked Gregor in an innocent tone, taking her hand and looking over his shoulder at her. From the expression on her face, *something* was surprising her. "Lord Vorkosigan's mutations have driven him mad, everyone knows that! He's been sulking around muttering like that for years. Of course, I trust him no further than I can throw him—"

Thanks, Gregor. I'll remember that line.

"—but as long as he feels he can further his interests by furthering ours, he'll be a valuable ally. House Vorkosigan has always been powerful in Barrayaran affairs. His grandfather Count Piotr put my grandfather Emperor Ezar on the throne. They'd make an equally powerful enemy. I should prefer us to rule Barrayar with their cooperation."

"Their extermination would do as well, surely." Cavilo glared at Miles.

"Time is on our side, love. His father is an old man. He, is a mutant. His bloodline-threat is empty, Barrayar would never accept a mutant as emperor, as Count Aral well knows and as even Miles realizes in his saner moments. But he can trouble us, if he chooses. An interesting balance of power, eh, Lord Vorkosigan?"

Miles bowed again. "I think much on it." So *have you, apparently.* He spared a quelling glance at Elena, who had fallen off her station chair somewhere around Gregor's word-picture of Miles's mad soliloquies, aside at state banquets no doubt, and was now sitting on the floor with her sleeve jammed in her mouth to muffle the shrieks of laughter. Her eyes blazed, over the grey cloth. She got control of her stifled giggles and scrambled back into her seat. *Close your mouth, Arde.*

"Then, Cavie, let's join my would-be Grand Vizier. At that point, I will control his ships. And your wish," he turned his head to kiss her hand, still resting in his grasp on his shoulder, "will be my command."

"Do you really think it's safe? If he's as psycho as you say."

"Brilliant—nervous—skittish—but he's all right as

long as his medications are adjusted properly, I promise you. I expect his dose is a little off at the moment, due to our irregular travels."

The transmission time-lag was much reduced, now. "Twenty minutes to rendezvous, sir," Elena reported, off-sides.

"Will you transfer in your shuttle, or ours, sire?" Miles inquired politely.

Gregor shrugged carelessly. "Commander Cavilo's choice."

"Ours," said Cavilo immediately.

"I will be waiting." *And ready.*

Cavilo broke transmission.

CHAPTER SIXTEEN

Miles watched through the vid link as the first space-armored Ranger stepped into the *Ariel's* shuttle hatch corridor. The wary point-man was followed immediately by four more, who scanned the empty passageway, converted into a chamber by the closed blast doors sealing each end. No enemies, no targets, not even automatic weapons threatened them. An utterly deserted chamber. Bewildered, the Rangers took up a defensive stance around the shuttle hatch.

Gregor stepped through. Miles was unsurprised to see that Cavilo had not provided the Emperor with space armor. Gregor wore a neatly pressed set of Ranger fatigues, minus insignia; his only protection was his boots. Even they would be quite inadequate, if one of those heavy-armored monsters stepped on his toe. Battle armor was lovely stuff, proof against stunners and nerve disrupters, most poisons and biologicals; resistant (to a degree) to plasma fire and radioactivity, stuffed with clever built-in weaponry, tac comps, and telemetry. Very suitable for a boarding expedition. Though in fact, Miles had once captured the *Ariel* himself with fewer personnel, less formidably armed and totally unarmored. He'd had surprise on his side, then.

Cavilo came through behind Gregor. She wore space armor, though for the moment she carried her helmet tucked under her arm like a decapitated head. She stared around the empty corridor, and frowned. "All right, what's the trick?" she demanded loudly.

To answer your question . . . Miles pressed the button on the remote-control box in his hand.

A muffled explosion made the corridor reverberate. The flex tube tore violently away from the shuttle hatch. The automatic doors, sensing the pressure drop, clapped shut instantly. A bare breath of air escaped. Good system. Miles had made the techs make sure it was working properly, before they'd inserted the directional mines in the shuttle clamps. He checked his monitors. Cavilo's combat shuttle was tumbling away from the side of the *Ariel* now, thrusters and sensors damaged in the same blast that propelled it outward, its weapons and reserve Rangers useless until the no-doubt-frantic pilot regained attitude control. If he could.

"Keep an eye on him, Bel, I don't want him coming back to haunt us," Miles spoke into his comm link to Thorne, on deck in the *Ariel's* tactics room.

"I can blow him up now, if you like."

"Wait a little. We're a long way from sorted out, down here." *God help us now.*

Cavilo was snapping her helmet on, her startled troops in defensive formation around her. All dressed up, and nothing to shoot. Let them settle down for just a moment, enough to prevent spinal-reflexive fusillades, but not enough to think. . . .

Miles glanced around at his own space-armored troops, six in number, and closed his own helmet. Not that numbers mattered. A million troops with nuclears, one guy with a club; either would suffice when the target was one unarmed hostage. Miniaturizing the situation, Miles realized sadly, had made no qualitative difference. He could still screw up just as big. The main difference was his plasma cannon, sighted down the corridor. He nodded to Elena, manning the big weapon. Not normally an indoor toy, it would stop charging space armor. And blow out the hull beyond. Miles figured that, theoretically, they could blow away, oh, one out of Cavilo's five at this range, if they came on at a dead run, before all became hand-to-hand, or glove-to-glove.

"Here we go," Miles warned through his command channel. "Remember the drill." He pressed another control; the blast doors between his group and Cavilo's began to draw back. Slowly, not suddenly, at a rate carefully calculated to inspire dread without startling.

Full broadcast on all channels plus loudspeaker. It was absolutely essential to Miles's plan that he get in the first word.

"Cavilo!" he shouted. "Deactivate your weapons and freeze, or I'll blow Gregor to atoms!"

Body language was a wonderful thing. It was amazing, how much expression could come through the blank shining surface of space armor. The littlest armored figure stood openhanded, stunned. Bereft of words; bereft, for precious seconds, of reactions. Because, of course, Miles had just stolen her opening line. *Now what do you have to say for yourself, love?* It was a desperate ploy. Miles had judged the hostage-problem logically insoluble; therefore, clearly the only thing to do was make it Cavilo's problem instead of his own.

Well, he'd obtained as much as the *freeze* part, anyway. But he dared not let the standoff stand. "Drop it, Cavilo! It only takes one nervous twitch to convert you from Imperial fiancee to no one of importance at all. And then to no one at all. And you're making me *real tense.*"

"You said he was safe," Cavilo hissed to Gregor.

"His meds must be further off-dose than I thought," Gregor replied, looking anxious. "No, watch—he's bluffing. I'll prove it."

Hands held out open to his sides, Gregor walked straight toward the plasma cannon. Miles's jaw fell open, behind his faceplate. *Gregor, Gregor, Gregor . . . !*

Gregor gazed steadily into Elena's faceplate. His step never quickened or faltered. He stopped only when his chest touched the beaded tip of the cannon. It was an enormously dramatic and arresting moment. Miles was so lost in appreciation, it took him that long to move his finger an imperceptible few centimeters and hit the button on his control box that closed the blast doors.

The shield hadn't been programmed for slow-closure; it banged shut faster than the eye could follow. Brief noises, from the other side, of plasma fire, shouts; Cavilo screaming at one of her men just in time to stop him from the fatal error of firing a mine at the wall of a closed chamber he himself occupied. Then silence.

Miles dropped his plasma rifle, tore off his helmet. "God almighty, I wasn't expecting *that.* Gregor, you're a genius."

Gently, Gregor raised a finger and moved the tip of the plasma cannon aside.

"Don't worry," said Miles. "None of our weapons are charged. I didn't want to risk any accidents."

"I was almost certain that was the case," Gregor murmured. He stared back over his shoulder at the blast doors. "What would you have done if I'd been asleep on my feet?"

"Kept talking. Tried for various compromises. I had a trick or two yet . . . behind the other blast door, there's a squad with live weapons. In the end, if she didn't bite, I was prepared to surrender."

"That's what I was afraid of."

Some peculiar muffled noises penetrated the blast doors.

"Elena, take over," said Miles. "Mop up. Take Cavilo alive if possible, but I don't want any Dendarii to die trying. Take no chances, trust nothing she says."

"I have the picture." Elena waved a salute, and motioned to her squad, which broke up to insert weapons-charges. Elena began to confer over the command-channel headset with the leader of the twin squad waiting on Cavilo's other side and with the commander of the *Ariel's* combat shuttle, closing in from space.

Miles motioned Gregor along the corridor, removing him as swiftly as possible from the region of potential messiness. "To the tactics room, and I'll fill you in. You have some decisions to make."

They entered a lift-tube, and rose. Miles breathed easier with every meter he increased the range between Gregor and Cavilo.

"My biggest worry," Miles said, "till we spoke face-to-face, was that Cavilo really had done what she thought she had, fogged your mind. I didn't see where she could be getting her ideas except from you. Wasn't sure what I could do in that case, except play along till I could hand you over to higher experts on Barrayar. If I survived. I didn't know how fast you'd see through her."

"Oh, at once," shrugged Gregor. "She had the same hungry smile Vordrozda used to get. And a dozen lesser cannibals, since. I can smell a power-hungry flatterer at a thousand meters, now."

"I yield to my master in strategy." Miles's armored hand made a genuflecting motion. "Do you know you rescued yourself? She'd have taken you all the way home, even if I hadn't come along."

"It was easy." Gregor frowned. "All that was required was that I have no personal honor at all." Gregor's eyes, Miles realized, were deathly, devoid of triumph.

"You can't cheat an honest man," said Miles uncertainly. "Or woman. What would you have done, if she'd got you home?"

"Depends." Gregor stared into the middle distance. "If she'd managed to get you killed, I suppose I'd have had her executed." Gregor glanced back, as they stepped out of the tube. "This is better. Maybe . . . maybe there's some way to give her a fair chance."

Miles blinked. "I'd be very careful about giving Cavilo any kind of a chance at all, if I were you. Even with tongs. Does she deserve it? Do you realize what's going on, how many she's betrayed?"

"In part. And yet . . ."

"Yet, what?"

Gregor's tone was so low as to be nearly inaudible. "I wish she had been real."

". . . and that's the present tactical situation in the Hub and Vervain local space, as far as my information goes," Miles concluded his presentation to Gregor. They had the *Ariel's* briefing room all to themselves; Arde Mayhew stood guard in the corridor. Miles had begun his speed-precis as soon as Elena reported that the hostile boarders had been successfully secured. He'd paused only to peel out of his ill-fitting armor and back into his Dendarii greys. The armor had been hastily borrowed from the same female soldier who'd lent him kit before, and the plumbing perforce left unconnected.

Miles froze the holovid display in the center of the table. Would that he could freeze real time and events the same way, at the touch of a keypad, that he might halt their terrible rush. "You'll notice our biggest intelligence holes are in precise information about the Cetagandan forces. I'm hoping the Vervani will plug some of those gaps, if we can persuade them we're their allies, and the Rangers may yield more. One way or another.

"Now—sire—the decision lands on you. Fight or flight? I can detach the *Ariel* from the Dendarii right now, to run you home, with little loss to this hot and dirty wormhole fight. Firepower and armor, not speed, are going to be at a premium there. There's not much doubt which course my father and Illyan would vote for."

"No." Gregor stirred. "On the other hand, they aren't here."

"True. Alternately, going to the opposite extreme, do you wish to be commander-in-chief of this mess? In fact, as well as name?"

Gregor smiled softly. "What a temptation. But don't you think there's a certain . . . hubris, in undertaking field leadership without a prior apprenticing in field followership?"

Miles reddened slightly. "I—hem!—face a similar dilemma. You've met the solution, his name's Ky Tung. We'll be conferring with him when we transfer back to the *Triumph,* later." Miles paused. "There are a couple of other things you might do for us. If you choose. Real things."

Gregor rubbed his chin, watching Miles as he might a play. "Trot them out. Lord Vorkosigan."

"Legitimatize the Dendarii. Present them to the

Vervani as the Barrayaran pickup force. I can only bluff. Your breath is law. You can conclude a legally binding defensive treaty between Barrayar and Vervain—Aslund too, if we can bring them in. Your greatest value is—sorry—diplomatic, not military. Go to Vervain Station, and deal with these people. And I do mean deal."

"Safely behind the lines," Gregor noted dryly.

"Only if we win, on the other side of the jump. If we lose, the lines will come to you."

"I would I could be a soldier. Some lowly lieutenant, with only a handful of men to care for."

"There's no moral difference between one and ten thousand, I assure you. You're just as thoroughly damned however many you get killed."

"I want to be in on the fight. Probably the only chance I'll have in my life for real risk."

"What, the risk you run every day from lunatic assassins isn't enough thrill for you? You want more?"

"Active. Not passive. Real service."

"If—in your judgment—the best and most vital service you can give everyone else risking their lives here is as a minor field officer, I will of course support you to the best of my ability," said Miles bleakly.

"Ouch," murmured Gregor. "You can turn a phrase like a knife, you know?" He paused. "Treaties, eh?"

"If you would be so kind, sire."

"Oh, stop it." Gregor sighed. "I will play my assigned part. As always."

"Thank you." Miles thought of offering some apology, some solace, then thought better of it. "The other wild card is Randall's Rangers. Who are now, unless I miss my guess, in considerable disarray. Their second-in-command has vanished, their commander has deserted at the start of the action—how was it the Vervani let her make an exit, by the way?"

"She told them she was going out to confer with

you—implied she'd somehow added you to her forces. She was going to jump her fast courier to the hot side immediately thereafter, supposedly."

Hm. She may have inadvertantly paved our way—is she denying involvement with the Cetagandans?"

"I don't think the Vervani have caught on yet about the Rangers opening the door to the Cetagandans. At the time we left Vervain Station they were still putting the Rangers' failures to defend the Cetagandan-side jump down to incompetence."

"Probably with considerable supporting evidence. I doubt the bulk of the Rangers knew about the betrayal, or it couldn't have stayed secret this long. And whatever inner cadre that was working with the Cetas, were left in the dark when Cavilo took off on her Imperial tangent. You realize, Gregor, you did this? Sabotaged the Cetagandan invasion singlehandedly?"

"Oh," breathed Gregor, "it took both hands."

Miles decided not to touch that one. "Anyway—if we can—we need to lock the Rangers down. Get them under control, or at least out from behind everyone's backs."

"Very well."

"I suggest a round of good-guy-bad-guy. I'll be happy to take the part of bad guy."

Cavilo was brought in between two men with hand tractors. She still wore her space armor, now marred and scarred. Her helmet was gone. The armor's weapons packs had been removed, control systems disconnected, and joints locked, turning it into a hundred-kilo prison, tight as a sarcophagus. The two Dendarii soldiers set her upright near the end of the conference table and stepped back with a flourish. A statue with a live head, some Pygmalion-like metamorphosis interrupted and horribly incomplete.

"Thank you, gentlemen, dismissed," said Miles. "Commander Bothari-Jesek, please stay."

Cavilo rolled her short-cropped blond head in futile resistance, the limit of physically possible motion. She glared furiously at Gregor as the soldiers exited. "You snake," she snarled. "You *bastard.*"

Gregor sat with his elbows on the conference table, chin resting in his hands. He raised his head to say tiredly, "Commander Cavilo, both my parents died violently in political intrigue before I was six years old. A fact you might have researched. Did you think you were dealing with an *amateur?*"

"You were out of your league from the beginning, Cavilo," said Miles, walking slowly around her as if inspecting his prize. Her head turned to follow him, then had to swivel to pick up his orbit on the other side. "You should have stuck to your original contract. Or your second plan. Or your third. You should, in fact, have stuck to *something.* Anything. Your total self-interest didn't make you strong, it made you a rag in the wind, anybody's to pick up. Now, Gregor—though not I—thinks you should be given a chance to earn your worthless life."

"You haven't got the balls to shove me out the air lock." Her eyes were slitted with her rage.

"I wasn't planning to." Since it clearly made her skin crawl, Miles circled her again. "No. Looking ahead—when this is over—I thought I might give you to the Cetagandans. A treaty tidbit that will cost us nothing, and help turn them up sweet. I imagine they'll be looking for you, don't you?" He fetched up before her and smiled.

Her face drained. The tendons stood out on her slender neck.

Gregor spoke. "But if you do as we ask, I will grant you safe passage out of the Hegen Hub, via Barrayar, when this is over. Together with any surviving remnant of your forces that will still follow you. It will give you a two-month head start on the Cetagandan vengeance for this debacle."

"In fact," put in Miles, "if you play your part, you could even come out of this a heroine. What fun!"

Gregor's glower at him was not entirely feigned.

"I'll get you," Cavilo breathed to Miles.

"It's the best deal you'll get today. Life. Salvage. A new start, far from here—very far from here. That, Simon Illyan will assure. Far away, but not unwatched."

Calculation began to edge out the rage in her eyes. "What do you want me to do?"

"Not much. Yield up what control you still have of your forces to an officer of our choice. Probably a Vervani liaison, they're paying for you, after all. You will introduce your replacement to your chain of command, and retire to the safety of the *Triumph's* brig for the duration."

"There won't be any surviving remnant of the Rangers when this is done!"

"There is that chance," Miles conceded. "You were going to throw them all away. Note, please, I'm not offering a choice between this and some better deal. It's this or the Cetagandans. Whose approval of treason is strictly limited to those who deal in their favor."

Cavilo looked like she wanted to spit, but said, "Very well. I yield. You have your deal."

"Thank you."

"But you . . ." her eyes were chips of blue ice, her voice low and venomous, "you will learn, little man. You're riding high today, but time will bring you down. I'd say, just wait twenty years, but I doubt you're going to live that long. Time will teach you how much *nothing* your loyalties will buy you. The day they finally grind you up and spit you out, I'm just sorry I won't be there to watch, 'cause you're gonna be *hamburger.*"

Miles called the soldiers back in. "Take her away." It was almost a plea. As the door closed behind the prisoner and her porters, he turned to find Elena's eyes upon him.

"God, that woman makes me cold." He shivered.

"Ah?" Gregor remarked, elbows still planted. "Yet in a weird way, you seem to get along with each other. You think alike."

"Gregor!" Miles protested. "Elena?" he called for a counter-vote.

"You're both very twisty," said Elena doubtfully. "And, er, short." At Miles's tight-lipped look of outrage she explained, "It's more a matter of pattern than content. If you were power-crazy, instead of, of . . ."

"Some other kind of crazy, yes, go on."

"—you could plot like that. You seemed to kind of enjoy figuring her out."

"Thank-you-I-think." He hunched his shoulders. Was it true? Could that be himself in twenty years? Sick with cynicism and unvented rage, a shelled self thrilled only by mastery, power games, control, armor-plate with a wounded beast inside?

"Let's get back to the *Triumph,*" he said shortly. "We've all got work to do."

Miles paced impatiently across the short breadth of Admiral Oser's cabin aboard the *Triumph.* Gregor leaned hip-slung on the edge of the comconsole desk, watching him oscillate.

". . . naturally the Vervani will be suspicious, but with the Cetagandans breathing down their necks they'll have a real will to believe. And deal. You'll want to make it as attractive as possible, to close things up quickly, but of course don't give away any more than you have to—"

Gregor said dryly, "Perhaps you'd like to come along and operate my holoprompter?"

Miles stopped, cleared his throat. "Sorry. I know you know more about treaties than I do. I . . . babble when I'm nervous, sometimes."

"Yes, I know."

Miles managed to keep his mouth shut, though not his feet still, until the cabin buzzer blatted.

"Prisoners as ordered, sir," came Sergeant Chodak's voice over the intercom.

"Thank you, enter." Miles leaned across the desk and hit the door control.

Chodak and a squad marched Captain Ungari and Sergeant Overholt into the cabin. The prisoners were indeed just as Miles had ordered; washed, shaved, combed, and provided with fresh-pressed Dendarii greys with equivalent rank insignia. They also looked palpably surly and hostile about it.

"Thank you, Sergeant, you and your squad are dismissed."

"Dismissed?" Chodak's eyebrows questioned the wisdom of this. "Sure you don't want us to at least stand-to in the corridor, sir? Remember the last time."

"It won't be necessary this time."

Ungari's glare denied that airy assertion. Chodak withdrew doubtfully, keeping his stunner-aim steady on the pair until the doors closed across his view.

Ungari inhaled deeply. "Vorkosigan! You mutinous little mutant, I'm going to have you court-martialed, skinned, stuffed, and mounted for this—"

They had not yet noticed quiet Gregor, still leaning on the comconsole and also wearing courtesy Dendarii greys, though without insignia, there being no Dendarii equivalent for emperor.

"Uh, sir—" Miles motioned the dark-faced captain's eye toward Gregor.

"Those are such widely shared sentiments, Captain Ungari, that I'm afraid you might have to stand in line and wait your turn," Gregor remarked, smiling slightly.

The remaining air went out of Ungari unvoiced. He braced to attention; to his credit, the uppermost of the wildly mixed emotions on his face was profound relief. "*Sire.*"

"My apologies, Captain," said Miles, "for my high-handed treatment of you and Sergeant Overholt, but I judged my plan for retrieving Gregor too, uh, delicate for, for . . ." *your nerves,* "I thought I'd better take personal responsibility." *You were happier not watching, really. And I was happier not having my elbow jogged.*

"Ensigns don't have personal responsibility for operations of this magnitude, their commanders do," Ungari snarled. "As Simon Illyan would have been the first to point out to me if your plan—however delicate—had failed. . . ."

"Well, then, congratulations, sir; you have just rescued the emperor," snapped Miles. "Who, as your commander-in-chief, has a few orders for you, if you will permit him to get a word in edgewise."

Ungari's teeth closed. With visible effort, he dismissed Miles from his attention and focused on Gregor. "Sire?"

Gregor spoke. "As the only members of ImpSec within a couple million kilometers—except for Ensign Vorkosigan, who has other chores—I'm attaching you and Sergeant Overholt to my person, until we make contact with our reinforcements. I may also require courier duties of you. Before we leave the *Triumph*, please share any pertinent intelligence you may possess with Dendarii Ops; they're now my Imperial, uh . . ."

"Most obedient servants," suggested Miles under his breath.

"Forces," Gregor concluded. "Consider that grey suit," (Ungari glanced down at his with loathing) "regulation wear, and respect it accordingly. You'll doubtless get your greens back when I get mine."

Miles put in, "I'll be detaching the Dendarii light cruiser *Ariel* and the faster of our two fast couriers to Gregor's personal service, when you depart for Vervain Station. If you have to split off on courier duties, I suggest you take the smaller ship and leave the *Ariel* with Gregor. Its captain, Bel Thorne, is my most trusted Dendarii shipmaster."

"Still thinking about my line of retreat, eh, Miles?" Gregor raised a brow at him.

Miles bowed slightly. "If things go very wrong, someone must live to avenge us. Not to mention to make damn sure the Dendarii survivors get paid. We owe them that much, I think."

"Yes," Gregor agreed softly.

"I also have my personal report on recent events for you to deliver to Simon Illyan," Miles went on, "in case I—in case you see him before I do." Miles handed Ungari a data disk.

Ungari looked dizzy at this rapid reordering of his priorities. "Vervain Station? Pol Six is where your safety lies, surely, sire."

"Vervain Station is where my duty lies, Captain, and perforce yours. Come along, I'll explain it all as we go."

"Are you leaving Vorkosigan loose?" Ungari frowned at Miles. "With these mercenaries? I have a problem with that, sire."

"I'm sorry, sir," said Miles to Ungari, "that I cannot, cannot . . ." *obey you,* but Miles left that unsaid.

"I have a deeper problem with arranging a battle for these mercenaries and then not showing up for it. A difference between myself and . . . the Rangers' former commander. There must be some difference between us, maybe that's it. Gre—the Emperor understands."

"Hm," said Gregor. "Yes. Captain Ungari, I officially detach Ensign Vorkosigan as Our Dendarii liaison. On my personal responsibility. Which should be sufficient even for you."

"It's not me that it has to be sufficient for, sire!"

Gregor hesitated fractionally. "For Barrayar's best interests, then. A sufficient argument even for Simon. Let us go, Captain."

"Sergeant Overholt," Miles added, "you will be the Emperor's personal bodyguard and batman, until relieved."

Overholt looked anything but relieved at this abrupt field promotion. "Sir," he whispered aside to Miles, "I haven't had the advanced course!"

He referred to Simon Illyan's mandatory, personally conducted ImpSec course for the palace guard, that gave Gregor's usual crew that hard-polished edge.

"We all have a similar problem here, Sergeant, believe me," Miles murmured back. "Do your best."

The *Triumph's* tactics room was alive with activity, every station chair occupied, every holovid display bright with the flow of ship and fleet tactical changes. Miles stood at Tung's elbow and felt doubly redundant. He bethought of the jape back at the Academy. *Rule 1: Only overrule the tactical computer if you know something it doesn't. Rule 2: The tac comp always knows more than you do.*

This was combat? This muffled chamber, swirl of lights, these padded chairs? Maybe the detachment was a good thing, for commanders. His heart hammered even now. A tac room of this caliber could cause information overload and mind-lock, if you let it. The trick was to pick out what was important, and never, ever to forget that the map was not the territory.

His job here, Miles reminded himself, was not to command. It was to watch Tung command, and learn how he did it, his alternate modes of thinking to Barrayaran Academy Standard. Miles's only legitimate point of overrule might come if some external political/strategic need took precedence over internal tactical logic. Miles prayed that event would not arise, because a shorter and uglier name for it was *betraying your troops.*

Miles's attention sharpened as a little jumpscout winked into existence at the throat of the wormhole. On the tactics display it was a pink point of light in a slowly moving whirlpool of darkness. On a telescreen, it was a slim ship against fixed and distant stars. From its own wired-in pilot's point of view, it was some strange extension of his own body. In yet another vid display, it was a collection of telemetry readouts, numerology, some Platonic ideal. *What is truth? All. None.*

"Sharkbait One reporting to Fleet One," the pilot's voice came over Tung's console. "You have ten minutes' clearance. Stand by for tight-beam burst."

Tung spoke into his comm. "Fleet commence jump, tight by the numbers."

The first Dendarii ship waiting by the wormhole jockeyed into place, glowed brightly in the tac display (though it appeared to do nothing in the televid), and vanished. A second ship followed in thirty seconds, pushing the safety limit of time margins between jumps. Two ships trying to rematerialize in the same place at the same time would result in no ships and a very large explosion.

As the Sharkbait's tightbeam telemetry was digested

by the tac comp, the image rotated so that the dark vortex representing (but in no way picturing) the wormhole was suddenly mirrored by an exit vortex. Beyond that exit vortex an array of dots and specks and lines represented ships in flight, maneuvering, firing, fleeing; the hardened Homeside battle station of the Vervani, twin to the Hub-side station where Miles had left Gregor; the Cetagandan attackers. A view of their destination at last. All lies, of course, it was minutes out of date.

"Yech," Tung commented. "What a mess. Here we go . . ."

The jump klaxon sounded. It was the *Triumph's* turn. Miles gripped the back of Tung's chair, though intellectually he knew the feeling of motion was illusory. A whirl of dreams seemed to cloud his mind, for a moment, for an hour; it was unmeasurable. The wrench in his stomach and the godawful wave of nausea that followed were anything but dreamlike. Jump over. A moment of silence throughout the room, as others struggled to overcome their disorientation. Then the murmur picked up where it had left off. *Welcome to Vervain. Take a wormhole jump to hell.*

The tac display spun and shifted, shunting in new data, recentering its little universe. Their wormhole was presently guarded by its beleaguered Station and a thin and battered string of Vervani Navy and Vervani-commanded Ranger ships. The Cetagandans had hit it once already, been driven off, and now hovered out of range awaiting reinforcements for the next strike. Cetagandan re-supply was streaming across the Vervain system from the other wormhole.

The other wormhole had fallen fast, the only way to fly from the attacker's viewpoint. Even with complete surprise on the Cetagandans' side for their massive first strike, the Vervani might have stopped them had not three Ranger ships apparently misunderstood their orders and broken off when they should have counterattacked. But the Cetagandans had secured their bridgehead and begun to pour through.

The second wormhole, Miles's wormhole, had been better equipped for defense—until the panicked Vervani had pulled everything that could be spared back to guard the high orbitals of the homeworld. Miles could scarcely blame them; it was a hard strategic choice either way. But now the Cetagandans boiled across the system practically unimpeded, hopscotching the heavily guarded planet, in a bold attempt to take the Hegen wormhole, if not by surprise, at least at speed.

The first method of choice for attacking a wormhole was by subterfuge, subornment, and infiltration, i.e., to cheat. The second, also preferring subterfuge in its execution, was by an end-run, sending forces around by another route (if there was one) into the contested local space. The third was to open the attack with a sacrifice ship laying down a "sun wall," a massive blanket of nuclear missilettes deployed as a unit, creating a planar wave that cleared near-space of everything including, frequently, the attack ship; but sun walls were costly, rapidly dissipated, and only locally effective. The Cetagandans had attempted to combine all three methods, as the Rangers' disarray and the filthy radioactive fog still outgassing from the vicinity of their first conquest testified.

The fourth approved approach for the problem of frontally attacking a guarded wormhole was to shoot the officer who suggested it. Miles trusted the Cetagandans would work around to that one too, by the time he was done.

Time passed. Miles hooked a station chair into clamps and studied the central display till his eyes watered and his mind threatened to fall into a hypnotic fugue, then rose and shook himself and circulated among the duty stations, kibbitzing.

The Cetagandans maneuvered. The sudden and unexpected arrival of the Dendarii force during the lull had thrown them into temporary confusion; their planned final attack on the strained Vervani must needs be converted on the fly into yet another softening-up round of hit-and-run. Expensive. At this point the Cetagandans had few ways of concealing their numbers or movements. The defending Dendarii had the implication of hidden reserves (who knew how unlimited? Not Miles, certainly) concealed on the other side of the jump. A brief hope flared in Miles that this threat alone might be enough to make the Cetagandans break off the attack.

"Naw," sighed Tung when Miles confided this optimistic thought. "They're too far into it now. The butcher's bill's too high already for them to pretend they were only fooling. Even to themselves. A Cetagandan commander who packed it in now would go home to a court-martial. They'll keep going long after it's hopeless, as their brass tries desperately to cover their bleeding asses with a flag of victory."

"That is . . . vile."

"That is the system, son, and not just for the Cetagandans. One of the system's several built-in defects. And besides," Tung grinned briefly, "it's not as hopeless as all that yet. A fact we will try to conceal from them."

The Cetagandan forces began to move, their directions and accelerations telegraphing their intention for a pounding pass. The trick was to try for local concentrations of force, three or four ships ganging up on one, overwhelming the defender's plasma mirrors. The Dendarii and Vervani would attempt an identical strategy against Cetagandan stragglers, but for a few bravura captains on both sides equipped with the new imploder lances playing an insane game of chicken, trying to put a target within the weapon's short range. Miles also tried to keep one eye on the Rangers' dispositions. Not every Ranger ship had Vervani advisors aboard, and battle arrays that put the Rangers in front of the Cetagandans were much to be preferred to ones that put Rangers behind Dendarii backs.

The quiet murmur of techs and computers within the tactics room scarcely changed pace. There ought to be a flourish of drums, bagpipes, something to herald this dance with death. But if reality broke in at all to this upholstered bubble, it would be sudden, absolute, and over.

A vid-comm message interrupted, intra-ship—yes, there was still a real ship encasing them—a breathless officer reporting to Tung. "Brig, sir. Watch yourselves up there. We've had a break-out. Admiral Oser's escaped, and he let all the other prisoners out too."

"Dammit," said Tung, glared at Miles, and pointed to the comm. "*Handle* that. Jack up Auson." He turned his attention back to his tactics display, muttering, "This wouldn't have happened in *my* day."

Miles slipped into the comm chair, and paged the *Triumph's* bridge. "Auson! Did you get the word on Oser?"

Auson's irritated face appeared, "Yeah, we're working on it."

"Order extra commando guards to the tactics room, engineering, and your own bridge. This is a real bad time for interruptions down here."

"Tell me. We can see the Ceta bastards coming." Auson punched off.

Miles began monitoring internal security channels, pausing only to note the arrival of well-armed guards in the corridor. Oser had clearly had help in his escape, some loyal Oseran officer or officers, which made Miles wonder in turn about the security of the security guards. And would Oser try to combine with Metzov and Cavilo? A couple of Dendarii imprisoned for disciplinary infractions were found wandering the corridors and returned to the brig; another came back on his own. A suspected spy was cornered in a storeroom. No sign yet of the truly dangerous . . .

"There he goes!"

Miles keyed in the channel. A cargo shuttle was breaking out of its clamps, away from the side of the *Triumph* and into space.

Miles overrode channels, found fire control. "Don't, repeat, *Do not* open fire on that shuttle!"

"Uh . . ." came the reply. "Yes, sir. Do not open fire."

Why did Miles get the subliminal impression that tech hadn't been planning to open fire in the first place? Clearly a well-coordinated escape. The witch-hunt later was going to be nasty. "Patch me through to that shuttle!" Miles demanded of the comm officer. *And, oh yes, send a guard to the shuttle hatch corridors . . .* too late.

"I'll try, sir, but they're not answering."

"How many aboard?"

"Several, but we're not sure exactly—"

"Patch me through. They've got to listen, even if they won't reply."

"I have a channel, sir, but I have no idea if they're listening."

"I'll try it." Miles took a breath. "Admiral Oser! Turn your shuttle around and come back to the *Triumph*. It's too dangerous out there, you're running headlong into a fire zone. Return, and I will personally guarantee your safety—"

Tung was looking down over Miles's shoulder. "He's trying to make it to the *Peregrine.* Dammit, if that ship pulls out, our defensive array will collapse."

Miles glanced back at the tac comp. "Surely not. I thought we put the *Peregrine* in the reserve area precisely because we doubted its reliability."

"Yes, but if the *Peregrine* pulls out I can name three other captain-owners who will follow it. And if four ships pull out—"

"The Rangers will break despite their Vervani commander, and we'll be cooked, right, I see." Miles glanced again at the tac comp. "I don't think he's going to make it—Admiral Oser! Can you read me?"

"Yike!" Tung returned to his seat, absorbed in the Cetagandans once again. Four Cetagandan ships were combining against the edge of the Dendarii formation, while another attempted to penetrate the center, clearly trying to close the range for a lance attack. Casually, in passing, a Cetagandan plasma gunner from it picked off the stray shuttle. Just bright sparks.

"He didn't know the Cetagandans were making their attack run till his stolen shuttle cleared the *Triumph,*" Miles whispered. "Good plan, rotten timing. . . . He could have turned around, he chose to try and run for it. . . ." Oser chose his death? Was that the comforting argument?

The Cetagandans did not so much break off their attack run as complete it, in depressingly good order. The score was slightly in the Dendarii's favor. A number of Cetagandan ships had been badly chewed, and one blown up entirely. Dendarii and Ranger damage control channels were frantic. The Dendarii had not lost ships yet, but had lost firepower, engines, flight control, life support, shielding. The next attack run would be more devastating.

They can afford to lose three to our one. If they keep

coming, keep nibbling, they must inevitably win, Miles reflected coldly. *Unless we are reinforced.*

Hours passed, while the Cetagandans formed up again. Miles took short breaks in the wardroom provided for that purpose off the tactics room, but was too keyed up to emulate Tung's amazing fifteen-minute instant naps. Miles knew Tung wasn't faking relaxation for morale effect; nobody could simulate such a disgusting snore.

It was possible to watch the Cetagandan reinforcements coming on across the Vervain system in the televid. That was the time tradeoff, the risk. The longer the Cetas waited, the better-equipped they could be, but the longer they waited, the better the chance that their enemies would recover too. There was doubtless a tac comp aboard the Cetagandan command ship that had generated a probability curve marking the optimum intersection of Us and Them. If only the damned Vervani would be more aggressive in attacking that supply stream from their planetary base . . .

And here they came on again. Tung watched his displays, his hands unconsciously clenching and unclenching in his lap between jerky, thick-fingered dances on his control panel, sending orders, correcting, anticipating. Miles's fingers twitched in tiny echoes, his mind trying to get around Tung's thought, to absorb everything. Their picture of reality was getting lacy with hidden holes, as data points dropped out due to damaged sensors or senders on various ships. The Cetagandans flew through the Dendarii formation, pounding . . . a Dendarii ship blew apart, another, weapons dead, tried to scramble out of range, three Ranger ships broke away as a unit . . . it looked bad. . . .

"*Sharkbait Three* reporting," an abrupt voice overrode all other comm channels, making Miles jump in his seat. "Hold this worm-hole *clear.* Help coming."

"Not *now,*" snarled Tung, but began to attempt a rapid redeployment to cover the tiny volume of space, keep it clear of debris, missiles, enemy fire, and most of all enemy ships with imploder lances. Those Cetagandan ships that were in position to respond seemed almost to prick their ears, hesitating as Dendarii ship movements telegraphed *changes coming.* The Dendarii might be in retreat . . . some exploitable opportunity might be about to open up. . . .

"Whatinhell's *that?*" Tung said, as something huge and temporarily indecipherable appeared in the throat of the wormhole and began instantly to accelerate. He punched up readouts. "It's too big to be that fast. It's too fast to be that *big.*"

Miles recognized the energy profile even before the televiewer yielded up a visual. *What a shakedown cruise they're having.* "It's the *Prince Serg.* Our Barrayaran Imperial reinforcements have just arrived." He took a dizzy breath. "Did I not promise you . . ."

Tung swore horribly, in pure aesthetic admiration. Other ships followed, Aslunder, Polian Navy, spreading out rapidly into attack—not defensive—formation.

The ripple in the Cetagandan formations was like a silent cry of dismay. An imploder-armed Cetagandan ship dove bravely at the *Prince Serg,* and was sliced in half discovering that the *Serg's* imploder lances had been improved to triple the Cetagandans' range. That was the first mortal blow.

The second came over the comm link, a call to the Cetagandan aggressors to surrender or be destroyed—in the name of the Hegen Alliance Navy, Emperor Gregor Vorbarra and Admiral Count Aral Vorkosigan, Joint Commanders.

For a moment, Miles thought Tung was about to faint. Tung inhaled alarmingly, and bellowed with delight, "Aral Vorkosigan! Here? Hot damn!" And in an only slightly more private whisper, "How'd they lure him out of retirement? Maybe I'll get to meet him!"

Tung the military history nut was one of Miles's father's most fanatical fans, Miles recalled, and until and unless firmly suppressed could rattle off every public detail of the Barrayaran admiral's early campaigns. "I'll see what I can arrange," Miles promised.

"If you can arrange *that*, son . . ." With an effort, Tung pulled his mind away from his beloved hobby of studying military history and back to his (admittedly, closely related) job of making it.

The Cetagandan ships were breaking, first in panicked singles and then in more coordinated groups, trying to organize a properly covered retreat. The *Prince Serg* and its support group did not waste a millisecond, but followed up instantly, attacking and disordering attempted self-covering arrays of enemy ships, worrying the resulting stragglers. In the ensuing hours the retreat became a true rout when the Vervani ships protecting their high planetary orbitals, encouraged, at last broke orbit and joined the attack. The Vervani reserve was merciless, in the terror for their homes the Cetagandans had instilled in them.

The mopping-up in detail, the appalling damage control problems, the personnel rescues, were so absorbing that it took Miles those several hours to gradually realize the war was over for the Dendarii fleet. They had done their job.

CHAPTER SEVENTEEN

Before departing the tactics room, Miles prudently checked with the *Triumph's* security to determine how their roundup of escaped prisoners was progressing. Missing and still unaccounted for remained Oser, the *Peregrine's* captain and two other loyal Oseran officers, Commander Cavilo, and General Metzov.

Miles was fairly certain he had witnessed Oser and his officers converted to radioactive ash in his monitors. Had Metzov and Cavilo been aboard that fleeing shuttle too? Fine irony, for Cavilo to die at the hands of the Cetagandans after all. Though—admittedly—it would have been equally ironic had she died at the hands of the Vervani, Randall's Rangers, the Aslunders, the Barrayarans, or anyone else she'd double-crossed in her brief, cometary career in the Hegen Hub. Her end was neat and convenient if true, but—he didn't like to think that her last, savage remarks to him had now acquired the prophetic weight of a dying curse. He ought to fear Metzov more than Cavilo. He ought to, but he didn't. He shuddered, and borrowed a commando guard for the walk back to his cabin.

On the way, he encountered a shuttle-load of wounded being transferred to the *Triumph's* sickbay. The *Triumph,* in the reserve group (such as it was) had taken no hits its shields couldn't handle, but other ships had not been so fortunate. Space battle casualty lists usually had the proportions reversed from planetary, the dead outnumbering the wounded, yet in lucky circumstances where the artificial environment was preserved, soldiers might survive their injuries. Uncertainly, Miles changed course and followed the procession along. What good could he do in sickbay?

The triage people had not sent minor cases to the *Triumph.* Three hideous burns and a massive head injury went to the head of the line, and were whisked off by the anxiously waiting staff. A few soldiers were conscious, quietly waiting their turns, immobilized with air bag braces on their float pallets, eyes cloudy with pain and painkillers.

Miles tried to say a few words to each. Some stared uncomprehendingly, some seemed to appreciate it; he lingered a little longer with these, giving what encouragement he could. He then withdrew and stood dumbly by the door for several minutes, awash in the familiar, terrifying odors of a sickbay after a battle, disinfectants and blood, burnt meat, urine, and electronics, until he realized exhaustion was making him thoroughly stupid and useless, shaky and near tears. He pushed off from the wall and stumped out. Bed. If anyone really wanted his command presence, they could come find him.

He hit the code-lock on Oser's cabin. Now that he'd inherited it, he supposed he ought to change the numbers. He sighed and entered. As he stepped inside he became conscious of two unfortunate facts. First, although he had dismissed his commando guard upon entering sickbay, he had forgotten to call him back, and second, he was not alone. The door closed behind him before he could recoil into the corridor, and he banged into it backing up.

The dusky red hue of General Metzov's face was even more arresting to the eye than the silver gleam of the nerve disrupter parabola in his hand, aim centered on Miles's head.

Metzov had somehow acquired a set of Dendarii greys, a little small for him. Commander Cavilo, standing behind Metzov, had acquired a similar set, a little large for her. Metzov looked huge and furious. Cavilo looked . . . strange. Bitter, ironic, weirdly amused. Bruises marred her neck. She bore no weapon.

"Got you," Metzov whispered triumphantly. "At last." With a rictus smile, he advanced stepwise on Miles till he could pin him to the wall by his neck with one big hand. He dropped the nerve disrupter with a clatter and wrapped the other hand around Miles's neck, not to break but to squeeze it.

"You'll never survive—" was all Miles managed to choke out before his air pinched off. He could feel his trachea begin to crunch, crumpling, his head felt on the verge of dark explosion as his blood supply was cut off. No talking Metzov out of *this* murder. . . .

Cavilo slipped forward, crouching, soundless and unnoticed as a cat, to take up the dropped nerve disrupter, then step back, around to Miles's left.

"Stanis, darling," she cooed. Metzov, obsessed with Miles's lingering strangulation, did not turn his head. Cavilo, clearly imitating Metzov's cadences, recited, " 'Open your legs to me, you bitch, or I'll blow your brains out.' "

Metzov's head twisted round then, his eyes widening. She blew his brains out. The crackling blue bolt hit him square between the eyes. He almost snapped Miles's neck, plastic-reinforced though those bones were, in his last convulsion, before he dropped to the deck. The blistering electrochemical smell of nerve-disruptor death slapped Miles in the face.

Miles sagged frozen against the wall, not daring to move. He raised his eyes from the corpse to Cavilo. Her lips were curved in a smile of immense satisfaction, satiated. Had Cavilo's line been a direct and recent quote? What had they been doing, all the long hours they must have been waiting in the hunter's blind of Oser's cabin? The silence lengthened.

"Not," Miles swallowed, trying to clear his bruised throat, and croaked, "not that I'm complaining, mind you, but why aren't you going ahead and shooting me too?"

Cavilo smirked. "A quick revenge is better than none. A slow and lingering one is better still, but to savor it fully I must survive it. Another day, kid." She tilted the nerve disrupter up as if to flourish it into a holster, then let it hang pointed down by her side in her relaxed hand. "You've sworn you'll see me safe out of the Hegen Hub, Vor lord. And I've come to believe you are actually stupid enough to keep your word. Not that I'm complaining, mind you. Now, if Oser had issued more than one weapon between us, or if he'd given the nerve disruptor to me and the code to his cabin to Stanis and not the other way around, or if Oser'd taken us with him as I begged . . . things might have worked out differently."

Very differently. Very slowly, and very, very carefully, Miles inched over to the comconsole and called security. Cavilo watched him thoughtfully. After a few moments, coming up on the time they might expect the reinforcements to storm in, she strolled over to his side. "I underestimated you, you know."

"I never underestimated you."

"I know. I'm not used to that . . . thank you." Contemptuously, she tossed the nerve disruptor onto Metzov's body. Then, with a sudden baring of her teeth, she wheeled, wrapped an arm around Miles's neck, and kissed him vigorously. Her timing was perfect; Security, Elena and Sergeant Chodak in the lead, burst through the door just before Miles managed to fight her off.

Miles stepped from the *Triumph's* shuttle through the short flex tube and on board the *Prince Serg*. He stared around enviously at the clean, spacious, beautifully lit corridor, at the row of smart and gleaming honor guards snapping to attention, at the polished officers waiting in their Barrayaran Imperial dress greens. He stole an anxious glance down at his own Dendarii grey-and-whites. The *Triumph,* key and pride of the Dendarii fleet, seemed to shrink into something small and gritty and battered and used.

Yeah, but you guys would not look so pretty now if we had not used ourselves so hard, Miles consoled himself.

Tung, Elena, and Chodak were all goggling like tourists too. Miles called them firmly to attention to receive and return the crisp welcoming salutes of their hosts.

"I'm Commander Natochini, executive officer of the *Prince Serg,*" the senior Barrayaran introduced himself. "Lieutenant Yegorov, here, will escort you and Commander Bothari-Jesek to Admiral Vorkosigan for your meeting, Admiral Naismith. Commodore Tung, I will be personally conducting your tour of the *Prince Serg,* and will be pleased to answer any of your questions. If the answers aren't classified, of course."

"Of course." Tung's broad face looked immensely pleased. In fact, if Tung grew any smugger he might implode.

"We will join Admiral Vorkosigan for lunch in the senior officers' mess, after your meeting and our tour," Commander Natochini continued to Miles. "Our last dinner guest there was the President of Pol and his entourage, twelve days ago."

Certain that the mercenaries understood the magnitude of the privilege they were being granted, the Barrayaran exec led the happy Tung and Chodak off down the corridor. Miles heard Tung chuckle under his breath, "Lunch with Admiral Vorkosigan, heh, heh . . ."

Lieutenant Yegorov motioned Miles and Elena in the opposite direction. "You are Barrayaran, ma'am?" he inquired of Elena.

"My father was liege-sworn Armsman to the late Count Piotr for eighteen years," Elena stated. "He died in the Count's service."

"I see," said the lieutenant respectfully. "You are acquainted with the family, then." *That explains you,* Miles could almost see him thinking.

"Ah, yes."

The lieutenant glanced down a little more dubiously at "Admiral Naismith." "And, uh, I understand you are Betan, sir?"

"Originally," said Miles, in his flattest Betan accent.

"You . . . may find the way we Barrayarans do things to be a little more formal than what you're used to," the lieutenant warned. "The Count, you understand, is accustomed to the respect and deference due his rank."

Miles watched, delighted, as the earnest officer

sought a polite way of saying, *Call him sir, don't wipe your nose on your sleeve, and none of your damned Betan egalitarian backchat, either.* "You may find him rather formidable," Yegorov concluded.

"A real stuffed shirt, eh?"

The lieutenant frowned. "He is a great man."

"Aw, I bet if we pour enough wine into him at lunch, he'll loosen up and tell dirty stories with the best of 'em."

Yegorov's polite smile became fixed. Elena, eyes dancing, leaned down and whispered forcefully, "Admiral, behave!"

"Oh, all right." Miles sighed regretfully.

The lieutenant glanced gratefully at Elena, over Miles's head.

Miles admired the spit and polish, in passing. Besides just being new, the *Prince Serg* had been designed with diplomacy as well as war in mind, a ship fit to carry the emperor on state visits without loss of military efficiency. He saw a young ensign, down a cross-corridor that had a wall panel apart, directing some tech crew on minor repairs—no, by God, it was original installation. The *Prince Serg* had broken orbit with work crews still aboard, Miles had heard. He glanced back over his shoulder. *There but for the grace of God and General Metzov go I.* If he'd kept his nose clean on Kyril Island for just six months . . . he felt an illogical twinge of envy for that busy ensign.

They entered officers' country. Lieutenant Yegorov led them through an antechamber and into a spartanly appointed flag office twice the size of anything Miles had seen on a Barrayaran ship before. Admiral Count Aral Vorkosigan looked up from his comconsole desk as the doors slid silently back.

Miles stepped through, his belly suddenly shaking inside. To conceal and control his emotion he tossed off, "Hey, you Imperial snails are going to go all fat and soft, lolling around in this kind of luxury, y'know?"

"Ha!" Admiral Vorkosigan stumbled out of his chair and banged around the corner of his desk in his haste. *Well, no wonder, how can he see with all that water standing in his eyes?* He enfolded Miles in a hard embrace. Miles grinned and blinked and swallowed, face smashed against that cool green sleeve, and almost had control of his features again when Count Vorkosigan held him out at arm's length for an anxious, searching inspection. "You all right, boy?"

"Just fine. How'd you like your wormhole jump?"

"Just fine," breathed Count Vorkosigan back. "Mind you, there were moments when certain of my advisors wanted to have you shot. And there were moments when I agreed with 'em."

Lieutenant Yegorov, cut off in mid-announcement of their arrival (Miles hadn't heard him speaking, and he doubted his father had either), was standing with his mouth still open, looking perfectly stunned. Lieutenant Jole, suppressing a grin himself, arose from the other side of the comconsole desk and guided Yegorov gently and mercifully back out the door. "Thank you, Lieutenant. The Admiral appreciates your services, that will be all. . . ." Jole glanced back over his shoulder, quirked a pensive brow, and followed Yegorov out. Miles just glimpsed the blond lieutenant drape himself across a chair in the antechamber, head back in the relaxed posture of a man anticipating a long wait, before the door slid closed. Jole could be supernaturally courteous at times.

"Elena." With an effort, Count Vorkosigan broke away from Miles to take both Elena's hands in a firm brief grip. "You are well?"

"Yes, sir."

"That pleases me . . . more than I can say. Cordelia sends her love and her best hopes. If I saw you, I was to remind you, ah—I must get the phrase exact, it was one of her Betan cracks—'Home is where, when you have to go there, they have to take you in.'"

"I can hear her voice," smiled Elena. "Tell her thank you. Tell her . . . I will remember."

"Good." Count Vorkosigan pressed her no further. "Sit, sit." He waved them at chairs, which he snugged up close to the comconsole desk, and sat himself. For an instant, changing gears, his features relaxed, then concentrated with attention once again. *God, he looks tired,* Miles realized, for a split second, almost ghastly. *Gregor, you have much to answer for.* But Gregor knew that.

"What's the latest word on the cease-fire?" Miles asked.

"Still holding nicely, thank you. The only Cetagandan ships that haven't jumped back where they came from, had damaged Necklin rods or control systems or injured pilots. Or all three. We're letting them repair two of them and jump them out with skeleton crews, the rest are not salvageable. I estimate controlled commercial travel could resume in six weeks."

Miles shook his head. "So ends the Five-Day War. I never once saw a Cetagandan face-to-face. All that effort and bloodshed, just to return to the status quo ante."

"Not quite for everyone. A number of Cetagandan senior officers have been recalled to their capital, to explain their 'unauthorized adventure' to their emperor. Their apologies are expected to be fatal."

Miles snorted. "Expiate their failure, rather. 'Unauthorized adventure.' Does anyone believe that? Why do they even bother?"

"Finesse, boy. A retreating enemy should be offered

all the face he can carry off. Just don't let him carry off anything else."

"I understand you finessed the Polians. All this time, I expected it would be Simon Illyan to show up in person to haul us lost boys home."

"He longed to come, but there was no way we could both leave home at the same time. The wobbly cover we'd put over Gregor's absence could have collapsed at any moment."

"How did you pull that one off, by the way?"

"Picked out a young officer who looked a lot like Gregor, told him there was an assassination plot afoot against the Emperor and that he was to be the bait. Bless him, he volunteered at once. He—and his Security, who had the same tale told them—spent the next several weeks leading a life of ease down at Vorkosigan Surleau, eating off the best plates—but with indigestion. We finally sent him off on a rustic camping trip, as inquiries from the capital were getting pressing. People will twig soon, I'm sure, if they haven't already, but now we've got Gregor back we can explain it away any way we like. Anyway *he* likes." Count Vorkosigan frowned an odd brief frown, odd because not wholly displeased.

"I was surprised," said Miles, "though very happy, that you got your forces past Pol so fast. I was afraid they wouldn't let you through till the Cetagandans were in the Hub. And then it would be too late."

"Yes, well, that's the other reason you got me instead of Simon. As Prime Minister and former Regent, it was perfectly reasonable for me to make a state visit to Pol. We came up with a quick list of the top five diplomatic concessions they've been wanting from us for years, and suggested it for an agenda.

"It being all formal and official and aboveboard, it was then perfectly reasonable for us to combine my visit with the *Prince Serg*'s shakedown cruise. We were in orbit at Pol, shuttling up and down to official receptions and parties," (his hand unconsciously rubbed his abdomen in a pain-warding motion) "with me still trying desperately to talk our way into the Hub without shooting anybody, when word of the Cetagandan surprise attack on Vervain broke. At that point, getting permission to proceed was suddenly expedited. And we were only days, not weeks, away from the action. Getting the Aslunders to lie down with the Polians was a trickier matter. Gregor astonished me, handling that. The Vervani were no problem, they were highly motivated to seek allies by then."

"I hear Gregor is now quite popular on Vervain."

"He's being feted in their capital even as we speak, I believe." Count Vorkosigan glanced at his chrono. "They've gone wild over him. Letting him ride shotgun in the *Prince Serg*'s tac room may have been a better idea than I thought. Purely from a diplomatic standpoint." Count Vorkosigan looked rather abstracted.

"It . . . astonished me, that you permitted him to jump with you into the fire zone. I hadn't expected that."

"Well, when you came down to it, the *Prince Serg's* fleet tac room had to have been among the most tightly defended few cubic meters anywhere in Vervain local space. It was, it was . . ."

Miles watched with fascination as his father tried to spit out the words *perfectly safe,* and gagged on them instead. Light dawned. "It wasn't your idea, was it? Gregor ordered himself aboard!"

"He had several good arguments to support his position," Count Vorkosigan said. "The propaganda angle certainly seems to be bearing fruit."

"I thought you'd be too . . . prudent. To permit him the risk."

Count Vorkosigan studied his own square hands. "I was not in love with the idea, no. But I once swore an oath to serve an emperor. The most morally dangerous moment for a guardian is when the temptation to become a puppet-master seems most rational. I always knew the moment must . . . no. I knew that if the moment *never* came, I should have failed my oath most profoundly." He paused. "It was still a shock to the system, though. The letting-go."

Gregor faced you down? Oh, to have been a fly on the wall of *that* chamber.

"Even with you to practice on, all these years," Count Vorkosigan added meditatively.

"Ah . . . how're your ulcers?"

Count Vorkosigan grimaced. "Don't ask." He brightened slightly. "Better, the last three days. I may actually demand food for lunch, instead of that miserable medical mush."

Miles cleared his throat. "How's Captain Ungari?"

Count Vorkosigan twitched a lip. "He's not overly pleased with you."

"I . . . cannot apologize. I made a lot of mistakes, but disobeying his order to wait on Aslund Station wasn't one of them."

"Apparently not." Count Vorkosigan frowned at the far wall. "And yet . . . I'm more than ever convinced the regular Service is not the place for you. It's like trying to fit a square peg—no, worse than that. Like trying to fit a tesseract into a round hole."

Miles suppressed a twinge of panic. "I won't be discharged, will I?"

Elena regarded her fingernails and put in, "If you were, you could get a job as a mercenary. Just like General Metzov. I understand Commander Cavilo is looking for a few good men." Miles nearly meowed at her; she traded a smirk for his exasperated look.

"I was almost sorry to learn that Metzov was killed," remarked Count Vorkosigan. "We'd been planning to try and extradite him, before things went crazy with Gregor's disappearance."

"Ah! Did you finally decide the death of that Komarran prisoner way back when during their revolt was murder? I thought it might be—"

Count Vorkosigan held up two fingers. "Two murders."

Miles paused. "My God, he didn't try and track down poor Ahn before he left, did he?" He'd almost forgotten Ahn.

"No, but we tracked him down. Though not, alas, before Metzov had left Barrayar. And yes, the Komarran rebel had been tortured to death. Not wholly intentionally, he apparently had had some hidden medical weakness. But it was not, as the original investigator had suspected, in revenge for the death of the guard. It was the other way around. The Barrayaran guard corporal, who had participated in or at least acquiesced to the torture, though over some feeble protest, according to Ahn—the corporal suffered a revulsion of feeling, and threatened to turn Metzov in.

"Metzov murdered him in one of his panic-rages, then made Ahn help him cook up and vouch for the cover story about the escape. So Ahn was twice tainted with the thing. Metzov kept Ahn in terror, yet was equally in Ahn's power if the facts ever came out, a kind of strange lock on each other . . . which Ahn at last escaped. Ahn seemed almost relieved, and volunteered to be fast-penta'd, when Illyan's agents came for him."

Miles thought of the weatherman with regret. "Will anything bad happen to Ahn now?"

"We'd planned to make him testify, at Metzov's trial . . . Illyan thought we might even turn it to our favor, with respect to the Komarrans. Present that poor idiot guard corporal to them as an unsung hero. Hang Metzov as proof of the Emperor's good faith and commitment to justice for Barrayarans and Komarrans alike . . . nice scenario." Count Vorkosigan frowned bitterly. "I think we will quietly drop it now. Again."

Miles puffed out his breath. "Metzov. A goat to the end. Must be some bad karma, clinging to him . . . not that he didn't earn it."

"Beware of wishing for justice. You might get it."

"I've already learned that, sir."

"Already?" Count Vorkosigan cocked an eyebrow at him. "Hm."

"Speaking of justice," Miles seized the opening. "I'm concerned over the matter of Dendarii pay. They took a lot of damage, more than a mercenary fleet will usually tolerate. Their only contract was my breath and voice. If . . . if the Imperium does not back me, I will be forsworn."

Count Vorkosigan smiled slightly. "We have already considered the matter."

"Will Illyan's covert ops budget stretch, to cover this?"

"Illyan's budget would burst trying to cover this. But you, ah, seem to have a friend in a high place. We will draw you an emergency credit chit from ImpSec, this fleet's fund, and the Emperor's privy purse, and hope to recoup it all later from a special appropriation rammed through the Council of Ministers and the Council of Counts. Submit a bill."

Miles fished a data disk from his pocket. "Here, sir. From the Dendarii fleet accountant. She was up all night. Some damage estimates are still preliminary." He set it on the comconsole desk.

One corner of Count Vorkosigan's mouth twisted up. "You're learning, boy. . . ." He inserted the disk in his desk for a fast scan. "I'll have a credit chit prepared over lunch. You can take it with you when you depart."

"Thank you, sir."

"Sir," Elena put in, leaning forward earnestly, "what will happen to the Dendarii fleet now?"

"Whatever it chooses, I presume. Though they cannot linger, this close to Barrayar."

"Are we to be abandoned again?" asked Elena.

"Abandoned?"

"You made us an Imperial force, once. I thought. Baz thought. Then Miles left us, and then . . . nothing."

"Just like Kyril Island," Miles remarked. "Out of sight, out of mind." He shrugged dolefully. "I gather they suffered a similar deterioration of morale."

Count Vorkosigan gave him a sharp look. "The fate of the Dendarii—like your future military career, Miles—is a matter still under discussion."

"Do I get to be in on that discussion? Do they?"

"We'll let you know." Count Vorkosigan planted his hands on his desktop, and rose. "That's all I can say now, even to you. Lunch, officers?"

Miles and Elena perforce rose too. "Commodore Tung knows nothing of our real relationship yet," Miles cautioned. "If you wish to keep that covert, I'm going to have to play Admiral Naismith when we rejoin him."

Count Vorkosigan's smile turned peculiar. "Illyan and Captain Ungari must certainly favor not breaking a potentially useful cover identity. By all means. Should be fascinating."

"I should warn you, Admiral Naismith is not very deferential."

Elena and Count Vorkosigan looked at each other, and both broke into laughter. Miles waited, wrapped in what dignity he could muster, till they subsided. Finally.

Admiral Naismith was painfully polite during lunch. Even Lieutenant Yegorov could have found no fault.

The Vervani government courier handed the credit chit across the homeside station commandant's comconsole desk. Miles testified receipt of it with thumbprint, retina scan, and Admiral Naismith's flourishing illegible scrawl, nothing at all like Ensign Vorkosigan's careful signature. "It's a pleasure doing business with you honorable gentlemen," Miles said, pocketing the chit with satisfaction and carefully sealing the pocket.

"It's the least we can do," said the jumppoint station commandant. "I cannot tell you my emotions, knowing that the next pass the Cetagandans made was going to be their last, nerving to fight to the end, when the Dendarii materialized to reinforce us."

"The Dendarii couldn't have done it alone," said Miles modestly. "All we did was help you hold the bridgehead till the real big guns arrived."

"And if it had not been held, the Hegen Alliance forces—the big guns, as you say—could not have jumped into Vervani local space."

"Not without great cost, certainly," Miles conceded.

The station commandant glanced at his chrono. "Well, my planet will be expressing its opinion of that in more tangible form quite shortly. May I escort you to the ceremony, Admiral? It's time."

"Thank you." Miles rose, and preceded him out of his office, his hand rechecking the tangible thanks in his pocket. *Medals, huh. Medals buy no fleet repairs.*

He paused at a transparent portal, caught half by the vista from the jump station and half by his own reflection. Oseran/Dendarii dress greys were all right, he decided; soft grey velvet tunic set off with blinding white trim and silver buttons on the shoulders, matching trousers and grey synthasuede boots. He fancied the outfit made him look taller. Perhaps he would keep the design.

Beyond the portal floated a scattering of ships, Dendarii, Ranger, Vervani, and Alliance. The *Prince Serg* was not among them, being now in orbit above the Vervani homeworld while high-level—literally—talks continued, hammering out the details of the permanent treaty of friendship, commerce, tariff reduction, mutual defense pact, & etc, among Barrayar, Vervain, Aslund and Pol. Gregor, Miles had heard, was being quite luminous in both the public relations and the actual nuts and bolts part of the business. *Better you than me, boy.* The Vervani jumppoint station was letting its own repairs schedule slacken to lend aid to the Dendarii; Baz was working around the clock. Miles tore himself away from the vista and followed the station commandant.

They paused in the corridor outside the large briefing room where the ceremony was to take place, waiting for the attendees to settle. The Vervani apparently wished the principals to make a grand entrance. The commandant went in to prepare. The audience was not large—too much vital work going on—but the Vervani had scraped up enough warm bodies to make it look respectable, and Miles had contributed a platoon of convalescent Dendarii to fluff up the crowd. He would accept on their behalf, in his speech, he decided.

As Miles waited, he saw Commander Cavilo arrive with her Barrayaran honor guard. As far as he knew, the Vervani were not yet aware that the honor-guard's weapons were lethally charged and they had orders to shoot to kill if their prisoner attempted escape. Two hard-faced women in Barrayaran auxiliary uniforms made sure Cavilo was watched both night and day. Cavilo did a good job of ignoring their presence.

The Ranger dress uniform was a neater version of their fatigues, in tan, black, and white, subliminally reminding Miles of a guard dog's fur. *This bitch bites,* he reminded himself. Cavilo smiled and drifted up to Miles. She reeked of her poisonous green-scented perfume; she must have bathed in it.

Miles tilted his head in salute, reached into a pocket, and took out two nose filters. He thrust one up each nostril, where they expanded softly to create a seal, and inhaled deeply to test them. Working fine. They would filter out much smaller molecules than the vile organics of that damned perfume. Miles breathed out through his mouth.

Cavilo watched this performance with an expression of thwarted fury. "*Damn* you," she muttered.

Miles shrugged, palms out, as if to say, *What would you have of me?* "Are you and your survivors about ready to move out?"

"Right after this idiot charade. I have to abandon six ships, too damaged to jump."

"Sensible of you. If the Vervani don't catch on to you soon, the Cetagandans, when they realize they can't get at you themselves, will probably tell them the ugly truth. You shouldn't linger in these parts."

"I don't intend to. If I never see this place again it will be too soon. That goes double for you, mutant. If not for you . . ." She shook her head bitterly.

"By the way," Miles added, "the Dendarii have now been paid three times for this operation. Once by our original contractors the Aslunders, once by the Barrayarans, and once by the grateful Vervani. Each agreed to cover all our expenses in full. Leaves a very tidy profit."

She actually hissed. "You better *pray* we never meet again."

"Goodbye, then."

They entered the chamber to collect their honors. Would Cavilo have the iron nerve to accept hers on behalf of the Rangers her twisted plots had destroyed? Yes, it turned out. Miles gagged quietly.

The first medal I ever won, Miles thought as the station commandant pinned his on him with embarrassingly fulsome praise, *and I can't even wear it at home.* The medal, the uniform, and Admiral Naismith himself must soon return to the closet. Forever? The life of Ensign Vorkosigan was not too attractive, by comparison. And yet . . . the mechanics of soldiering were the same, from side to side. If there was any difference between himself and Cavilo, it must be in what they chose to serve. And how they chose to serve it. *Not all paths, but one path. . . .*

When Miles arrived back on Barrayar for home leave, a few weeks later, Gregor invited him for lunch at the Imperial Residence. They sat at a wrought-iron table in the North Gardens, which were famous for having been designed by Emperor Ezar, Gregor's grandfather. In summer the spot would be deeply shaded; now it was laced with light filtering through young leaves, rippling in the soft airs of spring. The guards did their guarding out of sight, the servants waited out of earshot unless Gregor touched his pager. Replete with the first three courses, Miles sipped scalding coffee and plotted an assault on a second pastry, which cowered across the table linen under a thick camouflage of cream. Or would that overmatch his forces? This had it all over the contract-slave rations they'd once divided, not to mention Cavilo's doggie chews.

Even Gregor seemed to be seeing it all with new eyes. "Space stations are really boring, y'know? All those corridors," he commented, staring out past a fountain, eye following a curving brick path that dove into a riot of flowers. "I stopped seeing how beautiful Barrayar was, looking at it every day. Had to forget to remember. Strange."

"There were moments I couldn't remember which space station I was on," Miles agreed around a mouthful of pastry and cream. "The luxury trade's another matter, but the Hegen Hub stations did tend to the utilitarian." He grimaced at the associations of that last word.

The conversation wandered over the recent events in the Hegen Hub. Gregor brightened upon learning that Miles had never issued an actual battle order in the *Triumph's* fleet tac room either, except to handle the internal security crisis as delegated by Tung.

"Most officers have finished their jobs when the action begins, because the battle transpires too rapidly for the officers to affect it," Miles assured him. "Once you set up a good tac comp—and, if you're lucky, a man with a magic nose—it's better to keep your hands in your pockets. I had Tung, you had . . . ahem."

"And nice deep pockets," said Gregor. "I'm still thinking about it. It seemed almost unreal, till I visited sickbay afterwards. And realized, such-and-such a point of light meant this man's arm lost, that man's lungs frozen. . . ."

"Gotta watch out for those little lights. They tell such soothing lies," Miles agreed. "If you let them." He chased another gooey bite with coffee, paused, and remarked, "You didn't tell Illyan the truth about your little topple off the balcony, did you." It was observation, not question.

"I told him I was drunk, and climbed down." Gregor watched the flowers. ". . . how did you know?"

"He doesn't talk about you with secret terror in his eyes."

"I've just got him . . . giving a little. I don't want to screw it up now. You didn't tell him either—for that I thank you."

"You're welcome." Miles drank more coffee. "Do me a favor in return. Talk to someone."

"Who? Not Illyan. Not your father."

"How about my mother?"

"Hm." Gregor bit into his torte, upon which he had been making furrows with his fork, for the first time.

"She could be the only person on Barrayar to automatically put Gregor the man before Gregor the emperor. All our ranks look like optical illusions to her, I think. And you know she can keep her own counsel."

"I'll think about it."

"I don't want to be the only one who . . . the only one. I know when I'm out of my depth."

"You do?" Gregor raised his brows, one corner of his mouth crooking up.

"Oh, yes. I just don't normally let on."

"All right. I will," said Gregor.

Miles waited.

"My word," Gregor added.

Miles relaxed, immeasurably relieved. "Thank you." He eyed a third pastry. The portions were sort of dainty. "Are you feeling better, these days?"

"Much, thank you." Gregor went back to plowing furrows in his cream.

"Really?"

Crosshatches. "I don't know. Unlike that poor sod they had parading around playing me while I was gone, I didn't exactly volunteer for this."

"All Vor are draftees, in that sense."

"Any other Vor could run away and not be missed."

"Wouldn't you miss me a little?" said Miles plaintively. Gregor snickered. Miles glanced around the garden. "It doesn't look like such a tough post, compared to Kyril Island."

"Try it alone in bed at midnight, wondering when your genes are going to start generating monsters in your mind. Like Great Uncle Mad Yuri. Or Prince Serg." His glance at Miles was secretly sharp.

"I . . . know about Prince Serg's, uh, problems," said Miles carefully.

"Everyone seems to have known. Except me."

So that *had* been the trigger of depressive Gregor's first real suicide attempt. Key and lock, click! Miles tried not to look triumphant at this sudden feat of insight. "When did you find out?"

"During the Komarr conference. I'd run across hints, before . . . put them down to enemy propaganda."

Then, the ballet on the balcony had been an immediate response to the shock. Gregor'd had no one to vent it to. . . .

"Was it true, that he really got off torturing—"

"Not everything rumored about Crown Prince Serg is true," Miles cut hastily across this. "Though the true core is . . . bad enough. Mother knows. She was eyewitness to crazy things even *I* don't know, about the Escobar invasion. But she'll tell you. Ask her straight, she'll tell you straight back."

"That seems to run in the family," Gregor allowed. "Too."

"She'll tell you how different you are from him—nothing wrong with your mother's blood, that I ever heard—anyway, I probably carry almost as many of Mad Yuri's genes as you do, through one line of descent or another."

Gregor actually grinned. "Is that supposed to be reassuring?"

"Mm, more on the theory that misery loves company."

"I'm afraid of power . . ." Gregor's voice went low, contemplative.

"You aren't afraid of power, you're afraid of hurting people. If you wield that power," Miles deduced suddenly.

"Huh. Close guess."

"Not dead-on?"

"I'm afraid I might enjoy it. The hurting. Like *him.*"

Prince Serg, he meant. His father.

"Rubbish," said Miles. "I watched my grandfather try and get you to enjoy hunting for years. You got good, I suppose because you thought it was your Vorish duty, but you damn near threw up every time you half-missed and we had to chase down some wounded beastie. You may harbor some other perversion, but not sadism."

"What I've read . . . and heard," said Gregor, "is so horribly fascinating. I can't help thinking about it. Can't put it out of my mind."

"Your head is full of horrors because the *world* is full of horrors. Look at the horrors Cavilo caused in the Hegen Hub."

"If I'd strangled her while she slept—which I had a chance to do—none of those horrors would have come to pass."

"If none of those horrors had come to pass, she wouldn't have deserved to be strangled. Some kind of time-travel paradox, I'm afraid. The arrow of justice flies one way. Only. You can't regret not strangling her first. Though I suppose you can regret not strangling her after. . . ."

"No . . . no . . . I'll leave that to the Cetagandans, if they can catch her now that she has her head start."

"Gregor, I'm sorry, but I just don't think Mad Emperor Gregor is in the cards. It's your *advisors* who are going to go crazy."

Gregor stared at the pastry tray, and sighed. "I suppose it would disturb the guards if I tried to shove a cream torte up your nose."

"Deeply. You should have done it when we were eight and twelve; you could have gotten away with it then. The cream pie of justice flies one way," Miles snickered.

Several unnatural and sophomoric things to do with a tray full of pastry were then suggested by both principals, which left them laughing. Gregor needed a good cream pie fight, Miles judged, even if only verbal and imaginary. When the laughter finally died down, and the coffee was cooling, Miles said, "I know flattery sends you straight up a wall, but dammit, you're actually good at your job. You have to know that, on some level inside, after the Vervain talks. Stay on it, huh?"

"I think I will." Gregor's fork dove more forcefully into his last bite of dessert. "You're going to stay on yours, too, right?"

"Whatever it may be. I am to meet with Simon Illyan on just that topic later this afternoon," said Miles. He decided to forgo that third pastry after all.

"You don't sound exactly excited about it."

"I don't suppose he can demote me, there is no rank below ensign."

"He's pleased with you, what else?"

"He didn't look pleased, when I gave him my debriefing report. He looked dyspeptic. Didn't say much." He glanced at Gregor in sudden suspicion. "You know, don't you? Give!"

"Mustn't interfere in the chain of command," said Gregor sententiously. "Maybe you'll move up it. I hear the command at Kyril Island is open."

Miles shuddered.

✧ ✧ ✧

Spring in the Barrayaran capital city of Vorbarr Sultana was as beautiful as the autumn, Miles decided. He paused a moment before turning in to the front entrance to the big blocky building that was ImpSec HQ. The Earth maple still stood, down the street and around the corner, its tender leaves backlit to a delicate green glow by the afternoon sun. Barrayaran native vegetation ran to dull reds and browns, mostly. Would he ever visit Earth? Maybe.

Miles produced proper passes for the door guards. Their faces were familiar, they were the same crew he'd helped supervise for that interminable period last winter—only a few months ago? It seemed longer. He could still rattle off their pay-rates. They exchanged pleasantries, but being good ImpSec men they did not ask the question alight in their eyes, *Where have you been sir?* Miles was not issued a security escort to Illyan's office, a good sign. It wasn't as if he didn't know the way, by now.

He followed the familiar turns into the labyrinth, up the lift tubes. The captain in Illyan's outer office merely waved him through, barely glancing up from his comconsole. The inner office was unchanged, Illyan's oversized comconsole desk was unchanged, Illyan himself was . . . rather tireder-looking, paler. He ought to get out and catch some of that spring sun, eh? At least his hair hadn't all turned white, it was still about the same brown-grey mix. His taste in clothes was still bland to the point of camouflage.

Illyan pointed to a seat—another good sign, Miles took it promptly—finished whatever had been absorbing him, and at last looked up. He leaned forward to put his elbows on the comconsole and lace his fingers together, and regarded Miles with a kind of clinical disapproval, as if he were a data point that messed up the curve, and Illyan was deciding if he could still save the theory by re-classifying him as experimental error.

"Ensign Vorkosigan," Illyan sighed. "It seems you still have a little problem with subordination."

"I know, sir. I'm sorry."

"Do you ever intend to do anything about it besides feel sorry?"

"I can't help it, sir, if people give me the wrong orders."

"If you can't obey my orders, I don't want you in my Section."

"Well . . . I thought I had. You wanted a military evaluation of the Hegen Hub. I made one. You wanted to know where the destabilization was coming from. I found out. You wanted the Dendarii Mercenaries out of the Hub. They'll be leaving in about three more weeks, I understand. You asked for results. You got them."

"*Lots* of them," Illyan murmured.

"I admit, I didn't have a direct order to rescue Gregor, I just assumed you'd want it done. Sir."

Illyan searched him for irony, lips thinning as he apparently found it. Miles tried to keep his face bland, though out-blanding Illyan was a major effort. "As I recall," said Illyan (and Illyan's memory was eidetic, thanks to an Illyrican bio-chip) "I gave those orders to Captain Ungari. I gave you just one order. Can you remember what it was?" This inquiry was in the same encouraging tone one might use on a six-year-old just learning to tie his shoes. Trying to out-irony Illyan was as dangerous as trying to out-bland him.

"Obey Captain Ungari's orders," Miles recalled reluctantly.

"Just so." Illyan leaned back. "Ungari was a good, reliable operative. If you'd botched it, you'd have taken him down with you. The man is now half-ruined."

Miles made little negative motions with his hands. "He made the correct decisions, for his level. You can't fault him. It's just . . . things got too important for me to go on playing ensign when the man who was needed was Lord Vorkosigan." *Or Admiral Naismith.*

"Hm," Illyan said. "And yet . . . who shall I assign you to now? Which loyal officer gets his career destroyed next?"

Miles thought this over. "Why don't you assign me directly to yourself, sir?"

"Thanks," said Illyan dryly.

"I didn't mean—" Miles began to sputter protest, stopped, detecting the oblique gleam of humor in Illyan's brown eyes. *Roasting me for your sport, are you?*

"In fact, just that proposal has been floated. Not, needless to say, by me. But a galactic operative must function with a high degree of independence. We're considering making a virtue of necessity—" A light on Illyan's comconsole distracted him. He checked something, and touched a control. The door on the wall to the right of his desk slid open, and Gregor stepped through. The emperor shed one guard who stayed in the passageway, the other trod silently through the office to take up station beyond the antechamber. All doors slid shut. Illyan rose to pull up a chair for the emperor, and gave him a nod, a sort of vestigial bow, before reseating himself. Miles, who had also risen, sketched a salute and sat too.

"Did you tell him about the Dendarii yet?" Gregor asked Illyan.

"I was working around to it," said Illyan.

Gradually. "What about the Dendarii?" Miles asked, unable to keep the eagerness out of his voice, try though he might for a junior version of Illyan's impassive surface.

"We've decided to put them on a permanent retainer," said Illyan. "You, in your cover identity as Admiral Naismith, will be our liaison officer."

"Consulting mercenaries?" Miles blinked. *Naismith lives!*

Gregor grinned. "The Emperor's Own. We owe them, I think, something more than just their base pay for their services to us—and to Us—in the Hegen Hub. And they have certainly demonstrated the, er, utility of being able to reach places cut off to our regular forces by political barriers."

Miles interpreted the expression on Illyan's face as deep mourning for his Section budget, rather than disapproval as such.

"Simon shall be alert for, and pursue, opportunities to use them actively," Gregor went on. "We'll need to justify that retainer, after all."

"I see them as more use in espionage than covert ops," Illyan put in hastily. "This isn't a license to go adventuring, or worse, some kind of letter of marque and reprisal. In fact, the first thing I want you to do is beef up your intelligence department. I know you're in funds for it. I'll lend you a couple of my experts."

"Not bodyguard-puppeteers again, sir?" Miles asked nervously.

"Shall I ask Captain Ungari if he wants to volunteer?" inquired Illyan with a suppressed ripple of his lips. "No. You will operate independently. God help us. After all, if I don't send you someplace else, you'll be right here. So the scheme has that much merit even if the Dendarii never do anything."

"I fear it is primarily your youth, which is the cause of Simon's lack of confidence," murmured twenty-five-year-old Gregor. "*We* feel it is time he gave up that prejudice."

Yes, that had been an Imperial We, Miles's

Barrayaran-tuned ears did not deceive him. Illyan had heard it as clearly. The chief leaner, leaned upon. Illyan's irony this time was tinged with underlying . . . approval? "Aral and I have labored twenty years to put ourselves out of work. We may live long enough to retire after all." He paused. "That's called 'success' in my business, boys. I wouldn't object." And under his breath ". . . get this hellish chip taken out of my head at last. . . ."

"Mm, don't go scouting surfside retirement cottages just yet," said Gregor. Not caving or backpedaling or submission, merely an expression of confidence in Illyan. No more, no less. Gregor glanced at Miles's . . . neck? The deep bruises from Metzov's grip were almost gone by now, surely. "Were you still working around to the other thing, too?" he asked Illyan.

Illyan opened a hand. "Be my guest." He rummaged in a drawer underneath his comconsole.

"We—and We—thought we owed you something more, too, Miles," said Gregor.

Miles hesitated between a *shucks-t'weren't-nothin* speech and a *what-did-you-bring-me?!* and settled on an expression of alert inquiry.

Illyan reemerged, and tossed Miles something small that flashed red in the air. "Here. You're a lieutenant. Whatever that means to you."

Miles caught them between his hands, the plastic collar rectangles of his new rank. He was so surprised he said the first thing that came into his head, which was, "Well, that's a start on the subordination problem."

Illyan favored him with a driven glower. "Don't get carried away. About ten percent of ensigns are promoted after their first year of service. Your Vorish social circle will think it's all nepotism anyway."

"I know," said Miles bleakly. But he opened his collar and began switching tabs on the spot.

Illyan softened slightly. "Your father will know better, though. And Gregor. And, er . . . myself."

Miles looked up, to catch his eye directly for almost the first time this interview. "Thank you."

"You earned it. You won't get anything from me you don't earn. That includes the dressing-downs."

"I'll look forward to them, sir."

Author's Afterword

The Warriors Apprentice was my second novel. I began it in the fall of 1983, just six or so weeks after sending the manuscript of my first novel, eventually named *Shards of Honor,* off to a New York publisher, in blind hope and without a literary agent, in what is called, variously for unpublished writers, "on spec(ulation)," "over the transom" or "into the slushpile." The character of Miles Naismith Vorkosigan was a gleam in my eye when I began the story of his parents in that first book; by the time I had finished it, he'd already begun to take more substantial form. In the beginning I knew only three things about Miles: he was born crippled in a militaristic society, he was very bright, and he was extremely energetic. Since one of my own chronic complaints is that I never have enough energy, this last aspect of his character can legitimately be classified as author's wish-fulfillment fantasy.

Miles's first name was stolen from the character of Miles Hendron, in Mark Twain's *The Prince and the Pauper.* I was at the time innocent of the fact that "miles" means "soldier" in Latin, but I'll bet Twain wasn't. Miles's vaguely posited physical handicaps acquired a real-life template from a certain hospital pharmacist I used to work with; the height, the hunch, the head, the chin-tic and the leg braces were all lifted from this brilliant man. I took at least one of Miles's subtler psychological qualities from T.E. Lawrence. Lawrence had to a marked degree what one of his more prominent biographers, John Mack, described as a power of "enablement"; somehow, people around him in many different contexts found themselves doing more and better for the strength of his example and encouragement than they might have on their own. On a still deeper level of characterization, Miles's "great man's son syndrome," the fountain of so much of his drive and therefore my plots, owes much to my relationship with my own father. It is a curious comment on our culture that this particular psychological profile, which to my observation appears in both genders, is never called a "great man's daughter's syndrome." I wish that were only an artifact of the power of alliteration.

By the time I'd finished *Shards* I'd also developed the much more unexpected character of Konstantine Bothari. Bothari and Miles were a magnetic pairing. The very first image I had for the book that eventually became *The Warrior's Apprentice* was the death of Bothari, initially visualized defending Miles from some yet-to-be-conceived enemy on a shuttleport tarmac, far from home. The subsequent challenge to Miles, to survive without Bothari's quasi-parental support, was inherent in that initial vision. So while the book was written, largely, from beginning to end (a method I'd learned to prefer while writing *Shards),* it was generated from the inside out. I've described my usual writing process as scrambling from peak to peak of inspiration through foggy valleys of despised logic. Inspiration is better—when you can get it.

I began *Warrior's* exactly where it starts now; I made very few revisions to that first scene later. In the very first draft, however, Miles had a younger sister. Elena Bothari was originally named Nile, after the character of Nile Etland in a couple of James H. Schmitz stories I'd read back in *Analog* magazine in the '60s. The sister was deleted before I got to Chapter 3, as I realized she and Elena/Nile occupied the same ecological niche. Test readers eventually convinced me that the name Nile for my heroine and Miles for my hero would be a copy-editor's nightmare later, if I ever achieved publication, so I regretfully gave up the name. Elena was never quite the same after the change, though. I'm still saving the name Nile.

Over the years I've found my book titles sometimes appear simultaneously with their book ideas, sometimes partway through, and sometimes, worst of all, never—books arrive at publication still sporting some dippy working title which then must be hastily changed. I've had two or three different books with the working title of *Miles to Go* over the years. *The Warrior's Apprentice,* happily, is one of the first and best category. It is, of course, a pun on the old folk tale "The Sorcerer's Apprentice," so title, plot, and theme were all there from the first.

So I had set myself a comic plot structure with a tragedy at the heart of its maze. How many screwball comedies have the sequence of the little white lie that grows and grows out of hand? It was also, I discovered shortly, a theological romance, since sequence by sequence Miles was challenged by his then-three besetting sins: pride, imprudence, and despair. With these maps and compasses to guide me through the foggy valleys, I began writing my way to the shifting center.

Writing *Warrior's* also taught me some important

lessons about how to both use and ignore critique. I have some strong ideas about the importance of the reader in the story process. I've always used test-readers; I write to communicate a vision, and I always like to check and try to see if the message-received sufficiently resembles the message-sent. I twice earnestly re-wrote my way down wrong turns, when two trusted professional-level critiquers made suggestions which, in both cases, would have been fatal to the book and the series that eventually followed it. One, under the impression that I was writing standard commercial space opera, suggested I get rid of the entire opening sequence, including Miles's grandfather, and "start with the action" of the Beta Colony encounters; another had for personal reasons a view of the character of Bothari that was utterly hostile, and wanted a different version of his death. Trying to be a good little reviser, I finished these, sat back, and twitched for days. Then tore them both out and put back my first visions.

The fundamental substance of a book, if you are writing a real book, in your own blood, is not optional. The thematic vision often cannot be communicated—or even realized, if (as in my own case) the writing itself is a process of self-discovery—in partial sections. The whole must be present to become greater than the sum of the parts. Test readers, however useful in some areas (spelling! grammar! continuity! O please yes!) can become a hazard when they begin, on the basis of incomplete information, trying in all good faith to help you to write some other book than the one you intend. For example, the death of Miles's grandfather was based in a very oblique way on the death of one of my own grandfathers; cutting that sequence felt like chopping off my arm for very good reasons. Zelazny's dictum, "Trust your demon," meaning, follow your own inner vision, eventually became a mantra for me.

Once past the center, the book went more quickly. Even the return of *Shards* rejected from its first submission couldn't stop Miles's forward momentum by that time. I created *Warriors* final submission draft in the fall of 1984, turned back to an edit of *Shards* based on some editorial comments in its rejection letter (all of two sentences), and then began *Ethan of Athos*.

Seven *months* later *Warrior's* was returned *unread* from its first submission, because they'd decided not to take the revised *Shards* and didn't want to break up the set. This was devastating at the time, but I was in fact grateful later. An editor at a second publisher read the first fifty pages, decided it was a juvenile, and kindly suggested I try a Young Adult publisher.

The YA publisher disagreed with this evaluation; the book was bounced with a form rejection. (I don't know what percentage of it *they* read.) It was now late summer of 1985. My writer-friend Lillian Carl suggested I try it on Betsy Mitchell at a new publisher called Baen Books, because she'd met Betsy on the science fiction convention circuit, and thought she might give it a good read and, at the very least, a more useful and informative rejection letter than the cryptic ones I'd got so far. So I did.

I never got the useful rejection letter, though. In August the book passed the first reader, in September it passed Betsy, and in mid-October Jim Baen telephoned me and offered for all three completed books, two of which he had not yet seen. *My God,* I thought, after I stopped hyperventilating, *a publisher that operates in real time!* (Warning to aspiring writers: this was twelve years ago now. Baen's slush piles were *much smaller* then.)

I then began *Falling Free,* as a conscious attempt at a "more serious" form of SF than Miles's "space opera." (I care much less about such labels nowadays.) By chance, during a pause in the middle of it, Betsy at Baen called me up and invited me to contribute a Miles story to an anthology of mercenary novellas she was editing, as a result of which I wrote "The Borders of Infinity." I finished *Falling Free*, then went on to write *Brothers in Arms*.

Miles's potential as a series character was acquiring a serious kinetic wallop by this time. I was conscious that I was a rather slow writer by commercial standards. Both because I had very much enjoyed the novella form, and because it would allow me to produce a book in two-thirds my usual time, I'd suggested as part of my next three-book contract to recycle the "Borders" tale and add two more novellas to it, making an all-Miles volume. So I wrote "The Mountains of Mourning" next, followed by "Labyrinth," incidentally establishing a pattern of writing at will anywhere in Miles's timeline, and accidentally setting up the subsequent perpetual readerly argument of whether it is better to read the Miles stories in publication order or by internal chronology. In these omnibus volumes you are getting them by internal chronology, by the way—until I wreck the nice arrangement by writing another prequel someday.

I can name where many of the elements of "Mountains" came from; Fat Ninny was based on a real horse, and I share Miles's love of the semi-wild country. Ma Mattulich was an extreme version of a certain female type I knew from real life, both victim and enforcer of her culture's life-denying mores. The river of roses might seem to have wandered in from some fairy-tale, sign and signifier of transformations to come, but I have met those wild roses in person, in banked-up masses, while riding in the Ohio fields of my childhood. I borrowed the title from a friend's working title of a fantasy, *The*

Mountains of Morning, that she didn't use for her story's final version. "Mountains" was a contrary story, based on the "What's the worst possible thing we can do to this guy?" plot-generator, taking my new-minted Ensign Miles, his face to the stars, and forcing his head around to take a look at what his feet were planted in. At the time I was having an amiable debate with Jim Baen whether the series should be called "Miles Naismith Adventures" or "Miles Vorkosigan Adventures"; "Mountains" was in some degree the last word in this argument. It won me my first Hugo award, and my second Nebula, for best novella of 1989.

The third book in my three-book contract had been sold on what I fancied was the world's shortest synopsis: one word, "Quaddies." I really had intended when I'd finished *Falling Free* to write its sequel, but when I came to it, I still was not ready. (I am now even less ready.) It was very apparent, though, looking at the Miles tales I'd already written, that there was an important gap between "Mountains" and "Labyrinth." I knew how Miles had left the Dendarii Mercenaries, but I didn't know how he'd got back to them. I did know it couldn't have been simple. A lot must have happened in the three years Miles was tied down in military school, and such responsibility and respect weren't the sort of thing the military powers-that-be on Barrayar were likely to voluntarily give to the young ensign we'd last seen in "Mountains." Jim Baen meanwhile had primed the pump by sending me a copy of B.H. Liddell-Hart's *Strategy,* which I read primarily because Captain Liddell-Hart had also been an admirer of Lawrence in his day. Ah, connections.

As long as my novels of character were being packaged as military SF anyway, I figured I might as well take a whack at the sub-genre more nearly head-on. So I set out to make the book which became *The Vor*

Game as military as I could, as a sort of delayed present to Jim for raising me out of the slush-gutter back in '85. Unusually, I can describe exactly the moment at which the ideas came together in my head for the book's opening sequence. I was standing at my kitchen sink doing the dinner dishes, and listening to an Enya tape which contained a song sung in Latin titled "Cursum Perficio." What the actual lyrics of the song may be about I have no clue, but somehow its rhythms sounded both military and ecclesiastical to me, and I was put in mind of an early Christian martyr tale I'd once run across called "The Forty Martyrs of Sebastiani." The fast-forward version of this goes: a certain Roman legion was wintering in Dacia, up beyond the Black Sea, at a period when the high command was flip-flopping over the acceptability of this new religion. Orders came down for the Christians to recant. Forty men refused, and were ordered to stand out naked on the ice of a frozen lake until they changed their minds. Only one man broke. A watching Roman officer was so impressed with their fortitude, he went out to join them, to make up their round lot again, and they all froze to death. It seemed a very Barrayaran sort of tale to me, somehow.

I had also read T.E. Lawrence's *The Mint*, an account of his basic training when he re-enlisted in the British Army *after* World War I, under a pseudonym, as an enlisted man. Now, admittedly ex-Colonel Lawrence was not in the best psychological shape at this point in his life, but the account was nonetheless relentless in its description of the brutality and banality of training camp life.

Hanging on the wall of my father's home office for years, and now on mine, was a print titled "Alaskan Outpost," an almost art-deco stylized scene of an arctic weather station, with a parka-clad man out collecting data from his instruments, a snow-covered glacier sliding down the mountain in the background. It was a gift dated 1952 from his colleagues at the Battelle Memorial Research Institute, where he worked as a physicist and engineer till moving to his teaching post at the Ohio State University. In addition to his research and teaching, my father moonlighted as the second television weatherman in the United States, at Channel 10 Columbus, Ohio; most of the many Central Ohioans who knew him as "Bob McMaster, TV Weatherman," had no idea of his professorial day job. When the show first appeared, the weather segment used to be fifteen minutes long and he would always get in a short meteorology lesson as well as the forecast. He was so good, the Strategic Air Command pilots at Lockbourne Air Force Base used to call him up for pre-flight weather reports, in preference to their less reliable military weather sources, till their command caught up with them and made them stop.

So somehow, between one dish and the next, Enya; *The Mint,* "Alaskan Outpost," *Strategy,* the Forty Martyrs, and Miles all crashed together in my head, and came out the opening section of *The Vor Game.* Boom. The rest was mere logic, fine-tuning the connections.

I had set out to return Miles to the Dendarii fleet, but when that blasted dead body turned up in the drain in Chapter 3, the book tried very hard to turn into a military murder-mystery of some kind, set wholly on Kyril Island. The packet Miles retrieved had originally contained money, which had my test-readers jumping up and down in anticipation of all sorts of chicanery; I finally had to transmute the contents to *cookies,* dammit, *cookies,* to get them to shut up about it. For the information of those who worry about such things, *The Vor Game* was *not* an extension or continuation of the novella version, "Weatherman"; the novella segment was the original planned front end, cut off and cycled over to *Analog* magazine for some welcome extra cash and exposure. There is nevertheless a shift in tone between the two sections of the tale, between the darker *The* Mint-influenced opening and the rather, er, sunnier later Strategy-inspired sections which leads me to sometimes regret not splitting it into two separate novels. But *The Vor Game* went on to win me my second Hugo, my first for Best Novel, so I would hardly dare mess with it now.

And oh, Enya gets in her bit at the end of the book as well, for balance; for reasons only known to my backbrain, the triumphant arrival of the *Prince Serg* in the wormhole battle has for its associated music "Cu Chulainn," an instrumental piece from her self-titled album.

The stories in *Young Miles* are not as closely connected as those in its companion omnibus volume *Cordelia's Honor,* whose components *Shards of Honor* and *Barrayar* are truly two halves of one book. But the three pieces assembled here are held together by more than just chronology and the glue on the spine. Together, they form the story of Miles as an apprentice adult, from his naive beginnings to a solidly forged journeyman's place in his world. My favorite literary pattern is the spiral, where we come back around to where we started, but on a much higher plane and with a profoundly different perspective. Miles's time of true and tempered mastery will come later, as he discovers with age that "the questions are the same, but the answers change"—and that sometimes, that corkscrew line from beginning to end is a powder train.

Miles Vorkosigan/Naismith: His Universe and Times

Chronology	Events	Chronicle
Approx. 200 yrs before Miles's birth	Quaddies are created by genetic engineering.	*Falling Free*
During Beta-Barrayaran War	Cordelia Naismith meets Lord Aral Vorkosigan while on opposite sides of a war. Despite difficulties, they fall in love and are married.	*Shards of Honor*
The Vordarian Pretendership	While Cordelia is pregnant, an attempt to assassinate Aral by poison gas fails, but Cordelia is affected; Miles Vorkosigan is born with bones that will always be brittle and other medical problems. His growth will be stunted.	*Barrayar*
Miles is 17	Miles fails to pass physical test to get into the Service Academy. On a trip, necessities force him to improvise the Free Dendarii Mercenaries into existence; he has unintended but unavoidable adventures for four months. Leaves the Dendarii in Ky Tung's competent hands and takes Elli Quinn to Beta for rebuilding of her damaged face; returns to Barrayar to thwart plot against his father. Emperor pulls strings to get Miles into the Academy.	*The Warrior's Apprentice*

Chronology	Events	Chronicle
Miles is 20	Ensign Miles graduates and immediately has to take on one of the duties of the Barrayaran nobility and act as detective and judge in a murder case.	"The Mountains of Mourning" in *Borders of Infinity*
	Shortly afterwards, his first military assignment ends with his arrest. Miles has to rejoin the Dendarii to rescue the young Barrayaran emperor. Emperor accepts Dendarii as his personal secret service force.	*The Vor Game*
Miles is 22	Miles and his cousin Ivan attend a Cetagandan state funeral and are caught up in Cetagandan internal politics.	*Cetaganda*
	Miles sends Commander Elli Quinn, who's been given a new face on Beta, on a solo mission to Kline Station.	*Ethan of Athos*
Miles is 23	Now a Barrayaran Lieutenant, Miles goes with the Dendarii to smuggle a scientist out of Jackson's Whole. Miles's fragile leg bones have been replaced by synthetics.	"Labyrinth" in *Borders of Infinity*
Miles is 24	Miles plots from within a Cetagandan prison camp on Dagoola IV to free the prisoners. The Dendarii fleet is pursued	"The Borders of Infinity" in *Borders of Infinity*

Chronology	Events	Chronicle
	by the Cetagandans and finally reaches Earth for repairs. Miles has to juggle both his identities at once, raise money for repairs, and defeat a plot to replace him with a double. Ky Tung stays on Earth. Commander Elli Quinn is now Miles's right-hand officer. Miles and the Dendarii depart for Sector IV on a rescue mission.	*Brothers in Arms*
Miles is 25	Hospitalized after previous mission, Miles's broken arms are replaced by synthetic bones. With Simon Illyan, Miles undoes yet another plot against his father while flat on his back.	*Borders of Infinity*
Miles is 28	Miles meets his clone brother Mark again, this time on Jackson's Whole.	*Mirror Dance*
Miles is 29	Miles hits thirty; thirty hits back.	*Memory*
Miles is 30	Emperor Gregor dispatches Miles to Komarr to investigate a space accident, where he finds old politics and new technology make a deadly mix.	*Komarr*
	The Emperor's wedding sparks romance and intrigue on Barrayar, and Miles plunges up to his neck in both.	*A Civil Campaign*

Chronology	Events	Chronicle
Miles is 32	Miles and Ekaterin's honeymoon journey is interrupted by an Auditorial mission to Quaddiespace, where they encounter old friends, new enemies, and a double handful of intrigue.	*Diplomatic Immunity*